War God

GRAHAM HANCOCK

War God

CORONET

First published in Great Britain in 2013 by Coronet
An imprint of Hodder & Stoughton
An Hachette UK company

First published in paperback in 2014

4

A CIP catalogue record for this title is
available from the British Library

ISBN 978 1 444 73440 9

Typeset by Palimpsest Book Production Ltd, Falkirk, Stirlingshire

Printed and bound by CPI Group (UK) Ltd, Croydon, CR0 4YY

Hodder & Stoughton policy is to use papers that are natural, renewable
and recyclable products and made from wood grown in sustainable forests.
The logging and manufacturing processes are expected to conform to the
environmental regulations of the country of origin.

Hodder & Stoughton Ltd
338 Euston Road
London NW1 3BH

www.hodder.co.uk

For Santha

Graham Hancock on Facebook:
www.facebook.com/Author.GrahamHancock

Graham Hancock on Twitter:
@Graham__Hancock

Graham's website: www.grahamhancock.com

Nights of the Witch

'The Mexica . . . never at any point referred to themselves, or their city states, let alone their empire as "Aztec" . . . At the time of the Spanish conquest they were [rightly] referred to by the Spanish as "Mexica" – hence the name for modern Mexico.'

Colin McEwan and Leonardo López Luján, *Moctezuma: Aztec Ruler* (2009)

'The Mexica were the cruellest and most devilish people that can be imagined.'

Father Diego Duran, *The History of the Indies of New Spain* (first published 1581)

'Take care that they do not escape . . . Feed them well; let them be fat and desirable for sacrifice on the day of the feast of our god. Let our god rejoice in them since they belong to him.'

Priestly regulations, c. 1519, for securing and preparing victims for sacrifice in the Mexica capital city of Tenochtitlan

Part I

18–19 February 1519

Chapter One

Tenochtitlan (Mexico City), Thursday 18 February 1519

Moctezuma loved eminences, for to stand on any high place was to be reminded that he was the greatest and most magnificent of men, wielding the power of life and death over all he surveyed. Yet of the countless high places in his kingdom, none offered him a deeper and more abiding sense of ownership, or clearer evidence of his own importance, than the summit platform of the colossal pyramid on which he now perched, soaring three hundred feet above his glorious capital city Tenochtitlan, which in turn stood on an island in the midst of a vast lake at the centre of an immense valley surrounded by lofty, snow-capped mountains.

Moctezuma's gaze ranged out to those mountains and volcanoes – there Iztaccihuatl and there Popocatépetl – crowned with snow and wreathed with smoke.

Lower down, old-growth forests of tall trees carpeted the slopes, giving way in the floor of the valley to a gigantic patchwork of farmed fields shining green with new maize. The fields marched in to the edge of the great lake, its shores embellished with his vassal states, Tacuba, Texcoco, Iztapalapa, Coyoacan, Atzcapotzalco, Tepeyac and many more, its blue waters alive with fish, dotted with the bright colours of floating gardens planted with fruits and flowers, woven by the wakes of canoes, traversed by mighty causeways.

Moctezuma allowed his gaze to follow the causeways from the south, west and north where they led into Tenochtitlan, passing thousands of houses, whole districts, entire neighbourhoods standing out above the lake on stilts connected by a perfect geometrical grid of intersecting canals filled with busy water traffic. These gave way to streets lined

3

with noble stone mansions, where flowers bloomed from every rooftop, interspersed by market squares and pyramids and temples and imposing public buildings, beneath which the contours of the original island on which the Mexica capital had been built could still just be discerned.

Closer still, surrounded and protected by the city as the nest of an eagle safeguards its egg, lay the vast square of the sacred precinct, defined by its massive enclosure wall, oriented to the cardinal directions, measuring seven hundred paces along each side and decorated with reliefs depicting huge bronze, green and blue serpents, their gaping jaws set with long fangs and their heads plumed with crests of feathers. The wall was penetrated by four giant gates, one each in the midst of its north, south, east and west sides, opening onto the polished limestone paving of the grand plaza and aligned with the north, south, east and west stairways of the great pyramid. Measuring three hundred paces on each side at its base, the pyramid rose up from the centre of the plaza in four successive levels, painted respectively green, red, turquoise and yellow, narrowing to fifty paces on each side at the summit where Moctezuma stood in possession of the very heart of the world. 'Come Cuitláhuac,' he said. 'See how inspiring the view is this morning.'

Obediently his younger brother strode forward to join him at the top of the northern stairway, the hem of his scarlet cloak flapping around his large bare feet. Moctezuma wore purple, a colour reserved for the Great Speaker of the Mexica empire alone, his feet were shod with golden sandals and his head was adorned with the elaborate diadem of the monarch, studded with gold and jewels and enriched with precious feathers.

They were both tall, gaunt men but, looking at Cuitláhuac, Moctezuma thought, was like looking at himself in a poorly made obsidian mirror, for every aspect of their appearance was almost but not quite the same – the same fine bone structure, the same high, flat brow, the same liquid brown eyes, larger and rounder than was usual amongst the Mexica, the same sculpted cheek bones, the same long, prominent nose, the same delicate chin and the same full lips turned down disapprovingly at the corners. In Moctezuma these features were just as they should be and combined to create an aura of severe beauty and divine

4

charisma fully justifying his powerful name, which meant 'Angry Lord'. But in poor Cuitláhuac they were all very slightly awry – distorted, twisted and roughened in such a way that he could never hope to appear regal or commanding or ever live up to his name which meant 'Eagle over Water' but which could, with the deliberate mispronunciation of a single syllable, be made to mean 'Heap of Excrement' instead.

He looks so much older than me, Moctezuma thought, which was gratifying because at forty-eight, Cuitláhuac was in fact five years his junior. Better still, he was loyal, stolid, unambitious, unimaginative, predictable and dull; in this ill-omened year of One-Reed, when dangers long prophesied threatened to manifest, such qualities made him invaluable. After Moctezuma himself and his deputy Coaxoch, now away on campaign in the mountains of Tlascala, Cuitláhuac ranked third amongst the lords of the nation and was a potential rival since he was of royal blood. There was, however, no danger he would ever seek to seize power for himself. On the contrary, Moctezuma could be absolutely certain of his brother's steadfast support through whatever trials and turmoils lay ahead.

A shiver of apprehension ran down his spine and he glanced superstitiously over his shoulder at the tall, dark edifice that towered behind them. Dominating the summit platform of the pyramid, with its fantastic roof comb and brutal reliefs of serpents and dragons and scenes of battle and sacrifice, this was the temple of Huitzilopochtli, 'Hummingbird', the much-feared war god of the Mexica and Moctezuma's patron deity.

War was a holy pursuit and by means of it, under Hummingbird's guidance, the Mexica had risen in just two centuries from a wandering tribe of despised nomads to become the absolute masters of an enormous empire stretching from the eastern to the western oceans and from the lush jungle lowlands of the south to the high deserts of the north. After subjugating neighbouring states such as Tacuba and Texcoco and harnessing them to Tenochtitlan in a ruling alliance, Mexica armies had gone on to conquer ever more distant cities, peoples and cultures – Mixtecs, Huaxtecs, Tolucans, Cholulans, Chalcans, Totonacs and so many others. One by one, they had all been forced to become tribute-paying vassals offering up huge annual treasures in

5

gold, jewels, maize, salt, chocolate, jaguar skins, cotton, slaves and a thousand other goods, including myriad victims for the human sacrifices that Hummingbird unrelentingly demanded.

There remained only a few pockets of resistance to this otherwise unstoppable advance. Of these, because of its central position in the ruling alliance, Moctezuma had to admit he was somewhat vexed by the recent turn of events in Texcoco, where he had ousted Ishtlil, the eldest son of the late King Neza, and placed Cacama, Neza's youngest son, on the throne instead. This had been necessary because Ishtlil had proved to be a free thinker, showing signs of rejecting his vassal status, whereas Cacama was compliant and could be relied upon to do as he was told. The surprise was that the impertinent Ishtlil had refused to accept the coup and had staged a rebellion, leaving the lakeside city of Texcoco and its valley provinces in Cacama's hands but taking the highland provinces out of the alliance.

It was a declaration of war and there had already been bloody clashes. To punish the affront to his dignity and authority, Moctezuma had laid careful plans to have Ishtlil poisoned. His death would have been spectacular and agonising, with massive haemorrhaging from all major organs. Disturbingly, however – since it meant a resourceful spy must be at work in Tenochtitlan – a warning had reached the rebel prince just in time. A military solution was now being prepared, although not on so grand a scale as the campaign currently underway in the fiercely independent mountain kingdom of Tlascala, the other main sector of resistance to the spread of Mexica power.

Unlike Texcoco, where normal relations would have to be restored with all provinces after Ishtlil was smashed, it pleased Moctezuma for the stubborn Tlascalans to remain free so he could wage all-out war on them whenever he wished in a manner that would have to stop if they submitted to vassalage. His goal, confided to no one except Coaxoch when he had sent him into battle at the head of a huge field army, was to bring a hundred thousand Tlascalan victims to Hummingbird this year. The mission had been crowned with early success and Coaxoch had already sent back hosts of new captives to be fattened for sacrifice.

As the god of war, Hummingbird was thought to favour male victims, which was why four of the five fattening pens distributed around the edges of the sacred precinct and visible from the top of the great pyramid were exclusively reserved for men. Only one at present held women prisoners. This latter was positioned in the northwest corner of the precinct, in the shadow of the enclosure wall and adjacent to the palace of Moctezuma's late father Axayacatl. Moctezuma's own far larger royal palace, with its extensive gardens and its elaborate zoo featuring the House of Panthers, the House of Serpents, the House of Hunting Birds and the House of Human Monsters, stood to the east of the great pyramid.

'Truly an uplifting sight, eh, Cuitláhuac?' Moctezuma said.

'Indeed, lord,' his brother replied.

Down below, at the foot of the northern stairway, the fifty-two victims for this morning's special ceremony were being assembled under the directions of Ahuizotl, the high priest. They were all young Tlascalan men, the finest specimens, the fittest, the strongest, the most beautiful, the most intact of the prisoners sent back by Coaxoch.

Moctezuma licked his lips. 'I think,' he said, 'I will perform the sacrifices myself today.'

Chapter Two

Tenochtitlan, Thursday 18 February 1519

Tucked in a secret pocket inside her filthy blouse, Tozi carried two *atl-inan* leaves rolled into delicate little tubes, crimped at each end and filled with the sticky red paste of the *chalalatli* root. The medicine, obtained by barter from an unscrupulous guard in a dark corner of the women's fattening pen, was for her friend Coyotl, so Tozi kept her hand protectively over the pocket as she threaded her way through the crowds of prisoners, acutely conscious of how easily the tubes would be broken if anyone bumped into her.

Consisting of two interconnected wings, each a hundred paces long and thirty paces deep, set at right-angles to one another like an arm crooked around the northwest corner of the sacred precinct, the fattening pen had held just four hundred women when Tozi first arrived here seven months previously. Now, thanks to Moctezuma's recent wars with the Tlascalans, it held more than two thousand, and droves of new captives were still arriving every day. The rear of both wings was built of solid stone, and formed part of the larger enclosure wall of the sacred complex as a whole. The flat roof, also of stone, was supported by rows of giant stone columns. On its inner side, facing the great pyramid, the pen was open, except for a final row of stone columns and the stout bamboo prison bars that filled the gaps from floor to ceiling between them.

Tozi was near the back of the northern wing, making her way towards the western wing where she'd left Coyotl, when she saw five young Tlascalan women clustered in her path. Her heart sank as she recognised Xoco amongst them, a cruel, hulking, brute of a girl, a couple of years older than herself. She tried to dodge but the crowd was too dense and Xoco lunged forward, shoving her hard in the chest with both hands. Tozi reeled and would have fallen, but two of the others caught her and pushed her back at Xoco again. Then Xoco's fist slammed into her belly and drove the air out of her lungs with a great whoop. Tozi stumbled and fell to her knees but, even as she gasped for breath, an instinct she could not suppress sent her hand searching inside her blouse for the medicine tubes.

Xoco spotted the movement. 'What you got in there?' she screamed, her face writhing with greed.

Tozi felt the outline of the tubes. They seemed bent. She thought one of them might be broken. 'Nothing,' she wheezed as she brought out her hand. 'I . . . I . . . just . . . wanted to find out what you'd done . . . to my ribs.'

'Liar!' Xoco spat. 'You're hiding something! Show me!'

The other four girls jeered as Tozi arched her back and loosened the ties on her blouse exposing her flat, boyish chest. 'I don't have anything to hide,' she panted. 'See for yourself.'

'I see a *witch*,' said Xoco. 'A crafty little *witch*! Hiding something from me.'

The rest of the gang hissed like a basket of snakes. 'Witch!' they agreed. 'Witch! She's a witch!'

Tozi was still kneeling, but now a heavy kick to her ribs knocked her sideways. Someone stamped on her head and she looked into her attackers' minds and saw they weren't going to stop. They would just go on beating and kicking and stamping her until she was dead.

She felt calm as she decided she would use the spell of invisibility. But the spell itself could kill her, so she needed a distraction first.

Curling her body into a ball, ignoring the kicks and blows, she began to sing a dreary song, deep down at the bottom of her voice – *Hmm-a-hmm-hmm . . . hmm-hmm . . . Hmm-a-hmm-hmm . . . hmm-hmm* – raising the pitch with each repeated note, summoning forth a fog of psychic confusion and madness.

It wasn't a fog anyone could see, but it got into the girls' eyes and minds, making Xoco screech and turn furiously on her own friends, grabbing a handful of hair here, clawing a face there, interrupting the attack long enough for Tozi to surge to her feet.

9

She was already whispering the spell of invisibility as she stumbled away, turning her focus inward, slowing the urgent beat of her heart, imagining she was transparent and free as the air. The more strongly and vividly she visualised herself in this form, the more she felt herself fade, the fewer the hostile glances she received and the easier it became to penetrate the crowd of onlookers.

The spell had always hurt her.

Always.

But never really badly unless she held it for longer than a count of ten.

One . . .

Gaps opened up and she flowed through them.

Two . . .

No solid obstacle could now block her path.

Three . . .

It was as though she were Ehecatl, god of the air . . .

Four . . .

The spell was very seductive. There was something wonderful about its embrace. But when Tozi reached five she stopped the magic, found a patch of shadow and slowly faded back into visibility again – just a grimy, snot-nosed, lice-infested fourteen-year-old girl, quietly minding her own business.

First she checked her pockets and was relieved to find the two little tubes of *chalalatli* still mercifully intact.

Then she felt her ribs and face and satisfied herself that nothing was broken despite the beating.

Better still, she realised, the price of the fade was nowhere near as high as it might have been – indeed no more than a punishing headache and flashing lights and wavy lines exploding intermittently before her eyes. She knew from past experience the visual effects would soon subside but the headache would continue, gradually diminishing in intensity, for several days.

Until then it would be dangerous to use the spell again.

But she had no intention of doing so.

She gave a bitter laugh. *Witch?* she thought. *I'm not much of a witch!*

* * *

10

Tozi could send out the fog, she could read minds and sometimes she could command wild animals, but a real witch would have been able to make herself invisible for long enough to escape the fattening pen, and she couldn't do that. Ever since she could remember she'd been able to speak the spell of invisibility, but if she faded for more than a ten count, she paid a terrible price.

The last time she'd risked it was the day her mother was taken by surprise and beaten to death in front of her. It had been one of those times when the priests had whipped Tenochtitlan's masses into a frenzy of fear and hatred against witches, and her mother was amongst those who'd been named. Tozi had been seven years old then and she'd faded just long enough – no more than a thirty count – to escape the rampaging mob and hide. It had saved her life, but it had also paralysed her arms and legs for a day and a night, filled her body with raging fire and burst something in her brain so that her head felt hacked open, as though by a blunt axe, and blood poured from her ears and nose.

After that, fending for herself on the streets of the great city, she'd not had the courage to try a fade for many years, not even for a five count. But since being seized along with other beggars by the temple catchers and thrown in the pen to be fattened for sacrifice, she'd been working on the problem again, working on it every day. She'd even experimented with a fade from time to time, just for brief instants when it could most help her, slowly feeling her way through the deep tangled magic her mother had begun to teach her in the years before the mob. Sometimes she thought she was close to a solution, but it always vanished like a wisp just as it came within her grasp.

Meanwhile there were some, like Xoco and her gang, who'd become suspicious. They simply couldn't understand why Tozi was never amongst those selected for sacrifice when the priests came for victims, why again and again it was always others who were taken and this unlikely ragged girl who remained. That was why they suspected witch-craft, and of course they were right, but why did it make them want to hurt her?

If it wasn't so tragic, their vicious stupidity would almost have been funny, Tozi thought. Had the girls forgotten that just outside the sacred plaza, and presently going about the daily business of their capital city, the Mexica waited to hurt them all, very, very badly – in fact to murder them? Had they forgotten that they would all, sooner or later, be marched up the great pyramid and bent backwards over the execution stone where their hearts would be cut out with a black obsidian knife?

Simultaneous with the thought, Tozi's own heart quickened and she felt a wave of apprehension. A big part of being invisible wasn't magic at all, but common sense. Don't stand out. Don't offend anyone. Don't get yourself noticed. But now she saw she had been noticed! Despite the fade, which should have thrown off all pursuit, a girl who'd lurked in the background during Xoco's attack had followed her. She might be eighteen, this girl, or perhaps twenty, tall and lithe with glowing skin, full, sensual lips, big, dark eyes and straight black hair that fell almost to her waist. She didn't look like a Tlascalan, and she was older than the rest of Xoco's gang, but Tozi wasn't taking any chances. Without a backward glance she ducked into the crowd and ran.

And ran.

And ran.

The other girl couldn't keep up with her – definitely not a Tlascalan then! – and Tozi very soon gave her the slip, crossing the whole width of the pen from the rear wall to the bamboo bars at the corner of the north and west wings, and burrowing in amongst hundreds of women who had gathered there to stare out through the bars across the smooth paving of the plaza towards the steep northern stairway of the great pyramid.

Even though the routine dawn sacrifices had already been carried out, Tozi sensed the familiar mood of ominous anticipation in the air, her flesh prickled and the pounding pain in her head grew worse.

Just ten days previously the old year, *13-Tochtli*, 'Thirteen-Rabbit', had come to an end and the new year, *1-Acatl*, 'One-Reed', had begun, taking its turn again for the first time in fifty-two years, as was the case for each one of the fifty-two named years that danced the circle of the great Calendar Round. There was something special about One-Reed, however – something terrifying for all devotees of the war god Hummingbird, but most notably for the rulers of the Mexica themselves. As everyone knew, One-Reed years were linked inextricably to Quetzalcoatl, god of peace, Hummingbird's great antagonist. Indeed it had long ago been prophesied that when Quetzalcoatl returned he would do so in a One-Reed year.

In Nahuatl, the language spoken by the Mexica, the name Quetzalcoatl meant 'Feathered Serpent'. Ancient traditions maintained that he had been the first god-king of the lands now ruled by the Mexica. Born in a One-Reed year, he had been a god of goodness who was said to have stopped up his ears with his fingers when addressed on the subject of war. The traditions described him as tall, fair-skinned, ruddy complexioned and richly bearded. The traditions also told how Hummingbird and Tezcatlipoca, that other god of violence whose name meant 'Smoking Mirror', had plotted against Quetzalcoatl and succeeded in driving him out of Mexico – and how he had been forced to flee across the eastern ocean on a raft of serpents. This, too, had happened in a One-Reed year. Before departing from the Yucatán coast, Quetzalcoatl had prophesied that he would return many years in the future, once again in a One-Reed year. When that time came, he said, he would cross back over the eastern ocean, 'in a boat that moved by itself without paddles', and would appear in great power to overthrow the cults of Hummingbird and Tezcatlipoca. All those who followed them would be cast down into Mictlan, the shadowy realm of the dead, a wicked king would be overthrown and a new era would begin when the gods would once again accept sacrifices of fruits and flowers and cease their clamour for human blood.

For the ten days since the inception of the current One-Reed year, there had been rumours that a new cycle of sacrifices was planned, a spectacular festival of blood to appease and strengthen Hummingbird against the possible return of Quetzalcoatl. Guessing the commotion at the pyramid must be connected with this, Tozi decided Coyotl would have to wait a few more moments while she found out. Holding her hand over the pocket where the medicine tubes lay, she wormed forward through the crowd until her face was jammed against the bars.

As usual the pyramid impressed itself upon her as forcefully as a blow to the face. Towering in the midst of the plaza, glowing poison-ously in the sun, its four levels were painted respectively green, red, turquoise and yellow. On the summit platform, tall, narrow and dark and seeming to eat up the light that shone down on it, stood Hummingbird's temple.

Tozi gasped when she saw that Moctezuma himself, dressed in all his finery, was amongst the black-robed priests clustered round the altar in front of the temple. Less surprising was the presence of fifty, she counted them – no, fifty-two! – lean and beautiful young Tlascalan men, daubed with white paint, dressed in paper garments, who were trudging with heavy feet up the steep steps of the northern stairway.

Tozi had seen many deaths in the past seven months, inflicted in many ingenious and horrible ways. Despite all her efforts to stay alive she was constantly afraid she might be snatched aside by the priests and murdered at any moment. Still she could not rid herself of the pain she felt whenever she saw others climbing the pyramid to die, and she gasped as the first young man reached the top of the steps.

At once a drum began to beat.

Four burly priests flung the victim on his back over the killing stone and took position at each of his arms and legs, holding him down tight, stretching his chest. Then, with the jerky, ungainly movements of a puppet, Moctezuma loomed over him, clutching a long obsidian knife that glinted in the sun. Tozi had seen it all before but still she watched, rooted to the spot, as the Great Speaker raised the knife and plunged it to the hilt in the victim's sternum. He cut upward, urgent but precise. When he found the heart he sliced it vigorously from its moorings, snatched it out amidst fountains of blood, and placed it, still beating, on the brazier in front of Hummingbird's temple. There was a great hissing and sizzling and a burst of steam and smoke rose up at the top of the pyramid. Then the victim's body was rolled off the stone and Tozi heard hacking and rending sounds as skilled butcher priests fell on it and amputated the arms and legs for later consumption. She saw the head being carried into the temple to be spitted on the skull rack. Finally the torso was sent rolling and bouncing down the pyramid steps, leaving bloody smears all the way to the plaza below where it would soon be joined in a rising heap by the unwanted remains of all the other docile young men presently climbing the northern stairway.

Tozi knew from seven months of witnessing such scenes that the pile of torsos would be gathered up in wheelbarrows after nightfall and trundled off to feed the wild beasts in Moctezuma's zoo.

The Mexica were monsters, she thought. So cruel. She hated them! She would never be their docile victim!

But evading them was becoming more difficult.

Three searing beats of pain shook her head, and a burst of flashing lights exploded before her eyes. She clenched her teeth to stop herself crying out.

It wasn't just that she'd started to be noticed by some of the other prisoners – though that was dangerous enough. The real problem was caring for Coyotl, a huge responsibility that she knew she could not hope to sustain in these conditions. The only solution was to find a way to fade for longer than a ten count without having a massive physical collapse. Then she could get them out of here.

Tozi edged back and took her eyes off the pyramid, distracted for a moment by the way the morning sun poured through the bamboo prison bars creating stripes of deep shadow and stripes of intense, brilliant light, filled with swirling motes of dust. Suddenly she thought she saw the tall, beautiful woman again, gliding through the haze like a ghost. She blinked and the woman was gone.

Who are you? thought Tozi. *Are you a witch like me?* She felt the cool, packed earth of the floor under her feet and sensed the warmth and odours of the other prisoners all around her. Then, like an evil spirit, a breeze smelling of blood blew up out of the southeast and the screams of Moctezuma's next victim filled the air.

Normally the high priest wielded the obsidian knife, and Moctezuma would not become involved except on the most important State occasions. It followed that only something very significant could explain his presence here this morning.

With a shudder Tozi turned her back on the pyramid and moved swiftly through the crowd, disturbing no one, to the place where she had left Coyotl.

Chapter Three

Santiago, Cuba, Thursday 18 February 1519

Pepillo was halfway along the larger of the two piers jutting out into Santiago Harbour. He felt stunned and confused by the bustle and the noise. Every berth on both sides of the pier was filled with carracks, caravels and brigantines, and every ship was loading supplies at a feverish, almost frantic, pace – bags of cassava, barrels of wine and water, barrels of salt pork and dried fish, live pigs squealing and protesting, horses, guns, troops of grim-looking men . . .

A drunken sailor with the face of an ape made a sudden grab for one of the two huge leather bags Pepillo was carrying. He dodged back and the sailor lost his balance and fell heavily to the cobbles. 'You little whoreson,' he roared, 'I'm going to kill you for that.'

'For what?' Pepillo squeaked, backing away, still clutching the bags.

With horrible grunts the sailor levered himself onto one knee, struggled upright and lurched forward with his hands outstretched. Pepillo was already running. He heard footsteps closing rapidly behind him, then a sudden change in rhythm, and as he turned to look back over his shoulder he saw the drunk stumble, lose his balance and tumble to the cobbles again. There were hoots of derision, jeers and roars of laughter from the growing crowd of onlookers and the sailor glared up in fury at Pepillo.

Short, small-boned and delicately built for his fourteen years, Pepillo kept hoping for a growth spurt that would make him tall, robust and formidable. Now, he thought, as the sailor spat curses at him, would be an excellent moment to gain a span or two in height, and an arroba or two of solid muscle in weight. It would also be good if his hands doubled in size and quadrupled in strength in the process. He would not object to facial hair, and felt that a beard would endow him with an air of authority.

His arms aching, his fingers stiff, Pepillo hurried on, weaving through the thick crowds thronging the pier until his drunken attacker was lost from sight. Only when he was sure he was not pursued did he allow himself to set down the two enormously heavy bags. They clunked and clanged as though they were filled with hammers, knives and horseshoes.

How strange, Pepillo thought. It was not his business to wonder why his new master would travel with more metal than a blacksmith, but for the twentieth time that morning he had to suppress an urge to open the bags and take a look.

It was just one of the mysteries that had exploded into his life after Matins when he had been informed he would be leaving the monastery to serve a friar who was not known to him, a certain Father Gaspar Muñoz who had arrived that night from the Dominican mission in Hispaniola. There had been some sort of dispute with Customs officials, and after it Father Muñoz had gone directly to another vessel waiting in the harbour, a hundred-ton carrack named the *Santa María de la Concepción*. Although Pepillo could not yet really believe his good luck, it seemed he and the Father were to sail in this vessel to bring the Christian faith to certain New Lands recently discovered lying to the west. Pepillo was to present himself to Muñoz on board ship, after first passing the Customs House and collecting four leather bags, the good Father's personal belongings that had been detained there.

Pepillo flexed his fingers and looked at the bags with hatred before he picked them up again. He hadn't been able to carry all four at once, so there were two more exactly like them he would have to return for when these were delivered.

As he walked he scanned the dockside through the milling, noisy, crowd. There was no breeze, and a cloying smell of fish, decay and excrement clung thick in the muggy morning air. Above, in the cloudless blue sky, seabirds wheeled and shrieked. There were sailors and soldiers everywhere carrying sacks of supplies, tools, weapons. Gruff Castilian voices shouted abuse, instructions, directions.

Pepillo came to a big three-masted carrack that loomed to his left like the wall of a fortress. Five massive cavalry horses were being led up a rickety gangplank onto the deck, where a noble lord, dressed out in great finery, with a mane of blond hair falling to his shoulders, was directing operations. Pepillo squinted to read the ship's faded nameplate: *San Sebastián*. Then, beyond it on the right, almost at the end of the pier, he spotted another even larger carrack with jibs and derricks set up all around it and teams of men loading supplies. Pepillo walked closer. This ship had a high aftcastle and the new design of low-slung forecastle for better manoeuvrability against the wind. Another few steps and he made out the name: *Santa María de la Concepción*.

A gangplank sloped up to the deck right in front of him. With trepidation, holding his master's bags tight, Pepillo stepped on to it.

'Who are you? What do you think you're doing here?'

'I'm . . . I'm . . .'

'Tell me your business here!'

'I'm . . . I'm . . .'

'You're a puking dog breath.'

Pepillo didn't know whether he should laugh or take offence. The boy he confronted was a year or two older than him, at least a foot taller, much broader across the chest and made all the more formidable by a completely shaven, gleaming head. He was also black as tar from head to toe.

Pepillo had encountered Negroes before, but they'd all been slaves. This one didn't behave like a slave and was much too big to fight, so he forced a laugh. 'OK, yeah, great,' he said. He pretended to wipe tears of mirth from his eyes. 'Very funny . . .' He held out his hand: 'The name's Pepillo . . .' He laughed. 'Pepillo Dogbreath!' Another laugh. 'And you are?'

'Melchior,' said the other boy. He ignored the proffered hand.

'Melchior,' repeated Pepillo. 'Right. Good to meet you.' He awkwardly withdrew his hand: 'Look . . . You asked me my business here and it's very simple. I'm trying to find my master's quarters.' He indicated the two large leather bags he'd been lugging on board the *Santa María de la Concepción* when Melchior had confronted him. He'd dumped them on deck at the end of the gangplank, right below the forecastle. 'My master's belongings,' Pepillo explained. 'He came in from Hispaniola this morning and they were held up in the Customs House. I'm supposed to bring them to his cabin . . .'

An angry frown contorted Melchior's face. There was something ferocious about this frown. Something hateful. Perhaps even something frightening. 'This master of yours,' he spat. 'He have a name?'

'Father Gaspar Muñoz.'

'Muñoz!' The frowned deepened, became a grimace.

'Yes, Muñoz. You know him?'

'He got stick legs, this Muñoz? Like a crow? He got a little fat belly? How about his front teeth? Look like he been sucking too hard on something he shouldn't?'

Pepillo giggled at the crude image: 'I don't know,' he said. 'I've never seen my master before.'

'Huh?'

'I was assigned to him this morning and—'

'—Assigned? Assigned you say? That's a pretty word . . .'

'I was sent straight to the Customs House for his bags. There's two more I still have to fetch . . .'

A shadow distracted Pepillo and he glanced up to see a heavy brass cannon soaring overhead in a cat's cradle of ropes. With raucous shouts, and much squealing of pulleys, a gang of sailors manoeuvred it into the deep shadows of the hold.

'That's one of the lombards,' said Melchior. A note of pride crept into his voice: 'We've got three of them with the fleet. You can settle a lot of arguments with guns like that.'

'Are we expecting a lot of arguments?'

'Are you kidding?' Melchior sneered. 'After what happened last year?'

Pepillo decided not to bluff: '*What* happened last year?'

'The Córdoba expedition?'

Pepillo shrugged. It meant nothing to him.

'Hernandez de Córdoba led a fleet of three ships to explore the New Lands, see what trade was to be had there and bring the word of Christ to the Indians. He had a hundred and ten men with him. I was one of them.' Melchior paused: 'Seventy of us got killed.' Another pause: 'Seventy! Córdoba himself died of his wounds and we barely had enough hands on deck to sail back. It's been the talk of Santiago ever since. How can you not know anything about it?'

'I've been living in a monastery . . .'

'So?'

'We don't get much news there.'

Melchior laughed. It was a big, easy laugh, as though he was genuinely amused. 'You a monk?' he asked eventually. 'Or some such?'

'Not a monk,' said Pepillo. 'The Dominicans took me in when I was orphaned, taught me to read, taught me to clerk, taught me to keep numbers.'

'Ah, that would be why they chose you to serve Father Muñoz.'

'I don't understand.'

'He's our Inquisitor,' said Melchior. 'He'll need numbers and letters and clerking to keep track of all those people he's going to burn.' He leaned down, put his mouth close to Pepillo's ear: 'Muñoz was with us on the Córdoba expedition too,' he whispered. 'People used to say he was "vigilant for God". Vigilant for the devil's closer to the truth! It was him as caused all the trouble.'

As Melchior told the story, Muñoz had been so 'vigilant for God' during his time as Inquisitor with the Córdoba expedition that he had burned whole Indian villages to the ground and consigned their entire populations – men, women and children – to horrible deaths in the flames.

'But why would he do that?' asked Pepillo. He felt outraged.

'We brought them the word of Christ,' said Melchior, 'and they accepted conversion, but when we moved on some of them returned to the worship of their old gods.' He lowered his voice: 'Can't blame them really. They didn't think they'd see us again, but we came back and Muñoz rooted out the heretics and burnt them . . .'

'Didn't he give them a second chance? People like that who were new to the faith?'

'Never. Sometimes he tortured them first to make them name other heretics so he could burn them too. But I never saw him give anyone a second chance. Maybe that's why he brought the wrath of God down on our heads . . .'

'Wrath of God?'

'Thousands of angry Indians, driven mad by his cruelties, hell-bent on revenge. We had to fight our way out. Those of us that lived . . . we all hate Muñoz.'

There was an earsplitting crash as a massive ramp dropped into place and half a dozen trembling, sweating cavalry horses were led on board to makeshift stalls further aft. They neighed and snickered. One of them deposited an enormous heap of dung. Their iron hooves rang on the deck.

'You been to sea before?' Melchior asked.

Pepillo said he'd sailed with the Dominican mission from Spain to Hispaniola when he was six and again on the much shorter journey from Hispaniola to Cuba when he was nine.

'And since then?'

Pepillo told Melchior he'd lived in Cuba for the last five years, most of that time spent here in Santiago, helping old Rodriguez in the monastery library, assisting Brother Pedro with the accounts, running errands for Borges the quartermaster, and doing odd jobs for anyone who asked.

'Sounds boring,' prompted Melchior.

Pepillo remembered how he'd secretly yearned for freedom from the drab routine of his life and dreamed of stowing away on a ship and sailing to distant lands. Now, unexpectedly, it seemed his dreams were about to come true and it was all thanks to his new and as yet unknown master, the increasingly mysterious Father Gaspar Muñoz. Melchior might be right that he was a nasty piece of work, but for the moment Pepillo simply felt overjoyed to be on board this great vibrant ship, to feel its timbers move beneath his feet, to hear the shouts of the sailors in the rigging and the creak of the towering masts and to know that, very soon, he would be going . . . somewhere.

Anywhere . . .

Which wasn't the library.

Hurrah!

Which wasn't counting beans in Don Pedro's windowless cell.

Hurrah again!

The *Santa María* was a hundred feet in length, big enough, Pepillo thought, to serve as flagship for what was obviously a major expedition.

21

Judging from the other ships – surely at least ten of them! – also loading supplies, weapons and soldiers along the dock, something much more than preaching the faith was going on here.

'All these preparations,' Pepillo asked. 'All these soldiers. What are they for? Where are we going?'

Melchior scratched his head. 'You mean you really haven't heard?'

'I told you. I've been living in a monastery. I don't hear anything.'

Melchior drew himself up to his full height and pointed theatrically due west: 'If you sail in that direction for four days,' he said, 'you come to the mainland we explored last year with Córdoba. It's a beautiful land, and there seems to be no end to it. There are mountains, and navigable rivers, and great cities and fertile fields there, and gold and many precious things.

'And that's where we're going?'

'Yes, God willing . . . It's a fine land. We can all become rich there.'

Melchior had been so hostile just moments before, but he already seemed much more likeable. In this alien world of ships and warriors, Pepillo thought, was it too much to hope he might have found a friend?

'You're thinking I might become your friend,' said Melchior. 'Don't waste your time. It's never going to happen.'

'I'm not thinking any such thing,' said Pepillo. He was surprised at how indignant he managed to sound, and how disappointed he felt. 'I don't want to be friends with you. It was you who started talking to me.' He picked up the bags: 'Just tell me which way to go for my master's cabin.'

'I'll show you,' said Melchior, 'but you must not vex me with friendship.'

'Look, I already told you I don't want your friendship! I've got my job to do. I'm sure you've got yours . . .' Pepillo paused, realising he hadn't yet asked. 'What *is* your job by the way?'

Melchior's chest visibly swelled: 'I'm manservant to the caudillo,' he said.

'The caudillo?'

'Cortés himself.'

Cortés . . . Cortés . . . Another name Pepillo was apparently supposed to know.

22

'He bought me after the Córdoba expedition,' Melchior continued, 'and then he set me free.'

'And you stayed with him? Even after he gave you freedom?'

'Why wouldn't I? He's a great man.'

Melchior had led Pepillo to the rear of the ship and now pointed to the twin doors at the back of the navigation deck below the aftcastle. 'All the rest of us bunk on the main deck,' he said, 'but those are the cabins for your master and mine. It used to be one big stateroom with two doors, but my master partitioned it into two rooms to accommodate your master.' Melchior looked furtively around: 'Muñoz hasn't come on board yet,' he sniffed. 'I expect he's up to no good in town.'

'Hasn't come on board? He's supposed to have been here since before dawn . . .'

'Not my problem. Like I say, he'll be up to no good in town.'

'That sounds sinister . . . and a bit mysterious.'

'He's a sinister man, your master.' Melchior leaned closer, lowered his voice to a whisper: 'There's something you have to know about him . . .'

But Pepillo had suddenly remembered the second pair of bags. 'Tell me later,' he interrupted. 'I have to go back to the Customs House right now!' He put down the bags he was carrying: 'Will you stow these in my master's cabin? I beg you. I've got no one else to ask.'

Melchior nodded. 'I'll stow the bags,' he said, 'and here's my advice. Whatever you need to do at the Customs House, make it snappy. Cortés has itchy feet.' He lowered his voice still further: 'A lot of supplies have been brought aboard at night. I think he's about to pull a trick on Velázquez.'

Velázquez! Now there was a name Pepillo did know. Diego de Velázquez, the conqueror and governor of Cuba, the most powerful man on the island whose word was law. 'The governor?' he asked, realising how stupid he sounded even as he said it. 'He's involved in this?'

'Of course he's involved! He's the one who gave Cortés command of the expedition. He's paid for three of the ships out of his own pocket.'

'So why would Cortés want to pull a trick on him?'

Once more Melchior glanced shiftily around. 'Rumour has it,' he whispered, 'that Velázquez grows jealous. He imagines all the gold Cortés will win in the New Lands and wants it for himself. There are those who say he will relieve Cortés of command and put someone else he's better able to control in charge.'

'He can't control Cortés then?'

'Never! Cortés has always been his own man.'

'So why did he appoint him in the first place?'

'There was bad blood between them in the past. Something about Cortés getting the governor's niece pregnant and then refusing to marry her. It all happened a couple of years ago and I don't know the details, but maybe Velázquez felt sorry about the way he treated Cortés then. He put him in jail for eight months, threatened him with death and only pardoned him when he agreed to marry the girl. Maybe he gave him the expedition to keep him sweet after all that . . .'

Pepillo whistled: 'And now he wants to take it away from him again?'

'Which Cortés won't accept! I'd say he's a man who would sail with the fleet even before it's properly loaded. He's quite the lawyer, and if he never gets the order relieving him of command then he won't be breaking any rules.'

Pepillo felt a knot of fear in his stomach.

It was a new fear.

He feared the unfamiliar world of the ship, but now he feared even more an enforced return to the familiar prison of the monastery.

He told himself he was being ridiculous – that this caudillo called Cortés was still in the midst of loading his fleet and couldn't possibly be ready to embark for at least another three days. Muñoz wasn't on board, after all, and surely the fleet would not sail without its Inquisitor? Even so, Pepillo couldn't shake the feeling of lurking dread. With a shout of thanks to Melchior, he charged down the aft gangway onto the pier, swerved to avoid a water-seller, dodged around a butcher's cart, stretched out his legs and ran.

He was still daunted by the chaos and confusion of the piers and the harbour, but he didn't think it would be difficult to find his way back to the Customs House. All he had to do was retrace, in reverse, the route he had taken this morning.

The *San Sebastián* now lay on his right and, as Pepillo approached

24

the big carrack, he saw a mounted herald on the dockside, waiting at the foot of a gangplank. The herald was dressed in the scarlet and gold livery of the governorate and his splendid black horse wore a trapper of the same design.

Pepillo ran on, arms and legs pumping, not wanting anything to slow him down. But when he was twenty paces past the herald he heard a sound like a cannonade and turned to see another rider on an even bigger horse charging down the gangplank from the deck of the *San Sebastián*. The horse was white, like a vision from a legend, and Pepillo recognised the flying blond hair and the fine clothes of the noble lord he'd glimpsed earlier. Then the herald's horse bolted and both men rode past him at full gallop, one on either side, shaking the earth under their iron-shod hooves and filling his ears with thunder.

Pepillo's legs felt momentarily weak – the monstrous horses had seemed certain to trample him – but he kept on running towards the Customs House, intent on extracting his master's bags and getting back to the *Santa María* in the shortest possible time.

He sensed something in the air, like a bowstring stretched to breaking point, like a great storm about to burst.

Melchior was right.

This fleet was poised to sail.

Chapter Four

Moctezuma set down the obsidian knife, wiped blood from his eyes and took stock of the remaining victims on the northern stairway.

It was as he thought. He had killed forty-one and eleven were left. Just eleven!

And the war god showed no more sign of appearing to him now than at any other time in the past five years.

Clearly it had been a mistake to begin with only fifty-two victims, even if they were the pick of the crop from the war with the Tlascalans. The priests had said Hummingbird would be pleased with such a number, symbolic of a complete cycle of years in the Calendar Round. But if that was true, then wouldn't he have been even more pleased with five hundred and twenty?

An idea was beginning to take shape. Perhaps the god grew bored with male victims? Perhaps females would entice him to appear?

Five hundred and twenty ripe and fertile young females.

Moctezuma shrugged off his blood-drenched robes, let them drop with a heavy slap to the floor, stepped away naked but for a loincloth, and took up the knife again.

The next victim had already been forced down onto the sacrificial stone where he lay gasping with fear, his whole body trembling, his eyes rolling wildly. Such behaviour was not seemly for a warrior and Moctezuma took pleasure in castrating the man before slicing him open from groin to breastbone, dragging forth some loops of his intestines, puncturing his stomach, rummaging around in the mess for his spleen and, finally, amidst a crescendo of screams, ripping out his heart. A great, hot gush of blood spurted up and came spattering down again like a rainstorm as the corpse was rolled away.

Some victims, Moctezuma had noticed, just seemed to have more blood than others. Why was that?

He killed another man. And another. Sticky clots clung around his fingers where he gripped the knife. There was blood in his eyes, in his mouth, clogging his nose.

He rested a moment while the assistants prepared the next victim, and beckoned Ahuizotl, his high priest, whose bulging yellow eyes, blotchy skin, gaping nostrils, crooked teeth and lecherous monkey features greatly resembled those of the manipulative and vicious species of water monster after which he was named. The high priest was his man, bought and paid for, and he strode forward now in his black, blood-smeared robes.

'You did not give me good advice,' Moctezuma told him. His voice was soft, but there was a deliberate edge of implied threat and Ahuizotl looked worried.

As well you might, thought Moctezuma. *As well you might. I could have you strangled in your sleep.*

Ahuizotl kept his eyes downcast: 'I humbly apologise to Your Magnificence if I have failed you in any way. My life is yours to dispose of.'

'Your life is always mine to dispose of . . .'

Ahuizotl began to bare his breast but Moctezuma reached out a bloody hand to stop him: 'Spare me the theatricals. I don't want your heart. Not yet anyway.' He looked up at the sun which was high in the sky, standing close to noon. 'The god does not appear to me,' he said, 'because we have not offered an adequate basket of victims. I expect you to remedy this situation, Ahuizotl. Be back here in two hours with five hundred and twenty young women for me to kill.'

'Five hundred and twenty!' Ahuizotl's mournful face registered shock. 'In two hours? Impossible.'

Moctezuma's voice grew softer: 'Why is it always your instinct to say "no", Ahuizotl?' he asked. 'Learn to say yes if you wish the light of my presence to shine upon you.'

'Yes, Magnificence.'

'Very good. So I shall expect five hundred and twenty young women then?'

'Yes, Magnificence.'

'The younger the better. I do not insist that they be virgins. I don't expect you to perform miracles, you see. But I want them here in two hours.'

Dumb witness to this exchange, still stretched across the sacrificial stone and awaiting the first cut, the next victim trembled. Nonetheless, Moctezuma noted approvingly, he continued to hold himself under some sort of control. That took courage. He raised the obsidian dagger and plunged it deep into the man's bare chest, delighting in his screams as he sawed the blade savagely upwards, splitting the breastbone and exposing the palpitating heart.

'Watch and be thankful as the Great Speaker of the Mexica takes your life,' whispered Moctezuma. He began to cut again, busy now, with his nose in the gaping chest cavity, working close-up with the knife, soaked in streams of blood, severing the thick vessels that encircled the beating heart until the whole quivering, dripping organ came loose in his hands and he flung it on the brazier where it hissed and smoked.

Priests rolled the body away; even as they were butchering it, a new victim was dragged into place over the sacrificial stone.

Out of the corner of his eye Moctezuma saw Ahuizotl leaving the summit of the pyramid with three of his black-robed entourage – no doubt to round up the women he'd demanded for sacrifice.

'Wait,' he called after them.

Ahuizotl turned to look back.

'Before you bring me the women,' said Moctezuma, 'you will bring me the Flesh of the Gods.'

Sometimes, an hour or two before being sacrificed, specially favoured victims were fed the mushrooms called *teonanácatl*, the 'Flesh of the Gods', which unleashed fearsome visions of deities and demons.

More rarely, the sacrificer himself would partake of the mushrooms.

After he had killed the last of the fifty-two young men, Moctezuma received a runner sent by Ahuizotl, who had climbed the pyramid to bring him a linen bag containing seven fat, finger-length mushrooms. Their silver-grey fish-belly skins gave way to shades of blue and purple around the stems. They exuded a faint, bitter, woody aroma.

Seven big *teonanácatl* amounted, Moctezuma knew, to a sizeable, probably terrifying, dose, but he was prepared to eat them to engineer an encounter with Hummingbird, war god of the Mexica, whose representative on earth he was. In the early days of his reign the god had come to him often as a disembodied voice speaking inside his head, present at every sacrifice, giving him commands, guiding him in every decision he took, but as the years passed the voice became fainter and more distant and, for the last five years, as the ominous year One-Reed slowly approached, he had not heard it at all.

Priests were still hovering round him but Moctezuma ordered them away, telling them he required two hours of perfect peace before the next bout of sacrifices began.

He watched as they filed down the steps. When complete silence fell he stripped off his sodden loincloth and advanced naked into the shadows of Hummingbird's temple, clutching the bag of mushrooms.

The temple, which was built on the broad summit of the pyramid, was a tall stone building. Its two principal rooms were luridly illuminated by the guttering flames of burning torches.

Moctezuma put a mushroom in his mouth and began to chew. It tasted of death, of decay. He added two more and walked into the first room.

Lined up on both sides of the wall, skewered from ear to ear on long horizontal poles, taking their place amongst other, older trophies, were the dripping heads of the fifty-two men he'd spent the morning killing. He remembered some of their faces. Their wide, staring eyes. Their mouths frozen as they screamed their last.

He confronted one of the heads, pushed right up to it, glared into the vacant eyes, wiped blood from the high cheekbones and thin lips.

It made him feel powerful to encounter the so-recently living.

He moved on, into the second room.

Here, curiously patterned in the light and shadow cast by the flickering torches and the high, narrow windows, with a huge serpent

29

fashioned from pearls and precious stones coiled about its waist, was Hummingbird's squat and massive idol. Carved from solid granite, its eyes, tusks, teeth, claws, feathers and scales glittered with jade, polished horn and obsidian and the most precious gold and jewels; a golden bow was clutched in its right fist, a sheaf of golden arrows in its left, and a necklace of human hearts, hands and skulls was strung around its neck. The idol's snarling mouth was smeared with gore and lumps of meat where priests had forced the half-cooked hearts of the victims through it into the reeking receptacle beyond.

Moctezuma sat down cross-legged on the floor in front of the great idol and slowly and methodically ate the rest of the mushrooms.

For a very long time nothing happened. Then at last the disembodied voice he thought had deserted him was back inside his head:

'Do you bring me hearts?' the voice asked.

Chapter Five

Tenochtitlan, Thursday 18 February 1519

'This medicine is bitter,' complained Coyotl. 'Why must I finish it?'

'Because I say you must finish it,' said Tozi. 'I who obtained it for you at great expense. It will take away your pain.'

'How great was the expense, Tozi?' The little boy, who should have been born a merchant, was always inquisitive about anything to do with barter and exchange.

'It was very great, Coyotl.' *Greater than you can possibly know.* 'Pay me back by finishing it.'

'But I hate it, Tozi. It tastes of . . . uggh – bird shit!'

'So you're some kind of expert on the taste of bird shit?'

Coyotl giggled: 'It tastes like this medicine you are forcing me to eat.' Despite his protests, he had already swallowed almost the whole first dose of the noxious-smelling red paste. He was stretched out quite comfortably on the ground, with his head in Tozi's lap, and he now unwillingly ate the rest of the drug.

Coyotl was six years old. He was in the women's pen, rather than amongst the males, because his genitals had been hacked off in infancy by his parents, leaving only a slit. This had been done as an offering to Tezcatlipoca, 'Smoking Mirror', Lord of the Near and the Nigh. Four days ago those same loving parents had dedicated the rest of their son to the war god Hummingbird, whose temple stood on the summit of the great pyramid, and had delivered him to the fattening pen to await sacrifice. The other women in the pen had shunned him, as they did all freaks and oddities, but Tozi had taken him under her wing and they had become friends.

'You need to sleep now!' she said. 'Give the medicine a chance to do its work.'

'Sleep!' Coyotl's response was high-pitched and indignant. 'I don't think so.' But his eyes were already drooping closed.

Tozi was seated cross-legged. She blinked, rubbed her aching temples and yawned. She felt dizzy, perhaps a little sick. Though she had sustained it only for a five count, her brief, intense fade had exhausted her more than she'd realised. Her head nodded forward, sleep overmastered her and she dreamed, as she often did, of her mother the witch. In the dream, her mother was with her still, comforting her, teaching her and then, strangely, whispering in her ear, 'Wake up, wake up . . .'

'Wake up!'

It was not her mother's voice! The moment of confusion between dream and reality passed and Tozi, now fully alert, found herself face to face with the beautiful young woman who'd haunted her earlier. 'You . . .' she began.

Then she choked back her words.

Behind the woman, less than fifty paces away, four of the black-robed priests of Hummingbird had entered the pen, followed by armed enforcers, and were hauling fresh victims aside.

Although momentarily preoccupied with other prisoners, the priests were moving fast and making straight for them.

'Are you going to let them kill us?' the woman said. She spoke in a throaty whisper, her voice low and filled with urgent power. 'Or are you going to make us disappear?'

Tozi winced as a burst of pain struck her head. 'Us?' she said as the spasm passed. 'What us?'

'You, me and the little one,' said the woman. She glanced down at Coyotl, who stirred and grumbled in his sleep. 'Make us disappear the way you make yourself disappear.'

'If I could make myself disappear, do you think I'd still be in this prison?'

'That's your business,' the woman said. 'But I saw what happened this morning. I saw you fade. Then you were gone.'

The woman was crouched next to her, her sleek black hair shadowing her face, her body emanating a warm, intense musk, and for the second time that day, Tozi felt the dangerous pull of a connection, as though she had known her all her life. Making no sudden movements that might attract unwelcome attention, she looked round, taking stock of their predicament, automatically tuning in to the feverish agitation of the crowd, probing to see if there was something she could use.

Whatever it was, it could not be another fade. She cursed herself for employing the spell of invisibility earlier, when it had not been a matter as desperate as this. But with her head pounding so very badly, Tozi knew it would be at least another day, perhaps two, before she dared risk it again.

The pen was massively overcrowded and the sudden arrival of the priests at this unexpected hour had sparked off a mindstorm of fear. Most prisoners knew not to bolt – that was the fastest way to be selected for sacrifice – but there was a general cringing and drawing back, as from the approach of a savage beast.

Tozi recognised the high priest Ahuizotl in the lead, a vigorous, evil-looking, mean-mouthed old man with mottled skin. His black robes and thick, shoulder-length grey hair glistened with oozing curds of freshly clotted gore, and his blunt, bestial face was set in an expression of thunderous rage. Flanked by his three assistants, also copiously smeared and splashed with blood, he cut a swathe across the crowded floor of the pen, selecting women – all young – whom he pointed out with furious jabs of his spear. Armed enforcers at once restrained the protesting, terrified, screaming victims and led them off.

'I can only hide two of us from them,' Tozi volunteered abruptly, 'but I can't hide three. So it's you, or the kid.'

The woman pushed back her hair and a ray of sunlight, lancing deep into the prison through some crack in the roof, caught flecks of jade and gold in her irises and set her eyes ablaze. 'You must save the child of course,' she said.

It was the right answer.

'I lied,' Tozi whispered to the woman, 'I think I can get all three of us out of this. Anyway I'm going to try.'

'But . . .'

33

'Stay still. Whatever happens, you have to stay still. You have to stay quiet.'

Tozi glanced up. Ahuizotl was pushing towards them, just twenty paces away, every angry lunge of his spear nominating another victim. This was a man who'd taken countless lives for Hummingbird and Tozi sensed his blood power. He would not be easy to deflect or confuse.

Neither were the younger priests to be underestimated, with their cruel sneers and long, lean fingers.

So she scanned groups of prisoners milling nearby and her eyes fell, with a feeling of real gratitude, on Xoco and two of her gang. They were off to the left, trying, like everyone else, not to attract the attention of the priests.

Tozi started to sing. '*Hmm-a-hmm-hmm . . . hmm-hm . . . Hmm-a-hmm-hmm . . . hmm-hmm.*' The sound was so low as to be almost inaudible. But it didn't matter how quiet or how loud you sang it. What mattered was the sequence of the notes, the tempo of their repetition and the intent of the singer.

Tozi's intent was to save herself, and poor Coyotl and this strange, mysterious woman. She cared nothing for Xoco. '*Hmm-a-hmm-hmm . . . hmm-hm,*' she sang. '*Hmm-a-hmm-hmm . . . hmm-hmm.*' She kept winding up the tempo, as her mother had taught her, and felt the fog flowing out of her, invisible like breath, unsettling the senses and lightening the heads of everyone it touched. People stumbled, collapsed, barged into one another, became aggressive and reckless, and the priests of Hummingbird spun round seeking the source of the commotion. Then the mental fog slammed into Xoco who started up from the floor where she was crouching and charged straight at Ahuizotl. He was too surprised to avoid her and when she hit him with all her weight he went down hard, smashing his head into the ground.

Chaos erupted as priests fought to subdue and shackle Xoco. She seemed supernaturally strong and howled like a demon. There were not enough enforcers to stop the many other fights spreading like wildfire through the crowd.

'Now we get out of here,' said Tozi. She swept up Coyotl, still in a deep sleep, and signalled to the woman to follow her.

Chapter Six

The hill was steep, filled with hollows and overgrown with tall, feathery grass. That was why Shikotenka had been drawn to it. He'd found a deep crevice about halfway up the slope and snaked his lean, hard-muscled body into it just as dawn was breaking, hiding himself completely from view to observe the Mexica as they converged in the vast natural amphitheatre below. There were four regiments, each at their full strength of eight thousand men, and he counted them in as they approached one by one through passes in the surrounding hills, a huge and fearsome war machine the size of a city, mustering here as the day wore on to bring murder and mayhem to Tlascala.

Dressed only in a loincloth and sandals, his thick black hair drawn back from his brow in long, matted braids, Shikotenka's chest, abdomen, legs and arms, now pressed tightly into the soil and rock of his home-land, were criss-crossed with the scars of battle wounds received in hand-to-hand combat against the Mexica. At thirty-three years of age he had already been a warrior for seventeen years. The experience showed in the flat, impassive planes of his face and the determined set of his wide, sensual mouth, which masked equally the cold cruelty and calculation of which he was capable as well as the bravery, resolve and inspired flights of rash brilliance that had led to his election, just a month before, as the battle king of Tlascala. A man of direct action, he had not thought of delegating a subordinate for today's assignment. The very survival of his people depended on what happened in the next day and night and he would trust this task to no one else.

Eyes narrowed, he watched as teams from the first of the enemy regiments used ropes and pegs to mark out the perimeter of a great

35

circle on the open plain. The circle was then divided into four segments. Thereafter as each regiment arrived it was directed to its own segment of the circle, and the men at once set about pitching tents that varied in size from compact two-man units to enormous marquees and pavilions, where the standards of leading officers were raised. Meanwhile scouts were sent out in small, fast-moving squads to comb the nearby hills for spies and ambushes. Five times already, men beating the bush had passed uncomfortably close to where Shikotenka lay hidden.

Was it possible, he wondered, to hate an entire people as intensely as he hated the Mexica, and yet still admire them?

Their organisation, for example. Their toughness. Their efficiency. Their obsidian-hard will. Their absolute, ruthless, uncompromising commitment to power. Their limitless capacity for violence.

Weren't these all admirable qualities in their own right?

Moreover, here in force, in their tens of thousands, he had to admit they made a stunning impact on the senses.

His vantage point was five clear bowshots from the edge of their camp, yet his nostrils were filled with the reek of copal incense and putrid human blood, the characteristic stink of the Mexica that clung about them like a half-articulated threat wherever they gathered in large numbers.

Also rising off them was a tremendous cacophony of sound – drums, flutes and songs, the buzz of fifty thousand conversations, vendors shouting their wares in four makeshift markets that had sprung up across the plain like strange exotic growths.

With thousands of porters, water-carriers and personal slaves, and a ragged host of camp followers including butchers and tailors, astrologers and doctors, cooks and odd-job men, vendors of all manner of foodstuffs and services, and a parallel army of gaudily dressed pleasure girls, Shikotenka calculated the total numbers in the Mexica camp as somewhere close to sixty thousand. Despite the rigid military lines where the regiments were setting out their tents, the overall impression on the eye was therefore as much that of a country carnival as of a great army pausing on its march. Nor did the masses of soldiers detract from this impression of gaiety, for the Mexica rewarded success in battle with uniforms of feathers and gold and richly dyed fabrics that sparkled and glimmered in the sun, merging into waves and spirals of startling greens, yellows, blues, reds and deep purples, interspersed with expanses of dazzling white.

More than any other factor, what determined a man's worth amongst the Mexica was the number of captives of high quality taken alive in the heat of battle and sacrificed to their ferocious war god Huitzilopochtli, an entity of surpassing depravity and ugliness, whose name, somewhat incongruously, meant 'Hummingbird'.

All those of whatever age who had not yet taken a captive were considered novices. They signified their lack of achievement by wearing nothing more than a white loincloth and a plain white sleeveless jacket of padded cotton armour. There were a great many novices in this army, Shikotenka noted with interest, far more than normal in a force of such size.

More experienced fighters also used the armour but it was concealed beneath uniforms appropriate to their status.

Those who had taken two prisoners wore a tall conical headdress and a matching bodysuit. The shimmering colours of both cap and suit – most often crimson or yellow, but sometimes sky blue or deep green – came from thousands of tiny feathers painstakingly stitched to the underlying cotton garments. Men entitled to wear this uniform were usually the largest block in any Mexica army, but in three of the four regiments here today they were outnumbered by novices.

Next came warriors who had taken three captives. Shikotenka spotted companies of them distributed across the whole mass of the army, recognisable by their long armour and butterfly-shaped back ornaments made of purple and green feathers stitched to a wicker frame.

Still higher up the chain of honour, and again distributed everywhere across the army, were those who had been admitted to the military orders of the Jaguar and the Eagle. These might be the sons of nobles, in some cases unblooded but trained for war in one of the great military academies, or commoners who had taken four prisoners in battle. The jaguar knights wore the skins of jaguars and ferocious, garishly painted wooden helmets in the form of snarling jaguar heads. The eagle knights wore cotton bodysuits embroidered with the feathers of golden eagles, and wooden helmets in the form of eagle's heads.

A mass of warriors, their hair cut to a distinctive crest dividing the scalp, marked concentrations of men with more than six captives to their credit, who fought in pairs and had taken a vow never to retreat once battle had begun.

Even more formidable were the Cuahchics, their scalps shaved except for a lock of hair braided with a red ribbon above the left ear. Each Cuahchic's head was painted half blue and half red, or in some cases half blue and half yellow. They, too, had taken at least six captives, but they had also performed twenty acts of conspicuous bravery in battle.

Shikotenka grimaced, recalling previous occasions when he'd faced the Cuahchics. He would prefer not to face them again tonight if he could possibly avoid it.

But whatever would be would be. He dismissed the painted warriors from his mind and turned his gaze towards the centre of the camp. Teams of porters and labourers had been working there since morning to fit together the huge billowing pavilion of the Snake Woman, commander-in-chief of this colossal field army – who was, of course, a man.

Indeed, as far back as anyone could remember, it was an unexplained mystery that the revered Snake Woman of the Mexica, their highest-ranking official after the Great Speaker, always was and always had been a man.

The present incumbent, Coaxoch, now in his early fifties and enormously fat, had once been a renowned warrior. Moctezuma had appointed him soon after he became Speaker sixteen years ago and Coaxoch had remained his closest adviser and confidant ever since. A blow against Coaxoch was therefore a blow against Moctezuma himself and thus against the pride of the Mexica nation. It would evoke an immediate and, Shikotenka hoped, rash response. That was why he was here, on this grassy hill, crammed into this rocky crevice, watching and counting. If the gods were with him and blessed his plan, the result would be spectacular harm to the enemy.

A surge of movement in the southwestern quadrant of the camp caught his attention. He squinted. Shaded by splendid umbrellas of quetzal feathers, a procession of nobles and knights was advancing towards the centre. Shikotenka narrowed his eyes again and this time clearly made out the corpulent form of Coaxoch amongst the feathers, sprawled on a litter carried on the shoulders of half a dozen brawny slaves.

Conspicuous in the procession were four high-ranking nobles attired with spectacular radiance in elaborate rainbow-plumed headdresses and mosaic face masks of costly jade. On their backs, jutting an arm's-length above their heads, they wore the green triple-pennant standards of regiment generals. Shikotenka bit back the roar of loathing that rose automatically to his lips as he recognised Coaxoch's sons, promoted far above their station on account of their father's influence with Moctezuma, and already infamous for their foolishness and cruelty. The year before he'd met and instantly detested Mahuizoh, the eldest of them, when he'd led the Mexica delegation at so-called 'peace talks' with his people. How could he forget the man's bombastic, bullying manner and his loud-mouthed threats of rapine and ruin if his exorbitant demands for tribute were not met? Shikotenka uttered a silent prayer to the gods to put Mahuizoh under his knife tonight.

More movement in the northeast marked the location of a second procession, also advancing on the centre. It was made up of several hundred warrior priests dressed in tall headdresses and bodysuits embroidered with a background of black feathers to represent the night sky and patterns of white feathers to represent the stars. With them, bound together at the neck by heavy wooden halters, they dragged a hundred captives daubed with chalk paint and dressed in ungainly clothes of white paper.

The two processions converged in front of Coaxoch's pavilion. There, with much burning of copal, blaring of conches and beating of gongs and drums, the priests set up their altar and a carved wooden idol of Hummingbird. Propping himself on one elbow, conversing with his sons who had gathered close around him, Coaxoch looked on from his litter.

Shikotenka didn't doubt that every one of the prisoners who were about to be sacrificed were Tlascalans like himself. For, unlike the host of other free kingdoms that had once flourished in the region, Tlascala had always rejected the offers of vassal status and the payment of extortionate annual tributes to the Mexica in return for peace; as a result, it was the target of continuous raids by Moctezuma's armies. These attacks were intended to punish Tlascalan defiance and provide an object lesson to neighbouring peoples of the costs of independence. But their larger purpose was to ensure a steady supply of prisoners for sacrifice to the bloodthirsty pantheon at the apex of which sat Hummingbird, the divine source of all Mexica violence, who was reputed to have said in the long ago: 'My mission and my task is war. I will watch and join issue with all manner of nations, and that without mercy.'

In the past three months some terrible sense of urgency, some looming supernatural threat that called for a great mass offering to Hummingbird, had aroused the Mexica to new heights of cruelty. Shikotenka's spies thought the whole matter might be connected to the appearance of a small band of mysterious white-skinned beings, possibly deities, who had arrived in the lands of the Maya some months before, in immense boats that moved by themselves without paddles, fought and won a great battle using devastating, unknown weapons and then returned to the ocean whence they had come. Much about this strange encounter suggested the legends of the Feathered Serpent, Quetzalcoatl, and his oft-prophesied return, something that Moctezuma as a devotee of Hummingbird would certainly have cause to fear and attempt to delay or even prevent by offering extravagant sacrifices to the war god. This was only a theory at this stage, but it seemed plausible to Shikotenka in the light of Moctezuma's famously superstitious nature, and it would certainly explain why Coaxoch's thirty-two thousand warriors had been diverted from other duties and put in the field with the exclusive task of gathering in huge numbers of new victims. They had already ravaged a dozen Tlascalan cities, seized thousands of young men and women and dragged them off to the prison pens a hundred miles away in Tenochtitlan, the Mexica capital, to be fattened for the coming holocaust. Typical of the Mexica, however, a few of the captives – like these poor wretches now being dragged to the altar – had remained with the armies to be sacrificed at important staging posts on the march route.

The conches blared again and the snakeskin drum began to beat. Shikotenka clenched his fists as the first screams of pain went up, but there was nothing he could do for his brothers and sisters now suffering under the Mexica knife. The only satisfaction came from the thought of his own elite corps of fifty warriors waiting for his orders an hour's hard run to the south.

While the sacrifices were performed, the frothing heart blood collected and drunk by the most senior nobility, and the bodies of the victims butchered for the cooking pot, swarms of workers continued to put the finishing touches to the Snake Woman's pavilion. Not until mid-afternoon, however, when he'd witnessed the death of the last victim and drunk his share of the blood, did Coaxoch allow himself to be carried into the huge structure. He was followed by a dozen voluptuous slave girls, dressed in body-hugging tunics woven from yellow and green parrot feathers. Moments later his litter-bearers emerged but the women remained. From time to time other slaves continued to come and go carrying food and drink.

Suppressing his rage, Shikotenka stayed where he was in the rocky crevice, not moving a muscle, observing everything that was going on down below. For a while he became lost in thought, calculating distances, comparing a variety of possible entrance and exit strategies, quietly figuring out how he was going to get his warriors into Coaxoch's pavilion tonight and do the maximum damage there.

It was obvious that each man must go by a different route. In groups of even two or three they would attract attention but alone, dressed in a variety of captured Mexica battle uniforms, they'd have the best chance of blending in with the enormous crowd of warriors and camp followers. If all went well they would reassemble in front of the pavilion by the idol of Hummingbird and go straight into a devastating attack that the overconfident Mexica would not be expecting and would not have guarded against.

So much for the easy part of the plan.

Where things got difficult was the escape from the midst of an alerted and maddened foe.

But Shikotenka had supreme confidence in the battle skills of his fifty. They would have the advantage of surprise and momentum, of superior organisation, of their thirst for retribution and of the love of the gods. They would burst through the Mexica ranks like a flood and be off and away into the mountains before anyone could stop them.

They would of course be followed.

But that, too, was part of the plan . . .

Shikotenka's daydream of revenge was cut short by a sound.

A little, scraping, scratching sound.

He stayed frozen, unmoving, every sense alert.

Scratch . . . scrape . . . scratch . . . scratch . . .

The source was just twenty paces upslope and moving stealthily down towards him.

Scrape, scrape, scratch . . .

It was one man, Shikotenka thought, a soldier wearing heavy-duty battle sandals – not an experienced tracker, or he wouldn't have heard him at all, but someone crafty and determined enough to work his way round above him and get this close without detection.

Were there others with him? Perhaps further up the slope, out of earshot?

If yes, Shikotenka knew he was done for.

If no, there was still a chance.

He drew his knife.

Chapter Seven

Tozi led the woman away from the priests and rapidly back through the crowd to the massive rear wall of the pen. There was a negotiable ribbon of space here, where people did not want to be crushed against the wall. Tozi slipped into the gap, clutching Coyotl. The woman was right behind them.

'What do we do now?' she asked. She looked flushed and excited.

'We go this way,' said Tozi.

The prison was big enough to vanish in; indeed Tozi had spent the last seven months doing precisely that. So she was drawing on deep experience when she led the woman on the rat run along the rear wall, away from the priests, and back eventually into a far-off sector of the crowd.

She found a clear area of floor and sank down with Coyotl, his feverish, damp forehead resting on her shoulder.

The woman sank down beside them. 'You did really well,' she told Tozi. 'In fact I'd say you're amazing.'

'I didn't make us disappear like you thought I would.'

'But what you did was just as clever. Another kind of magic. What's your name?'

'I'm Tozi . . .'

'I'm Malinal,' the woman said. Then unexpectedly she leant forward and wrapped Tozi and Coyotl in a warm embrace that went on for an embarrassingly long time. When it was over she said: 'Are we safe now?'

Tozi shook her head. 'They're not going to go away quietly after such a riot. They're going to be all over us looking for ringleaders, taking more of us for sacrifice.' As she spoke she set Coyotl down on his side, arranging his hand for a pillow. He mumbled but did not awake.

'He sleeps a lot, the little one?' queried Malinal.

'I gave him *chalalatli* root,' said Tozi, 'for head pains and fever.'

'Ah, then he'll sleep through anything . . . Though only the gods know where you obtained such a medicine.'

Tozi ignored the comment. She reached out and touched Malinal's face – those wide oval eyes, that full mouth, that perfect skin. 'Your beauty is your strength,' she said, 'but it works against you in here—'

'I don't . . .'

Tozi frowned at the interruption: 'No, it's true. Being beautiful makes you stand out and that's dangerous. The first rule of staying alive is not to get noticed.'

Malinal spread her hands: 'So what should I do?'

'We'll start by cutting your hair.' From one of her hidden pockets Tozi produced a flint, about the length of a man's middle finger. The flint had razor-sharp serrated edges and narrowed to a needle point.

'Where did you get that?' Malinal gasped.

Tozi grinned. 'I'm a finder,' she said, 'and a keeper.' She signalled Malinal to sit in front of her.

The older woman hesitated.

'There's no TIME,' Tozi yelled.

With a shrug Malinal sat and presented her head to Tozi, who at once began to shear off her long thick hair in great clumps. A woman passing by stopped a few paces away to stare at the growing pile of fallen tresses. Her eyes were dull and her flesh had the pudgy, tortilla consistency of those who ate their fill of the rich diet of the fattening pen. 'Can I take some hair?' she asked. She had a stupefied look, as though her brain were already dead, anticipating the sacrifice of her body.

'Take as much as you want,' said Tozi.

Human hair was a valuable commodity in the pen: threads and fibres were made from it, clothes were repaired with it; it could be used to improvise pillows. To cheat the sacrificial knife one prisoner had recently hung herself with a rope of woven human hair. Under less threatening circumstances, therefore, Tozi would have guarded

44

such a treasure fiercely for use or barter, but there was no time for that today. As other women approached she invited them all to help themselves and they gathered it up in their aprons and dresses.

'You're generous with my hair,' said Malinal.

'We don't want the priests to find a single strand. Might make them think someone was trying to change her looks. Do you know a better way to get rid of it?'

Malinal laughed: 'You're very smart, Tozi. Tell me about yourself.'

'What about myself?'

'Like your home town. Let's start with that. Where do you come from?'

'Oh, here and there.'

'Here and there? What does that mean? Are you Mexica? Are you Tlascalan?'

'Not Mexica. Not Tlascalan.'

'Hmm, a puzzle. I like puzzles. You speak Nahuatl like a native. But with a certain . . . accent. Are you perhaps Tepanec? Acolhua? Xochimilca?'

'I belong to none of those peoples.'

'Quite the girl of mystery then . . .'

A bolt of pain shot through Tozi's head. 'Look,' she said. 'I've lived in Tenochtitlan since I was five, OK? My mother brought me here. I never knew my father. My mother died when I was seven. She said we came from Aztlán. That's all I know.'

The enchanted realm of Aztlán needed no further explanation. There lay the Seven Caves of Chicomoztoc, where masters of divine wisdom and workers of the highest magic were said to have concealed themselves from common sight. It was the home of the gods and the mystic place of origin of the Mexica, the Tlascalans and all other Nahuatl-speaking peoples.

But no one came from Aztlán any more. No one had come from Aztlán for hundreds, perhaps even thousands, of years. Indeed no one today even had the faintest idea where it was.

'The people who came from Aztlán called themselves the Aztecs,' remembered Malinal.

'So I suppose that makes me an Aztec,' said Tozi. Wanting to divert attention from herself she asked, 'And you? Where do you come from? You speak Nahuatl like a native too.'

Malinal laughed: 'I have a gift for languages but my mother tongue is Maya.'

Tozi had finished the haircut. 'So how come you ended up here?' she asked as she stood back to admire her handiwork.

Before Malinal could answer they both became aware of a commotion in the crowd, a ripple, a wave of disturbance, screams. 'We need to run again,' Tozi said. She stooped to lift Coyotl but Malinal was ahead of her: 'I'll carry him awhile. You lead the way.'

As Malinal supported the little boy's bony bottom with her right forearm, manoeuvring his floppy head to rest on her right shoulder, he woke up, looked her in the eye and asked drowsily, 'Who are you?'

'I'm a friend,' said Malinal.

'Excuse me, but how do I know that?'

Tozi appeared at Coyotl's side, mopped his damp hair back from his brow. 'Her name is Malinal,' she told him. 'She is truly our friend.'

'Well . . . If Tozi says you're a friend then I know you're a friend,' said Coyotl. He closed his eyes, dropped his head back on Malinal's shoulder and was instantly asleep again.

Tozi walked fast but she hadn't gone two hundred paces when movement ahead stopped her. She heard more screams and a hoarse, muffled shout. A line of priests was approaching from that direction as well! She shot off at a tangent, looking back to see that Malinal was still following with Coyotl, but within a hundred paces she was brought to a halt again by more priests and enforcers. Clearly a massive cull was in progress and victims were being rounded up in every part of the prison.

She tried twice more in different directions but always with the same result. A ring of priests and enforcers was closing in and there would be no escaping it.

'Very well then,' said Tozi. There was no point in even trying the fog with so many priests coming at her. 'We'll just have to stay here and not be seen . . .'

'You mean disappear?' Malinal said hopefully.

'I mean not be seen.' Tozi looked around. 'We need mud,' she said. '*Now*.'

46

Malinal rubbed at the dry earth with her toe. 'There is no mud,' she said.

Tozi lifted her skirt, squatted and let loose a stream of urine. When she was finished she plunged her fingers into the damp puddle and began to knead the earth, churning a few handfuls of it into mud. She looked up at Malinal: 'Brace yourself,' she said, 'this is for you.'

'Me!' Malinal choked. 'Why me?'

'Because I'm dirty enough already. So is Coyotl. But your clean skin's going to get you noticed. We need to filthy you up. It's a matter of life or death. Are you OK with that?'

'I guess I'm OK with that.'

'Then squat right there and make us some more mud.'

After she had thoroughly smeared Malinal with the wet earth, got it all over what was left of her hair, rubbed it into her forehead, left long streaks of it down her face, and daubed it on the exposed parts of her legs and arms, Tozi looked the older woman up and down. 'Much better,' she said. 'You're a real mess . . .'

'Thank you . . .'

'You're still beautiful, of course, but you're filthy and you smell bad. Let's hope that's enough.'

There were more screams. A wild-eyed, frantic woman charged by, another blundered past, bleeding from the scalp. All around prisoners were murmuring fearfully and trying to sidle away. 'What's happening?' asked Malinal. 'What do we do?'

Tozi sat down cross-legged. 'We do nothing,' she said. She lifted Coyotl's head into her lap and beckoned Malinal to sit beside her.

The priests had approached to within fifty paces and were cutting through the crowd directly towards them. They were followed by their teams of enforcers, armed with heavy wooden clubs, who seized the victims they nominated and marched them off – presumably for immediate sacrifice.

Tozi didn't intend to find out. 'Think of yourself as ugly,' she whispered to Malinal. 'You are hunched and wrinkled, your breasts are flat, your stomach sags, your teeth are rotten, your body is covered in boils . . .'

'What good can that possibly—?'

'Just do it.'

As the line of priests came on, Tozi's heart sank to see Ahuizotl again in the lead. There must be scores of priests inside the pen now, so was it just bad luck, or was it some malign intelligence that kept sending the sharp-eyed old killer straight to her? She noticed with some small satisfaction that the left side of his face was badly swollen after Xoco's attack and he walked with a limp, using his spear as a crutch. Four big bodyguards were clustered round him. They weren't armed with clubs but with *macuahuitls*, the wooden battle swords, edged with obsidian blades, favoured by Mexica knights. Obviously no repetition of the Xoco incident would be permitted.

The priests were forty paces away now, then thirty, then twenty. Under her breath, Tozi began to whisper the spell of invisibility, but for a few moments longer she held to the hope that the disguise would work; that, smeared and dirty as they were, Ahuizotl would simply pass by without seeing them, that inconspicuousness would indeed prove to be the better part of concealment and that there would be no need for her to risk her life in a rash adventure into magic.

Yet as the high priest continued to advance, some magnetism, some connection, seemed to be drawing him remorselessly towards them, and Tozi saw that he was gazing fixedly at Malinal. Suddenly it dawned on her that he recognised this beautiful, shorn, mud-streaked woman – that he knew her very well and that he had already singled her out from the crowd long before.

He wasn't fooled. He wasn't misled. He was here for her!

Realising there was no alternative, Tozi turned her mind inward, slowed the urgent beat of her heart, and imagined she was transparent and free as the air. She found she was holding Malinal's hand, and that it was firm and warm. 'You can make us disappear,' Malinal whispered. 'I know you can . . .'

Ignoring a further savage burst of pain across her temples, speaking so quietly the words could not be heard, Tozi brought her focus to the spell and willed it into life.

Chapter Eight

Tlascala, Thursday 18 February 1519

The rocky crevice sank almost horizontally into the side of the hill.
Shikotenka had shoved himself into it feet first until it swallowed him,
leaving only his eyes visible in the narrow opening as he spied on the
Mexica army.

Scratch . . . scratch . . . scrape . . .

He was baffled that anyone had found him in such a well-chosen
hiding place, but the man on the slope above, stealthy and careful,
could be there for no other reason. All that mattered now was whether
he was alone or whether he was part of a squad.

'I say,' came a voice, 'you there, skulking in that hole . . . Care to
crawl out and fight me for your life?'

The man spoke Nahuatl, the shared mother tongue of the Mexica
and the Tlascalans, but with the distinctive sneering drawl only affected
by the top rank of Tenochtitlan's nobility. This was some primped-up
prince, Shikotenka realised with a flash of annoyance, maybe even a
member of Moctezuma's close family. It didn't make him any easier to
kill – Mexica aristocrats were superbly trained from childhood in all
the warrior arts – but it should mean that a long-established knightly
code would govern what happened next.

Shikotenka's hopes began to rise that he faced only one enemy. He
clenched the long flint blade of his battle knife between his teeth,
leaving his hands free to propel himself from the crevice. He felt no
fear and a surge of energy coursed through his body.

The Mexica was speaking again. 'Why not just surrender to me?'
he said. 'I'd think about it seriously if I were you. It'll make your life

much simpler and you'll avoid the terrible beating I'll have to give you if you put up any kind of fight.'

Much simpler! thought Shikotenka.

Much shorter was the truth.

Because if he once even breathed the words 'I surrender', he would absolutely be obliged to become this Mexica's prisoner, would be bound by the code of honour to attempt no escape, and would be sacrificed to Hummingbird on the appointed day, his heart sliced out and his thigh-meat eaten by his captor in a stew with chillies and beans.

'We will fight,' said Shikotenka from the crevice.

'Ah-ha, the ground speaks,' said the Mexica.

'But I have two questions for you . . .'

'A man in a hole facing a man with a spear is in no position to ask questions.'

'Unless the man with the spear is a noble and honourable lord of the Mexica . . . But perhaps I am mistaken . . .'

'I am Guatemoc, nephew of the Great Speaker himself. Is that noble and honourable enough for you?'

Guatemoc!

Shikotenka had heard much about this young man. He was rumoured to be a hothead but brave and skilful. According to some accounts, he had captured eleven high-ranking warriors in battle for sacrifice to Hummingbird – an impressive total. No doubt he was here to increase his score to twelve.

'I was going to ask if you are alone,' said Shikotenka, 'but now I know the answer. The warrior pride of the great Guatemoc would never allow him to seek help to capture a solitary enemy.'

'And who is this solitary enemy who speaks to me from beneath the ground?'

'I am Shikotenka, son of Shikotenka.'

There was a long silence. 'Shikotenka!' Guatemoc said finally, 'Prince of Tlascala.' He gave a low whistle: 'Well, I must say I'm impressed. When I spotted you here amongst the rocks I thought you no more than a humble spy, good for a few hours' entertainment at most. Instead you turn out to be the highest-ranking captive I've ever taken. You'll make a noble sacrifice when I bring you to the temple.'

'You think you're going to bring me to the temple just like that,' said Shikotenka. 'You think you're going to defeat me. But here's my second question – what if we fight and I win?'

'You? Win? Frankly, that's most unlikely.'

'When I come out of this hole I'm going to be in full view of your army. If we fight and I kill you or take you prisoner, thirty thousand of your warriors are going to see it. I'll have no chance at all of getting away.'

'Should I care?'

'Of course! It's meaningless to invite me to fight for my life if I'm going to be killed whether I win or not.'

'Hmm . . . I suppose I see your point.'

A moment's silence followed before Guatemoc spoke again. 'There's a hollow thirty paces above us,' he said. 'I came through it on my way down. It's deep enough to hide us from view. I'll saunter up there now and you can follow – you know, crawling in the grass. You won't be seen and I won't give you away.'

Shikotenka heard the shuffle and scrape of footsteps retreating up the hill. He forced himself to count slowly to ten, then thrust himself out of the crevice and into the light.

Chapter Nine

At one level Moctezuma knew he was sitting cross-legged on the floor of Hummingbird's temple, his hands folded in his lap. He still held the empty linen bag in which Ahuizotl had sent him the seven *teonanácatl* mushrooms. Rearing above him, as though about to stoop down and devour him, casting monstrous shadows in the flickering flames of the torches, the idol of the god gleamed with gold and jewels.

But in his mind Moctezuma was quite somewhere else, transported to some far-off battlefield strewn with corpses. Strangely, he noted, all the dead were Mayan warriors. Some bore upon their ruined bodies the marks of the fangs of beasts, some were utterly crushed and destroyed, some decapitated, some torn limb from limb, some trampled, some burst apart into unrecognisable fragments of flesh and bone. Through this shambles, his feet bathed in blood, Moctezuma walked side by side with Hummingbird himself.

The god had chosen to manifest in the appearance of a strong, tall man of middle years, very handsome and commanding with golden hair and dazzling bright skin. He wore a robe of hummingbird feathers and a garland of human hearts, hands and skulls. 'It's been long since we last talked,' he said to Moctezuma, 'but I've been watching you.'

The Great Speaker of Tenochtitlan trembled: 'Thank you, lord. You are gracious . . .'

'I am disappointed. I had high hopes when I raised you to the throne sixteen years ago that you would find new and ingenious ways to serve me . . .'

'My lord, I have done everything in my power—'

'NO!' thundered Hummingbird, 'you have *not*, by any *means* done *everything* in your power! I wanted sixteen years of innovation. You've given me sixteen years of more of the same.'

'But have I not served you faithfully, lord? Have I not continued to bring you hearts?'

'Hearts?' said Hummingbird. 'I suppose you have.' He yawned, showing his large, even teeth. 'And today? We've had such a dismal start. Let me guess what's in store . . .' The god's red tongue, strangely pointed, flicked out between his lips, and his eyes rolled up until only the whites were visible. 'Ah . . . How completely predictable . . . Virgins.' His nostrils flared and he sniffed the air. 'The hearts of five hundred and twenty sweet young virgins.'

Moctezuma suffered a moment of acute anxiety. 'I cannot promise virgins, lord, though I hope some will be intact . . .'

'So, not even virgins then . . .' The god's irises, black as obsidian beads, rolled back into view: 'What's this *splendid* offering in honour of?'

Moctezuma was transfixed by the glittering eyes. They seemed to swallow his soul. Finally he summoned the courage to speak. 'Most vengeful lord,' he said, 'two years ago dark omens began to be witnessed, unexplained visitations, terrible signs . . . And now the year One-Reed has returned.'

Another cavernous yawn from Hummingbird. 'Tell me of these omens and signs.'

'A great column of flame, lord, that seemed to bleed fire, drop by drop, like a wound in the sky. It was wide at the base and narrow at the peak, and it shone for a year in the very heart of the heavens . . .'

'Ah,' said Hummingbird. 'My fiery messenger . . . I suppose you're going to tell me about the temple struck by lightning next?'

'The temple of Tezcatlipoca was indeed struck, lord, and there came a violent agitation of our lake until it washed against half the houses of the city. A man with two heads appeared. We captured him and imprisoned him, but he vanished from the prison without a trace. A woman was heard lamenting, passing nightly through our streets, but she was never seen. A fisherman found a strange bird. The bird was brought to me. It was somewhat like a crane, with feathers the colour of ashes. A mirror, pierced in the centre like a spindle whorl, was set into its head and in the face of this mirror the night sky could be seen. The hour was noon, lord! Noon! Yet I saw clearly, as in the deepest night, the *mamalhuaztli* and other stars. Of course I had the fisherman strangled . . .'

'Of course . . .'

'Then I looked in the mirror again. The stars were gone, the night was gone and I saw a distant plain. A host of beings moved across it in ranks, warriors armed with metal weapons, dressed in metal armour. Some seemed like humans but bearded and with light skin, as the companions of Quetzalcoatl are described in our ancient scriptures. Some also had golden hair like yours, lord. Others seemed part-human, part-deer and ran ahead very swiftly . . .'

'I sent you that mirror,' said Hummingbird. 'Return it to me now.'

'I cannot, lord,' Moctezuma sobbed. 'I tore it from the bird's head and destroyed it.'

'Like the violent, petulant child you are.'

'I could not bear the visions it showed me . . .'

'Yet the visions were true, were they not? Isn't that really why you're here today?'

Moctezuma lowered his eyes: 'For a year after I destroyed the mirror, there were no more signs. I began to believe that all was well in the one world, that my kingship would again flourish under your blessing . . .'

Hummingbird uttered a harsh laugh, like the bark of a coyote.

'. . . But four months ago,' Moctezuma continued, 'with the birth of year One-Reed looming close, I received tidings from the land of the Chontal Maya. Strange beings had emerged from the eastern ocean. They resembled humans but they were bearded and light-skinned like the beings I saw in the mirror, lord – like the companions of Quetzalcoatl! They wore metal armour and used powerful metal weapons that belched fire. They worshipped a god who they said had been killed and returned to life, and they forced some tribes of the Maya to worship this god. Others refused and there was a great battle. The beings numbered little more than a hundred, lord, but they defeated a Mayan army of ten thousand! Then they returned to the sea, climbed onto three floating mountains and were carried away eastward by the wind.'

'So naturally you were puzzled,' said Hummingbird, 'and wanted my advice. Your thoughts turned to victims and to sacrifices to appease me . . .'

'I made war on the Tlascalans, on the Huexotzincos, on the Purupechas. I levied extra tribute on the Totonacs. My armies brought many prisoners to Tenochtitlan. We have fattened them here, prepared them for you. Truly, lord, I have a great feast of victims ready for the knife . . .'

'What do you ask of me in return?'

'Knowledge of the beings who emerged from the eastern ocean . . .'

'These are not tidings you will wish to hear,' said Hummingbird.

'Still I beg you to tell me, lord.'

'Very well,' said the god. 'These beings were the first scouts of a great army that gathers across the eastern ocean to sweep you away. Soon you will hear they have returned in their floating mountains. Before the year is out they will be at the gates of Tenochtitlan.'

The whole concept was so impossible, intolerable and extraordinary, yet also somehow so inevitable and so long foretold, that it made Moctezuma's head spin. 'I fear them, lord,' he confessed. 'Are they gods or men? Is this perhaps the One-Reed year when the ancient prophecy is to be fulfilled and the god Quetzalcoatl will appear in his power to walk amongst us again?'

Hummingbird didn't answer directly. Instead he said: 'You have nothing to fear, for I fight at your side . . . I will bring you victory.'

Moctezuma's mood soared and he felt suddenly inflated with joy and confidence: 'Tell me what I must do . . .'

'First finish your work here,' said the god and vanished like a dream at dawn.

Moctezuma looked up.

Ahuizotl had entered the temple. He held a terrified young girl pinned under each of his arms. 'The women are ready, Magnificence,' he said with a horrible leer. 'The sacrifices can begin.'

Chapter Ten

Despite his fifty-five years and his tough reputation, Diego de Velázquez, the conqueror and governor of Cuba, seemed on the verge of tears. A blush suffused his pale pasty skin and his jowls, grown fat and heavy of late, wobbled with every movement of his oversized head.

'Ah, Pedro,' he said, 'my *friend*.' He put a menacing edge on the last word and thrust out his double chin with its neatly trimmed spade beard streaked with yellow tobacco stains. 'Something's going on.' He set his lips in a line so mean and thin that they became almost invisible. 'I have to know where you stand on it.'

Velázquez's notoriously bad temper was popularly attributed to haemorrhoids the size of grapes. He sat in obvious discomfort on a mahogany throne behind a massive square mahogany writing table in the midst of an echoing, high-ceilinged marble audience chamber. Pedro de Alvarado had met the governor frequently, but never here and never before in the ceremonial robes he wore today. He guessed with annoyance that the events of the last two hours – the herald, the summons, the gallop from the docks to the palace, the insultingly long wait in a sweltering, heavily-guarded corridor, this huge formal room with its imposing furniture and even Velázquez's robes of office – were all part of an elaborate set-up designed to intimidate him.

Alvarado stood opposite the governor on the other side of the table, with his right hand open, long fingers resting lightly on his sword belt. He was thirty-three years old, broad-shouldered and strong but light on his feet with the easy grace of a practised fencer. His thick blond hair hung to his shoulders and an extravagant blond moustache, elaborately curled and waxed, decorated his upper lip. Fine featured, with a firm chin, a long straight nose, bright blue eyes and a duelling scar that he found rather fetching running from his right temple to the corner of his right eye, he was a man who had broken many women's hearts. He was also rich in a small way, having prospered in Cuba these past five years thanks to lands, mines and Indian slaves granted him by Velázquez.

'My herald told me you were loading heavy hunters on board that carrack of yours,' the governor said suddenly. 'The *San Jorge*?' His right eye twitched, as though in sympathy with Alvarado's scar.

'The *San Sebastián*,' Alvarado corrected. What game was Velázquez playing here? Did he really not remember?

'Oh yes. Of course. The *San Sebastián*. A fine ship, which my generosity helped you buy. So my question is . . .' A long, silent pause. That weird twitch again. 'Since our expedition to the New Lands is purely for trade and reconnaissance, what possible use do you have for cavalry horses?'

The last words came out in a rush, as though Velázquez were embarrassed to raise the matter, and Alvarado launched smoothly into the lie he'd rehearsed with Cortés just that morning – the lie that half the fleet already knew by heart. 'For self-defence,' he said. 'Córdoba's men took such a beating last year because they didn't have the advantage of cavalry. We're not going to be caught out the same way.'

Velázquez sat back in his throne and drummed on its arms with thick, ring-encrusted fingers. 'I want to believe you, Pedro,' he said. 'You came with me from Hispaniola and you've been a loyal ally to me all these years in Cuba. But I still don't understand why you were loading the horses today or why another six were seen going on board the *Santa María* at the same time. Why load the horses now when you're not sailing for another week?'

Alvarado spoke in his most honeyed tones, as though reassuring a lover: 'What your informants saw was a routine training exercise, Don Diego! Nothing more sinister than that. If the horses are to serve us we must be able to get them on and off our ships quickly without broken legs. It's an exercise we'll practise daily until we sail next week.'

There was another long silence during which Velázquez visibly relaxed. Finally he made a horrible attempt at a smile. 'I knew you wouldn't be involved in anything dishonourable, Pedro,' he said. 'That's why I called you here. I need a man I can trust.' He rang a little bell and from a curtained doorway a native Taino Indian, clad in a white tunic, appeared carrying a wooden chair. He crossed the audience chamber with a peculiar bobbing motion and the slap of bare feet, placed the chair behind Alvarado and retreated. Alvarado sat down but his flesh crawled at the proximity of the indigene. These creatures were, in his opinion, barely human.

Velázquez reached beneath the table and with a grunt pulled out a bulging silk moneybag, opened its drawstrings and poured the gleaming, jingling contents in a flood onto the table. The river of gold was heavy and bright. Involuntarily Alvarado leaned forward in his chair, his eyes widening as he tried to estimate its value.

'Five thousand *pesos de oro*,' said Velázquez, as though reading his thoughts. 'It's yours if you will assist me in a certain matter.'

Five thousand pesos! A small fortune! Alvarado's love of gold was legendary. He licked his lips: 'What do you want me to do?'

'You're a close friend of Don Hernando Cortés?'

'Yes, he's my friend. Since we were boys.'

'That's what I hear. But is your friendship with Cortés more important to you than your loyalty to me?' Velázquez began to sweep the golden pesos back into the bag.

Alvarado's eyes followed the money. 'I don't understand.'

'He's planning to betray me,' stormed the governor, 'though God knows I've loved him as if he were my own son.' Once again his face had taken on the congested look of a man about to burst into tears. 'Believe me, Pedro, what I have learnt this past day has been like a thousand daggers through my heart.'

Alvarado feigned shock: 'Cortés? Betray you? I don't believe it . . . He's told me many times he loves you like a father.'

'Words, mere words. When the fleet reaches the New Lands I have sure intelligence he will no longer act as my viceroy but will declare the expedition his own. Too late by far for anyone to stop him! So I need your help now.' Velázquez drew the strings of the moneybag closed and rested his hands proprietorially on top of it. 'But first I must know . . . Can I trust you? Do I have your loyalty? Will you deliver your *friend* to me if I ask you to do so?'

'Friends come and go,' said Alvarado smoothly, 'but gold is a constant companion. If you don't trust me, trust gold . . .'

'If you do *exactly* what I ask,' said Velázquez, 'then all this is yours.'

Alvarado sat back in the chair, his eyes fixed on the bag. 'Ask me,' he said.

'Invite Cortés to join you for dinner on the *San Sebastián* late this evening. Shall we say around ten p.m.? Make some pretext, something private you want to discuss. Get him intrigued . . .'

'Why so late?'

'Fewer people around, less chance for things to go wrong.'

'What if he's otherwise engaged?'

'Then you must move the invitation to tomorrow instead. But do all you can to persuade him to join you tonight. Dine in your stateroom. Serve him wine.' Velázquez searched in his robes and brought out a little glass phial containing a clear, colourless liquid. 'Pour this first into the wine you will give him. Within an hour he will be . . . indisposed.'

'Dead?'

'No! I want the blackguard alive! The draft will make him puke his guts out, run a high fever, sweat like a lathered horse. You'll send a man to fetch a doctor – Dr La Peña. You know him, yes?'

Alvarado nodded. La Peña was a turd. He wondered how much Velázquez was paying him for his part in the plot.

'He'll come at once,' the governor continued. 'Whatever time of night it is. But when he examines Cortés he'll say he can't treat him on board ship and he must be brought to his hospital in town . . . The doctor's own carriage will take him there.'

'Cortés's people aren't going to like that.'

'They'll have no choice. Their master will be ill, close to death . . .'

'Some of them are going to want to ride with him.'

'No matter. When the carriage is clear of the harbour, a squad of my palace guard will be waiting for it at the roadside. Anyone with Cortés will be killed; he'll be brought to me here for questioning; and you, my dear Pedro' – Velázquez patted the bag – 'will be an even richer man than you are already.'

'You have thought of everything, Don Diego.'

Perhaps detecting a little of the scorn buried deep in Alvarado's tone, Velázquez frowned: 'It's underhand but necessary,' he explained. 'Cortés has become powerful since I gave him command of the fleet. If I arrest him openly there's going to be a fight . . .'

Alvarado hastened to agree. 'He's recruited more than five hundred men, signed them up with bribes and promises and dreams. Their loyalty is to him before anyone else . . .'

'That's exactly why he's so dangerous! That's why this poison has to be rooted out now!'

'But I see one great weakness in your plan.'

Velázquez bristled: 'Weakness? What weakness?'

'It only works if I'm the sort of man who would betray Cortés for five thousand pieces of gold.'

Velázquez was hunched forward now, an ugly scowl making him look suddenly monstrous. 'And are you not such a man?' he said.

It seemed a good moment for some drama, so Alvarado sprang to his feet, sent his chair crashing back and towered over the table, his right hand resting on his sword belt. 'Five thousand pesos is a paltry price to betray a friend.'

'Ten thousand then.'

'Twenty thousand, not a peso less.'

Velázquez made a strangled sound: 'It's a lot of money.'

'You'll lose a thousand times more if Cortés does what you fear.'

Alvarado could see the idea of paying out such a huge sum was almost too horrible for the old man to contemplate. For a moment he wondered if he had gone too far, asked too much. But then Velázquez reached under the table again and with great effort pulled out three more large moneybags, setting them down beside the first. 'Very well,' he coughed. He seemed to have something caught in his throat, 'twenty thousand it is. Do we have a deal?'

'We have a deal,' said Alvarado. As he spoke he sensed danger and spun round to find the governor's personal champion, bodyguard and bullyboy, a gigantic warrior named Zemudio, looming silently over him. The man was as big as a barn door, bald as the full moon and stealthy as a cat. He'd been in Cuba for less than a month, joining the governor's service direct from the Italian wars where he'd won a fearsome reputation. As yet he'd fought no bouts in the islands.

'My, my,' said Alvarado, annoyed that he had to crane his neck like a child to see Zemudio's stubborn, oafish face. 'Where did you come from?' *Another of those creepy curtained doors,* he thought. He looked the champion up and down. The brute wore light body-armour – knee-length breeches and a sleeveless vest, both made of padded cotton with hundreds of small steel plates riveted into the lining. He was armed with an old-fashioned falchion that was exceptionally long and heavy in the blade. Though crude, and unsuited to a gentleman, this cutlass-like weapon wielded by a strong, experienced hand could do terrible damage.

For a moment Alvarado locked stares with the champion, testing his will. Small, brown, patient eyes glared back at him, unblinking, flat as buttons, filled with stupid self-confidence.

As the aura of threat between the two men became palpable, Velázquez spoke: 'It's all right, Zemudio. Don Pedro and I have reached an accommodation.'

At once the huge bodyguard stepped back.

Alvarado retrieved his chair and sat down. 'Why was any of that necessary?' he asked. His neck and shoulders prickled under Zemudio's violent stare, but he refused to acknowledge him.

'I couldn't be sure you'd deal,' said the governor. 'If you didn't . . .' He drew his hand meaningfully across his throat.

'You'd have had me killed?'

'Of course. But all that is behind us now. You give me Cortés, I give you these twenty thousand gold pesos . . .'

'Who leads the expedition – when Cortés is gone?'

'Your question is to the point,' said the governor. He pulled a sheet of vellum from a thick heap on the table in front of him, dipped a quill in an inkwell and began to write in a small, spidery hand. As the quill grated across the calfskin, Alvarado tried to read the words upside down but couldn't make them out. Velázquez frowned with concen-tration, pushing the tip of his tongue out between his lips like a schoolboy in an examination.

When the governor was done, he read through what he had written, blotted the page and placed it in a document wallet. A motion of his finger was sufficient to bring Zemudio surging to his side. 'Go at once to Narváez. Give the wallet to him. He'll know what to do.'

As the bodyguard placed the wallet in a leather satchel and strode from the room, Velázquez turned back to Alvarado. 'I've chosen a man I can trust to lead the expedition,' he said. 'My cousin Pánfilo de Narváez. Zemudio takes my orders to him now.'

Narváez! A complete ass! Incompetent, vainglorious and foolish! In every way the antipodes of Cortés! But Alvarado kept these thoughts to himself and instead asked slyly, 'Who will be second in command?'

'I thought perhaps you, Don Pedro, if you agree.'

Alvarado didn't hesitate: 'Of course I agree. It will be an honour and my privilege to serve under a great captain like Narváez.'

Velázquez grasped one of the fat moneybags, rose from his throne and walked round the mahogany table. Alvarado also stood and the governor passed the bag to him. 'A quarter of your payment in advance,' he said. 'You'll get the rest when you've delivered Cortés.' He awkwardly embraced Alvarado and told him to return at once to his ship. 'Send your invitation to Cortés. Make ready for tonight.' He clapped his hands and the great formal doors of the audience chamber were swung open by two iron-masked guardsmen armed with double-headed battle-axes.

Alvarado didn't return to his ship.

When he'd passed the last of the governor's guards and made certain no one followed him, he led his white stallion Bucephalus out from the palace stables, secured his gold in a saddlebag and rode at full gallop after Zemudio.

The only way to get to Narváez's estate lay across dry, hilly country, partially overgrown with groves of acacia trees and intercut by a series of shallow ravines. The champion had left a trail a three-year-old could follow, so quite soon Alvarado started to get glimpses of him – that broad back, that bald head, that air, obvious even from afar, of unshakable self-confidence.

Let's see how confident you really are, thought Alvarado. He touched his spurs gently to Bucephalus's flanks; the great war horse thundered forward as fast as a bolt from a crossbow, and the distance began to close rapidly.

62

Chapter Eleven

A glance at the sun told Pepillo it was well past two in the afternoon, perhaps nearer three. He felt bone weary, his arms already protesting at the weight of the two big leather bags he'd finally retrieved from the Customs House after hours of frustration and confusion involving five different officers, three different batches of paperwork and a lengthy temporary misplacement of the bags themselves.

Which he still had to carry to the pier!

He groaned. The distance was close to a mile! Worse still, this second pair of bags was even heavier than the first, but they clunked and clanged in the same way, as though filled with metal objects.

The road thronged with people coming and going between the town and the harbour. For the most part they were Spaniards but there were Taino Indians amongst them and Pepillo passed a file of Negro slaves, naked but for loincloths, marching up from the docks with huge bundles balanced on their heads. An open coach drawn by a pair of horses sped by carrying a young noblewoman and her retinue of giggling favourites. Then an ox slowly plodded past, pulling a cart. It had ample space for a passenger and his baggage, but when Pepillo tried to steal a ride, a ferocious dog jumped back from the driver's platform and threatened him with bared teeth.

Pepillo resigned himself to walking. He had walked this morning and he would walk again this afternoon, but he did hate the way the bag in his right hand kept banging against his shin. The assortment of loose metal objects that Muñoz had packed it with seemed maliciously placed to bruise him and make him miss his step. 'Aargh!' he grunted as the bag smacked into him again. In a fit of temper he dropped it and threw its companion down after it.

The clasps of the second bag burst open as it hit the ground.

Inside the bag were steel knives – tiny knives so sharp that their blades cut at the slightest touch, hooked and barbed knives, butchers' knives the size of small swords, knives like saws, daggers with jagged edges, stilettos, cleavers, spikes, skewers . . .

Pepillo realised immediately he was in a dangerous situation. Santiago was a tough town, filled with fighting men, and there were weapons here that any fighting man would want to possess. As he crouched by the bag, struggling to close it, hastily rearranging its contents, fumbling with its catches, he noticed some strips of dried skin, with hair attached, lying inside. How extremely strange!

Pepillo looked back and saw a figure approaching, a shimmering black ribbon silhouetted by the sun. He felt threatened. The knives mustn't be seen! With a flurry of effort he succeeded at last in closing and relocking the bag just as a man materialised at his side and stood over him.

'Is there a problem here?' the man asked. He was Castilian. His voice was subtle, pleasant, educated, but pitched high and with perhaps the slightest hint of a lisp.

Pepillo looked up and was reassured to see the stranger wore a friar's habit. No knife-stealing ruffian this! 'I had an accident, Father. I dropped my master's bags, one of them came open, but everything seems to be in order now.'

The friar still had the sun behind him and his face was hidden in deep shadow. 'Do you know what your master keeps in this bag?' he asked.

Some instinct made Pepillo lie: 'I don't know, Father, I just fumbled it closed again as quickly as I could.'

'You'd better thank Providence you did!' the friar suddenly shouted. He punched Pepillo hard in the face, knocking him on his back, then ran forward and kicked him in the ribs. '*That's for dropping my bags,*' he yelled.

As a bolt of pain exploded in his side, Pepillo understood what he should have realised at once. This was Father Muñoz he'd run into!

And at the worst possible moment! Father Muñoz returning from his mysterious, day-long absence – where he'd been up to no good if Melchior was any judge.

Pepillo lay curled on the road in a defensive ball, wincing at the thought of another kick as he looked at the Father's large, dirty feet and cracked, broken toenails strapped into heavy-duty hobnailed sandals. Muñoz wore the black habit of the Dominicans, which he'd hitched up to his knobbly knees for walking, exposing scrawny ankles and calves overgrown with short black hairs and crosshatched with small blue veins.

Stick legs like a crow, Pepillo thought.

The little fat belly that Melchior had described was also there. It bulged through the Father's woollen habit and overhung the length of rope tied round his waist as a belt.

Muñoz was thirty-five or forty years old, sallow-skinned and clean-shaven, with a broad forehead and a thick crown of greasy black hair encircling the dome of his tonsure. His two upper front teeth protruded, much as Melchior had described, and his upper lip, which was red and moist, was drawn back around them in a fixed snarl. He had a receding chin and rather chubby cheeks that made his face look weak, but his large nose with its prominent bridge and wide nostrils sent the opposite message. There was the same ambiguity about his eyes. At first glance they were warm, kindly, wrinkled at the edges by smile lines, but when he turned to meet Pepillo's furtive stare, they emptied of emotion in an instant and became hooded and cold.

Muñoz drew his foot back. 'What are you gawping at?' he barked.

'You, Father,' said Pepillo. 'You're my master then?'

'So it seems. Though I must confess I don't see the point of a runt like you.'

'I can read, Father, I can clerk, I can keep numbers—'

'Splendid . . . splendid . . . But can you carry bags?' Muñoz had moved round behind Pepillo and now kicked him low in the back. 'Well, can you? It doesn't look like you can. And if you can't even carry bags, then what use are you to me?'

Although his tongue bled where he'd bitten down on it, Pepillo felt stubbornly proud that he hadn't cried out. He rolled onto his stomach, slowly, laboriously, got to his feet and picked up both bags.

He could do this.

He shuffled his left foot forward, then his right, felt the bag bang into his shin. Left, right, bang, he did it again. He picked up the pace, blinked his eyes and focussed on the distant pier. He thought he could see the booms and derricks around the *Santa María* and the high sides of the *San Sebastián*. The ships were still far away, but not impossibly far. If he could just keep putting one foot in front of the other, he would get there in the end.

Without warning, Muñoz unleashed another kick. This time the foot in its heavy sandal connected with Pepillo's buttocks like a blow from a sledgehammer, lifted him bodily off the ground and sent him sprawling on his face, losing his grip on both bags. He struggled to stand but Muñoz toyed with him, kicking his arms and legs from under him, making him collapse repeatedly.

'Why are you torturing me?' Pepillo asked.

Muñoz was all over him, straddling him, whispering in his ear. 'You think this is torture? I'll show you what torture is.'

'But why?' For an instant Pepillo's resolve broke and he let out a strangled sob. 'What have I done to you?'

'You searched my bag,' said Muñoz.

'I didn't! I swear!'

'I saw you with your filthy hands in it.'

'You're mistaken, Father . . .'

A pause. Heavy breathing. 'Swear it on the Holy Book!'

Pepillo must have hesitated because quick as a flash Muñoz rolled him on his back, reached down a long bony hand and seized him by the nostrils, applying painful, grinding pressure with his thumb and forefinger. Pepillo refused to cry out, but his eyes watered profusely and the pain got worse. He felt something twist, then break, high up near the bridge of his nose, and blood gushed down his face and filled his mouth. He spluttered, felt the blood enter his windpipe and began to cough and choke. How silly! He was drowning in his own blood! He struggled to turn his head to the side, wanting the stream to flow out of his body and into the ground, but Muñoz still held him fast by the nose and glared down at him with the light of madness dancing in his eyes.

Pepillo gagged and spluttered, but it hurt to struggle and anyway there was no strength left in his body. His sight grew blurred, a tremendous weariness stole over him and a great ringing filled his ears.

Chapter Twelve

When Shikotenka propelled himself out of the crevice he was ready for anything, his knife back in his hand and a snarl on his lips. To be sure, it had been agreed this was to be a matter of honour between knights, but he still half expected to be bludgeoned into unconsciousness. He'd long since learned the bitter lesson that any treachery was possible when dealing with the Mexica.

But Guatemoc hadn't betrayed him. Draped in a shimmering cloak of turquoise *cotinga* feathers, the prince was strolling up the hill and singing, passably enough if somewhat out of tune, the lyrics of 'I Say This'.

The song was well chosen. As famous amongst the Mexica as it was amongst the Tlascalans, it had been composed by Shikotenka's ancient father Shikotenka the Elder and it contained an embarrassing reference to Shikotenka himself, which Guatemoc now recited: 'My young son, you leader of men, a precious creature.'

Guatemoc looked back over his shoulder and gave Shikotenka a mocking smile. 'Behold,' he said, 'the precious creature has emerged from its burrow. Creep in my tracks if you wish, oh leader of men, the long grass will hide you.'

Guatemoc was a head taller than Shikotenka, broader in the shoulder, heavier through the body and about five years younger, perhaps twenty-seven to Shikotenka's thirty-three. He wore a mahogany helmet, painted gold, in the form of an eagle's head. The jutting beak framed his handsome face, which was also eagle-like with a hooked nose and cruel mouth and bright, predatory eyes. His black hair tumbled down over his shoulders from beneath his helmet. In his right hand, held loosely, almost carelessly, was a long spear with a leaf-shaped obsidian blade. Strapped to his back, lodged inside a leather scabbard with only its handle protruding above the collar of his cloak, was his *macuahuitl*, the obsidian-edged broadsword used both by Mexica and Tlascalan knights as their primary battle weapon. Shikotenka had come here to spy, not to fight, and for that reason was without his sword, but he didn't worry unduly about the imbalance. The *macuahuitl* was an instrument for killing and dismembering opponents. If Guatemoc opted to use it he would be unlikely to end the fight with a live prisoner to offer to Hummingbird.

Shikotenka put his knife back between his teeth again and snaked silently on his belly through the tall, feathery grass that covered much of the hillside. It was a manoeuvre he had practised in a thousand training sessions, so it was an easy matter to circle past the Mexica prince and get ahead of him.

When Guatemoc reached the hollow, Shikotenka was already there.

'I'm not going to ask you how you did that,' said Guatemoc. He stood at the edge of the grassy circle in the bottom of the hollow, ten paces from Shikotenka.

'Put it down to my superior military training.'

'If Tlascalan military training is in any way superior, then why do we Mexica so often defeat you in battle?'

'I'd say it's because you breed like rabbits and outnumber us ten to one,' said Shikotenka. 'On the rare occasions when it's a fair fight with equal numbers, we Tlascalans always win.'

Guatemoc smiled but there was no humour in it. 'I see one Mexica and one Tlascalan here,' he said, 'so let's put your theory to the test.' He removed his helmet and placed it on the ground, set down his spear and cast off his shimmering turquoise cloak. As well as his great advantage of height, Guatemoc had the broad, muscular chest, narrow waist and powerful sculpted legs of an athlete. He wore no armour, only a simple white loincloth and battle sandals. 'We're even dressed the same,' he observed. 'What could be fairer than that?'

'You still have your *macuahuitl*,' Shikotenka pointed out.

'Ah yes. Of course.' Guatemoc shook off the leather shoulder straps that held the scabbard to his back and laid the weapon down on the grass. In the same smooth movement he snatched a long, double-edged flint dagger from its sheath at his waist. 'Knife to knife then,' he said.

'Knife to knife,' said Shikotenka. He raised his own double-edged blade in a mock salute. 'But will you tell me something first?' he asked. 'Something I'm curious about . . .'

'By all means.'

'How did you find me? I chose that crevice carefully. I was well hidden inside it. You shouldn't have been able to see me there . . .'

'Do you have a sweetheart?' Guatemoc asked.

'What?' said Shikotenka. He couldn't understand the sudden change of subject.

'A sweetheart. Do you have one?'

'You're talking about a woman?'

'Yes. Or a man if you're that way inclined. A sweetheart. Someone who loves you.'

'Well yes. I do . . .'

'Girl? Boy?'

Shikotenka laughed. 'Girl.'

'And her name?'

'Zilonen.'

'Beautiful name. She's the one that gave you to me . . .'

Shikotenka perceived an insult and his blood instantly boiled, but Guatemoc held up an appeasing hand: 'Don't worry, that's not what I mean!'

'What do you mean?'

'I'm picturing a tender moment. After a night of passion Shikotenka and Zilonen are saying their goodbyes. Shikotenka is a daring sort of fellow and he's off on a dangerous mission to spy on the Mexica. Zilonen says, "Wear this charm for me, my love", and gives him a silver amulet she has worn since childhood. She weaves it into Shikotenka's hair. "It will keep you safe" she says.'

Shikotenka's hand went to his long braided hair. He'd forgotten about the little amulet, but it was still there, still intact, *still shiny*, exactly where his wife Zilonen had placed it. He'd been a fool not to remove it immediately, but he'd felt sentimental about it. Now he saw how it had put his life in danger. 'It was reflecting the sunlight,' he said.

'Like a signal.'

'Really elementary mistake on my part,' admitted Shikotenka.

'That's how I found you,' said Guatemoc. And while he was still speaking, giving no hint or warning of his intent, without even a change of facial expression, he launched himself at Shikotenka across the ten paces that separated them, his dagger gripped point-down in his right fist, its long blade hissing through the air in a blur of criss-crossing diagonal slashes.

Shikotenka was unimpressed. He'd survived enough knife fights to know that speed, strength and technique were all very well, but what really counted was having the sheer malicious will to do as much harm as possible to your enemy. By all accounts Guatemoc was brave and cruel in battle, but Shikotenka knew there were limits to the damage he would want to do today when his overriding concern must be to win honour by bringing in a high-ranking living captive for sacrifice.

Shikotenka had no such distractions. He would not take Guatemoc prisoner. His only interest, the entire focus of his will, was to kill him now, quickly and silently, and continue with his mission. So he weaved and ducked before the furious assault, keeping his own knife hand back, not yet committing himself to a counterattack, waiting for the right moment.

'It must be difficult for you,' he said conversationally as they circled.

Guatemoc blinked: 'Difficult? What?'

'To be the most accomplished warrior in Coaxoch's army and yet see his windbag sons raised above you as regiment generals.'

'They're welcome to the job,' laughed Guatemoc. 'I fight for honour not position, and I take my orders only from our Speaker.'

'Oh yes, of course, your uncle! But tell me – as a brave Mexica, how can you possibly endure the leadership of *that* stuffed tunic? Why even Coaxoch is a better man than him!'

'Moctezuma is the greatest Speaker ever to lead the Mexica nation.'

'Come off it, Guatemoc! You don't really believe that, do you? The man's an arse. I know he's an arse. You know he's an arse. Why not just admit it?'

'He's a great man.'

'He's an arse. He's going to put you all in the shit if you don't get rid of him soon. That's what arses do.'

'I'll not hear your filthy insults against my Speaker!' Guatemoc feinted as though about to strike upward and predictably stabbed down, aiming to disable Shikotenka with a wound to the thigh.

Shikotenka danced away from the blade. 'Perhaps the rumour about the Lady Achautli is true?' he suggested. He made the face of a man who has tasted something sour. 'It would explain your insane loyalty.'

'You dare speak of my mother!'

'Not I, Guatemoc, not I, but every gossip on every street corner, every merchant, every fruit-seller, every masturbating schoolboy speaks of your mother – and of your mother's loins . . .'

A thunderous look had settled over Guatemoc's brow. 'You go too far!' he warned.

'Apparently those loins of hers were famously loose—'

'*Too far!*' Guatemoc roared, and lashed out with his knife – a curling right hook that whistled past Shikotenka's neck, missing him by the breadth of a finger.

Shikotenka danced away another few paces. He could feel the joy of battle rising in him. 'Apparently,' he said, 'the Lady Achautli wasn't just bedding your father Cuitláhuac – that poor cuckold! – when you were conceived. The hot little hussy was also bedding his brother Moctezuma. Five times a day I'm told, when she could get it. So no wonder you're loyal to him! He's not just your uncle, he's your father as well!'

As Guatemoc charged, making strangled, choking sounds, drawing his dagger up into a brutal overhead strike, time seemed to slow for Shikotenka, and muscle memory from many battles took over. He slid his left foot forward, punched his blade into his opponent's exposed flank, scraped it across his ribs and swung it up to parry his strike.

The knives clashed and locked a span above Shikotenka's head, and the two men strained against each other, muscles knotted, grunting like animals. Shikotenka found himself close enough to Guatemoc to see the mad cruel Mexica arrogance in his eyes and smell the distinctive metallic reek of human blood on his breath. *Which of my brothers?* he thought. *Which of my sisters?*

Knife fighting was all about deception, so Shikotenka allowed Guatemoc to use his superior height and weight to bear down on the fulcrum of the two blades, wanting him to focus his mind there. He waited . . . waited . . . until he felt the point of balance shift, then abruptly swept his own blade clear, letting the big man's momentum carry him forward and down. Guatemoc rolled as he hit the ground, bounded back to his feet and came circling in again, but he was slower than before, blood was streaming from the wound in his side and he seemed to notice the injury for the first time.

Did he still seriously imagine he was going to take a captive here?

Guatemoc lunged and Shikotenka blocked, slid his left leg forward, trapped Guatemoc's right knee behind his left knee, sliced the blade of his knife thrice through the soft flesh of Guatemoc's right forearm to disable his knife hand and in a flurry of activity stabbed him in the chest and throat five times in rapid succession – Tac! Tac! Tac! Tac! Tac!

In an instant the bottom of the hollow had become a butcher's shambles and Guatemoc was on his back on the grass.

A bright bubble of blood at the corner of his mouth, the faint rise and fall of his chest and the pulse of the big artery in his neck – miraculously still intact – were evidence that life still clung to his body.

Shikotenka stooped, knife in hand, whispering a brief prayer of gratitude that his enemy's heart still beat. Ilamatecuhtli, aged goddess of the earth and death, required no temple or idol and would surely be pleased to receive such an exalted offering.

True the victim was no longer in perfect physical condition . . .

But while he lived he could be sacrificed.

Like the helpless Tlascalans sacrificed this morning. The smell of their blood still lingered on Guatemoc's falling breath.

Cold, implacable rage seized Shikotenka as he remembered the slaughter and his impotence as he witnessed it. He positioned himself to split the prince's breastbone, raised his knife and was about to make the first deep incision when a wet, choking rattle rose in Guatemoc's throat, a great convulsion shook his body and his heels drummed out a furious tattoo on the ground. Blood spewed from his mouth and, with a final hideous groan, his breathing ceased, the pulse of the artery in his neck slowed and stopped and the spirit left him.

Unbelievable! Even in defeat the strutting Mexica had found a way to escape the rightful vengeance of Tlascala! It would have been justice to tear his palpitating heart from his chest, but now it was too late.

One could not meaningfully sacrifice the dead.

Keeping his knife in his fist, Shikotenka dropped to his haunches while he decided what to do. The thought occurred to him that he might cut out Guatemoc's heart anyway and leave it on the grass beside his corpse. It would send a potent message to Moctezuma of Tlascalan contempt. There was a risk the body would be found in the coming hours, putting the Mexica army on high alert with potentially disastrous consequences for tonight's raid, but that risk would be there whatever Shikotenka did. With so much blood about already it would be point-less to try to hide the body, so he might as well have the pleasure of inflicting this final humiliation upon it.

Again he raised his knife, and again lowered it.

The problem was he found no pleasure at all in the prospect of further humiliating Guatemoc.

Quite the opposite.

As he looked down at the still, broken corpse of the prince, his handsome face peaceful and almost boyish in death, Shikotenka realised that what he felt was . . .

This could be my brother.

This could be my friend.

To be sure, Guatemoc was Mexica, and belonged to the family of the hated Speaker. That was his birth. That was his fate. But he had also shown courage, chivalry, intelligence and ingenuity and had been, in his own way, amusing.

He'd not been as good a knife fighter as he'd imagined, though.

With a grunt of displeasure, Shikotenka stood, cast around and snatched up Guatemoc's *macuahuitl* from where it lay nearby. He strapped it to his back, strode to the rim of the hollow, dropped on his belly and began to crawl furiously through the long grass towards the top of the hill a few bowshots above.

Dust filled his nostrils as he snaked upward. He passed through further hollows and gullies that hid him completely from view, but there were other stretches where the cover was thin and he felt dangerously exposed.

Shikotenka risked a glance back as he reached the summit and saw nothing to suggest he'd been detected by the Mexica army below. He crawled a few body-lengths down the other side of the hill to be sure he was out of sight, then stood and broke into a run. Soon he settled into the loping, long-distance stride that would carry him effortlessly over the ten miles of rough country to the forest where his squad lay hidden.

His spirits soared.

If things had gone according to plan he would have waited until nightfall to do this run, hidden by darkness from Mexica scouting parties.

But war was the art of improvisation.

Chapter Thirteen

Tenochtitlan, Thursday 18 February 1519

After the priests had gone, Malinal was dazed and silent, not wanting to speak as she tried to make sense of what had just happened, reliving the events scene by scene:

> She's seated on the ground beside strange, powerful little Tozi. She holds Tozi's hand. She's aware that Tozi is whispering under her breath, but the words are so quiet and so fast she can't make them out. On the other side of Tozi, with his head nestled in her lap, Coyotl sleeps the sleep of the innocent so he cannot see Ahuizotl approaching or the murderous intent that oozes from every pore of the high priest's face.
>
> What Malinal hasn't told Tozi yet is that Ahuizotl knows her – knows her very well – and if he sees her he will certainly select her and anyone with her for sacrifice. She feels bad for putting Tozi and Coyotl at additional risk this way, but there's no alternative. Her only realistic hope of staying alive is to continue to harness the girl's astonishing skills and learn from her extensive and ingenious knowledge of the prison.
>
> All that, however, has become irrelevant now that Ahuizotl is here, limping towards her. Since he's using his spear as a crutch he points the index finger of his left hand at the victims he chooses for the knife. He singles them out with grim intensity, sometimes stopping to peer into a woman's eyes as his finger consigns her to death, sometimes making her stand and perform some repetitive physical task before selecting or rejecting her as a victim.
>
> He's less than twenty paces away now, ripples of fear spreading

out ahead of him through the terrorised crowd. Malinal has her eyes downcast, praying he'll somehow pass her by, trying to think of herself as ugly, imagining herself flat-chested, hunched, wrinkled, covered in pustules and boils, as Tozi suggested. It's difficult because she has lived all her life with the knowledge that she is beautiful, but she works hard at it, is even beginning to believe it, when she starts to notice a burning sensation at the centre of her brow. A reflex movement that she can't control makes her look up and she sees Ahuizotl staring intently at her, his jaundiced water-monster eyes glittering with malice.

He limps closer until just five paces separate them and it's clear he's not fooled. There was never any point trying to hide from a man as evil as this. A sly, triumphant smirk comes and goes on his wicked face. He raises his left arm, his long bony finger snakes out and he inscribes a circle in the air encompassing Malinal, Tozi and Coyotl, consigning all three of them to death.

As the enforcers stride forward to grab them, Tozi's whisper changes pitch and her voice seems to deepen and roughen, becoming almost a snarl or a growl. Malinal suddenly feels her hair stand on end, feels it crackling and sparking with an inner fire. Tozi and Coyotl are struck the same way. At the same instant a transparent, filmy screen seems to form itself around them, as though they're on the inside of a bubble.

Ahuizotl's jaw drops. He blinks stupidly. He rubs his eyes with the back of his hands. He has the look of a man in the path of a whirlwind. His four bodyguards wear the same amazed, bemused, disbelieving expression. And they've all stopped in their tracks.

What are they seeing?

Or not seeing?

Malinal can only guess until Ahuizotl utters a single, high-pitched shout of pure frustration and limps forward, leaning on his spear. To her astonishment he passes right through her and through Tozi without any impact or collision. One of the bodyguards tramples Coyotl and again there's no damage. All Malinal's senses tell her the three of them are still on the prison floor. Yet some strange transformation seems to have taken place and they've become no more substantial than the mist of a summer morning.

Ahuizotl looks back and it's obvious he still can't see them. He slashes the broad blade of his spear through the air, by chance passing it twice through Malinal's body, but she feels nothing, suffers no injury, and he does not detect her presence.

A crowd of priests and enforcers have gathered round now. They're all staring at the place where Malinal, Tozi and Coyotl still are but they too do not see them.

Ahuizotl glares at his underlings. 'Tell me what you observed here,' he snaps at a junior priest.

'Venerable one. I saw you select three victims. Then they disappeared! They vanished before our eyes. It is surely an omen.'

'Wrong!' roars Ahuizotl. 'I selected no victims. No victims disappeared. There is no omen . . .'

The young priest looks uncertain: 'But venerable one, I saw it with my own eyes . . . We all did.'

Suddenly Ahuizotl makes a lunge with the spear. Despite his injured leg it's a forceful, vicious thrust at close range. The heavy flint blade plunges into the priest's throat and smashes out through the vertebrae at the base of his skull, almost decapitating him. 'You saw nothing,' says Ahuizotl to the corpse. He wrestles his spear free. 'No victims disappeared.'

Twenty other priests and enforcers stand watching and Ahuizotl turns slowly on the spot, holding the dripping spear, looking from man to man. 'What did you see?' he asks.

One by one they reply that they have seen nothing.

'Very well,' says Ahuizotl. He claps his hands.' We've not yet filled our quota for this afternoon's sacrifice.' He smiles, exposing his gums. 'I suggest we continue.'

Despite his bravado, Malinal can see he's a worried man.

As well he might be, since she's miraculously vanished into thin air just when she seemed most completely in his power! He'll be wondering if some god is aiding her, where she might turn up next and whom she might talk to. She knows too much for him ever to feel safe while she lives.

He begins to work his way through the prisoners again, casually assigning death to them with every jab of his finger. Screams and wails go up from the women in his path as they are dragged off by the enforcers. Ahuizotl doesn't deviate left or right but ploughs straight ahead. He's moving fast and soon he's a hundred paces away, then two hundred. The screams become more distant. After some time they stop completely. Ahuizotl and his entourage can no longer be seen and silence falls.

Once every part of the floor was busy with captives, but so many have been taken that there are now large gaps and empty spaces. It's fortunate that such a gap has opened up where Malinal sits with Tozi and Coyotl, because suddenly the magic is over. The tempo of Tozi's whispers changes, the static goes out of their hair, the filmy screen that has surrounded and concealed them withdraws, and they are back.

With so much to think about, Malinal stayed silent for a long while after the priests were gone.

Finally she turned to Tozi. 'I've got something to tell you,' she said.

That was when she realised how pale and beaten Tozi looked and noticed for the first time that blood had streamed from her left ear and run in a line down her neck.

Chapter Fourteen

Santiago, Cuba, Thursday 18 February 1519

As Pepillo regained consciousness he heard a man's voice: 'Come, come, Father.' The voice was deep, faintly reproving and filled with calm, confident authority. 'This is no way for a religious to behave on the public highway. Has the heat overmastered you? Have you lost your reason?'

With tremendous gratitude and relief, Pepillo discovered that he had been released from the crushing grip on his nose. He rolled over and pushed himself onto his knees, head down, coughing and gurgling, clearing a torrent of blood and phlegm from his windpipe. Over the sounds he was making, he heard Muñoz speaking through clenched teeth: 'Where I choose to discipline my page is not your business, sir.'

'Hmmm. Perhaps you're right. But you're a man of God, Father – a *man* – and this boy is little more than a child, and does not the Good Book say that the Kingdom of Heaven belongs to ones such as these?'

Pepillo was breathing freely again. Some blood was still running from his nose, but not enough to choke on. He scrambled to his feet and saw his rescuer mounted on a big chestnut stallion, towering over Muñoz and himself.

'"Withhold not correction from the child"', Muñoz suddenly thundered. '"Thou shalt beat him with the rod, and shalt deliver his soul from hell."'

The man on the horse nodded his head. 'Proverbs 23,' he said, 'verses 13 and 14 . . . But I still prefer the words of Christ our Saviour: "Whoso shall offend one of these little ones which believe in me, it were better for him that a millstone were hanged about his neck, and that he were drowned in the depth of the sea . . . " Matthew 18:6, if I remember correctly.'

'You dare to tell me my scriptures!' Muñoz snapped.

'The word of God is for all, Father.'

By now Pepillo very much liked the man on the horse, not only for saving him from a painful beating, or because he had the nerve to quote the Bible at Muñoz, but also because he looked splendid and warlike and must surely be a great lord. He wore long leather boots, a fine Toledo broadsword strapped over his rich purple doublet, a black velvet cloak with knots and buttons of gold, and a large gold medallion suspended from a thick gold chain around his neck. On his head, tilted at a jaunty angle, was a broad-brimmed leather hat with a plume of feathers. Perhaps thirty-five years old, but radiating an air of worldly experience that made him seem far older, he was deeply tanned with a long oval face, a generous forehead and black hair cropped short, military style. A beard followed the firm edge of his jaw and covered his chin; a long moustache decorated his upper lip. Disconcertingly, his eyes were different sizes, shapes and colours – the left being large, round and grey, the right being smaller, oval, and so dark it was almost black.

'The word of God is indeed for all,' said Muñoz gruffly, 'but most do not merit it and fewer truly understand it.' He signalled Pepillo. 'Pick up the bags, boy. We still have a long way to go.'

Pepillo jumped to obey but the horseman said, 'Hold!' and raised his gauntleted right hand. He turned to Muñoz. 'I see you wear the habit of the Dominicans, Father. But the monastery is that way' – he pointed to the town – 'back the way you came. There's nothing but ships up ahead.'

Muñoz sighed. 'I am here to take passage on one of those ships. I am appointed Inquisitor of the expedition of Diego Velázquez, which is soon to set sail to the New Lands.'

'By which you must mean the expedition of Hernando Cortés.'

'No. It is the expedition of Diego de Velázquez, governor of this island . . . He it was who conceived of it, financed it, supplied the ships. Cortés is merely its captain. A hired hand.'

The man on the horse gave Muñoz a cold smile. 'You will find,' he said, 'that I am much more than a hired hand.' He took off his hat, swept it down in a salute: 'Hernando Cortés at your service. Velázquez sent me word to expect you. I've set aside a cabin for you on my flagship.'

'Then you must have known all along who I am!' An angry grimace crossed Muñoz's face as the implications dawned. 'You've been playing me for a fool, sir.'

'I've been learning about you, Father . . .'

'And what have you learned?'

'That you are Velázquez's man. It's something I will think on.'

'Aren't we all Velázquez's men?'

'We're all the king's men and his loyal subjects, Father.' Cortés looked down at Pepillo and winked, his mismatched eyes giving him an oddly quirky and cheerful look. 'Pass me those bags,' he said. He indicated hooks hanging from both sides of his saddle.

Pepillo swung towards Muñoz, seeking permission, but the Dominican said loudly, 'No!' There was an edge of something like panic in his voice.

'Nonsense!' said Cortés as he spurred his horse round Muñoz, kicking up a cloud of dust and stooping down low to snatch the two bags and secure them to his saddle. 'My manservant Melchior will have these waiting for your page to collect when you come on board,' he told the friar. He touched the spurs to his horse's sides again and galloped towards the pier where, in the distance, the *Santa María de la Concepción* was still loading.

'But . . . but . . . but . . .' Pepillo opened and closed his mouth, feeling shocked, not sure what to expect next.

Muñoz turned towards him with a terrible blank stare.

Chapter Fifteen

Cuba, Thursday 18 February 1519

Zemudio was riding a piebald heavy hunter a full eighteen hands high. Its huge hooves threw up curtains of dust and the low hills, shallow ravines and stands of acacia trees provided excellent cover so Alvarado was able to gain ground rapidly without being seen.

His hand went to his rapier and he felt a flush of excitement as he caressed the guard of interlaced steel rings that surrounded the hilt. The weapon had been made for him by Andrés Nuñez of Toledo, reckoned by many to be the greatest swordsmith in the world. Over the years Alvarado had purchased eleven blades by Nuñez including two double-handed longswords and three broadswords. The rapier brought his collection to twelve and had been delivered only yesterday. It was very long, light and flexible, and culminated in a deadly needle tip claimed by Nuñez to be able to punch through the toughest chain mail and even penetrate plate armour. But unlike most other such weapons, designed primarily or exclusively for lunging and stabbing, this sword also had a strong double-edged cutting blade. The combination of these virtues was made possible by new techniques for tempering steel that were known only to a few, of whom Nuñez was one.

Bucephalus was much faster than the heavy hunter; the distance had closed to less than a bowshot and still Zemudio did not look back. Alvarado drew the rapier, liking the heft of it in his hand, raised it above his head and rose up in his stirrups to add force to the blow. He hoped to decapitate the man with a single stroke. If he could get the positioning right he was confident this curious new blade could do it, but if he failed it would quickly come to steel on steel – his long thin blade against the champion's massive falchion.

He'd not yet been able to test the rapier in such a match.

Or against such a dangerous opponent.

But what was life without risks?

Alvarado drew within three lengths of Zemudio, then two, then one, and began to overhaul him. Surely he must hear the thunder of Bucephalus's hooves and the bellows of his breath as he galloped? But even now the man seemed not to notice he was being followed!

As he drew parallel, Alvarado's arm came lashing down to deliver a powerful scooping, scything strike, but annoyingly, at the last moment, Zemudio wasn't there. With unexpected speed and dexterity he ducked low across the heavy hunter's neck, letting the blade hiss over his head, and immediately lashed out a counter-blow with the wicked-looking falchion that had somehow miraculously sprung into his hand.

Alvarado swerved Bucephalus to avoid being hacked in half and lost momentum for an instant before resuming the pursuit at full gallop. Obviously Zemudio wasn't as stupid as he looked. He must have known all along he was being followed and he'd been ready for the attack.

There was a real danger that the champion might yet prove formidable.

With a sigh because he hated to waste good horseflesh, Alvarado spurred Bucephalus to a burst of speed that the other animal could not match, came within striking distance of its rump, thrust the tip of his rapier with tremendous force a cubit deep into its anus and twisted the blade as he jerked it out.

The effect was breathtaking.

The heavy hunter was, in an instant, mad and out of control, leaping and bucking, whinnying wildly, blood gushing as though some major artery had been severed. Alvarado didn't think that even he could have stayed in the saddle of such a huge, crazed animal for very long and, sure enough, within a few seconds, Zemudio was thrown. He came crashing down on his muscular buttocks, roaring with rage, still clutching his falchion and, Alvarado noted with satisfaction, still holding tight to the leather satchel containing Velázquez's orders for Narváez.

Alvarado wheeled Bucephalus, threw his reins over a low-hanging branch of a nearby tree and dismounted.

A few paces away, Zemudio's horse lay on its side, snuffling and kicking in a widening pool of blood.

A little further off, Zemudio himself was on his feet. He seemed undamaged by the fall and held the falchion out before him ready to do mischief. 'That's a good horse dying there,' he said. His voice was curiously soft and high. 'A fine horse. He was with me in Italy. Rode him in many a battle.'

'You can ride him again in Hell,' said Alvarado. He flicked his wrist, sending a bead of blood flying from the tip of the rapier towards Zemudio's eyes.

Chapter Sixteen

Malinal had been so deep in her own thoughts she'd missed the alarming change that had come over Tozi. Looking closer she saw that blood, now clotting, had run from both the teenager's ears and also from her nose where she'd made a half-hearted attempt to wipe it away. Her eyes were open but unresponsive, as though focussed on events in some distant place, and her face was almost unrecognisably slack and blank.

'You did it!' Malinal whispered. 'You actually did it!' She reached out and embraced Tozi: 'You made us invisible! You saved us again!' But the girl sat hunched, impervious to praise, silent and closed off. Her body trembled, filled with a fierce, feverish heat. After a moment a groan started somewhere deep down in her chest, forced its way to her throat and burst from her mouth as a stifled scream.

Coyotl had slumbered peacefully through everything else but now he lifted his head from Tozi's lap and sat up. His eyes opened wide as he saw the blood around her ears and nose. 'Tozi!' he shouted. 'What happened? Why is there blood?'

'Be quiet!' hissed Malinal, suddenly alert to a new danger, fear making her voice harsh. The population of the pen had been much reduced, leaving wide patches of the once-crowded floor empty, but many prisoners still remained and, by great bad fortune, Tozi's scream had drawn the attention of two of the girls who'd attacked her this morning. They had been sitting quietly, facing in the opposite direction just forty paces away on the edge of a large group of Tlascalans, but now they were working themselves into a frenzy of pointing and glaring and general ill will. They sidled over to an older woman

86

whose lower lip and earlobes were extended by the blue ceramic plugs that signified married status in Tlascala, and began talking to her urgently.

'Uh-oh,' whispered Coyotl. 'Those girls don't like Tozi.'

'You know them?'

'They bully us.' The little boy looked proud, then anxious. 'Tozi always finds a way out.'

'They beat her up this morning when she was bringing medicine to you,' Malinal said softly. 'But she was really clever and she escaped . . .'

'She always escapes,' said Coyotl wistfully. 'Always.'

They both glanced at Tozi but she remained absolutely unresponsive, and Malinal's spirits plunged as the dire implications for their survival came home to her. Gone was the tough, decisive, fierce, enchanted, quick-thinking teenager who'd saved her life and who always knew what to do. In her place was a helpless, crumpled, clenched-up, withdrawn shell of a girl from whose throat, very faintly, could be heard a low, continuous moan, as though of pain or misery.

Malinal stayed seated, but out of the corner of her eye she saw the big Tlascalan woman scramble to her feet and march the short distance across the open earth floor of the prison. She looked around thirty, tall with very heavy thighs, massive hips and shoulders, a small, out-of-proportion head and the sort of lean, nervous hatchet face that would have been just as ugly on someone half her weight. Something about her said she was one of those women who loved to fight. She loomed over Malinal, glowered down at her and pointed a fat aggressive finger at Tozi. 'Friend of yours?' she asked.

'Sure she's my friend,' said Malinal. 'You got a problem with that?'

'I have a problem with witches,' said the Tlascalan. She jerked her finger at Tozi again. 'And she's a witch.'

Malinal showed her scorn. 'A witch? What a stupid idea!' She'd already prepared the next move in her mind and now jumped to her feet, stepped in to crowd the other woman and thrust her face forward until their eyes were separated by less than a span. 'She's just a *child*,' Malinal yelled. She put great emphasis on the last word. 'A poor, sick *child!*'

'Some people say differently.' The Tlascalan seemed unmoved. Her absurdly stretched lower lip hung down over her chin, exposing teeth blackened in the latest fashion and giving her a macabre, permanently astonished look. 'Some people say *you're* a witch too,' she added, spite putting an edge on her voice.

Malinal laughed it off. 'So there's two of us now!' Praying Tozi would stay calm and silent until she could get her to some corner of the prison where she wouldn't be noticed, she turned to indicate Coyotl. 'I suppose next you'll be saying this little one is a witch as well.'

They were still standing nose to nose, but now the Tlascalan backed off a couple of paces. She seemed to consider the question. 'I'm told it's neither male nor female,' she said, sucking her teeth, 'so most likely it's a witch.'

Silently the two girls from this morning's attack had come forward and placed themselves on either side of the older woman. The girl on the left, lean as a rattlesnake, was glaring at Tozi with undisguised hatred and fear. 'That's the dangerous one,' she warned. 'She gets inside people's heads. She drives them mad.'

'Better kill her now,' said the second girl, 'while we have the chance.'

Other Tlascalans, maybe fifteen, maybe twenty, had detached themselves from the large group and were pressing closer to watch the unfolding drama. It would take very little to make them join in; Malinal knew she had to act fast before murder was done.

She stooped, flung Tozi's arm round her shoulder and tried to lift her, but her small body seemed rooted to the floor. 'Help me, Coyotl,' Malinal grunted, and he darted forward to support Tozi's elbow. It still wasn't enough to budge her; it was as though she were actively resisting.

Now three things happened very fast.

First, the big Tlascalan barged Malinal aside, stooped over Tozi, placed her arms under her shoulders and tried to drag her to her feet.

Second, Tozi screamed again. It was an unearthly, truly witchlike sound, Malinal had to admit, a sound loud enough to wake all the dead in Mictlan. The Tlascalan released her as though she were in flames and stumbled back making the sign of the evil eye.

Third, Tozi toppled over sideways where she'd been sitting cross-legged and began to thrash and kick the floor. Spit foamed at the corners of her mouth, her teeth snapped, drawing blood as she bit her own lips and tongue, and she shook her head from side to side, smashing her skull violently against the ground, her mouth spraying flecks of pink foam.

Coyotl was fast. He grabbed hold of Tozi and clung to her, wrapping his hands and arms around her head, his legs around her body, using his small frame in every way he could to stop her hurting herself.

Malinal whirled to confront the Tlascalans.

Chapter Seventeen

Cuba, Thursday 18 February 1519

Zemudio inclined his head and the glob of horse blood from the tip of the rapier missed his eyes and spattered across his cheek and ear.

'Didn't think you'd fall for that old trick,' Alvarado said. *But I'd still prefer to fight you with blood in your eyes.* He was slowly circling; the rapier was angled slightly up. Now suddenly, with a huge explosion of breath, he threw himself into a lunge, right knee bent, left leg fully extended, surging forward with tremendous power, his whole weight behind the blade, driving its tip like an awl through Zemudio's light upper body-armour to finish the fight right here, right now . . .

Except . . .

. . . Zemudio rolled his wrist and the heavy falchion battered the flimsy rapier aside – a surprisingly fast and agile parry. It looked as though he would follow through at once with a thrust to the belly, and Alvarado was already moving to block and counterstrike when Zemudio surprised him again. Instead of the obvious thrust, he swept the falchion down, trapped the rapier against his own right thigh where the steel plates in the lining of his breeches protected him from its edge, took a huge stride forward with his left foot and clamped his massive left hand – *God's death, how could this be happening?* – into the thick hair at the back of Alvarado's head. It was all done so fast, with such enormous strength and flowing momentum, and was so unlooked-for a piece of artistry from this ox of a man, that Alvarado found himself spread-eagled, bent over Zemudio's left knee, his head jerked hard back by the hair like a lamb to the slaughter and the big blade of the falchion searing through the air towards him, chopping down on his exposed throat.

The blow came in spectacularly fast, but Alvarado caught hold of

Zemudio's massive, strangely hairless arm with his left hand, stopping the blade a finger's-width from his windpipe. The champion was so sure of himself that he was no longer blocking the rapier, perhaps because it was too long to be a threat at such close range. But Alvarado wasn't thinking about the blade. The heavy hilt embedded in its guard of interlaced steel rings was also a weapon and he smashed it viciously backwards into Zemudio's groin.

Clunk! It felt as though he'd hit a fork in a tree, not a man, but – 'Ooof!' – it forced a human enough grunt out of Zemudio, making him double over and release his grip on Alvarado's hair. Any normal man would then have obliged by staying doubled over, mewling with pain, gasping for breath and easy to kill. Not so this monster, who straightened at once, his face expressionless, and came right back swirling the falchion. Alvarado scrambled for balance and stumbled. It was an undignified moment, but somehow, more by accident than design, he succeeded in hacking his blade across Zemudio's right shin and deep into his calf between his breeches and the top of his boots.

The counterstrike came too fast to parry with the rapier, or block with his left, but Alvarado was an accomplished gymnast and threw himself into a desperate backflip. He landed on his feet, heart soaring as he thought he'd made it, then felt an explosion of savage pain as the big blade of the falchion connected with his left forearm like an axe biting into a tree. Only after he'd skipped sharply back five paces, keeping Zemudio at a safe distance with the tip of the rapier, could Alvarado confirm that his left hand was still attached to the end of his arm. A livid welt had appeared a span above the wrist and his fingers were numb from the shock of the blow, which must have come from the thick heavy back of the falchion. As he circled Zemudio again he tried to make a fist and found he could not. Annoyingly, it seemed his left arm was broken.

The champion bared his big yellow teeth and nodded at the injured limb. 'Does that hurt, pretty boy? Fetched you a fair knock, didn't I?'

'Hmm. Yes. Can't deny it.' Alvarado cast a glance at Zemudio's leg, rivulets of blood welling from the wound and spattering over his heavy boots, leaving thick wet drops in the dust. 'But first blood to me, I think.'

Zemudio made a gesture of acknowledgement in a way that said it meant nothing to him. 'I've killed seventeen men in single combat. Sometimes they blood me first, sometimes I blood them first. Makes no difference in the end. They always die.'

Alvarado took care not to let the agony he felt in his arm show on his face. 'That's quite a pile of bones you've left behind you,' he said. But what he was thinking was: *Seventeen! Shit!* He was genuinely impressed. Other than the Taino Indians of Hispaniola and Cuba, whom he'd slaughtered in quantities so huge he'd long since lost count of the total, he'd fought nine real duels with white men – six Spaniards, a Genoese, a German and a very tricky Russian – and killed them all.

Of course Zemudio's boast of near twice that total might not be true; he was a bit of an unknown quantity having never before fought a bout in the islands. But he'd brought a big reputation with him from Italy, and Alvarado had seen enough to believe he'd earned it. Zemudio was a clever, experienced, skilful warrior, and not by any means the stupid, overconfident thug he appeared to be.

As he and Zemudio circled, neither yet ready to commit to a renewed attack, the agonising pain in Alvarado's left arm, and its floppy, useless weakness, kept nagging at his attention like an anxious wife.

He felt no fear. He had heard this emotion described and he had often observed its effects on others, but he had never known it himself and he did not know it now.

Still, he was a practical man, and the odds in the fight had turned against him the moment his arm was broken. It was even possible – though unlikely – that he would be defeated, in which case Zemudio would carve him up with the falchion like a butcher dressing a pig.

As he grappled with this repellent image, a strategy that he knew Cortés would approve of began to take shape in Alvarado's mind. 'Hey, Zemudio,' he said, looking along the blade of the rapier, 'what's Velázquez paying you?'

The champion frowned: 'None of your concern.'

'Two hundred pesos a year plus bed and board?' guessed Alvarado. 'Three hundred at the most?'

He could see immediately from the other man's eyes that it was less. Much less. 'Oh dear . . . A hundred? Is it just a hundred? A fighter of your skills and talents and the richest man in Cuba pays you just a hundred a year?' A pause – as though it were a sudden insight or intuition, a completely new idea, then: 'Come and work for me instead! I'll pay you five hundred a year plus bed and board and you'll share in the booty we take in the New Lands. You'll be a rich man if the expedition goes well. What do you say?'

'I say you're all piss and farts, pretty boy.' Zemudio lashed out with the falchion, forcing Alvarado to jump back. 'I say you're a coward trying to buy me off because you know you're beaten . . .'

'Of course you say that. What else would a swine say when pearls are strewn at its feet?' As he spoke Alvarado stepped in, making a series of exploratory lunges, trying to feel his way past the whirling falchion, failing to make a hit but adjusting his own style more closely to the other man's technique. There were certain repeated patterns and sequences that seemed strangely familiar and just as he thought, *Maybe I can turn those to my advantage*, he remembered exactly where and when he'd seen this weird swirling, rotating-blade style before.

Zurich in the year of '02 at the school of Feichtsmeister Hans Talhoffer.

Alvarado had spent three months there as a visiting student at the age of seventeen – the time when his own abiding interest in swords and swordsmanship was beginning to take form. One of the classes he'd been obliged to attend had been in falchion combat – except the Swiss called the falchion a *messer* – and it was in this class that he'd seen defence sequences in the style Zemudio was now deploying against him.

A class in which every fight was a weird sort of dance.

Alvarado recalled despising the *messer* as a peasant's weapon, more suited to felling trees than combat, and had scorned the flowing, paradoxically dainty moves it was put to in the Talhoffer style.

But that had been in training sessions.

It was quite a different matter to be at the receiving end in a real fight when a giant has one hand in your hair, a long blade as heavy as an axe in the other, and is about to take your head.

Still they circled, flexible rapier and rigid falchion clashing with a song of steel, the rapier sinuously bending, seeming almost to caress and wrap itself around the bigger weapon. Alvarado's attention stayed locked on Zemudio, trying to second-guess his next move, but part of him noticed this new, unexpected, in some way feminine and seductive quality of the Nuñez blade and he thought, *Hmmm . . . Interesting.*

The blood had not stopped guttering from Zemudio's leg and lay in damp trails and widening puddles all around them. Was he slowing down, just a little? Was he close to bleeding out? Alvarado was just beginning to think, *Maybe yes*, when he saw the faintest hint of a glitter in those shuttered-off brown eyes, and in complete silence the champion attacked him again, all momentum and mass like a charging bull, the falchion slicing blurred figures of eight out of the air in front of him.

Alvarado didn't hesitate. Shutting his attention off completely from the new burst of agony in his broken arm, he threw himself headlong against the raw force of the other man's onslaught, meeting him blade for blade, advancing on him in a series of mighty lunges, aggressively crowding him, forcing him to retreat until Zemudio abruptly broke off the engagement and they were circling at swordpoint once again, each more wary and focussed than before, each seeking out the gaps, testing the weaknesses in the other's defences.

'You're good with that little pricker of yours,' said Zemudio with a grudging nod at the rapier.

'If I can't talk sense into you, I'm going to have to kill you with it,' said Alvarado. 'You'll leave me no choice.'

'Because of what's in here?' Zemudio tapped the leather satchel hanging at his side.

Because you're an ugly piece of shit, Alvarado thought. *Do I need any other reason?* But he said: 'You're carrying orders from Velázquez for Narváez. I don't want Narváez to get those orders. Why don't you just hand them over to me now? Join me? I'll make you a rich man.'

Zemudio laughed, and it was a peculiar, squeaky, high-pitched giggle. 'Señor Alvarado,' he said, 'you must think me a fool.'

'I do think you're a fool. Who else but a fool would die for Velázquez for a hundred pesos a year?'

Zemudio had lost so much blood from his leg that his swarthy complexion was turning pale and his skin had a waxy sheen. *All I need do is keep walking round him a little longer and he'll drop where he stands*, Alvarado thought, and simultaneously the champion staggered. It was an almost imperceptible misstep, and well hidden, but Alvarado saw it.

It was obvious Zemudio would want to end the fight fast, with some killer blow, before he bled out. That was why he was talking again now, some nonsense about being a man of honour, about his master entrusting him with this and that, blah, blah, blah, spinning distractions. But Alvarado wasn't listening. Hit them before they hit you was his simple motto, so he slammed in his own attack first, felt the falchion block the rapier as he'd expected, felt the rapier come alive in his hand as it whipped partially round the big heavy blade, sensed the moment he'd planned arrive.

He dipped his wrist.

Now!

Chapter Eighteen

Hernán Cortés stretched and yawned in the hammock he'd slung across a corner of the long, narrow cabin that was laughably still referred to by the crew as his stateroom.

His boots lay on the bare boards of the floor where they'd fallen as he'd thrown them off. Beside them was a heavy, triple-locked sea chest. His selection of richly embroidered jerkins and capes, some decorated with gold and silver thread, the best embellished with pearls, hung suspended in a makeshift cupboard alongside hose, codpieces and brocade shirts. His purple doublet was folded over the back of a chair together with his thick gold chain and its medallion of Saint Peter holding the keys of heaven.

The cabin's single porthole was open to admit the stink of the harbour as well as a splash of sunlight and a cooling late afternoon breeze.

To the right of the porthole, fixed to the wall and somewhat in shadow, was a large wooden crucifix on which a pale-skinned Christ, one-third life size, writhed in pain, the crown of thorns lacerating his bloody brow, iron nails transfixing his bloody palms and feet.

Positioned directly beneath the porthole, where the light was best, stood a heavy oak table. Those parts of its surface that were visible were scuffed and deeply scored with knife cuts, burnt in places and smeared with dried candlewax, but mostly it was covered with maps and nautical charts pinned down under navigational instruments – a compass, a mariner's astrolabe, a quadrant, a nocturnal and a glittering armillary sphere.

The sphere was Cortés's pride and joy, a gift from his father Martin who had won it during the conquest of Granada in '92. Save the ring defining the equinoctial colure, which was broken, the costly device was in perfect working order.

Slap!

For the third time in as many minutes Cortés heard the sound of flesh striking flesh followed by the suppressed whimper of a child in pain.

The sounds were coming from the far side of the partition that divided the flagship's original capacious stateroom into two equal halves, one half of which Cortés now found himself uncomfortably crammed into. The other half, on urgent orders received from Velázquez only yesterday, had been assigned to the abominable Father Muñoz. Through the thin pine partition, the best the ship's carpenter had been able to rig at such short notice, it was impossible not to hear Muñoz trampling about, or the harsh words he barked at his young page, or the intensifying sounds of blows and cries.

Cortés sighed. He'd intervened on the harbour road because the Inquisitor's bizarre and bullying behaviour was unseemly in public and unhelpful for the good name of the expedition. But if Muñoz wanted to beat his page in the privacy of his own cabin, there was really nothing to be done about it.

Even if he beat the boy to death?

Even so, Cortés admitted. Even so.

Because it was a sad fact of life in today's Cuba that a Dominican Inquisitor with the favour and support of the governor could get away with literally anything, even murder, if it pleased him to do so.

Indeed, there were rumours about the page who'd accompanied Muñoz on the ill-fated Córdoba expedition. His relationship with his master had been strange – everyone had noticed – and, one night, the boy had disappeared at sea, presumed lost overboard. Perhaps his death had been an accident? Perhaps suicide? Or perhaps, as some of the survivors whispered, Muñoz was a violent sodomite with a taste for adolescent boys who'd killed the page to silence him?

Cortés had scorned the whispers, refusing to believe a man of God could ever commit such crimes; but what he'd witnessed this afternoon had changed his mind. Rarely had he taken so instant or so extreme a dislike to anyone as he had to Muñoz! It was bad enough that the

Dominican had been foisted on him at the last moment by Velázquez – undoubtedly as much to spy on him and confound him as to attend to the spiritual wellbeing of the expedition. But what added insult to injury was the foul unnatural air of this Inquisitor! Recalling the scene on the harbour road, it was the perverted *pleasure* Muñoz had taken from inflicting pain on his little page that stood out.

Cortés swung down off the hammock, padded barefoot over to the table below the porthole, and retrieved his well-thumbed Bible from beneath a heap of maps and charts. It was one of the new mass-produced editions, printed on paper by the Gutenberg press, and as he opened its leather covers he felt again, as he always did, the magic and the mystery of the word of God.

He turned to the New Testament, the Book of Matthew, and after some searching found the passage he was looking for in Chapter Seven. 'Beware of false prophets,' he read, 'which come to you in sheep's clothing, but inwardly they are ravening wolves.'

A false prophet! It was amazing how often you could find the exact thought you wanted in the Good Book – and this was a thought that seemed to fit Muñoz very well. Outwardly the respectable sheep's clothing of the Dominican habit, inwardly a ravening wolf . . .

There came another *slap* from beyond the partition, another cry, a tremendous, incoherent yell from Muñoz, a loud crash as of a body thrown against a wall, and then silence.

Cortés started upright in his hammock – Jesu in Heaven, surely the boy was not already dead? Then he heard that thin pitiful whimper again and a surge of fierce anger and revulsion shook him.

His powerful impulse was to find any excuse to have Muñoz removed from the expedition. But if he did that it would draw unwelcome attention from Velázquez at just the time when he most wanted the governor to stay away.

So instead Cortés closed his eyes and forced his tensed muscles to relax. The key to health in these climes, he had discovered, was to take a siesta of at least one hour's duration in the afternoon. It wasn't always possible; he completely understood that. But when it was possible he gave it as much priority as prayers or alms.

Sleep embraced him.

Chapter Nineteen

The two girls who'd attacked Tozi this morning were mischief-makers, not leaders, and the other Tlascalans snooping around also seemed to be waiting for someone to tell them what to do. So it was the big woman with the black teeth and the rubber lip who was the main danger. Deal with her and the others would fall into line.

Maybe . . .

Malinal had been sheltered from violence by noble birth. When she was sixteen her fortunes fell but, even in the five strange and terrible years she'd spent as a slave since then, she'd been protected by the high value placed on her beauty by powerful men. The result, in her twenty-one years, was that she'd never once had to fight for her life. Her strengths were sensuality, flattery, dissimulation and subtle influence; she was not well equipped to use force.

Black Teeth had been stopped in her tracks by Tozi's nightmarish scream, and stood gazing at her with fear, but also with something unexpectedly like pity as she thrashed and snapped her teeth on the floor, while Coyotl fought desperately to keep her from harm. With a flash of intuition, Malinal stepped to the big Tlascalan woman's side, laid a long slim hand gently on her shoulder and said in a hushed tone: 'She's no witch. She's just a poor sick child. Aren't you a mother yourself? Can't you see that?'

Black Teeth's massive body twitched. 'I am a mother.'

'And your children? Where are they now?'

'The gods only know. The Mexica raided my village. I was captured, my two children were snatched away from me, I haven't seen them since.'

'Would you tell me their names?'

The Tlascalan woman's brutal manner suddenly dissolved and to Malinal's surprise she sobbed. 'Huemac,' she said, 'he's five. And then there's Zeltzin. She'll be fourteen this summer.'

'Zeltzin . . . Beautiful.' The name meant 'delicate' in the Nahuatl tongue. 'She and Tozi are almost the same age . . .'

'Tozi?'

'This child –' Malinal looked down at Tozi, still thrashing on the ground – 'whom you believe is a witch but who really is just sick and in need of help and love.'

Black Teeth grunted and wiped away a tear. 'Why should I care what she needs?'

'Because in this world of pain the gods see to it that what we give out is what we get back. Wherever they may be today, perhaps in another fattening pen, perhaps slaved by some merchant, don't you hope someone will care for your own children's needs – if they're sick, if they need help like poor little Tozi?'

Black Teeth looked round at the girls whose provocations had sparked this trouble. 'It's them as told me she's a witch,' she said.

'And they attacked her this morning, and got the worst of it, and now they're trying to use you to get revenge.'

On the floor Tozi was quieter, her struggles less desperate, her features calmer. The two Tlascalan girls began to edge towards her but Black Teeth called out 'Wait!' and they hesitated, scowling at Malinal.

'You have children yourself?' Black Teeth asked.

'No. I've not been blessed. The Mexica slaved me, used me for sex. I fell pregnant twice but they forced me to drink *epazote* and I miscarried.'

The woman spat. 'Brutes. How they use us!'

Malinal pressed home her advantage. 'We're all their victims. Why do we fight and kill each other when the Mexica persecute us all? They're the real witches and sorcerers – not innocent children like poor Tozi.'

Black Teeth looked doubtful. 'If she's not a witch, then what is she? How is it that she's never selected for sacrifice?'

Malinal had her answer ready. '*Yollomimiquiliztli*,' she said gravely, invoking the Nahuatl word for epilepsy. 'Perhaps she who cursed her also protects her.'

Everyone knew that the terrible affliction of epilepsy, which caused fits exactly like the one that Tozi had just suffered, was the work of the fickle goddess Cihuapipiltin. And everyone also knew that in return for the suffering she caused Cihuapipiltin sometimes gave magical gifts to her victims.

Black Teeth thought about it for what seemed like a long time as Tozi's shaking and foaming at the mouth gradually ceased and she lay still. Finally the big Tlascalan woman nodded to Malinal. 'What you've told me makes sense,' she said. She turned to the other Tlascalans and spoke up: 'This child is not a witch. Poor one! She has been touched by Cihuapipiltin. We should leave her alone.'

One of the troublemakers clenched her fists and gave a little scream of frustration, but Black Teeth silenced her with a glare.

Within a few moments all the Tlascalans withdrew, leaving Malinal alone with Tozi and Coyotl.

Perhaps an hour later Tozi opened her eyes. Linking arms with Coyotl, Malinal helped her sit up. 'You OK?' she asked. It seemed such an ordinary question after all the extraordinary things that had happened, but it was what she wanted to know.

'I'm OK,' said Tozi.

'Me too,' said Coyotl. 'Malinal saved us from the bad girls.'

Tozi was looking at the nearby group of Tlascalans. 'We had trouble?'

'Yes, but it's over. Everything's going to be fine.'

'Good,' said Tozi, 'because I'm all used up.' Her eyes were bright but the whites were jaundiced, her skin was grey with fatigue and there was a sheen of sweat on her brow.

'What happened to you?' Malinal asked.

'I'm trying to remember . . . For how long did I fade us when Ahuizotl came?'

Malinal thought about it. 'I don't know,' she said. 'Maybe a two hundred count, maybe a three hundred count?'

Tozi gave a low whistle. 'I didn't even know I could do that.'

'I don't understand.'

'When I fade for more than a ten count I get sick. Really sick. Something breaks inside my head. If I faded us for a two hundred count, I'm lucky to be alive.'

'You were in a bad way.'

'I'm still in a bad way.'

Malinal reached out and brushed her fingers down Tozi's pale, exhausted face. 'You'll get better,' she said, but it was more a hope than a statement of fact.

'I'll get better,' Tozi echoed dully, 'but I won't be able to fade us again. Not today. Not tomorrow. It always takes me a long time to get my strength back.'

'Don't worry about that,' said Malinal. 'Don't worry about anything. I'll take care of you.' She ruffled Coyotl's hair. 'And you too, little one.'

She knew it was a hollow promise, even as she made it.

Thanks to Black Teeth they were, for the moment, probably safe from further accusations of witchcraft, but the threat of sacrifice had not receded and, beyond the bars of the prison, Ahuizotl still lurked. He would not forget or forgive how badly he'd been embarrassed by Tozi's magic.

Realising anew the endless horror of their predicament, Malinal felt all her strength and resolve ebb away.

Then Coyotl tugged at her hand, gazing up at her with his big serious eyes.

'Do you know how to fade us?' he said.

Chapter Twenty

Cuba, Thursday 18 February 1519

When Alvarado dipped his wrist, Zemudio predictably followed the flow of force, and thrust down hard, sliding the falchion along the blade of the rapier, grinding out the keening song of steel, sending sparks of hot metal flying. Alvarado had invited this savage cut with the heavier weapon. It was a standard move in the Talhoffer system of *messer* combat – engage, slide the blade, pivot to misdirect your opponent's force, hack off his arm at the elbow. But the blow was ill matched against the Nuñez rapier with its guard of steel rings spun round the hilt. The falchion skidded over the guard and, as Zemudio whirled into the pivot, Alvarado trapped the thick blade between two of the rings, deftly twisted the weapon from his grip and cast it to the ground.

It all happened so fast – *like disarming a child!* – that Zemudio was taken completely by surprise. He made a clumsy grab for the fallen weapon but Alvarado got his boot under it and kicked it out of reach. Zemudio put his head down and charged, hands outstretched, and Alvarado reacted instinctively with a clean, straight, powerful lunge, rapier and right arm extended, right leg sliding ahead, left leg and left arm stretched out behind, propelling his body forward. The needle point of the rapier pierced the padded outer fabric of Zemudio's vest where it covered his belly, glanced off the overlapping steel tiles sewn into the lining, slid a span, found a tiny gap and – *ooof!* – punched deep into the champion's body. Alvarado was unstoppable, all his power and weight behind the lunge, and as he went to full extension he felt the point ripple through Zemudio's guts and burst out of his lower back. There was slight resistance as it hit the armour at the rear of the vest but again, like a worm, the flexible blade found a way through, and the champion was spitted.

Alvarado was close to him, very close, close as lovers. Wrapped in the rapier's guard, his fist was right against the dying man's belly and the tip of the blade stood out a cubit from his back. Ecstasy! A kind of ecstasy! Zemudio's little pig eyes gazed into his own with more puzzlement than anger, his stupid oafish mouth gaped, and he groaned like a woman being pleasured.

'Still think I'm all piss and farts, do you?' yelled Alvarado. He sawed the blade of the rapier back and forth.

Zemudio gasped.

'Still think I'm a pretty boy?'

'Aaaah . . .'

The mist of death was clouding Zemudio's eyes. Alvarado could always recognise it. With a yell of triumph and a vicious twist of his wrist, he hauled out the rapier, drenched with gore, and stepped back.

He expected Zemudio to fall, but the great ox of a man just stood there blinking, blood oozing through the front of his vest, guttering out of the gaping wound in his leg and dropping *pitter-patter, pitter-patter* into the dust at his feet.

'Very well,' said Alvarado, 'if that's how you want it.' The rapier still needed more trials with armour and now was as good a time as any. Throwing his right foot forward he slid into another lunge, easily found another weak point and ran the man through. He withdrew, lunged again, slight resistance from the armour, quick workaround, found a gap and – *ooof!* – another healthy dose of steel administered direct to Zemudio's vitals.

As Alvarado stood back to inspect his handiwork, Zemudio shouted something indistinct and collapsed to his knees.

'What was that?' said Alvarado, taking a step closer.

Another incoherent yell.

Alvarado frowned. 'What?'

Zemudio looked up at him in mute appeal, mouth gaping.

'What?' Alvarado took another step, put his ear to Zemudio's lips.

'Bastard,' whispered Zemudio.

'Biggest bastard this side of the Ocean Sea,' agreed Alvarado. He straightened, swept the rapier up over his right shoulder, swung it almost lazily down and hacked the razor edge of its clever Nuñez blade into the side of Zemudio's thick, muscular neck. There was a smacking sound, almost like a slap, a spray of blood as the jugular was severed, some resistance and a grinding sensation as the blade cleaved vertebrae, then much more blood and a tremendous acceleration as the sword flashed out on the other side of his neck, taking his head clean off.

It bounced when it hit the ground, rolled twice and came to rest upside down against a rotten tree stump, the surprised, reproachful eyes still glaring.

'*Yes!*' Alvarado shouted, because somebody had to praise that perfect *coup de grâce*.

Such precision. Such elegance. Such economy of effort.

He doubted if there were three other swordsmen in the world, maybe not even two, who could have matched the blow.

Though headless, Zemudio was still on his knees and the satchel containing the Velázquez documents still hung by its strap around what was left of his neck. Blood was bubbling up, getting everywhere, already completely drenching the satchel, but Alvarado was a one-armed man now. He first wiped the blade of the rapier clean on Zemudio's body, and sheathed it, before he stooped over the corpse and pulled the dripping satchel away.

The buckles were slippery and proved near impossible to open with only one functioning hand, until Alvarado had a brilliant idea. He turned back to Zemudio's kneeling corpse, kicked it over in the dust and used the cloth on the ample seat of the champion's breeches to clean the satchel and his own fingers. When he was satisfied he'd done enough, he turned back to the buckles, opened them easily and peered inside.

The document wallet was there, safe and dry, no blood yet staining its contents. Alvarado fished it out and opened it.

Inside was the single page of vellum on which Velázquez had scrawled his orders for his loathsome favourite Pánfilo de Narváez – *Captain-General* Narváez, no less! – the despicable fool who was supposed to take Cortés's place. As he read, Alvarado's face darkened, but when he'd finished he put his head back and laughed for a long time. 'Sweat of the Virgin,' he said as he slid the page back into the wallet. All that trouble to kill a man and at the end of it he'd learned nothing more than Velázquez had already told him. Still, Cortés was going to be impressed to see the proof in writing.

Alvarado pushed the wallet into Bucephalus's saddlebag alongside his gold, and was about to mount up and ride for Santiago when he remembered Zemudio's falchion.

It had turned out to be a damn fine weapon.

Indeed Alvarado could imagine situations – a crowded battlefield, a press of combatants – where it would be the best weapon a man could possibly have and where a rapier might be useless. He looked around the blood-smeared scene and a ray of late-afternoon sunlight glanced off the big blade where it lay in the dust. He walked over and picked it up. It felt heavy and unwieldy, yet Zemudio had handled it as though it were a tin toy! It would take some getting used to, Alvarado supposed, but he had yet to encounter an edged weapon he couldn't master.

He glared down at Zemudio's headless body – *so much for the hero of the Italian wars!* – and paused to give the corpse one more kick. 'Who's the bastard now?' he yelled. Then he stuffed the falchion into his sword belt, marched to Bucephalus and climbed into the saddle.

The sun was sinking into the west and it was an hour's ride back to Santiago, with visibility falling and evening coming on. Alvarado spurred the great war horse into a reckless gallop.

Chapter Twenty-One

Santiago, Cuba, Thursday 18 February 1519

Cortés was dreaming.

Strangely he was both within the dream and an external observer of it.

Stranger still, it seemed he could change aspects of the dream simply by thinking about them!

For example, he was at this moment walking through a green meadow covered in lush grass laid over firm turf. He thought, *Perfect riding country*, and at once found himself on the back of the grey mare, Altivo, which he'd ridden when he was a boy in Extremadura. All the sensations were completely realistic – the smell and the feel of the horse, the sun on the grass, the wind in his hair.

Then, inexplicably, Altivo vanished, the scene changed, and he found himself inside a giant Gothic vault, all delicate ribs and soaring arches like the great vault of the Cathedral of Plasencia, but made entirely of dazzling white crystal and enclosing a vast space that seemed filled, flooded, engorged with the purest and most perfect light. Cortés was at the centre of the nave. Rows of empty pews, likewise of crystal, surrounded him, their ranks marching two hundred paces forward to the edge of the transept. Straight ahead, on the left side of the crossing, where the nave, transept and choir all met, was a pulpit, full five fathoms high, approached by a slender spiral stairway, sculpted, it seemed, from a single mass of transparent ruby.

At the pulpit, but almost too blinding for the eye to tolerate, stood a figure, human yet not human, from whose body rays of intense white light burst forth in splendour.

Do I gaze on God Himself in his Heavenly Church? Cortés thought.

And he remembered Moses on the Mount, who had also seen God face to face, and he felt fear.

It wasn't like battlefield fear, which he'd learned to master better than most. It was something else, something he could not name, something arising from the tremendous radiant power emanating from this being of light who seemed to reach out and entrap him as though in an invisible net and then draw him forward.

Cortés watched the crystal floor of the nave slipping by beneath his feet, hints of buried rainbows swirling in its depths, but felt no physical contact, seemed to be floating as much as walking – which was strange until he remembered this was a dream. He tried to change the setting again but the trick wouldn't work this time and he was pulled irresistibly towards the base of the pulpit.

As though the wick of a lamp had been lowered, the radiance surrounding the figure dimmed as Cortés drew closer, becoming more bearable to the eye, finally revealing a tall and robust man standing in the pulpit. He had a rugged demeanour, more like a soldier or a labourer than a cleric. He was clean-shaven and fair-haired, perhaps forty years old and dressed in a simple hemp tunic, yet he projected an unassailable aura of charisma and authority – that quality of exceptional personal presence and spiritual power that the Moors call *Baraka*.

'I've been watching over you all your life,' said the man. 'I've seen that you've done well . . .' His voice was quiet and his tone intimate – as a father speaking to a son, or a friend to a friend – yet it seemed effortlessly to fill the entire vault, and there was something about it that was arresting, unsettling, almost physically probing.

Cortés came to a halt at the edge of the crossing and gazed up at the extraordinary ruby pulpit poised in space thirty feet above him, and at the awesome and terrifying man who stood in it. 'Who are you?' he asked. He fought down his fear. 'Are you God? Are you an archangel?'

'You already know who I am . . .'

'I do not know you, sir, I swear it. But give me some hint, some clue, and I will place you . . .'

The man laughed and it was a deep, rich sound. 'You had an episode of sickness as a child, Cortés, do you remember?'

'I remember.'

'A fever of the lungs brought you close to death, a priest was called, the last rites were spoken?'

'Yes.'

'But your nurse called down heavenly help.'

It was true. She'd been called Maria de Esteban and she had called on Saint Peter to save the dying child who miraculously recovered.

Even as Cortés gasped, suddenly getting it, he had to remind himself again that this was a dream. Only a dream. 'You are . . . the blessed Saint Peter?' he asked.

'I am the rock on whom Christ built his Church and the powers of Hell cannot prevail against me . . . Your own patron saint, Cortés – yet only now you know me!'

'But why? How . . . ?'

'Never mind all that. What I need you to remember, is that all of this' – his voice suddenly boomed – '*is by no means only a dream*. On the contrary, Don Hernando, all of this is very real. All of this is very serious. You are to do God's work.'

'Thank you, Father,' said Cortés. 'I have tried to do God's work in these islands.'

'And with great success! The Taino were too deeply sunk in idolatry and superstition for their souls ever to be saved . . .' Peter hesitated. 'I see, though, that some still live?'

'Only those who willingly accepted the faith and were ready to serve us . . .'

'Oh well, good then. Very good. Besides . . . a far greater task lies ahead of you . . .'

'In the New Lands, Father?'

A faraway look had come into Peter's eye. 'You will be the sword of God there, Don Hernando. Overthrow the heathens and the devil-worshippers, bring them the word of Christ and you will be rewarded in this world and the next.' The saint turned, descended the ruby stairway, his simple tunic hitched up over bare feet, and he came to stand opposite Cortés in the midst of the crossing. His eyes were utterly black, calm, steady, like deep pools of midnight, but his skin was pale and somehow bright, even dazzling, as though lit from within by the heat of some immense banked-down fire.

He placed his huge, calloused hands – soldier's hands, labourer's hands – on Cortés's shoulders. 'I have great plans for you,' he said.

'I am honoured, Father, and ready to serve.'

'But there is a condition.' Peter's eyes held Cortés prisoner. 'The friar Muñoz has a part to play in this. You must set aside your dislike for him. He is rough and crude in his ways but a tireless worker for God. Heaven will not bless your expedition without him.'

Chapter Twenty-Two

His name was Shikotenka, he was a king and the son of a king, and a ten-mile run was nothing to him, so much part of his usual routine that he didn't even break a sweat. The sun was low in the sky now, edging down towards setting, and though the day was still warm there was a breeze in the mountains, blowing off the snowbound shoulder of Popocatépetl, which kept a man cool. The early evening air caressed his skin, and the rugged green peaks of Tlascala spoke to him of freedom, filling his heart with joy.

Shikotenka could keep this pace up for two days if he had to, but he wouldn't have to. Already he could see the great forest where his fifty lay waiting, and his mind began to move ahead to the bloody work they must do together tonight . . .

If Guatemoc's body had not been found . . .

If no special alarm had been raised . . .

If they were blessed with the luck of the gods.

His hand went to his hair and he tugged out the little silver amulet that had betrayed his position this afternoon. It was a sensual, naked figure of Xochiquetzal, goddess of love, female sexual power, pleasure and excess.

Zilonen's favourite deity, of course.

Shikotenka pressed the amulet into a fold of his loincloth, where it should have been all along, and looked ahead.

Now less than a mile away down an open grassy slope, the forest was a huge imposing presence on the landscape, abundant with hidden life, a place of refuge and a place of mystery. Above, the leafy canopy was still lit a brilliant green by the dying sun, but down amongst the trees there was already a mass of shadow – as though night was not something that fell but something that rose from the ground like a black mist.

Shikotenka allowed himself to focus on the image – was there a song in it? – until a short, thin spear whistled past his ear, followed a heartbeat later by another that sliced a shallow groove into the flesh of his left thigh. Both weapons buried themselves in the ground with tremendous force and he saw as he ran by that they were *atlatl* darts launched from spear throwers.

He risked a quick glance over his shoulder, ducked as a third dart whooshed past, threw himself into a somersault to avoid a fourth and came up running, zigzagging left and right, losing much of his forward momentum.

Shikotenka was being hunted by three Mexica scouts. Quite how they'd crept up on him, he couldn't understand, because he'd been constantly on the lookout for precisely such a threat. But their shaved heads painted half yellow and half blue announced their rank as Cuahchics, the best of the best.

Two of them were armed with *atlatls* and had hung back to aim and throw their darts to maximum effect. The third was a runner . . .

A very *fast* runner.

Over longer distances he probably wouldn't amount to much, but he looked to be absolutely lethal as a mid-distance sprinter. Having to evade the darts was slowing Shikotenka down. Less than half a mile remained to the cover of the forest, but it was obvious the Cuahchics would catch him before he made it.

He was still zigzagging. Two more darts came in, both near-misses, slowing him further. He sensed without wasting time looking back that he'd lost most of his lead and thought – *might as well get up close and personal*. At least that would stop those cursed darts, since presumably the other Cuahchics wouldn't want to spear their brother-in-arms?

Would they?

Shikotenka heard footsteps behind him, closing fast, skidded to a halt and in one fluid movement whirled, drew Guatemoc's beautifully balanced *macuahuitl* from its scabbard at his back, and brought it crashing down on his pursuer's head.

The only problem was that the man's *macuahuitl* got in the way first.

As the obsidian teeth in the wooden blades of the two weapons clashed, there was an explosive spatter of broken pieces and it was luck that one of the larger fragments pierced the Mexica's right eye . . . He had a hard will, no doubt, this fearsomely painted Cuahchic, but the splinter of obsidian distracted him long enough for Shikotenka to catch him with a swooping blow that took off both his legs just above the ankles.

The Cuahchic went down hard, as one does with no feet, but continued to crawl around on his knees on the ground, spurting blood, roaring curses and lashing out with his *macuahuitl*.

Pointless stubborn pride, thought Shikotenka, as he hacked off the man's ugly blue and yellow head. *Utterly pointless*.

Out of the corner of his eye he'd been watching the other two Mexica. They'd abandoned the spear-throwers, as he'd expected, and were closing in fast.

The forest was invitingly near but Shikotenka knew he wouldn't make it. He took a strong two-handed grip on the hilt of the damaged *macuahuitl* and stood ready for battle.

Chapter Twenty-Three

For routine purposes, with a hundred sacrifices or fewer, victims approached their deaths only up the north stairway of the great pyramid of Tenochtitlan.

When greater numbers were required, as was the case today, the south, east and west stairs were also opened and a team of trained sacrificers – a knifeman and his four helpers who held the victims down – waited at the top of each staircase.

But on certain very special occasions, as when eighty thousand victims had been harvested to inaugurate the great pyramid in the time of Moctezuma's grandfather, up to forty additional killing teams would be deployed working back to back all around the summit platform.

Regardless of whether one, or four, or forty teams were at work, it had been discovered through repeated trials that each team was capable of processing approximately one victim every two minutes. There were uncertainties and imponderables that could make extraction of the heart and the elements of butchery a few seconds shorter or longer in some cases, but on average it was a two-minute operation, with each team killing thirty victims per hour. Sacrificers typically became exhausted after two hours of relentless effort and began to lose efficiency, but fresh teams stood by to take over smoothly without causing any interruption in the flow.

All afternoon, at the rate of thirty per stairway per hour, the five hundred and twenty women Moctezuma had called for, some sobbing, some silent, some hysterical, had climbed in four miserable columns to meet their deaths.

Moctezuma was outraged to hear their complaints. They should feel honoured to offer their hearts, their lives, *everything* they had, to so great a god as Hummingbird! They should be rushing to the sacrificial stone with excitement and joy, not inviting bad luck on all concerned by voiding their bowels and dragging their feet.

Moctezuma led the team at the top of the northern stairway but, unlike the knifemen of the other teams, he'd refused to take a break. The sorcery of the *teonanácatl* mushrooms still coursed through his veins and he felt tireless, ferocious, superhuman – his energy seeming to swell with every life he took.

After this morning's ceremony with fifty-two male victims, all of whom he had despatched personally to Hummingbird, he'd been killing women nonstop since the mid-afternoon. He'd been enjoying the work so much it was hard to believe nearly four hours had passed, but the sun had been high in the sky then and now lay just a few degrees above the horizon. In the great plaza at the foot of the pyramid the shadows of evening were growing long and deep, and priests were busy lighting hundreds of lanterns. But as he plunged the obsidian knife into yet another breastbone, and plucked out yet another pulsing heart, enough daylight remained to show Moctezuma that the entire northern stairway where he'd been at work was drenched in a slick and dripping tide of dark blood, through which his last victims, goaded by their guards, were being forced to wade wretchedly upward.

He giggled. The steps would be slippery. Someone might get killed!

Moctezuma's assistants spread out the next victim in front of him, a pretty screaming young thing with barely a wisp of pubic hair.

As he fell on her and tore out her heart, the power of the mushrooms, which had been coming and going in waves all afternoon, surged through him again, this time with enormous force, like the current of some great river or the career of a whirlwind. He had the feeling that he'd left his body – or rather, as he had felt earlier in Hummingbird's temple, that he was both in his body and out of it at the same time. So at one level he could see exactly where he was and what he was doing. He was on top of the great pyramid of Tenochtitlan, cutting women's hearts out. But at another level he again experienced himself to be elsewhere, transported high and far away into a rarefied empyrean zone, and once more in the presence of bright-skinned Hummingbird himself . . .

The god licked his lips. 'That last was a virgin,' he said. 'Quite tasty . . .' He made a sad face: 'But unfortunately most of the victims you've sent me this afternoon have not been of this quality. One or two have even been grandmothers. There were three prostitutes. Once again I'm disappointed in you . . .'

Moctezuma had already opened the chest of his next victim. He stopped abruptly, slipped out the sacrificial knife and smashed its heavy pommel into his own forehead, splitting the skin and drawing a burst of blood. 'I beg your forgiveness, master,' he said. He was aware that to his assistants, to Ahuizotl and to the other priests in attendance, he must appear to be addressing an invisible figure. 'We will find virgins for you, lord,' he promised. 'A thousand virgins – ten thousand if you require.' He eyed Ahuizotl, who was looking alarmed. 'It may take a little time, lord, that is all . . .'

'Time . . . ? I see . . . You speak to me of time?'

'Yes, master.'

'So you have time to wait, while enemies more powerful than you can possibly imagine raise forces against you? You don't care that wild beasts fight beside them in battle, some carrying them faster than the wind, others with monstrous teeth and jaws that tear men apart? You have no urgent need of knowledge of these enemies? Of their mastery of unknown metals? Of their terrible Fire Serpents that vomit lightning?'

Moctezuma trembled. Exactly as he had feared, these were not men Hummingbird was describing but an army of *tueles* – of gods. The fabled Xiuhcoatl, the Fire Serpent, was the magical weapon of the gods, able to strike men dead and dismember their bodies at a distance. Likewise who but gods could enchant wild beasts and turn them to their purpose?

'It is my desire and my responsibility, lord, to know all you have to teach about these enemies. Are they the companions of Quetzalcoatl, come to overthrow my rule? Tell me, I beseech you, what can I do to satisfy you?' Moctezuma bent to his victim again. He'd ripped her chest wide open with the first incision but she was still alive, eyes fluttering in pain and terror. Oblivious to her pleas he extracted her heart, placed

116

it sizzling on the brazier, and turned to the next woman. The process had become automatic and he was able to carry out his duties while keeping his attention focussed almost exclusively on Hummingbird, whose body had somehow vanished but whose face had grown to enormous size.

'It's very simple,' the god said, 'a straightforward transaction. Raid the Tlascalans, for their young girls, raid the Huejotzingos, raid the Otomis, *bring me virgins*, and I'll give you the help you seek . . .'

Moctezuma feared to repeat himself but it seemed there was no choice. 'It will take time, lord,' he said, 'My army is already in the field harvesting more victims, but I cannot give you a large basket of virgins tonight . . . Even so, I beg you to help me now on this matter of the strangers.'

Hummingbird seemed to think about it. 'I help you now,' he said, as though clarifying some point of argument, 'and you give me virgins later? That's the proposition?'

'Yes, lord, that is what I ask.'

There was a long silence before the god said finally: 'I believe that's acceptable.' He paused again as though for thought. 'But I'll need a down-payment . . .'

'Anything within my power . . .'

'The women's fattening pen isn't empty yet . . .'

'You are right, lord.'

'So empty it. Empty it tonight! Before I help you I want all those women's hearts. Every one of them.'

The visionary realm and the here and now were both equally present to Moctezuma and, in some strange juncture between the two, Hummingbird's immense face began to fade and melt downward, seeming gradually to dissolve into the mass of flickering orange lanterns that filled the great plaza below. The lanterns were in motion, dancing, swirling, coalescing into clumps and blots of light, spiralling apart again, leaving ghostly trails to mark their paths. The face of the god continued slowly to fade until soon there was nothing left of him but his two gigantic eyes, the whites stark as bone, the obsidian irises black as night – and they called Moctezuma down into their depths with a terrible seductive power. He felt a compulsion to jump from the top

117

of the pyramid, dive into those cool, black pools in the midst of that glimmering orange sea and merge himself forever with Hummingbird, but then a hand took his elbow and his whole body jerked like a man wakened suddenly from sleep.

'Are you all right, sire,' asked a familiar voice. He looked round to see that it was his own good and virtuous brother Cuitláhuac who had taken his arm. Glancing down, Moctezuma discovered, to his horror, that he had walked away from the sacrificial stone and now stood tottering right on the edge of the precipitous northern stairway. The twenty victims he had yet to process from this afternoon's sacrifices were lined up on the steps below, staring at him with . . . what?

Horror?

Hope?

Because for a moment there, Moctezuma realised, he must have come very close to leaping to his death.

'Thank you, Cuitláhuac,' he said, allowing the other man to draw him back to safety. 'I grow weary.'

'You must rest, brother. Let me or Ahuizotl take over from you here. Only a few victims remain.'

'No. I cannot rest. None of us can rest. I have been in the presence of the god!'

Cuitláhuac gasped, suitably impressed.

'I have been in the presence of the god,' Moctezuma repeated, 'and he has ordered more sacrifices tonight.'

Ahuizotl had been skulking in the background – *he would have been pleased to see me fall*, thought Moctezuma – but now came scuttling forward. 'More sacrifices tonight?' the high priest yelped. 'Surely we must rest, lord? All the teams are tired. Tomorrow we can begin again . . .'

'We will not rest!' roared Moctezuma. 'The sacrifices must continue through the night! The god himself has ordered this.' He lowered his voice: 'Do not thwart me, Ahuizotl,' he hissed, 'or you will be the first to die.'

The high priest gulped, nodded his understanding.

'Take two hundred of my palace guard,' said Moctezuma, 'and round up all the women still in the fattening pen. None must remain. You're to bring them all to the pyramid.'

Ahuizotl blinked. '*All*, Your Majesty?'

'Yes. All.'

'Do you realise their numbers, Majesty?'

'Does it matter?'

'After this afternoon's sacrifices, themselves not even complete' – Ahuizotl glared at the line of terrified victims still waiting on the steps – 'more than one thousand seven hundred women remain in the pen. Many are disorderly and belligerent – I myself was attacked this afternoon – and we faced severe problems martialling even five hundred and twenty of them. At least give me until tomorrow if I must bring seventeen hundred to the knife. I don't have sufficient enforcers to do this in a single night.'

'You will do this, Ahuizotl, and you will do it tonight.'

The high priest subsided into a glowering silence.

'You have two hundred of my palace guard to help you marshal troublesome prisoners,' Moctezuma reminded him. He lowered his voice again. In his opinion it was this troublesome priest who needed to be marshalled. 'Give me one more excuse,' he said, 'and I'll have you flayed alive.'

Ahuizotl stiffened. 'Please accept my abject apologies, lord. I will go immediately to the pen. I will bring all the women . . .'

'Of course you will,' said Moctezuma. He turned his back and looked at the patterns of orange lights swirling down below in the great plaza. He couldn't see Hummingbird's whirlpool eyes any more, not even a hint of them, but then right in his ear he heard the god whisper. '*Eat more* teonanácatl *and I will come to you again in the night.*'

'Oh Ahuizotl,' Moctezuma called after the high priest who was lifting the hem of his robes and about to attempt a descent of the slippery northern stair, 'those *teonanácatl* you sent me earlier . . .'

'Yes, Majesty . . .'

'I require more. I have great work ahead of me.'

'My servant will bring you the mushrooms, lord.'

'Good,' said Moctezuma. 'Very good.' He remembered he still held the obsidian knife. Dismissing Ahuizotl from his mind, he looked to the sacrificial stone where the next victim lay splayed, awaiting his attention.

Chapter Twenty-Four

Tozi sat with her face pressed against the bars of the fattening pen, looking out into the great plaza. Priests had lit hundreds of flickering orange lanterns and were carrying them through the steps of a complicated, flowing dance, long lines and interwoven processions coming together and pulling apart, fantastic shapes and patterns briefly forming and dissolving.

At the centre of this swirling, undulating sea of light, sending up a cacophony of drumbeats and conch blasts, squatting in a dark, malignant mass like some monstrous suppurating tumour, reared the great pyramid.

From her vantage point Tozi could see the summit and both the north and west faces clearly, and what was striking was how all these areas were not just blood-smeared as usual when sacrifices were underway, but seemed to be thickly covered everywhere with a wet, oozing crust of blood.

It was as though the pyramid itself were bleeding.

And down at its base, amongst the spiralling lanterns, swept by attendants into great heaps to either side of the stairways, were huge numbers of butchered torsos.

Tozi's head reeled.

Armies of shadows and darkness were on the march, encroaching everywhere, light fast leaching from the heavens, true night beginning to fall, but it was easy enough to count the twenty bedraggled women lined up on the north stairway waiting to climb the last few steps to their deaths. A similar number were in sight on the west stairway. Tozi couldn't see the east and south stairways, but she was sure they too were in use in the vast engine of human sacrifice that had been set in motion today. Out of the hundreds of victims seized this afternoon, only around eighty – twenty on each of the four stairways – remained alive.

The moon was already in the sky, but the last rays of the setting sun still lingered on the summit platform of the pyramid, illuminating a tall, naked man, covered from head to toe in blood, who balanced unsteadily at the top of the northern stairway, brandishing an obsidian knife.

He'd looked different this morning in his robes, but there was no doubt in Tozi's mind who this was. She nudged Malinal. 'That's Moctezuma,' she whispered, pointing at the naked figure, 'the Great Speaker himself.'

Malinal and Coyotl sat on either side of her, no more able than she was to tear their eyes away from the nightmarish spectacle of the great pyramid. Attracted by a growing commotion from the plaza, they'd left their place near the back of the prison and walked past Black Teeth and her group. They'd not been molested but were acutely conscious of the hateful stares of the two troublemakers from Xoco's gang as they made their way here to join other morbid spectators already gathered by the bars to watch the sacrifices.

Coyotl's usually happy features were set in a deep frown. 'If the Great Speaker is not careful,' he said, 'he will fall down the stairs.'

'Then let us hope,' said Malinal, 'that for once in his evil, useless life he's not careful.'

A woman sitting nearby, who seemed unaware that accusations of witchcraft had been made against Tozi, giggled raucously: 'Let's hope!' she agreed. 'Maybe if we all hope together we can make it happen?'

Maybe we can, Tozi thought. The idea seemed perfectly reasonable to her – worth trying, anyway – and as though on cue two more women joined in, then a third, chanting low and urgent: 'Fall! Fall! Fall! Fall!' Others round about began to take up the chorus, but were quickly silenced when the imposing figure of Cuitláhuac, younger brother of the Great Speaker, thrust himself forward beside Moctezuma, took his arm and guided him away from the top of the stairs.

The two men paused and spoke animatedly. They were still in sight on the summit platform, close to the sacrificial stone where the next victim lay spreadeagled, arms and legs braced by the assistant priests, waiting for death. Then a third figure came into view beside them, and Tozi's heart lurched. 'There's Ahuizotl,' she told Malinal. 'The high priest.'

'I know who he is,' said Malinal. An uncomfortable silence followed while she seemed to think things over. 'In fact, I know him personally.' Her eyes were downcast. 'There's stuff I have to tell you about myself.'

Tozi shrugged. She had seen the look of recognition Ahuizotl had fixed on her friend, but she'd not yet attempted to read Malinal's mind and she felt no desire to pry. 'I know you're a good person. I know you're brave. I know you've stuck by me and Coyotl. Nothing else matters . . .'

'But . . .'

'Save it for when we get out of here.'

'I might be putting you in danger—'

'Save it! It's not going to change anything. We're friends now. We stick together. That's what friends do, isn't it, Coyotl?'

'We stick together,' confirmed the little boy, 'and we help each other.'

'Good,' said Tozi. 'I'm glad we're all agreed.' She felt a fresh trickle of blood dripping over her upper lip, raised her cupped hand, blew her nose loudly into it and threw the blood and snot to the ground.

'Better not to blow,' Malinal suggested. 'Just makes nosebleeds worse.' She leaned forward, holding out her thumb and forefinger. 'May I?' she asked.

Tozi nodded and tilted back her head. A lot more blood was running from her nose, and now it started to pour down the back of her throat as well.

'No,' said Malinal. 'Don't lean back, lean forward.' She reached out and gripped Tozi's nostrils, pinching them closed with a firm, gentle pressure. 'Breathe through your mouth,' she said.

Tozi breathed, Malinal held her nose and, over Malinal's fingers, Tozi saw Coyotl's big bright eyes looking up at her, filled with concern.

My friends, she thought.

It was the best feeling she could remember having for a very long time.

When Tozi's nosebleed stopped, full night had fallen, but outside in the plaza hundreds of black-robed priests continued their slow processional dance of lights. Swinging loosely from their hands, their orange lanterns sent an unearthly glow flickering up the sides of the pyramid, and this seemed to be collected and reflected back by the lurid flames of the sacrificial braziers on the summit platform and the rows of guttering torches set up in front of the temple of Hummingbird. The great snakeskin drum, which had fallen silent, was beating again – a mournful, hollow, gut-wrenching sound. A conch blew, somewhere a flute trilled, and Tozi saw Moctezuma back at work at the sacrificial stone, wielding the knife, cutting out hearts. Lined up on the stair beneath him fewer than ten victims remained, and amongst them was one – she seemed no more than a child – who was screaming in terror again and again the words: '*Mama, Mama, Mama* . . .'

'Poor kid,' whispered Malinal. 'All afternoon being beaten and shoved by Mexica guards, climbing the pyramid, seeing all that blood, hearing all those cries, guessing what's coming to her in the end . . .'

'That's how they want us,' said Tozi. 'They want us mad with fear when they feed us to their gods. They think we taste better that way.'

Coyotl had been very quiet but now he began sobbing and sniffling. 'I don't want to be fed to their gods,' he said.

Tozi wrapped her arms round him, held him tight, told him, 'You will *not* be. No matter what happens, I'll protect you. I'll never let them hurt you.'

'Besides,' said Malinal – she pointed to the priests with their lanterns, to the pyramid, to the few remaining victims – 'surely it's over for tonight?'

Sometimes, even when she didn't want to, Tozi couldn't help seeing inside other people's minds. That was how it was now when the sight came on her unbidden, and in an instant she knew things about Malinal. Knew that she had been a slave but prized for her beauty, highly trained in the arts of love and privileged despite her captivity. Knew that noble and powerful men had paid her owner fortunes to enjoy her. As though she were viewing swimmers at the bottom of a murky pool, Tozi saw that many of the leaders of Tenochtitlan had crossed Malinal's path – here was Itzcoatl, here was Coaxoch, here Zolton, here Cuitláhuac, here Maxtla. And here? Whose was this mean face, this mottled face hidden in the deeps of the seeing-pool, if not Ahuizotl himself, high priest of the Mexica, a man sworn on pain of death to lifelong celibacy?

That was when the seeing ended with a flicker, as abruptly as it had begun, and Tozi found Malinal shaking her by the shoulders, peering into her eyes, saying: 'Are you all right?'

Ahuizotl! Tozi thought. *So that's what you were trying to tell me.* But instead she said: 'I've survived in here for seven months and I've not been through a day like this before. I've seen them sacrifice thirty, fifty, sometimes even a hundred often enough. But never so many victims as went under the knife today, and the Great Speaker leading the killing from morning to night? There has to be a special reason for that.'

Malinal's beautiful face had become sombre and thoughtful. 'There is a reason,' she said.

Tozi gave her a long, level look. 'And you know it?'

'Something happened late last year. Something that's never happened before. I think it's made Moctezuma crazy . . .'

From the top of the pyramid they could both hear the screams of a woman in terrible fear, abruptly silenced by the *thud* of the obsidian knife.

'Four months ago,' said Malinal, 'strangers appeared in the Yucatán, in the lands of the Chontal Maya. They were bearded and white-skinned, they came from across the eastern sea in boats as big as mountains and they made their way to the town of Potonchan near the mouth of the Tabasco river. They had great powers, these strangers. They were few in number – about a hundred – but they possessed fearsome weapons and they defeated an army of ten thousand before they returned to the sea. Some thought they were human beings, some thought they were gods, maybe even the retinue of the god Quetzalcoatl himself, come to herald his return – it's still not settled.' She lowered her eyes. 'I am of the Chontal Maya,' she confided, 'and I was born in Potonchan. My people fear Moctezuma. They're not his vassals, they don't pay him tribute, but they like to please him. They sent word to him, paintings on bark, and an eyewitness to describe the strangers with a full account of the battle . . . That's how I came to know about this . . .'

'From the witness?'

'He spoke only Maya, and when the Great Speaker wanted to question him I was summoned to interpret. I've been a slave in Tenochtitlan for five years but I have a gift for languages and I've learnt fluent

Nahuatl.' Malinal paused, looked at Tozi, then at Coyotl: 'Does it seem odd to you that a slave such as I was chosen for so important a task rather than some diplomat?'

Coyotl was indignant. 'No! You were chosen because you're beautiful . . . I bet the diplomats are all ugly!'

Malinal tousled his hair. 'Thank you!' she said. 'That's very sweet!' Her manner changed. 'But I think the real reason I was chosen was because I was expendable. Anyway, this is what happened. The witness and I were bound hand and foot and forced to kneel in the audience chamber of the palace, in front of an empty throne, until Moctezuma came in and was seated. We saw just his feet, his clean brown feet in gold sandals, and the hem of his robe. We were told we must not look at his face, must keep our eyes downcast at all times, or we would die. Then the guards left the room. The voice of the Great Speaker is soft but very cold. He told me that the witness should describe the strangers – their appearance, their manner of speech, their manner of dress and their weapons. The witness gave his report, described their beards and their white skins and the deadly weapons they used. I interpreted and all the time I felt the atmosphere changing, becoming very dark, very heavy, like a funeral. Twice, just for a heartbeat, I risked a glance and I saw that fear had come upon the Great Speaker as he received the news. Believe me! I saw it! His jaw hanging loose! His hands shaking! His eyes sliding from side to side. You don't expect the Speaker of the Mexica to be a coward, Tozi, but that's what Moctezuma is, a coward – even though the witness did tell a terrifying story! I put it faithfully into Nahuatl and when I'd given it all, Moctezuma groaned. He clutched his belly! His bowels turned to water!' She let go a peal of laughter: 'He just shat right there, Tozi, in front of us! There were terrible farts and . . . you know . . . other sounds. The most awful smell . . .'

Tozi was laughing too; some of the other women around joined in. Coyotl giggled, but Malinal's voice had become serious again. 'After he was done,' she said, 'he moved about, I think he was cleaning himself but we didn't dare look. Then we heard him talking at the door. Soon afterwards a group of guards and priests entered. The poor witness never knew what hit him; he was strangled on the spot. The executioner turned to me, put his hands round my throat. I thought I was done for

125

until Ahuizotl came storming in and stopped him. "No!" he said. "I want this woman for sacrifice!" There was no one to overrule him – Moctezuma had left the room – and in this way I was set aside.'

'But,' said Tozi, 'obviously not for sacrifice . . .'

'Not at first. Ahuizotl used me for sex these past four months . . . Uggh! His breath smells of carrion.' Malinal made a face and blushed. 'This is what you told me you didn't need to know,' she said apologetically, 'but here we are back at it in a roundabout way.' She shrugged. 'So he used me for four months then, last night, guards took me from the house where he kept me prisoner and threw me in here. He'd had what he wanted from me, I suppose, so he sent me for sacrifice.'

'You're a knife at his throat,' said Tozi, 'as long as you're still alive.'

Malinal nodded. 'Because of his vows . . . I know. He'd be afraid I'd bear witness against him. But really – celibate priests! Believe me, it's a joke! It's easier to find a virgin in a whorehouse than a celibate in the Temple.'

Tozi made a habit of being aware of people in her surroundings at all times, so she noticed immediately that the two hellions from Xoco's gang had followed her here. They would never give up, it seemed! They were whispering to other Tlascalans around them, and some who'd been friendly enough moments before were now giving them ugly glances. Tozi heard the word 'witch'. Coyotl heard it too and huddled closer. Malinal looked scared but calm somehow.

'Witch! Witch! Witch!'

It's all starting again, Tozi thought wearily. She tried to marshal her strength and found she had nothing left to give. If these Tlascalans decided to tear them to pieces now, she knew she would be helpless.

But then there came a commotion, the swaying, undulating dance in the plaza abruptly ceased, some of the lanterns fell to the ground, the gates of Moctezuma's palace swung open and a phalanx of heavily armed soldiers marched out.

A lot of soldiers!

They cut across the plaza, straight towards the fattening pen.

At their head, flanked by his two acolytes, was Ahuizotl.

Chapter Twenty-Five

From the direction of the forest a storm of arrows whirred around Shikotenka in the dusk, passed him on both sides and smashed the Cuahchics down before they could close with him.

He turned with a broad grin. All fifty of his men were out of the trees and coming on at a run, a second volley of arrows already nocked to the string. But they lowered their bows and slowed to an easy walk when they saw the Cuahchics were no longer a threat. Two were dead and the third writhed on the ground, bristling with arrows and filling the air with screams and curses.

'A nice surprise,' called out Shikotenka. 'I thought I was on my own.'

The plan had been to meet three hours later by a sweet-water spring in the depths of the forest. There was no reason for his men to be here.

Panitzin was out in front. He was nicknamed 'Tree' for his massive size, stolid features, dark skin the colour of *ahuehuete* bark and long, wild hair. 'Too many mosquitos at the spring,' he growled as they embraced.

'No reasonable man could be expected to stand it,' agreed dagger-thin Acolmiztli, who'd jogged up right behind Panitzin. At forty-two he was the grandfather of the squad, but had proved his worth in countless battles and could outrun warriors fifteen years his junior.

'So you just decided to wait here instead?'

Tree spoke again, which was unusual for such a taciturn man. 'Yes,' he said. 'More comfortable.'

'And close to the path,' added Shikotenka's cousin Tochtli, 'so we would spot you as you entered the forest.'

Tochtli, whose name meant 'Rabbit', was the newest and by far the

127

youngest member of the squad. His smooth complexion, slight stature and soft brown eyes contributed to a gentle, almost womanly manner that exposed him to constant ridicule. Perhaps to compensate for this, and to win the approval of the more experienced fighters, he'd taken what Shikotenka considered to be unnecessary risks during both the prior skirmishes with the Mexica in which he'd so far been engaged.

Shikotenka frowned. 'Spot me as I entered the forest, eh?' He snorted and spat. 'That sort of plan usually goes wrong . . .'

Tochtli's face immediately fell and he looked round uncertainly at Tree and Acolmiztli.

'But today it went right!' Shikotenka laughed, taking the pressure off his cousin. 'If you'd stayed where you were supposed to, I might have had my work cut out here.'

As the rest of the squad milled around, laughing and joking, Tree unslung his great mahogany war club, strolled over to the surviving Cuahchic and dealt him a single massive blow to the head. His screams stopped abruptly as his shaved skull shattered, spattering warriors standing nearby with fragments of brain and bone, provoking roars of complaint.

'All that yelling was giving me a headache,' Tree explained with an apologetic shrug.

Shikotenka clapped him on the shoulder: 'Looks like you gave him a worse one,' he said.

The squad was formed of five platoons of ten, with Tree, Chipahua, Etzli, Acolmiztli and jade-nosed Ilhuicamina as the platoon leaders. They were battle-hardened, clever, calculating men, but they were also independent and argumentative and the death of Guatemoc had provoked controversy.

'I don't see the problem,' said Tree, who liked nothing better than a good battle. 'You fought Guatemoc and you killed him. Dead men don't tell tales.'

Shikotenka was repairing the broken obsidian teeth of Guatemoc's *macuahuitl* from the squad's stock of spares. 'Sometimes they do,' he said as he slotted another of the razor-sharp blades into place. 'If the Mexica find his body it'll put them on high alert. They'll have search parties out combing the area. Our task tonight was hard enough anyway. I fear this will make it much harder.'

'Do you want to call it off?' asked Chipahua. His bald head was as big as a chilacayohtli gourd, smooth and domed on top, narrowing somewhat at the temples but widening again to accommodate his prominent cheekbones and full fleshy face.

'No,' said Shikotenka. 'We can't call it off.'

'Then all this is empty talk.' A brace of white-tailed deer roasted on spits over the banked-down fire and Chipahua reached out, worked loose a steaming chunk of bloody meat and transferred it to his mouth. He chewed slowly, almost lecherously, smacking his sensual, sneering lips and making a great show of sucking his fingers. 'Reckon that's ready to eat,' he said.

The entire squad was gathered round the fire and now everyone dived into the feast. There had been an element of risk in cooking it, but the men needed their strength for the trial that lay ahead. They'd found a place a mile into the forest, boxed in tightly by great stands of trees and undergrowth, where there was almost no chance a fire would be seen. The roasted meat would more likely be smelled, but there was nothing to be done except bolt it down quickly.

Acolmiztli's eyes glittered and the planes of his narrow face caught the glow of the fire, emphasising his usual hollow-cheeked and ghoulish appearance. 'If they've found Guatemoc the whole camp's going to be buzzing like a hornet's nest,' he complained. 'We'll not get anywhere near Coaxoch's pavilion, let alone inside it to kill him.'

Etzli was with him. 'We should think again. We're fifty but they've got four regiments. With surprise on our side we might have pulled it off; without, we don't stand a chance.'

'Perhaps the death of Guatemoc will make things easier for us?' Tochtli dared to offer. He'd been watching the older warriors, his eyes shifting eagerly from man to man, obviously summoning up the courage to make his voice heard. 'The Mexica won't know exactly what happened, or who knifed their prince. Could be just the distraction we need.'

'Quiet, little Rabbit,' snarled Etzli, showing teeth filed to sharp points. 'What do you know, who's fought in only two battles?' Etzli's name

129

meant Blood and, despite his caution this evening, he was a seasoned, brutal killer. It must have taken some nerve, Shikotenka realised, for Tochtli to contradict him.

But support came from Ilhuicamina who looked scornfully at Acolmiztli and Etzli. 'You're both turning into old women,' he snapped. A livid scar where a *macuahuitl* had struck him traced a thick, puckered, horizontal track from left to right across the middle of his face. His prosthetic nose, fashioned from small jade tiles to cover the most hideous part of the injury, glittered eerily in the firelight. 'The boy's right. We can still do this.'

'I'm certain we can do it,' agreed Shikotenka. 'But the risk will be great.'

'For a chance to kill a piece of shit like Coaxoch,' said Ilhuicamina, 'I'll take that risk.'

Shikotenka's men were sworn to follow him even into death, and in return he gave them the right to speak their minds. The time had come to tell them the truth about this mission. The stakes were higher than any of them knew. 'To be honest,' he said, his face deadpan, 'if this was just about Coaxoch, I'd call the attack off.'

Ilhuicamina blinked. Even Tree sat up and paid attention.

'But Coaxoch is only the bait.' Shikotenka lowered his voice so everyone had to lean a little closer, and in the fire's glow he told them the plan.

130

Chapter Twenty-Six

Shielded from view by three large coils of rope and piles of canvas sheeting he'd arranged around himself, Pepillo lay on his back in the aftcastle of the *Santa María de la Concepción*, trying to decide what to do. Here he was well away from the whirl of activity on the main deck, where bales and barrels were still being loaded. He heard men shouting, seemingly arguing. Others sang a vulgar song in unison as they hoisted some great burden. He heard roars of laughter. The horses brought on board earlier stamped and snuffled in their stalls. Far below he heard the slap, slap, slap of wavelets lapping against the hull of the great ship.

He could run, he thought bleakly, if his legs would carry him after the beating he'd taken. But then what? If he returned to the monastery, the brothers would bring him straight back here and hand him over to Muñoz again. And if he tried to hide, where would he shelter, how would he find food? He didn't have a centavo to his name.

Pepillo groaned. His body was a mass of pain. His buttocks ached from the repeated kicks Muñoz had delivered to them. His nose, where Muñoz had broken it, was swollen and inflamed and still hurt more than he could believe. His scalp stung as though scalded where Muñoz had wrenched a clump of hair out by the roots. His head pounded because Muñoz had repeatedly punched him, and a tooth at the front of his lower jaw had been knocked loose. His side, chest and arms were horribly bruised from being thrown against the cabin walls by Muñoz. There was a red stripe across his shin, another diagonally across his belly and three more on his thighs where Muñoz had struck him with a bamboo cane. Finally, in a crescendo of rage, Muñoz had

131

seized Pepillo by the shoulders, savagely bitten his left ear, hurled him across the cabin again and told him to get out.

He'd been hiding on the deck of the aftcastle since then, watching early evening dusk edge into night. Now the first stars were showing amongst scudding clouds and he hoped Muñoz was sleeping deeply.

In fact Pepillo hoped Muñoz was sleeping so deeply he would never wake up.

But then he thought how wrong it was to wish death on any human being, particularly a religious, so he whispered, 'Dear God forgive me', and returned to his gloomy concerns about the future.

He could not run; there was nowhere to run to. Besides – he felt the great carrack bob beneath him, heard the creak of its rigging in the freshening breeze – he very much wanted to stay. Truth was, he wanted this adventure more than anything else in the world. To sail into unknown waters with brave men, to explore fabled New Lands, to bring the faith to benighted heathens, even perhaps to earn some gold – he could not imagine anything he would rather be doing. All his dreams seemed poised on the verge of coming true.

Except for Muñoz.

No position in which Pepillo put his body was comfortable and now, with a grunt of pain, he rolled onto his stomach to ease the distress in his back. As he turned, brushing against the canvas sheeting, he heard the sound of a stealthy footstep on the navigation deck below, where the whipstaff that steered the great ship was mounted. There was a beat of silence, then another step – this time plainly on the stair up to the aftcastle.

Fear gripped Pepillo by the throat, and then at once relief as he heard Melchior's voice. 'So there you are! Come down to the main deck, Pepillo Dogbreath. Food's a'cooking – fish stew and beans.'

'Thank you,' said Pepillo. 'But I can't come just now . . .'

'Otherwise engaged are you, your lordship?' Lanterns burned bright on the main deck so the loading could continue, but little light reached the aftcastle and Pepillo lay behind the coiled ropes in a pool of deep shadow. 'Too important to eat with the common herd?' Melchior asked, looming over him. His tone suddenly changed. 'What are you doing down there anyway?'

With some difficulty and pain because his injuries were stiffening,

Pepillo rolled on his side and forced himself to sit. 'Muñoz beat me up,' he said.

A backwash of lantern light from the main deck fell across his face, his bloody nose, his torn ear, and Melchior dropped into a crouch beside him. 'That devil!' he said. 'I expected something like this. Just not so soon.'

Pepillo was startled. 'You *knew*? Why didn't you warn me?'

'I did try to warn you but you ran off to the Customs House . . . Look, there's no good way to tell you but I'd say you're lucky this stopped at a beating. Most of us who sailed on the Córdoba expedition think Muñoz murdered his last page . . .'

'Murdered?' Pepillo's voice was a squeak . . .

'That's what I said.'

'But why?'

'The *peccatum Sodomiticum*,' Melchior whispered.

Pepillo had learned Latin in the monastery. 'The sin of Sodom . . .' he translated. He felt himself blushing: 'You can't mean . . . ?'

'That Muñoz is a sodomite? That he likes his pages' arses? That he kills them to keep them silent. I certainly can mean that! And I do!'

'But . . . But . . .' With this horrible new thought, Pepillo had completely forgotten about his aches and pains.

'Did he grope you?' asked Melchior. 'Did his fingers get in private places?'

'No . . . *No!* Of course not. Nothing like that.'

'Are you sure?' said Melchior.

'I'm sure.'

But Pepillo's hand went unconsciously to his ear. He'd not been groped, but he'd been bitten! It was so unexpected and so astonishing a thing that he might almost have convinced himself it had never happened if it wasn't for the torn flesh of his earlobe and his vivid memory of the wet, soft, heat of Muñoz's lips . . .

The prospect of being confined on board ship with such a monster, constantly at his beck and call, exposed to his every cruel or perverse whim, was almost more than Pepillo could bear. But the prospect of *not* sailing in the *Santa María* and of missing his chance for the adventure of a lifetime seemed even worse.

133

A pulse of pure hatred shook him and he clenched his fists. This time he wouldn't ask God's forgiveness. 'I wish Muñoz would die,' he whispered.

Melchior was just a shadow, crouching in the darkness. Now he stretched his back, looked up at the stars. 'People die all the time,' he said. 'Even big, important people like Muñoz. They go overboard or they get killed and eaten by savage tribes, or they mysteriously fall from the rigging and break their necks. Accidents happen. They're expected. Usually no one digs too deep.'

'What are you suggesting?'

'I'm not suggesting anything, you silly mammet. I'm stating facts. Fact One – accidents happen. Fact Two – most people don't like Muñoz.' Melchior sauntered to the railing surrounding the aftcastle and rested his elbows on it, leaning out over the pier.

In the distance, but coming closer at speed, Pepillo heard an urgent drum roll of galloping hooves on the cobbles. He stood and limped to the railing. It sounded like an entire squadron of cavalry was thundering towards them but, moments later, scattering the crowds still thronging the pier, a single rider, blond hair flying about his shoulders, exploded out of the night. He brought his huge white horse to a rearing halt beside the *Santa María*, leapt down gracefully, handed the reins to a dumbfounded guard and stormed up the gangplank onto the ship.

'That's Don Pedro de Alvarado,' Melchior said. 'He does like to make a dramatic entrance.'

Chapter Twenty-Seven

Santiago, Cuba, Thursday 18 February 1519

Smash! Thud! Crash! Bang! Cortés awoke in hot darkness, sweat lathering his body, his mind sluggish, a stunning headache addling his brains. Trapped! He was trapped in some thundering Hell! *Smash! Crash! Thud!* His arms and legs were tangled, every movement seemed to constrict and bind him further and for a few terrifying, vertiginous seconds he had no idea where or even who he was. Then he heard *Bang! Bang! Bang! Crash! Thud!* – hammer blows following one another in quick succession – and suddenly it all came back to him. He was tangled in his hammock in his stateroom on the *Santa María*. He had overslept his siesta. Night had fallen. And a few paces away, on the other side of the partition, Muñoz was still beating his page. Thud! Smash! Bang! Bang!

Enough! thought Cortés. With a mighty effort he wrestled himself free of the hammock and dropped barefoot to the floor. He was about to pound on the partition and yell some insult when he remembered his dream. He hesitated, heard further loud banging and a gruff voice shouting 'Cortés, wake up!', and realised with relief the noise wasn't coming from Muñoz's quarters at all. Cursing as he stubbed his toe in the darkness on the corner of his sea chest, he strode to the door, slid back its heavy bolts and flung it open.

'Ah,' said Alvarado, 'at last! It's like trying to wake the dead.' He was holding a lantern and brushed past Cortés into the much-reduced stateroom. 'Dear God!' he said, waving the lantern at the partition. 'What happened here?'

Cortés held up a warning finger. 'Next door is my guest, Father Gaspar Muñoz. He'll sail with us as the expedition Inquisitor.'

Alvarado made the face of a man sucking a lemon and mouthed, 'Velázquez?'

Cortés nodded yes.

Alvarado grinned. 'There's trouble at the Customs House,' he boomed. 'They've impounded our whole consignment of falconets. You need to come now.'

Cortés knew that all the expedition's small cannon, including the falconets, had already been safely loaded, but made appropriately disbelieving and infuriated noises as he dressed in haste, tugged on his boots and sword and marched out onto the navigation deck with Alvarado, calling for his horse to be saddled and brought down to the pier. The two men talked of nothing but falconets and Customs duties until they rode off, but when they reached Alvarado's ship they reined in, dismounted and went quietly on board. The moon was up now, and the sky bright, making them visible from the *Santa María*, but no one seemed to be watching.

The *San Sebastián* was built to the same design as the *Santa María*, with the stateroom abaft the navigation deck occupying the whole of the stern beneath the aftcastle. On the *San Sebastián*, however, there had been no need to partition the captain's quarters to make space for a black-robed friar and Alvarado had the full, generous, well-lit area to himself. 'We can talk safely here,' he said. He reached into his jerkin and pulled out a single sheet of vellum. 'First you need to read this.'

Cortés took the sheet but deliberately ignored it as he moved to one of the two stuffed chairs with which Alvarado had furnished the stateroom. He sat down, noticing for the first time that there was something odd about the manner of his oldest and closest friend. He was holding his left arm in an awkward, delicate way, his hair was wildly dishevelled, and there were streaks of what looked like dried blood – apparently not his own – on his jerkin and hose. He wore one of the new Toledo rapiers in a scabbard on his hip, but also carried a huge single-edged falchion, thrust into the front of his sword belt.

'Isn't that Zemudio's blade?' Cortés asked. He'd been in and out of the governor's office more times than he'd care to count in the past month and the bodyguard was always there.

Alvarado grinned like a puppy waiting to be praised. 'I just killed Zemudio,' he said.

Cortés frowned. Knowing his friend as he did, he had no difficulty in believing him. Still he had to ask: 'Why would you do such an insane thing?'

'To get that sheet of vellum you're holding in your hand.' Alvarado was bouncing up and down with impatience: 'Read it now! It proves everything.'

'Proves what?'

'Just read it!'

From the Hand of His Excellency Don Diego de Velázquez, Governor of Cuba

To Don Pánfilo de Narváez

This 18th day of February, Year of our Lord 1519

Don Pánfilo,

The matter of our previous discussions has now reached its crisis and all is to proceed as we have planned. Tonight I will relieve Don Hernando Cortés of command of our expedition to the New Lands and appoint you as captain-general in his place. Cortés will be arrested discreetly, late at night, so as not to excite resistance from his supporters. So, prepare yourself my friend! When we have him in chains I will send for you.

May God bless this night's operations, and our expedition, which I am certain will be lucrative and crowned with success for us both.

Yours in Christ,

Diego de Velázquez

After Cortés had read the letter, turning over in his mind all the layers of bad faith and betrayal between him and Velázquez, Alvarado flopped down in the armchair opposite him. 'The discreet arrest he talks about,' he said with a knowing wink, 'that involves me.'

Cortés sighed: 'What's he paying you?'

'Twenty thousand gold pesos. I was actually able to get five thousand up front . . . Mine to keep, I reckon. Spoils of battle and all that . . .

Anyway, I'm to invite you to dinner at ten o'clock tonight here on the *San Sebastián* and pour this in your wine,' Alvarado fished in his pocket and produced a little glass vial containing a colourless liquid. 'An hour later you start puking your guts out and running a deathly fever. I'm to send for Dr La Peña – another one of Velázquez's stooges. He'll ship you off to his hospital in a horse-drawn carriage, but you won't ever get there. Velázquez's guards will detain you on the road, you'll be flung in jail in his palace and, when the drug wears off, you'll be questioned under . . . I think the term is "extreme duress"?'

'I take it,' said Cortés, 'since you're telling me all about it, that none of this is going to happen.'

Alvarado grinned again: 'Of course it's not going to happen! You're a winner! I want to sail with you, not that ass Narváez. Besides, you're my friend.'

'You're giving up a lot of money for friendship.'

'Fifteen thousand gold pesos to be exact. But I'm a businessman. I expect to make that back many times over with my friend Hernán Cortés in command of the expedition.'

'And you fought Zemudio . . . To the death.'

'Well . . . We needed to see Narváez's orders, didn't we? Had to know what was in them.'

'Thank you, Don Pedro,' said Cortés. He felt touched and deeply grateful for his friend's loyalty, and wanted to reward him. 'I'll not forget this.'

Another big grin from Alvarado: 'I'll not let you forget it.'

'You realise we'll have to sail?' said Cortés. 'Tonight.'

'Are we ready?'

Ready? Cortés thought. *Ready enough.* He'd been preparing for such a sudden, unscheduled escape since the moment he'd first talked Velázquez, with honeyed words and grand promises, into giving him command of the expedition three months earlier. It was to be his ultimate revenge on the old monster for forcing him to wed Catalina. And revenge, as everyone knew, was a dish best served cold. The months he'd spent rotting in jail on trumped-up charges until he'd finally given in to Velázquez and married his hell-bitch niece rankled constantly in his memory. But if this colossal gamble paid off, if he could steal the expedition and get away with it, and most of all if the rumours of the fabulous wealth of the New Lands turned out to be true, then he would be rich beyond all imagining and the name of Cortés would be honoured by history, while Velázquez would be cut to the quick in his pride and his pocket and remembered by no one within a generation. The only danger – the one that had now come to pass – was that the governor would guess the plan before they were ready to sail. This was why Cortés had done everything fast and lied about progress, making it seem that much more time would be needed before the ships were fully loaded when, in truth, apart from a few items, they were stocked and ready to sail tonight. All crews, horses, dog teams, and almost all the enlisted men were boarded and ready to go at a moment's notice, and those who were not were in the taverns of Santiago where they could be easily found.

'Are we ready?' Alvarado repeated.

'Sorry,' said Cortés. 'A lot on my mind. Yes . . . we're ready. Almost. But there's one pressing need we can't neglect. With soldiers and ships' crews added together, we've more than six hundred mouths to feed, and Córdoba's experience proves we can't count on friendly natives to supply us. We're well stocked with staples but we must have meat for our men – fresh meat for the voyage, preserved meats and more live-stock on the hoof to sustain us until we're self-sufficient in the New Lands.'

Alvarado raised an eyebrow: 'Tonight? Where?'

'The slaughterhouse. They have enough to feed the city. Let's send a squad over there on the double to bring us everything they've got.' Cortés paused, lowered his voice: 'The other captains must know nothing of this until it's done. I raised five good private soldiers to ensign rank yesterday. They're grateful to me and they'll do what we ask without question. One of them sails with you – Bernal Díaz, do you know him?'

'I know him,' said Alvarado with a sneer. 'He's a peasant. Not officer material.'

'He's literate. He keeps a daily journal.'

Alvarado shrugged. 'So?'

'It speaks of a certain seriousness of mind, don't you think, a certain dedication when one of his class reads and writes? You judge by surface appearances, Pedro. I've looked deeper and I see great potential, high intelligence, unusual abilities, all gathered together in this young man. Send for him, please.'

Moments later heavy footsteps sounded on the navigation deck. There came a loud knock at the door and Bernal Díaz del Castillo clumped into the stateroom. He was twenty-seven years old, tall, heavy-built, with solid labourer's muscles like a ploughboy and a big, sallow-skinned face that was all bony planes and angles. How very unsure of himself he was, how out of place he obviously felt, how overwhelmed at his elevation to ensign, and how desperately he wanted to please.

Cortés beckoned him closer: 'Welcome lad,' he said. He rubbed his hands vigorously together. 'I've got a job for you to do and it's got to be done fast . . .'

After Díaz had repeated his orders and lumbered off to carry them out, Cortés turned to Alvarado: 'How long have we got until Velázquez realises you've played him false? Four more hours? Five? Let's think this through.'

An Amsterdam clock stood in the corner of the stateroom. 'No use looking at that,' said Alvarado. 'It's been stopped for a year. But it's around eight of the evening now. Sun's been down for a couple of hours.'

Cortés nodded. 'Velázquez told you to organise the dinner for ten o'clock. He'll be expecting, what? That you'll poison my wine within the first hour?'

Alvarado nodded in agreement: 'Seems reasonable.'

'In which case I'll be expected to be showing symptoms by midnight. Agreed?'

'Agreed.'

'So around midnight we raise the hue and cry on the *San Sebastián*, and send a messenger to fetch Dr La Peña. It will take at least an hour for the messenger to reach him and bring him to the harbour. That would mean it's one o'clock, maybe half past, when La Peña comes on board – around the time of tonight's high tide. Velázquez won't be surprised if the doctor stays on the ship for an hour before bringing his patient out, so I'd guess that makes us safe from interference until, well . . . let's say two o'clock. We must sail no later than that; the ebb tide will aid our departure.'

'What about the other captains?' Alvarado asked. 'They're going to want to know why we're embarking so suddenly. Some of them definitely won't be ready, or will say they aren't, and some of them are loyal to Velázquez – Juan Velázquez de León is his cousin for God's sake; he'll not stand by and let us steal away with the fleet.'

'Cristóbal de Olid is also Velázquez's man,' said Cortés, naming another of the captains of the expedition, 'and Diego de Ordaz used to be his major-domo. Velázquez put him here to keep an eye on me and stop me doing precisely what we're about to do tonight. It just means we're going to have to tell a careful story when we call the captains together.'

'Do you have something in mind?'

Cortés leaned forward in his chair and rubbed his aching back. 'Someone,' he said. 'Specifically Pedrarias. This afternoon my shipping agent returned from Jamaica. He brought word Pedrarias has assembled a fleet there twice the size of our own and hurries to stake his claim to the New Lands before we do.'

'Damn the man!' shouted Alvarado theatrically. 'We have to beat him to it!' He lowered his voice: 'It's not true, is it?' he asked.

Pedro de Arias Dávila, Pedrarias for short, had earned a fearsome reputation in the Granada campaigns and during the Italian wars. He had arrived in Hispaniola in 1513 and sailed on with a small force to establish the colony of Castilla del Oro in Darién in 1514. There he had spread such ruin, rapine and mayhem that the colony had had to be abandoned in 1517, but he was still in the region and known to be looking for new ways to get rich by force of arms.

'Fortunately it's not true,' Cortés laughed, 'but it *could* be true, and that's what matters. Olid, Ordaz and Velázquez de León all have as much at stake in the expedition as we do and none of them will want Pedrarias to snatch the prize. If they believe me they'll all see why we have to set sail at once or risk losing precedence. We can't wait another week, or even another day, to finish equipping and loading the fleet.

Everyone will understand the haste, the urgent departure by night, even emptying the city slaughterhouse – it'll all make perfect sense to them by the time I'm finished . . .'

Alvarado's mind seemed to be elsewhere. 'Damn,' he exclaimed. 'I've just remembered something . . .'

'What?' Cortés felt the slightest stir of anxiety.

'Velázquez's palace guard! He's going to have a squad stationed on the harbour road to grab you from La Peña's carriage. Those boys are pretty stupid, but even they'll get suspicious if they see our men herding swine and cattle to the docks at one in the morning . . .'

Cortés was relieved. 'That's the least of our worries,' he said. 'I'll send my scouts out to watch the road. They'll tell us where the guardsmen have stationed themselves and in what numbers. We'll deal with them.' He grinned. 'But first we've got to sell all this to the captains.'

Chapter Twenty-Eight

Though she had nothing left to give, Tozi tried to fade the three of them when the soldiers entered the fattening pen, but the power had deserted her. Something had broken in her head. She could no longer even send the fog.

So they ran, and kept on running, dodging through the thinning crowds, hiding sometimes in pools of deeper darkness where the soldiers' torches did not penetrate, then running again, always running, Malinal carrying Coyotl on her hip, as the prisoners were gathered in and herded remorselessly towards the gate. Tozi had no sense of the passage of time but at a certain point, quite suddenly, like water poured from a pot, the last of her strength flowed out of her. 'I can't go on,' she said, halting near the bars where their flight had started. The pain in her head was unbearable. 'I'm done in.'

Malinal, still with Coyotl on her hip, reached out and wrapped her in a warm embrace. Coyotl also flung his arms round her neck. *My friends*, thought Tozi again.

'Let's just stay here,' said Malinal. 'It's as good a place to be as any.' She gestured at the lines of soldiers with their guttering torches, working their way through the prison, tightening the net, efficiently rooting out fugitives from every corner and shadow. 'They're not going to stop until they've taken all of us, so running makes no difference, hiding makes no difference. Whatever we do they're going to catch us. Maybe it's time we accepted that.'

'I never accept I'm going to get caught,' flared Tozi. She felt threatened by the very idea. 'Not today! Not ever!'

'Well, let's hope you're right.' Malinal set Coyotl on his feet. 'But, honestly, we're out of options.'

Through her own sickness and exhaustion, Tozi saw that Malinal too was close to breaking point. The strain of the last hours had taken a terrible toll on them both – and on poor Coyotl. 'You're the one who's right,' Tozi said after a moment's thought. 'There's no point in running any more. Whatever the gods have in store for us, we'll discover it soon enough.'

She sank down on her haunches and sat cross-legged. Malinal and Coyotl sat on either side of her and the three of them gazed out through the bars at the extraordinary spectacle evolving in the great plaza, their ears numbed by the shrieks and cries that echoed there and the loud, discordant music of the ritual.

Tozi looked up at the bright moon, close to full, approaching the heart of heaven and shedding an eerie luminescence over the two faces of the pyramid – the north, and the west – that were visible from the fattening pen. With this, and with the dance of the lanterns that had now resumed in the plaza, and the blaze of the torches and braziers at the summit of the pyramid, the whole scene was lit almost as bright as day. Tozi saw that hundreds of wailing and lamenting women, kept in line by guards armed with short spears, occupied every step of the north and west stairways and queued in the plaza below. It would be the same, she was sure, on the east and south sides of the pyramid. Those Moctezuma had killed earlier had only been a taster for the much bigger sacrifice now under way.

She wrapped her arms round Malinal and Coyotl, and realised with a flood of emotion how deeply connected to them she felt. It was as though they'd been together all their lives, or in lives before this life, but certainly not for just a few hours or days.

Even in the midst of evil, Tozi thought, *good still flourishes.*

When at last the soldiers came for them they'd already decided not to resist – might as well resist a mountain or the ocean – and silently obeyed the harsh barks of the Mexica officers. In this way they soon found themselves herded together with the last five hundred women remaining in the pen. The whole group was then marched out of the gates and into the plaza, where they were greeted by a horrible, disorienting clamour of cries and screams, conches, tambourines, horns, whistles and the mournful, gut-churning beat of the snakeskin drum.

Tozi had witnessed countless sacrifices and knew what to expect next. Jeering guards surrounded the women and made them strip naked, leering at their bodies, roughly shoving and goading them into compliance. Poor Coyotl clutched his little hands to his mutilated genitals – as if any of that mattered now, thought Tozi as she shrugged off her own filthy rags. Malinal stood tall and proud, firm-breasted, her head held upright.

'I'm afraid,' said Coyotl in a small voice.

'Me too,' said Tozi.

'This is so hideous,' said Malinal. 'What are they going to do to us now?'

'They're going to paint us,' Tozi said.

It was already happening. Up ahead the women were being harried into a line where slaves armed with brushes daubed their bodies with a thick chalk plaster, turning them ghostly white. Some cried out, hunched over, but it only delayed the inevitable – they were forced upright and the plaster was applied. Other functionaries were at work hurriedly painting their eyelids black and their lips red, anointing the crowns of their heads with molten rubber and pluming them with turkey feathers. Finally they were dressed in crude paper garments and herded onwards towards the looming pyramid.

Tozi, Malinal and Coyotl stuck close together as their turn came, submitting passively to the painting and feathering. Although Tozi had never admitted to herself that she would ever become a victim, there was a strange, dreamlike way, as she donned the paper loincloth and the paper blouse, in which she found she was ready to admit it now. Perhaps it was because she was so tired, her body so punished, her head hurting so much, her spirit so beaten down, but after months of relentless struggle to stay alive, always alert, always suspicious, always afraid, she began at this moment to see death as a welcome release from the hell-world the Mexica had created.

A fat priest in black robes, blood-matted hair down to his waist, stepped onto a low platform and addressed the women, most of whom

were from Tlascala and other more distant lands, as they trudged past
him towards the pyramid:

> *We welcome you to this city of Tenochtitlan*
> *Where reigns the god Hummingbird.*
> *Do not think that you have come here to live;*
> *You have come here to die,*
> *To offer your chests to the knife.*
> *Only in this way, through your deaths, has it been your fortune*
> *To know this great city.*

'Such arrogance!' whispered Malinal. A wind had come up while the
priest spoke, a warm, damp wind swirling round the plaza, plucking
at their flimsy garments. Tozi looked to the sky. Thick clouds had
begun to build there, though the moon still shone clear, casting its
cold glamour over the whole hellish scene – the swirling orange patterns
painted by the lanterns in the plaza, the torsos and heaps of human
offal piled up at the base of the pyramid, the hideous glistening cascades
of blood through which the victims must climb, the diabolical flare
and flicker of the torches and braziers on the sacrificial platform before
the temple of Hummingbird, and Moctezuma himself still wielding
the obsidian knife at the top of the northern stairway.

Coyotl was clinging tight to Tozi's hand as the panicked crowd
jostled round them, great shivers and tremors shaking his body. She
stooped, uncertain if she had the strength to lift him, but Malinal got
there first. 'Let me carry him,' she said, hoisting Coyotl up onto her
hip again. 'He's not heavy.'

The little boy looked her straight in the eye. 'I'm still afraid,' he said.

'We're all afraid,' said Malinal. She smiled wearily at Coyotl: 'Rest a
bit, little one,' she told him, and he obediently put his head on her
shoulder.

Again Tozi felt a wash of gratitude for her new family. If the struggle
was truly over and the end came for all of them under the sacrificial
knife, it was a comfort to know they would pass to the next world
together.

With loud whistles and shouts and repeated kicks and punches, the guards kept the women moving forward in a mass towards the pyramid through swirling, grimacing lantern dancers whose faces were painted red as boiled lobsters. Somewhere ahead, but close, Tozi heard loud shouts and high-pitched screams. Standing on tiptoe she saw a squad of brute-faced soldiers armed with *macuahuitls* dividing the prisoners into two lines.

The line that forked left led to death at the top of the northern stairway.

The line that forked right led to death at the top of the western stairway.

As she approached the fork, Tozi saw Ahuizotl pushing his way towards them through the dancers, his face busy with malign intent. He seemed to have recovered from whatever hurt Xoco had done to his leg and was no longer using his spear as a crutch.

His eyes were fixed on Malinal. He marched right up to her, leaned in and whispered, loud enough for Tozi to hear, 'I don't know how you and your friends did that vanishing act today but now you're going to disappear for ever.' Recoiling from the venom in his tone, or perhaps the stink of blood that rose from him, Coyotl whimpered on Malinal's shoulder and the high priest's hand shot out, snatched the child by the hair and jerked his head violently back, half pulling him from Malinal's arms.

'NO!' Coyotl screamed – a single word, filled with terror. An instant later Tozi sank her teeth into Ahuizotl's wrist and Malinal went for his face. He shook them off as the soldiers piled in, there was a flurry of movement and, at the end of it, the high priest held Coyotl triumphantly clamped under his arm.

'*Tozi!*' Coyotl wailed.

Ahuizotl barked orders to the guards to bypass the line and take Malinal and Tozi forward at once to the foot of the northern stairway. His face set in a horrible, mocking leer; he then hurried off, still clutching the struggling child.

Tozi found a burst of strength and tried to follow, but a soldier smashed his fist into the side of her jaw, sending her sprawling on her face on the hard paving of the plaza. A vast new pain exploded in her head, confounding her senses. She dimly heard the sounds of shouting and struggle, shrill screams from Coyotl, blows, then Malinal landed on top of her, knocking the breath from her body.

'*Tozi . . . Help me! . . .*' Coyotl's voice was filled with terror, abandonment, loss, violation and pain – everything that a child should never know or feel. '*No No No . . . Owwwwwww! No, no . . . To-ziiii!*'

Then soldiers were hauling Malinal to her feet, half stunned, eyes rolling drunkenly, lips split and bleeding from a blow to the face. Tozi drew in a great whooping breath as her friend's weight came off her, and felt rough hands gripping her arms, forcing her to stand. 'Tozi . . . Help me!' Coyotl screamed again. His voice was fainter, moving away. 'You said you wouldn't let them hurt me. You *promised!* Toziiii!'

But it was a promise she could not keep. As Ahuizotl carried the little boy all the way to the foot of the western stairway and tossed him down, Tozi was swarmed over by guards prodding her with the obsidian points of their spears, beating her thighs, whooping and whistling at her, dragging her forward to the foot of the northern stairway. Right in front of her in the line, still reeling from the blow she'd taken, and forced to mount the first step, was Malinal.

Coyotl's screams were faint now, barely audible. Tozi heard, 'You *promised*' one more time, fluttering on the breeze like a butterfly, then the little boy was swallowed up amongst the other victims and his voice fell silent.

Chapter Twenty-Nine

As the great ship gently rocked beneath him, and the lanterns on the wall flared and flickered, Cortés sat alone at the map table in Alvarado's spacious stateroom, looking round the ten empty seats soon to be filled by his captains, considering how best to get what he wanted from these men. Some of them were his already, some he was in the process of making his, and some would never be his. He could only hope he had done enough to tip the balance in his favour.

Since Cortés had taken command of the expedition three months previously, and begun to make all necessary preparations, Diego de Velázquez had constantly interfered, insisting on appointing many of the captains himself. Of these, Cortés was most offended by the glowering Juan Escudero – the very man whom Velázquez had sent to arrest him two years before over the matter of Catalina. Escudero had looked down his long nose at Cortés as though he was a criminal then – and nothing had changed today.

There would be no accommodation with him, but other Velazquistas had proved easier to subvert with gold, or flattery, or friendship.

Juan Velázquez de León, for example, appeared on the surface to be completely loyal to his cousin Diego. Of a naturally loud, harsh and vulgar temperament, this ox of a man with his angry green eyes, bushy black beard and aggressive chin was quiet and unusually servile in the governor's presence. But Cortés had discovered that his outward deference concealed simmering bad blood. De León felt bitter that his powerful kinsman had not given him sufficient land, or Indians to work it, when he came to Cuba. Cortés had poured subtle poison in his ear almost daily during the past three months, stoking his already

149

fierce resentment of Velázquez and filling his mind with new suspicions and rancour. He had also extended a generous personal loan of two thousand gold pesos to De León to refit his ancient, leaking caravel, telling him that if the expedition was a success, as he expected it to be, he would not ask him to pay the money back.

Still, it was by no means clear which way Velázquez de León would jump if he was forced to choose sides, and the same was true of many of the others. Indeed out of the ten captains, there were only three whom Cortés counted as firm and reliable friends – the well-placed aristocrat Alonso Hernández Puertocarrero, Juan de Escalante and, of course, Pedro Alvarado.

Cortés stepped out onto the navigation deck and looked up at the moon, close to full and riding high, its pale glare casting baleful shadows through the masts and rigging of the *San Sebastián*, reflecting off the black water of the harbour, filling the sky with light. It would be about nine o'clock and down below on the pier, right on schedule, he heard voices and saw a large group of men approaching – Alvarado with, it seemed, all the captains. Most of them were in their mid-thirties – around Cortés's own age – and all were veterans who'd fought their way through the Italian wars and the conquest of Hispaniola and Cuba. Juan de Escalante was the youngest of them at thirty-one, Diego de Ordaz the oldest at forty-three. Cortés had also sent orders with Alvarado for one of his newly appointed junior officers to attend, twenty-two-year-old Gonzalo de Sandoval.

When all the captains were seated, with Sandoval left standing for want of a chair, Cortés launched right into things, bluntly, with no preamble. 'Gentlemen,' he said, 'we must leave Santiago tonight. We sail on the ebb tide five hours from now.'

He did not immediately elaborate and there was a beat of stunned silence. Juan Escudero's lantern jaw gaped comically for a moment before he snapped it shut. 'Sail to where?' he asked.

'To the New Lands, of course, but a week early.'

'This is highly irregular,' objected Ordaz. He had the strong, stubborn face of a miller or a mason. 'Does the governor know what you intend?'

'He does not,' said Cortés, meeting the man's thoughtful, grey-eyed stare. 'And if he did he would not permit our departure this night.'

'But then surely we must not leave?' proposed Velázquez de León. He flashed Cortés an apologetic glance as though to say: *You and I know how I really feel, but I have to be seen to defend my kinsman's interests.*

'We will not leave!' thundered Escudero, slapping his hand on the table. 'Cortés is nothing more than a thief. He would steal the expedition from the governor.'

Cortés pushed back his chair and stood, half drawing his sword. Escudero looked startled, as though he really wasn't expecting this, and scrambled to his feet, knocking his own chair over with a loud crash. 'I'll not be called a thief,' Cortés said. 'Apologise now or we step outside and settle this man to man.'

'Gentlemen, gentlemen,' said Puertocarrero, his red beard twitching. 'How can we hope for victory in the New Lands if we're already fighting among ourselves?' He turned his moist brown eyes on Cortés: 'Please, Hernán, put away your sword. If Juan is too pig-headed to apologise to you, I will apologise on his behalf, but we must not fall to killing each other, don't you agree?'

Cortés thought about it, but only for an instant. Everything that was impulsive, violent and vengeful in his nature yearned to run Escudero through. That was what had got him out of his chair. But his more rational side saw no gain in killing the man while they were still in the port of Santiago and subject to the governor's jurisdiction. A better opportunity was sure to present itself. 'Very well,' he said, 'we will not fight.' He sheathed his sword and sat down again. *Now make a virtue of necessity.* He smiled. 'Instead, I have a suggestion. Let us agree that all of us around this table may trade insults tonight as we wish, without any man's honour being impugned. That way' – he looked at Escudero – 'we may speak our minds freely and be satisfied as to the truth.'

There was a rumble of assent from the captains.

'Which of course does not mean,' added Cortés, 'that we're *obliged* to insult each other.' A ripple of laughter ran round the table. 'I for one intend to remain civil even if some do not . . . Now, Don Juan, you suspect me of stealing the expedition from our patron Diego de Velázquez, but the truth is I wish to save it for him. Will you hear me out?'

'Be my guest,' sneered Escudero with a wave of his hand. 'Given enough rope, you're bound to hang yourself.'

Cortés smiled again. *When we reach the New Lands*, he thought, *we'll see which one of us hangs*. But instead he said: 'Something's come up – a great danger to us that we must deal with at once. Under such circumstances our official Instructions, written by Don Diego himself, vest full emergency powers in me to take whatever actions I decide are in the best interests of the expedition.' He brought out a scroll from his pocket, pushed it into the middle of the table. 'Clause twenty-three,' he said. 'It's on this basis, though I hold him in the highest personal regard, that I've decided not to consult Don Diego tonight. Neither the interests of the expedition, nor his personal interests, will be served by involving him. What's needed now is swift action, but he's the governor of Cuba, busy with a thousand things, and if we put this to him he'll bog us down for days. We all know he's a man who doesn't make decisions quickly . . .'

'I'll second that,' said Cristóbal de Olid. He was short, squat and gnome-like, with a wild black beard and twinkling blue eyes. 'Takes him three months to sign a simple requisition sometimes.'

'I've waited three years for a proper grant of Indians,' complained De León.

Puertocarrero agreed: 'What Velázquez promises and what gets done are two different things.'

Cortés moved swiftly to capitalise on his gains. 'You touch upon my exact point, Alonso. This emergency is such we can't waste a single minute waiting for His Excellency to make up his mind. *We have to sail tonight!*' He leaned forward over the map table, his voice low and urgent. 'My shipping agent, whom I trust with my life, has returned this afternoon from Santiago de La Vega on the island of Jamaica. He reports that Pedro de Arias has installed himself there, recruited close to fifteen hundred men – the scum of the earth, so it seems – and gathered together a mixed fleet of twenty good carracks and caravels. They're bound for the New Lands.' He paused for effect. 'Nigh on ready to sail. If we don't beat them to it, there'll be no prize left for us to win.'

'Oh very good, Cortés, very good,' said Escudero, performing a slow handclap, 'but you don't seriously expect us to believe any of this, do you?'

'I see nothing to disbelieve,' snapped Juan de Escalante. A lean, rangy, blue-eyed man, he wore his black hair straight and long to his shoulders, framing a wolfish, heavily bearded face and concealing the sword wound from the Italian wars that had deprived him of the top two-thirds of his right ear. 'We all know what Pedrarias did in Darién. We all know he's been gathering men. We all know he's looking for fresh pickings. Why not the New Lands?'

'There's a way to settle this we'll all believe,' said Ordaz. His cold grey eyes rested on Cortés again. 'Simply produce your shipping agent and have him repeat his story to us . . .'

It was Cortés's experience that some truth in a lie makes the lie stronger, and he would have told a different lie if his shipping agent, Luis Garrido, had not in fact returned from Jamaica that very afternoon. It helped that Garrido was himself an accomplished liar, having sworn falsely on Cortés's behalf in many business disputes. He had also recently fallen into debt – a problem that Cortés could help him solve. Best of all, Garrido had met Pedrarias the previous year and was able to describe him.

'I'll be happy to oblige,' Cortés answered Ordaz. 'He'll be down on the main deck taking his dinner.' He signalled to Sandoval. 'Would you go and fetch him please? Ask for Luis Garrido. Any of the crew will know him.'

Sandoval was short with a broad, deep chest. His curly chestnut hair had receded almost to his crown, making him look peculiarly high-browed, but as though to compensate he had grown a curly chestnut beard, quite well maintained, that covered most of the lower half of his face. Although he presently owned no horse, lacked the means to purchase one and had enlisted as a private soldier, Cortés noted that his legs were as bandy as his own – the legs of a man who'd spent most of his life in the saddle.

* * *

When fat, perspiring, moustachioed Garrido entered the stateroom, he was in the midst of heaping complaints on Sandoval, wringing his hands and lamenting that he'd already told his story to Cortés and only wanted to finish eating his dinner and have a good night's sleep.

Several of the captains had met Pedrarias, and others were familiar with the anchorage where he was supposedly mustering ships and men, but Garrido didn't wilt under their close questioning, even naming and describing most of the vessels in his fleet. There was a danger of being caught out here – Garrido need only mention a single carrack or caravel that one of the captains knew for sure was not in Jamaica and his credibility would fall into doubt. Get two wrong and the whole exercise would become a fiasco. But so complete was the agent's knowledge of shipping movements in the region, so accurate the details he reported and so fresh his recollections, that his imaginary fleet proved unsinkable.

Bravo, Cortés thought as Garrido left the stateroom to return to his dinner. *A masterful performance.* And, looking round the table, where an excited buzz of conversation immediately ensued, he could see that most of the captains were swaying his way – that escaping tonight on the ebb tide, to get a foothold in the New Lands and be the first to stake a claim there, was suddenly beginning to make sense to them.

In the end Escudero was the only Velazquista who still felt the matter should be reported to Velázquez. But he accepted the decision of the majority, and the authority of Cortés under clause twenty-three of the Instructions, to sail at once without informing the governor. 'Under duress I accompany you,' he said, 'and under duress I stay silent. But what we are doing is not right. I fear we will all pay a price for it.' He turned on Cortés. 'You, sir,' he said, 'have no more conscience than a dog. You are greedy. You love worldly pomp. And you are addicted to women in excess . . .'

At this last remark, which seemed so irrelevant to the matter in hand, Alvarado burst out laughing. 'Addicted to women in excess! What's wrong with that, pray tell? If it's a sin then I'd guess a few around this table are guilty of it! But what would you know or care of such things, Juan, when I'm told your own preferences run to little boys?'

Crash! Over went Escudero's chair again and he was on his feet, lurching round the table towards Alvarado, his sword drawn, his knuckles white on its hilt. He didn't get far before Puertocarrero, Escalante and Ordaz piled on top of him and disarmed him. Alvarado stayed where he was, one eyebrow sardonically raised.

'Don Juan,' Cortés said. 'It seems you have forgotten.'

'Forgotten what?' Escudero was still struggling with his captors.

'The agreement we all made an hour ago. Tonight we may trade insults with no man's honour at stake. You have just insulted my conscience, for example, but do you see me at your throat with my sword?'

Escudero must have known he was trapped. 'My apologies,' he choked finally. 'In my anger I forgot myself.' He looked up at Alvarado: 'But if you say such a thing tomorrow, I will kill you.'

'Tomorrow is another day,' said Cortés. He motioned to Sandoval. 'Go and bring two of the men from the main deck, then take Don Juan below and lock him in the brig.'

'The brig?' Escudero spluttered. His face was suddenly purple. 'You can't do that to me!'

'I think you'll find I can,' said Cortés. He unrolled the Instructions scroll, made a show of reading it. 'Ah yes,' he said, 'here it is. Clause seventeen: "Captain-General may, on his sole discretion, restrain and if necessary incarcerate any member whose conduct becomes disruptive or threatens the success of the expedition . . . " To my mind, attacking Don Pedro with a sword in his own stateroom is disruptive and threatens our success.'

De León tried to intervene. 'Please, Captain-General. Your point is made. Surely it's not necessary to—'

'It is,' said Cortés, 'absolutely necessary.'

Ordaz also seemed about to object but Cortés waved him down: 'I'll risk no distractions! Don Juan will be released in the morning. He can resume command of his ship then.'

Cortés had been expecting at least token opposition from the other captains, but Escudero was not well liked. Now that the decision had been made to embark immediately, it seemed no one wanted to speak up for him.

With an inner sigh of relief, Cortés realised his gamble had paid off. His authority over this unruly group had prevailed – at least for tonight.

'Gentlemen,' he said, 'thank you for your support. I'm heartened by it. We're embarking upon a great and beautiful enterprise, which will be famous in times to come. We're going to seize vast and wealthy lands, peoples such as have never before been seen, and kingdoms greater than those of monarchs. Great deeds lie ahead of us; great dangers, too, but if you've got the stomach for it, and if you don't abandon me, I shall make you in a very short time the richest of all men who have crossed the seas and of all the armies that have here made war.'

Everyone liked the idea of getting rich, so the speech went down well.

As the last of the captains hurried from the stateroom to make their ships ready to sail, Sandoval returned from locking up Escudero.

'Ah,' said Cortés. 'Is the prisoner settled?'

'Settled is not the word I'd use,' said Sandoval. 'He's shouting and pounding on the walls of the brig.'

Cortés shrugged. 'He can pound until dawn if he wants to; nobody's going to take a blind bit of notice.' He grinned: 'Now listen, Sandoval, I'm glad you're here. I've got soldier's work for you to do tonight.'

Chapter Thirty

Santiago, Cuba, Thursday 18 February 1519

Gonzalo de Sandoval was from a respected hidalgo family, albeit one impoverished in recent years by a property dispute. He was born and bred a cavalier and university educated – natural officer material on every count. He was also from Medellín, Cortés's home town in the north of Extremadura, and the Extremenos were famous for sticking together.

All these things, thought Bernal Díaz, made it easy to understand why Cortés had singled Sandoval out for responsibility yesterday, despite his obvious youth.

What made less sense – indeed, so *much* less sense he feared an elaborate practical joke – was that at the same ceremony, Cortés had also singled out Díaz himself, a man of poor family and almost no education, and elevated him from common *soldado* to *alferez* – ensign – the same rank he had bestowed on Sandoval.

Now, tonight, hard on the heels of his unexpected promotion, Díaz had been given his first command – not a very glamorous or prestigious command, to be sure, but one that was important and worthwhile.

Respectable work that made sense to him.

Cortés and Alvarado had entrusted him with the fabulous sum of three hundred gold pesos with which he was to purchase the entire contents of Santiago's slaughterhouse – all the butchered meat and all the animals awaiting slaughter. In the unlikely event that three hundred pesos did not prove sufficient to buy everything, then Díaz was to commandeer whatever remained, carrying it away by force if necessary, but leaving a promissory note to cover payment.

'Any problems with that?' Cortés had asked.

'I don't want to get arrested, sir!'

'You have my word that won't happen. We are God's soldiers, Díaz, doing God's work and God's work won't wait . . .'

'But if there's trouble, sir?'

'No need to call me "sir". Don Hernando will do. Hernán when you get to know me better. I like to keep things informal if I can. As to trouble, there won't be any – and if there is, I'll protect you. You have my promise.'

It seemed Cortés was a man who made promises easily. But he was also the caudillo, captain-general of this great expedition to the New Lands, and Díaz's best hope for finding wealth. So he'd shrugged and said, 'That's good enough for me . . . Don Hernando.'

He was having second thoughts now, though, as he stood in the middle of the slaughterhouse floor, his boots soiled with blood and straw, carcasses of pigs, cattle and sheep suspended from hooks all around him, night insects throwing themselves suicidally into the torches that lit up the whole room. In front of him, Fernando Alonso, the director of the slaughterhouse, was so angry that spit sprayed from his mouth and a vein in his right temple began to throb conspicuously. 'No, I will not sell you any meat!' he yelled. 'Not for three hundred pesos or for three thousand pesos. I have a contract to feed the city.'

'But with respect, sir,' Díaz persisted, 'we *must* have this meat. And all your livestock on the hoof as well.'

'Livestock on the hoof! So you'll have the whole of Santiago go hungry not only tomorrow but for the rest of the month! What kind of men are you?'

Díaz sought around for an answer and remembered what Cortés had told him. 'We are soldiers of God,' he said, 'doing God's work. Would you have us go hungry as we do it?'

'I would have you *honest*,' shouted Alonso, unleashing another geyser of spit. He had one of those personalities that made him seem physically bigger than he was, but in reality he was a small, bristling, bald man with rather long hairy arms, hefting a big cleaver in his right hand and wearing a bloody apron. Díaz had been surprised to find him already at work, slaughtering beasts and butchering them for Santiago's breakfast; he had hoped at this time of night he could deal with some junior who wouldn't know what he was doing.

Now, whether he liked it or not, he was into a full-fledged confrontation. Alonso put two fingers to his mouth, gave a piercing whistle, and five more men in bloody aprons made their way forward through the curtains of hanging carcasses.

Seeing they all carried cleavers and carving knives, Díaz glanced back over his shoulder to the door. He'd been given twenty men to move the meat and livestock. But he preferred persuasion to force so he'd left them outside and come in alone with the money.

Foolish hope!

'La Serna,' he yelled at the top of his voice, 'Mibiercas! At the double, please!'

'Look, for goodness' sake please accept the money.' Although it was Alonso and his five assistants who'd been trussed up, bruised and dishevelled on the floor, by Díaz's soldiers, it was somehow Díaz who was pleading.

'It's not enough,' said Alonso with conviction. 'Even if this were a legal purchase, three hundred pesos is a joke. I'll need at least fifteen hundred pesos to cover my costs and lost business.'

'Then take the three hundred and I'll write you a promissory note for the other twelve hundred. Don Hernando Cortés himself will cash it.'

'Tonight?'

'Yes. This very night. Come to the harbour within the hour and you'll be paid.'

The men were released, quill, ink and paper were found, and Díaz wrote a note for one thousand two hundred pesos, payable by Cortés.

'Come soon,' Díaz told Alonso. 'We'll not wait for morning to sail.'

He left the slaughterhouse with his men, and began a forced march back to the harbour with two wagonloads of fresh and preserved meats and close to two hundred sheep, pigs and cattle on the hoof.

He didn't know whether he'd done well or not and could only hope Cortés would be pleased.

Chapter Thirty-One

'I must take you into my confidence,' Cortés had told Gonzalo de Sandoval. 'I trust I shall not regret doing so.'

The man's charisma and charm were infectious and Sandoval was looking for adventure. 'You'll not regret it,' he'd said.

The upshot was that he now knew much more about how things stood between Cortés and the governor than he wanted to, understood very clearly that what was happening tonight was indeed a coup against Velázquez, and had still allowed himself to be soft-talked by Cortés into participating.

Dear God! What was he thinking? He was taking the first step in what he'd always imagined would be an illustrious and honourable career, and he was quite likely to end up being hanged, drawn and quartered for it! For a moment Sandoval considered resigning his commission but immediately dismissed the idea from his mind. Whether or not he now regretted it, the fact was he'd given his word to Cortés, and a gentleman does not take his word back.

A scout had found the place, closer to the harbour than the city, where a squad of Velázquez's palace guards lay in waiting. Cortés had not told Sandoval who they intended to ambush, only that there were twelve of them and that they were a threat to his plan – entrusted to Bernal Díaz – to supply the fleet with meat and live animals from the slaughterhouse. So much traffic on the road late at night was bound to arouse suspicion, and the guards couldn't be permitted to disrupt the operation in any way, so Cortés had asked Sandoval to deal with them.

'Deal with them, Don Hernando?'

'We're going to the New Lands to do God's work,' Cortés had said with a fierce light in his eyes, 'so I want those guardsmen off the road fast and no longer threatening our meat supply – or our departure. Try to persuade them to join us. I'd prefer that. Bribe them – a few gold pesos can make all the difference. But if none of that works, then disarm them and tie them up – I'll leave the details to you. They may put up a fight. Kill the lot of them if you have to. I won't shed any tears.'

'Will you be giving me men who'll be prepared to kill fellow Spaniards . . . if we have to?' Sandoval had asked, the question sticking in his gullet. He'd been through military academy in his youth, when his family still had money and position. He'd trained with the broad-sword, the longsword and the cavalry sabre, he was judged a skilful horseman and had won top honours in the joust, but he'd never killed anyone before – let alone a Spaniard.

'I'm giving you twenty-five of my best men,' Cortés had replied. 'They'll kill anyone you tell them to kill.'

'What if we're caught? Taken prisoner? Arrested?'

'Then I'll protect you,' said Cortés, looking him straight in the eye. 'You have my promise.'

Wondering again what fatal enchantment had led him to agree to such a risky venture, Sandoval looked back at his twenty-five men. They marched silently, in good order, keeping a square of five ranks of five.

Their sergeant, the only one he'd talked to so far, was García Brabo, a lean grey-haired Extremeno with a hooked nose and a permanently sour expression, but the man you'd want beside you in a fight, Cortés had said. All the others looked like hardened killers too. Ferocious, stinking, hungry predators in filthy clothes, they wore strange combinations of scratched and battered plate and chain mail, and equally scratched and battered helmets, but were armed with Toledo broadswords and daggers of higher quality than their dress and general deportment would suggest. Many had shields – mostly bucklers, but also some of the larger, heart-shaped Moorish shields called *adarga*. Many carried additional weapons – halberds, lances, battle-axes, hatchets, war-hammers, maces, clubs. Five had crossbows and five were armed with arquebuses, the slow and cumbersome muskets that everyone was now raving about.

All in all, Sandoval thought, they were a formidable squad, his twenty-five, and he was stunned, amazed and perplexed not only that Cortés had given him command of them in the first place, but also that they had so far obeyed him without question. The fact that he had no experience – unlike them – of killing men made him feel like a fraud. Worse still, he'd never even been in a skirmish before, let alone a proper battle against trained troops like the governor's palace guard.

He prayed silently it would not come to that, but if it did he prayed he would not prove himself a coward.

Esteban, the wiry little scout, held up a warning hand, and Sandoval felt fear grip his belly like a fist. Reasons not to continue with this mad venture began to parade through his mind.

The plain truth was the moon was against them, two days away from full, shining brilliantly in a cloudless, tropical sky, flooding the winding road and the surrounding slopes with light. In an ideal world they would wait until after moonset to make the attack, but tonight that wasn't an option. The guards had to be dealt with before the meat and livestock could be brought from the slaughterhouse and the fleet must sail at two o'clock in the morning. These were the facts, this was the emergency, and he was going to have to handle it frighteningly soon.

Loping along thirty paces ahead of the rest of the squad, Esteban reached a sharp bend where the road wound about a tall outcrop of rock. He stopped, crouched, peered round the corner and waved his hand urgently behind him, signalling to Sandoval to bring the men to a halt.

'If I may suggest, sir,' whispered García Brabo, his breath reeking of garlic, 'you might think of going forward and striking up a conversation with the officer in charge of those guards. Likely he'll be the same class of gentleman as yourself.'

'A conversation . . .'

'That's right, sir. Bright young ensign newly out from Spain, making his way to Santiago, would naturally stop to pass the time of night. All very innocent and above board. Just keep him talking as long as you can. While you do that, me and half the men will have a go at climbing this lot.' He pointed to the rocky outcrop rearing above them. 'The scout says he knows a way over the top of it so we can get round behind them. I'll leave Domingo' – he gestured to another bearded ruffian – 'in charge of the rest and we'll come at them from both sides.'

'It should put the fear of God in them when they see our numbers,' said Sandoval, sounding, he thought, more enthusiastic than he felt. His palms were damp, his bowels were in a knot and his heart was thudding irregularly. Funny that – how you never really knew you had a heart until a time like this.

'With a bit of luck we won't have to fight at all,' Brabo said. He cupped his hands to his mouth and emitted a sound remarkably like the call of one of the local night birds. 'I'll do that three times when we're in place behind them,' he said, 'loudly enough for Domingo to hear as well, then we'll move in at the double – all subject to your agreement, of course, sir.'

Sandoval felt uneasy, but Brabo's plan sounded more likely to succeed than simply charging round the corner *en masse*, which was the only other strategy that came to mind. *Dear God*! This was actually happening. He was in it up to his neck and there was no way out now. 'Very well,' he said, 'let's get on with it.'

'Halt! Who goes there?'

'Ensign Gonzalo de Sandoval, off duty from the fleet and on his way to Santiago for some entertainment.'

'Come forward then.'

Clearly visible in the moonlight, the guards had taken up position about two hundred paces ahead – twelve big men, all decked out in their ostentatious formal uniforms despite the night's heat. They'd made no attempt to hide but sat in plain view, occupying a little clearing on sloping, lightly forested ground overlooking the road. If this was an ambush, Sandoval thought, it was a very strange one.

He didn't hurry to cover the two hundred paces. Every second he could delay here gave more time for Brabo to climb the outcrop and get round behind them. But the guardsmen were instantly suspicious.

'Don't dawdle!' yelled their officer, leaping to his feet. There was a rattle of swords and armour as all the others stood too, and quite suddenly the atmosphere of the encounter turned sinister.

Overcoming an overwhelming urge to turn tail and run, Sandoval stepped forward briskly. 'My apologies,' he said. 'The sight of so many armed men unnerved me.'

'If your business is legitimate you have nothing to fear . . .'

'My business is at the Moor's Head,' Sandoval said, naming a famous tavern in Santiago's red light district. He was close enough now to see the three gold roundels blazoned on the cuirass of the clean-shaven middle-aged officer doing the talking. A colonel. Surprisingly high rank to be leading such a small squad. There was something familiar about him and, as he entered the clearing, Sandoval recognised the tall, upright, square-shouldered, self-important stance, and the malicious, mean-spirited features of Francisco Motrico, commander of the palace guard, yet another of the governor's many cousins to have found high office.

A Velázquez loyalist to the core.

Sandoval had been in Cuba less than three weeks, and in that time he had visited the governor's palace only twice, but he already knew enough about the way things worked here to realise it was pointless to try to bribe or recruit this man. Judging from the stony expressions of the rest of his squad, all mature, hard-eyed soldiers, there'd be no compromise with them either.

Quite possibly they were all related to Velázquez!

'So you're with the governor's fleet,' said Motrico gruffly. 'Which vessel? Which commander?'

'*Santa María de la Concepción*,' Sandoval replied without thinking, 'the captain-general's vessel.'

There was a peculiar shuffling and exchange of glances amongst the guards, one of them sniggered and Motrico said 'detain him' in a tone so soft and conversational that Sandoval didn't fully understand it referred to him until two guardsmen twisted his arms behind his back, forced his head and neck down, removed his sword and frog-marched him over to the colonel.

'What's this about?' Sandoval protested. His heart was now jumping so fast it threatened to burst forth from his chest. His mouth felt dry, his bladder was painfully full and his whole body was suddenly drenched with sweat. 'By what authority do you detain me?'

'By the authority of the governor of Cuba and the Crown of Spain. Orders have been given for the arrest of Don Hernando Cortés. We're here to carry them out.'

'Well, don't let me delay you, please.' Sandoval's mind raced: 'I want no part of this. I'm on my way to Santiago for a few drinks and a girl.'

'You're a filthy spy for Cortés,' snarled Motrico.

'I'm no such thing,' protested Sandoval. 'If I was, why would I tell you I'm sailing with him?'

'You are what I say you are, and I say you're Cortés's spy.' The colonel bit his lower lip and the moonlight revealed an uncompromising glint in his eye. 'Under normal circumstances I'd just detain you, take you back to the palace and find out more about you, but unfortunately for you these aren't normal circumstances. All my men are required for tonight's purpose, I don't have the people to guard you or even a rope to bind you, so I'm afraid I'm going to have to execute you.'

The statement was so out of proportion, so shocking and so sudden that once again Sandoval only grasped its significance after the two guardsmen at his shoulders shoved and kicked him down to his knees. While one stayed behind him, trapping his arms, the other stepped round in front of him, took a tight grip on his hair, pulled his head violently forward and exposed his neck.

Sandoval's bowels, already in uproar, seemed to turn a somersault. 'Execute me?' he yelled. 'God in heaven, man, that's preposterous!'

'Nothing preposterous about it,' said the colonel. His tone was measured, as though all that was at stake was a point of argument. 'Just can't risk you running back to Cortés and telling him we're here.'

Struggling mightily, Sandoval forced his head up to look Motrico in the eye. 'You won't get away with this,' he shouted. He felt another terrifying lurch of his bowels. 'I'm a brother Spaniard and an innocent man.'

'You're a spy and as guilty as sin.' With a loud swish and a blur of reflected moonlight, the colonel drew his sword and raised it ceremoniously above his head as the guard tightened his grip on Sandoval's hair, forcing his head down again.

Almost simultaneously – and never more welcome – came the call of a night bird repeated three times, the sharp clunk as a crossbow was fired and the thump of the bolt striking home. There was a beat of absolute silence followed by the wild roars of battle cries, the sound of a mass of men charging through the trees and into the clearing, the sounds of weapons being drawn and blows struck. Sandoval felt the grip on his arms suddenly loosen and found himself free.

So this was war, he thought, strangely rational now. He struggled to his feet in the midst of a maelstrom of fighting and saw that Motrico was down on his knees, a crossbow bolt transfixing his neck. The colonel's hands were fluttering around the projectile, one at the barbed head, the other at the base, seeming to caress its leather vanes. Sandoval spotted the glint of his sword where it lay on the ground and snatched it up as a panicking, wild-eyed guardsman came at him. He parried the blow and whirled, letting the man stumble past, stabbing him in his unarmoured flank just as he'd been taught in fencing school. He knew the strike was perfectly executed as he drove it home, but what he wasn't prepared for, what no amount of teaching could ever have prepared him for, was the bony, muscular resistance of a living human body to the blade, the squelching suction of the guts as he withdrew it, and the screams and rolling eyes of a fellow man in unendurable pain. As much to end those terrible screams as anything else, and since no one seemed about to attack him, Sandoval stabbed the point of the sword down repeatedly into the fallen man's face, smashing his teeth, caving in his nose, reaming out his eyes, splitting his skull until there was nothing human left of him at all.

'Make you feel better, sir?' asked Brabo, appearing silently at his side, his face grim and smeared with gore, a dripping sword in his hand.

Sandoval thought about it, looked down at the ruin at his feet. 'I don't know what I feel. I've never killed a man before . . .'

'You've certainly killed this one, sir. Was it your first battle?'

'It was. I felt afraid.'

'Everyone feels fear. It's what we do with it that matters. You did well, sir! You should be proud of yourself.'

Sandoval took a deep breath and looked round the clearing where moments before he had faced execution. Brabo's men had made the first assault, saving his life; Domingo and the other half of the squad had arrived a few moments later and finished things off. As fast as it had begun, the fighting was over and all the guardsmen were dead. 'Thank you, Brabo,' he said.

'For what, sir?'

'For saving my life!'

'The caudillo told me to keep an eye on you, sir. "Through thick and thin", was how he put it. Would have been more than my job's worth if I'd let that ape Motrico take your head.'

Sandoval looked up, trying to judge the time. From the position of the moon he guessed midnight had already passed.

'Come on, men,' yelled Brabo. 'Let's get these bodies dragged back into the trees. I don't want any of this visible.' But even as he gave the order, the sergeant paused, cupped his hand to his ear and peered down the road where it vanished amongst shadows in the direction of Santiago.

Sandoval did the same.

Faint but clear on the night air, he heard men approaching.

Chapter Thirty-Two

Swords that had been cleaned and sheathed only moments before hissed from their scabbards again, but then came nervous laughter, smiles, a few curses, and Sandoval felt Brabo's big calloused hand clapping him on the shoulder. At the point where the road from Santiago emerged from the shadows into the full glare of the moonlight, a large drove of pigs had appeared and numbers of sheep, goats and cattle followed behind them. Herding the whole menagerie forward with curses, kicks and blows from the butts of their spears were fifteen or twenty men. At the rear were two heavily loaded waggons drawn by bullocks. Right at the front, unmistakable in his size and solidity, Sandoval recognised Bernal Díaz, the young soldier who'd received his commission as ensign yesterday in the same ceremony as himself.

He stepped out from the clearing as the bleating, oinking, snuffling mass of animals approached. 'Well met, Díaz,' he called.

'Well met, Sandoval. What are you doing here?'

With pigs and goats swirling round them, the two men embraced and Sandoval briefly explained.

'I see,' said Díaz, 'so the caudillo told you the whole story but me only part of it.' He sounded offended.

'Believe me, my friend,' said Sandoval. 'He *didn't* tell me the whole story! I knew these men were here' – he gestured to the guardsmen's corpses being dragged into concealment amongst the trees – 'but not *why* they were here. They were a threat to your mission, that's all he said, and we were sent to clear the road of them . . .'

'Sirs,' said Brabo, 'get used to it. It's the habit of the caudillo to tell you only what you need to know.'

'So how much,' Díaz asked, 'did he tell you?'

'Everything,' said Brabo. 'But then I've been with him a long time . . .' He grinned. 'Anyway, he only wanted this kept quiet until we'd dealt with things here, so I suppose I can let you in on it now.' He shouted directions to the clean-up squad in the trees and continued: 'This afternoon Cortés got word of a plot to kidnap him and take him in chains to Velázquez. These guards were part of it . . .' He paused as the sound of a rider was heard approaching at a gallop from the direction of the port and waved cheerfully at the man as he thundered past. 'I was expecting him,' he explained, 'but it won't be long before a hospital carriage comes by in the other direction.' He sniffed. 'Might raise all kinds of suspicions if that carriage were to pass us on the road, so what the caudillo wants us to do now, gentlemen, is get our arses and these animals back to the ships at the double . . . All subject to your agreement, of course.'

'Of course,' said Sandoval.

'Of course,' said Díaz.

The last of the bodies were dumped out of sight amongst the trees, a flock of goats was driven through the clearing to erase all signs of the fight, and the column of men and animals surged forward again towards the harbour.

Sandoval felt a shadow pass overhead and looked up to see a wisp of cloud blowing across the face of the moon. A wind stirred and, despite the night's heat, he shivered. Something cold in that unexpected wind, he thought; something dark in that unpresaged cloud blowing in out of a clear sky.

Without consciously choosing to do so, he found he was thinking about the man he had killed back in the clearing. He might have had a family, children, a beloved wife to hold close each night, and he must surely have had ambitions and dreams. But now everything he ever was or would be had ceased. All his thoughts and all his hopes had come at last to nothing. His story was over and it was Sandoval who had ended it.

A terrible regret clenched his heart as he walked and he was haunted

169

by images of what he'd done to the guard, a memory of the way the sword had lodged in his vitals, echoes of his screams, the nightmare of his face . . .

'Have you ever killed a man?' he asked Díaz.

Some emotion – was it wariness, was it sorrow? – seemed to shake the big ensign. 'I was with Pedrarias in Darién,' he said softly, 'I sailed with Córdoba. Of course I've killed men.'

'But have you killed Spaniards?' Sandoval persisted.

Díaz didn't answer.

Soon afterwards a second man on horseback appeared, this time riding from the direction of Santiago. Díaz recognised Fernando Alonso, and when Sandoval ordered him to be stopped to discover his business on the road, Díaz said, 'No. I can vouch for him. He's the director of the slaughterhouse on his way to claim payment from Cortés.'

'You didn't pay for these animals?'

'Not nearly enough. The caudillo gave me three hundred pesos. The price was one thousand five hundred. I was made to feel a fool, then a thief – so I ended up writing a promissory note.'

'Think Cortés will honour it?' Sandoval's tone suggested he didn't believe there was the remotest chance he would.

'He'd better,' said Díaz. 'I'll lose all faith in him if he doesn't.' He laughed bitterly. 'Not that anyone cares for the opinion of an uneducated idiot like me!'

A powerful gust of wind ran its fingers through his hair, tugged at his clothes, whispered amongst the trees. He'd been conscious for some while of a change in the weather, of a restlessness in the air, but looking up he was surprised to see a turbulent mass of clouds already swarming over the sky.

He still couldn't get Cortés off his mind and, soon afterwards, as they reached the Customs House, he turned to Sandoval: 'There must be a reason why the caudillo chose us to do his dirty work,' he said. 'I mean you and me rather than anyone else.'

In the next moments they were occupied herding the animals into the port through the archway that straddled the road. The few Customs officers on duty so late at night had been arrested, and the building was held by a squad of expeditionaries, known to most of them, who waved them through with many ribald comments about the differences between soldiers and farm boys.

Díaz thought Sandoval had forgotten his question, but it seemed he'd been considering it. 'I think it's clear,' he now said. 'There was nobody else Cortés could trust or spare to do it, but he could be sure two rookies like us would leap at the chance to please him.'

'I know he's a great man,' said Díaz, 'but I think he uses people – and he makes promises too easily. He told me he'd protect me if I got arrested for raiding the slaughterhouse. I hope he would have kept that promise, yet part of me doubts him.'

'He told me the same thing when he sent me to kill fellow Spaniards. I don't know . . . maybe it's all just words – I'm filled with doubts too, Bernal – but there's something inspiring about the man that sweeps all that away. If anyone can bring us victory in the New Lands, it's Cortés.'

'That's why I signed on,' said Díaz. 'But I still don't trust him.'

They spilled out onto the harbour road to confront a scene of intense activity where the fleet was still loading. Lanterns blazed in the rigging and men scurried around the ships like swarms of insects. Reflecting off the water, the intense, almost white light of the moon made everything seem as bright as day until a bank of thick dark cloud scudded over it, plunging the world into instant night. The gusts of wind continued to grow stronger and ever more frequent, blowing always from the east, and Díaz sensed the electric excitement – and dread – of a coming storm.

'Not good weather for sailing,' he said, thinking aloud. The moon had come out from behind the clouds again and if even the sheltered water of the harbour had grown so choppy, then what would the open sea be like?

'We've no choice now,' Sandoval said. His voice was grim. 'We've killed twelve of the governor's guardsmen, we've raided the city slaughterhouse. It's you and me who did that, Bernal – not Cortés, not his friend Alvarado, but you and me – and if we get stuck here it'll be you and me dancing a jig at the end of the gallows . . .'

'But Cortés . . . ?' said Díaz. He realised too late that a tone almost of pleading had crept into his voice.

'Will protect us?' Sandoval completed his question and looked worried as another ferocious gust of wind hit them. 'I hope we haven't bet our lives on that.'

Up above, the cloud masses thickened, covering ever more of the sky.

They marched deep in their own thoughts for a while, and had drawn close to the clamour and frenetic movement of the pier when they heard a loud clatter of hooves behind them and a rumble of iron-clad wheels.

Out of the night loomed four black horses, drawing a tall black coach that swept by so fast and so close they had to jump to the side of the road.

The messenger had been sent shortly after midnight and, right on schedule, at one o'clock in the morning, amidst the freshening storm, Dr La Peña came thundering down the pier in a big medical carriage drawn by four horses. 'Very nice,' said Cortés, meaning the horses, 'we'll have those.'

'And the good doctor himself,' Alvarado reminded him.

They retreated into the stateroom. La Peña knocked, Alvarado invited him to enter and Cortés confronted him just inside the door. 'Good evening, doctor,' he said, 'or rather, good morning. Thank you so much for coming.'

La Peña stood, apparently dumbfounded.

'You'll have been expecting to find me on my sickbed, of course,' said Cortés, 'but as you can see I am perfectly well.' He paused for effect. 'Naturally I know everything about Velázquez's plan . . .'

At this the doctor's eyes darted rapidly several times from side to side, as though he were seeking a way out.

'And I know about your part in it,' Cortés added.

'My part in what?' spluttered La Peña.

'You know, pretend I'm sick, spirit me away from here in your carriage supposedly to take me off to your hospital but in reality to hand me over to the governor's palace guard . . .'

La Peña squealed and turned to run, but Cortés caught him before he reached the door and backhanded him twice, knocking him to his knees.

'Don't kill him!' protested Alvarado in mock horror. He looked down at his left arm, bound in a makeshift sling. 'I need someone to fix this.'

After La Peña had joined Escudero in Alvarado's brig, Cortés returned to take charge of his own ship. Hours before, he'd sent orders to prepare for an urgent departure. Everything seemed ready as he came on board.

With sailors rushing here and there around him, he felt the fresh blast of the wind on his face, listened to its keening as it whipped through the rigging, and looked up with growing disquiet to see armies of cloud now occupying much of the sky and frequently shrouding the moon. At first when the wind had risen he'd felt nothing but joy – for it was a fair wind that would drive them out of the trap of Santiago's anchorage and west across the ocean to the New Lands.

But *dear God in Heaven*, Cortés thought, *is nothing ever simple?* Not only did he have to contend with so treacherous and dangerous an adversary as Velázquez, but now it seemed the very elements were turning against him as well.

His mood darkening he climbed the steps to the navigation deck and found not one, not two, but three men waiting for him outside his half of what had once been the *Santa María*'s stateroom. The first, he saw with a shiver of disgust, was Muñoz, directly responsible for the present, reduced state of his accommodations. Second was Antón de Alaminos, pilot and chief navigator of the fleet. Third was someone he did not know, a small bald man with a somewhat battered face and a large black bruise forming round his right eye.

It was this latter who now rushed forward, thrusting a sheet of paper at him.

'Do you wish to ruin me, Cortés?' he yelled. 'My slaughterhouse has been emptied in your name and there'll be no meat in Santiago for days. None at all! I'll be forced to breach contracts to the army, to the government, to the monasteries, to the taverns. In every case there's a financial penalty. Citizens will be up in arms and I'll be blamed. To add insult to injury your men beat me' – he pointed to his eye – 'and paid me just three hundred pesos – *three hundred pesos, I say* – for my entire stock.' A look of outrage congested his face. 'Which is worth one thousand five hundred pesos at least . . .'

'What?' said Cortés. 'One thousand five hundred pesos! That's a king's ransom.'

'That's a fair price for my stock and your officer Díaz agreed upon it. See here . . .' Again he waved his paper at Cortés, who this time took it from him, held it up to a swinging lantern and read, to his horror, in a clear firm hand, that he was indeed obligated to pay this man, Fernando Alonso, a further one thousand two hundred gold pesos . . .

There came the clump of booted feet on the stairs leading up to the navigation deck and Sandoval appeared. Díaz was right behind him. 'Ah,' said Cortés. 'Speak of the devil. Did you sign this piece of usury, Díaz?' With a withering glance he handed the paper to the tall ensign.

Díaz took it to the lantern to read it. 'Yes sir,' he said, 'I did. On your instructions. You gave me three hundred pesos and told me to leave a promissory note if it wasn't enough . . .'

'I know, I know, but did you not think to bargain, man?'

'No, sir. We've bought and are loading two hundred head of livestock and two wagonloads of fresh and salted meats. One thousand five hundred pesos doesn't seem excessive . . .'

'The price is fair,' said Alonso. 'You have my stock. I won't leave your ship until I have my money.'

Cortés felt cornered. Díaz seemed somehow to be judging him. Even Sandoval was looking at him in a new way and he felt the chill, flat stare of Muñoz's dead-fish eyes on him too.

Not too late to change tack. 'We won't fall out over the amount,' Cortés told the slaughterhouse director smoothly, 'but I don't have that sort of cash to hand. To compensate you for the delay I'll up the amount on your promissory note to two thousand pesos payable at the end of the expedition. We're about to sail—'

'What? What's that?' Still as a tombstone in the shadows, emanating an almost tangible aura of ill will, Muñoz suddenly stirred. 'Did you say we're about to sail?'

Alonso spoke over him, directly to Cortés. 'You insult me, Don Hernando. I repeat, your men have beaten me and humiliated me. All my stock has been stolen. I do not want your promises. I want my money! Only when I have it will I leave your ship.'

'And I demand to know what treachery's afoot here,' insisted Muñoz, thrusting himself forward, his prominent Adam's apple bobbing in his throat. 'What are all these hasty preparations? Why is the fleet about to sail? And at dead of night – without the governor's knowledge or permission, I'll warrant!'

Cortés turned on the friar with a snarl. 'You will mind your tongue, Father, and your business.'

Muñoz drew himself up to his full height, looming over Cortés. 'All the business of the fleet is the business of the Inquisitor,' he thundered, 'and you'll not sneak away from Santiago like a thief in the night while I'm here to guard the interests of God and Don Diego de Velázquez.'

'God and Velázquez?' Cortés exploded. 'You name both in the same breath, Friar?'

'I do. Don Diego is a right holy man and you, sir, are the devil's imp. Embark without the governor's blessing and I swear to you I will call down the wrath of heaven on this fleet and all who sail in it.'

Cortés glanced at the soldiers and crew on the main deck and didn't like what he saw. Those about to embark on a sea voyage tend naturally to superstition and, as the wind howled in the rigging and the lanterns swung, it was obvious the Inquisitor's holy fury was having a chilling effect. Some of the men crossed themselves, Alaminos amongst them. Even Sandoval and Díaz looked alarmed. Matters must not be allowed to deteriorate further! But at the same time Alonso was still sounding off at the top of his voice, pacing back and forth in front of Cortés, contemptuous of his authority and thoroughly distracting his attention.

There was, at least, an easy way to be rid of the tiresome butcher.

Turning his back on Muñoz, Cortés swept his thick gold chain over his head, carefully removed and placed in his pocket the heavy gold medallion of Saint Peter that hung from it, and handed the chain to Alonso with a flourish. 'That should more than cover your costs,' he said. 'And whatever surplus you've left over, you may keep for your troubles.'

In no hurry now, his expression of aggrieved entitlement never wavering, the slaughterhouse director examined the chain and bit it in two places before concealing it in some fold of his garments. Then, without a further word, not even of thanks, he turned his back, clattered down the stairs to the main deck and thence made his way by the gangplank to the pier where his horse was held waiting.

Once in the saddle he found his voice again. 'Hey Cortés,' he yelled, 'a word with you.'

Cortés was already regretting the impulsive piece of showmanship that had separated him from a chain worth at least two thousand pesos, wondering if there was some way he could get it back and realising with a sour stomach there probably wasn't. He looked over the rail of the navigation deck at Alonso. 'You've been paid,' he said coldly. 'What more do you want?'

'To give you something to think about, you knave. Before I rode over here I sent my messenger to the governor. Thought I should let him know his fleet is leaving tonight in a hurry. I expect you'll be hearing from him soon.'

He laughed and spurred his horse away.

'I expect you lick the governor's arse!' Cortés yelled after him.

At the back of his mind he was aware that Muñoz's complaints, threats and curses had never ceased and he made three quick decisions. First the Inquisitor's loud imprecations were bad for the morale of his crew, doubly so on a stormy night like this. Second, he wanted his stateroom back and wasn't prepared to share it for a moment longer. Third there was the matter of his dream – his fingers went unconsciously to the medallion in his pocket – which could not safely be dismissed. Most likely it was just a dream, but suppose it was more? Suppose it really was Saint Peter who'd told him Heaven would not bless the expedition without Muñoz?

Cortés wanted to think further on all these matters, but first he had to get the fleet safely out of Santiago. So he told Díaz and Sandoval to escort Muñoz discreetly along the pier to the *San Sebastián*. 'Throw him in the brig when you get there,' he said. 'He'll be in good company.'

'You can't do that to me!' roared Muñoz.

'I've looked into it,' said Cortés, 'and in circumstances like these I can do pretty much anything I like.' He leaned closer, lowered his voice to a whisper. 'You might unsettle the men with your curses, but don't imagine any of them will rush to support you. You're not well liked after the Córdoba expedition, Muñoz. In fact, I'd go so far as to say you're hated.' He smiled pleasantly, lowered his voice still further: 'Then there was that terrible business with your last page.' An almost inaudible whisper now. 'Tell me, is it true, did you murder him to stop him witnessing against you?'

He had the satisfaction of seeing Muñoz's face turn ashen-white. 'Take him away,' he told Díaz and Sandoval.

When they were gone, Cortés was alone on the navigation deck with the pilot Antón de Alaminos, an experienced explorer of these waters since his youth when he'd sailed as a cabin boy on Columbus's fourth voyage. The wind was howling without let-up, whipping around them, rattling the sails in the rigging. Alaminos shrugged his shoulders and held both his hands palm out in a gesture of surrender. 'You understand we can't sail in this,' he told Cortés, 'it would be suicide . . .'

Buffeted by the storm, Cortés knew Alaminos was right, and yet could only think of one thing. All tonight's careful planning and manoeuvring – the snatching of the meat supply, the foiling of the plot with La Peña – now lay in ruins. That bastard Alonso had sent a messenger and Velázquez was sure to act on it. The sands were running through the hourglass at a terrifying rate, and even now the governor would be galloping towards them with a strong force of his guard to appeal to his friends amongst the captains and stop the fleet from sailing.

'Come come, Alaminos,' Cortés chided. 'Has easy living stolen your courage? You've sailed in worse gales than this!'

Chapter Thirty-Three

Tlascala, small hours of Friday 19 February 1519

'Where am I?' Guatemoc asked.

'This is Aztlán,' a man's voice replied. 'Homeland of your people and of the gods. You are in the caves of Chicomoztoc.'

Guatemoc looked around. He was in a vast underground cavern, illuminated by a soft but pervasive glow that seemed diffused everywhere. The domed ceiling overhead glittered with a thousand stalactites of pure transparent crystal. From the floor, made of the same substance and towering above him, soared a forest of stalagmites. He felt no pain and looked down at his body to find he was uninjured and dressed in a robe of simple white cotton loosely belted at the waist.

Everything about this was very strange. There had been a fight, though he could not remember with whom, then darkness and now he was here.

'Who speaks to me?' he asked.

An arm's length in front of his face, the air of the cave rippled and swirled. It was as though a pair of great curtains, hitherto unseen, had been momentarily whisked apart revealing a blank void. And out of that dark and empty gap, out of that nothingness, there came a blur of wings, and suddenly a small hummingbird with a long, dagger-sharp beak and feathers of iridescent blue and yellow burst forth, making Guatemoc throw himself back with a gasp of surprise.

'I am Huitzilopochtli,' the creature said, flying a rapid circle around him, 'the Hummingbird at the left hand of the Sun.' Though it was tiny, its voice was strong and deep.

The resolute voice of a warrior.

The commanding voice of a god.

Guatemoc dropped to his knees. 'Lord Hummingbird,' he said. 'Is it truly you?'

There came another shimmer of the air, the hummingbird was gone and a man stood before him. A perfect man in the prime of life, beautiful and strong, tall, with sculpted muscles and glowing skin and golden hair and brutal soldier's hands, wearing a blue loincloth and armed with a long, wickedly sharp killing knife fashioned from some deadly metal. 'Yes, Prince,' he said. 'I have work for you to do.'

'Work, lord?' Guatemoc glanced up to see the god towering above him, to see that gleaming, murderous knife raised high, poised over his head. 'I am here to serve you.'

'And serve me you will.'

'Tell me what I am to do,' Guatemoc said. The god's eyes, he noticed, were black as night, black as obsidian, and yet shone with a fierce inner fire.

'You must return to the land of the living,' Hummingbird replied. 'You must return at once.'

And suddenly everything that had happened came back to Guatemoc in a rush. He remembered every move, every moment, every mistake of his fight with Shikotenka, remembered the icy chill, the tearing agony, the fatal heaviness, as the Tlascalan's knife entered his viscera, remembered how he had been bested and vanquished with contemptuous ease, as a child might be slapped down and put in his place by a grown man. 'But I was killed, lord,' he said. 'How can I return when I am dead?'

'Because this is not your time to die,' said Hummingbird. 'Because I have made you live again that you might do the work you were brought into the world for. Because a great battle lies before your nation, but the weakling Moctezuma is not competent to fight it.'

Then, in a flash, the god's arm came lashing down and the blade clasped in his huge hand smashed through the top of Guatemoc's skull, admitting an explosion of light . . .

It was deep night, and a big moon feathered with clouds was riding high as Guatemoc regained consciousness in a pool of his own blood. Two images superimposed themselves in his mind – Shikotenka stabbing him to death and Hummingbird stabbing him back to life again. Which was real and which a dream?

He dragged himself forward out of the cold, coagulating mass, but the effort required to move was great and he lay prone, gasping like a fish on a riverbank, still uncertain if he was alive or dead, a freshening wind blowing through the grass and over his body. Finally he accepted that by some miracle, perhaps indeed worked by Hummingbird, he was still amongst the living, that Shikotenka's knife, which had struck him so often and so fast, had somehow spared his vital organs, and that he must raise the alarm. The battle king of the Tlascalans would not have been here, doing his spying in person, unless something deadly and spectacular was planned . . .

Six bowshots down the steep slope, almost directly beneath the hollow where Guatemoc lay, was the camp's south gate, little more than a line of thorn bushes drawn across the wide, lantern-lit thoroughfare running two thousand paces due north to Coaxoch's pavilion. Uninjured, Guatemoc could have reached the gate and alerted the sentries in minutes but now, as he struggled to rise, his strength failed again. He couldn't even get off his knees! He tried to call out but his voice was no more than a whisper and the wind was strong.

He had to get closer to those sentries! It was the only way. He formed a mental picture of the straight route to them, lowered his head and began to slide on his belly. The movement opened his wounds and had him lathered in fresh blood in an instant. More agony followed as he slowly worked his way downhill, now crawling, now shuffling on his buttocks through the long grass, unable to see exactly where he was going, the camp a lake of light and voices far below, always luring him on.

Guatemoc knew himself to be savagely injured. Despite Hummingbird's intervention – whether real or imagined – he would surely die if he couldn't reach the royal surgeons soon; nonetheless the pain that burned him deepest was his shame at the easy, contemptuous way Shikotenka had destroyed him in combat. The Tlascalan prince wasn't just better than him. He was massively, consummately better. Guatemoc remembered boasting and strutting before the fight, trying to put the other man down. But now it was he who was down, a crawling cripple, while Shikotenka was free to go where he pleased and do what harm he wished.

Swallowing his pride, Guatemoc continued his slow, determined downhill crawl, grateful for the steady cooling breeze. He suffered a shattering bolt of pain as he dropped into a shallow crevice. He pulled himself out and lay stretched on his back on the hillside, glaring at the moon around which great mountains of cloud were now gathering. When he found the strength to lift himself again and look down at the camp, he realised to his horror that he'd strayed from the straight route that would have taken him to the sentries at the south gate. Instead, in his confusion, he'd followed a meandering course across the slope and made his journey much longer.

Gritting his teeth, he once more turned directly downhill. It meant he wouldn't reach the perimeter at the south gate, but further round to the east. The sentries here were separated by intervals of a hundred paces. He aimed as best he could for the nearest of them.

As he crawled, Guatemoc dreamed of the moment when he would meet Shikotenka again and exact revenge for his humiliation today. He would make the Tlascalan battle-king his prisoner; he would treat him as his honoured guest, and then he would lead him up the steps of the great pyramid and offer his heart to Hummingbird.

He had the scene very vividly fixed in his mind, so that it was almost more real than real – the pyramid looming above them, the rope in his hand looped around Shikotenka's neck, and Shikotenka himself, daubed with white paint, dressed in a paper loincloth, humbly mounting the steps to meet his death. All this was very satisfying and correct, and Guatemoc found he was able to watch the imaginary scene unfold in his mind's eye while simultaneously tracking his own crawling progress towards the sentry. 'Help!' he tried to shout. 'Help!' But the word wouldn't emerge, not even a whisper. 'Help!' He tried again, but Shikotenka's knife had taken his voice.

Guatemoc kept crawling. Suddenly he was on the flat ground at the foot of the hill and the sentry was just a hundred paces away, while in his head Shikotenka was still trudging up the steps of the pyramid, the sculpted muscles of his thighs moving under his brown skin. As his captor, Guatemoc enjoyed the exclusive right to Shikotenka's thighs, which would be cooked for him in the time-honoured fashion in a stew with chillies and beans. He licked his lips, then remembered that none of this was real, no matter how real it seemed. The great pyramid of Tenochtitlan was two days' hard march from here. There would be no sacrifice. He would not be feasting on Shikotenka's thighs tonight.

He looked up through tussocks of waving grass as the moon emerged, redoubled in brilliance, through a gap in the clouds. He saw the sentry clearly, just fifty paces from him with his back turned, his moon-shadow reaching out like an admonishing finger. 'Help!' Guatemoc cried. 'Help!'

Nothing . . .

But then he heard footsteps in the grass, coming on at the double. Praise the gods, he had been found!

The sentry was beside him now, looming over him. 'Drunkard,' he exclaimed in a coarse regional dialect. Judging from the bone through his nose, this was one of the Otomi rabble recently hired by Moctezuma. Guatemoc had opposed the policy but now here he was in his time of need being rescued by one of them! It was too much to expect that a lowly mercenary would actually know who he was, and he wore only a loincloth which gave no indication of his rank, so he tried to introduce himself: 'My good man, I am Guatemoc, a prince of the Blood. Send a messenger for Lord Coaxoch at once.'

But the words wouldn't come and the Otomi just stared at him, finally seemed to notice his injuries and said, 'What? I can't hear you.'

Guatemoc tried again. 'Danger!' he said. 'Now! Tlascalans. Coaxoch must be told!'

But still he couldn't produce the words.

The Otomi stood straight, heaved a great sigh of what sounded like annoyance and called out to the next sentry post – 'Hey, I need help. I've got an injured man over here.'

'I am Guatemoc. Summon Coaxoch at once.'

This time the words came. Just the faintest, croaking whisper.

But the Otomi wasn't listening.

Chapter Thirty-Four

While the rest of the fifty sat on their haunches, breathing evenly after their ten-mile night run, Shikotenka led Chipahua and Tree to the ridge. The moon was just off full, shedding its brilliant silvery light through scudding cloudbanks, and the long grass swayed in a strong breeze as the three of them peered downslope to the huge amphitheatre amongst the hills where the Mexica had set their camp. Ablaze with flickering fires and lanterns, a chaotic and ill-disciplined scene presented itself. To their amazement, despite the lateness of the hour, thousands of the enemy were still on the move, wandering in noisy, guffawing groups from sector to sector of the immense armed camp, frequenting the hawkers' stalls and brothels, bartering with merchants for cloth, or pulque, or tobacco.

'Doesn't look like they've found Guatemoc,' said Chipahua. 'Or missed him.'

'Doesn't even look as though they're here to fight a war,' said Tree. 'Looks like a party.'

'They're too used to winning,' Shikotenka mused, profoundly relieved that the matter of Guatemoc had gone no further. The prince's body must still be lying in the grassy hollow where they had fought. 'They've forgotten they can lose.' He narrowed his eyes, noting the sentries spaced at intervals of a hundred paces all round the enormous perimeter, and the avenues of lanterns that marked out the principal thoroughfares. These ran north–south and east–west, intersecting at Coaxoch's pavilion in the dead centre of the camp. 'That's where we have to get to . . .' He showed them the pavilion. 'Any thoughts?'

'Fly?' said Chipahua.

'Wait for clouds to cover the moon,' suggested Tree, who was studying the increasingly stormy sky. 'It won't be long. Then we just go straight in.' He pointed to the southern end of the north–south axial avenue which lay almost directly beneath them at the foot of the hill. Pairs of sentries were stationed along its entire length at intervals of twenty paces.

'And the sentries?' asked Chipahua.

'Kill them,' said Tree.

'I prefer stealth,' said Shikotenka. 'That's what these are for.' He tugged the sleeve of his uniform, taken from the body of a Mexica jaguar knight he'd killed a few months earlier. All the rest of the squad were similarly attired. 'They don't have enough sentries round the perimeter, so when the moon's behind cloud we'll be able to slip between them without being seen. We'll split up into small groups, blend in with the crowds and make our way to Coaxoch's pavilion. When we're all there we'll go straight into the attack.'

Chipahua and Tree exchanged a concerned glance, which Shikotenka ignored. He knew his plan was full of holes, but he had put his faith in the gods and there was no going back.

With the moon still bright, and dancing in and out of cloud, Shikotenka had his men take cover in the long grass and crawl down the hill by the same route he'd used going up it this afternoon. They reached the hollow where he'd fought Guatemoc and found it trampled and flattened, scabbed pools of congealed blood everywhere, but no sign of the prince himself. One particularly wide and obvious track, as of someone crawling or sliding, led out of the hollow and down in the direction of the Mexica encampment.

Acolmiztli was studying the fresh blood in the track and glaring accusingly at Shikotenka: 'I thought you said you killed him?'

'I thought I had. I got my knife in him six times.'

'You should have made certain. He's still bleeding so he's still alive but the good news is it doesn't look as if anyone found him here. He's on his own and he's not been gone long. Let's get after him.'

Leaving the rest of the squad under Tree's command in the hollow, the two of them shot downhill on their hands and knees. Acolmiztli moved fast with a weird, scuttling, spider-like gait and easily stayed ahead of Shikotenka, who caught up with him on the flat, lying low amongst the undulating grass.

'Hush!' signed Acolmiztli.

Up ahead, very close, they heard a shout over the sound of the wind: 'Hey, I need help. I've got an injured man over here.'

Shikotenka pushed his head above the grass and saw a sentry less than a hundred paces away. At his feet lay a crumpled, bloodstained figure.

Another sentry charged up and Shikotenka ducked out of sight.

There came the sound of more shouting, the new arrival yelling at the top of his voice: 'Don't you realise who this is? Don't you even have the *faintest idea*?'

A mumble: 'Just looks like some sot got himself stabbed.'

'This is Prince Guatemoc, you idiot!'

More sentries had come running now, at least five or six, and several took up the shout: 'Guatemoc! Guatemoc!' Somebody blew a whistle. A drum started to beat. 'Prince Guatemoc has been attacked! Call the surgeons! Call out the guard!'

Shikotenka and Acolmiztli watched open-mouthed as chaos deteriorated into pandemonium, hundreds of the Mexica rushing to where Guatemoc lay. In the last moments before an immense mass of cloud covered the moon, they saw to their astonishment that even the sentries guarding the camp's principal thoroughfares had left their posts and were flocking to the side of the wounded prince.

The long avenue connecting the southern gateway to Coaxoch's pavilion appeared, for the moment, to be completely unguarded.

Shikotenka and Acolmiztli grinned at one another in disbelief. Then they were running, hidden by darkness, the moon now entirely lost to view in dense cloud. With no need to crawl through the grass any more, they went up the hill at a sprint and in moments reached the hollow where the fifty were waiting.

Tree was at the ridge with the men ready behind him in full battle order. 'So we just go straight in?' he said. 'Like I wanted to do at the beginning?'

'We go straight in,' said Shikotenka with a grim smile.

How fickle were the gods, he thought, and how inscrutably they meddled in the lives of men.

Chapter Thirty-Five

Tenochtitlan, small hours of Friday 19 February 1519

As Malinal's head began to clear from the beating she'd taken in the plaza, she discovered she had somehow already reached the great pyramid and begun to climb the wide northern stairway. On both sides, stationed at every third step, were guards holding guttering torches, and she saw she was part of a long line of prisoners ascending between them. She felt a helping hand pressed into the small of her back and turned to find Tozi right behind her. 'Coyotl?' she asked, her voice cracking.

'Gone,' Tozi said. Her chalk-white face was smeared with blood. 'Ahuizotl put him in the other line. I've lost sight of him.'

'It's my fault!' sobbed Malinal. Though she hardly knew Coyotl, the intensity of the last hours was such that she was overwhelmed to be separated from the anxious, intelligent little boy, and filled with guilt for her part in what had happened. 'Ahuizotl did it to spite me. If I hadn't been holding Coyotl, he wouldn't have taken him.'

'It's not your fault that Ahuizotl is an evil, hateful old man,' said Tozi. 'You gave Coyotl love. That's what you should remember.'

They were climbing very slowly, sometimes standing in place for a long count before shuffling up another step or two and halting again. The warm wind that had risen earlier was blowing more strongly now; overhead thick clouds raced across the face of the moon, and round Malinal's feet a foaming, clotting tide of human blood flowed from the summit platform and rolled ponderously down the steep, narrow steps. It was slippery and treacherous. It accumulated in shallow pools spreading out across the plaza at the base of the pyramid. It filled the air with a sour, terrifying stink.

Malinal's stomach cramped and heaved and bile rose in her throat. Though the cruelty and excess of the Mexica were nothing new to her, she was overwhelmed by the horror and depravity of this vast pageant of murder. Her stomach cramped again; this time she couldn't hold it back, and she threw up in a hot, spattering, choking gush.

'What a hero she is!' yelled one of the guards sarcastically.

'How brave!' sneered another. 'A whiff of the knife and she spews her guts!'

There came the thumping, rumbling sound of flesh striking stone as priests threw a pile of a dozen bleeding torsos over the edge of the summit platform. They tumbled down the steps like clumps of viscid fruit fallen from some evil tree, trailing streamers of guts, rolling and bumping wildly until they came to rest in the plaza below. Something heavy and wet had brushed against Malinal's leg as they went past, and now her stomach heaved uncontrollably again; she doubled over, dry-retching, gasping for breath, to the general hilarity of the guards.

As the spasm passed, she straightened and spat, hatred scourging her like acid. What a vile, vicious race these Mexica truly were – a race of arrogant, strutting, loud-mouthed bullies whose greatest pleasure was the desecration of others.

A race whose wickedness and cruelty knew no bounds.

Malinal was filled with impotent rage, wanting to punish them, to visit retribution upon them, to make them experience the same humiliations they inflicted, but she knew at the same time that none of this could ever happen, that she would continue to climb the pyramid, passive and unresisting as a dumb animal on its way to slaughter, and that when she reached the top she would be killed.

A soldier approached, carefully descending the steps, picking his way through the blood. Slung round his neck he carried a huge gourd containing some liquid and into it he dipped a silver cup that he offered to each prisoner in the line.

Most drank.

When it came to Malinal's turn she asked the soldier, who had a big, plain, honest, sunburned face, what he was offering her.

'Why it's *Iztli*, of course.'

'*Iztli*?'

'Obsidian-knife water.' He glanced towards the summit of the pyramid, less than fifty paces above them, reverberating with the agonised screams of the next victim. 'Drink!' He held out the silver cup. His tone was almost beseeching, his eyes level and kind, wrinkled with laughter lines. 'Drink, beautiful lady.'

'What will it do?'

He looked meaningfully again to the summit of the pyramid, then back down. 'It will dull your pain, lady.'

As Malinal reached out, Tozi lunged up from the step below and knocked the cup aside. 'It's not about dulling pain! Listen to those screams! They don't give a shit about our pain. They use *Iztli* to dull our wits. They use it to make us docile so we're easier to bring under the knife.'

The kind eyes of the soldier had turned indifferent. 'Your loss,' he shrugged, refilling the cup and moving down past Tozi to the next victim, who drank greedily.

Malinal was thinking, *Maybe I don't mind being docile so long as there's no pain when the knife opens my chest.* She was about to call the soldier back, but Tozi silenced her with a glance and whispered: 'No! We have to stay alert. This isn't over yet.'

Malinal looked closer and saw that something was back in the girl's eyes, a spark, a fire, that had fled after the fade and her subsequent catastrophic fit in the pen.

There was another outburst of horrific screams and the whole line, like some monstrous centipede, shuffled two steps closer to the summit.

'What are we going to do?' Malinal asked. The heart that was soon to be ripped from her chest was pounding against her ribs; the blood that was soon to be drained from her body was coursing through her veins and beating in her ears.

Tozi suddenly smiled and Malinal caught a fleeting glimpse of unsuspected depths in her strange new friend – of a sweet, otherworldly innocence beaming through the chalk and charcoal, and through the deeper disguise of the tough, streetwise beggar girl in which she concealed her witchiness. 'I thought all my powers were gone,' she said, 'maybe gone forever. But right after they took Coyotl, something started to come back . . .'

The line trudged another dreadful step upward.

'I don't know what it is yet,' Tozi continued. 'But there's something there! I can feel it!'

'Will you try to fade us again?'

'No! It's not that.'

'Why so sure?'

'I've tried already – before we started climbing the steps, just for a second or two – but it didn't work.'

'Is it the thing you call the fog?'

Tozi shook her head: 'No, not the fog.'

'Then what?'

'I don't know! I wish I did! But there's something there I can use. I'm sure of that. I just have to find it.'

More screams went up from the summit of the pyramid, close now, though still out of sight because of the steep slope of the stairway. There was the distinct wet *crack* that the obsidian knife makes when it splits a human breastbone, followed by a high-pitched gurgling screech and a sudden pulse of blood gushing over the top of the steps.

Ahead of them, her swaying pendulous buttocks pitifully uncovered by a flimsy paper loincloth, a young Totonac woman who had likewise refused the *Itzli* suddenly turned in her tracks, reached out her hand and gripped Malinal's shoulder. 'I can't bear this!' she screamed. Her eyes were rolling. 'I can't stand it any more.' She gave Malinal a forceful shove, almost dislodging her from the slippery step and said, 'Jump with me right now! You and me together! Let's throw ourselves down. The fall will kill us. It's better than the knife . . .'

A death chosen rather than a death inflicted? Malinal could see the point of that. And it would have the added advantage of cheating the bloodthirsty gods of the Mexica.

But such a death was not for her while there was still hope, and Tozi had given her hope. She swayed, pulled her shoulder free of the Totonac's grip. 'Jump if you must,' she told her. 'I won't try to stop you but I won't go with you.'

'Why not? Don't you understand what will be done to us there?' The woman turned her face up to the summit of the pyramid, still hidden by the gradient.

'I understand,' said Malinal, 'and it's OK. You take care of your death and I'll take care of mine.'

With groans of fear, whispered prayers, and the slack, dull faces of *Iztli* intoxication, the prisoners continued to shuffle upwards, pausing for long moments, then climbing again. Only those near the very top could see the altar and the sacrificial stone, but the butchered torsos of women who'd climbed the steps moments before continued to be thrown down by the priests, a constant reminder of what was to come.

Up a step. Stop.

Up two steps. Stop.

Though the moon was again behind cloud, the whole summit was brightly lit by torches and braziers, and Malinal began to see first the heads, then the shoulders, then the upper bodies of the team of sacrificers on the summit platform.

Ahuizotl was there!

How could he not be, since he'd want to gloat over her death?

Her fingers curled into claws.

Beside the high priest was Cuitláhuac who had also shared her bed.

And there, nude, bathed from head to toe in blood, working with furious efficiency, his face fixed in an ecstatic grin, was the coward Moctezuma, who she'd seen shit himself with fear.

Whack! Crack! In went the obsidian knife again, saturating the white paper garments of the next victim with bright red blood in an instant. Arteries were severed, more blood fountained into the air, and with a horrible, rending squelch, the heart was out.

Malinal distinctly heard Moctezuma say, apparently to thin air: 'Welcome, Lord. All this is for you.' Then at once another victim was stretched over the sacrificial stone and the Totonac woman climbed the final step to the summit platform and stood waiting, watching the killing team busy with their tasks. As the knife rose and fell she turned with a sad smile on her face, stretched her arms out beside her like wings and stood poised over the plunging stairway.

Cuitláhuac saw the danger first and barked an order for her to be held, but as the guards closed in she grappled with one of them, somehow unbalanced him, and tumbled with him over and over down the steep stairs, rolling and bouncing, their bodies pounded and broken into bloody shards long before they reached the bottom.

Malinal knew Moctezuma to be a superstitious man.

An ignominious suicide, carried out in his presence, snatching a beating human heart from Hummingbird's grasp, could never be anything other than a very bad omen indeed – one for which Ahuizotl as high priest must surely be held responsible. The snakeskin drum, the conches, the trumpets all instantly ceased their din and in the ghastly silence that followed the only sound to be heard came from Tozi. It was that same soft, insistent whisper she'd used when she'd faded them in the pen – and in the same way it now rose in intensity, seeming to deepen and roughen, becoming almost a snarl or a growl.

Ahuizotl took a step forward. His eyes found Malinal but drifted past her. He seemed shocked and disoriented.

Was he imagining the terrible ways Moctezuma would punish him?

Or was Tozi getting inside his head?

Malinal was beginning to hope her friend really had got her powers back when she felt Moctezuma's blood-rimmed glare drill into her skull as his four helpers grasped her by the arms and legs and threw her down on her back over the sacrificial stone.

Chapter Thirty-Six

Tenochtitlan, small hours of Friday 19 February 1519

It was truly a night of the gods, torn by winds and storm. Thunder rolled and huge black clouds harried the fleeing moon, sometimes reducing her to a flicker of balefire, sometimes allowing her furious and jaundiced face to peer through, sometimes shutting off her light entirely as though a door in heaven had closed.

Moctezuma had been killing since morning but now, in the depths of the night, his work illuminated by flickering torches and glowing braziers, he felt no fatigue. He had consumed two more massive doses of *teonanácatl* and the god-power of the mushrooms coursed through his veins, making him ferocious, vigorous and invulnerable. Far from tiring him, each new blow he struck with the obsidian knife seemed to animate him further. Should the priests find him five thousand more victims, he would kill them all. Ten thousand? Bring them on! There was nothing he would not do for his god.

Moctezuma felt preternaturally aware of everything.

Everything.

Of this world of blood and bone, and of that other shadow world where he had met and talked with Hummingbird.

The god had been absent for many hours while the new batch of sacrifices offered themselves to the knife, but now he returned, with so little fanfare it seemed he'd always been there. He stood between Cuitláhuac and Ahuizotl unnoticed by them, his face sly and amused.

'Welcome, lord,' Moctezuma said, holding up a palpitating heart. 'All this is for you.' He threw the streaming organ on the brazier, where it steamed and smoked, and immediately turned to the next victim, tore her body open and plucked her heart out too.

Everything was going wonderfully well, Moctezuma thought. He couldn't stop himself grinning and cackling. And why should he? The god was with him again, the down payment on his price was being made in hearts and blood, and now he could expect divine help against the powerful strangers. No matter if they possessed fire serpents that could kill from afar! No matter if wild animals fought beside them in battle! With Hummingbird leading the way the Mexica were certain of victory, and even if the strangers were the companions of Quetzalcoatl himself they would be vanquished! There was no other conceivable outcome.

The dream was sweet until Moctezuma heard Cuitláhuac shout, 'Grab her!' and the scuff of bare feet behind him. He whirled round as the bloody corpse on the sacrificial stone was dragged aside to be butchered and witnessed something extraordinary and unbelievable. Instead of submissively waiting to take her place under his knife, the next victim was standing at the edge of the summit platform, her paper garments flapping in the wind, her arms stretched out beside her like wings, poised to throw herself down the northern stairway. This must not under any circumstances be allowed to happen, for it would bring the displeasure of the god. Moctezuma's heart pounded against his ribs and anger surged through him. He would have Ahuizotl's skin if the woman went through with it. Time seemed to race as guards moved towards her. One reached her. They wrestled on the edge of the abyss and then slowly, with the impossibility of a thing never seen before, both figures tumbled from view . . .

An awful sound broke the shocked silence that followed – an eerie, rough, whispering snarl that had the rhythms of magic. Moctezuma saw at once that its source was a dirty little female with wild hair. She was waiting second in the line of prisoners near the top of the stairway and staring straight at him.

Nobody looked the Great Speaker of the Mexica in the eye!

Yet this filthy child, whose heart he would soon cut out, showed no fear as she calmly met his gaze.

And she wasn't alone! One step above her stood another defiant figure. Tall, plastered chalk-white, hair roughly shorn, in the paper clothes of her humiliation, this woman looked nothing like a victim and stared him down with the same predatory anticipation as the child, throwing him further into turmoil.

Panic seized him as he sensed everything falling apart. The terrible omen of the suicide followed at once by the bizarre behaviour of these two females threatened to unman him completely. He sought out Hummingbird, fearing his anger, yet filled with a hopeless yearning for absolution, but the god who had been so present only moments before had vanished again, as silently and as mysteriously as he had appeared.

'Aaaah! Aaaah!' Moctezuma's bowels cramped and loosened, cramped and loosened, an ancient curse returning to haunt him, but he could not evacuate here at the top of the pyramid in full public view. It was simply unthinkable.

He clenched, tried to bring his emotions under control, and a renewed surge of the god-power of the mushrooms pulsed through him, shoving a fist of vomit into his mouth, forcing him to swallow and gulp like a frog. The tall woman smiled.

Smiled!

How dare she?

Anger triumphed over fear and he began to think clearly again. The suicide was the worst form of sacrilege, yet amends could be made. The god had deserted him again, but he had done so before and there was still hope that the harvest of victims would lure him back. The only answer was to put all distractions aside and continue with the sacrifices as if nothing had happened.

Moctezuma signalled to the musicians to resume play as his four helpers seized the tall woman by the arms and legs, spun her round with practised economy of effort, and cast her down on her back on the sacrificial stone. He raised the obsidian knife, gripping its hilt in both hands, and muttered the ritual prayer – 'Oh lord, Hummingbird, at the left hand of the Sun, accept this my offering.'

He was about to plunge the knife down when the voice of the god, loud and unexpected, boomed inside his head: 'No! I do *not* want this offering. You must *not* kill this woman.'

Moctezuma froze in place, the knife poised. 'But, lord, you told me to bring you hearts.'

'You must still bring me hearts, Moctezuma, but not this heart. I have chosen this woman *and she must not be harmed*. I have work for her to do.'

'You have . . . chosen her, lord?'

'Just as I chose you.'

Suddenly the tenor of the divine voice changed and Moctezuma found himself once more in the presence of Hummingbird. It was as though they were both looking down on the victim from a great height. The war god's skin glowed white hot. 'Set her free,' he commanded.

Moctezuma hesitated. Was he understanding correctly? Could there be some mistake? 'Set her free?' he babbled.

The god sighed. 'Yes. Free. Must you repeat every word I say?'

And at the same instant, in the world of blood and bone, Moctezuma felt Ahuizotl at his elbow, whispering alarm in his ear. 'You must *not* free her, Magnificence! This woman must die! She must die! The god will not forgive us if she walks from the stone.'

Moctezuma remembered that he alone conversed with Hummingbird, while for Ahuizotl and others it must seem he was talking to himself. 'Be silent!' he roared.

'But lord . . .'

'You know *nothing*, Ahuizotl! I will have your *skin* for failing me this night.'

The high priest cowered and trembled, stammering apologies and then, unbelievably, the woman on the stone spoke. Her voice was rich and throaty, somehow familiar, and she seemed to look deep into Moctezuma's eyes: 'Your priest is corrupt,' she told him. 'He broke his vow of chastity and took me to his bed . . .'

'Lies!' Ahuizotl screamed. 'Lies! Lies!'

But Cuitláhuac had stepped close now and was examining the woman's face, rubbing at her chalk-white mask, revealing ever more of her skin. 'Malinal!' he suddenly exclaimed. 'This is Malinal, Lord Speaker! She was your interpreter when the messenger from the Chontal Maya brought tidings of the gods to you. You ordered her execution.'

'Ahuizotl disobeyed the Lord Speaker,' the woman said. 'He keeps a secret house in the district of Tlatelolco. He took me there from your palace four months ago. He used my body . . .'

196

'Lies!' Ahuizotl shrieked again. 'All lies!'

'There's more here than meets the eye,' Cuitláhuac said. He was known to be a stickler for rules and regulations, an enemy of Ahuizotl and a strong advocate of priestly celibacy. 'The charge is grave. We must question the woman further and discover the truth.'

'No!' snarled Ahuizotl. 'Kill her!'

Moctezuma's eyes darted back and forth between the two men and down to the prone, spread body of the woman.

Yes, he remembered her. His stomach cramped and his bowels rumbled. She had witnessed his shame and he had ordered her death; yet here she was, four months later, still alive.

How could that be if her story was not true?

As another devastating cramp gripped his stomach and a bubble of sour air burst from his mouth, he made his decision. No questions could be asked. He would deal with Ahuizotl later, but the woman knew his secret and she must die with it now.

Her eyes, huge and dark, gazed up at him, catching and magnifying the flickering flames of the torches and the fiery glow of the braziers, seeming to burn into his soul. Resisting a powerful urge to recoil, even to run from her, Moctezuma jerked the dripping knife above his head, felt a thrill of pleasure as her pupils dilated with fear, and put all his force into a killing blow.

That never landed.

That never even began.

'You pathetic grubby little human,' boomed the voice of Hummingbird. Unseen and unheard by all the others, the god was still at his side, radiant as a volcano. 'You will free this woman at once. You will send her from this city unharmed. I have spoken.'

Moctezuma struggled, tried to move his knife hand and discovered that it was paralysed in place above his head. 'Release her, or die,' said the god. 'In fact, why don't you just die anyway? I think I prefer Cuitláhuac for your role.'

'Bu ... bu ... bu ...' Moctezuma tried to speak, but could not, tried to breathe but could not.

'Interesting, isn't it,' said the god, 'this business of dying? Fun when you're dishing it out, not so nice when you're at the receiving end.'

Moctezuma gaped, his chest heaved, and yet no breath would come. It was as though a huge hand covered his nose and mouth.

'You are desperate to breathe,' the god continued. 'It gets worse. Very soon fear will overwhelm you, you will lose all control of your body and you will void your bowels. Tut tut! *Where will your secret be then?*'

'Gahhh, ahhh, gaargh . . .'

Moctezuma felt it coming now, felt death all over him like a swarm of bees, was shaken by another terrifying cramp and tried desperately to signal his surrender.

The god's smile was malevolent. 'What?' he said. 'What was that?'

'Gnahh, aargh . . .'

'Ah. You agree? Is that what you're saying? You will release the woman?'

His head spinning, his knees rubber, Moctezuma nodded his assent.

'Hmmm,' said the god. 'I rather thought you would. Well, I suppose I shall give you another chance. Grooming Cuitláhuac to play your part would be such a bore.'

At once the sense of a hand clamped to Moctezuma's face was gone and he could breathe again. Gasping, heaving, his vision steadying, he turned on his four assistants. They held the woman stretched over the sacrificial stone, gripping her by her wrists and ankles, terror and confusion squirming on their faces. 'Release her!' he roared.

After she'd struggled to her feet, Moctezuma ordered the woman to be taken from the pyramid, given clothes and sent on her way out of Tenochtitlan. The god had said she was to leave the city. The god had said she was not to be harmed. The god must not be denied.

Yet she refused to go!

Instead, looking him straight in the eye as though she were his equal, this woman, this Malinal, as Cuitláhuac had named her, made a new demand.

'I was brought here with my friend,' she said, indicating the wild-haired girl at the top of the steps. 'I won't leave without her.'

Moctezuma turned to Hummingbird, but the god had again deserted him.

He looked for Ahuizotl. The high priest too had vanished.

He looked to Cuitláhuac, who knew Malinal, and to the other nobles. They stood in groups around the vacant sacrificial stone, whispering to one another.

Whispering sedition.

'I remember our last meeting,' Malinal said quietly. She looked pointedly at Moctezuma's belly. 'It seemed the royal person was unwell. Allow me to express the hope that you have fully recovered your health.' As she spoke, Moctezuma felt the eyes of the woman's little ragged friend on him, heard the whisper of magic still pouring from her lips and helplessly doubled over as another agonising cramp struck him.

'Take her,' he gasped. 'Take her. I free you both.'

Smeared with chalk and blood, Malinal seemed more demon or ghost than human flesh and blood.

'Wait!' she said. 'There's one more thing.'

Chapter Thirty-Seven

Santiago, Cuba, small hours of Friday 19 February 1519

The man was whip-thin. Caught in the swaying lantern light, his clever, weather-beaten face was lined with worry. 'You understand we can't sail in this,' he told Cortés, 'it would be suicide . . .'

Melchior had gone about his master's business soon after Alvarado's arrival, but Pepillo remained hidden in the aftcastle, nursing his wounds. Then Alvarado and Cortés left the ship and clattered off along the pier on horseback. Time passed. Pepillo had some sense of it from the gradual westward track of the moon across the increasingly crowded and stormy heavens. He dozed for a while. When he awoke the wind had grown stronger, whistling and rattling through the rigging, and down below on the navigation deck he heard voices raised in anger.

With a feeling of dread he recognised one of them as Muñoz.

He heard Cortés and another voice he did not recognise. It was an argument about money. There was a sudden bustle of activity, heavy footsteps pounded on the deck and down the gangplank. More shouting – it seemed the fleet would sail tonight without the governor's blessing! – then a thunder of hooves as a horse took off at a gallop.

Taking care not to make a sound, Pepillo crawled out from behind the piled ropes, snaked forward on his belly, wincing at his bruises, and found a spot where he could look down on the navigation deck without being seen.

Five men stood there – Cortés, Muñoz and three others he did not know. It was obvious at once from the tension in their bodies that the argument was far from over, and now Muñoz shouted, 'You can't do that to me!'

Cortés said strongly that he could do anything he wanted, then lowered his voice. Amidst gusts of wind, Pepillo heard only the words, 'Córdoba expedition', 'terrible' and 'page', before Cortés leaned closer and whispered in Muñoz's ear. He must have said something frightening because the Dominican gasped, blanched and stumbled back. Then the impossible happened. In a tone of disgust, Cortés said, 'Take him', and two of the other men leapt forward. Pepillo's breath caught in his throat and hope surged through him as they seized Muñoz by the arms and frogmarched him from the ship. The Inquisitor's strident protests continued but were soon snatched by the wind and lost to hearing as he was led off along the pier.

In this way Cortés was finally left alone with the thin, weather-beaten man, who at once told him that to sail this night, in this weather, would be suicide – advice the caudillo clearly did not want to hear.

'Come come, Alaminos,' he said. 'Has easy living stolen your courage? You've sailed in worse gales than this!'

'I have,' the man called Alaminos admitted. He looked to the troubled sky now overcast from horizon to horizon, the light of the moon entirely swallowed. 'But we're only at the birth of the storm. It's going to get worse. Much worse.'

'If the month were August or September I'd agree with you,' Cortés said cheerfully. 'But this is February, man. February! Think about it. Since you sailed with Columbus, how many great storms have you witnessed in these waters in February?'

'None,' Alaminos admitted.

'March then, or April? Even May? Come now, be honest. Have you ever seen a real storm hit Cuba or any of the islands before the month of June?'

Again Alaminos was forced to admit he had not. 'But there's always a first time,' he said, 'and I have a bad feeling about this storm, Don Hernán. A very bad feeling. I'm a pilot, and a good one—'

'A great one!' Cortés interrupted.

Alaminos ignored the compliment and pressed on: '. . . because I trust my feelings. That's why I've never lost a ship. If you insist on sailing this night then I give you fair warning – you will sink your entire fleet and drown every one of us with it.'

'Fie, man! Don't say such things!'

'It's not the saying that matters, but the hearing, Don Hernán. Hear me well, I beg you! Delay our departure until the storm clears.'

Cortés walked to the rail of the navigation deck and stared out over the darkened harbour, across the agitated waters, into the teeth of the wind. He stood silent, his head held high, like a hero of old, like a Caesar or an Alexander. Seeing him like that, indomitable, fearless and strong, Pepillo believed in his heart what Alaminos doubted – that this great caudillo would vanquish the storm in the same confident way he had vanquished Muñoz.

'I'm grateful for your advice,' Cortés now said, still gazing into the night. 'It is good advice and well meant, but mine is the burden of command and there are other matters you know nothing of that I must consider.' He turned and walked back to join Alaminos, who was standing by the whipstaff that steered the great ship; he clapped him heartily on the shoulders. 'Besides,' he said, holding up a finger to the gale, 'this is a strong wind, but a fair one in my judgement – it's blowing our way. Once we're free of the harbour and out on the open sea, it's going to take us straight to the New Lands.'

'So we sail then?'

'Posthaste, Alaminos. The ebb tide will speed our departure. Don't you see how everything is going our way?'

Alaminos still looked gloomy.

'Well?' said Cortés. 'What is it, man? Speak your mind.'

'Even if we're not sunk,' said the pilot, 'you can be sure the fleet will be scattered. I have to plot a course to a rendezvous point and the course must be shared with all the captains before we sail or we'll never find each other again.'

'I've been giving thought to that. There was an island you visited with Córdoba in sight of the coast of the New Lands. Friendly natives, you said. Plentiful game. Sweet water. Sounds like just the spot for us.'

'The natives call it Cozumel,' Alaminos answered immediately. 'The island of swallows, or some such meaning, as best we could understand it through signs and pointing. It's a good place.'

'Quick about it then! Plot a course for Cozumel. Make copies for each of the captains. I'll have a rider standing by to distribute them across the fleet and then we sail.'

The ship had become a hubbub of rapidly increasing noise and activity, with sailors swarming in the rigging and working together on ropes to complete a hundred different bewildering tasks that Pepillo couldn't understand. So far, however, the aftcastle wasn't the focus of any of this, so he crawled back to his hiding place and tried to make a plan.

One thing was sure – Muñoz was no longer on board the *Santa María* and therefore posed no immediate threat to him. Pepillo realised he could now walk about freely, if he wished, without risking another beating. But if he did that, then might not he too be thrown off the ship? After all, what use was a page without a master?

He heard Cortés's voice again, now on the main deck, shouting for a despatch rider. A little later a horse galloped off and all the time the frenetic pace of preparations continued. Pepillo knew no way to make himself useful in any of this, even if he weren't a mass of bruises and pain, so all in all, he decided, the best thing he could do was stay exactly where he was, stowed away behind the coiled ropes.

Once out at sea he couldn't be sent back.

He was beginning to think he might actually get away with it, when he heard men climbing from the main deck to the navigation deck, heavy footsteps and a stream of foul oaths.

'Where's those bloody ropes?' someone said.

Chapter Thirty-Eight

Tlascala, small hours of Friday 19 February 1519

Acolmiztli and Tree sprinted downslope to the unguarded thorn barrier and tore it apart, opening the way for the rest of the squad to stream through in a compact mass.

No turning back now, Shikotenka thought. He stretched out his legs and took the lead, flashing past neat ranks of tents and bivouacs ranged east and west of the wide central avenue. Glancing at young Tochtli running proudly beside him, he felt for the first time the full weight of the danger he'd asked his men to face and the threat of imminent failure. Tlascalans were the greatest runners in the world, and these were the best of the best, but even they would need three minutes or more to cover the two thousand paces to Coaxoch's pavilion.

All round them harsh shouts and cries of alarm filled the air and torches flared and guttered in the rising wind. The moon, troubled by clouds, still shed enough light to show hosts of warriors, intermingled with a rabble of camp followers, merchants and pleasure girls, crowding through the tented alleys towards the edge of the southeastern sector where Guatemoc lay. Drawn by the commotion, many more were surging across the avenue from the southwestern sector, but none seemed to suspect the rapidly advancing Tlascalans in their guise as jaguar and eagle knights, simply making way for them as they pounded past.

It was an astonishing dereliction of duty, yet another sign that the Mexica were falling short of the legendary discipline Shikotenka so much admired – almost all the sentries along the avenue had left their posts to join in the general melee. Here and there, a few were still in place, novices conspicuous in their white cotton armour, who stood around awkwardly clutching their spears and casting anxious glances towards the southeast. Several actually saluted the Tlascalans and Shikotenka heard Chipahua snigger, 'Mexica arseholes!'

Five hundred paces out from the pavilion, a heavy burst of rain spattered down like an avalanche of small stones, soon settling into a drenching, insistent downpour, and in the same instant the last gap in the clouds closed, completely obscuring the moon and plunging the camp into darkness. *Perfect*, thought Shikotenka. Further evidence that the gods indeed blessed his plan. Campfires and torches were quickly doused to dull red points by the squall, but the great pavilion towered directly ahead, bright as a beacon, its walls of thick maguey-fibre sheeting, and its soaring conical roof stretched over a frame of poles lit up brilliantly from within by a multitude of lanterns.

There was a sudden shouted challenge and a troop of Mexica spearmen, silhouetted against the pavilion's glow, loomed out of the dark. There were no more than twenty of them, perhaps thirty, all novices judging from their uniforms, but still enough to put up a fight and hinder the attack. 'Step aside, fools!' yelled Shikotenka at the top of his voice. He disguised his Tlascalan accent and summoned his most regal tones. 'We're here to protect the Snake Woman.'

'Let's just kill them,' hissed Tree.

'Maybe we won't have to,' said Shikotenka, his mind working furiously, and as they closed with the other group he brandished Guatemoc's *macuahuitl* and yelled again: 'Step aside! Tlascalan attack in the southeast quadrant. We're here to protect the Snake Woman!'

He wasn't even surprised when the ruse worked. In this army of novices, the uniforms of jaguar and eagle knights commanded immense respect, and with hair and faces hidden by their distinctive wooden helmets, there was nothing to identify his squad as the enemy. After only the slightest hesitation, the block of spearmen divided before them, some of them raising their right arms in hasty salutes as the Tlascalans shot through the gap. 'Reinforce the southeast quadrant at the double,' Shikotenka yelled back through the rain. 'Heavy fighting there. Prince Guatemoc's been killed!'

Chipahua gave another snigger. 'Arseholes,' he said again. The word boomed emphatically inside his eagle-beaked helmet.

Yes, thought Shikotenka. *Arseholes. A whole host of arseholes.* Come rain or shine there should be hundreds of sentries around the Snake Woman's pavilion, blocking every road. Instead it seemed that Coaxoch was so confident of his power, so secure in the midst of this huge army, that he'd not thought to take additional precautions.

The pavilion's entrance was a great square, twice the height of a man, veiled with gaudy curtains and approached under an immense awning borne up on rows of gilded wooden pillars, thick as tree trunks. Protected from the rain by the awning, each pillar supported a guttering lantern; by the light of these, Shikotenka saw that a dozen men had taken shelter here. They wore the distinctive yellow and black livery of the Snake Woman's personal guards and were peering out into the storm, plainly disturbed by the general commotion in the camp, but apparently not yet aware of what had happened because their spears were held at rest and their *macuahuitls* still sheathed. Better still, Shikotenka realised, the lanterns that made the guards so visible to him must make him and his squad invisible to them.

He didn't need to give orders. His Tlascalans all knew instinctively what to do and bore down on the pavilion at a dead run, the sound of their footfalls muffled by the driving rain. They were less than twenty paces out when they were spotted, so close the guards had no time to deploy their weapons.

The slaughter began.

A big Mexica charged with clawed hands, yelling defiance, his teeth bared, but Shikotenka brought his *macuahuitl* crashing down on the man's head, spilling his brains. Tugging the weapon free he glimpsed Tree flailing about mightily to left and right with his huge war club, and Acolmiztli jerking his knife out of a guard's stomach followed by a coil of guts. Tochtli whirled his *macuahuitl* in a classic training-ground manoeuvre; he struck off another guard's leg above the knee and half severed his neck as he fell, abruptly silencing his screams. With fifty against twelve the fight was over in seconds. Shikotenka saw Etzli slip in a pool of blood and the last Mexica still standing thrust a spear down at him as he hit the ground. The Tlascalan rolled to avoid the blow and, as the guard thrust again, Tochtli sprang into his path, deflected the spear with his *macuahuitl*, drew his dagger left-handed and stabbed the man repeatedly through the chest.

Etzli picked himself up and clapped Tochtli on the shoulder. 'Good work, little Rabbit,' he said. 'You'll make a warrior yet.'

Nicely done, cousin, Shikotenka thought. To win a compliment from Etzli was no easy task and brought Tochtli one step closer to the recognition and acceptance he craved.

Chipahua and Ilhuicamina were checking the bodies of the foe. They found three who were injured but not dead and swiftly slit their throats.

The rain still poured down, a torrential, rumbling flood beating on the sagging awning overhead and on the glowing lantern-lit walls of the great pavilion, alive with silhouettes. From within came the sounds of wild music and laughter, and quite clearly and unmistakably Shikotenka heard the high-pitched groans and gasps of a woman approaching orgasm.

'Bet she's faking it,' commented Chipahua sourly.

'You're just jealous,' growled Ilhuicamina.

Amazingly no one inside the pavilion seemed to have heard the sounds of struggle at the entrance. No alarm had yet been raised. What sounded like a party in full swing, even an orgy, simply continued unchecked.

Shikotenka signalled his platoon commanders to gather round. 'Tree, Acolmiztli, you and your men are with me. We go straight in through the front entrance and remember – we're here only for Coaxoch and his sons and we can't risk more than a two-hundred count to get the job done. Kill everyone who gets in our way but *don't waste time on anyone else*. Same goes for you, Chipahua – take your ten round the west side of this monstrous tent and cut your way in. Ilhuicamina – you get the east side. Etzli – you get the north. We meet in the middle – that's where Coaxoch will be.'

'What if he isn't?' said Etzli.

'He'll be there – surrounded by sycophants and arse-lickers. He's too fat to miss.'

Shikotenka was less sure of this than he pretended to be. The pavilion was massive – there could be dozens of inner rooms and it wasn't inevitable that Coaxoch would be holding court. He might be sleeping. He might be fornicating. He might be taking a bath.

But it was too late now – much too late! – for any such concerns.

With slow, deliberate movements Shikotenka removed his helmet, shrugged loose his long Tlascalan locks and stripped off his jaguar knight uniform until he wore only a loincloth, weapons, waterskin and sandals. He signalled everyone else to do the same. 'No more disguises,' he said. 'They have to know who we are.'

Chapter Thirty-Nine

Tenochtitlan, small hours of Friday 19 February 1519

Tozi understood the new power she had found. It was the power to magnify others' fears.

She had directed it at Moctezuma and magnified his fear that his bowels would betray him.

She had directed it at Ahuizotl, who feared his deceit would be exposed, and driven him into a frenzy of terror.

But she was under no illusions about Moctezuma's decision to free Malinal from the killing stone. It had not happened because of anything she had done.

In the highly charged moments that had passed since she'd attained the summit of the pyramid, Tozi had experienced a revelation. It was often said by the Mexica that their Great Speakers were in direct communication with Hummingbird and served as his agents and instruments on earth, but she'd always suspected such statements of being little more than boastful propaganda. Now she knew she had been wrong, for her witch gift had allowed her to see something dreadful lurking there amongst the priests and lords clustered round the killing stone, something that no one except Moctezuma was meant to see – the true spiritual source of all the horror and wickedness the Mexica inflicted upon the world.

The war god himself.

And to see him was to witness the apparition of ultimate evil incarnate in a phantasm of immense beauty – not a body of flesh and blood, Tozi had understood at once, but a vision-body, tall and powerful with luminous skin and a nimbus of golden hair and black, black eyes, and a sly, cruel smile delighting in fear and misery and pain.

Delighting even in the fear and misery of the Great Speaker, whom he toyed with and taunted and confused by coming and going, slipping away through rifts in the fabric of the night into some invisible realm that lay beyond, only to return to pull the strings of his human puppet again and enforce his will upon him.

It was this demonic entity, this god of the dark places of the human soul, who had ordered Malinal freed, who had held back the obsidian knife, who had clamped his phantom hand over Moctezuma's nose and mouth and stifled his breathing and forced him to release her from the stone and then vanished again as though his work was done.

Tozi would not have believed it if she had not seen it with her own eyes. But having seen it she was still left with the fundamental question.

Why?

Why would such a being, nourished by the hearts of the victims Moctezuma offered him, have wanted *anyone* released?

And why Malinal in particular?

And was Tozi's own freedom, which her friend had so courageously and selflessly required, also part of some diabolical plan?

Malinal's manner towards Moctezuma had been almost . . . intimate. But as Tozi ran to her side her voice snapped out like a whip. 'Wait!' she said, as though the Great Speaker were of no more consequence than a household slave. 'There's one more thing . . .'

Tozi was acutely conscious of how the nobles gathered on the summit platform, the killing crew and the priests were all standing round with their mouths gaping in disbelief watching this impossible exchange.

'There's a boy,' Malinal continued. 'A little boy. He was imprisoned amongst the women in error. Ahuizotl sent him to the western stairway for sacrifice. If he still lives I want to take him with us.'

All eyes turned towards the western altar. After the dramatic events of the past few moments the sacrifices there had ceased, as they had ceased also at the eastern altar – both these points being plainly visible in the bright light of torches and braziers, and less than a hundred feet distant from their present position.

'A boy?' said Moctezuma.

'Yes,' said Malinal. 'A boy. I would take him with me. You must give the order.'

Tozi focussed her power and read the squirming mind of the Great Speaker. He was trying to guess if it was the god who wanted this, or only the impertinent woman whom the god had so inexplicably favoured? He also very much wished not to appear weak in the presence of the nobles. He played for time while he struggled to decide: 'Why must I give such an order?'

'*Because the god wills it*,' hissed Tozi. Though unseen she felt the presence of Hummingbird again, horribly close, looming over her, and heard a voice, thick and triumphant, whisper in her ear the words, '*You're mine now.*' In that same fleeting instant, a great bolt of lightning cracked down out of the storm-tossed sky and struck the roof-comb of the temple, bathing the whole structure in a glory of flickering blue flame. Tozi watched, hypnotised, as a tongue of the witch fire licked out towards her, touched her, and was gone, leaving her astonished she was unhurt, her whole body reverberating as though she were a bell struck by some great hammer. A colossal roll of thunder shook the pyramid like an earthquake and Moctezuma groaned and stiffened. 'Take the boy!' he shrieked. 'Cuitláhuac – see to it!'

As Cuitláhuac escorted them round the side of the temple towards the western altar, Tozi's breath came in short, sharp gasps and she heard herself muttering – *Gods let us be on time. Gods let us be on time.* Reflected in the evil glow of the brazier, where a dozen hearts lay smoking, she saw the cruel hooked nose and sneering lips of Namacuix, Ahuizotl's deputy. Clutching a long obsidian knife loosely in his right hand, he stood back from the killing stone where his assistants held a small struggling body stretched out ready for sacrifice.

'*Coyotl*,' Tozi bellowed rushing forward, only to discover as she drew closer that the victim was a young girl whose terrified face she half remembered from the fattening pen. Namacuix seemed to be in a trance, gazing up with rapt attention at the roof of the temple where the lightning bolt had struck, but Tozi's frantic approach snapped him out of it. He turned on her with a roar of fury, knife raised.

211

'Stay your blade, Namacuix,' barked Cuitláhuac. 'She's not to be harmed.' He indicated Malinal: 'That one too. Moctezuma himself has ordered their release.' As he spoke more lightning flickered amongst the clouds, thunder growling up there like some monstrous beast, and a few heavy drops of rain spattered down.

The anger drained from Namacuix's face. Puzzlement replaced it. 'What's this all about?' he asked Cuitláhuac. 'The Great Speaker offering sacrifices from morning to night, a suicide on the northern stairway, the temple of Hummingbird struck by lightning, prisoners released. I've known nothing like it in twenty years as a priest.'

'Neither have I, my friend,' said Cuitláhuac. 'Neither have any of us.' He lowered his voice: 'There's sorcery at work.' He looked at Malinal and Tozi again and made a gesture of disgust. 'They say they have a friend who was brought to the western stair for sacrifice – a little boy. He's to go free also. Have you seen him?'

Namacuix's puzzlement deepened. 'The Speaker ordered only females sacrificed. The fattening pen was emptied. No males have come under my knife.'

'His *tepulli* and *ahuacatl* had been hacked off,' Tozi snarled. 'Many mistake him for a girl. Did you see such a one?'

'Insolent cockroach!' Namacuix was furious again. 'How dare you address *me*?'

'Answer her question,' Malinal snapped, 'unless you prefer to answer to the Great Speaker.'

'It would be wise to answer,' suggested Cuitláhuac. 'Could one of your victims have been a mutilated boy?'

Namacuix nibbled his lower lip. 'How can I know?' he said after a moment's thought. 'I'm here to kill them not examine them.' He pointed his knife at a heap of butchered torsos stacked five deep and four wide, like logs at the edge of the summit platform ready to be thrown down. 'The last ones I harvested are still there. See for yourselves.'

Tozi fell on her knees in the pool of gore before the grisly mound of human remains. Behind her, on the sacrificial stone, she heard a wail of renewed terror. Below, the captives waiting their turn for sacrifice occupied the bloody steps in a long line that stretched down through the deep shadows enveloping the lower reaches of the pyramid and emerged beyond into the lantern-lit plaza.

Tozi put her hands on the first of the slick, glistening bodies – a woman's body, full breasts obscenely divided by a wide, dripping gash where the heart had been torn out. The others next to it were also those of mature women. She groaned with effort and horror as she shoved them aside to reach the layer below.

'Don't,' Tozi heard Malinal say. 'This is more than any human can bear.'

'I have to know. I promised I'd protect him . . .' Tozi bowed her head and one by one examined every blood-smeared cadaver, but Coyotl was not amongst them.

When she was done she felt a gentle hand on her shoulder. 'Come,' Malinal said quietly. She was holding a flickering torch. 'Perhaps he's still somewhere in the line.'

As they moved to the steps, Cuitláhuac sighed with impatience and urged them to make haste, but Malinal held the torch up to the tired, terrified, sometimes defiant faces of every waiting victim. Each time a child of approximately Coyotl's age and size was illuminated by the flames, Tozi peered closer, only to stand back again in disappointment and continue the slippery, precipitous journey.

About halfway down, the torch light reflected in the *Itzli*-dulled eyes of one of the Tlascalan girls from Xoco's gang who'd persecuted Tozi since the morning. 'Well if it isn't the witch,' she slurred. 'Walking free again, are you?'

Tozi didn't explain. 'We're looking for Coyotl,' she said.

The girl gave a crafty, knowing grin: 'You mean that little eunuch of yours?'

A surge of hope. 'Yes. Have you seen him?'

'Might have done. Then again I might not.'

Tozi moved closer. 'If you've seen him, please tell me.'

The girl cast a sideways glance at Cuitláhuac. 'Get this great lord to free me,' she said, 'then I'll tell you.' But Tozi was already inside her head and saw at once she knew nothing. Without a backward glance she resumed the descent.

'I've seen him all right,' the girl suddenly shouted, high-pitched, furious. 'He was crying out for you! I dealt him a few slaps but he wouldn't shut up, so I shoved him off the steps. He fell and died! That's what happened to him.'

Tozi ignored her, continued to examine the faces in the line. 'It's not true,' she said to Malinal.

'How do you know?'

'I just know. It's not true. She hasn't seen Coyotl.'

When they reached the foot of the stairway there were more hideous piles of torsos piled on both sides, the remains of victims already sacrificed and thrown down the pyramid. Tozi felt drawn strongly towards the huge mound of hundreds of bodies on their right but Malinal's hand touched her shoulder again. 'There isn't time,' the older woman said, her voice urgent. 'You've done all you can but this is hopeless. We have to get out of here, *now*, before Moctezuma changes his mind.'

Chapter Forty

Cuitláhuac led Malinal and Tozi across the plaza, where gangs of enforcers surrounded the prisoners who had not yet begun to climb the pyramid, keeping them in order with goads and whips. Malinal had held onto the torch and Tozi insisted that these last victims, too, must be examined by its light, but Coyotl was not amongst them.

Huge numbers of priests were still present, clutching their flickering orange lanterns. No longer dancing, they stood solemnly in place, their red-painted faces set in expressions of bemusement, even fear. No drums beat, no conches blared, and even the wind, which had blown so wildly before, seemed to have fallen still. Indeed, since the dramatic pause in the sacrifices, the extraordinary behaviour of the Great Speaker, and the bolt from heaven that had struck the temple, a deadly uncertainty had settled upon the proceedings.

Cuitláhuac strode directly towards the northwest side of the plaza. He seemed to be making for the fattening pen where they'd so recently been held. Malinal stiffened: 'What's this?' she demanded. 'We're to be set free.'

'You will be,' said Cuitláhuac grimly, 'though I'd prefer otherwise. If this was my decision I'd find out what you know about Ahuizotl and then have you killed. But Moctezuma has spoken. I have no choice but to obey.'

'Why would you wish me dead, Cuitláhuac? Don't you remember our nights together?'

'I remember them – to my shame. But at least I'm not a priest sworn to celibacy.'

'You were dull and clumsy,' Malinal recalled.

'And you're a whore,' Cuitláhuac said, 'a whore and a witch. You were meant to die four months ago and you lived. You were meant to die tonight and yet you live again.'

Tozi was walking quietly along beside them, deep in thought. 'It's because the gods will it,' she now said. 'Don't you know the gods always get their way?'

Adjacent to the women's fattening pen, but towering above it, was the empty palace of Axayacatl, Moctezuma's father. It now became clear that this was where Cuitláhuac was heading – not to the imposing main entrance, which stood directly opposite the western face of the pyramid, but to a small door at the northern end of the huge building.

On either side of this door stood two hulking spearmen wrapped in long cloaks.

Again Malinal hesitated, still mistrusting Cuitláhuac's intentions, and he sighed with exasperation. 'You *will* be freed!' he repeated. 'I may not agree with the Speaker's decision but I'm a man of the law. You and your friend will go safely from our city. You have my word on it.'

He snapped a command to the spearmen, who swung open the door, admitting them to a long, narrow corridor smelling faintly of mildew overlaid with copal incense. The door closed again behind them, leaving the spearmen outside, and Cuitláhuac hurried forward. 'Quick now,' he growled. 'I don't have all night.'

Malinal cast a sideways glance at Tozi, who was once more lost in reflection, her head down and her eyes half closed. No doubt the teenager was grieving for her lost friend Coyotl, but she seemed to sense no danger and that was surely a good sign. Besides, the more Malinal thought about it, the more confident she became that Cuitláhuac was telling the truth. He was a dogmatic advocate of the lawful procedures and hierarchy of Mexica society, at the apex of which sat Moctezuma. Others, like Ahuizotl, might be willing to frustrate the Speaker's will, but not this nit-picker.

Most reassuring of all, however, as she now recalled from previous visits to Axayacatl's palace – which members of Moctezuma's close family were sometimes permitted to use for entertaining – was that a secret postern at the rear of the grand building led via a narrow alley directly onto the Tacuba causeway, the principal western exit from Tenochtitlan. It seemed that Cuitláhuac had chosen a quick and discreet route to get them out of the island city.

Though kept unoccupied since Axayacatl's death, the grand banqueting halls of the palace, its audience chambers and countless bedrooms and living areas were all fully furnished. A permanent staff of servants and slaves maintained the facilities, and it was even rumoured that Axayacatl's royal treasure was still kept somewhere on the premises, walled in to a secret chamber on Moctezuma's orders.

Cuitláhuac led Malinal and Tozi to the palace kitchen, barked instructions at the pair of elderly male retainers on duty there and abruptly left the room, saying he would be back within the hour. One of the retainers scuttled off, leaving the other watching them fearfully, but soon returned accompanied by a team of eight female slaves carrying huge tubs of steaming, scented water. With eyes averted, the slaves offered to bathe Malinal and Tozi and plucked off their torn and bloodied paper garments. Not a word was said to them during the entire process, and neither did they speak to each other, but Malinal watched Tozi in amazement as the layers of gore and grime and paint were washed from her skin and hair. What emerged was much more than a skinny fourteen-year-old waif. The events of the last day, she realised, had transformed her friend into a young woman – a beautiful, fey young woman whose dark eyes glittered with a deep and formidable inner strength.

At all times avoiding looking them in the face, the slaves offered them towels, then brought in piles of skirts and blouses of the finest quality, sturdy sandals and heavy travelling cloaks, signalling them to take their pick. When they had finished dressing, they were given backpacks filled with fresh and dried provisions suitable for a long journey. Finally Cuitláhuac reappeared, raised an eyebrow at their changed appearance, and told them once again to follow him.

Minutes later they exited the postern and found themselves in the darkened alley behind the palace. The wind had risen again and thunder still rolled ominously overhead. Cuitláhuac gripped Malinal's upper arm. 'Before I let you go,' he said, 'I want you to tell me the exact location of the secret house where you say Ahuizotl kept you prisoner.

'Why don't you ask him yourself?'

The nobleman hesitated. 'I can't. He fled the pyramid and we don't know where he is. But if your story's true then he's committed sacrilege.'

Malinal found herself filled with fierce pleasure at the prospect of the terrible death she hoped would very soon be inflicted on the high priest. 'My story's true all right,' she said. 'He's holding five other women captive. They'll back me up. Search street seventeen in the district of Tlatelolco – about halfway along, I'd say. Big house, all of stone, three storeys, an orchard in the garden. It shouldn't be too difficult to find.'

Cuitláhuac gave her a harsh shove and released her arm. 'Whore,' he growled, as she stumbled and rebounded off the wall of the alley. 'You've been told to leave Tenochtitlan, so leave it. Now! If you or your little friend ever return to our city I'll hear about it and, mark my words, I'll have you killed.' He spat, turned his back on her, stooped through the postern into the palace, and was gone.

Tozi rushed to Malinal's side and they embraced. Tozi was trembling, though whether with fear or anger Malinal could not tell.

As they emerged from the alley and joined the throng of human traffic moving in both directions on the two-mile length of the Tacuba causeway, the rainstorm that had been threatening all evening broke at last and a heavy downpour began, soaking them to the skin. The crowds commuting across Lake Texcoco between Tacuba and Tenochtitlan were still numerous, despite the late hour, but now rapidly thinned, with only the most determined still braving the deluge. All the rest ducked into doorways and under the awnings of the countless shops and homes built up on stilts along the causeway's flanks.

Sturdily constructed of stone, and wide enough for ten people to pass comfortably abreast, the causeway was raised twice the height of a man above the surface of the lake. Approximately every three hundred paces, however, intervals occurred where the stone paving was replaced by bridges of thick wooden planks. These were designed to be removed quickly in the unlikely event that any of the Mexicas' enemies were foolish enough to use the causeway to mount an attack on Tenochtitlan. Guardhouses two storeys high loomed over every bridge. Approaching

218

the first of these, Malinal's heart beat faster. She reached out and clutched Tozi's hand but, as they crossed the bridge amidst a cluster of housewives, merchants and servants in too much of a hurry to take shelter, they saw that all the sentries had been driven within by the rain.

'It's all right,' whispered Tozi. 'You're still afraid Moctezuma will change his mind and order our arrests, but I've been thinking about it and I don't believe he will. Not tonight anyway. He was scared out of his wits. He had to let us go.'

'You saved our lives,' Malinal exclaimed, putting all the gratitude and awe she felt into her voice. 'I still can't believe what you did to him!'

'I did nothing,' Tozi replied.

'What do you mean you did nothing? You said your powers had come back – and they did! I *saw* what happened. Only magic could have done that.'

'Maybe so,' Tozi allowed, 'but it wasn't my magic. I couldn't even find Coyotl! It was the magic of Hummingbird that saved us.'

Malinal frowned in puzzlement and wiped rain from her eyes. 'Hummingbird? I don't understand you.'

'He was there. I saw him. Moctezuma was talking to him. Hummingbird ordered you freed and he touched me with his flame. He chose us, Malinal, and he protected us!'

'But that makes no sense!'

'It's not easy to make sense of what the gods do, but there's only one possible answer. Hummingbird has a plan for you . . . And for me too.'

Malinal fell silent, her mind reeling. Her years in Tenochtitlan had left her in no doubt about the nature of the Mexica war god. He was a being of pure evil. So if he had a plan for them, as Tozi said, then it followed that only evil could come of it.

The very idea made her feel nauseous, and utterly helpless. Tozi must be imagining all this. It could not – it must not! – be real.

They came to another bridge. As they crossed it she squeezed her friend's hand tightly, but once again there was no challenge. Only a few people walked alongside them now, their heads bowed and their shoulders hunched. The rain hissed down and the wind churned the waters of the lake into angry waves that beat against the solid mass of the causeway. Thunder groaned in the heavens, the heavy clouds flickered and glowed, lit from horizon to horizon by great sheets of lightning; in the distance behind them, carried through the storm on a gust of wind, they heard the leaden beat of the snakeskin drum and the blare of conches announcing that the sacrifices had resumed.

They both turned, as though forced by some giant hand. The hulking silhouette of the palace of Axayacatl reared up behind them, dark as a breach in the night. Beyond it, dwarfing every other structure of Tenochtitlan and blazing with the eldritch glow of braziers and torches that no earthly downpour could extinguish, the summit of the great pyramid seemed to threaten even the sky.

When they reached the end of the causeway, they walked through almost deserted streets into the main square of Tacuba. The rain was still sheeting down and, other than a few beggars hunched beneath awnings, the square was deserted.

As they took shelter under a projecting roof, Tozi said fiercely: 'We've got to put a stop to it. Don't you agree?'

'Put a stop to what?'

'The Mexica, what they're doing. We have to put a stop to their sacrifices or they'll damn this land forever.'

Malinal laughed, and the sound was hollow in her ears. 'Stop the sacrifices? Sweet one, you might as well try to stop this rain, or the wind blowing, or the sun rising tomorrow. The Mexica are addicted to sacrifice. It's their drug. No one will ever be able to stop them.'

'Hummingbird stopped us being sacrificed today and he's the worst and most evil of the gods . . .'

'Which means he must have had an evil reason for doing it,' Malinal said, giving voice to the fear that had gripped her the moment Tozi had mentioned this horrible idea on the causeway. But even as she spoke she thought, *It's not real. It cannot be real.*

'Maybe so . . .' Tozi continued oblivious. 'But at least it proves the gods can stop any sacrifice if they want to.'

'Well, yes . . . I suppose they can – since it's in their name that all the sacrifices are made.'

'But there's one god who never demanded human sacrifices – who condemned all sacrifices, except of fruits and flowers.'

'Quetzalcoatl,' Malinal said. And suddenly she got a glimpse of where Tozi was taking this strange conversation.

'Exactly! Quetzalcoatl – who, it was long ago prophesied, would return in a One-Reed year to overthrow the rule of wickedness forever.'

'Yes,' Malinal breathed. 'So it was prophesied.'

'And are we not now,' Tozi asked triumphantly, 'in a One-Reed year?'

Again Malinal could only agree. 'The year One-Reed has just begun,' she said.

'And didn't you tell me today,' Tozi continued, 'that the retinue of Quetzalcoatl was seen four months ago emerging from across the eastern ocean to herald his return? Didn't they come ashore in the lands of your own people, the Chontal Maya, and isn't that why you were called to interpret when the messenger of the Chontal Maya came to Moctezuma?'

'Yes,' said Malinal distractedly, beginning to believe this madness of Tozi's. 'Yes. It's true. That is why I was called.'

'Moctezuma was very afraid, was he not?' Tozi gave a harsh laugh. 'He actually soiled himself, I think you said.'

Malinal laughed too, although her memories of what had happened afterwards were terrible ones. 'It's true. He soiled himself with fear.'

'So if Quetzalcoatl were really to return, can you imagine what would happen to Moctezuma?'

Malinal could imagine it all too well. 'It would mean the end of his rule,' she said slowly, 'the end of human sacrifice, even the end of Hummingbird himself.'

'Exactly, my dear! Exactly!' Tozi stepped out from under the shelter of the roof and began to dance in the rain. 'Surely you must see now that we're playing our parts in a great plan, that Moctezuma too is playing his part, and that even the wicked and deluded god he serves must play his part.'

'I don't know,' Malinal said. 'I don't understand any of this.'

'You don't need to understand it, beautiful Malinal. This is the year One-Reed and you just have to play your part.' Tozi was half chanting, half singing. 'Don't you see it's not an accident that you are of the

Chontal Maya and that those who came to herald the return of Quetzalcoatl first appeared in the land of your people, and in Potonchan, the very town where you were born? None of this is an accident, Malinal. That's why you must go back to Potonchan now, without delay. That's why you must start your journey at once.'

Malinal was dismayed. 'I can't go back there,' she cried. 'I can't ever go back! It was my own people – my own mother! – who sold me into slavery to the Mexica. It's a long story, but if I return to Potonchan it's certain I'll be arrested. At best I'll be made a slave again. At worst I'll be killed on the spot.'

Tozi's face was ferociously set. 'It doesn't matter!' she said. 'Don't you see, it doesn't matter? You simply have to go back and the plan will begin to unfold. Trust the plan, Malinal. Trust the plan . . .'

Now Tozi began to strip off her fine clothes – cloak, blouse, skirt, underwear – and hung them folded over her arm.

'What are you doing?' Malinal yelled and strode out into the rain.

'I'm doing what has to be done,' said Tozi. 'I'm playing my part. And you must play yours. Go to your homeland *now!*' Her voice had risen suddenly to a commanding shriek. It pierced Malinal's head like a lance and stopped her in her tracks. 'Go now,' Tozi said more softly. She gestured towards the glow of the great pyramid still faintly visible two miles distant across the causeway. 'Go to Potonchan and bring Quetzalcoatl here and we'll put a stop to all that.'

Taking off her sturdy sandals, Tozi walked naked and barefoot to a beggar girl who sat nearby, crouched under an awning. There was a brief murmur of conversation and then the girl, too, began to undress.

'What are you *doing*?' Malinal cried again. She tried to step forward to stop this foolishness but found she was rooted to the spot.

'I told you,' said Tozi, who was already dressing herself in the girl's threadbare skirt and blouse. 'I'm playing my part and you must play yours. Go to Potonchan *and bring Quetzalcoatl!*'

'And what about you?' Malinal called. 'Where will you go?'

'Back to Tenochtitlan, of course, to work harm on Moctezuma and to find Coyotl.'

'Coyotl is dead, Tozi! Any other thought is madness. You must accept this.'

'I won't accept it!' Tozi said defiantly. 'We didn't see his body. I don't believe he even climbed the pyramid. Somehow he still lives. I'm sure of it.'

And without a further word she whirled and ran off towards the causeway. Again Malinal tried to follow and again she found she could not. The rain was heavy in the thick darkness, and Tozi vanished into it as suddenly and as completely as if she'd regained the power to fade.

Only when she had gone was Malinal once more able to move.

She turned in the opposite direction, her mind made up.

No matter the dangers, she would do as her friend asked. She would return to Potonchan and the memories that awaited her there.

And if Quetzalcoatl should appear, as Tozi in her madness claimed he would, then she would bring him to Tenochtitlan.

Chapter Forty-One

Tlascala, small hours of Friday 19 February 1519

As befitted the man who bore the official title of Snake Woman, and ranked second only to Moctezuma himself in the entire, vast Mexica power structure, Coaxoch travelled into battle in the greatest possible luxury, surrounded not only by the thirty-two thousand warriors of his field army, but also by cohorts of servants, personal attendants, clerks, bodyguards, cooks, masseurs, doctors, tailors, entertainers and pleasure girls. The presence of his four sons, ranked as regiment generals, each with their own retinue of assistants, staff officers and concubines, further added to the scale of the vast mobile court assembled within the giant pavilion that Shikotenka had watched being assembled during the course of the day. Consisting of acres of heavy-duty maguey-fibre sheets secured around a framework of poles and struts, it formed a square cage measuring perhaps a hundred paces along each side. The whole edifice was roofed by further acres of sheeting, hung and tied over an ingeniously constructed dome of cantilevered spars soaring to a height of thirty feet. The delights of Tenochtitlan might be two days' hard march away, but this vast structure somehow managed to summon up, encapsulate and symbolise all the pomp and ceremony of the Mexica capital, all its boastfulness and arrogance, all its cruelty and danger.

Tochtli was trembling but bright-eyed at the prospect of battle and a chance to prove himself further. Shikotenka once again felt a moment of apprehension. The boy might die tonight on this insane mission. They all might die! But if they succeeded, if they could kill Coaxoch and his sons, they would strike a mortal blow against Mexica pride and power and, Shikotenka hoped, set in motion a chain of events that would make all the risks worthwhile.

'We go,' he said, 'right now!' With Tochtli bounding along beside him, and Tree and Acolmiztli and the rest of their twenty right behind, Shikotenka charged through the front entrance of the pavilion, hoping for a clear avenue running north to south to the great banqueting hall at its centre. Instead he found himself in an east–west corridor, wide enough for three men to pass abreast, confronted, as he had feared, by a second wall of sheets running parallel to the external wall. He immediately raised his hand to signal a halt, his men pressing in behind him, crowding one another in an unruly scrum, bristling with weapons and pent-up battle rage. He hesitated. Seeming to emanate from some point nearby, the barbaric sounds of drums, stringed instruments and trumpets were much louder than they had been outside, while beyond the sheets forming the inner wall of the corridor, the groans of a woman being pleasured, and the grunts of the man pleasuring her, were rising rapidly to a crescendo.

Shikotenka raised Guatemoc's *macuahuitl*, slashed a great rip in the sheeting of the corridor and shot through the gap. His eyes fell immediately on another *macuahuitl* and two flint knives, all sheathed. They lay amidst a heap of discarded clothing at the foot of a camp bed where a hefty Mexica male, supporting himself on his hands, muscular buttocks glistening with sweat, was vigorously coupling with some slender female. The woman – Mexica also, judging from her hairstyle – was not too far gone in pleasure to fail to notice the intrusion, and gave vent to an ear-piercing scream as Shikotenka brought his *macuahuitl* crashing down on the man's spine, cutting him almost in half.

Freeing the weapon with a sharp tug, he rushed onwards across the little room followed by the rest of his crew, slashed open the opposite wall and burst into a much larger chamber beyond. There he found himself in the midst of a fragrant mass of women – forty of them at least – some naked, some dressed in revealing tunics, some still prone amongst cushions, some struggling to their feet, most already standing, their confusion and evident fear rapidly escalating into panic as the heavily armed Tlascalans barged into them.

The sound of so many women shrieking in unison was deafening, and suddenly a furious, heavy-set matron, her face red, her eyeballs bulging, popped up in Shikotenka's path, howling abuse at him and wagging an admonishing finger. Without breaking momentum he simply bowled right over her, smashing her to the ground. Tree then gave her a thorough trampling, and the rest of the gang followed as Shikotenka reached the next wall and cut a gaping slash in it through which they all streamed.

Gods! It seemed that Coaxoch had assembled a whole city with its different districts and neighbourhoods inside this immense pavilion, for the room they now entered was huge and quite different in character from the outer chambers. There were musicians on a podium and a few dozen dancers still milling on the floor, but all were alert, terrified, many already running. Some armed men – a small detachment of Coaxoch's guard, a handful of nobles who'd drawn their weapons – attempted resistance, but the Tlascalans were gripped by battle rage and cut them down in a shambles of blood and hacked-off limbs.

Shikotenka paused to get his bearings. They'd entered the pavilion through its southern portico and cut their way northward from there, spearing towards the centre of the huge structure where they hoped to find Coaxoch and his court. It was difficult to estimate how far they'd come – perhaps halfway? – but Shikotenka took it as a sign they were headed in the right direction when he spotted Iccauhtli, the youngest of Coaxoch's four sons, a pampered nineteen-year-old raised by influence to the rank of regiment general. The brawny, moon-faced youth threw himself to the ground, wriggling beneath the podium, and Shikotenka went after him, grabbed his feet and hauled him out kicking and bawling for help. 'If you want to live,' he said, 'take us to your father.' But as he spoke he sensed a flicker of movement out of the corner of his eye and dived sideways on pure instinct, pulling Iccauhtli back to the ground with him. Some sort of projectile whizzed over their heads and he looked up to see a dwarf – Coaxoch kept a team of them, trained as acrobats, to amuse his court – drawing a ludicrously tiny bow. A second arrow, no doubt poisoned, was already notched to the string when Tochtli appeared out of nowhere, grabbed the halfling around the legs, lifted him bodily and hurled him across the room where he fell in a crumpled heap.

Iccauhtli was struggling mightily, lashing out with his fists. He was heavily built and reputedly had fought some engagements, taken some prisoners, but he was no match for Shikotenka, who smashed the hilt of his *macuahuitl* viciously into his face as he dragged him to his feet again. 'Your father!' he roared. 'Lead us to him.'

'Never!' spat Iccauhtli, teeth dropping from his mouth.

'Then die,' hissed Shikotenka, taking a rapid step backward, swinging his *macuahuitl* through a half-circle and decapitating the thickset youth. As he struck the blow he noticed five more Mexica guards barrelling into the room, their javelins taking flight even as the peculiarly spherical head of their boy general went rolling and bouncing across the floor.

They were good these guards, steady on their feet as they launched, and the Tlascalans suffered their first casualties, amongst them Tochtli, Shikotenka's own cousin, who took a javelin in the belly. Though such a wound was not immediately fatal, it meant Tochtli would be unable to flee the pavilion after the raid and must therefore certainly die.

Most of the Tlascalans still carried their bows over their shoulders. In an instant a dozen had unslung and fired, sending a dense volley of arrows at the guards, killing all but one of them who emerged miraculously unscathed but died under Tree's club a moment later. With that, all opposition in the dance chamber ceased. Shikotenka's heart was heavy to see Tochtli on his knees, struggling to withdraw the spear, but there could be no help for any of the injured tonight, no kindness or love or sentiment, and he rushed past his cousin without glancing back, calling Tree and Acolmiztli to rally their men.

It was taking too long to find Coaxoch, who surely must know by now what was happening, must already be fleeing? But just as Shikotenka admitted this depressing possibility, he heard sounds of battle, saw an alley heading north through the maze of sheeting and followed it at a dead run into a great open space in the heart of the pavilion. There a force of the Snake Woman's personal guard had formed a protective circle around Coaxoch and his three surviving sons. Fewer than twenty of the guards remained on their feet, their numbers dwindling rapidly as they were picked off with arrows and cut down by the *macuahuitls* of the other Tlascalan platoons under Chipahua, Etzli and Ilhuicamina.

'What kept you?' said Chipahua as Shikotenka, Tree and Acolmiztli jogged up beside him and immediately threw their men into the fight, bringing a decisive advantage of numbers and instantly transforming what had been a battle of attrition into a massacre. In less than a minute all the guards were down and two more of Coaxoch's sons were dead. Ilhuicamina held a knife to the throat of Mahuizoh, the last and eldest of them, but, on Shikotenka's orders, had so far restrained himself from killing him. Coaxoch, his fat jowls dripping with tears, was on his knees at Shikotenka's feet, begging for mercy.

There was no mercy in Shikotenka's heart, only the sense of time slipping away too fast – for undoubtedly many had fled the pavilion to spread the alarm and Mexica reinforcements must be on the way. He pointed at Mahuizoh. 'We'll let that one live,' he said.

'Why?' demanded Ilhuicamina. He was angry, his prosthetic jade nose giving him a strange, almost inhuman appearance.

'I want him to bear witness to what happened here. You can cut off *his* nose if you like but keep him alive.'

Shikotenka turned back to Coaxoch. 'You fat turd,' he said. 'You used to be a man once but look at you now, blubbering like a woman. Stand up! *Stand up I say!*'

With great difficulty Coaxoch clambered to his feet. 'What do you want of me?' he asked sullenly.

Shikotenka had been holding Guatemoc's *macuahuitl* loosely in his left hand. Now he clamped his right hand to its hilt and swung the weapon up between Coaxoch's legs with savage force, hacking through his pubic bone, rending his abdomen to the navel and finally twisting the weapon as he pulled it out so that the Snake Woman's intestines, swollen and stinking, spooled to the ground at his feet. To his credit he did not cry out in death, perhaps recovering some of the warrior composure he'd been famed for in his youth, and as he dropped to his knees a ghastly smile stiffened his corpulent features.

Hearing a sudden shriek behind him, Shikotenka spun and saw Mahuizoh bent almost double by Tree who had twisted his arms behind his back. Ilhuicamina loomed over the struggling general, holding a fat knob of flesh and gristle in his hand which he now threw with disgust to the ground. 'Well,' he said defensively, 'you did say I could cut off his nose.'

'It's the least he deserves,' said Tree as Mahuizoh roared and tried to pull free but was unable to break his grip, 'the very least.'

Shikotenka swung the *macuahuitl* again, decapitating Coaxoch, then walked over to Mahuizoh, the head dangling by its hair from his fist. 'Do you remember me?' he said.

An incoherent roar from Mahuizoh.

'*Do you remember me?*' Shikotenka repeated, louder this time, and Tree twisted the captive's arms tighter, extracting a gasp of pain.

'I remember you,' Mahuizoh replied, his voice gurgling through blood and horribly distorted. 'You are Shikotenka, battle king of Tlascala. You've killed my father. You've killed my brothers. Why don't you go ahead and kill me?'

'Because you're more useful to me as a messenger,' sneered Shikotenka. 'Run off home to Tenochtitlan now and tell Moctezuma how the nation of Tlascala humiliated Coaxoch and his phony generals tonight.'

Like his late father, Mahuizoh was a big man with a torturer's cruel face but, where Coaxoch had run to fat, the son, still less than thirty years of age, was all solid muscle, a towering square slab whose tunic had come awry showing massive thighs and a heavy wrestler's body glistening with sweat. He didn't have Tree's height and couldn't match his enormous strength but, even injured, with his arms bent forcefully behind his back, he was putting up a creditable fight.

Mahuizoh laughed – a hideous, liquid, choking sound. 'You'll not leave this camp alive,' he said, 'and when I go to Moctezuma I'll be wearing your skin.' Over the blood pouring from the cavity that had once been his nose his eyes burned with hatred.

That's right, thought Shikotenka. *Hate me. Hate me with all your foul heart. It's exactly what I want you to do.*

Tree dealt the general a stunning blow to the temple, knocking him to the ground while Shikotenka turned on the balls of his feet, his eyes urgently searching the great tented hall. He'd gambled on Coaxoch keeping the armoury of his personal guard close, so it was with a sense of vindication that he spotted racks of spears, *atlatls*, bows, *macuahuitls*, clubs and shields stacked in neat rows to one side. 'Every man grab a shield,' Shikotenka yelled, and the blood-smeared Tlascalans, who'd started the raid armed only with offensive weapons to maximise their speed and killing power, scrambled to obey.

In moments they all had circular bucklers fashioned from heavy hardwood, covered in leather painted in yellow and black stripes, and studded with flint, strapped to their forearms. Shikotenka, who had also snatched up a long spear, reviewed his squad with approval. The expressions on their faces were hard to read. 'Well?' he yelled. 'What are you waiting for? The whole Mexica army's coming our way. Time we got out of here.'

Running back south, they soon reached the dance chamber. Shikotenka paused by Tochtli, who had failed to free the javelin from his belly and was curled up in a ball around its shaft. 'I'm sorry, little Rabbit,' he said as he gently slit his cousin's throat. 'You were brave tonight, and skilful. I wish this had ended better for you.'

Chapter Forty-Two

Santiago, Cuba, small hours of Friday 19 February 1519

Cortés was striding about the main deck, willing the storm to abate whilst supervising the loading of the last supplies. In his imagination he pictured the governor and a squadron of his guards thundering down the road from Santiago. Should they reach the port before the fleet sailed, all would be lost.

Yet even as he counted the minutes, he refused to lose his nerve, and kept a calm countenance, issuing orders without panic or obvious hurry. Everything must be done that should be done for, if it was not, even if they got to sea in time, the expedition would surely fail.

The *Santa María*'s share of the pigs, goats and cattle brought by Díaz from the slaughterhouse were already billeted in the forward hold, squealing and bleating in the pens hastily knocked up for them. Meanwhile, here on the main deck, the four excellent carriage horses that Dr La Peña had so generously donated to the expedition were even now being led on board and tethered into slings alongside the six fine chargers loaded earlier and stamping nervously in their stalls. With the five good mounts that Alvarado was transporting, and three more on Puertocarrero's ship, the expedition could field a force of eighteen cavalry. Cortés would have preferred more – fifty, even a hundred! – but he was reasonably sure the natives of the New Lands would never have faced battle against mounted troops. They would likely be as overawed and demoralised by the experience as the Indians of Cuba and Hispaniola.

'Caudillo . . . Excuse me.' Cortés felt a tug at his sleeve and turned to confront Nuno Guiterrez, a bearded brute of a sailor, one of the team he'd ordered moments before to prepare the *Santa María* to be warped out from the pier.

'Yes, Nuno? What do you want?'

'We've found a stowaway, sir.'

'Stowaway?' Cortés glanced down, saw that the sailor's massive paw was clamped around the small frail shoulder of Muñoz's unfortunate page, and nodded in recognition. 'Oh,' he said. 'Him.' The boy's nose was red and painfully swollen, and the mass of cuts and bruises on his skinny body stood out like accusations in the yellow light of the ship's lanterns. 'He's no stowaway. He serves our Inquisitor. Where did you find him?'

'Hiding in the aftcastle,' said Guiterrez, who had a voice like pebbles being shaken in a sieve. 'Burrowed down amongst the springlines.'

'Very well. Be about your business. You can leave him with me.'

Guiterrez had the peculiar rolling gait of those who'd been too long at sea. As he moved aft, Cortés saw that the boy was afraid – who wouldn't be with a master like Muñoz? – but trying not to show it.

'What's your name, lad?'

'I am Pepillo, sir.'

'And what's your opinion of your master, young Pepillo?'

A look of caution came into the boy's eyes. 'I'm sure I can't say.'

'Can't say? Or won't say?'

'It's not my place to speak of my master, sir.'

'He beats you. Do you know why?'

'I know nothing, sir. I'm his page. I must serve him. He may do with me as he wishes.'

Diplomatic little fellow, Cortés thought. 'So . . . You were hiding in the aftcastle, eh?'

Pepillo nodded.

'In which case, I expect you know already that your master's no longer aboard the *Santa María*.'

Another nod. 'You sent him to Don Pedro Alvarado's ship.' Was there just the slightest hint of vindication in the boy's tone? 'You ordered him placed in the brig, sir.'

'And do you know what the brig is?'

'A kind of prison, sir.'

'Think he belongs there?'

Pepillo looked uncomfortable again, as though he feared a trap. 'That's not for me to say, sir.'

232

'You're careful with your words, boy. I like that. What other skills do you have?'

'I can read and write Castilian well' – a note of pride – 'and in a fine hand. I have some Latin. I know ledgers and numbers.'

Useful, Cortés thought. An idea had occurred to him and now he voiced it impulsively. 'I'll be needing a first-class secretary on this trip. My usual man's in Santiago and I haven't the time to fetch him to the ship before we sail. What would you say if I were to offer you his job?'

Hope lit up the boy's face like a beacon and was immediately doused.

'I don't think Father Muñoz would agree, sir . . .'

'But Father Muñoz is in the brig – remember?'

'Oh . . . Yes.'

'So here's the thing. I'm going to be writing letters as our expedition proceeds. A great many letters. I'll be writing them in Castilian, of course, but they're likely to be rather long with frequent corrections and crossings out. Would you be able to make fair copies of those letters in that fine hand you say you have? Copies good enough to be read by the king of Spain?'

The boy's jaw dropped. 'The king himself, sir?'

'Yes. His Sacred Majesty, our sovereign, Don Carlos, the most high and powerful Caesar, ever august Holy Roman Emperor and king of Spain.'

Pepillo's little frame had been drooping for much of the interview, but now his head was up and his eyes were clear. 'I was judged the best copyist in my monastery, sir. I believe my work will be good enough even for the king.'

'Very well then. I'll give you a try. And don't worry yourself about Father Muñoz. I'll be ordering him freed from Don Pedro's brig tomorrow, but I'll make your new appointment right with him first.'

A huge smile broke out on Pepillo's face. 'Thank you, sir! Thank you! Thank you!'

'I'll expect you to earn your keep. Now run along and find my manservant Melchior. You know who he is?'

Pepillo nodded vigorously. 'He showed me to my master's – my former master's – cabin when I first came on board, sir.'

'Well that's very much to the point, because what I want the two of you to do now is tear down the partition that was put across my state-room to make Muñoz's cabin. I'm going to need all the space for myself, so clear out the good Father's bags and possessions, stow them some-where dry and we'll transfer them over to the *San Sebastián* tomorrow. He'll be sailing with Don Pedro for the rest of the voyage.'

For a moment Pepillo just stood there looking dazed.

'Get on with it, lad!' Cortés said gently. 'When I say I want a thing done, it means I want it done at once.'

While he'd been talking to the boy, Cortés had kept his eyes and ears open. Some expanses of clear sky had opened up amongst the clouds, the moon was shining through brightly and the storm appeared to be slackening. He hurried up to the navigation deck where Alaminos was looking out to sea. 'Well,' he said to the navigator, 'what do you think?'

'A little better, Don Hernán, but I still don't like it. Can I not persuade you to delay?'

'God hath not given us the spirit of fear,' Cortés quoted cheerfully, 'but of power, and of love, and of a sound mind.' He rubbed his hands together: 'Gird up thy loins like a man, Alaminos! We sail. Now!'

'Very well,' said the pilot, 'and may God save us.' He barked a command to Guiterrez and his mates who stood ready with the uncoiled springline they'd brought down from the aftcastle. All business now, they looped one end of the line round a sturdy cleat nailed to the side of the ship near the front of the navigation deck, while two of the team swarmed down the mooring ropes, cast them off and looped the other end of the springline round a stanchion on the pier.

Holding a powerful lantern fuelled with whale oil, a lookout named Inigo Lancero stood waiting in the crow's-nest at the top of the main-mast. 'Ahoy there, Inigo,' Cortés bellowed, cupping his hands to his mouth to attract the man's attention over the wind. 'Do you hear me well?'

'I hear you, Caudillo,' came the faint reply.

'So hear this. The fleet sails now! The fleet sails now! Give the signal.'

For a few seconds nothing happened, then the lantern flared in Inigo's hands and the flare rapidly blossomed, steadying and sharpening into a brilliant effulgence that would carry for miles. At once Cortés pounded up the stairs to the aftcastle and hurried to the starboard rail. The crow's-nests of the rest of his fleet were visible from here, and he stared out anxiously into the moonlit night, waiting for the answering signals. He counted 'one . . . two . . . three . . . four . . . five . . . six . . . seven . . .' Before he reached eight he saw the signal blaze to life atop Alvarado's carrack – then Escalante's, then Puertocarrero's, then Montejo's, then Ordaz's, then Morla's, and then all the others in rapid succession. It seemed that not even the most ardent Velazquistas were using the storm as an excuse to stay in port!

Cortés pounded back down the stairs to the navigation deck. The warping team were applying their weight to the springline now, pulling it rapidly round the cleat to put leverage on the stanchion while Alaminos leaned on the whipstaff, turning the steering hard shoreward. Responding to these opposing forces, the bow of the *Santa María* began to swing ponderously out from the pier, while deckhands swarmed over the masts, unleashing the sails. First the spiritsail, the small square sail attached to the bowspirit, came down, and almost at the same moment the larger foresail and the lateen mizzen sail aft. Then, finally, with a tremendous cracking and lashing of canvas the huge mainsail unfurled. The small topsail, however, which was usually set above the mainsail in fine weather, was left rolled up lest the fierce gusts of wind snatch it away. At the last moment, the two men still on land loosed the springline from the stanchion, leapt across the rapidly widening strip of water between the ship and the pier, grabbed dangling ropes and hauled themselves on board.

'That was well done,' Cortés said to Alaminos, clapping the navigator on the shoulder. But the man made no response and was staring back to land.

Cortés followed his gaze. A mounted troop of the governor's palace guard was galloping hard along the pier. At their head, dressed in full armour and quite unmistakable in the moonlight for his bulk and girth, was Velázquez himself.

With a sigh Cortés gave the order to lower sails, there was a flurry of activity as the crew obeyed, and the *Santa María*'s forward dash slowed and stopped.

Chapter Forty-Three

Santiago, Cuba, small hours of Friday 19 February 1519

Pepillo could not believe his ears as he heard Cortés give the command to lower the sails, could not believe his eyes as the great ship wallowed to a halt, and was utterly perplexed and dumbfounded as the caudillo then called for a skiff to be lowered, showing every sign of getting into it himself and returning to the pier where the governor and his men waited – most certainly to arrest him!

Unnoticed in the hive of activity, Pepillo and Melchior had made their way to the rear of the navigation deck and now stood at the door of the stateroom, hammers and saws in hand, ready to demolish the partition as their master had ordered.

Pepillo had not told Melchior that he, too, now worked for Cortés – and in such an exalted position as the great man's secretary. He worried that the Negro, who seemed to have a high opinion of his own abilities, might take the news badly. So he had stuck to the simplest part of the truth, namely that Cortés had assigned both of them to remove the partition.

'Muñoz doesn't object to you doing this work?' Melchior had asked. 'Because if he does, I don't really need your help.'

Pepillo hastened to reassure the older boy that Muñoz was presently in no position to object. 'He can't! While I was up on the aftcastle, the caudillo had him marched over to Don Pedro Alvarado's vessel and thrown in the brig. I think he'll let him out tomorrow.' He couldn't bring himself to add that the Dominican wouldn't be returning to the *Santa María*. Once he revealed that, he thought, he'd be more or less obliged to cough up the rest of the story and he felt reluctant to do so without preparing the ground.

So there he and Melchior stood, at the door of the stateroom, divided by a secret, while Cortés seemed poised to hand the expedition back, without a struggle, to the man he'd been about to steal it from. 'Why's he doing this?' Pepillo whispered as crewmen hurried to lower the boat.

Melchior raised a sardonic eyebrow. 'Doing what?'

'Returning to the pier. Delivering himself to the governor.'

'No chance of that!' Melchior scoffed. 'It's like I told you this morning – there's an old quarrel between these two. I expect my master wants the last word . . . Come on, let's watch from the rail.'

The wind had risen again, adding to the swell, and as the skiff reached the water it banged repeatedly against the *Santa María's* towering flank. A ladder was rolled down and Cortés strode to it, telling Guiterrez to bring the oars and follow. Then they both climbed on board, Cortés cast off the line and Guiterrez at once began to row towards the pier, the little boat rolling perilously, throwing up wings of foam as it breasted the waves. The moonlight still shone fitfully through the clouds, reflecting off the angry water, and Pepillo could see Cortés gesticulating to Guiterrez, who suddenly began to thrust back on one oar while pulling hard with the other. The flimsy craft turned, almost foundering in the process, and was soon bumping against the *Santa María* again. *Thank goodness,* Pepillo thought as the ladder was once more rolled down, *the caudillo has come to his senses.*

Cortés was shouting something now, standing up as Guiterrez held the skiff in place, pointing to the navigation deck; pointing, it seemed, directly at Pepillo and Melchior who were peering down over the rail.

'My master wants me to accompany him,' said Melchior, swelling with pride.

He ran to the main deck where the ladder was positioned, but returned in moments with a thunderous face. 'It's not me my master wants,' he told Pepillo. There was resentment and hurt in his voice. 'It's you.'

'Come on,' Cortés boomed as Pepillo climbed down into the wildly bucking skiff. 'Quick about it. I need you to keep a proper record of what passes between me and the governor. What's said now will have a place in history.'

Much troubled by Melchior's reaction, Pepillo was now doubly dismayed. 'I have no writing materials, sir . . .' A plunge of the skiff all but pitched him into the sea and he fell back hard on a bench that stretched from side to side across the stern of the little boat. Cortés sat down next to him. 'Of course you don't have writing materials, lad! I don't expect you to perform miracles. But your memory will suffice. Mark well what's said and jot it down when we get back to the ship.'

The *Santa María* had dropped anchor about three hundred feet from the pier, not a great distance, Pepillo thought at first. Yet the wind was blowing strongly out to sea and it was quickly obvious that the skiff was making poor headway, despite a great deal of rowing, splashing and blaspheming by Guiterrez. What seemed like an age passed before they came within thirty feet – and hailing distance – of the pier, and Cortés at last ordered the little boat held still, a feat that seemed to require even more mighty efforts and curses. 'Watch your tongue, man!' he snapped as the sailor took the Lord's name in vain for perhaps the twentieth time. 'We're here to parlay with the governor, not break the third commandment.'

'Sorry, sir,' said Guiterrez. 'But these waves. They're terrible, sir. Like to capsize us, they are.'

Velázquez had dismounted and stood on the edge of the pier, which towered a full fifteen feet above the heaving waterline. Raised up on this eminence and silhouetted by the setting moon, his massive, armour-clad figure seemed monstrous in Pepillo's eyes. Most of his men, perhaps as many as twenty, had also dismounted and stood around him, glaring down at the little boat. Only four remained on horseback and one of the great beasts now reared and pawed the air as a streak of lightning crashed across the sky. At this Guiterrez paused from plying the oars to cross himself – a singularly useless thing for such a blasphemer to do, Pepillo thought. But Cortés, too, seemed moved by the scene: 'Behold a pale horse,' he said quietly, 'and his name that sat on him was Death, and Hell followed with him.'

The governor cupped his hands to his mouth and shouted something, but the words were snatched away on the wind.

'Get us closer,' Cortés ordered Guiterrez.

'Closer, sir? I'm not sure that's wise.'

Cortés's face was set. 'Closer, please.'

Guiterrez heaved at the oars again, thrusting the skiff through the waves, the pier loomed ever higher above them and suddenly they could hear the governor. 'Why is it, Don Hernán, that you sail in such haste?' he bellowed. 'Are we not friends? Are we not business partners? Is this a courteous way for you to take your leave of me?'

Cortés stood up in the lurching boat, his feet spread wide, somehow keeping his balance, and made an elaborate bow: 'Forgive me, Don Diego, but time presses and this was something that needed to be done rather than talked about. Has Your Excellency any final commands?'

'Yes, you wretch,' Velázquez shouted. 'I command you to accept my authority and return to shore where I'll give you the hanging you deserve.'

'My deepest regrets, Excellency,' Cortés said with another mocking bow, 'but that is something I can never accept. This expedition sails on the authority of God and of His Majesty the King alone to conquer new lands and bring wealth and honour to Spain. I cannot permit such high purposes to be subordinated to the whims of a mere provincial governor.'

'Then accept *this*,' Velázquez spluttered, and two men, previously unseen, suddenly stepped through the ranks of his guard and raised long devices to their shoulders in the manner of crossbows – devices in which smouldering embers seemed to be embedded. Pepillo had never seen crossbows such as these, but he felt sure they would harm Cortés, so without further thought he propelled himself forward, wrapped his arms round his master's knees and knocked him down into the bottom of the boat. Simultanously he heard two loud reports, projectiles whizzed and whined through the air just above his head, and Guiterrez began to row like a madman back towards the *Santa María*. The wind was with them now and they moved much faster than they had before.

'Forgive me, master,' Pepillo heard himself yelling. He felt sure he had made some terrible mistake. His career as the caudillo's secretary was over before it had begun.

Cortés struggled upright and peered back over the side of the skiff at the rapidly receding pier. Then he started to laugh. 'Forgive you, lad?' he said. 'I was having such fun baiting Velázquez, I didn't see the muskets. I think you've just saved my life!'

Ten minutes later, the *Santa María* was under way, every sail bending before the wind.

The signal lights of the rest of the fleet were visible far ahead of them, shining like shooting stars, proceeding through the narrow, mile-long inlet that connected Santiago harbour to the open ocean.

The weather had turned truly foul and, despite the shelter afforded by the inlet, huge waves rolled under the ship, sending it caroming and tumbling from crest to trough. Alaminos and Cortés both had their hands on the whipstaff, which jumped and quivered as the racing seas shook the rudder.

Pepillo heard banging and crashing sounds coming from the state-room, where he found Melchior at work by lamplight, demolishing the partition with a sledgehammer, delivering every blow with grim, focussed attention. A huge splintered gap was now open between what had formerly been the cabins of Cortés and Muñoz, and since Melchior had coldly refused his help, Pepillo walked through, lit a lantern and began to collect up various items of Muñoz's property that the Dominican had set out on the bed and the table. On the latter he found parchment, a quill and an inkwell and, remembering his instructions, sat down to write out the words that had passed between Cortés and Velázquez at the pier.

The keening of the wind in the rigging, the crack and whip of the sails, the alarming groaning of the timbers, the concussion of the waves and the increasingly tumultuous rearing and plunging of the ship made the task burdensome, and Pepillo realised he was beginning to feel quite sick. Still he persevered. He had just reached the point where the caudillo said that the expedition had sailed on the authority of God and the king of Spain alone when the *Santa María* heaved over violently to starboard and took on a great mass of seawater that foamed and boiled thigh-deep across the floor of the stateroom. Helpless to resist, Pepillo was dragged from his chair by the flood and sluiced towards the open door.

Chapter Forty-Four

Shikotenka judged his squad's losses to be light. Only cousin Tochtli and three others had died in the raid and nine more were injured, none too seriously to disrupt the next phase of the plan. Alarms were being raised everywhere and the vast Mexica camp seethed with noise and anger, drums beating, conches blaring, warriors boiling forth from every quarter, responding to the threat with all the instinctive fury and blind aggression of a disturbed ant colony.

The Tlascalans streamed out of the pavilion's south portico to confront a baying mob, already many hundreds strong, illumined by the flickering glare of firebrands and armed with spears, *macuahuitls*, daggers and clubs, the vanguard less than fifty paces away. Shikotenka had expected worse. The Mexica were advancing, shrieking their rage, milling across the great southern avenue, spreading out to left and right into the makeshift city of tents on either side, but they were poorly coordinated, not yet in military order, still barely able to believe that a strike had been made against their leader.

The bad news was that the rain which had concealed the Tlascalans' approach had stopped as quickly as it had begun, giving way to a soft drizzle, and now they had to run a gauntlet of two thousand paces back to the camp's southern gateway before they could seek the refuge of the hills.

The good news was that the Mexica were in a state of obvious disorder and confusion, with huge groups of men visible in the shadows running in a dozen wrong directions, not towards the pavilion but away from it! Off to the southeast a great glow of torchlight showed the distraction created by Guatemoc was still working its magic.

Detailing Tree, Chipahua and three of the biggest, most hardbitten foot soldiers in the squad to form the head of the Tlascalan battering ram, Shikotenka placed himself in the second rank alongside Acolmiztli, Etzli and Ilhuicamina, with the rest of the men in eight ranks behind. As the whistling and hooting mob surged towards them he gave the signal, and the tight, disciplined phalanx charged as a single, deadly unit, the ground trembling beneath their feet.

Arrayed close and deep, shields interlocking, bristling with spears and *macuahuitls*, they hit the chaotic mass of the enemy at a dead run, crashing into them where they were most numerous and ploughing brutally through them. Right in front of him, Shikotenka heard Tree roar and saw the muscles of his enormous shoulders ripple and flex as he thrust his heavy shield into screaming faces, spraying blood, demolishing warriors as though they were of no more substance than baked clay, crushing heads with hammer blows from his great club. By his side Chipahua laughed cruelly, swinging his shield in a scything arc, sweeping three Mexica novices off their feet and trampling them in the remorseless momentum of the onslaught, while Shikotenka and the other platoon commanders, all armed with spears, used the longer reach of their weapons to kill and maim and spread the contagion of dismay three and four ranks deep in the disordered rabble pressing round them. The technique here was the high overhand jab, into an eye, into a throat, into a belly, jerking the blade loose again as soon as the blow was delivered so the spear was not snatched away. Shikotenka saw with approval how the same tactic was being used by the men in the inner ranks, all along the length of the phalanx, while the outer ranks with their shields, clubs and *macuahuitls* battered aside the waves of attackers attempting to close with them.

Still they were hard-pressed, fighting for their lives, but Tlascalan training and discipline and sheer bloody resolve were second to none, and soon the squad had broken through the press, outpaced the pursuit and was left free to run for a hundred count with no more encumbrance than a few wild, uncoordinated attacks by small groups of warriors and desultory arrows and *atlatl* darts that were easily deflected by their shields.

'These Mexica aren't what they once were,' scoffed Chipahua as he struck down a single jaguar knight who ran yelling at him out of the darkness.

'Like doing battle with babes,' Acolmiztli agreed.

And Shikotenka thought, *We're going to get away with it*, his heart exultant despite the sad loss of Tochtli, daring to hope now that he might extract his squad from the midst of this badly led rabble without further casualties. Where the Mexica should have thrown thousands of men across their path, only handfuls continued to challenge them, and the howling throng they'd broken through outside the pavilion was far behind them now.

The distance left to run to the foot of the hills had been cut to just five hundred paces before the second wave of Mexica warriors came in, a whole company of Cuahchics this time. They had the muddled look of men roused suddenly from their sleeping mats, and many were unarmed, yet they threw themselves at the Tlascalans with suicidal ferocity, slowing them while others hastily snatched up weapons and joined the attack.

The fight quickly became vicious. A giant of a Cuahchic, whirling a huge war club, smashed Chipahua's shield to splinters and dealt him a hard blow full in the mouth that shattered his front teeth and mashed his lips to bloody pulp. Chipahua just gave an ugly laugh and hacked the man down with a great slash of his *macuahuitl*, charging on over his fallen body and killing a second attacker on the upswing. Tree seemed invulnerable, yelling defiance and laying about left and right with his own blood-spattered club, using his shield to batter through a wall of Cuahchics, opening the way for the rest of the squad to follow.

Again escape seemed within their grasp, the hillside beckoning, but as the phalanx rushed on, Shikotenka was tackled by four wild-eyed young warriors, grimly determined to capture him for sacrifice, and Etzli died screaming, impaled on a stabbing spear as he came to the rescue. Now more Cuahchics saw the prize, drawn to him like flies to meat, and Acolmiztli and Ilhuicamina piled in, not just out of loyalty, Shikotenka realised, but because they knew his survival was essential. As battle-king of Tlascala, the plan required that he must not only leave the field alive but be *seen* to leave it alive; for him to be taken prisoner would be the worst of all possible outcomes. He'd lost his spear and his shield, and his *macuahuitl* was still in its scabbard over his back, but he squirmed like an eel, the sweat and blood covering his body making him slick, and twisted his right arm free from the brawny fanatic who clung to it. He stabbed him once between the ribs with the dagger drawn from the scabbard at his waist, and then *tac, tac, tac*, punched three holes in the next man's heart, killing him instantly, while Acolmiztli and Ilhuicamina slaughtered the rest of the little knot of attackers.

Then they were running again. The squad, which had rallied round to defend Shikotenka, had taken terrible punishment and was reduced, he thought, to fewer than thirty men. But now they were at last away, free, no Mexica able to catch them. Not even the Cuahchics, for all their formidable reputation, could keep pace with trained Tlascalan runners, and the shattered remnant, legs pumping up the long hill above the camp, at last began to put serious distance between themselves and the shrieking, howling pack that hunted them.

Though he knew that nothing could be taken for granted, Shikotenka had calculated that if he could stage a sufficiently provocative raid on Coaxoch's army, then a large force would be detached from it and sent after him. This would be a force of sufficient magnitude – he hoped for a whole regiment – to conduct immediate and spectacular reprisals against Tlascalan towns and villages after it had hunted him down. The character of the Mexica was such that any lesser reaction was simply unthinkable, and in this way the great field army – one of six of similar size at Moctezuma's command – would be divided and weakened, an objective that formed the essence of the broader Tlascalan strategy. Shikotenka's intention all along had therefore been to slaughter Coaxoch and every one of his sons in a manner so insulting it would drive the Mexica into a blind, unthinking rage. Only at the last moment had it occurred to him that this purpose might be even better served if he left Mahuizoh alive.

The eldest son of the Snake Woman was pompous and arrogant, conceited and self-glorifying, puffed up with pride and accustomed to being flattered – a strutting, posturing bully who'd come to believe he would always triumph over others, and that no man was his equal. It was not difficult to predict that seeing his father and brothers butchered before his eyes, and his own nose sliced from his face and thrown in the dust, was likely to produce a massive reaction – especially since it was Shikotenka himself, battle-king of the despised Tlascalans, who'd brought him to such ignominy.

The rain had not returned, the gaps in the cloud were rapidly widening, and the moon burst brightly through again. Shikotenka thought to profit from this as he neared the top of the hill, aiming to draw out as many of the enemy as possible by parading his squad along the ridge in full view of the camp. But when he turned and looked back, he saw the taunt was hardly needed. A vast river of fire poured from the heart of the Mexica army, streaming with surprising speed up the hillside like some immense, unnatural lava flow – men running with torches, many more than he'd hoped for. It looked very much as though half of the whole fighting force, two complete regiments, each eight thousand strong, had been sent after them.

Not slowing his pace, Tree took a swig from his waterskin. 'Gods in Mictlan,' he breathed. 'We've certainly got the buggers stirred up.'

Yet the most dangerous part of the game was still to come. Days of careful planning with Shikotenka's aged father Shikotenka the elder, the chief of all Tlascala's civil affairs, and with venerable Maxixcatzin who served as deputy to them both, had persuaded the ruling Senate of the nation – by a majority of a single vote! – to accept this risky, high-stakes gambit and grant the men they needed to carry it through.

More men – close to a hundred thousand – than Tlascala had ever before put into the field at one time.

Enough to ensure victory in a pitched battle against Coaxoch's entire field army.

But that victory would be all the more certain, Shikotenka had reasoned, and all the less costly, if the Mexica force could be divided, put through a night of alarms and excursions, and a great part of it run to exhaustion, while those who stayed behind in the main camp were distracted and disoriented by a devastating assault on their leadership.

There were many in the Senate who did not believe it could be done – and if the raid on Coaxoch's pavilion had failed the whole attack would have been called off and the Mexica brought to battle in some other place on some other day. But the attack had not failed. On the contrary, Shikotenka had carried out the first part of the plan to perfection, with better results than anyone could have hoped for.

Even now the spies who'd taken up position along the ridges after nightfall would be hurrying to carry word of what had happened to Maxixcatzin, who should be no more than ten miles away, advancing by forced march under cover of darkness with sixty thousand elite Tlascalan warriors. Other messengers, fresh and strong, would be flying fleet of foot across the twenty miles of mountainous terrain to the hidden valley where Shikotenka the elder had gathered a further thirty thousand warriors to destroy whichever fraction of Coaxoch's army pursued Shikotenka and his squad.

Fraction? Shikotenka thought. No one had imagined that half the Mexica force would be sent after him. Even so, his father's thirty thousand were more than enough to annihilate them, especially so since the Mexica regiments would be run ragged and exhausted by the time they reached the killing ground. The only thing left to do to make victory certain was to keep his squad in sight of their vanguard at all times. Leave them too far behind and they would lose them; let them get too close and they would be overtaken and engulfed – a delicate balance to maintain over such a great distance.

The moonlight helped, for much of the course would be run in darkness as they slogged up the barren, snow-covered slopes of Iztaccihuatl, that grand volcano whose name meant 'White Woman', and crossed the high pass separating Iztaccihuatl from Popocatépetl. They would then have to negotiate a dozen mountain torrents and descend a long downslope of treacherous scree before reaching the foothills that would bring them at last to the canyon where the ambush had been set.

Malinal was walking fast, as fast as she could go in fact, through a night loud with cicadas and filled with the sweet scents of tuberose and dragon fruit flowers. The lightning storm was long since over, leaving its own rich fragrance lingering in the air, the rain had stopped and the moon shone brightly again in the sky from which most of the looming cloud mass had now cleared.

There was nothing sinister about any of this; on the contrary Malinal felt overwhelmed by its beauty. Nonetheless, as she made her way along the deserted track that led from Tacuba, around the southern shore of Lake Texcoco and thence east towards the distant mountain range connecting the twin peaks of Iztaccihuatl and Popocatépetl, she couldn't shake the unpleasant feeling that she was being followed.

Perhaps Moctezuma had changed his mind and sent enforcers after her to bring her back to Tenochtitlan? Or perhaps it was Cuitláhuac. Might he have been so outraged and offended by the way she'd been set free that he'd overcome his natural obedience to the Great Speaker's orders and arranged to have her killed on the road?

Yet if either of these two were involved, then why was she being followed in such a cautious and secretive way? Just a scrape of a sandal on gravel every now and then, followed by nothing for ages but her own footsteps, the beat of her heart and the song of night insects. Mexica enforcers would have taken no such precautions. If her arrest or murder had been ordered, they'd come after her at the double and got the job done. They wouldn't drag it out forever like this.

Slowly Malinal began to convince herself that she must be imagining the whole thing – that the horrors she'd been through had made her see danger everywhere when in fact there was none. She flexed her shoulders under her heavy backpack and looked east towards the mountains, shivering at the thought of the cold she must endure as she crossed that high range, and at the splendid beauty of the moonlight on the snowcapped peaks of the two great volcanos.

The Mexica, who could be strangely poetic and even romantic despite their bloodlust, believed that Popocatépetl and Iztaccihuatl had once been a handsome warrior and a beautiful young princess who were deeply in love. They had planned to wed against the wishes of Iztaccihuatl's father, who sent Popocatépetl to war in Tlascala to delay the marriage and then falsely reported to his daughter that the young man had been killed in battle. The princess's sorrow was so great that she fell mortally ill and died of a broken heart. Popocatépetl, on returning victorious to Tenochtitlan, went mad with grief, seized the body of his beloved and carried her off to the highlands, where he too died as he sat in watch over her. Moved by their tragic end, the gods turned the young lovers into mountains and covered them both with snow so their story would be remembered for ever – and indeed, Malinal thought, the white contours of Iztaccihuatl, gleaming in the moonlight, did resemble the form of a woman stretched out on her back, while it required only a slight leap of imagination to see the brooding hump of Popocatépetl as the hunched figure of the grief-stricken prince keeping vigil over her.

Would she too die up there amongst the snows? For, in her desire to stay as far as possible from the Mexica on her way to the coast, in this mad quest that Tozi had set her on to seek out Quetzalcoatl, Malinal had chosen to avoid the easy and well-travelled thoroughfare used by the merchant caravans to carry the rich trade between Tenochtitlan and the Maya lowlands. Instead she would cross the mountain pass between Iztaccihuatl and Popocatépetl, within the encircled but still free state of Tlascala, and travel onwards to the Yucatán from there using side roads and byways.

Not that her experiences in the fattening pens had given her any reason to expect help in Tlascala! But Malinal knew from bitter experience that female slaves were amongst the items most prized by Mexica merchants, and that a woman of her beauty, travelling alone, would be at great risk. Better to take her chances with the Tlascalans than end up a prisoner of the Mexica again before she got within a hundred miles of the coast.

She was trying not to think about the even greater dangers that awaited her if she did get to the Yucatán and did succeed in making it all the way back to her home town of Potonchan – dangers posed by the Chontal Maya, her own people – when she heard a sudden rush of footsteps behind her and someone crashed hard into her back. She lost her balance and was knocked flat, just managing to get her hands under her to break her fall. A knee pinned her buttocks, long fingers snaked round her neck and a face was thrust down beside her own.

Even before he spoke she recognised her attacker from the foul smell of his breath and the reek of blood in his hair. 'You witch,' snarled Ahuizotl. 'You've ruined me. Now you're going to die.'

* * *

Pepillo couldn't swim and had never had reason to learn, but now discovered an abject fear of drowning. Tumbling and choking in the flood, his mouth and nose full of seawater, he gasped for air as he surfaced and found he'd been sluiced completely clear of the stateroom and out onto the navigation deck which sloped to starboard, steep as a roof, awash with solid debris. The water was shallower here, no more than a couple of spans deep, but it rushed and foamed down the slope carrying him with it. He saw Cortés and Alaminos clinging for their lives to the whipstaff, felt hope and absurd gratitude when Cortés pulled a hand free to grab his sleeve, then terror as the sleeve ripped from his jacket.

His helter-skelter plunge continued. Some large object slammed into his side and a barrel pitched by, rolling end over end, narrowly missing his head before crashing through the railings at the edge of the deck where the roaring flood poured back into the deep. Dazed, numbed, helpless to arrest his fall, Pepillo shot feet first through the jagged void the barrel had torn in the railings. He was swept over the streaming precipice, and had already consigned his soul to God, when a hand seized his hair in a firm, strong grip and jerked him to an abrupt halt. An instant later the careening ship righted itself, then tilted violently to port and spilled both him and his rescuer back across the deck where they ended up in a tangle of limbs, wrapped around the whipstaff at the feet of Cortés and Alaminos.

A spasm shook Pepillo's body and seawater spewed from his mouth. Lifting his head, he saw that the hand still locked in his hair belonged to Melchior. 'Thank you,' he tried to say as the older boy released him.

'Don't think this makes you my friend,' coughed Melchior.

With a vast creaking of timbers, the *Santa María* settled on an even keel, shook herself like a wet dog, and ploughed on before the raging wind through blasts of icy spume.

Melchior jumped to his feet and Pepillo followed, though he felt sick and faint. Every part of his body, already battered and bruised from the beating Muñoz had given him, was filled with new pain from his fight with the sea.

'Better get some rope and tie yourselves to a cleat, lads,' Cortés advised cheerfully. 'Looks like we've got a rough night ahead of us.'

* * *

Shikotenka had to admit the Cuahchics were good. A hundred of them were running vanguard for the Mexica regiments and, despite the punishing terrain, they'd reduced the Tlascalan lead to less than three hundred paces. Some of them were armed with *atlatls* and knew how to use them, but so far none of their darts had hit their mark because they were climbing the steep flank of Iztaccihuatl and the gradient worked against them. That would change to the disadvantage of the Tlascalans when they came to a downslope, and Shikotenka knew they must cross three deep transverse gullies before reaching the pass.

He took a long cool draught from his waterskin. Weariness was beginning to tell on him, to seep into his muscles and his bones, sapping his strength. It seemed he'd been running and fighting, running and fighting since the beginning of the world, and ten miles still lay ahead before they brought the Mexica to the killing ground.

He reached a decision. Something had to be done about those Cuahchics.

The mountainside was all loose gravel and boulders interspersed with ancient, crumbling lava flows, and as the squad beat their way up, he'd noticed how their sandals constantly set off avalanches of little stones. Might not a greater avalanche be started? Already the sky was lightening in the east, more of the features of the landscape were becoming apparent, and Shikotenka began to look around for something he could use.

Malinal heard the hiss of Ahuizotl's knife being drawn from its scabbard, and felt his fingers scrabble at her forehead and dig into her eyes as he jerked her head back to expose her throat to the blade. The thing she hated the most, after all she'd been through, was that she was to be slaughtered here on her belly like a deer in a huntsman's trap and couldn't even spit in her killer's face as she died.

She screamed with rage and defiance but the blow never came. Instead she heard a hard, hollow thump, like the sound a coconut makes when it falls from the tree, and Ahuizotl slumped forward over her with a terrible groan. Then someone she couldn't see dragged his limp body to the side, not completely clear of her but enough so she could begin to squirm out from under his weight, and there was another hollow thump followed by a loud *crack* and a series of ugly, wet squelching sounds.

As she sat up she saw the strangest thing – a hefty lump of rock seemingly moving by its own power, smashing repeatedly down on the high priest's head. Then there was a shimmer in the air and Tozi, in her beggar's clothes, became visible out of nothingness, and Malinal understood that she was the one who was making the rock move, gripping it tight between her two hands, stooping over Ahuizotl and pounding his brains to pulp. His evil face, turned sideways, was already barely recognisable, one eye hanging loose, his skull, crushed and deformed, leaking matter and blood.

'Tozi,' Malinal said after a few more moments of this. 'I think he's dead.'

'Just making sure,' her friend replied. 'With people as beastly as this it always pays to be sure.' She examined her handiwork, nodded with satisfaction and tossed the stone aside.

'Thank the gods you came,' said Malinal. She frowned. 'But you faded for a long time and you didn't get sick. Are you all right?'

'I've never felt better,' said Tozi. She lowered her voice, a confidential tone: 'I told you, Malinal. Hummingbird showed himself to me on the pyramid. He spoke to me, he touched me with his fire, and he made me strong.'

Shikotenka had found what he was looking for – a group of large boulders, two as high as a man, three others almost equally massive, that had rolled together in a cluster from somewhere higher up the lava-strewn ribs of Iztaccihuatl.

The squad had put on a sprint, opening up their three-hundred pace lead on the Cuahchics to somewhere closer to a thousand. Now they came to a halt, gathered in the shelter of the boulders, unslung their bows and looked down at their pursuers.

Dawn was very close; with every minute that passed the sky grew brighter, revealing more of the long rugged slope below. They saw the Cuahchics moving fast, rapidly narrowing the gap again, and beneath them, spread out across the mountainside, the torches of the two pursuing regiments creating great pools of light, yellow and sulphurous as the fires of Mictlan. Some large groups of warriors were hard on the heels of the vanguard, others were as many as two thousand paces behind them, but all in all they were doing well, Shikotenka thought – well for Mexica, at any rate, who could not match the level of training in long-distance running that was so much a part of the Tlascalan way of life. As he'd expected, rage and the thirst for revenge were driving the mass of the soldiers on to feats that were really beyond their capacity. He smiled. That was good, very good, for it meant that many of them would be exhausted, some perhaps even too exhausted to fight, when they came to the killing ground.

Tree and the ten most muscular members of the squad were already at work rocking and loosening the boulders as the Cuahchics below closed the distance to less than three hundred paces again. They threw an experimental volley of *atlatl* darts, all of which fell short – technically they were within range but, as with their earlier shots, the incline defeated them. The opposite was the case for the Tlascalan bows. On the flat, the range would still have been too great, but they had the advantage of targeting an enemy downslope and their first flight of a dozen arrows fell squarely amongst the Cuahchics, leaving three either dead on the ground or too badly injured to rise again and inflicting debilitating wounds on five more. A second volley was in the air before the first had struck and a third immediately followed, bringing the number of Cuahchics killed or injured to around thirty before they were at last near enough to unleash a storm of *atlatl* darts that flew true and forced the Tlascalan archers to duck for cover.

'Now!' Shikotenka yelled, and the archers downed bows and joined Tree and his men heaving at the boulders. Around eighty of the Cuahchics were still coming at them, bounding uphill in a concentrated mass, their glistening red and blue head-paint clearly visible in the rising light, their war cries exultant as they tasted victory. For a moment Shikotenka feared he'd miscalculated, until Tree, who had squatted low, his hands under the largest boulder, great cords of knotted muscle standing out on his shoulders and thighs, gave a roar of triumph. There was an explosive sound of rending and cracking and the huge rock broke away from its roots in the earth and went tumbling downslope in a tremendous cloud of dust and debris, closely followed by the other four which the squad had already loosened and which now required only a final heave to set in motion.

The effects were stunning. As the avalanche crashed into them, the mass of the Cuahchics, uttering terrible screams, were mowed down – fifty or sixty of them dead in an instant, all the rest broken and scattered. Nor was that the end of the devastation, for the three biggest boulders were not stopped but only slowed by the multiple impacts and soon picked up speed again as they thundered onward, tumbling and bouncing high into the air before smashing into the much larger mass of warriors below and ploughing a deadly red swathe through their ranks before finally coming to a halt.

When the dust settled, Shikotenka turned to Tree. 'What do you think?' he said. 'Three hundred, maybe four hundred?'

'Maybe more,' said Tree dourly. 'But that still leaves fifteen and a half thousand of them on our tail.'

'You're right,' said Shikotenka. He looked up. Dawn had broken and, although it would not climb over the enormous shoulder of the volcano for another hour at least, the sun had already risen and was flooding the sky with light. A thousand paces above, the snowline glimmered and glittered. A thousand paces below, the furious cries of the Mexica rang out.

A new vanguard was already streaming up towards them.

'Let's go,' Shikotenka yelled. 'No time to be standing around gawping.'

'I know you told me,' said Malinal, 'but I didn't understand you. I thought it was the terror we've been through that made you say that. I thought it was the pain. I didn't think you meant it.'

'I meant it,' Tozi said gravely. 'Hummingbird showed himself to me, and he spoke to me, and he's as real as you and I are, Malinal. He's – I don't know – ugly and beautiful at the same time. He's sly and stealthy and cruel and he touched me with his fire, but I didn't understand what he'd done to me – I didn't really understand – until I left you in the square at Tacuba and spotted Ahuizotl watching you from a corner. It was obvious he meant you harm, so I took a risk and tried a fade and nothing bad happened to me – nothing at all! It was easy to follow him, Malinal! I just waited for my chance . . . and . . . well, you saw the rest.'

It was soon after dawn and the sun wasn't hot yet, but clouds of fat blue flies were already buzzing industriously around the bloody ruin of the high priest's head. Malinal felt a heavy sense of foreboding but decided not to speak of it.

'My dear little Tozi,' she said, forcing a smile. 'You're really amazing, do you know that? You didn't even embrace me when we parted in the square and yet here you are, as though by magic, saving my life again.'

'I know you think it's bad,' Tozi said looking her in the eye, 'that Hummingbird made me stronger.'

'I don't know what I think,' Malinal admitted. 'All I know is that I'm glad it's me who's alive and Ahuizotl who's dead and not the other way round.' Without another word she reached out and wrapped her arms round her strange friend, seeing the lice crawling in the beggar's clothes she wore and not caring, just delighted to hold her close again and feel her warmth and sense her strange power.

When they stepped apart, Malinal asked, 'What now?' But she already knew the answer.

'Nothing's changed,' Tozi confirmed. 'You must go to the coast to find Quetzalcoatl and bring him to Tenochtitlan to end the rule of the Mexica.'

'And you? Are you still determined to stay in that depraved city?'

'Yes, that's my part. I owe it to Coyotl.'

'But it's not safe there. You'll never be safe!'

Tozi smiled, a strange, lopsided smile. 'I wasn't much of a witch before, in the fattening pen, even though everyone believed I was, but I think I've become one now. I know how to look after myself.'

They embraced again. 'Very well,' said Malinal. 'I'll see you in Tenochtitlan. I promise I'll be back and, if Quetzalcoatl exists, I promise I'll bring him.'

'He exists,' said Tozi. 'He's already crossing the eastern ocean. His boat moves by itself without paddles, just as the prophecy foretold. It's all coming true, Malinal. Every word of it. You'll see!'

Shikotenka's lungs were tortured, his muscles failing, his waterskin, which he'd replenished above the snowline, again nearly empty. His

254

squad had already run many miles the previous evening, fought a hard fight in the pavilion and made a difficult escape. The only consolation was that the hundred highly trained Cuahchics who'd formed the new Mexica vanguard must be in equally bad shape – maybe worse. They'd left the camp in such a hurry that very few carried waterskins. Nonetheless, they'd pressed the Tlascalans hard in the hour after the avalanche, rarely trailing them by more than a thousand paces and several times drawing close enough in the rising daylight to harass them with *atlatl* darts. Shikotenka lost two more men that way, and another two had simply dropped with fatigue and were left to their fate while the rest of the squad struggled on.

The punishment of the long run over mountainous terrain had slowed everyone – the Tlascalans, the Cuahchics and the two regiments following behind. The five thousand fastest Mexica were hot on the heels of the vanguard but the rest, numbering more than ten thousand, were now spread out over almost three miles of the rugged downslope on the east side of the pass between Iztaccihuatl and Popocatépetl. No one had any breath for war cries so there were no more furious hoots and whistles, just grim silence and the scrape and slide of feet.

The dry scree of the pass was already giving way to bushes and greenery at these lower altitudes, and stands of trees, at first stunted but soon increasingly dense and tall, grew out of folds and gullies in the land. Shikotenka heard birdsong as he ran, a beautiful sweet melody, strangely at odds with the terrible business at hand, and he felt the fresh breath of the early morning on his face and the kiss of the rising sun.

A glance over his shoulder showed him the Cuahchics had closed the gap to less than two hundred paces and were gaining ground at alarming speed. They'd stopped using their *atlatls*, no doubt because they scented victory and hoped to take him prisoner with what was left of his squad, drag them back in dishonour to Tenochtitlan and put them to sacrifice. Mahuizoh's thirst for revenge had driven this mad chase all through the long night, and the pursuers were so numerous, and so confident of their own supremacy, that it seemed none yet suspected an ambush. Still, the prey was very far from being in the pot. Even if the Cuahchic vanguard could be held off until Shikotenka's exhausted men reached the canyon where his father waited with thirty thousand warriors, and even if the ambush went undetected until then, the real danger now was the ten thousand Mexica stragglers, who would still be outside the killing ground when the trap was sprung.

There was too much here for Shikotenka's weary mind to grapple with. He only knew that everything he had done would be fruitless if the Cuahchics were to overtake him. Whatever else might unfold he could not – he must not! – allow that to happen. He looked ahead. Less than a mile downslope the land levelled out into thickly forested foothills; leading into the hills, still masked by morning shadows, yawned the dark mouth of the canyon they sought. Yet even as he spotted it, and his heart soared, another of his stalwart Tlascalans stumbled and fell, bringing down two more men, and the foremost Cuahchics were on them in seconds.

Pedro de Alvarado examined himself in the costly Venetian mirror affixed to the wall of his stateroom. God's wounds but he was a handsome man! Thanks to La Peña's ministrations (the doctor was already proving to be a most useful addition to the expedition), his broken left arm was comfortably bandaged and splinted, but he could still use the long, elegant fingers of his right hand to twirl the ends of his moustache. *Dashing*, he thought, *very dashing*. He adjusted his lion's mane of blond hair – how the women loved it! – and smiled at his own somehow devilish reflection. *A handsome man, to be sure, a rakish and scornful man whom no one could upstage, but also a dangerous one. Let there be no mistake about that!*

With a last approving glance at himelf he strolled out onto the deck of the *San Sebastián* to count the distant sails of the scattered ships all now rallying to his signal. People talked about the calm before the storm, but he was, on this morning of Friday 19 February 1519, quite content to enjoy the relative calm *after* the storm. There was a fair wind blowing, whipping up the sparkling blue waters into little wavelets – but nothing like the gigantic rollers that had threatened to send the entire fleet to the bottom of the sea the night before.

It was a miracle that only one of the eleven vessels was missing, but unfortunately that vessel was the *Santa María de la Concepción*, Cortés's own flagship.

'Oh dear, Hernán,' Alvarado said quietly to himself. 'Where have you got to?'

Tree and Acolmiztli ran to Shikotenka's left, Chipahua and Ilhuicamina to his right, and behind them in four thin ranks pounded the other survivors of the squad. Fifty men had honoured the gods at the start of the night but now, in this bright morning, just twenty-two were still in the race.

'*Run!*' Shikotenka yelled. '*Run for your lives!*'

The Mexica had their skills, no one could deny them that, but when it came to long-distance running, when it came to stamina, when it came to sheer heart and nerve, they had always been outmatched by the Tlascalans, and so it proved now. The Cuahchics had left the binding of the fallen prisoners to the mass of foot soldiers who followed them, and had closed the gap to twenty paces, but on Shikotenka's command his men found resources of training and strength deep within themselves, conquered their fatigue and redoubled their pace, leaving their pursuers behind. Breath drawn in quick, harsh snatches, every muscle trembling, faces burned out and grey, they nonetheless soon opened their lead to thirty, forty, fifty, then sixty paces and, as they entered the cool, shadowed mouth of the canyon, they were once again close to two hundred paces ahead.

Shikotenka had thoroughly scouted the killing ground in the days before and knew what to expect. Narrow at its mouth and fifty feet deep between steep walls of weirdly striped and patterned red rock, the great box canyon rapidly widened to half a mile across and a hundred feet deep, curving sharply west, then north, before terminating after two miles in sheer, unscalable cliffs. Flash floods had carved out a series of criss-crossing gullies along the midline of its otherwise generally flat and stony floor, but off to the sides, near the canyon walls, there were stands of acacia trees and brushwood thick enough to conceal the huge Tlascalan ambushing force.

A mile in, Shikotenka drained the last drops from his waterskin and put on a final burst of speed, looking quickly left and right, hoping to catch some sight of his father's men. 'Are you sure we've got the right canyon?' Chipahua croaked through his cracked, bloody lips.

Shikotenka nodded, saving his breath. This was the right place, but he had to admit the forests at the foot of the canyon walls did seem eerily quiet and empty. He could see others in the squad casting about anxiously, and doubt gripped him for an instant as he ran on. Had something gone terribly wrong?

Their painted skulls glistening in the sun, the Cuahchics of the vanguard were relentless, running silent and determined, spread out across the canyon floor. Sometimes twenty or thirty of them, bunched close together, would disappear into a gully, only to bound back into view, closer than before. Next came a block of the fastest footsoldiers from the Mexica regiments, a few hundred at most, followed by thousands more in a loose, disordered throng stretching all the way back to the canyon mouth and filling it from side to side almost as far as the strips of forest.

Shikotenka was too busy ensuring he didn't stumble on the treacherous, rutted ground to risk more than a quick glance over his shoulder but, as the track veered sharply north and the final desperate leg of the race began, he saw that perhaps half the Mexica force had now passed through the entrance. It wasn't enough, not nearly enough, but the cliffs that blocked the northern end of the canyon loomed ahead and there was no time left.

The last half-mile passed in an exhausted blur. Sweat poured into Shikotenka's eyes, thirst parched his throat, all the strength seemed to have drained from his muscles, his legs ached and trembled. Tree was not a man to show weakness but he, too, looked nearly done in, twice almost losing his footing so that Chipahua had to steady him with a hand to his elbow. 'No more running,' the big man said finally, and staggered to a halt a few hundred paces short of the acacia thicket at the foot of the cliffs.

'We'll make our stand here,' Shikotenka agreed, stopping beside him. It was the right place, out in the open, and would allow the ambushers to stay concealed until they chose to show themselves.

If the ambushers were there.

The squad needed no orders to know what to do next. There was just time to make a defensive circle, bristling with spears, before their pursuers were on them.

*　*　*

Malinal felt sad and bewildered and terrified all at once. The gods were real in all their glamour and power. Sorcery was real and Tozi was a witch of great magic who could kill invisibly, and who had saved her life.

Ah Tozi . . . Tozi.

To her surprise, Malinal discovered she missed her frightening little friend already, missed her with a great ache in her heart, and at the same time was filled with apprehension at the undertaking Tozi had set her on – to return to her homeland, to return to Potonchan, alone, without magical support, to face and overcome the demons awaiting her there.

The demon who was her own mother, the woman who had given birth to her yet who had nonetheless bowed to the will of her demon stepfather and sold her into slavery in the interests of the demon boy the two of them had conceived together after the sudden and unexplained death of Malinal's beloved father, the late chief of Potonchan.

These were the demons of Malinal's own family. Of course they were not demons at all in the supernatural sense, but they had nonetheless destroyed her life to steal her inheritance, and would certainly do so again if she showed herself amongst them, an unwelcome reminder of the truths they'd tried to hide, a ghost best left buried in the past.

So it was into this toxic mess, this stew of family rivalries and danger, that Tozi had sent Malinal, alone, relying only on her own resources, to seek out the god Quetzalcoatl.

Well, she thought, *I shall do it. I shall not falter. I shall not fail.* Regardless of the schemes of supernatural gods and all-too-human demons, her story could never be complete if she did not master and overcome her own dark legacy.

She squared her shoulders, settled her load more comfortably upon her back and strode forward into the morning. Having covered the ground before when she'd first been brought as a slave to Tenochtitlan, Malinal had a good idea of the length of the journey. If she could walk all day, every day, then it would take her thirty days, more or less, to reach Potonchan. And even though she must walk off the beaten track, she knew that there were many villages along the way, and even some great towns and cities.

Malinal was only a woman, but she was a beautiful woman, practised in the arts of flattery and seduction. She would rely on the kindness of strangers, she resolved, and somehow she would survive.

There was no immediate attack. Instead the Cuahchics formed a loose ring around the Tlascalans at a distance of thirty paces. A few of them, winded, actually threw themselves to the ground. Many stooped over, gasping. All the rest stood panting, some leaning on their spears, sweat dripping from their bodies, faces set and impassive.

For a two-hundred count nothing happened, the silence between the two groups of warriors broken only by the sound of birdsong.

'What's their game?' whispered Ilhuicamina. 'Why don't they just annihilate us with *atlatl* darts and get it done with?'

'They want us for sacrifice,' said Acolmiztli. 'Obviously.'

Tree summoned up the energy to brandish his war club. 'Women!' he shouted. 'Come and get us if you have the guts for it.'

'They're just catching their breath,' Chipahua suggested sourly. He turned to Shikotenka. 'Where's your father?' he asked. 'Now would be a good time for him to show himself.'

'Don't expect any help yet,' Shikotenka said. He looked back down the canyon in the direction they had come; thousands of Mexica foot soldiers were streaming towards them. 'My father will wait until we have more fish in the net.'

'If your father's even here,' Chipahua gave voice to Shikotenka's own fears. The forested sides of the canyon presented a bosky scene. Birds flew in and out amongst the treetops, calm and unruffled. 'Never seen thirty thousand warriors lie so low,' Chipahua added, his sneer horribly distorted by his smashed mouth and the jagged stumps of his teeth.

'They're supposed to lie low,' objected Tree. 'Wouldn't be much of an ambush if they didn't.'

Shikotenka nodded. 'They're Tlascalans, and they're here. Count on it.'

He was surprised how sure he managed to sound, but in the solitude of his thoughts the worm of doubt was gnawing . . . gnawing.

Suppose another of Moctezuma's armies was in the field and had mounted a simultaneous raid on Tlascala when all eyes had been on Coaxoch? If so, his father would have been obliged to divert his warriors to confront it.

Or suppose the Senate had intervened disastrously at the last moment? Half the senators had opposed Shikotenka's election as battle-king and voted against this plan. Could some terrible betrayal have been engineered in the past day and his father overruled? *No! Surely not! Gods forbid it!* He shook his head from side to side to clear away the unwelcome thought and asked: 'Anyone got any water left?'

Some of the men still had a few drops in their waterskins, which they willingly shared as the hundred Cuahchics, with no more than a dozen empty skins amongst them, looked on greedily. Studying the members of the elite Mexica force, Shikotenka saw just how close to the limit of their endurance the Tlascalans had run them, and could only guess at the condition of the rest of the enemy footsoldiers staggering up to reinforce them. More than a thousand had already reached the outer edges of the Cuahchic encirclement, but most of them now lay stretched out on the ground, chests heaving in abject exhaustion.

'Tosspots!' said Ilhuicamina with an insulting gesture along the canyon. 'Mexica can't run to save their lives.'

Tree seemed much restored by the water and the fury of battle was glinting in his eyes. *'Women!'* he taunted the Cuahchics again. 'If by chance there's a man hiding there amongst you, I offer you single combat.' He stepped to the edge of the Tlascalan circle and smacked his club menacingly against the huge palm of his left hand.

The Cuahchics had removed their insignia of rank and run the final miles in loincloths and sandals only, but it was obvious who their commander was. A short, squat warrior of about thirty, with the left side of his head and face painted yellow and the right side blue, masses of knotted muscle standing out on his thighs, arms and belly, he stood calmly with his eyes fixed on Tree. 'Bluster all you wish, Tlascalan,' he replied, his voice rasping like a saw cutting wood. 'We'll soon enough show you what men we are.'

Chipahua gave a loud belch. 'Men have balls, but your breechclouts look empty. Send your wives to us and we'll show them what they've been missing.' Around him the Tlascalan squad laughed while the Cuahchics chafed and murmured. Swinging his club, Tree ran forward to stand alone in no man's land. 'Single combat,' he shouted again. 'Single combat now.'

Shikotenka reluctantly decided to see how his friend's act of bravado played out. It was a useful distraction while the canyon behind the Cuahchics continued to fill up with Mexica footsoldiers – at least ten thousand of them now and counting. Every minute the ambush was delayed meant more of them would fall into the trap.

As three of the Cuahchics darted forth to answer Tree's challenge, their leader barked a command and they stopped in their tracks while they were still out of range of the big man's whirling club, then slunk back to the protection of their squad in a way that was almost comical. '*Cowards!*' Tree roared. 'Three not enough? Send six. Send twelve. I'll kill you all!'

More murmurs of fury from the enemy ranks were answered by further stern rebukes from the thickset officer. 'Nobody fights,' he was yelling, while he held one of his men by the scruff of the neck and knocked another to the ground with a great blow of his fist. 'Nobody dies! Not until General Mahuizoh gets here.'

Suddenly Shikotenka understood the Cuahchics' strange behaviour. *Ah*, he thought as he sent Chipahua and Acolmiztli to drag Tree back to the Tlascalan circle. *Now it all makes sense.*

Mahuizoh arrived within the hour, more than enough time for every man of the two Mexica regiments to enter the killing ground. Stripped down to his loincloth like all the rest, a thick brown poultice covering the ruin of his nose, breathing noisily and blowing bubbles of blood through his mouth, pale and shaking with pain, you had to admire the dedication of the general, Shikotenka reflected; you had to admire the resolve; you had to admire the sheer violence of the hatred that had driven him across mountains, up and down steep gradients and along the length of this canyon to extract vengeance for what had been done to his father and his brothers.

And there was no doubt his revenge would be terrible, as cruel and as hideous as anything the wicked imaginings of the Mexica could devise . . .

If the Tlascalan ambush was not in place.

Flanked by four strutting Cuahchic bodyguards, Mahuizoh advanced to within a dozen paces of the Tlascalan circle and sought Shikotenka out, fixing him with an inflamed glare. 'You, Shikotenka!' he said, his voice wet and bubbling. 'Tell me the name of your man who cut me.' He turned towards Ilhuicamina whose prosthetic nose of jade mosaic tiles glittered in the morning's brilliance.

'He'll tell you himself,' Shikotenka replied.

Ilhuicamina laughed and lifted the mask from his face, exposing the gaping bone beneath. 'I am Ilhuicamina,' he said. 'It was I who cut you. Do you wish to thank me for making you as lovely as myself?'

'I will thank you with this,' said Mahuizoh. He produced a long-bladed obsidian knife from his waistband and held it up to the sun. 'My gratitude will be beautiful to behold and will require much time to express.' He turned back to Shikotenka. 'I told you I will go to Moctezuma wearing your skin,' he said. A choking cough shook him and blood sprayed from his mouth. 'I will make your own men flay you alive before I take your heart.'

Shikotenka didn't reply but turned to his captains. 'When my father attacks,' he said, with more assurance than he felt, 'we go straight for Mahuizoh. Cut the heart out of the Mexica resistance. Agreed?'

'Agreed,' said Chipahua.

'Agreed,' said Ilhuicamina.

'Agreed,' said Acolmiztli.

'Agreed,' said Tree. 'We cut out their heart.'

Shikotenka glanced again at the strips of forest at the base of the canyon walls and at the coming and goings of the birds. Once again the shadow of doubt fell over him, but then the great war conch blew a triumphant blast and the birds scattered up to heaven amidst a flurry of wings. Thirty thousand Tlascalans erupted from their hides amongst the acacia and brushwood to engulf their hated enemies in a howling, vengeful tide.

The look on Mahuizoh's evil face made every agonising moment of the last day and night worthwhile. Shikotenka surged forward and, as

Tree's club and Chipahua's *macuahuitl* and the knives of Acolmiztli and Ilhuicamina struck down the astonished bodyguards, he closed with the general and *tac, tac, tac, tac, tac,* he took his vile and vicious life.

By noon, when there was still no sign of the *Santa María*, Alvarado looked out at the rest of the fleet gathered around his own magnificent carrack, *San Sebastián*, and shrugged his shoulders.

The only thing to do, under the circumstances, was to sail at once to Cozumel. Cortés had the coordinates. If he'd survived they would meet him again there.

And if not . . . well . . . Alvarado smiled. The expedition would just have to find a new leader, and he was ready to step up to the mark.

Part II

19 February 1519 to 18 April 1519

Chapter Forty-Five

Huicton sat on his begging mat in his usual spot at the junction where the Tepeyac causeway branched off from the Azcapotzalco causeway in the northern quarter of Tenochtitlan. Invisible, insubstantial, able to pass unseen wherever and whenever she wished, Tozi approached him without making a sound and waited for a moment when there was a suitable gap in the crowds. Then, quite suddenly, giving no warning, she faded back into visibility right in front of him.

He gasped in surprise, blinked rapidly twice and put his old hand to his chest, but very soon recovered his composure. 'Tozi!' he said, with real joy in his voice. 'I knew you'd be back . . . You're not one to give yourself up to the knife.' His brow furrowed. 'But how long have you been standing here invisible waiting to shock me?' He beckoned her to sit down beside him on the mat, rested his hand on her shoulder. 'You've not harmed yourself with this fade?'

'No, Huicton, I have not harmed myself. I've gone through many changes since we last met.'

There was a secret that Tozi had kept to herself during her months in the fattening pen. She'd told Coyotl and Malinal that her mother had brought her to Tenochtitlan when she was five years old; that she'd died two years later, leaving Tozi to fend for herself from the age of seven until she was grabbed off the street by Moctezuma's catchers, who had brought her to the fattening pen when she was fourteen. That was all true, but she'd not told them her mother had been murdered by a mob of commoners whipped up into a frenzy against witches, or that they'd have murdered Tozi, too, if she hadn't cast the spell of invisibility and faded for a thirty count to escape them.

And she'd said nothing about Huicton, the poor, blind beggar with milky-white eyes who'd been there on the street corner when it happened. After the mob surged on in search of other victims, he'd looked for her and rescued her from the hole she'd crawled into where she lay helpless, stunned and bleeding from the effects of the fade.

Because Huicton wasn't really blind.

And when he passed through the streets of Tenochtitlan tapping with his stick, seeming to feel his way, he saw everything that went on.

He wasn't really a beggar, either. In that disguise, he'd explained to Tozi as he nursed her back to health all those years ago, he served as a spy for King Neza of Texcoco who was nominally Moctezuma's vassal but pursued many independent policies.

'How long have you known how to make yourself invisible?' Tozi remembered Huicton asking. His voice was low, with a strange nasal drone, almost like a swarm of bees in flight, and he'd smiled – such a nice, warm, *conspiratorial* smile – adding almost shyly: 'A spy with such a skill would be truly valuable.'

There was something trustworthy about him, so Tozi had told him the truth – that it was a gift she'd been born with but that it had to be harnessed by the spell of invisibility. Her mother had begun training her in the use of the spell from her earliest childhood, but it was difficult, and by the age of seven Tozi had only succeeded in mastering it for very short periods. Huicton had seen for himself how close it brought her to death when she sustained a fade for longer than a few seconds.

She remembered the close, intelligent way he'd studied her face through his clouded, deceptive eyes. 'You have other gifts, I think?' he'd said finally. She wasn't sure if it was a question or a statement, but in the years that followed they had often worked together. Her job was to lead him through the streets like a dutiful granddaughter, attracting sympathy and alms from passers-by, and as they walked, or sat on their mats and begged, he'd talk to her constantly about many things. Little by little she came to realise that these conversations were lessons – a sort of school – and that Huicton's purpose was to teach her to look deep within herself and find her gifts. He claimed no magical abilities of his own, but without his encouragement and advice, Tozi knew she would never have had enough confidence to learn how to send the fog, or read minds, or command animals.

He was not always with her. Sometimes the cunning old spy would vanish from Tenochtitlan for days on end as completely as if he did, after all, possess some magic. He never gave any explanation or warning. He was just gone – she presumed to take the intelligence he'd gathered to King Neza in Texcoco.

It had been during one of these periods of absence, much longer than usual, that Moctezuma's catchers had seized Tozi and put her in the fattening pen. But now, the morning after the terrible orgy of sacrifices on the great pyramid of Tenochtitlan, she was back and reunited with Huicton.

'I'm so sorry I was gone when you were taken,' he hastened to tell her. 'My master King Neza died and problems arose. His eldest son Ishtlil should have become king in his place but Moctezuma preferred the younger son Cacama and put him on the throne instead.'

Even in the fattening pen, Tozi had heard rumours of the recent events in Texcoco. 'So do you serve Cacama now?' she asked.

'No! Certainly not! Cacama is a yes-man who does whatever Moctezuma tells him. But Ishtlil has a mind of his own – like his father. Rather than accept the new state of affairs, he broke away, seized control of Texcoco's mountain provinces and declared a rebellion. He's at war with both Cacama and Moctezuma, and that war has grown bloody in the months you've been imprisoned.' Huicton glanced uneasily at the crowds passing by on the causeway and his voice fell to an almost inaudible whisper. 'I support the cause of Ishtlil,' he confided. 'He's become my new master and I do my spying for him now . . . A dangerous task – much more dangerous than before.'

Tozi understood the need for discretion. Numbering in their thousands, Moctezuma's secret police walked the streets of Tenochtitlan in plain clothes, listening and watching for any hint of sedition. They could be in any crowd, at any time. Even here. 'It was this change of circumstances,' Huicton continued, 'that kept me away from Tenochtitlan for so long and when I returned you'd been taken.' An apologetic grimace: 'I looked for you, I discovered what had happened, I even learned where they were keeping you, but there was nothing I could do except work for the destruction of Moctezuma. He tried to poison Ishtlil, you know. At least I managed to foil that plot! And I continued to have faith in you, my little Tozi, and to believe that somehow you would make yourself free. You always had great powers . . .'

'Not great enough to escape from the fattening pen!' Tozi whispered. 'I would have died yesterday on the killing stone but Hummingbird saved me. Hummingbird himself!'

Consternation crossed the old man's face. 'I don't understand you, child. What do you mean, Hummingbird saved you?'

'I couldn't escape from the pen,' Tozi said, 'no matter how hard I tried. I could never fade for long enough, so I was with all the other women victims brought for sacrifice yesterday. Last night I reached the top of the great pyramid. Moctezuma wielded the obsidian knife. But Hummingbird intervened to save me, he showed himself to me, he whispered in my ear as I whisper in yours now, he touched me with his fire when lightning struck his temple, and I was spared . . .'

Huicton's frown deepened. 'What did the god say to you?' he asked.

'He said "*You're mine now*".'

'You're sure of this?'

'Sure as I sit here alive beside you! The god saved me from Moctezuma's knife, Huicton, and he gave me the power to fade whenever I wish to. I don't even need the spell of invisibility any more! But I'm *not* "his" and I never will be "his"! I discovered my purpose when I was up there on the pyramid – and it's to destroy him not to serve him.'

The old man looked suddenly weary. 'The road to Mictlan is paved with good intentions just like that,' he said. 'When you accept a gift from the gods, there's always a price to pay.'

'At any other time you would be right,' said Tozi, 'but Hummingbird is just one god amongst many and his reign is nearly over.' She gripped the bent old man by the shoulders: 'This is the year that has been foretold,' she whispered, 'the year One-Reed in which Quetzalcoatl will return with all his host. Even now he journeys across the eastern ocean to overthrow Hummingbird and end the rule of Moctezuma forever. I can see you doubt me! Of course you do! I don't blame you. But what

I say is true. I have sure knowledge of this. Human sacrifices will end, torture will end, slavery will end, pain and suffering will end, and we who are alive at this time will witness the dawn of a new age. Will you not believe me?'

'You sound so certain,' said Huicton. There was hope in his voice, but also sadness.

'I am certain! This is the year One-Reed! All those who are with Moctezuma will fall and all those who are against him will rise. Your new master Ishtlil of Texcoco will rise. The Tlascalans will rise. The power of the Mexica will be broken.'

On the busy causeway, few of the prosperous passers-by even glanced at the beggars who were too far beneath their contempt to be noticed. Tozi put her lips close to Huicton's ear. 'I could kill Moctezuma,' she whispered. 'I could enter the palace without being seen, pass easily through the walls of his bedchamber and cut his throat while he sleeps.'

The old man thought about it for a while, staring straight ahead over the waters of Lake Texcoco with his milky, deceptive eyes. Finally, speaking so quietly Tozi had to strain to hear him, he said: 'It's tempting but I advise against it. And for two reasons. First, you have magic – I've always known that and I can see that it's more powerful now than ever before. But Moctezuma is surrounded by his own sorcerers, who work to protect him from magical attacks of the kind you're contemplating. Some of them may be stronger than you have become, even with this gift you've received from Hummingbird . . .'

Tozi shook her head vigorously. 'Their strength cannot match mine,' she said, not boasting but simply expressing the quiet confidence she felt.

Huicton looked at her with disapproval: 'Never be too sure of yourself,' he said. 'In this world of the strong and the weak there is always someone stronger than ourselves. If you encounter such a one in your invisible form, it might be you, not Hummingbird, who is destroyed . . .'

She began to voice an objection, but he held up his hand palm outward to silence her. 'I know you do not imagine this could happen, but Tozi, please believe me when I say that it can and that you – even you! – can be snuffed out like the flickering flame of a lamp or

271

imprisoned in some sorcerous realm from which you can never escape. How then would you work for the return of Quetzalcoatl? What then would be the fate of the good you hope to accomplish with your powers?' Again he waved her to silence. 'Besides,' he continued, 'there's a second reason to leave Moctezuma alive and this is simply that he's the worst Speaker the Mexica have had in a hundred years. If you were to succeed in killing him, it's a plain fact that anyone else they might put on the throne when he's dead – Coaxoch, Cuitláhuac, even Guatemoc – would do a better job than him. If we're truly to bring the Mexica and their evil god down, and if you're willing to use these new powers of yours in ways you may not have thought of yet, then Moctezuma's weaknesses and failings, his superstitions and his fears can be made to serve our interests . . .'

Tozi thought about it and decided that what Huicton was saying made a strange kind of sense.

'You're right,' she agreed after a moment. 'Maybe the fool is more use to us alive than dead!'

'He is,' said Huicton. 'You will see. Now come . . . We need to plan this carefully. I have a place where we can talk without risk of being overheard.'

Hummingbird did not appear again after Moctezuma freed the woman and the girl and he began to fear that – despite the great harvest of victims he had offered – he had somehow lost the favour of the god.

Sure proof of this was not long coming.

On the morning of the second day after the holocaust, a royal messenger spattered with dirt and blood and, in the last stages of exhaustion, stumbled into Tenochtitlan along the Iztapalapa causeway. He was brought directly to the palace where he prostrated himself on the floor of the audience chamber in the normal manner, but was overcome by emotion and stammered uncontrollably.

'I . . . I . . . There has been . . . The Lord Coaxoch has . . .'

'Speak, man!' Moctezuma urged. 'You have nothing to fear . . .'

The messenger sobbed and attempted to grasp the royal feet with his grimy hands, producing a stern rebuke from Cuitláhuac who was also present in the chamber.

'You have nothing to fear,' Moctezuma said again. 'Give us your report.'

It took a long while, and many such reassurances, before the messenger was sufficiently calm to speak. The giant field army mobilised by the Serpent Woman with the ambitious goal of seizing a further hundred thousand Tlascalan victims for sacrifice was no more. Two of the regiments, sixteen thousand men, had been lured away by a clever ruse and massacred in the eastern foothills of Iztaccihuatl. The other two regiments, together with tens of thousands of camp followers, had been surrounded at the muster point and annihilated. Inevitably some Mexica had escaped the fighting, and were presently limping back to Tenochtitlan, but their numbers were not thought to exceed three thousand. About a thousand more had been taken prisoner and reserved for sacrifice. It was clear, however, that the Tlascalans' primary goal was not to accumulate captives but to kill great numbers of their enemies on the battlefield. In this they had succeeded.

'Who were the Tlascalan generals?' Moctezuma asked, his voice sounding strangely thin and cold in his own ears.

'Shikotenka the younger, lord,' the messenger stammered, 'his father Shikotenka the elder, and the Lord Maxixcatzin.'

Moctezuma sat silent on his throne. These were no mere generals but the three most powerful men in Tlascala, the younger Shikotenka being the battle-king, the older Shikotenka being the civil king and Maxixcatzin being the deputy to both.

'And what of the Serpent Woman? What of his sons?'

'All amongst the dead, lord.'

Cuitláhuac stepped forward and addressed the messenger directly. 'My own son Guatemoc was with the Serpent Woman's army,' he said. 'Do you know his fate?'

'He lives, lord, though badly wounded and, I regret to report, close to death. Some of his men survived and carried him away from the battlefield. He is with them now, returning to Tenochtitlan in a well-protected caravan attended by surgeons, may the gods preserve him.'

'May the gods preserve him,' echoed Cuitláhuac.

Seeing his brother's expectant look, Moctezuma, too, repeated the time-honoured formula. The truth was, though, he'd never cared for his warrior nephew. Guatemoc was handsome, charismatic and virile. These qualities already made him a threat to the succession since Moctezuma had many daughters by his wives and many sons by his concubines, but only one legitimate son, the sickly boy Chimalpopoca, who was not yet four years old. Worse, the high esteem in which Guatemoc was held by the public and his wild, ambitious nature – so different from Cuitláhuac's stolid loyalty and complete lack of personal popularity – made him a threat to Moctezuma himself. All in all, therefore, it would have been better if the Tlascalans had succeeded in killing him. Still, with luck, he would die on the journey. 'You've done well,' he told the messenger. 'You may go.'

The wretched man crawled gratefully backwards out of the audience chamber. Moctezuma waited until the door closed behind him before he turned to Cuitláhuac. 'You have my permission to go to your son,' he said. 'Meet him on the road, speed his journey and bring him to the royal hospital. My surgeons can work wonders.'

Cuitláhuac bowed. 'Thank you, brother. I will leave at once.'

'Yes, yes, of course. But before you go,' Moctezuma ordered, 'kindly arrange to have that messenger strangled. We have lost an entire field army. I cannot forgive the bearer of such terrible news.'

During the next days, as the survivors of the carnage in Tlascala straggled back to Tenochtitlan and the Mexica began to count the cost of their first real defeat in battle, Moctezuma became ever more deeply convinced that all his problems were connected to the powerful strangers who had appeared on the coast of the Yucatán four months before. They must indeed be the retinue of Quetzalcoatl and it must therefore be true that the bearded god was about to return – and in this very year One-Reed, as had long ago been prophesied. Since the Mexica had strayed far from his ways, it was not to be wondered that he had given the Tlascalans so significant and unprecedented a triumph. Even so, the fact remained that Hummingbird had driven Quetzalcoatl out from the land of Mexico in times gone by and Moctezuma clung to the hope that he would do so again. He remembered the promise the war god had made to him in the temple: 'You have nothing to fear for I fight at your side . . . I will bring you victory.'

It seemed unlikely that promise would still be kept, now he had lost Hummingbird's favour. But might there not be something he could do, some great sacrifice he could make, that would win back the approval of the god?

Moctezuma's attempts to meditate on the problem and find the right solution were constantly interrupted by the more mundane distractions of running his empire with all its dangers and rivalries.

On the morning of the fourth day after the battle with the Tlascalans, Cuitláhuac brought Guatemoc into the city and installed him in a richly furnished room in the royal hospital. Moctezuma summoned Mecatl, his personal physician, who informed him from the floor of the audience chamber that the upstart prince would live.

'Live, you say? I heard he was close to death.'

'He is young, sire, he is strong, and Lord Cuitláhuac took three of my best surgeons with him to meet the caravan.' The fool swelled with pride. 'I trained them personally, sire. They did their jobs. Undoubtedly the prince will live.'

'Come closer, Mecatl,' hissed Moctezuma.

A worried expression crossed the fat surgeon's face as he shuffled on his knees to the side of the throne. 'Have I offended you, sire?'

Moctezuma ignored the question. 'Know this,' he said, 'and know your life depends on your silence. It is better for the peace of the realm if young Guatemoc does not live.'

Mecatl gasped. His shiny bald head glistened. A pulse of body odour rose from beneath his robes. 'Yes, sire . . . Do you wish me, then, to . . . ?'

Moctezuma placed his thumb and forefinger beneath his nostrils to block the smell of fear wafting from the surgeon. 'Nothing drastic, Mecatl. Nothing sudden. Nothing like the haemorrhaging venom we planned for Ishtlil. Nothing that would arouse suspicion. Some subtle poison that will sap Guatemoc's strength little by little, would be my recommendation, so that his relapse is gradual, spread over days, and his death, when it comes, appears a natural thing. Poor boy. His injuries were grave. He struggled mightily but in the end he was overcome . . . You get the idea?'

Mecatl gulped. 'Yes, sire.'

'And you can administer such a poison?'

'Yes, sire, but Lord Cuitláhuac has told us he will stay by Guatemoc's side until he has more fully recovered. He has ordered that a bed be brought for him into the prince's chamber. His presence will make it more difficult to do what you ask.'

'We are in a time of crisis,' Moctezuma said. 'Lord Cuitláhuac has urgent State duties to perform that will stop him playing nursemaid to his son. We will allow him that privilege today but from tomorrow I'll see to it he's kept busy with other things.'

'Thank you, sire.'

'I hope you understand me well, Mecatl?'

'I . . . I . . . I think so, sir.'

'Do what I have commanded, work the death of Guatemoc so it seems natural, and I will reward you. Fail in this task, allow anyone else to know of our little arrangement, raise the slightest suspicion, and you will die.'

Mecatl gulped again.

'Go now,' said Moctezuma, still holding his thumb and forefinger beneath his nose. 'Report progress to me daily.'

He felt a moment of quiet satisfaction as he watched the perspiring surgeon leave. He even began to hope things would soon start to go his way again. But within an hour his spies brought news to the palace of the recurrence of an omen of impending doom that had first troubled him a year earlier – a woman had passed through the streets of Tenochtitlan during the night, lamenting loudly, heard by many but seen by none. A year ago there had only been the sound of her weeping, but last night as she passed she had cried out in a terrifying voice, 'My children, we must flee far away from this city . . . My children, where shall I take you?'

On the morning of Tuesday 23 February, the fifth day after the expeditionary fleet had made its hasty departure from Santiago, the lookouts sighted a large island. Those who had been here before with the Córdoba expedition immediately recognised it as Cozumel. Beyond it to the west, stretching away into the hazy distance, lay a mainland of vast size and proportions.

276

Observing the prospect from the navigation deck of his great carrack, the *San Sebastián*, Pedro de Alvarado felt a quiet sense of satisfaction. It was unfortunate Cortés was not here to share this moment, but the fact was the discovery of the New Lands had begun. As to Cortés, God only knew what had happened to him. Had he been sent to the bottom of the sea in the storm? Was he drowned? Was he shipwrecked? Was he lost? Only time would tell. Meanwhile the conquest must go on, and Alvarado intended to make certain it did.

He turned to his good friend Father Gaspar Muñoz, whom he'd freed from the brig on their first day at sea and with whom he was now getting along famously. Not that Alvarado cared much for religious types but the Father was an exception – a hard man, no doubt, even a cruel man, if his reputation was anything to go by, but in many ways a man after his own heart. 'Looking forward to your return, Father?' he asked. 'I'm told you converted the whole population when you came with Córdoba.'

Muñoz was glaring at the island, his eyes screwed up against the spears of bright sunlight reflecting off the water. 'I had some success when our soldiers were amongst them,' he said. 'But that was last year. I shall wish to discover if they've stayed true to Christ since we left.'

Alvarado nodded. He'd heard how Muñoz treated converts who lapsed back to paganism and he thoroughly approved. You had to take a tough line with savages. Still, he was curious. 'Forgive me for asking, Father,' he said, 'but how can you be sure you've converted the heathens at all when they don't speak our language and you don't speak theirs? You had no interpreters on the Córdoba expedition.'

Muñoz gave him a strange look. It was a look, Alvarado thought, that a lesser man might even have found . . . chilling. 'It is a matter my order has studied,' the friar said eventually. 'As you can imagine, we frequently find ourselves as missionaries in lands where there is no common tongue. We have developed certain methods, certain techniques and signs, to overcome these difficulties. Naturally we require our converts to destroy their idols.' A fanatical glint appeared in Muñoz's eye. 'The zeal with which they do this – or their lack of it – speaks volumes. Then there are the symbols of our own faith. If they accept the cross and an image of the Virgin with glad hearts, we take it as sure evidence of conversion and after we are gone the sacred symbols continue to work wonders.'

'So these Cozumel Indians – they were happy to destroy their idols?'

'Most happy. And they understood they must desist in future from the vile cult of human sacrifice – did you know it is the practice of the Indians throughout these New Lands to cut out men's hearts and offer them to the devils they worship as gods?'

'So I had heard,' conceded Alvarado.

'I ended that abomination on Cozumel and afterwards we had the savages whitewash the blood from the walls of their temple and put the cross and an image of the virgin in the place where their principal idols had stood.' That fanatic gleam again. 'It will anger me if there has been any relapse.'

'It will be all the easier to detect relapse,' Alvarado offered, 'and make fresh converts now we have our own interpreter.' He nodded in the direction of the main deck, where the Indian kidnapped during the Córdoba expedition sat hunched in conversation with the young ensign Bernal Díaz, the farmboy whom Cortés had promoted above his station to the rank of ensign.

'Interpreter?' Muñoz said. His moist upper lip retracted to expose protruding yellow teeth as he sneered at the Indian. 'That creature has no Castilian at all, so I fail to see how he can interpret anything.'

Perhaps a slight exaggeration, Alvarado thought. During the creature's enforced stay in Santiago, it had acquired a smattering of Castilian, but it frequently misused the few words it knew, and spoke with an accent so thick as to be almost unintelligible. Was it even fully human? It had crossed eyes and long greasy hair hanging in a fringe over a low, sloping brow. It walked with a deep stoop, its knuckles trailing apelike almost to the ground.

Still, it would have to serve. Muñoz might face problems getting it to convey the rarefied spiritual notions he dealt in, but as long as it could put the words 'bring out your gold' into the native tongue, the stinking creature would be some use to Alvarado.

The Indian's name was Cit Bolon Tun but the Spaniards – those few who spoke to him at all – called him 'Little Julian'. This shunning of the man, and his treatment by most as though he were lower than a dog, partly explained why he had learned so little of the Castilian tongue. But there was also, Díaz sensed, a stubborn, rebellious streak about him. Most likely he simply did not *want* to learn the language of his oppressors, preferring to sulk and slouch, his squint eyes locked on the tip of his own nose, watching everything but making as little effort as possible to become useful.

Díaz had done what he could to remedy this state of affairs on the four-day voyage from Santiago, making a concerted effort to add to Little Julian's vocabulary – 'this is called a "dog", this is a "horse", this is a "mast", those are called "waves", that bird there is a "seagull"', and so on and so forth. As a campaigner from the Córdoba expedition himself, Díaz had been present when Little Julian was captured during a great battle fought on the outskirts of a town named Potonchan, but other than that name, which stuck in his memory, and the name of Julian's tribe, the Chontal Maya, he knew next to nothing about the people and culture of the region, except that they were savages who practised the disgusting rite of human sacrifice. During the voyage, in return for the language lessons Díaz had given, Julian had added to this information, telling him that the Chontal Maya were just one part of a great confederation of Maya tribes. The land they inhabited, the 'Yucatán', another name Díaz recalled from the year before, was a very extensive country of jungles filled with wild beasts including deer – which Little Julian insisted were a species of horse – and panthers, as well as many other creatures large and small, fierce and timid, that were unknown to Spaniards. The jungles were interspersed by cultivated gardens and farms where the main crop, maize, was one that Díaz had already tasted in Cuba even before his part in the Córdoba expedition. As he had seen with his own eyes, there were also great towns and even cities in the Yucatán, of which Potonchan was one. There Julian's two wives and seven children awaited his return, and it was his hope, Díaz learned, that he would be allowed to rejoin his family if and when the present expedition once again made its way to Potonchan.

'Do they even speak your language here?' Díaz asked, pointing to Cozumel now less than five miles dead ahead. It would be their first port of call, just as it had been the first port of call for the Córdoba expedition.

'Cozumel peoples is Maya,' Julian replied. 'I speak them like my own home.'

'Good. Very good.' Díaz clapped the squint-eyed Indian on his narrow shoulder, then stood and walked forward to the forecastle for a better look at the island he had visited last year, now revealing itself as a large, tear-shaped landmass, narrowing to a point in the north but a good six miles wide in the south and twenty-five or thirty miles in length. Densely overgrown with lush green tropical forest, it appeared, for the most part, to be flat and featureless, but in the northeast a fair-sized town of whitewashed, flat-roofed dwellings was visible on a low hill. As was the case with the few other Indian towns that Díaz had visited with Córdoba, a stone pyramid surmounted by a squat dark temple stood at the highest point.

In the Díaz family's farmhouse near the Castilian town of Medina del Campo, there had hung a painting of the three famous pyramids of Egypt, inherited by Bernal's father from his great grandfather, who had in turn – so the story went – inherited it from an even more antique relative who had been on the crusades to the Holy Land and had, at some time, passed through Egypt. Bernal's own memory of the painting was faint, but it was enough to confirm for him that the pyramids of the New Lands belonged to the same general class of objects as the Egyptian pyramids. The latter, however, had no temples on their summits, which rose to a sharp point, whereas in these New Lands – and Cozumel was no exception – all pyramids were built in a series of steps with flat and spacious summits often accommodating large structures.

Díaz could not forget the dismembered bodies and blood-splashed temple walls that had confronted him when he had first climbed to the top of the great pyramid of Cozumel – a scene that was all the more surprising for being so at odds with the seemingly friendly nature and gentle character of the island's inhabitants. Equally terrible had been Muñoz's fury at this proof not only of idolatry but also of human sacrifice. In view of the brutal chastisement of the natives that had followed, it was little wonder they'd converted so quickly and so willingly to the faith of Christ. Díaz hoped for their sakes, now Muñoz was returning, that they'd not relapsed.

After two hours more easy sailing in a light following wind, the *San Sebastián* rounded a headland and Cozumel's good anchorage revealed itself at the foot of the hill on which the town was built. The protected bay edged by palm trees presented an idyllic scene, the long, crescent-shaped beach of white sand packed with brown-skinned natives, many as naked as the day they were born, the more senior men in breach-clouts, their women in simple blouses and skirts, and every one of them cheering and waving as though the Spaniards were long-lost brothers returning to the fold.

How sweet and innocent they were! So different from the warlike mainland tribes of the Yucatán encountered by the Córdoba expedition when it had sailed on from here last year – tribes like the Chontal Maya from which Little Julian hailed.

Díaz heard a scuffle of bare feet and turned to see the cross-eyed interpreter had come forward silently and joined him on the forecastle. But Julian wasn't looking ahead at the crowded beach. Instead he was looking back along the ship to the navigation deck, where Father Muñoz still stood side by side with Don Pedro de Alvarado.

A sudden epiphany afforded Díaz a glimpse of the captain and the friar as the Indian must see them now, both of them greedy and both hungry, the one for human souls, the other for gold – both of them monsters who would stop at nothing, who would have no compunction, who would do anything, anything at all, to gratify their desires.

Muñoz placed his hand on Alvarado's shoulder and moved his fingers down in a manner peculiarly intimate to touch the captain's broken left arm where it hung, bandaged and splinted, in the sling fashioned by Dr La Peña. Some wordless communication seemed to be exchanged, then the friar turned, strode down the steps to the main deck and climbed through the hatch into the hold, the black sackcloth of his habit merging seamlessly with the shadows below.

Above, the coarse yells and work songs of the sailors filled the air as the *San Sebastián* dropped anchor in the bay of Cozumel. Below, in the tiny dark prayer cell that Pedro de Alvarado had caused to be built for him in the bowels of the great carrack, Father Gaspar Muñoz knelt naked on the bare boards, repeatedly flagellating his own back with the knotted cords of a cat-tail whip, beating himself with such force that streams of blood poured down over his buttocks and thighs. Lacerations he had inflicted a few days before, and that had begun to scab over and heal, burst open again under the scourging, and new wounds opened up amongst them until his flesh was a mass of blood and bruises.

He welcomed the pain – welcomed it and embraced it like a lover – and when it reached its crescendo he experienced, as he always did, a sudden detachment of soul from body, and entered into a state of holy and mystical union with the divine. A luminescence flared in the darkness, spreading and opening like the petals of some great night-blooming flower, and out of its midst, floating towards him and crossing in an instant the impossible distance between heaven and earth, appeared the shining figure of Saint Peter.

Though gratified, Muñoz was not surprised, for the saint had chosen to commune with him in these moments of ecstasy, and sometimes in dreams, since his first visit to Cozumel last year. The purpose of their mystical encounters had been made clear from the outset. Muñoz had been called to do God's work in the New Lands and the work was so important that Peter himself, the rock on whom Christ built his church, had been sent to guide him.

Now, as his glowing form filled the darkened prayer cell, the saint laid his huge hand on Muñoz's head, the warm, calloused palm bearing down, sending a tingling vibration through the kneeling friar's tonsured crown, through his skull and into his brain, penetrating his spine with a liquid glowing heat that diffused rapidly to all parts of his body and rose to a delicious peak as it entered his member of shame.

'Are you ready,' asked the saint, 'to begin the great work?'

'I am ready, Holiness,' Muñoz murmured, 'yet I fear I am not worthy.'

'You are worthy, my son. I have told you this many times before.'

'But I have desires, Holy Father. *Unnatural desires*. Are they not sinful?'

'When you do the work of God,' said Saint Peter, 'there is no sin in it.'

'Yes, Holiness.' Muñoz laid the scourge by his knees on the floor and now peered with hope into the saint's coal-black eyes. 'May I go out then, tonight, and take a child?'

A glint of fire sparked in the black depths of those eyes. 'To take a child so soon after the fleet has anchored would excite suspicion even amongst your fellow Spaniards and that would not serve our interests. You must proceed with stealth and be seen to go about your normal business. Today you will inquire into the progress of our sacred faith since you first planted it here. You will find it has withered on the vine while the worship of idols and the cult of human sacrifice have flourished in your absence. Tomorrow you will punish these abominations. On the third day, in the uproar that follows, you may take a child. Afterwards wait a day, then take another.'

'Thank you, Holy Father. You are generous.'

'One thing further, my son . . .'

'Yes, Holiness.'

'I saved Cortés from the storm. Even now he makes sail for Cozumel.'

Muñoz was suddenly confused, his head spinning: 'You *saved* him, Father. Why? I had hoped I had seen the last of him. He is not the right man to lead this expedition! With Alvarado as captain-general, I would be so much better placed to do God's work in the New Lands.'

The pressure of Peter's hand on Muñoz's head increased. It was as though a great weight forced him down. 'Such matters are not for you to decide,' the saint said, 'or even involve yourself in.'

'But, Holiness, I must object . . .'

'*You object?*' Saint Peter's voice became a roar like thunder and wind. 'Take care, Muñoz, for you are a mere man and you enter deep waters here. Wade another step and you may drown . . .'

Muñoz whimpered. The pressure on his head was unbearable. He felt himself driven down through the rough planks of the floor. 'I am sorry, Holy Father. In my zeal for God I spoke beyond my station.'

The pressure was lifted as quickly as it had been applied. 'You are forgiven, my son. But you must reach an accommodation with Cortés. You and he are my sword and my shield in these New Lands. You have both been called according to God's purpose.'

A man like Cortés, Muñoz thought, *called to God's purpose? How can that be?*

'This is not given to mortal man to know,' replied Saint Peter, from whom nothing was hidden. 'It is a secret thing that belongs to the Lord our God.'

The saint's glow was beginning to fade, his immense spirit withdrawing to heaven whence it came. 'Know that I visit Cortés in his dreams,' he said as he slipped away, 'know that I speak with him. Know he loves me, even as you love me. And know that all things work together for good to them that love God . . .'

It was the afternoon of Tuesday 23 February, the fifth day since their departure from Santiago de Cuba. *Five days!* Cortés thought. *Five bloody days!* Alaminos had estimated that Cozumel lay not much more than three hundred nautical miles due west of Santiago, and under normal conditions it should have been possible to sail such a distance in four days. Instead here was Cortés's proud flagship the *Santa María*, quite alone in the midst of the ocean sea, and with at least two days' hard sailing still ahead of her!

It was the storm on that wild night of Thursday 18 February that had changed everything. Miraculously all the horses, braced in their stalls by slings under their bellies, had lived through it without serious injury, and only one man had been lost; the toll could have been so much higher! But once the wind and the waves had died down it became clear that the *Santa María* had been separated from the rest of the fleet and blown very far to the south of her original course – indeed so far south that the next morning, Friday 19 February, she lay within sight of the Spanish settlement of Seville on the north coast of the island of Jamaica. They'd been obliged to put in to this undesirable shanty town filled with rats, thieves and mosquitos while the ship's carpenter, Martin Lopez, made good the worst of the storm damage, including a raging leak below the waterline that would have sunk them in a few more hours if they'd attempted to sail on.

The repairs required two days to complete so they'd not finally been able to put to sea again until Sunday 21 February, and in the two days since then they'd made slow progress. The winds on the voyage had been variable, sometimes dropping away completely and leaving them becalmed, as was the case this afternoon, frustrating Cortés, filling him with impotent rage and leaving him prey to all manner of anxieties. His greatest fear was that the rest of his fleet had been destroyed in the storm, that his enterprise was therefore already over before it had begun, and that his remaining men might force him to return to Cuba where Diego de Velázquez waited to hang him.

The only refuge from these uncharacteristically pessimistic and negative thoughts was in sleep and, since there was little else to do, and a dour humour was upon him, Cortés had resorted to his hammock for what he hoped would be a lengthy siesta this afternoon of Tuesday 23 February.

At first, however, sleep eluded him, and after a short while he understood why. Although his stateroom had been restored to its original spacious dimensions since Pepillo and Melchior had smashed down and removed the central partition, the evil emanations of Father Gaspar Muñoz still clung about the place. In particular they seemed to arise from the friar's four large leather bags. Miraculously these had not been washed away when seawater had flooded in on the night of the storm, and Cortés had retained them with some vague notion that he might return them to the Inquisitor when and if they were reunited.

The bags were stacked side by side in a corner at the back of the stateroom, where a jumble of Cortés's own belongings – heaps of clothes, a rack of hanging cloaks, assorted weapons and miscellaneous sacks and valises – shielded them from common view. Now, with a sigh, he extricated himself from his hammock, strode over to the untidy pile, pulled the bags free from their hiding place – ye gods they were heavy! – and lined them up in the middle of the floor.

They were padlocked, but that was scant impediment and their owner, if not at the bottom of the sea, was too far away to object. Cortés found a short steel dagger and, after further searching, a slim crowbar. In less than a minute he had the bags open.

How strange! Here were flensing knives, slim and wicked, razor sharp; here scalpels, each fine blade in its own miniature leather sheath; here lancets, here stilettos, here bone saws, here hatchets, here a selection of butcher's knives as long as a man's forearm, the blades of some smeared and matted with dried blood; here cleavers, here daggers of many different designs, and here were instruments of torture – hooks, screws, spikes, steel garrottes, heretics' forks, tongue pliers, eye-gouges, hammers and many more.

Cortés could have believed, or could at any rate have persuaded himself, that all these ugly devices were possessed by Muñoz for the purposes of his work as Inquisitor – work for the Lord, it should not be forgotten – were it not for the trophies of human skin and hair that he also found in the bags, not even hidden away but simply lying there in plain view. These appeared to be strips cut from the scalps of Indians, judging from the hair – thank God not from Spaniards – and though some were desiccated, others seemed relatively fresh and exuded a mephitic stink.

Holding his hand over his nose, Cortés placed everything back inside the bags, closed them as best he could with the broken padlocks, concealed them once again at the rear of his stateroom and retired to his hammock with his mind in turmoil.

What on earth – or in heaven or hell for that matter – was Muñoz up to?

Even as this question crossed his mind, sleep stole up on Cortés – not with its usual gentle seduction but brutally and fiercely – and took possession of him like an enemy seizing a prisoner. As this happened and his eyelids fluttered closed, he felt the hair on the back of his neck rising, as though he were in the presence of danger, and became convinced at some deep level of his awareness that something intelligent, something that was not human and not friendly, had entered the stateroom and now stood over him where he lay in his hammock.

I'm dreaming, he thought. And though he slept – and absolutely *knew* that he slept – though his body lay paralysed and he *knew* he could not move a muscle, he also knew, with that same sense of complete certainty, that all his faculties of reason and memory remained intact and could be deployed to probe and perhaps even understand the high strangeness of the moment. He remembered his dream of a few days before when Saint Peter had appeared to him, and immediately recognised certain similarities and a familiar flavour to the experience, most notably the sense of being both within a dream and an external observer to it.

But there was nothing familiar about what happened next.

With the peculiar, sinuous, unfolding motion of a serpent shedding its skin, Cortés's hammock transformed itself into a great broad table upon which he lay immobilised by tight iron shackles fastened around his ankles, knees, wrists and elbows. An intense crackling, buzzing sound filled his ears and, instead of the timber ceiling of his stateroom, he found himself looking up at an immense flat object, completely covered in intricate geometrical patterns somewhat like a huge painting, that hung suspended over his body and occupied his entire field of vision. His eyes followed the patterns which he now saw were formed from very fine lines, or filaments, brick-red in colour, etched into or in some other way fixed upon an ivory background, forming boundaries or tracks, between which were placed multitudes of bone-white clock faces with strangely bent and twisted black hands pointing to hours and minutes.

It was terrifying, although Cortés could not at first understand why, until it came to him that this colossal, convoluted, labyrinthine, machine-like image was sentient and that its attention was focussed upon him in a manner hellish and menacing. He thought he glimpsed a hint of eyes and of vibrating antennae, like those of some great predatory insect, and he began to feel deeply uncomfortable and restless. But he was unable to struggle against the irons that held him in place.

Then – again subtly and sinuously – the scene began to change, the giant effigy faded from view and Cortés, who still felt himself to be both inside and outside the dream at the same time, a participant and yet also an observer, caught glimpses of the space in which he was confined. Whatever and wherever it might be, this vast and umbral chamber, its floor littered with the rusting hulks of strange engines, its smoke-blackened walls dimly lit by flickering sulphurous flames, was no longer his stateroom, no longer, perhaps, even of this earth, but a place of horror where hunched fiends darted towards him through the shadows, chattering furiously in unknown tongues as they surrounded the table on which he lay prone and immobile.

'Stop,' Cortés wanted to shout, 'Please stop this! Show me no more!' But the words could not escape his mouth. Instead, seeming to emanate from everywhere and nowhere within the colossal, echoing chamber, he heard a rumbling, portentous voice, deep and ominous, yet filled with a sort of malicious glee, that said to him plainly and clearly: 'You're mine now.' And as though this were a signal, the figures surrounding him fell upon him and he had the sense that his body was nothing more than some huge, bloated cocoon and that these hunched, faceless beings were all over it, tearing it apart, clawing away lumps of matter and throwing them aside, gaining access to the real Cortés, the hidden Cortés, the demonic, sinful, wilfully wicked Cortés that he had striven so hard for so many years to conceal from the world.

And he thought: *This is the place of absolute truth. This is the place where everything about me is known. This is the place where every thought and every deed throughout my whole life is utterly transparent. This is the place where I am to be weighed and measured and found wanting.* But at that very instant, as the last vestiges of his protective outer husk were stripped away, Cortés heard another voice clear and pure, strong and filled with joy, that announced in the tones of a proclamation at court: 'Now the great transformation will begin!' And suddenly Saint Peter was with him, Saint Peter his saviour, Saint Peter his protector, Saint Peter his guardian, and he felt himself swept up from that hellish table and that infernal realm into the high blue empyrean, up, up to some immeasurable height from which he looked down upon the green, sparkling ocean and there, far below him, dancing across the waves, sails billowing in a good following wind that must have sprung up while he slept, was his own fair and elegant *Santa María* speeding towards the New Lands.

'Come,' said Saint Peter, 'let me show you that all is well for those called to God's purpose,' and he cradled Cortés in his huge hands, and carried him off through the vault of the firmament, across the face of the ocean, and brought him down in the blink of an eye to a great green island and a sheltered sandy bay lined with waving palms. In the bay, safe at anchor, with Alvarado's *San Sebastián* in pride of place, bobbed the carracks and caravels and brigantines of the expeditionary fleet – all ten of the lost ships intact after the storm, though some were wave battered, their crews busy on deck, squads of soldiers in armour going ashore to be welcomed and presented with bright garlands by great crowds of smiling and seemingly friendly Indians.

Above the bay rose a low, wooded hill, skirted by fields and capped by a town of white-walled, flat-roofed houses. At the centre of the town loomed a great stone tower in the form of a pyramid and on its summit squatted a dark, ugly building. 'That,' said Saint Peter, 'is the temple of the heathens. And this man' – in a trice the saint brought Cortés down to the bay again where Father Gaspar Muñoz stood on the strand – 'is the cure for their idolatry.'

Tall and severe in his black robes, his face shining with the uncompromising light of faith, Muñoz held aloft the cross of Christ.

'By this sign you shall conquer,' Saint Peter whispered, and in a flash Muñoz, the bay, the ships all dissolved, as though they were no more substantial than mist, and Cortés awoke in his hammock in his stateroom, sweat pouring in rivulets from his body, his heart thudding in his chest and the light of late afternoon pouring in through the open window.

He sensed the onward rush of the ship, heard the creak of the masts and the flap of the sails in a fair following wind and knew that in some sense his dream had touched on true things.

But what did it all mean?

What was that terrible shadowy chamber he had found himself in, where his soul had been stripped bare? What spiritual horror had Saint Peter rescued him from? And was he to understand that not just the promise of a successful conquest, but the price of his own eternal salvation, was some accommodation with that foul creature Muñoz, whose bags of blood-blackened knives and grisly human trophies seemed to lurk in hiding like savage beasts in their corner of the stateroom?

Muñoz had been holding up the big wooden cross all afternoon, making it a rallying point for the men as they disembarked. Around a hundred and fifty of them had assembled behind him now, most wearing the colourful garlands of fragrant flowers hung around their necks by the happy crowds of welcoming islanders. Astonishingly, these bare-arsed Cozumel Indians were actually singing and dancing with joy at the sight of the Spaniards, and had already brought basketloads of food and drink to the beach for their refreshment. *Fools!* thought Alvarado. The smiles would be on the other side of their faces once everything of value they possessed had been transferred to him – but meanwhile, he had to admit, their naïve gentleness was useful and made his job easier.

The same could not be said for Muñoz, who had already commandeered that squint-eyed ape Little Julian, slouching near him on the sand, for what he clearly intended to be a major investigation of the health of the faith on Cozumel. That was all very well, of course – Alvarado had no philosophical objections – but experience on Hispaniola and Cuba proved that searches of temples, the destruction of idols and other such business of the Inquisition stirred up resentment in these native races, and that once resentful they were inclined to hide their gold.

Alvarado had already assembled two hundred soldiers, all eager for booty, and now strolled over to Muñoz and took him aside. 'I'll be needing these men,' he said with an eye to the column lined up awaiting the friar's orders, 'and the interpreter.'

'You may not have them,' said Muñoz somewhat pompously. 'I intend to search the temple. I must know the fate of the cross and the icon of the Virgin I left here last year. I can't do such work alone.'

'Your search of the temple can wait until tomorrow, Father. In Cortés's continuing absence I am captain-general here and my need is greater than yours.'

'Ha! What need?'

Alvarado looked up. The sun was distinctly in the western sector of the sky. It had taken much longer than expected to prepare the fleet for a full-scale landing at Cozumel and get sufficient men disembarked. There were now less than three hours of daylight left and he wanted every house in the town searched before darkness fell. 'Today we look for gold,' he said. 'Tomorrow I'll give you all the men you need to save souls.' He rested his hand on the hilt of the great falchion hanging in its scabbard at his waist. 'Don't try to gainsay me, Father,' he added somewhat sternly. 'I'll have my way on this with your agreement or without it.'

Díaz could feel the atmosphere changing, the islanders becoming more agitated and suspicious with every passing minute as the squads of conquistadors went from house to house turning everything upside down, often brutally, with vulgarity and anger. He did everything in his power to be polite, respectful, even apologetic as his own men played their sorry part in the searches, but the fact was that nothing like this had happened here last year and the Indians were unprepared.

'Not that everything was roses,' Alonso de La Serna reminded him. 'Muñoz gutted their temple and smashed their idols and generally gave them hell.'

'They were the lucky ones!' said Francisco Mibiercas, whose unusually broad shoulders and muscular arms were the result of hours of daily practice with the *espadón*, the long, two-handed sword that hung in a scabbard at his back. 'Compared with what he did down the coast at Potonchan, he was an angel of mercy here.'

La Serna rolled his eyes. He was a tall, clever, cynical young man with a mop of fair hair, his otherwise handsome face marked by the scars of an old smallpox infection, and like all of them he hated Muñoz. 'Compared with what he did at Potonchan,' he said, 'the devil himself would have seemed an angel of mercy.'

Díaz could only agree. The three of them had been together at Potonchan when Muñoz's excessive zeal had so provoked the Chontal Maya that they had risen in their thousands, killed more than seventy of Córdoba's conquistadors and fatally wounded Córdoba himself. But at Cozumel, which Córdoba had planned to cultivate as a safe haven, Muñoz had been kept on a short leash, and the soldiery had been strictly enjoined against looting.

All of which went to explain why the fleet had been welcomed earlier today and why looks of stupefaction, hurt and disappointment had wiped the glow from the Indians' faces. Sprawling over the island's only hilltop, its narrow streets running higgledy-piggledy between rows of simple whitewashed adobe homes, the town of Cozumel had perhaps two thousand inhabitants. Every one of them – men, women and children who not long before had been hanging garlands around the Spaniards' necks – now stood by, sullen and resentful, as their simple possessions, consisting mostly of bales of cloth, cotton garments and wall hangings of little value, crude ceramics, green-stone ornaments, and a few objects of copper, as well as a handful of trussed turkeys, were turned out, raked over and trampled into the dust.

'God help us if Cortés does not return,' said La Serna, with a nod towards Alvarado, who was storming through the streets, followed by his personal crew of hardened, brutal killers, demanding 'gold, gold, gold'. The blond-haired captain did not seem able to understand that a place like Cozumel could never be, and had never been, rich in that substance. 'I'm told he's a gifted swordsman,' said Mibiercas wistfully, 'but he's not the stuff of which a good captain-general is made.'

As they watched, Alvarado loudly cursed his broken left arm which hung uselessly in a sling, turned to Little Julian, who was doing his best to keep up with him, drew the big falchion he liked to carry and dealt the interpreter a hard blow to the buttocks with the flat of the blade. Julian squealed and jumped and Alvarado went after him, sheathing the cutlass and pummelling Julian about the ears so hard with his right fist that the Indian fell half stunned to the ground.

Díaz sighed and exchanged a weary look with Mibiercas and La Serna. 'I think I'd better go and see if I can restore some sanity to the situation,' he said.

Alvarado couldn't believe it! He'd come all this way, braved all manner of risks, even eschewed fifteen thousand pesos of the bribe offered him by Don Diego de Velázquez, only to discover at the end of it all that there was no gold here!

It didn't bear thinking about.

But to add insult to injury, it seemed that this monkey interpreter couldn't interpret to save his life. Only the hayseed farmboy Bernal Díaz seemed to have the faintest inkling of what he was saying. As a result, and it was intolerable, in order to communicate with the native chief he was obliged to state his demands in Spanish to Díaz, who would then put them into some sort of pidgin for Little Julian who then put them to the chief. The whole laborious process then began again in the other direction as the chief's replies were filtered through Julian and Díaz back to Alvarado and the end result was: 'Humble apologies, great lord, but we have no gold here on Cozumel.'

The chief's name, Alvarado had managed to establish, was B'alam K'uk or some such barbarism. Not that he cared two hoots what the tall, rangy, straight-backed, grey-haired savage with the hooked nose and the blue cotton loincloth called himself. He wasn't fit to polish boots, in Alvarado's opinion, and had confirmed this the moment they met by throwing himself down in front of the hovel he'd emerged from, scrabbling at the filthy earth of the street and stuffing a handful of it into his mouth. Dear God! Whatever next? But this was the sorry creature in charge of Cozumel and here he was, back on his feet again, insisting there was no gold. In a sudden fit of anger, Alvarado strode forward, thrust out his good right hand and gripped the subhuman by his scrawny throat. '*What do you mean there's no gold?*' he yelled.

Eventually the answer came back through Julian and Díaz. There really was no gold.

'Lies!' Alvarado stormed. 'Lies and mendacity.' He tightened his fingers around the man's windpipe and spoke slow and clear and loud: 'You,' he roared, 'will . . . deliver . . . up . . . all . . . your . . . gold . . . by . . . noon . . . tomorrow – or I will burn your miserable town to the ground and butcher every man woman and child . . . Do you understand?'

The threat went back via Díaz and Little Julian to B'alam K'uk, who squirmed and choked in Alvarado's iron grip.

'Yes,' the chief finally managed to reply. 'I understand. Tomorrow at noon there will be gold.'

Early in the morning of the sixth day, after the mass sacrifices on the great pyramid, Moctezuma's spies were back with reports not only that the weeping woman had been heard again but also of a new development. Certain elders living in different wards of the city had been overheard speaking to one another about identical dreams they had all shared during the previous two nights. It seemed these dreams touched upon the security of the Great Speaker's rule.

This smacked of treason!

Moctezuma summoned Cuitláhuac from his vigil at Guatemoc's hospital bed and gave orders for the individuals concerned to be rounded up and brought to the palace. It was late morning by the time they arrived and he had them wait in the audience chamber while he composed himself. How dare they question his reign? When he was ready he entered with Cuitláhuac by his side and saw four wrinkled old men and three ancient crones cowering on the floor.

They had about them the smell of age and sickness, which he could not abide. Since their dreams were shared, he instructed the women to nominate one of their number who would speak for the rest, and the men to do the same, and sent the others shuffling out backwards to wait in the courtyard.

The man spoke first. He was very small, bird-like, with thin wispy hair, a weather-beaten, deeply lined, toothless face and the lumps of some canker protruding from the bones of his skull. 'Powerful lord,' he said in a voice that was surprisingly loud and strong, 'we do not wish to offend your ears or fill your heart with anxiety to make you ill. However, we are forced to obey you and we will describe our dreams to you.'

'Proceed!' snapped Moctezuma. 'You have nothing to fear.'

'Know then,' the old man continued, 'that these last nights the Lords of Sleep have shown us the temple of Hummingbird burning with frightful flames, the stones falling one by one until it was totally destroyed. We also saw Hummingbird himself fallen, cast down upon the floor! This is what we have dreamed.'

Maintaining his composure with great difficulty, Moctezuma next ordered the old woman to speak. 'My son,' she said, 'do not be troubled in your heart for what we are about to tell you, although it has frightened us much. In our dreams we, your mothers, saw a mighty river enter the doors of your royal palace, smashing the walls in its fury. It ripped up the walls from their foundations, carrying beams and stone with it until nothing was left standing. We saw it reach the temple and this too was demolished. We saw the great chieftains and lords filled with fright, abandoning the city and fleeing towards the hills . . .'

'Enough of your ravings, woman!' Moctezuma snapped. The symbolism could not have been more obvious. He turned to Cuitláhuac: 'You know what to do.'

The fate of the elders had never been in doubt. They had, after all, engaged in a conspiracy of dreams! Cuitláhuac gave the command and the palace guards dragged all seven of them off across the courtyard. A small dungeon had been prepared for them a mile away in the northern quarter of the city, and they would be kept there without food or water until they shrivelled up and died.

Observing from a window, Moctezuma saw that the old man who'd spoken in the audience chamber was dragging his feet, protesting in his astonishingly loud voice. With a mighty struggle, revealing unexpected strength for one his age, he brought the whole procession to a halt as they reached the edge of the courtyard. 'Let the Lord Speaker know what is to become of him,' he harangued the guards. 'Those who are to avenge the injuries and toils with which he has afflicted us are already on their way!'

As he heard these awful words, Moctezuma's sense of impending doom deepened. He had put on a brave face for Cuitláhuac but it was all he could do to control himself now.

The guards beat the old man to the ground and carried him away, senseless, but what he had said seemed to linger, linger, in the sullen noontime air.

Around noon on Wednesday 24 February, the sixth day after the fleet's departure from Santiago, Cozumel's chieftain B'alam K'uk presented himself to Alvarado and Father Muñoz on the *San Sebastián* at the head of a delegation of four of the town's elders. There was much oohing and aahing, accompanied by fearful glances cast at the glowering Inquisitor, as the dignitaries, ferried out from shore in a longboat, were hauled up to the great carrack. Though they had of course seen Spanish ships when Córdoba called here, it seemed they had never before been on board, and the experience was so overwhelming for them that they threw themselves face down, as the chief had done yesterday, and attempted to gather and eat dust from the deck.

Disgusting, Alvarado thought. He turned to Muñoz. 'Shall I kick them to their feet,' he asked, 'or would you like to have that pleasure, Father?' But before the friar could respond, the Indians popped up again and stood there bobbing and grinning like monkeys. Unprompted, Little Julian said something in the local lingo, at which B'alam K'uk stuck a hand inside his sopping wet breechclout – wet from the sea, Alvarado hoped! – and pulled out a little cloth bundle, also wet. He proceeded to unwrap it, revealing a yellow gleam.

The bundle contained a few trinkets of poor-quality gold – a miserable necklace, two ear-spools, a figure of a bird no larger than a man's thumb and a little statue of a human being which, on closer examination, proved to be made of wood covered with gilt!

'A sorry start,' said Alvarado, keeping his voice even. 'Now show me the rest.'

The usual gibbering interchange involving Julian, Díaz and the chief followed, in which Julian looked increasingly frantic as Díaz kept plying him with questions while the chief and the elders answered with eyes downcast. Finally Díaz turned to Alvarado and said, 'I'm afraid that's all they have, sir.'

'All they have?'

'Yes, sir. Julian's Spanish is very hard to understand but he's clear enough on this. He says these islanders are very poor and anyway the Maya don't much value gold.'

'Don't value gold, eh? Bloody liars!' With a sudden rush of anger, Alvarado stepped in on the chief, grasped the waist of his loincloth, lifted him screeching from the deck, strode to the railing, threw him overboard, and watched with satisfaction as he hit the water with a tremendous splash. His only regret was that he hadn't had the use of both hands so he could have thrown the savage further and harder. 'Father,' he said to Muñoz. 'The time has come for you to attend to the souls of these poor benighted bastards. God help them, but if you find they've turned their backs on the Christian faith, you may do as you wish to them and their temple, and their gods. You have my blessing.'

Muñoz was in a holy rage. At last, *at last*, the time had come to strike!

But it was mid-afternoon before the three hundred conquistadors he'd asked for were mobilised and landed and the remainder of the force deployed to guard the ships.

Finally, with Alvarado at his side, the Inquisitor led the way up the hill into the maze of hovels of the Indian town. The streets were deserted and the reason why soon became clear. A babble of voices, hoots and cries, drums and whistles, was heard ahead and, as the phalanx of conquistadors entered the main square, a great throng of islanders, almost the whole population it seemed, surged forward to bar the approach to the pyramid.

'Do something about this, Alvarado,' Muñoz said, and watched with approval as the handsome captain ordered twenty musketeers forward in two ranks, one kneeling, one standing, and had them fire a salvo that cut a great swathe through the crowd and sent hysterical Indians running and screaming in all directions. When the smoke cleared the square was empty but for the dead. Muñoz raised his cross, shouted, 'God wills it!', and the conquistadors charged with a great yell.

The seventy-two steps were steep and narrow – one had to pick one's way with care – and as the Inquisitor reached the top of the pyramid only a little out of breath, he saw at once that Saint Peter had spoken true. The Indians had indeed reverted to their heathen abominations.

The first proof of this was the life-size stone sculpture of a man with leering face and jug ears that half sat and half reclined near the edge of the summit platform holding a stone plate across his chest. In the plate, surrounded by a thick puddle of blood, sat two freshly extracted human hearts, one it seemed still palpitating.

As the conquistadors gathered round with expressions of horror, Muñoz pointed an accusing finger at the idol. 'Who will do God's work?' he thundered, and immediately a dozen men put strong hands on the statue and began to rock it back and forth. It was heavy but, as Muñoz watched with approval, it was broken free of its plinth, lifted and then thrown forcefully down the steps. It rolled over and over, pieces breaking off it, cracking and smashing, gathering speed as it went, until it exploded into a thousand fragments in the plaza below, scattering the crowd that had once again begun to gather there and evoking from them a dreadful chorus of superstitious howls and groans.

Alvarado had already pressed on into the dismal, dark temple that crouched in the midst of the summit platform like some monstrous toad, its narrow doorway decorated with hellish carvings of fiends and devils. The single rectangular room, measuring perhaps ten paces in length and five in width, had a beastly stink about it, and as his eyes grew accustomed to the dim light he saw that a huge figure that was not quite human, arms outstretched, massy hands and fingers curled into claws, reared up close to the back wall. There came a sudden, unearthly screech, and out of the figure's towering shadow darted something hunched and capering with naked feet and long, matted hair, dressed in filthy black robes. Alvarado drew his falchion in a trice and, as this shrieking apparition plunged towards him, wielding what he now recognised as a long stone knife, he raised the point of his weapon and punched it forward into his attacker's face, catching him between the eyes so that it split his skull and drove deep into his brain.

The Indian – and it was an Indian – fell dead on the spot. So firmly lodged was the falchion that Alvarado had to brace his foot over the man's mouth in order to pull the heavy blade free.

He looked again at the enormous figure at the back of the room. For a moment he'd thought it was alive, but now his eyes, always quick to adjust, revealed the banal truth. It was just an idol, ugly and malformed like any other pagan mummery. The face, jaws and teeth were those of some species of dragon; the body, though scaled, was more or less human. At its feet sprawled the corpses of a young woman in her twenties and a girl child of perhaps six years of age, their breasts split open, no doubt to extract the hearts that had sat in the plate held by that other idol outside. Blood pooled on the floor, was smeared everywhere on the smoke-blackened walls of the chamber, and a flagon or two of it had been set aside in a large stone basin. Also laid out were assorted cloths, likewise sopping with blood, certain fruits and a collection of dried skulls and human bones.

Alvarado sheathed his falchion and placed his right hand over his nose. Gods! The smell of this place! He advanced into the gloom, kicked aside a pile of cloth to the right of the idol and quickly picked up and pocketed three gold objects that had been hidden there, one resembling a lizard, one fashioned in the form of a panther, and one representing an erect human phallus, rather short and thick. They were, he observed, of noticeably better quality than those the lying chief had brought to him this morning.

'So you have your gold?' said a sibilant, lisping voice behind him.

Alvarado whirled and saw Muñoz in his black habit silhouetted in the doorway.

'I do, Father, though precious little of it. Have you any objection?'

'Oh none,' Muñoz said. 'None at all. I am always ready to render unto Caesar the things which are Caesar's.'

Díaz, Mibiercas and La Serna were conscripted, along with many more of the soldiery, to take a hand in the destruction of the great idol of the temple. Díaz was willing enough; he prided himself on being as good a Christian as any of them. Still, he dreaded what must come next when the Indian town rose in outrage, as he knew it would, against the interlopers.

The business with the idol didn't go well. Fifty men dragged it forth from the temple with ropes, sweating and heaving, singing verses from the book of Numbers that Muñoz had taught them: 'You will drive out all the inhabitants of the land before you. Destroy all their carved images and their cast idols, and demolish their high places. And ye shall dispossess the inhabitants of the land, and dwell therein: for I have given you the land to possess it.' With a mighty effort, even while they still sang, the conquistadors brought the huge heathen statue, which must have weighed close to a ton, to the edge of the steps, where it tottered dangerously. Down below the square was now packed full with townsfolk, so that there was no room for them to move, no space for those at the base of the steps to flee even if they wanted to.

Díaz let go his rope and walked over to Muñoz. 'Father,' he said, 'we must wait to throw this vile thing down.' He pointed to the crowd standing in stupefied silence, the men, the women, the elders, the children of the town gazing up, horrified, frozen in place. 'If we throw it down,' Díaz added, 'people are going to die – a lot of people. Let me take a squad into the square and clear the Indians out of there. When they're gone, that's the time to smash the idol.'

'No,' said Muñoz, his buck teeth protruding beneath his moist upper lip.

'*No*, Father? Why in Heaven not?'

'Don't you *dare* invoke Heaven to me, boy!' Muñoz thundered.

'But this is not a Christian act, Holy Father! We cannot simply slaughter these innocents.'

'They are far from innocent!' Muñoz roared. 'You were here with me, were you not, when we came with Córdoba?'

Díaz nodded. 'I was here,' he admitted.

'Then you know these heretics accepted our faith. You know they accepted the destruction of their idols. You know they placed the cross of Christ and the icon of the Virgin in yonder temple behind us . . .'

'Yes, Father,' said Díaz wearily. 'I know these things.'

'Yet the cross is no longer there. The icon of the Virgin is no longer there. Instead we see this . . . this' – Muñoz turned his basilisk glare on the idol – 'this *enormity* in their place, this *vile thing*, this manifestation of evil. And it is they' – he was spraying spittle now as he pointed down at the massed Indians in the square – 'it is they alone, of their own wicked choice who have done this. So on their own heads be it!' And with a loathsome smile that would afterwards haunt Díaz in his nightmares, Muñoz gave the signal, and the conquistadors gathered around the idol, laughed with glee and gave it a final muscular heave – God save them – and it was launched on its journey down the steps, a ton of stone tumbling and bouncing, gathering speed, flying high into the air until it pounded down in the thick of the screaming, panicking crowd, smashing into a dense knot of people and transforming them in an instant into blood and bone and brain matter and smearing them like some obscene condiment over the flagstones of the plaza.

A shocked silence fell.

Then a wail of horror.

And then, as Díaz had expected, a roar of outrage and a surge of armed men up the steps.

There was only ever one possible outcome to the wild fighting that followed. The conquistadors were armoured, disciplined, ruthless, and equipped with vastly superior weapons, and with Alvarado leading them, his falchion dripping blood, they were merciless and profligate in their anger. By nightfall the Indians with their stone knives and primitive bows had suffered at least a hundred dead, large parts of the town were in flames, and the elders and the priests who served the temple had been captured.

On the morrow, Muñoz announced triumphantly, they would all be burnt to death for their sins.

* * *

'Let the Lord Speaker know what is to become of him,' the old man had warned. 'Those who are to avenge the injuries and toils with which he has afflicted us are already on their way!'

Moctezuma had brooded on these baleful words for the remainder of that day and the long, troubled night that followed.

Avengers? Already on their way?

In this fated year of One-Reed he could not ignore the possibility that here was yet another omen of the return of Quetzalcoatl. The next day, therefore, the seventh after the failed holocaust at the great pyramid, he sent Cuitláhuac to the dungeon to interrogate the elders again. Was it men or gods who were coming? What road would they follow? What were their intentions?

The interrogation should have lasted most of the morning, but within the hour Cuitláhuac was back bringing terrible news.

The prisoners had vanished during the night.

Every one of them.

'What of the jailers?' Moctezuma demanded.

Cuitláhuac had already caused them to be arrested, he said, but they most vehemently protested their innocence and, for what it was worth, he believed them. They were loyal men whom he himself had appointed to the task. The prison gates had been firmly locked and the bars were secure. Cuitláhuac had inspected the floor carefully but no tunnel had been burrowed through it – and besides, the elders would never have had the strength for such a task. The roof was intact. In short, the explanation offered by the jailers themselves – namely that the prisoners must have been powerful sorcerers who had used magic to make their escape – seemed the most reasonable one.

'What is to be the fate of the jailers, lord?' Cuitláhuac asked.

'Send them to kill the families of the sorcerers,' Moctezuma said. 'Husbands, wives, children – all are to be killed. They're to dig in the places where their houses stood until they reach water. All their possessions are to be destroyed.'

But it turned out that not one of the elders had any living family, most were in fact beggars, their houses were poor places barely worth destroying, and they had almost no possessions.

After ordering Cuitláhuac to have the jailers skinned alive,

Moctezuma fell into a black mood and retreated to his secret chambers in the depths of the palace. He took with him a basket of the sacred mushrooms called *teonanácatl*, 'Flesh of the Gods', which had proved so helpful in facilitating his audiences with Hummingbird.

Each day for seven days after she had been reprieved from death beneath the sacrificial knife, Tozi spent every moment she could spare from her work with Huicton flowing invisible and undetected amongst the prisoners in the fattening pens of Tenochtitlan, searching for Coyotl. The women's pen where she had been held was still quite empty, though slowly being restocked, and it required only a short visit to satisfy herself that Coyotl was not there. Then she turned to the four pens holding male prisoners, all of them stuffed to bursting point, and searched each one of them systematically, but again without result. Finally she moved on to the five further great pens scattered around the city outside the sacred plaza and crisscrossed each of these repeatedly, but never once did she see any sign of the little boy who had been so cruelly snatched away from her by Ahuizotl.

Yet, like a ghost who would not be laid to rest, Coyotl continued to haunt her.

Chapter Forty-Six

First light on the morning of Thursday 25 February, the seventh day since the *Santa María*'s departure from Santiago de Cuba, revealed the island of Cozumel less than four miles ahead. Eerily, the Indian town that perched on the low hill on the northeast side of the island was *exactly* as it had appeared to Cortés in his last dream of Saint Peter.

Exactly, that is, except for one thing – the thick pall of smoke that now rose above the whitewashed, flat-roofed houses like a symbol of divine wrath.

'What do you make of that, Don Antón?' Cortés asked the grizzled pilot who stood by his side leaning on the newly repaired oak rail surrounding the navigation deck.

Alaminos shrugged. 'Looks like trouble,' he said.

Cortés could only agree. Alvarado, whose love of gold was only exceeded by his love of violence, would have assumed the position of captain-general in his absence. And with a man like that in charge of this great expedition . . . Well, anything was possible.

Worse, Muñoz was also on board Alvarado's ship.

Cortés looked across the dancing waves to the pyramid that towered above the smoking town. Stepped, not smooth-sided like the famous pyramids of Egypt, it too was exactly as Saint Peter had revealed in his dream. Equally disturbing were the squat familiar contours of the dark stone edifice perching on the pyramid's summit. The saint had described it as 'the temple of the heathens' and had made a point of singling out Muñoz as 'the cure for their idolatry'.

Muñoz in his dark robes! Muñoz with his cross!

(And his bags of knives and gruesome trophies!)

Was Cortés never to be free of him?

Was he only to conquer, as Saint Peter had intimated, if he made an accommodation with that vile man?

As the *Santa María* rounded the headland, the other ten ships of the scattered fleet, about which Cortés had fretted for these past seven days, came into view in the sheltered bay, with Alvarado's *San Sebastián* placed closest to shore. All this, too, was exactly as it had been in the dream, but for the happy crowds of Indians with their garlands, who were nowhere to be seen on this bright morning, and that ominous pall of smoke looming above the town and sending down a rain of fine ash.

'It's good to be back on dry land,' Gonzalo de Sandoval said.

'Still feels like the deck's swaying under my feet,' replied García Brabo, the tough Extremeno sergeant whom Sandoval had begun to count as a friend since the battle with Velázquez's guards on the road outside Santiago harbour. Clearing his throat noisily, Brabo spat a copious gob of phlegm. 'Sea's not a natural place for a man to be,' he added. 'If it was, we'd be born with fins and scales like fish.'

'Reckon I'm going to learn to swim,' said Sandoval, who had always hated the ocean with its vast impersonal power and its raging unpredictable moods. He'd felt sure the *Santa María* would go to the bottom and he would drown, during the frightful storm that had battered them as they left Santiago. One great wave had washed completely over the ship, but by then he'd been clinging for dear life to the foremast and had survived – unlike the unfortunate soldier whom he'd seen swept overboard, his screams snatched away by the wind as the heaving vessel somehow ploughed on.

'Don't see the point of swimming,' Brabo said after a moment's thought. 'Ship goes down and you're dead anyway. Better drown fast and get it over with than drag it out for another day.'

The two men were marching side by side up the hill towards the burning Indian town. Wearing his steel cuirass and a broadsword strapped to his hip, the caudillo himself strode a few paces ahead, leading the way. Behind came the other eighty soldiers who'd survived the journey from Santiago. Left to guard the *Santa María* in the anchorage were Cortés's manservant Melchior, the young secretary Pepillo and the full crew of twelve sailors under the command of Alaminos. From words exchanged with sailors guarding the other ships, it seemed that there had been a major battle here in Cozumel the night before and that Don Pedro de Alvarado and Father Gaspar Muñoz had ordered almost the entire expeditionary force up to the town to witness some kind of 'punishment' that was about to be meted out to the local inhabitants.

As they reached the outskirts, the smell of burning became stronger and more pungent. There was a reek of roasting flesh that Sandoval had been trying to ignore as they'd climbed the hill, but that now began to impress itself on him forcefully. Suddenly nervous, no longer quite so happy to be on land, he peered ahead through wreaths of smoke. 'Think we're going to see any action here?' he asked Brabo as they entered a narrow street between two rows of simple flat-roofed houses, which appeared to be constructed of wattle and daub plastered over with adobe.

'Nah,' said the sergeant. 'We'd have heard it by now if there was still any fighting going on. It's all done and dusted. Look – there!' He pointed to the corpse of a small, thin Indian woman sprawled half in and half out of a doorway. Her throat had been cut. 'What the hell . . .' Sandoval muttered as more bodies began to emerge from the smoke – a grey-haired elder spread-eagled in the middle of the street with a massive head wound, two boys spitted by crossbow bolts, four young men who'd been badly mauled by sword blows, their guts hanging out, piled in a heap.

Up ahead, looming above the single-storey native dwellings, the temple on the pyramid came into view. Now cries of terror and gruff Spanish jeers began to rise up from that direction.

'With me, lads,' yelled Cortés, breaking into a run. 'At the double.'

Bernal Díaz was opposed in principle to the notion of burning human beings to death. He'd seen it done a number of times during his career as a soldier, and once in his youth in Medina del Campo, the region of Castile where he'd grown up, when a group of heretics, condemned by the Inquisition, had been burnt at the stake. Unlike his friends and fellow soldiers, who often relished such scenes, Díaz had always been sickened by them. Perhaps it was because he had an over-active imagination, whilst others often seemed to have none, but when he considered what was involved in death by burning – the slow, prolonged agony, the melting of the flesh from the bones, the body fat itself becoming fuel for the fire – he simply could not understand why anyone would wish to inflict such a terrible fate on others. Surely human kindness and Christian charity required quite the opposite – that one would rush to rescue the victims, no matter how hateful they might be or how disagreeable their views, rather than stoke the flames?

So Díaz felt acutely uncomfortable to find himself amongst the small army of conquistadors now gathered in the plaza at the base of the pyramid to witness the town's leaders and heathen priests being burnt at the stake. The rest of the population of two thousand – most had survived the night – had also been herded into the plaza and stood there under guard, shivering and crying out in fear.

Though Díaz had refused to participate in the lynch mob, five wretched Indians had already been chained and thrown into the embers of one of the buildings set alight around the plaza. Three of these unfortunates were still alive, their flesh slowly roasting, and as their screams rose to heaven some twenty more, including the chieftain B'alam K'uk and the man identified by Little Julian as the high priest, were tied to stakes and surrounded by a mountainous pile of logs. Meanwhile Muñoz marched up and down in front of them, holding an open Bible, loudly deploring the abomination of human sacrifice – but what was burning at the stake, Díaz wondered, if not a form of human sacrifice? – and declaiming some pious nonsense about how it fell to the Inquisitor to be a physician of souls, how heresy was a disease and how the flames were a specific remedy for it.

Positioned at the edge of the massed soldiery, Díaz stood amongst a small group of hardened veterans who, like him, had sailed with the Córdoba expedition and already knew all too well the trouble Muñoz was capable of causing. Turning to his friend Alonso de La Serna he whispered: 'It's all happening again.'

La Serna rolled his eyes: 'And there's still nothing we can do about it.'

306

Francisco Mibiercas was listening. 'Maybe there is something we can do,' he offered.

Díaz and La Serna both turned to him in surprise, but Mibiercas appeared unruffled. 'We're all agreed this friar's no good, right?'

'He's evil,' nodded Díaz.

'And he's going to get us killed,' added La Serna.

'So let's kill him first then.' Mibiercas quickly glanced around. 'Not here, obviously. Not today. But a chance will come and when it does we'll take it.'

As Díaz registered that the swordsman was completely serious, there came a commotion on the eastern edge of the plaza and a large group of armed men spilled out of a side street and came on at a run. At their head was Hernando Cortés. Just behind him Díaz recognised Gonzalo de Sandoval.

'What the hell's going on here, Pedro?' Cortés demanded. He walked right up to Alvarado and stood just inches away from him, his right hand on the hilt of his broadsword. He noticed that his old friend, whose left arm was in a sling, had likewise placed his right hand on the hilt of his sword – or rather cutlass, for he was wearing the falchion he'd taken from Zemudio.

'I would have thought it was obvious,' Alvarado replied innocently. 'I'm prosecuting the business of this expedition in your absence.' His blue eyes had a cold, dangerous glint but he smiled, showing white, even teeth. 'Welcome back, by the way. We've missed you, Hernando.'

Although Cortés was seething with rage, his mind was clear, quickly sifting through his options and making decisions. His intentions for Cozumel had been entirely peaceful – to win the hearts of the inhabitants and make them his allies so that he could fall back on the island as a place of safety if necessary. Instead he found himself confronted by a scene of murder and mayhem, with that strutting fool Muñoz about to burn a large group of Indians, apparently with Alvarado's full support.

The first and most important matter, Cortés realised, was to impose his own authority on this situation at once, otherwise he would lose face in front of the men, something that he could never allow. That meant publicly countermanding Alvarado. He was reluctant to humiliate such a good and true friend, but he was left with no alternative. Muñoz would also have to be humbled and Cortés felt some reluctance here too, on account of his strange dreams, but again he could see no other option.

'Don Pedro,' he said, speaking formally and in a loud voice, 'you have done wrong here and acted against my wishes.'

Alvarado's face flushed and he spoke in a whisper: 'What are you saying, Hernán? The men are listening. Don't make a fool of me in front of them.'

Ignoring the appeal, Cortés pointed to the piles of meagre booty lined up in the plaza, to the captive townsfolk and to the twenty who were about to burn. 'This no way to pacify a country,' he boomed so that everyone could hear, 'robbing the natives of their possessions, taking them prisoner, razing their town . . .' He turned to Muñoz who was standing frozen nearby: 'And you, friar! Is it really your plan to burn these poor Indians as though they were Bogomils or Albigensians?'

'They are filthy heretics!' screeched Muñoz. 'They accepted the faith when I came to this island with Córdoba, but they have relapsed.'

'I see no heretics here,' Cortés yelled back. 'I see ignorant savages in need of further teaching, in need of Christian love and understanding, not the flames.'

The Inquisitor raised the Bible and thrust it out in the direction of the condemned men, who gazed at him with fear and fascination like rabbits hypnotised by a snake. 'Light the fire,' Muñoz screamed at a soldier who stood by with a burning brand. 'Let us purge their souls in the flames so they may stand purified before the Lord on the day of judgement . . .'

The soldier moved the brand towards the kindling.

'Don't light that fire,' Cortés warned him. 'There'll be no burning today.'

The soldier looked around uncertainly.

'I speak as your Holy Inquisitor,' roared Muñoz. 'Light the fire, man!'

'And I speak as your captain-general,' said Cortés. 'Light that fire and I'll see you hanged.'

The soldier cursed and stepped back sharply, setting the brand down on the plaza. Muñoz rushed to pick it up but, at a nod from Cortés, García Brabo was suddenly in his path. 'Not so fast,' he said. 'You heard the caudillo. Nobody's getting burnt today.' Muñoz growled with frustration and tried to push past, but Brabo grappled with him, twisting his arm so sharply behind his back that he gasped with pain. 'I wouldn't struggle if I were you,' advised the lean, grey-haired sergeant. 'Just do as the captain-general says, there's a good friar.'

Cortés turned to Alvarado, speaking quietly now: 'You were too hasty, Pedro. You should have waited for me before taking such drastic action, and now you're going to have to make reparations to put everything right.'

'Reparations? What on earth do you mean?' From the thunderous look on Alvarado's face, Cortés half expected his friend to challenge him, but he pressed on. 'You can start by cutting those men loose from the stakes. It'll look better for you if you give the order than if I give it over your head.'

Alvarado's handsome face contorted in a furious grimace and his mouth worked as though chewing on a tough lump of meat, but at last he barked the command and soldiers scrambled over the heaped logs to free the elders. Cortés nodded with satisfaction. 'Free the townspeople you're holding under guard as well, please. All of them. There's been some killings I see?'

'Yes,' Alvarado admitted. 'We burned five –' he gestured towards a smouldering building – 'and a few score died in the fighting last night. It's their own fault. They should have surrendered.'

'Would you surrender, Pedro, if our home town was attacked?'

'That's different. We're Christians, they're heathens—'

'Heathens whom we need as allies, not as enemies. Heathens whose knowledge of the lands and peoples that lie ahead is of vital importance to us. We'll have to pay blood money to satisfy them on the dead. Work with Little Julian to find out what they'll accept.'

'Blood money for savages? Have you lost your mind?'

Cortés fixed Alvarado with a withering glare. 'It's your madness, not mine, that caused the problem here, Pedro. If you'd waited for my arrival, none of this would have happened and we'd have what I want at no cost.' He smiled: 'But they *are* savages. A small price in glass beads and shiny baubles will likely satisfy them.'

Alvarado had a brooding, sulky look, but seemed to brighten at the prospect of swindling the simple-minded natives. Cortés wasn't finished with him, however. 'Did you find gold?' he asked suddenly.

'No,' Alvarado replied a little too soon, his eyes hooded.

'Come, Pedro,' Cortés prompted. 'I know you too well.'

'There is some gold,' Alvarado scowled. 'A few pieces we found in the temple. A few more in the richer houses of the town. Nothing of great value. I have them on board my ship.'

'I want you to give them back,' Cortés said.

'But—'

'Don't beat around the bush! Everything goes back. Every piece of gold, every pot, every bale of cloth . . . Do this, Pedro, do it willingly and we won't fall out.'

As Alvarado set about his tasks, Cortés walked over to Muñoz who was seated on the lower steps of the pyramid, guarded by Brabo and Sandoval. 'Thank you,' Cortés said to the two soldiers. 'I'll handle things from here.' He remained outwardly calm, looking round the plaza as he waited for them to get out of earshot. Crowds of Indians were streaming back to their dwellings, and the elders he'd reprieved from the flames were gathered round Alvarado and Little Julian, engaged in what looked like a heated negotiation. All well and good, he thought, but what was he going to do about Muñoz? Under normal circum-stances he might have been inclined to arrange a fatal accident for the troublesome friar, but his dreams of Saint Peter gave him pause.

'My apologies if I've handled you roughly today, Father,' he said, 'but please understand that we're here to conquer and settle these New Lands. This is a military expedition, I am its leader and you are placed under my command.'

'That's not my understanding at all,' said Muñoz, his face mulishly set. 'As I had it from His Excellency Governor Velázquez, we are here only to trade, to explore and to spread the word of God. You may claim no special powers as a military commander, and in matters of evangelism – *and heresy* – I have a free hand.'

310

'You have been misinformed, Father,' Cortés insisted, working hard to keep the anger that he felt out of his voice. 'By all means evangelise. I want you to do that, and I shall help you. I share your desire to spread the word of God in these heathen realms. But you must never get in my way or create unnecessary hostility for us as you did today. No matter what you think you know, our mission *is* conquest and settlement. If you ever jeopardise that mission again, I'll crush you like a louse in a seam.'

'Big talk for a small man,' sneered Muñoz getting to his feet.

The friar had such an advantage in height that Cortés almost unconsciously found himself sidling up the first two steps of the pyramid so they were level. 'No mere talk,' he insisted as he completed this awkward manoeuvre. 'I have absolute jurisdiction in all military matters and you must defer to me.'

Muñoz just stared at him for a moment, his irises absolutely black and expressionless like two blank holes in his eyes, then he turned abruptly and began to walk away, his robes flapping.

'Hold,' barked Cortés. 'Our business is not done!'

Muñoz stopped and looked back, one bushy eyebrow quizzically raised: 'Yes?'

'You've bunked on the *San Sebastián* these past seven days. Kindly continue to do so.'

When the Inquisitor smiled, as he did now, there was something of the Barbary ape about him. 'No doubt you think to inconvenience me,' he said, 'but what you propose was my intention anyway. I find Don Pedro's company congenial. He would, in my opinion, make a far better captain-general than you. Send my page with my bags.'

'Alas that will not be possible. Your bags were washed overboard in the storm.'

Cortés wasn't sure why the lie had leapt so readily to his lips, except that in a strange way he felt pressured, *cornered*, by his dreams, which seemed to foist Muñoz upon him like an unwelcome house guest. Perhaps this ploy with the bags was his way of striking back. At the very least, he hoped, it would disconcert the Inquisitor, and he was pleased to see it did so.

'How dare you?' Muñoz blustered. 'You evict me from my cabin, imprison me on another ship – though God in his wisdom guided Don Pedro to release me – and now you tell me you have failed to guard property that was essential to my work as Inquisitor.'

Cortés shrugged. 'A great wave near sunk us and your bags were washed away. Nothing could be done to save them. Sincere regrets . . .'

Muñoz's frown deepened, his sallow features taking on a calculating look. 'My simpleton of a page should have protected them. Have him sent to me on the *San Sebastián*.'

'Unfortunately I cannot oblige.'

'Why? Was he washed away also?'

'No, but he's working for me now. I need the assistance of a secretary and he has the requisite skills.'

At this Muñoz actually stamped his foot: 'You cannot do this!' he shouted.

'Certainly I can,' said Cortés. Regardless of your opinion of me, I *am* the captain-general and I'll have whomever I like as my secretary.'

Muñoz came pounding back now, his sandals slapping on the stones of the plaza, and thrust his face with his protruding upper teeth next to Cortés's ear. 'It's not my opinion you should be concerned about,' he said in a strangely triumphant tone. 'You will be held accountable by a higher authority.'

Cortés laughed. 'If you mean your friend Velázquez, I don't give a fig what that oaf thinks or does.'

'Oh no,' said Muñoz. 'Not Velázquez.' He moved even closer, his breath moist and warm. 'Your patron saint is Peter. Am I not right?'

Though the day was sultry, Cortés felt a shiver run down his spine. 'Who told you that?' he asked, taking another step up the pyramid.

'He comes to me in dreams,' said Muñoz with a sinister smile. 'He speaks of your love for him.' Then he was gone again, scattering the crowd, the milling Indians stumbling fearfully out of his path.

Crouched side by side with Melchior at the corner of a side street looking onto the plaza, Pepillo gasped as Muñoz turned his back on Cortés for the second time and came striding straight towards them. 'Quick,' said Melchior, 'in here.' He grabbed Pepillo by the collar, dragged him a few paces along the street and through the low doorway of a half-burnt hovel. They ducked down behind the fire-blackened wall, the sun scorching them through a great hole in the collapsed roof. Pepillo's breath was coming in quick frightened gasps, but Melchior seemed calm. He held his finger to his lips. 'Be quiet,' he said. 'He won't see us.'

Cortés had expressly forbidden them to visit the Indian town when he'd led the soldiers up there this morning, telling them they must stay with the sailors to guard the ship. But Melchior had different ideas. 'I'm going to find out what's happening,' he'd told Pepillo. 'If there's some action, I want part of it. Want to come along?'

Matters between them had improved a little in the seven days since the *Santa María*'s departure from Santiago. It was as though by saving Pepillo's life in the storm, Melchior had somehow restored the dignity he felt he'd lost when Cortés had appointed the younger boy as his secretary. There was still some tension, however, which Pepillo very much wished to dissipate, so he'd suppressed his natural caution, put on a brave face, and agreed to Melchior's scheme.

They'd slipped overboard into the shallows and waded ashore – or rather Melchior had waded ashore with Pepillo perched on his shoulders – and made their way up the hill into a scene of horrors. Melchior professed indifference to the dead bodies they'd come across, but Pepillo felt he'd been plunged into a corner of hell and had vomited twice, receiving cuffs about his head from Melchior for his trouble.

By the time they reached the plaza, it was clear that Cortés had wrested control from Alvarado, and they watched as twenty elders who'd seemed doomed to be burnt at the stake were set free. Then all the other townsfolk were released as well and suddenly the streets, which had been deserted, were filled with Indians who wept and called out as they searched the shells of burnt buildings and took possession again of looted homes. 'Aren't we in danger here?' Pepillo asked as a group of dark-skinned youths rushed past, yammering in their strange tongue; but Melchior pointed to the hundreds of armed conquistadors still occupying the square. 'We're safe enough, you silly mammet,' he said.

They'd watched, fascinated, as the confrontation between Cortés and Muñoz unfolded. There was some shouting, though they were too far away to hear what was said, and the postures of both men expressed anger. 'Do you think the caudillo will arrest him again?' Pepillo asked. But before Melchior could answer, Muñoz was heading their way and they ducked out of view.

Now they heard his heavy footsteps approach. He slowed as he reached the door to their hiding place, then stopped. Pepillo tensed, his stomach lurched and he cast a terrified glance at Melchior, who was sweating, his eyes very wide. As though from nowhere a rusty dagger had appeared in his right hand and the muscles of his forearm bunched and knotted as he clenched his fist fiercely round its hilt.

'*Don't*,' Pepillo mouthed, shaking his head.

Melchior ignored him, rising to a crouch.

But then the Inquisitor's footsteps moved on, proceeding along the street away from the square, and the sense of looming threat lifted.

Pepillo collapsed against the wall, his heart pounding. He felt he couldn't breathe.

'Come on,' said Melchior, grabbing him again by the scruff of the neck and pulling him to his feet. 'Let's follow him. He's up to no good, I'm sure of it.'

Bernal Díaz had entertained doubts about Cortés's character since the night they'd left Santiago. The way the caudillo had ruthlessly made use of him to steal the entire stock of the slaughterhouse – and it *would* have been outright theft if Cortés could have got away with it – had disillusioned him greatly. And the easy, charismatic promises the man had made to him and to Sandoval to get them out of any trouble they faced on his behalf – trouble that could have seen them hung – had been wholly irresponsible and most unlikely to be redeemed if the worst came to the worst.

But the morning's events cast a new light on everything. The fact that Cortés had personally intervened to save Cozumel's elders and priests from the hideous fate of being burnt to death was enough on its own to raise him high in Díaz's estimation, but he'd gone much further than that, freeing all the captive Indians and ordering their property restored to them with reparations made to the families of those who'd been killed. These actions showed the caudillo to be a man who was prepared to do the right thing, even if he made powerful enemies such as Muñoz and Alvarado in the process – and such a man, Díaz now decided, deserved his loyalty; indeed he would follow him to the ends of the earth.

For some time after Muñoz walked away from him in the plaza, Díaz observed that Cortés stayed where he was, standing alone on the third step of the pyramid, seemingly deep in thought. But now, suddenly, he sprang into action, summoning Brabo, Sandoval and Díaz himself. 'Come, friends,' he said as they gathered round him – Sandoval and Díaz greeting one another like long-lost brothers – 'let's climb this heap of stones and take a look at the temple these heathens worship in. I've a mind to make it into a church.'

'We tried that before,' Díaz felt compelled to offer, 'when we came here with Córdoba. It didn't work. The Indians got rid of the cross and the image of the Virgin we gave them and went back to their idols after our departure. That's why Muñoz was so angry with them.'

'I'm not Muñoz,' said Cortés with a hard stare. 'He does everything with anger, by force; no wonder people reject his teachings.' He shaded his eyes against the sun and looked out, seemingly searching for someone in the huge crowd of Indians and conquistadors filling the plaza. 'Has anyone seen Father Olmedo?' he asked after a moment.

Sandoval volunteered to go and find him. 'Olmedo sails with us on the *Santa María*,' Cortés told Díaz while they were waiting. 'A right holy and modest friar. He sleeps on deck with the men – doesn't he, Brabo?, sharing their hardships and asking no special favours.'

'A good man,' Brabo concurred. 'Puts on no airs and graces, rolls up his sleeves and lends a hand when there's work to be done. Would that our Inquisitor had half his mettle.'

Cortés seemed preoccupied, Díaz thought, but he brightened when Sandoval returned, bringing with him a portly, rugged friar, aged perhaps forty, wearing the white robes of the Mercedarian order. 'Ah,' said Cortés, 'there you are. Come with us to the temple, Father, and we'll see about planting Christianity here.'

Olmedo's face was broad and round but with a strong bearded jaw and a straight nose, giving him a somewhat fierce look that was greatly softened on closer inspection by humorous brown eyes. Despite a full tonsure out of which rose the smooth and deeply tanned dome of his skull, his hair was unruly, reddish-brown in colour, thick and shaggy at the nape of his bull-like neck and somewhat overhanging his brow. His shoulders and chest were massive, and an ample stomach thrust comfortably forward through his habit. 'Oh dear,' he said, 'isn't that a job for our Inquisitor?'

'I fear he'd rather burn men than convert them,' Cortés said.

'I dare say he would,' agreed Olmedo, his eyes twinkling. He struck a posture that reminded Díaz powerfully of Muñoz in mid-harangue, and retracted his upper lip so that his front teeth protruded. 'Let us purge their souls in the flames,' he brayed, 'so they may stand purified before the Lord on the day of judgement . . .'

Somehow he succeeded in altering the timbre of his own deep voice to produce an excellent imitation of the Inquisitor's higher, more sibilant tones. Díaz, who'd heard more than enough of Muñoz holding forth on the voyage, felt a chuckle rising in his throat and tried to check it until Cortés too threw back his head and roared with laughter. Sandoval and Brabo joined in and Cortés clapped Olmedo on the back. 'You're quite the mimic,' he said. 'You've got him perfectly.'

The friar gave a little bow: 'One of my many skills when a man takes himself too seriously, as our friend the Inquisitor unfortunately does. We should all learn to laugh at ourselves' – his eyes twinkled again – 'lest others do it for us.'

They climbed the pyramid, sweating in the hot sun, swords and armour clanking, and stepped onto the summit platform with the temple looming before them, its door gaping like the mouth of hell.

Díaz explained that the bodies of two sacrificed Indians, a young woman and a child, had been found yesterday inside the temple, their hearts placed in a plate held across the breast of an idol that had stood at the top of the steps.

'It's beyond comprehension,' said Cortés. 'Truly the work of the devil.'

Sandoval's face was pale with horror. 'These are dangerous realms we enter,' he said in a hushed voice. 'Let's pray no Spaniard ever suffers such a fate.'

'I'd take my own life first,' Brabo growled.

As he led them into the single dark room of the temple, Díaz explained that it had contained a great idol but that it, and the other that had held the receptacle for hearts, had been thrown down the steps and smashed on Muñoz's orders.

'In that at least he did well,' Cortés growled. 'Don't you agree, Olmedo?'

The shadowy, low-ceilinged chamber, lit by guttering torches set into the walls, smelled of blood and rotting flesh. Holding the sleeve of his habit to his nose, Olmedo said, 'I am not certain that the immediate destruction of idols is the best way to proceed – any more than burning priests and elders at the stake. Such harsh actions do nothing to convince these poor souls that our faith is any better than theirs. If we wish them to become Christians, we should set an example of gentleness and tolerance, as Christ himself would have done.'

The corpses of the sacrificial victims had been removed, but there were still three skulls and a heap of human bones on the floor of the chamber and the walls were daubed with great splashes of dried blood. 'How can we tolerate this?' Cortés said, his voice rising. 'How can we be gentle when confronted by such wickedness?'

'Forgive them, lord?' suggested Olmedo quietly. 'For they know not what they do?'

'The words of Christ on the Cross,' mused Cortés. 'You make a good point and I'll think on it – but outside, yes? I can't stay a moment longer in this pit of the devil.'

They stepped out of the reeking temple into bright sunlight.

At the top of the steps stood a large group of Indians. Most were unarmed but several clutched stone knives, spikes of bone and other bizarre weapons that looked like stingray spines.

Muñoz pursued an erratic, wandering course through the streets, sometimes peering furtively into buildings. On one occasion he entered a group of houses, disappeared for several minutes and reappeared from another door. 'You've got to admit the man has balls,' Melchior said. 'After what he's done today you'd think he'd fear assassination.'

But the truth, Pepillo observed, was that the Indians were the ones

317

who were afraid, giving the Inquisitor a wide berth, scattering and running away at the first sight of his black robes.

'What's he after?' Pepillo asked as Muñoz continued his rapid investigation of the town, sniffing at doorways, peering through windows, darting into alleys.

'He's like a dog after a bitch in heat,' Melchior said grimly. 'What do you think he's after?'

Pepillo felt his face flush hot as they hurried along in pursuit. He guessed that Melchior was referring to sex but didn't really understand the details. He had to agree, though, that there was something hungry and animalistic about the way Muñoz kept casting around, now hurrying, now slowing down, now lurking at a corner looking this way and that before moving on.

It was as though he were following a trail . . . But of what?

Being built around the summit of a hill, the town's streets sloped steeply on all sides, giving way to mixed patches of woodland and open ground that in turn led down to the turquoise waters of the bay where the fleet bobbed at anchor. Striding along one of the narrow streets in the lower section of the town, Muñoz's pace suddenly quickened and he forked abruptly left into a side street. Pepillo and Melchior were a hundred paces behind and lost sight of him for a moment, but when they charged up to the corner where he'd turned, there he was again, still maintaining the same lead.

They also saw what had excited him, why his body strained forward so eagerly, why he was moving so fast.

Running just ten paces ahead of him, crying out in fear, was a little Indian boy, naked but for a string of coloured beads around his waist.

'Hurry!' said Melchior. Pepillo wasn't sure whether he was alarmed or relieved to see the rusty knife in his friend's hand again as the child bolted round the next corner and was lost to view, with Muñoz right behind him.

With an oath Melchior increased his pace and Pepillo scrambled to catch up. They reached the corner together and peered cautiously round it into a maze of hovels, some intact, some burnt and sprawling in smouldering ruins down the hillside to the edge of a large patch of woodland.

It was as though the earth had opened, swallowing Muñoz and the child – for there was no trace of them. Melchior cursed again and thrust his head into a doorway. Pepillo apprehensively peered into another. A group of Indians sat inside in the gloom and stared at him, saying nothing, with expressions he could not interpret. He mumbled a hasty apology, blundered out again and followed Melchior. The next house was burnt, the next deserted. They continued to search fruitlessly for a little longer, but increasing numbers of Indians were emerging onto the devastated streets and the atmosphere was becoming hostile. Agreeing it would be good to be back on board the *Santa María* before Cortés returned, Pepillo and Melchior began to make their way downhill in the direction of the anchorage.

Their route took them close to the copse, dense with knotted and gnarled strangler figs festooned with hanging vines, growing across the slope below the last of the dwellings. The sky remained clear blue, as it had all morning, but it was now early afternoon and the heat was dense, clammy, heavy with damp. As they skirted the wood a flock of bright green parrots shifted and squabbled in the leafy canopy and suddenly, like an evil spirit, Muñoz reappeared from amongst the trees a few hundred paces below them, raven black in his Dominican habit, his cowl raised, concealing his head and face. He did not look back but strode rapidly down the hill.

Without a word, Melchior dived into the forest. 'Where are you going?' Pepillo called, hastening after him, struggling with the rank undergrowth.

'To find out what that bastard's done,' said Melchior, plunging on ahead.

The going did not prove as difficult as it had seemed to Pepillo at first, and they found a trail, perhaps made by animals, perhaps by the people of the town, where they were able to keep up a good pace. The sun's light was much reduced as they forged deeper, filtered by the thick canopy into a dreamlike emerald dusk, but shone through again, harsh and dazzling, as they entered a small, irregular clearing where the trees had been felled leaving only rotten stumps.

'God and his angels,' breathed Melchior, staring across the clearing.

Pepillo blinked, seeing nothing.

'There!' Melchior's voice was thick with rage.

Pepillo looked again and this time he did see what had drawn his friend's attention – a pair of small, brown naked feet protruding from the undergrowth where the forest resumed.

It took them only moments to pull the body free. Still warm, but stone dead, it was the same little Indian boy, with the bright string of wooden beads round his waist, whom Muñoz had been following. There was blood on the child's scrawny buttocks and livid bruises marked his throat and neck. A wide patch of his scalp extending from his crown to his left ear was missing, crudely hacked away to expose the white and bloody skull beneath.

For the third time that day Pepillo vomited, but this time Melchior didn't cuff him.

Cortés, Sandoval, Brabo and Díaz all went for their swords but were somewhat reassured as Little Julian shouldered forward through the thirty or forty Indians crowded onto the summit platform. The stooped, cross-eyed interpreter was sweating and wheezing from the climb. Peering uneasily from beneath the fringe of his long greasy hair, he told Cortés: 'They not here crisis you sir; they say you are buffoon.'

As Cortés bristled at the insult – A buffoon? How dare they call him a buffoon? – the Indians launched into an extraordinary display. Those who were unarmed dropped to their knees, scrabbled at the paving stones with which the platform was surfaced and shoved their fingers into their mouths whilst smacking their lips. Those who carried weapons proceeded to slice or skewer their own flesh in a variety of painful but non-lethal places such as their lips, tongues, biceps, buttocks and outer thighs. In two cases penises were shamelessly produced from beneath loincloths, stretched forth and pierced with stingray spines.

'Dear God,' Cortés barked at Julian. 'What are they doing?'

'Eat great fear,' the interpreter said. 'Honour blood.'

'What?' Cortés couldn't make head or tail of the explanation. 'Does anyone understand what this idiot is talking about?'

'His Castilian is atrocious,' offered Díaz, who had sailed with Julian on the *San Sebastián*, 'pretty much non-existent, and what little he does know he gets all mixed up. Let me try and make sense of this.'

While drops of blood continued to spatter down on the platform and one of the Indians sawed a stingray spine back and forth transversely through his penis, with the Spaniards looking on in a mixture of fascination, amusement and horror, Díaz talked urgently with the interpreter. After a moment he turned back to Cortés. 'I think I've sorted it out now,' he said. 'He's trying to say *tierra*, "earth" – but his accent's so bad he makes it sound like *terror*, "fear". It's a custom amongst these people to show respect to those more powerful than themselves by eating earth in their presence. Same goes for the blood. They're honouring you, sir, by bleeding themselves. They do this before their idols as well. It's a kind of sacrifice.'

'Well tell them to desist immediately!' Cortés snapped. Díaz spoke urgently to Julian who in turn said something in the local language. The bloodletting stopped at once.

'By the way,' Cortés asked, 'why did they call me a buffoon?'

Díaz laughed. 'They didn't, sir. That's just Julian mixing up words again. He's saying *un gracioso* – "a buffoon, a funny man" – but what he means is *dar las gracias*, "to thank". The "crisis" bit is pretty clear too. What it boils down to is they're not here to cause us trouble but to thank us. As you might imagine, the priests and elders are much beholden to you for halting their execution.'

'Well, very good.' Cortés smiled. As he thrust his sword firmly back in its scabbard, one of the Indians, a tall elder in a blue cotton loincloth, made his way forward, his dignified presence only slightly compromised by the streaks of blood on his chin and chest from the wounds he'd made to his lower lip.

'The *cacique*, sir,' said Julian proudly, using the word for chief that the Spanish had adopted from the Taino Indians of Hispaniola and Cuba. 'Him name B'alam K'uk. He funny you say.'

During the encounter that followed, fuelled by general goodwill but constantly fogged and befuddled by Julian's poor grasp of Castilian, Cortés accepted the gratitude of the Indians, who belonged, they said, to a great confederation of peoples called the Maya. He in turn apologised for the cruel and unwarranted behaviour of his deputy, Alvarado, and said he hoped sufficient compensation had been offered. On impulse, as an additional gesture, he sent Sandoval down to the *Santa*

María to return with Spanish shirts for each of the elders and a chest containing a velvet doublet, mirrors, small brass bells and several strings of glass beads. These treasures Cortés bestowed upon B'alam K'uk, the chief, much to that worthy's apparent satisfaction.

Sandoval also brought a platoon of men with him carrying parasols, wooden stools, cushions and comfortable rugs, and a rather fine folding chair that Cortés had asked for and now proceded to sit in.

Once the parasols were erected to provide shade for himself and the other Spaniards on the summit platform, he invited the Indians to be seated and told them, to the limited extent that Julian was able to convey these ideas, that their idols were evil, not gods at all, but devils who would only lead their souls to hell. He would take it as a sign of friendship between them and his own people if they would see to it that every idol in every temple on the island was smashed within the next few days. At this Olmedo whispered fiercely in his ear, but Cortés ignored him and added that the idols must be replaced by images of the Virgin Mary and by wooden crucifixes which the Spanish would supply. He had been informed, he said, that a crucifix and a statue of the Virgin had been placed here in the temple when Spaniards had visited the island before. He professed sorrow and disappointment that these sacred objects had been removed and insisted this must never happen again. There was only one God, he said, the creator of heaven and earth and the giver of all things, and the cross and the Virgin Mary were amongst his most precious symbols.

As he spoke, Cortés was aware that very little of what he was saying was being understood, but he felt compelled to continue anyway. He had kept up a cheerful demeanour throughout the meeting, but the truth was that Muñoz's last words to him had thrown him into turmoil. That the Inquisitor had known about his special feelings for Saint Peter, and known Peter was his patron saint – these things were not in themselves surprising. He could have acquired the information from a variety of sources. Much harder to explain, however, was Muñoz's revelation that he too had dreamed of Saint Peter, who had spoken to him of Cortés – just as in dreams the saint had spoken to Cortés of Muñoz. This, surely, could not be mere coincidence!

For all these reasons, Cortés decided, he was going to have to think extremely carefully about how to handle the Inquisitor in the future, and find an accommodation with him as Saint Peter required. Meanwhile, although it had been essential to put Muñoz in his place, and prevent the *auto-da-fé* in the plaza, Cortés also felt it was right, notwithstanding Olmedo's more cautious counsel, that he should continue to support and enforce Muñoz's policies regarding the removal and smashing of idols and their replacement by Christian symbols.

He closed the meeting with a lengthy homily against human sacrifice, a foul practice, he told the Indians, that they must agree to abandon at once. If they did not do so, he warned, he might be unable to prevent his Inquisitor a second time from burning them at the stake. Some further confusion resulted here, since it seemed the chief and the elders laboured under the misguided impression that Muñoz had wanted to burn them as sacrifices to his God, and Cortés found it very hard to disabuse them of this repugnant notion which, to make matters worse, it appeared that both Díaz and Olmedo had some sympathy with! He soldiered on, however, patiently working round the execrable interpreting skills of Little Julian, making his points again and again in different ways, until he was reasonably sure he had been properly understood.

What happened next convinced Cortés he was on the right track and that, despite his harsh treatment of Muñoz, he did still have Saint Peter's blessing for his expedition.

As the elders were taking their leave, the chief – now dressed in the splendid doublet he had been given – put an arm round Cortés's shoulder, drew him to the edge of the pyramid and pointed northwest, towards the mainland. He then made a short speech in his own language, but interspersed within it was a familiar-sounding word – something like '*Castilan*' – repeated several times and with great emphasis. As he spoke, the chief rubbed his own hairless chin with his fingers and pointed to the beards of the Spaniards.

Intrigued, Cortés delayed the elders' exodus from the pyramid and inquired further. More excruciating difficulties of interpretation followed but, bit by bit, with Díaz's help, the story was teased out. Some days' journey away on the mainland, which the Indians called the 'Yucatán', it seemed there lived a bearded white man, much like the Spanish in appearance. He had been carried there a long time before in a boat and was held captive by a lord of that land. Apparently this white man called himself a '*Castilan*'. He had learned the language of the Maya and spoke it like a native.

Could it be, Cortés wondered, that God had delivered into his hands the very gift he now so obviously required, namely a shipwrecked Spaniard, a man of Castile, who might serve as a proper interpreter for his expedition? With growing excitement he asked the chief to send a messenger to the Yucatán requesting the release of the '*Castilan*' and offering rich gifts – which the Spanish would provide – in return.

The chief demurred. The men of the Yucatán, he said, were fierce and warlike and, moreover, cannibals; any messenger was likely to be killed and eaten. If Cortés wished to free this '*Castilan*', the only solution would be to send one of his own great boats and soldiers there to seize him by force of arms – in which case, the chief promised, he would be happy to assign two Indians who knew the way to accompany them.

Cortés needed no further urging. 'Sandoval,' he said as they descended the pyramid. 'I've got a little job for you.'

Chapter Forty-Seven

Tozi was in the royal hospital, invisible, standing by the bedside of Prince Guatemoc, hating his handsome sleeping face. She was thinking how easy it would be to slit his throat with the sharp little knife Huicton had provided for her, when Moctezuma's chief physician Mecatl, a famous man in Tenochtitlan, entered the room. He was fat and bald and wore his ornate robes of office, but there was, Tozi immediately detected, something odd about his manner.

Something secretive and jittery.

He seemed nervous, but what would he have to be nervous about in his own hospital?

Wiping a sheen of sweat from his brow, he peered out into the corridor, looking left and right as though seeking to ensure he would not be disturbed, then closed the door behind him and advanced on the bed, drawing a small ceramic bottle from his robes as he did so. He removed the bottle's rubber stopper, sniffed its contents, lifted Guatemoc's head from the pillow and muttered, 'You must drink this medicine, sire.'

The prince groaned and turned his head away. 'Not again! Can't you see I'm sleeping?'

'You must drink the medicine, lord.'

'Leave me *alone*, Mecatl. I'm not in the mood for any more of your foul brew.'

'Your life depends on it, lord. Drink now, please, I beg you. It's only a matter of a moment and then you may rest.'

'Come back later, damn you! Let me sleep!'

The doctor was persistent. 'I'm afraid, sire, that I must insist.'

Guatemoc's eyes fluttered open. 'You're a horrible fat worm, Mecatl. *Go away!*'

'I will not, great Prince. I am your doctor, appointed by the Lord Speaker himself. I cannot leave your side until you drink this medicine.'

Another groan. 'Damn it then, get on with it – if it's the only way for me to be rid of you!'

'Thank you, sire.' Mecatl lifted the prince's head again, put the bottle to his pale lips, nudged it between his teeth and upended it into his mouth. Tozi saw Guatemoc's throat working as he swallowed the draught, leaving a few drops of what appeared to be liquid chocolate on his chin, which Mecatl carefully wiped away with a cloth. The physician then restoppered the empty bottle, placed it and the cloth back inside his robes, stood looking down at the prince for a few moments until his breathing fell back into the regular pattern of sleep, then left the room as furtively as he had entered it.

Tozi followed.

Her connection with the stuff of the world was different, more complicated, when she was invisible. Her clothes and the contents of her pockets always faded with her, and she had learned she could spread the field of magic to other things, and the people around her, if she concentrated her will. She could pick up objects and use them if she chose to do so, but she was also able to make herself as insubstantial as thought and flow in this form even through solid matter. In every case, she had discovered, the keys to control were focus and intention, so she focussed now, flowed through the wall with no more resistance than passing through a light shower of rain, and stayed right behind Mecatl as he waddled along the corridor and into a lavishly furnished office. He went to a cupboard standing in a corner of the room, opened it, took out a large bottle, carried it over to a table, placed the small bottle from his robes beside it and refilled it from the large bottle with more of the same chocolate-coloured liquid. A drop spilled on the table and he carefully wiped it up with the cloth. Finally he placed both bottles and the cloth back inside the cupboard and left the room, closing and locking the door behind him.

When he was gone, Tozi remained invisible while she conducted a rapid search. Laid out on the table was a fine collection of obsidian surgical instruments, a large mortar and pestle and two human skulls. There were shelves stacked with medical books painted on maguey cloth and deerskin and folded zigzag fashion between wooden covers. None of this was of any use to her but on a ledge beneath the shuttered window she found a collection of empty bottles. She took the smallest of these, filled it from the larger bottle in the cupboard, which she then carefully replaced, tucked the smaller bottle inside her blouse, mopped up a few spilled drops with the cloth Mecatl had used, and closed the cupboard. She made a final inspection to ensure she had left no trace of her visit other than the missing bottle, which she hoped would not be noticed. When she was satisfied she flowed out through the wall directly into the gardens surrounding the hospital and thence back into the streets of Tenochtitlan. Finding a patch of shadow in a deserted alley, she re-emerged into visibility again and began to walk briskly northwards through the city.

An hour later Tozi and Huicton sat together on their begging mats, talking quietly, reviewing their progress.

Everyone knew the story of the weeping woman who'd haunted Tenochtitlan the year before, so it had been an obvious ploy for Tozi, shielded by invisibility, to play that part, passing through the streets these last six nights, heard but not seen, seeding doubts and fear in Moctezuma's mind.

It was Huicton who'd had the idea of the dreamers, rounding up a few lonely old tramps and invalids with the promise of a big reward from Ishtlil, and a comfortable retirement in the mountains, if they could pull it off. Of course there'd been a danger that Moctezuma would kill them on the spot, but the elders had decided the reward was worth the risk.

The scheme had worked better than they could have hoped. It had been an easy matter for Tozi to fade herself into the dungeon, slip the sleeping draught Huicton had procured into the guards' food, and set the prisoners free. The guards, naturally, had not admitted to falling asleep on duty and had told a story of magic and sorcery that had disturbed Moctezuma even further.

Next Tozi and Huicton decided to turn their attention to Cuitláhuac, who was not only the Great Speaker's brother but also his strongest supporter and closest adviser – the very man who had escorted Tozi and Malinal from the pyramid on the night of the sacrifices. Rumour had it he would be appointed to the high office of Snake Woman, now that Coaxoch had been killed in the Tlascalan wars, so he was an obvious target. And the fact that Cuitláhuac's own son Guatemoc had also been injured in Tlascala and lay in the royal hospital seemed to offer special opportunities for mischief.

So Tozi had entered the hospital early this morning and waited quietly and invisibly by Guatemoc's bed for Cuitláhuac to arrive. Surprisingly, however, despite his son's obviously grave condition, he had not come. Instead there had been the strange and sinister visit of Mecatl.

'He didn't behave like a doctor,' Tozi told Huicton. 'That's what made me suspicious, so I followed him.' She pulled the little bottle from her blouse and passed it over. 'This is what they're treating Guatemoc with,' she said. 'Any idea what it is?'

Moctezuma was in a state of morose despair. Despite consuming huge quantities of *teonanácatl* on each of the last four nights, and sacrificing a dozen small children, he'd been unable to make contact with Hummingbird again. The only good news came in the daily reports from Mecatl. Cuitláhuac was out of Tenochtitlan on a trumped-up mission to Texcoco and Tacuba, supposedly to seek assurances of their continued commitment to the alliance that united the three cities. In his absence the poison was being administered morning and evening and Guatemoc's condition was deteriorating at a satisfactory pace.

Mecatl had arrived from the hospital some moments earlier and now spoke from his usual position, face down on the floor of the audience chamber. 'Sire,' he said, 'I gave the prince a further dose this morning . . .'

'Good, good . . . How much longer, then, until he . . . ?'

'The poison is subtle, sire, as you requested, but at the present dosage I do not believe he can survive it for more than another eight days.'

Sitting on his throne, Moctezuma placed his index fingers together and twirled his thumbs around each other. 'That will be perfect,' he said finally. 'Much sooner and suspicions might be aroused. We would not wish that. But much later and there is the possibility that his father will remove him from your care. I can't keep Cuitláhuac out of Tenochtitlan forever.'

'If he can be kept away from the hospital for another two days, sire, it should be sufficient. By then the effects of the poison will be irreversible.'

Much as Mecatl had done this morning before giving the medicine to Guatemoc, Huicton pulled the rubber stopper from the bottle and sniffed the contents. 'Aha . . .' he said. He took another deep sniff. 'Interesting.' He poured a few drops of the liquid into the palm of his hand and tentatively dipped his tongue into it before spitting vigorously, leaving a brown smear on the paving of the causeway.

'Looks like chocolate,' Tozi said.

'Yes. Quite clever of Mecatl, that. It helps disguise the bitter taste. It would probably pass casual inspection because most medicines are bitter. But when you've been in this business as long as I have, you get to know your poisons, and I think I can say with certainty that the chief physician of our revered Great Speaker is presently poisoning Cuitláhuac's son.'

'I knew it!' Tozi exclaimed. 'I knew he was doing something wicked.'

Huicton sniffed the bottle again and placed the stopper firmly back in its mouth. 'Wicked indeed,' he said. 'This is dangerous stuff. Quite rare in these parts, by the way. It's made from the powdered body and wings of a butterfly that the Zapotecs call *cotelachi* – which means in their language "the butterfly that kills within a year". But actually it depends on the size of butterfly you use. A small, young *cotelachi* consumed entire will take about a year to kill you, a big full-grown one will do the job overnight and the medium-sized ones take ten or twelve days.'

'But why would Mecatl want to kill Guatemoc?'

'Oh, he won't be acting without orders from above. This whole thing has Moctezuma's cowardly stamp on it. I think I told you he would have poisoned Ishtlil if I hadn't got wind of the plot and managed to foil it?'

Tozi remembered.

'As to Guatemoc,' Huicton continued, the Speaker's motive is obvious. Easy way to get rid of a potential rival to the throne and make it look as if he died of his battle injuries. Question is . . . how best to turn this to our advantage?'

Tozi didn't have to think about the answer. 'If Moctezuma wants Guatemoc dead,' she said, 'then we might stir up some useful trouble by making sure he lives.'

That same night, very late, Tozi returned to the hospital and drifted invisibly through its gloomy passageways. Outside Guatemoc's chamber she spied the portly figure of Mecatl leaning forward, his ear pressed to the door, listening intently.

Tozi slipped through the wall and by the light of the lanterns that burned bright within, she saw a handsome matron, richly clad in fine linens, thick black hair streaked with grey, leaning over the prince, her face lined with grief and worry. At her side, a plain and dumpy younger woman stood crying, wiping tears from her eyes which she'd rubbed as pink as an albino rabbit's.

'Silence, sister,' said Guatemoc in a weak, dry whisper. 'If you wish me well then I beg you, give me no more sobs! Your laughter will serve me better.' But she merely wailed the louder. The prince turned to the older woman: 'Mother, can you not persuade her to stop? Give me music, give me laughter, give me dancing girls – something, anything to cheer me, but no more tears please.'

'You need to be at home with us,' said his mother, 'instead of wasting away in this hospital. Good food, the clear air of our estate, the care of our own doctors – these are what will save you . . . They say your recovery after the battle was almost miraculous – until your father brought you here!'

'This is the royal hospital!' The prince's lean features were grey with pain as he struggled to calm his mother's fears. 'What better place can there be for me? What better hope can I have? I'm under the care of Mecatl himself.'

'I don't trust that man,' the matron said, 'and I don't trust your uncle. Ahh, gods! If only your father were here! It's intolerable of Moctezuma to send him on some unimportant mission of diplomacy while you fight for your life . . .'

'To bind Texcoco and Tacuba to the triple alliance cannot be said to be unimportant, mother.'

'Yes, but *now*? He should have sent another—'

At that the door swung open and Mecatl bustled in, coming to a halt halfway across the room. 'Good evening, Lady Achautli,' he said smoothly, feigning surprise. 'I had not expected to see you here so late.'

'And why not?' she snapped. 'No one is more important to me than my son. I can't possibly think of any better way to spend my time than by his side.'

'Of course, of course,' Mecatl soothed as he turned to the younger woman. 'And you, my Lady Chalchi. I am sure your brother's strength rallies at the very sight of you.'

'He certainly does not rally with any of the treatments you're giving him here,' said Achautli.

'Well, so it may appear, my lady, but healing is a mysterious process. There are ups . . . and there are downs . . .'

'As far as I can see it's been all downs since he came under your care!'

'Oh mother, *please*,' sobbed Chalchi. 'I'm sure Mecatl is doing his best for poor Guatemoc. You're not helping my brother with all these complaints.'

The doctor's expression, Tozi thought, was a masterpiece of wounded virtue. 'I understand your concerns, Lady Achautli,' he said, as he glided across the room and positioned himself by the bed. 'I take no offence, I assure you, but the Lady Chalchi is right. I am doing everything possible for your son and this is why, since the hour is late, I must ask you to leave now. Sleep is a great restorative, and if the prince is to recover, he must get as much rest as possible.'

Achautli spluttered an objection but Chalchi put a hand on her arm. 'Come, Mother. The doctor knows best. We must let Guatemoc sleep.'

'Very well,' said the older woman. All the fight, suddenly, seemed to have gone out of her. She stooped over the bed and kissed her son: 'Until morning, Guatemoc.'

'Until morning, Mother. Don't fear for me. I'm stronger than you

331

think. I'll recover. You have my word on it.' The prince attempted a smile but his pallor was so bad and his skin stretched so thinly over his skull that the effect was ghastly.

With more floods of sobs from Chalchi, the two women hurried out, leaving Guatemoc with Mecatl, who crossed the room again, peered from the door to be sure they were gone, returned to the prince's bedside, made a show of examining his exhausted patient and began to change the bandages covering a series of hideous abdominal injuries. Tozi counted five individual puncture marks. They were all neatly stitched but they were suppurating and they gave off a bad smell. There was also a wound to his throat, but this seemed to have healed more completely than the others, and another on his right forearm.

The prince was wide awake, staring up at the ceiling while the doctor worked. 'Tell me honestly, Mecatl,' he said. 'How do you rate my chances?'

'I have the highest hopes for your complete recovery, sire, thanks to the new elixir I've been treating you with these past four days . . .'

'That vile brew! I shudder to think of it.'

'Even so, sire, it will make you well.' As Mecatl applied the last bandage he reached into his robes, sought in a pocket, brought forth the same small ceramic bottle he had used that morning and showed it to Guatemoc. 'The elixir has extraordinary regenerative properties and the power to heal every ill of the flesh. The supply is so restricted that I would limit any lesser man to a single dose a day, but the Lord Speaker has commanded that we spare no expense to make you well . . .'

'I suppose I should be grateful, but I'm not sure I can bring myself to drink another dose tonight.'

'I'm afraid you must, lord. It will give you rest, numb the pain of your injuries and work on your body as you sleep.'

Watching invisibly from the corner of the room, Tozi felt a powerful urge to rush at Mecatl and snatch the bottle from his hands, but she knew it would do no good and undo every advantage she had.

'Come sire,' the doctor said, 'let me help you.' Just as he had done that morning, he lifted Guatemoc's head and put the bottle to his lips. The prince innocently opened his mouth and swallowed.

'There, you leech!' he said with a grimace when he'd drunk every drop. 'Satisfied now?'

'Yes, lord. Completely satisfied.' Mecatl restoppered the bottle and put it back in his pocket in what Tozi was coming to recognise as his usual routine. 'Sleep now, sire,' he said, casting a glance over his shoulder as he walked towards the door. 'I'll bring your next dose in the morning.'

Tozi remained in the corner of the room until she was certain Guatemoc was asleep, then she moved silently towards his bedside. Mecatl had left the lantern burning and, by its light, she could see the rise and fall, rise and fall, of the prince's chest. It was obvious he had once been heavily muscled, but now he was weak and emaciated, indeed almost skeletal. Strangely, she felt something close to pity for him.

Remaining invisible, she reached out her hand and lightly brushed his forehead, finding it hot and clammy with sweat. 'The time has come for you to awake,' she said. As Huicton had instructed, and rehearsed with her relentlessly all afternoon, she deepened her voice, adding a sombre, ominous note.

Guatemoc sighed.

'Awake!' Tozi said. She leaned in and shook him. 'Awake, Prince Guatemoc.'

He rolled away from her and grumbled, 'Piss off, Mecatl,' followed by some meaningless slurred sleep talk.

'You may slumber no longer,' Tozi insisted. 'I visit you from Aztlán . . .'

'Aztlán?' Guatemoc's eyes came open and he blinked twice. 'Aztlán?' He appeared confused, and little wonder since Aztlán was the mystic home of the gods – the enchanted land where the Mexica and all other Nahua peoples were believed to have had their origin. Still prone, he blinked again, clearing his sight, and turned his head from side to side. 'Who visits me from Aztlán?' he croaked.

Veiled in invisibility, Tozi replied, 'It is I, Temaz, who stands before you. I bring you tidings from the world beyond.'

With a groan of pain, the prince levered himself up onto his elbows, his eyes sweeping the room. 'I do not see you,' he said.

'Because I do not choose to reveal myself.'

Guatemoc shook his head vigorously, in the manner of one clearing water from his ears, and slumped back on the bed. 'I am dreaming,' he said.

'This is no dream, Prince.'

'Then I've gone mad, or you are a phantom of the night.'

'I am she who is called Temaz, sweet Prince. Do you not know who I am?'

'I know the name of Temaz, goddess of healing and medicines. But you are not she! You are a phantom – a voice without form that speaks to me from the shadows!'

'I am the goddess of medicines, and their rightful use, the patron of doctors and of all who perform the healing arts. That is why I have journeyed from Aztlán to bring you a warning . . .'

Guatemoc levered himself up again. Although she knew he could not see her, his eyes were fixed on exactly the spot where she stood. Involuntarily, she took a step back.

'A warning?' he growled. Despite his injuries, he looked dangerous. 'Even if you are Temaz, why would you bring me a warning?'

'Because a doctor of this hospital seeks your death,' Tozi said quietly, 'and uses a false medicine to poison you. I cannot allow such unholy behaviour to go unpunished, let alone to succeed.'

Now she had the prince's attention! 'Which doctor do you speak of?'

'None other than Mecatl.'

'It cannot be!' said Guatemoc, but Tozi ignored him.

'He brings you a special medicine to drink,' she said. 'He brings it every morning and night. It is flavoured with chocolate but there's a strange bitterness to the aftertaste that is not the bitterness of chocolate.'

'How can you know this?' Guatemoc asked wonderingly.

'Mecatl tells you it is an elixir,' Tozi continued, 'that can cure all ills of the flesh, but its real purpose is to poison you slowly in such a way that no suspicion will be aroused . . .'

Conflicting emotions – doubt, belief, hope – wrote themselves on the prince's tortured, finely sculpted face. 'If you are truly the goddess Temaz,' he said finally, 'then show yourself to me!'

During the afternoon, as well as discovering the exact whereabouts of Cuitláhuac, Huicton had used his connections to obtain a rich green skirt and blouse for Tozi, a fine shawl decorated with tassels, and a headdress of cotton bands adorned with amaranth seeds – an outfit that would pass inspection as the sacred regalia of Temaz. He had also applied yellow *axin* pigment to her cheeks, black bitumen to her eyelids and a tincture of cochineal to redden her lips, giving her the appearance of a grown woman.

Satisfied she was well prepared, she now took two further steps back from the bed to stay out of reach and allowed herself to fade into full visibility.

Guatemoc gasped, and something that was not fear, but more closely akin to awe, showed in his eyes. 'I see you,' he said.

'And do you now believe me, Prince?'

'I believe you, gracious goddess.'

'Then here is what you must do. In the morning, when Mecatl comes to administer more of the poison, *you must not drink it.*'

Guatemoc's voice seethed with anger. 'I'll kill him.'

'No, Prince. Nothing so hasty. The plot against you goes deeper than Mecatl and you must not arouse suspicion. Make him believe you are too ill to drink the medicine, that your stomach revolts against it. Tell him you will attempt the evening dose but that the morning dose is beyond you. *Convince him*, until he leaves you in peace. Then summon the Lady Achautli, tell her everything I have told you, and persuade her to use all means at her disposal to have your father, who is in Texcoco, return at once to Tenochtitlan. Between the morning and evening visits of Mecatl, there is sufficient time for Cuitláhuac to cross the lake and reach the hospital . . .'

Guatemoc nodded. 'And if my father does return, then what?'

'He must lie in wait until Mecatl comes to you with the poison and he must catch him in the act of giving it to you. It's the only way to bring an end to this plot.'

'What if my mother doesn't believe me,' said Guatemoc, 'or if my father doesn't believe her? What if he thinks this story of poisoning is just a bad dream I've had.'

'The Lady Achautli will believe you because she is your mother. But if she is to persuade your father, you will need to give her this . . .'

Now came the most difficult and potentially dangerous part of the whole masquerade. Remaining fully visible, Tozi stepped forward, pulled from a pocket of her blouse the little ceramic bottle containing the *cotelachi* poison she had stolen that morning and held it out to the prince. 'Take it,' she said. 'It's the medicine Mecatl has been giving you. The poison it contains is called *cotelachi* and your mother will be able to find a physician to verify that.'

Lightning fast, Guatemoc's hand shot out and grasped Tozi's wrist. For a moment she thought he had seen through her disguise. But then he said: 'I am in your debt, Lady Temaz. For your kindness to me this night, I swear to you that when I am well I will make a pilgrimage to find the lost land of Aztlán and the Seven Caves of Chicomoztoc and speak there with the masters of wisdom and restore virtue to the realm.' He took the bottle from her, slipped it under his sheets and released her.

'Only do as I ask,' Tozi said. 'Defeat this plot against you, and find the one who is truly responsible for it.'

Then impulsively she stepped close to the bed and placed both her hands, very gently, over the bandages covering Guatemoc's stomach.

Chapter Forty-Eight

Friday 26 February 1519 to Saturday 27 February 1519

The storm that had scattered the fleet on leaving Cuba had damaged several of the ships, and their captains requested at least a week longer in the sheltered anchorage of Cozumel to carry out the necessary refitting and repairs. Juan de Escalante's carrack, with the expedition's entire supply of cassava bread in its hold, was in a particularly bad way, close to sinking, and had to be unloaded and dragged up onto the shore to be made sound.

But two of the smaller vessels, both brigantines, were found to be fully seaworthy. Cortés put them temporarily under Sandoval's command for the mission to seek out the bearded white man whom the natives called the '*Castilan*', and they sailed from Cozumel at dawn on Friday 26 February. Antón de Alaminos, who knew these waters better than any other Spaniard, was the pilot. García Brabo and the same squad of twenty-five ruffians who'd been with Sandoval in the battle against Velázquez's guards provided the main fighting strength. The guides were Yochi and Ikan, two wide-eyed Cozumel islanders, familiar only with local canoes, for whom the brigantines seemed, if Little Julian's interpreting was to be trusted, 'as large as mountains'. Last but not least, Cortés insisted that Sandoval also take along ten out of the expedition's complement of a hundred ferocious war dogs whose snarling, howling and snapping disturbed and terrified the islanders even though the animals, which they described as 'dragons', were securely caged on deck.

Despite their fears and bewilderment, Yochi and Ikan, whose names meant 'Hope' and 'Star', proved to be excellent guides. Hope was the older of the two, perhaps in his fifties, and Star was much younger

– barely out of his teens, Sandoval thought; both were fishermen who knew the Yucatán coast well. Meeting with approval even from Alaminos, they skilfully avoided powerful currents by guiding the ships steadily northward through the obstacle course of small islands lying just offshore.

During the night of Friday 26 February and the small hours of the morning of Saturday 27, Cortés was visited again by Saint Peter as he slept in his hammock. The dream came upon him suddenly in the midst of a jumble of meaningless, inconsequential images, and took him by compulsion to a place he did not know, an Indian town on a great river, at the centre of which, in the midst of a spacious plaza where a tall silk-cotton tree grew, stood a lofty pyramid rising in nine steep terraces and seeming to reach for the sky.

Saint Peter had appeared at first in his usual form as a tall and robust man, clean-shaven and fair-haired with the hands of a soldier. But then, as the aerial journey began, he transformed mysteriously into a hummingbird, brightly coloured with blue and yellow feathers, a blur of wings and a long, dagger-sharp beak. Exerting some powerful force, some magnetism, he drew Cortés in a swirling vortex of flight around the pyramid and whispered in his ear – or perhaps it was not a whisper, perhaps more a thought taking shape inside his brain – 'I require your presence here.'

'Holy Father,' asked Cortés, 'where is this place?'

'This is Potonchan,' said the hummingbird that was Saint Peter, hanging in the air. 'Here Christian forces led by your predecessor Córdoba suffered the humiliation of defeat at the hands of the Chontal Maya.'

'I have heard the story,' said Cortés. 'We all have.'

'That defeat must not go unavenged,' said Saint Peter. 'If you allow it to do so, all your work for God in the New Lands will fail.'

And with that the scene changed and Cortés again felt himself transported through the air with the hummingbird by his side. He was carried over jungles and wide rivers, crossed immense mountains wreathed in snow and at last found himself looking down upon a vast green valley with a great lake at its heart. At the heart of this lake, built upon the water like an enchanted vision, he saw a jewelled and shining city, and at the heart of the city towered a pyramid of pure gold so high and so bright that it caught his eye by force, and astonished him, and stupefied him with wonder.

'All these things God will give you,' said Saint Peter, 'when you have done the thing I require you to do.'

'Command me, Holiness, and I will do it.'

'You must punish the wicked ways of the Indians of Potonchan. You must lay my vengeance upon them. You must destroy them utterly until their dead lie thick upon the ground. Only then will you earn your reward.'

Early on the morning of Saturday 27 February, Sandoval's brigantines rounded Cape Catoche and came in under oar to a shallow lagoon, named Yalahau in the Mayan tongue, which Alaminos had visited the year before when the Córdoba expedition had passed a night at anchor here.

Protected on its north side from Atlantic storms and currents by a long narrow island that the guides called Holbox, the five-mile-wide lagoon was sheltered and peaceful, fringed by white sand and palm trees and home to tremendous populations of large and colourful birds including species familiar to the Spanish such as long-legged pink flamingos and white pelicans. On the lagoon's south side, where the Yucatán mainland stretched away into limitless distance, several villages were visible amongst the trees and, within minutes of the brigantines being sighted, great numbers of people had emerged to line the shore.

Sandoval ordered the crews to row closer and it soon became obvious the villagers were hostile. There were many women and children amongst them, but he also counted close to a hundred men waving spears and clubs. As the ships came within hailing distance, several flights of arrows soared up but fell short into the blue waters of the lagoon. 'I think we'll drop anchor here,' Sandoval said to Brabo, 'and give some thought to strategy while we're still out of arrow range.'

'Good idea, sir,' agreed the sergeant, shading his eyes with his hand and frowning at the Indians on the shore. 'But, if I may suggest, a few rounds of grapeshot fired into the midst of them would be likely to work wonders.'

Sandoval winced. Each brigantine was armed with two small cannon, one in the bow and one in the stern. With barrels four feet long, these weapons were called falconets because they fired metal or stone balls, similar in size to a falcon with its wings folded, weighing about a pound and lethal up to a range of a mile. They could also be loaded with canvas tubes containing clusters of smaller balls – somewhat like clusters of grapes in appearance – that broke up and spread out on firing and were utterly devastating against a massed enemy at close range. The Indians lined along the shore were less than five hundred feet away and if Brabo's suggestion were followed many of them would die.

'I'm not sure that will be necessary,' Sandoval said. 'Let's see if we can scare them off with some ball fired into the trees.' He turned to Alaminos: 'Did you use cannon when you were here with Córdoba?' he asked.

The pilot shook his head. 'We didn't land so there was no need.'

'Well and good then,' said Sandoval and gave the order for the falconets to be charged. 'Let's fire two rounds each from all four of them and see what happens.'

That same morning, Saturday 27 February, Cortés and Alvarado took breakfast together on board the *Santa María de la Concepción*.

'Well,' Cortés said with a smile, 'are we friends again?'

Alvarado still wore a sulky, somewhat wounded expression. 'You should not have shamed me, Hernán.'

'You shamed yourself, Pedro, with your haste and your greed. Please forgive me for being blunt but that's how I see it. Your actions here in Cozumel could have cost us dear . . .'

'Dear? How so? The Indians were heretics. They deserved to burn. And their gold was ours by right of conquest. Why should I not take it? Why should I have been compelled to give it back?'

Cortés sighed. 'Strategy, Pedro. Strategy . . . By making reparations we regained the trust that you had lost us, and because of that trust we were given vital intelligence. Nothing could be more central to our interests than a proper interpreter but I doubt the Indians would have breathed a word about this shipwrecked Spaniard if I'd left things the way I found them when I arrived . . .'

Alvarado sniffed. 'Ah yes, your mysterious *"Castilan"* . . . If he even exists, which I very much doubt. I'll wager you've sent Sandoval off on a wild goose chase . . .'

'Really? A wager? How much?'

Alvarado grinned: 'A hundred gold pesos.'

'Come come! A mere hundred? There's no sport in that!'

'Very well then, let's say a thousand.'

'Done!' agreed Cortés. 'If Sandoval comes back with this *"Castilan"* you'll pay me a thousand gold pieces; if he comes back empty handed you can take a thousand from me.'

Alvarado's spirits had lightened, as they always did at the prospect of a gamble, but he was still visibly sulking. 'A mere fraction of what you owe me,' he said. 'For your sake I passed up fifteen thousand gold pieces from Velázquez, risked my life and took an injury.' He stabbed his knife into a slice of roast pork and glanced down at his splinted left arm hanging uselessly in a sling across his chest. 'You conveniently forgot all that, Hernán, when you rebuked me in front of the men.'

'I forgot nothing, but I am in command of our expedition and I carry responsibilities that you do not.'

'You'd have no expedition to command if I'd done what the governor asked of me.'

Cortés slowly nodded his head. 'I'm in your debt for that,' he said. 'I don't deny it . . .'

'And that debt is about to deepen! Juan Escudero and the governor's cousin Velázquez de León paid me a quiet visit yesterday, you know. They've taken hope from our quarrel on Thursday. They can't imagine I'll ever forgive you for it, so they fancy I'm ready to join their side. They're hatching some plot to arrest you and hinted they'd offer me joint command with Escudero if I play along with them. I've agreed to meet them on my ship this afternoon to hear more . . .'

Cortés laughed. 'Somehow, old friend, I don't see you ever joining such swine.'

'I'm no Velazquista,' Alvarado agreed. It was the derisive term the two of them used between themselves for the clique of cavilling and complaining officers loyal to the governor of Cuba. 'And I'm no captain-general, either – "joint" or otherwise! Appearances to the contrary, I do know my limitations. I'm rash, hot-tempered, impatient; I like a fight, and frankly the burdens of command bore me. But I thought I'd string them along, find out more about what they want and give you a full report.'

'So I can still count on you, Pedro? Despite the harsh words we've exchanged?'

The atmosphere in the stateroom lightened further as Alvarado gave another big grin. 'You can count on me, Hernán. I'll keep the Velazquistas guessing and strengthen your hand against them, but I ask you this in return – respect my pride, give me enemies to kill and don't keep me too long away from gold!'

'You will have gold! More than even you could wish for. And battles too. We'll be refitting for a few more days here in Cozumel while Sandoval finds that shipwrecked Spaniard and brings him to us here—'

'If,' objected Alvarado, 'if . . .'

'Oh, he'll find him all right, and when he does, I tell you what, I won't even have my thousand pesos off you. You can keep it as a down payment on the fortune you'll make in the new lands. Then we'll sail the fleet north along the east coast of the Yucatán peninsula, round Cape Catoche – where Sandoval should be now, by the way – and thence south down the west coast of the peninsula to a place called Potonchan . . .'

'Where Córdoba took a beating?'

'Exactly. His defeat there sets a bad precedent.'

'Some would call routing an army of ten thousand savages with a hundred men a victory . . .'

'It was a defeat. Seventy Spaniards died in the fighting, the survivors fled back to their ships with their tails between their legs before the enemy could regroup, and Córdoba himself perished from his injuries on the return journey to Cuba. He was a brave man. All who were with him there were brave men; but, make no mistake about it, they were defeated, and they were seen to be defeated, and now those Indians know we can be killed. Such reverses happen on campaign, and they will happen to us, but if we are to conquer here then we cannot afford

342

to let any reverse go unpunished. That's why I intend to take revenge for Córdoba's defeat and do great harm to the Indians of Potonchan. I'll not hold you back there, Pedro, you have my promise. None will be spared until I receive their abject surrender, and we will have their gold, their silver, their jewellery – and their women for our beds.'

'Bravo Hernán!' roared Alvarado. 'Now you're talking.' His grin was wider than ever, his teeth bared in a wolfish snarl, and he slapped his uninjured right hand on the table. 'I'm not sure about their filthy women, though.'

Like all the Spaniards on board the brigantines, Sandoval was used to the crashing, explosive roar of cannon fire, to the pressure wave of the percussion as it struck the ears, to the whistle of the ball through the air, and to the foul, sulphurous smell of the clouds of smoke given off by the guns. So were the caged dogs, trained and habituated to war, and so also, though to a lesser extent, was Little Julian. But Hope and Star were completely new to the experience and threw themselves to the deck, their eyes rolling, their jaws slack, uttering high, keening wails of terror which drove the dogs into a frenzy, barking, snarling and pawing at the walls of their cage.

On shore the effects were even more dramatic. As the first four shots smashed into the dense trees that Sandoval had told the gunners to aim for, turning great swathes to matchwood in an instant, and as the shock of the explosions echoed round the lagoon, a tide of hysteria swept through the Indians, causing many to fall on their knees or their faces and many more to turn and run, barging into those behind them in what rapidly became a cascading, screaming, desperate stampede into the jungle. Within moments the white sand beach was empty, but for the fallen and the trampled, and very soon all the injured who were able to walk or drag themselves away were gone.

A ragged cheer went up from the Spaniards. 'Looks like you were right, sir,' said Brabo with a grim smile. 'That worked a charm.'

Cortés felt calm despite Alvarado's revelations about Escudero and Velázquez de León. Of course they were plotting against him! He had spies on their ships, and amongst the other Velazquistas too, and knew exactly what they were doing from day to day. They'd only implicate themselves further in their foolish meeting with Alvarado this afternoon and, when the right time came, he'd use all this evidence against them. There'd be some hangings then – mutiny was a capital offence, after all – and Escudero would be the first to dance at the end of the rope.

But for now there were other priorities. Cortés summoned his young secretary Pepillo, who had seemed pale and ill these past three days, and sat him down at the writing table with quill, ink and paper to take dictation of the letter he was in the process of composing to King Charles V of Spain. Despite Pepillo's apparent poor spirits, he was a clever boy, and had suggested this system of dictation, which Cortés quickly realised was an easier and more efficient way of arriving at a first draft than painstakingly writing it out himself.

'Where did we get to yesterday?' he asked.

'The fleet,' read Pepillo, 'was disposed according to the orders of Governor Diego de Velázquez, although he contributed but a third of the cost . . .'

'Ah yes. Very well, we continue.' Cortés, who was standing, now began to pace about the floor of the stateroom. 'And Your Majesty should also know,' he declaimed, 'that the third part contributed by Velázquez consisted in the main of wine and cloth and other things of no great value which he planned to sell later to the expeditionaries at a much higher price than he paid for them. So you might say he was investing his funds very profitably and that what he intended was more a form of trade with Spaniards, your Royal Highness's subjects, than a real contribution to the expedition.'

Cortés paused, thinking through what he wanted to say next. Technically, the whole enterprise had become illegal as a result of his precipitate departure from Cuba without Velázquez's permission. The only way to get round this was to win the direct support of the king, which would require some manoeuvring and some eloquence, to say the least! It was therefore essential to present the governor's behaviour in as unflattering a light as possible, while casting the best possible light on his own. 'I, on the other hand,' he continued, 'spent my entire fortune in equipping the fleet and paid for nearly two-thirds of it, providing not only ships and supplies but also giving money to those who were to sail with us who were unable to provide themselves with all they required for the journey.'

As Pepillo's hand moved rapidly across the page, there came a knock at the door. 'Yes,' Cortés said with a hint of irritation, 'come in.'

The visitors were Bernal Díaz and Father Olmedo. 'Good morning, gentlemen,' Cortés said, 'what can I do for you?'

A silence followed and both men glanced uncomfortably at Pepillo. 'Come on! Speak up!'

Olmedo took the lead. 'There's trouble in the town, Hernán. It seems two murders have been committed – both the victims are little boys no more than six years old. One was found in the forest on Thursday, the day of Don Pedro's ill-advised raid, and thought to be a casualty of the fighting. We paid blood price for him as we did for all the others killed and injured. But the second murder took place last night. It's hard to make head or tail of what's going on without our interpreter. They took me to see the bodies and' – a look of profound disgust crossed his face – 'both were sodomised. As far as we can tell, the Indians believe a Spaniard was responsible.'

'A Spaniard!' Cortés was horrified. 'No Spaniard would commit the abominable sin of sodomy.'

'There's something else sir,' said Díaz, stepping forward. 'The boys were scalped.'

'Scalped?'

'Yes, sir. Whoever killed and sodomised them also cut a strip of scalp from the victims' heads – in both cases between the crown and the left ear.'

With a sudden lurch of nausea, Cortés remembered Muñoz's bags, still lying hidden in the back of the stateroom, and pictured their contents – the knives, the peculiar strips of dried skin and hair – and knew immediately who the murderer was. But he fought hard to keep his face expressionless. 'I don't see what this proves,' he said.

'Sir, the same thing happened on the Córdoba expedition,' offered Díaz with a frown. 'Indian boys were murdered then as well and scalped in exactly the same way.'

'So what?' Cortés snapped. His heart was pounding and he felt – what was this? – almost *guilty*.

Díaz was looking at him with increasing puzzlement. 'But it's obvious, sir! It can only mean one thing. A Spaniard who was on the Córdoba expedition, and who's now here with us, is committing these murders.'

'Almost every survivor of the Córdoba expedition is in Cozumel, Díaz, including you yourself!' Cortés realised he was shouting and lowered his voice. 'Thirty men, more or less . . . Must I suspect all of them of sodomy and murder?'

'In theory, yes,' said Olmedo. 'All are suspects until they've been ruled out. This is a serious matter, Hernán. I urge you to authorise a full investigation at once.'

Cortés paced back and forth deep in thought. 'I'll do no such thing,' he said finally. 'Any open investigation could throw the whole expedition into turmoil. Look into it yourselves, if you must. You have my authority. But do it quietly . . .'

By the account originally given of it back on Cozumel, which Hope and Star repeated after recovering their composure, the town where the '*Castilan*' was being kept was named Mutul. It had more than a thousand inhabitants – 'every one of them cannibals, sirs,' translated Little Julian – and it was situated in the jungles of the interior some five hours' march south from Laguna Yalahau.

Newly converted to the merits of artillery, the guides urged Sandoval to bring the falconets; there was, they claimed, a good road cut through the jungle over which the weapons on their wheeled carriages could easily be manoeuvred. However, Brabo advised against it. 'Even if the road's as good as a king's highway, sir, the cannon will slow us down. It would be a different matter if we had fifty Indian bearers, but the fact is we don't and every minute we waste on the road is a minute longer for the enemy to make preparations against us. I say we move fast, get there before word of us reaches them, find our man and get out before the buggers know what's hit them . . . Besides, sir, look on the bright side! We have the dogs and they'll level the odds. I'm supposing you haven't seen them at work against men, being as you're newly out from Spain, but I've seen it often enough in the islands and believe me, it's a fearsome sight fit to turn the strongest stomach.'

Sandoval glanced at the slavering pack of wolfhounds, greyhounds and mastiffs, still excited by the recent commotion, pacing back and forth in the big cage on deck. Their keeper, a sullen, heavyset hunchback named Telmo Vendabal and his four filthy, foul-mouthed assistants were readying the animals' armour of viciously spiked collars, chain mail and even steel plate. Brabo was right, Sandoval reflected, he had never seen war dogs in action. He found himself hoping, fervently, that he would not do so today. 'Very well,' he agreed with a curt nod of his head, 'we leave the guns. Let's get on with it.'

With much shouting and cursing, frayed tempers and furious gesticulation, the launches were lowered into the surf from the decks of the brigantines and Sandoval, Brabo, the twenty-five members of Brabo's squad, Vendabal and his assistants, the ten dogs, Hope, Star and Little Julian were all landed.

Vendabal and his men each held two of the eager, straining hounds on chain leashes attached to their collars, but one of the men stumbled in the knee-deep water as he made his way up to the beach. With a roar a huge wolfhound broke free, charged across the sand, pounced on the body of an Indian who'd been trampled when the rest of the villagers took flight and plunged its fangs into his naked abdomen.

At least he's dead, thought Sandoval, but then the man suddenly howled and struggled to his feet, striking wildly at the dog's head, hauling it up with him, its teeth locked in his belly, blood gushing hither and yon.

The Indian was screaming now, a desperate, keening, pleading yowl as he struck again and again at the furious animal, his naked fists bouncing ineffectually off its armoured jowls and shoulders.

For a moment the man broke free, leaving some great steak of his flesh in the dog's mouth, which it gulped down in an instant before pursuing him, leaping through the air and attacking his naked upper right thigh, just below his breechclout, opening a ghastly wound and releasing another gouting spray of blood. The Indian went down on his face, still howling, high pitched and pitiful.

'In the name of God and all that's merciful,' Sandoval yelled at Vendabal, 'can't you stop this?' but the hunchback was watching with what looked like amusement – even pleasure.

'Then Hell take you!' exclaimed Sandoval, drawing his sword and advancing up the beach, intent on killing the dog, only to hear a rush of feet behind him and discover that a strong hand gripped his sword arm while another snaked around his neck. He heard Brabo's voice, smelt his garlic breath. 'Not so fast, sir,' said the sergeant. 'That's a valuable dog, sir, and not lightly to be wasted.'

His grip was iron. 'Unhand me, Sergeant,' Sandoval choked.

'With regret, sir, sorry, I can't do that.'

The Indian was still alive, still fighting. Somehow he tore himself loose from the wolfhound's jaws, rolled onto his back and tried to get his hands around the monster's armoured throat, but the effort was fruitless. His stomach already torn open, blood gushing onto the sand, the huge dog effortlessly shook off his grasp, worked its jaws into his belly and suddenly a heap of bloody intestines spooled out. A moment later the Indian's struggles ceased as the dog's massive head disappeared almost entirely inside his abdominal cavity.

Brabo loosed his grip on Sandoval's throat. 'They're trained to relish the flesh of the Indians, sir,' he explained. 'It's not a pleasant thing, but a time may come when you'll be thankful for it.'

No sooner had Olmedo and Díaz left the stateroom than Cortés turned to Pepillo: 'That's enough for today,' he said. 'You can go . . .'

'Go, sir?'

'Yes, go and help Melchior with the horses. You'll find him in the pasture. We'll work on the letter again tomorrow. I have other more urgent matters to attend to.'

Pepillo stood at the writing table for a moment, wrestling with his conscience. He and Melchior had said nothing to Cortés about the first murder. They'd been off the ship against his orders and had feared punishment. 'Besides,' Melchior had argued, 'he won't believe us anyway. It's our word against the word of a Holy Inquisitor. Who do you think will win?' He'd pulled out his dagger. 'We'll deal with Muñoz ourselves.'

Which was all very well, except they hadn't dealt with Muñoz and now murder had been done again.

'Sir . . .' Pepillo said as he shuffled the papers on the writing table into a neat pile.

'Yes?' A note of irritation.

Pepillo sought the right words. It was too late to report what he'd seen Muñoz doing three days ago. But might he not somehow hint, put an idea in the caudillo's mind? He gathered his courage: 'Sir . . . I couldn't help but overhear Father Olmedo and Don Bernal and I've been thinking, sir, that Father Muñoz was with Córdoba . . .'

'What's that boy? What are you suggesting?' Cortés's voice was suddenly hard and dangerous, and his features had contorted into an angry frown.

'. . . And Father Muñoz is very cruel,' Pepillo persisted, 'and . . . and—'

'Be silent, boy! I took your side against Muñoz but I'll not permit you to make such vile insinuations . . . He's here to do God's work, as are we all.'

Pepillo's heart fell. This wasn't going at all as he'd hoped. 'Yes, sir. I'm sorry, sir. I don't mean to cause offence . . . I just thought—'

'You're not here to think, boy!'

'No sir . . . It's just that . . .' Pepillo's voice trailed off. The fact was that he would never convince Cortés unless he was prepared to report what he'd seen and get himself and Melchior into terrible trouble – even worse trouble, now, than they would have faced if they'd reported it three days ago.

'It's just *what?*' Cortés roared, and Pepillo suddenly saw something monstrous in the caudillo's usually good-humoured features.

'Nothing, sir. I'm very sorry, sir, for speaking out of turn. I mean no harm.'

'Get out of my sight,' Cortés snapped.

And with that, filled with foreboding and self-loathing, Pepillo hurried off.

Below deck on the *San Sebastián*, Father Gaspar Muñoz lay naked, face down on the bare boards of his dark prayer cell in a state of sacred rapture. Last night he had sodomised and murdered a second young Indian boy. This morning, as penance, he had scourged himself severely, passed almost at once into communion with the divine, and now found himself in a vast, celestial chamber, flooded with supernal light, at the distant end of which Saint Peter sat in majesty on a great jewelled throne. The walls of the chamber were of mother-of-pearl, its lofty ceiling of diamonds and rubies, its floor of gold. Heavenly music, as though of a choir of angels, filled the air.

'Approach,' said the saint, his voice booming, and Muñoz felt himself drawn forward at tremendous speed so that an instant later he was before the throne.

'Kneel,' said the saint, and Muñoz knelt, his head bowed.

'You are troubled, my son,' said the saint.

'Yes, Holy Father.'

'Then unburden yourself . . .'

'The boys of the Indian tribe are dragons that lurk in hidden lairs to tempt the innocent. I was tempted, Holy Father, and I sinned again last night . . .'

'You do the work of God, my son. I have already taught you there is no sin in taking your reward on the bodies of the heathens.'

'I understand, Holy Father, but I am tempted to another and greater sin for which I seek your absolution . . .'

The saint leaned forward in his throne and tilted Muñoz's head up, forcing him to look into his eyes.

'Tell me, my son . . .'

Those eyes, like black whirlpools, seemed to suck Muñoz's brain out of his head. 'Holiness,' he said, 'you know my mind already . . .'

'Still I would hear you speak the words.'

'As you command, Holy Father. This matter concerns the blackamoor Melchior, who once before tempted me to carnal lust, and the page Pepillo. That little Judas! My own servant turned against me! Two days ago, when I was seeking out the first Indian child, I observed the pair of them watching me. Following me! I evaded them. But last night Melchior followed me again, this time alone . . .'

'And you evaded him once more and took a second child?'

'I did, Holy Father, but I cannot allow this spying to continue. I fear others will soon be informed of my . . . appetites. Melchior harbours a deep hatred for me—'

'Because you had carnal knowledge of him?'

'To my shame, Holiness . . . On the Córdoba expedition, my lust

350

for the blackamoor was great and he tempted me to the sin of Sodom.'

'The only sin is that you failed to kill him on the day you had him! I permit you these . . . pleasures, Muñoz, because you do God's work, but I expect you to be efficient. I expect you to be . . . discreet.'

'Will you absolve me then if I kill the blackamoor now, though he is a converted Christian? Will you absolve me if I kill the page Pepillo, also a Christian and reared amongst my own Dominican brothers?'

Muñoz felt the familiar warmth of a strong, calloused hand resting on his head. '*Ego te absolvo,*' the saint pronounced, '*a peccatis tuis, in nomine Patris, et Filii, et Spiritus Sancti.*'

The jungle chimed and trumpeted with birdsong and reverberated with the grunts and roars of wild beasts, while high above, long-haired black monkeys swung howling from branch to branch amongst the trees.

The road through this hostile, poisonous, alien realm was almost as astonishing as the jungle itself, somewhat raised above the surrounding ground level, two lances wide and surfaced, Sandoval discovered on investigation, with iron-hard limestone stucco over a stone and rubble fill. Brabo had joked earlier that even should it prove to be as good as a king's highway, it would not be practical to bring the cannon. Yet the workmanship of this *sacbe*, as Hope and Star called it – the word apparently meant 'white road' – was far superior to any of the great thoroughfares that Sandoval had travelled on in Spain and surely testified to the presence of a high civilisation with advanced engineering skills.

He found the thought a chilling one. The assumption had been made by Cortés that the Indians of the New Lands must be at the same low level of culture as the Taino of Cuba and Hispaniola; the first encounters made by Córdoba, and even this morning when the falconets were fired, had seemed to confirm this. Yet the *sacbe* sent a very different message.

Through the limited interpreting services of Little Julian, Sandoval attempted to question Hope and Star on the matter as the little group of expeditionaries pushed on at a forced march. His worry increased as he learnt that dozens of roads, just as well made as this, crisscrossed the Yucatán; however, the knots of tension that had settled at the base of his neck gradually began to dissipate as the guides explained that the *sacbes* had been built hundreds of years earlier by the ancestors of the Maya and that although they were still maintained and kept free of jungle growth, none of the tribes possessed the skills, organisation or technology to make such wonders today.

'Why?' Sandoval asked. 'What happened here to bring about this change?' But Hope and Star merely shrugged. Their ancestors, they said, were 'giants', but the gods had brought them low, and the Maya now inhabiting the Yucatán were ordinary mortals living simple lives, much as they themselves did on Cozumel, amongst the mighty memorials of their long-lost glory.

'We can be grateful for that at least,' Sandoval said to Brabo, and the sergeant nodded. 'Indeed, sir. Our numbers are small. It's the superiority of our arms and military discipline we must rely on to bring us victory.'

There was a chorus of agreement from the men and Miguel de La Mafla, the bright-eyed young adventurer who led the five musketeers in the squad, said, 'Don't worry, Sergeant, we'll see them off for you. Judging from what happened this morning, they'll run at the first sound of gunfire . . .'

'Just as well,' Brabo grinned, 'seeing as you boys can't hit a barn door at twenty paces!' He put his hand to the hilt of his broadsword: 'Until your aim improves, I'll put my trust in good Toledo steel.'

Rearing above them, the dense foliage of the great trees, overgrown with creepers, all but blotted out the sky, so the Spaniards marched in a deep emerald gloom through which the rays of the sun rarely penetrated directly. This made it difficult to know the time of day, but from his glimpses of the sun's position, Sandoval estimated it must already be an hour or more past noon. Despite the shade there was no refreshing breeze down here on the jungle floor, not even the slightest movement of air, and the heat and humidity were becoming insufferable. The armoured dogs, which led the column, straining at their leashes, panting, constantly snarling and snapping at the unfamiliar scents and sounds, were plainly distressed, their pink tongues lolling, saliva dripping from their fangs. Sandoval and Brabo came next, and behind them the twenty-five members of the squad marched in their customary square of five ranks of five. Several men had already stripped themselves of their armour, which they now carried awkwardly as they trudged onward, and Sandoval, itching and sweating, was seized by an over-whelming urge to unstrap his own heavy steel cuirass within which he imagined he was slowly baking like a crab in its shell.

'Stay alert, men,' Brabo warned casting a suspicious eye on the dense undergrowth hemming in the road on both sides. 'They say these savages use poison darts . . .'

'Which they bend over and blow out their arses at their enemies,' joked Diego Martin, a thickset, powerfully muscled crossbowman. As with the musketeers, there were five specialists with this weapon in the squad, and Martin had made a name amongst them for his accuracy and speed of reloading.

Esteban Valencia, one of the squad's two scouts, held a finger to his lips. 'Let's keep it quiet, boys,' he said. 'We've been marching nigh on five hours. Can't be far to where we're going now.'

Sandoval turned to Hope and Star and beckoned Little Julian closer. 'Ask them how far,' he said.

'Will know when get there,' came the answer after a muttered and urgent exchange in the Mayan language. 'Jungle all look same to them.'

Since they were in the midst of hostile territory, unknown except to the two fishermen (who had seemed lost themselves from the moment they left the sea behind), Sandoval had decided not to send the scouts ahead on the road. They were, in his opinion, more likely to be picked off than to return with any useful information. The strategy therefore remained much as Brabo had proposed it at the outset – move fast, hit the enemy hard in the hope of awing them into the same sort of panicked precipitous flight they'd provoked with the falconets on the beach, find the shipwrecked Spaniard and withdraw at a forced march to the waiting brigantines.

The likelihood of all this unravelling in dangerous and unpredictable ways was, of course, extremely high, but short of turning up here with the entire expeditionary force, which had never been an option as far as Cortés was concerned, Sandoval couldn't think of any better way to do things. He was brooding on what might go wrong, and constantly glancing left and right into the undergrowth, when he thought he

353

caught a flash of movement deep amongst the trees. The moment he focussed on the spot where he'd seen it, however, it was gone. Just leaves, thick bush, hanging creepers – nothing more.

Then . . . flash, flicker – there it was again on the other side of the road. This time he could have sworn he saw a human eye glaring at him out of the foliage, felt the shock of being watched, of a definite connection, but again when he focussed there was nothing there.

He might have gone on doubting himself if the dogs hadn't suddenly started baying all at once. Vendabal shouted a command, the handlers stooped to let a pair of heavy mastiffs off the leash, and with eager barks they bounded away, one to the left, one to the right, into the jungle. They were instantly lost to sight, crashing through the undergrowth, their course marked only by swaying branches; then there came a terrified yell, then another, followed by a horrible cacophony of snarling and snapping and men screaming in terror and pain from both sides of the road.

Vendabal was standing alert, listening, watching. It sounded as if the mastiffs had brought two of the spies down, but more crashing in the undergrowth revealed others trying to make their escape. Sandoval didn't hesitate: 'Put more dogs after them,' he yelled.

As the rest of the dogs sped left and right into the jungle, yapping with excitement, Brabo turned to Sandoval with a knowing leer. 'It's like I said, sir. They're trained to relish the flesh of the Indians.'

'Very well, Sergeant,' Sandoval said ruefully as more terrible screams rose up. 'I admit your point. I'm thankful for the presence of the dogs – and sooner than I expected to be . . .' He grimaced, and Brabo grinned, at a particularly hideous, gurgling cry from somewhere to the left of the road. 'Well, let's get after them and see what they've found.'

Brabo led a team of five men off to the left, Sandoval took another five to the right. He drew his sword and used it to push the dense green vegetation aside, sometimes having to hack through thick creepers and branches to clear a path, but the dogs and their victims were still making so much noise they were easily found.

There were two Indians here. The first was already dead and being disgustingly eaten by the two snarling mastiffs and the greyhound that had brought him down. The second, with only one dog on him, a big lurcher that had him by the shoulder, was a boy of barely fifteen years, and still very much alive. His thin body was naked but for a loincloth and his moon face, dotted with acne, daubed with stripes of green paint and framed by straight black hair, was contorted with terror as the beast shook him like a rag doll. One of Vendabal's handlers surged forward yelling staccato commands, striking at the dog with a whip. It released the boy and stood over him, its jaws dripping blood and saliva.

The youth was trembling, his eyes rolling in mute entreaty, as the conquistadors dragged him to his feet, bound his arms behind his back and marched him to the road. There Brabo had already rejoined the main squad with two more prisoners, both severely mauled, one with his throat so badly torn it seemed impossible he could survive.

'I suppose we'd better try and question them,' said Sandoval. 'If Little Julian's interpreting skills are up to it.'

Brabo nodded brusquely. 'Be nice to know what sort of reception's waiting for us ahead.' He barked an order and the Indians were forced to their knees in the middle of the road. Before Sandoval could stop him, the sergeant had drawn a dagger from his belt, seized the hair of the boy who'd been taken by the lurcher and sliced off his left ear, producing a spray of blood and horrified screams from the captive.

'What the hell . . . ?' Sandoval gasped.

'Just letting them know we mean business, sir,' said Brabo. 'If you don't have the stomach for this it'd be best to leave the interrogation to me.'

With feelings of shame, Sandoval shrugged helplessly and stood back while the horror unfolded. Did Little Julian even understand the questions Brabo put to him? Did he translate them correctly to the captives? Were they brave men, or simply confused when at first they didn't reply? And when speech finally tumbled from them as an eye was gouged out here, a hand hacked off there, were the answers they gave truthful and did Little Julian translate them accurately?

Within minutes all three of the Indians were dead and Sandoval knew what he could already have guessed – that refugees fleeing from the coast had brought warning of the approach of the Spaniards, that the town of Mutul was alert and prepared, and that two hundred warriors, armed and ready for battle, were waiting to annihilate them.

355

For a moment Sandoval considered the possibility of flight. But only for a moment. To return to Cortés without even having attempted to win the prize was too shameful an outcome to imagine. Better to die here than be branded a coward for the rest of his life. He took a long swig from his water bottle and turned to Brabo. 'What do you reckon?' he asked.

'Nigh-on thirty Spaniards and ten dogs against two hundred painted savages?' The sergeant's sneer said it all. 'I reckon we march right in and kill them all, sir.'

Chapter Forty-Nine

After a mile the jungle began to thin and Sandoval and his squad, all fully armoured again and ready for war, soon found themselves in open terrain obviously cleared by human hands. There were signs of recent slash and burn, with blackened tree stumps still standing out a cubit or two above the acres of charred waste that lined both sides of the road, but ahead lay regular fields with the first green shoots of new maize – a crop already known to the Spaniards from Cuba and Hispaniola – pushing through the earth.

Less than a mile away across the fields lay the town of Mutul, consisting for the most part of simple huts clustered round a towering stone pyramid with stepped sides, far larger than the pyramid of Cozumel. At the edges of the town Sandoval spied green patches that he took to be vegetable gardens, and an orchard planted with regular lines of tall, leafy trees. What most pressed upon his mind, however, was the great mass of people boiling from every quarter like ants out of a disturbed nest and, much nearer, at a distance of seven hundred paces, a disciplined force of about two hundred heavily armed warriors clad in loincloths and skins, arrayed in four ranks of fifty, and rapidly closing on the Spanish column.

'Orders, sir?' said Brabo. His voice was terse.

Sandoval was still haunted by guilt at the torture he'd witnessed and failed to stop, but at least the spies had spoken true and he'd had time to think through a strategy in the last mile of the march. His men were few in numbers, but the sheer shocking strangeness of their appearance, their armour, their dogs and their science of warfare offered powerful advantages over the Indians.

357

There were five archers in the squad and their Genoese crossbows were lethal killing machines. They had an effective range up to four hundred paces against unarmoured foes and, even at two hundred paces, the steel bolts they fired could penetrate plate armour. Sandoval also had five musketeers, armed with Spanish-made arquebuses that fired lead balls about the diameter of a man's thumb. These travelled much faster than crossbow bolts and often shattered on impact causing devastating wounds, but they were rarely effective at ranges beyond a hundred paces.

As to reloading, the muskets with their powder and ramrods and smouldering matchlocks, and the crossbows with their crannequins and windlasses to rewind the tough strings were equally cumbersome – both types of weapon requiring about a minute between shots. The great advantage of the muskets today, however, would come from the thunder and smoke of their firing. Since there had been no landing and no fighting when Córdoba's fleet had recced Laguna Yalahau, it was safe to assume the inhabitants of Mutul had never faced guns and most probably never even heard rumour of such weapons. With luck the effects would be spectacular.

'Crossbowmen and musketeers to the fore to form the first two ranks of the square,' Sandoval barked. 'Dogs and handlers stand to the side. Crossbowmen fire at two hundred paces, countermarch to the rear of the square and reload, musketeers fire at a hundred paces and countermarch to the rear. Then release the dogs.'

As they charged closer, the enemy began to shout war cries in their singsong language and to whistle and whoop in an eerie and disconcerting manner. When they were three hundred paces out, still beyond the effective range of the muskets, they deployed a weapon Sandoval was unfamiliar with – angled wooden sticks used to launch a hail of little spears that arched up into the sky and swooped down with alarming accuracy on the Spanish square. Reacting instinctively, the men in the rear three ranks raised their bucklers and big adarga shields to protect both themselves and the ranks in front. The barrage of darts, tipped with flint points, was easily deflected. Three of the dogs in the baying pack to the right of the square took direct hits, but their steel armour shattered the flint warheads leaving the hounds themselves unharmed. Then – *click . . . whoosh* – the crossbowmen let fly, and five of the onrushing enemy tumbled screaming to the ground, transfixed by the heavy steel bolts. As the crossbowmen stepped back through the square, a manoeuvre they had practised a hundred times, the musketeers fired a single massive, crashing volley into the heart of the enemy, now less than a hundred paces distant, and quite suddenly, through the thick clouds of foul smoke, Sandoval saw what he had been silently praying for, saw the Maya horde falter and stumble, saw the fear on their faces and their rolling eyes, heard their howls of terror.

On a European battlefield the toll taken by the guns would have been confined to those actually hit, and the charge would have continued unbroken, but here amongst savages who had never encountered firearms before, the effect was devastating beyond all proportion, almost as though the Spanish were not mortal men but gods throwing thunderbolts. The enemy front ranks instantly turned and ran, while the ranks behind, still carried forward by their own momentum, crashed into them in a jumbled, churning, panic-stricken scrum, upon which, snarling and baying, teeth snapping, armour gleaming, like demons released from hell, pounced the ten furious war dogs. Here a man's throat was torn out, there the great artery in another's thigh gushed blood, here a coil of guts spilled loose, there a wolfhound clamped a face in its massive jaws. Few of the Maya even tried to fight back against the onslaught, and those who did found their puny stone weapons unable to pierce the animals' armour.

Sandoval watched awestruck for a moment as the huge beasts ravaged the enemy, spreading chaos and terror, then Brabo whispered in his ear, 'Order the advance, sir.'

'We can't watch him all the time,' said Pepillo. 'You have your duties, I have mine, but Muñoz is free to move around as he pleases.'

'I followed him last night,' Melchior admitted suddenly.

'You followed him? Why didn't you tell me?'

'You were working with Cortés; the chance came and I took it.'

'Chance! Suppose he'd caught you? Are you mad?'

Melchior had a strange, sad look on his face. 'No. Not mad. I wanted to stop him . . . doing what he does. But he gave me the slip and sure enough he killed again.'

It was the afternoon of Saturday 27 February, and they were in the paddock where the expedition's eighteen precious cavalry mounts were penned. In the past two days, shaking off the stiffness and jitters that had afflicted them after the storm and the long journey from Cuba, the horses had thrived on the pastures of rich wild grass that grew plentifully around the foot of the low hill on which the town of Cozumel stood.

Melchior was an accomplished rider and spent several hours in the paddock every day, grooming and exercising Molinero, Cortés's dark chestnut stallion. This afternoon other manservants were also present doing the same work with Puertocarerro's silver-grey mare, Alvarado's white stallion Bucephalus, Escalante's light chestnut gelding with its three white feet, and Cristóbal de Olid's sorrel mare.

Pepillo watched Melchior as he patiently brushed Molinero's flank and realised he didn't fully understand the depth of the older boy's hatred for Muñoz. Of course the friar was evil! Of course he should be stopped before he murdered any more Indian children! But were he and Melchior the ones to do it, and what had driven his friend to take the awful risk of going after the friar alone? Even together, what chance did they really stand?

'The only mercy,' Melchior said after a long silence, 'is he's not going to find it easy to catch another child. There's uproar in the town after last night's murder, and the Indians are beginning to lose their fear of us.'

Pepillo thought about this while he held his hand under Molinero's whiskery lips and felt the horse's hot breath as he nuzzled him. He very much wanted to learn to ride and constantly pestered Melchior to allow him to climb up on the big animal's back, so far without success. 'Muñoz won't stop,' he said eventually. 'I saw what was in his eyes when he was beating me and I don't believe he'll ever stop.'

'You're right,' said Melchior with a fierce grimace, 'but he's not going to risk a murder when the sun's up like he did the first day. Tell you what. If Cortés has nothing for us tonight we'll sneak out and watch the *San Sebastián*. If Muñoz comes to shore we'll follow him.'

Pepillo's heart sank. Every instinct screamed this was a bad plan that could get them both into terrible trouble and possibly even dead. But he had to support his friend, didn't he? And he didn't want to seem a coward, so he nodded bravely and said yes.

As Sandoval broke into a run he heard himself yelling at the top of his voice 'Santiago and at them! Santiago and at them!'

Behind him, with a clank of armour and the rasp of steel as weapons were drawn, the square of twenty-five seasoned veterans surged forward, every man echoing the rousing war cry with which Spaniards had gone into battle for a thousand years. They fell mercilessly upon the disordered mass of the Maya, some retreating, some still attempting to advance, cutting them to pieces with swords and battle-axes, impaling them on pikes, clubbing them down with spiked maces and iron flails.

In the thick of it, Sandoval found himself face to face with a bellowing wild-eyed savage, dressed only in a loincloth, wielding a long wooden sword with thin flakes of some black stone set into its edges, and clearly ready to fight rather than run. The man was holding the weapon in a two-handed grip, slashing it madly through the air with tremendous power but no balance or style, so it was a simple matter for Sandoval to parry and deflect, slide his right foot forward as he had been taught, drive the point of his broadsword into the warrior's heart and withdraw. Again that pluck of innards on steel that he'd felt when he'd killed his first man less than ten days before, but this time there was no remorse – rather a sense of exultation – as his enemy crumpled at his feet in a spray of blood.

Brabo shouted, 'Behind you!', and Sandoval whirled into a massive blow from another wooden sword that smashed against his cuirass, shattering every one of the stone flakes along the edge of the weapon but doing him no damage at all. The new attacker was a lean, lank-haired Mayan youth whose eyes locked on his in frozen disbelief as Sandoval hacked him near in half in the riposte.

Moments later it was over and the last of the Mayan warriors were in full flight across the fields. The musketeers had reloaded and fired another volley after them and the baying dogs charged on towards the assembled townsfolk, who also turned and ran uttering wails of horror.

* * *

Don Pedro de Alvarado sat out on the navigation deck of the *San Sebastián*, a length of sailcloth rigged to give him shade from the afternoon sun, while Doctor La Peña examined his broken forearm, and set about rebinding the splints with bandages thickly coated in a mixture of egg whites, flour and pig fat that would harden in the next hours into a rigid cast.

Leaning on the rail surrounding the deck, supposedly waiting for La Peña's ministrations to various health needs of their own, but really here to further their other, more clandestine purpose, were lantern-jawed Juan Escudero and his massively bearded ally Juan Velázquez de León, the two ringleaders of the clique loyal to Diego de Velázquez, the governor of Cuba. Their approach to Alvarado the day before had come while he was still hurt and angry, indeed it had come precisely *because* he was hurt and angry, and they knew nothing of his reconciliation with Cortés this morning.

La Peña was also of the Velazquista persuasion, hence the plotters' willingness to speak in front of him. Indeed, after spending the first night of the voyage from Santiago sharing the brig with him, the kidnapped physician had clung to Escudero like shit to a shoe. *Repulsive little arse-licker*, thought Alvarado. The only saving grace was that the snivelling, deceitful, trouble-making doctor, whose outsized buttocks wobbled like jellies in his pantaloons as he busied himself preparing the bandages, was good at what he did. His skill with casts and poultices had undoubtedly speeded up the healing of Alvarado's broken arm and that was a small mercy to be thankful for. 'How long do you think now, La Peña? A week? Two . . .'

The doctor made insincere clucking noises – meant, presumably, to mimic concern. 'No, no,' he said. 'It's not yet ten days since your . . . err . . . accident. You'll have to wear the cast for at least another month. Maybe longer.'

'Another month! That's damned inconvenient. I'm a fighting man.'

'Indeed so, Don Pedro, and one whose prowess is legendary. But I should refrain from battle, if I were you, until that arm is fully healed . . .'

'It's my right arm does the fighting,' Alvarado glowered.

'And your left that holds the shield.'

'I've gone into battle without a shield before . . .'

'As you'll have to again if battle is imminent,' said La Peña. He glanced over the rail at the peaceful bay of Cozumel and added, 'But that does not appear to be the case.'

Escudero sniffed loudly and wiped a drop of clear mucus from the end of his long nose. 'We'll not be fighting fellow Spaniards, that's for sure.'

'Oh,' said Alvarado, 'were we expecting to?'

'All that nonsense about Pedrarias and a rival expedition to the New Lands,' Escudero growled. 'It's obvious now that Cortés was lying . . .'

'It was just a pretext to dupe us into leaving Santiago in an unholy rush without proper procedure,' complained Velázquez de León, scratching his huge black beard.

'Without the blessing of His Excellency the Governor,' added Escudero. He turned to fix Alvarado with a fanatical glare. 'You supported Cortés in that folly,' he said, 'and look what your loyalty to your so-called "friend" earned you. We all saw the shameful way he treated you over the matter of Cozumel. That's why, despite our differences, we thought it right to approach you yesterday with our proposal. I hope we were not mistaken.'

'Ah, yes, your proposal. But yesterday you beat about the bush somewhat, and I prefer straight talk – therefore tell me plainly what you want of me.'

Escudero paused to peer suspiciously around the deck and lowered his voice to a conspiratorial whisper. 'Why that you join us, of course, to save the expedition . . .'

'To make it legal again,' added Velázquez de León, with an emphatic thump of his fist on the rail, 'to bring it back under the jurisdiction of Don Diego de Velázquez . . .'

'Your cousin,' Alvarado noted.

'Yes, my cousin.' The tanned skin of the big man's face turned beetroot red in the few areas where it was not covered by hair. 'But also your patron for many years. Why, if my memory serves me right, he even advanced you the funds to purchase this great carrack of yours.'

'And besides, Don Diego is the governor of Cuba,' prompted

Escudero, 'the secular power throughout this region, appointed by His Majesty the King himself, whose will we flout at our peril.'

'So, to get back in his good books,' Alvarado said, 'you want me to help you arrest Cortés and ship him back in irons to Cuba. Excuse me for speaking plainly, but do I understand you correctly on this?'

Velázquez de León looked uncomfortable: 'Well, yes . . . More or less.'

Tsk, Tsk, from Escudero: 'No "more or less" about it. That's what we want you to do, Don Pedro, and because your role will be crucial in preventing a rebellion amongst Cortés's friends, we offer you joint command of the expedition thereafter. Now tell us, here and now, are you with us or are you against us? Are you in or are you out?'

Alvarado looked at the fat doctor who knelt at his side listening intently while pretending to fuss with his arm. 'What do you say, La Peña? Should I be with or against this cunning plot? Should I be in or should I be out?'

Escudero bristled at once. 'Don't toy with us, Don Pedro. This is a matter of life and death.'

Yes, thought Alvarado, *your death – if I know my friend Hernán well*. But he answered: 'I never toy, Juan. Cortés has offended me mightily, as you all observed, and I'm attracted by your offer. I'm just not sure this is the right time to strike.'

Now it was Escudero's turn to flush, quite an achievement since the man's skin had the pallid, lifeless quality of a five-day-dead cadaver. 'Not the right time? After you've made us show our hand to you in this way? By God, Don Pedro, you will join us or I'll see you dead.'

Alvarado pushed La Peña aside and stood up, his hand dropping to the hilt of his falchion. '*You'll* see me dead? Begging your pardon, Don Juan, but I think not. Even with only one arm, I'll cut you down in a trice should you be foolish enough to come at me.'

Escudero lunged forward but Velázquez de León stepped in his way. 'No! No! This is *not* what we planned, this is *not* what we came here to do. Don Pedro is our friend, our natural ally and much wronged by Cortés. If he says now is not the right time then let's at least hear his reasons . . .'

Fool, thought Alvarado, *weak, bearded fool*. But what he said was:

'I don't share your view about Pedrarias. For all we know his fleet could be within a day's sail of us now, either to land here and attempt to overwhelm us or strike direct for the mainland to beat us to its richest treasures. Either way, until we're sure of the matter, I don't think it's wise to fight amongst ourselves.'

'There *is* no Pedrarias fleet!' Escudero was practically foaming at the mouth. 'It's an invention of Cortés's, a clever fabrication, to suit his purposes.'

'Perhaps . . . Perhaps not. We must wait and see.'

Escudero was muttering about security risks, Alvarado knowing too much, a trap, a ruse . . .

'You'll keep what's been said here today to yourself?' Velázquez de León said anxiously.

'Yes of course,' Alvarado replied. 'I'm the soul of discretion. We'll watch and wait for another week or two. If the threat of Pedrarias fails to materialise, then feel free to approach me again. You'll find me much more amenable.'

Escudero stepped forward until his long ugly face was just a finger's breadth from Alvarado's. He said nothing, just stood there looking at him, then turned his back and stamped off, followed, like a tame dog, by Velázquez de León.

'Well,' said Alvarado half to himself, half to La Peña who was still pretending to be busy with the plaster cast on his arm, 'that was interesting.'

Ten minutes later, after La Peña had scurried off to join his masters, there came a clump of boots and Bernal Díaz climbed the steps from the main deck. The jumped-up farm-hand whom Cortés had promoted to ensign was followed by the swordsman Francisco Mibiercas, more a man of Alvarado's own class, and another young soldier named Alonso de la Serna. All three were carrying crossbows and quivers stuffed with bolts.

'Excuse us, Don Pedro,' said Díaz without preamble, 'but since we won't be sailing until the refits are finished, and that's going to be a few more days, we'd like your permission to take a bit of shore leave.'

Raising a quizzical eyebrow, Alvarado cast a glance across the bay and up the hill towards Cozumel. 'Shore leave? There're no taverns in this town, you know. No ladies of the night either.' He laughed: 'Unless you fancy tupping these Maya she-goats.'

'We want to do a bit of hunting,' said Mibiercas, holding forth his crossbow, 'but not for ewes. We're told there are big herds of deer grazing on the south side of the island. Thought we'd head down there this afternoon, camp out for a couple of nights and see what we can bag.'

'Not sure I should let you go. There's been a murder in the town.'

'I was told there had been two,' said Díaz.

'Seems the Indians are holding us responsible. There are those who think there might be trouble.'

'I doubt it,' interjected Mibiercas. 'The Indians don't have the stomach for it after the beating we gave them.'

'Agreed!' Alvarado grinned. He pointed to the hilt of the longsword jutting above Mibiercas's left shoulder: 'I hear you know how to use that, but how do you rate it against a broadsword, for example, or a good Toledo rapier?'

'I always say it's not so much the weapon that counts, as the man wielding it, but I like the range the longsword gives me.'

'Here, let me take a look,' said Alvarado, holding out his hand.

Mibiercas reached back across his shoulder, unsheathed the weapon and passed it over for the other man to examine.

'Nice weight,' Alvarado commented. 'Double fuller cross-section too, so it's strong. Good sharp point on it. You can put it through plate armour, I'd hazard?'

'Like a hot knife through butter, Don Pedro.'

'Well, very good then.' Alvarado passed the weapon back. 'Perhaps we'll do some sparring when this damned arm of mine is better.'

'I would be honoured,' said Mibiercas with a bow.

Díaz coughed. 'About the hunting, Don Pedro? Do we have your permission?'

'By all means yes. Be back on Monday. Enjoy yourselves, but half of what you bag goes in the communal pot.'

By Sandoval's count, some sixty of the Mayan fighters, with varying degrees of injury, had survived the carnage. Menaced by the musketeers and crossbowmen, they now sat hunched on the ground, miserable, vanquished and terrified, while the dogs – called back from inflicting further harm on the fleeing women and children – feasted on the flesh and offal of the dead.

Sandoval viewed the spectacle with disgust, but the animals needed to eat. He turned to Brabo and asked: 'What shall we do with the prisoners?'

The sergeant's face was expressionless. 'We're still outnumbered,' he said, 'they might turn on us at any time.'

'They don't look capable of turning on anybody.'

'No guarantee they'll stay that way.'

Sandoval sighed. 'I suppose we'd best tie them and leave them here.'

A sour look. 'I don't advise it, sir. The townspeople will return and free them when we're gone. They might come after us.'

'So what should we do?'

'Well, let's get them bound hand and foot to start with. The men will find it good sport to set the dogs on some of them and it won't take long to cut the throats of the rest.'

'You can't be serious.'

'I'm completely serious, sir. This is war.'

The worst of it was that Sandoval could see the logic of Brabo's position. In many ways killing these captives was the easiest and most sensible thing to do. But his guilt at permitting the torture of the spies still burned him and he was loath to add to it. 'Tie their hands for now and march them into the town,' he said in a firm tone that he hoped brooked no dissent. 'I'll make a decision later.'

Though it was mid-afternoon, the sun's rays could not penetrate the hot, fetid, claustrophobic prayer cell in the hold of the San Sebastián that Alvarado had given Father Gaspar Muñoz for his quarters.

The friar did not object. He had endured far worse in his rise through monastic orders. Of course the little cell was less grand than the accommodation he was to have enjoyed on Cortés's ship before his rift with that vile man. But the discomfort and the darkness were a form of continuous mortification – to say nothing of the lasting pains from this morning's flagellation! – like thorns in the flesh to buffet him lest he exalt himself too highly for the great works he was called to do.

A single candle burned in the darkness and, by its light, Muñoz repeatedly passed first one side then the other of the steel blade of his razor back and forth, back and forth, across a leather strop, from time to time testing the edge with his thumb. When he was satisfied it was fit for tonight's purpose, he folded the blade away into its bone handle and tucked the instrument into an inner pocket of his habit.

He snuffed the candle and got to his feet.

It was time to take a stroll on deck. Since it was Saturday he thought he might preach a sermon for the edification and improvement of any of the crew and soldiers who happened to be gathered there.

Mutul was a town of some four hundred hovels and shanties, for the most part consisting of a single room with walls of wattle and adobe, and roofs thatched with palm fronds. Even with the small force at Sandoval's command it was a simple matter to search them all but, except for a few of the aged and the sick, who had clearly been too infirm to run, every one of them was deserted. It seemed that all the inhabitants had fled into the surrounding jungle.

Then came a shout from Brabo, who was investigating a group of larger structures close to the base of the ancient pyramid. 'Better get over here, sir,' the sergeant yelled. 'Something you need to see.' Signalling Little Julian to follow, Sandoval broke into a run, feeling a surge of excitement, and found himself moments later in front of what appeared to be a prison containing about forty naked, ill-kempt inmates. Hope and Star had just reached the spot, Star gripping the bars and peering eagerly through them. Sandoval joined him and asked in Castilian: 'Is any one of you a Spaniard?' The prisoners cowered back in terror at his voice. '*Is any one of you a Spaniard?*' he repeated, louder this time, but again the only answer was a low murmur of fear.

Now Star was shouting something incomprehensible in his language and Sandoval saw a female prisoner looking up. She was perhaps twenty years of age with filthy hair and a mud-smeared body. Star shouted again, and beckoned. Beside him Hope also spoke, his voice low and urgent. The woman rose to a crouch, one hand covering her crotch, the other placed across her breasts, and sobbed repeatedly 'Ikan, Ikan' – Star's name! – then ran across the earth floor of the prison and embraced the young guide through the bars.

'What's going on here?' Sandoval asked Little Julian.

'Sir, Ikan find sister, sir.'

'His sister?'

'Yes, these cannibals peoples take her last year. Keep her. We don't come, next big moon they eat her.'

'Nobody told me Star had a sister.'

'Oh yes, sir, she daughter of Cozumel cacique.'

Which meant that Ikan must be the cacique's son! Sandoval mentally reviewed the events of the past two days – the all-too-plausible story about the 'Castilan', the insistence that a strong force would be required to free him, young Ikan offered as a guide – and realised in a flash how the Spanish had been played for fools. The wily old Cozumel chieftain had spun a clever web, and offered Cortés a lure he could not resist, with the sole objective of rescuing his own daughter!

'Well I'll be damned!' he muttered, restraining himself with difficulty from striking Little Julian, who must have been in on the scheme from the beginning. Turning his back on the squint-eyed interpreter he muttered, 'All this way, risking our lives, for some slip of an Indian girl.'

He was half resolved to leave her in the prison – with Star and Hope for company! – and march his men back to the brigantines posthaste when a flash of movement caught his eye.

There!

A tall Indian darted from the cover of one of the adobe longhouses near the base of the pyramid, sprinted across a patch of open ground and concealed himself behind a second structure. Fearing he was not alone but part of a new attacking force, Sandoval called a warning to Brabo and charged towards the Indian's position, skidded round the side of the longhouse brandishing his sword and was confronted by an unkempt, cowering, ragged apparition who held up large, grimy hands in supplication and croaked some words in his barbaric tongue. Sandoval had his sword at the man's throat as Brabo came running to join him. 'Julian!' yelled the sergeant, drawing his dagger. 'Over here at the double. We've got another spy to question.'

By now most of the conquistadors, drawn by the commotion, were gathering round and, as Brabo stepped in, the cowering Indian began to speak more rapidly, his croaking voice taking on almost the cadence and rhythms of a Latin prayer. *How odd*, Sandoval thought. A nagging suspicion troubled him and the more closely he looked at the man, filthy and lean, eyes like pale flames burning in the dark hearth of his face, the more strange and incongruous he seemed. He was naked except for a single sandal on his right foot and a squalid breechclout into which his left sandal, which appeared to be broken, was tied. His black hair hung lank and greasy to his shoulders and was braided over his forehead in the local fashion. He was beardless, as were all the Maya, but – another peculiarity – there was heavy stubble about his jowls and these were a people who seemed unable to grow facial hair.

Julian trotted up and Brabo put the tip of his dagger against the captive's face, breaking the skin under his right eye so that a line of blood guttered out and ran down his sooty cheek. 'Right, my lovely,' said the sergeant, 'I've got a few questions to ask you.' He turned to the interpreter. 'Julian, tell him. He answers us straight and he dies easy, he answers us false and he dies hard.'

'Wait!' Sandoval was surprised by the authority in his own voice. 'Not so fast.' He laid a restraining hand on the sergeant's thick wrist, drawing the dagger down.

'What now, sir?' Brabo sighed. 'Not more scruples, I hope? We don't have time for scruples.'

'No, not scruples. I believe you're about to torture the very man we've come to find. Back away from him. Give him space. I want to hear what he has to say for himself.'

The Indian stood panting, looking round at the hard, cruel faces of the conquistadors, the fingers of his right hand with their cracked blackened nails going to the cut beneath his eye, and a moan of fear – or was it something else? Was it frustration? – escaping his mouth. Several times he seemed on the verge of speaking, but only incoherent grunts and stammers emerged until suddenly he seemed to master himself and said in clumsy, somewhat halting Castilian: 'Gentlemen, are you Christians?'

A shocked silence followed which Sandoval was the first to break. 'We are Christians and Spaniards,' he confirmed.

The Indian burst into tears and fell to his knees: 'God and the blessed Mary of Seville!' he exclaimed. 'I am saved.'

Then, even stranger, he asked if it was Wednesday the twenty-fourth of February.

Sandoval informed him it was Saturday the twenty-seventh, at which the Indian said: 'I have kept a count of the days these past eight years. It seems I am not far out.' He then dried his tears, raised his hands and eyes and proclaimed: 'Thank you, God, oh thank you, thank you, thank you for saving me from these infidels and hellish men. Thank you, Lord, for restoring me to Christians and men of my nation.'

'Who are you?' Sandoval asked when the odd figure had finished his prayer.

All the conquistadors gathered there, pressed in close to hear his answer.

'Sir,' the man replied, 'I am Jerónimo de Aguilar of Ecija, and I am a castaway in this land.'

'You are a Spaniard!'

'I am, sir.' He turned towards Brabo. 'I understand why you thought me an Indian,' he told the sergeant. 'I've been amongst the heathens so long that at first I could not recall our tongue, but I'm a Spaniard born and bred and a good Christian.' As though to prove it, Aguilar pulled from some fold of his verminous loincloth a Book of Hours, very old and worn, which he opened and held above his head.

At once a flurry of cheers broke out from the conquistadors, a hubbub of conversation, and one by one the soldiers, Brabo first amongst them, stepped forward to clap the man on his naked back.

Aguilar's initial clumsy articulation of Castilian improved rapidly as he told his story, seeming less of an Indian and more of a Spaniard as every minute went by. He had been, he said, a slave of the cacique of Mutul. He had been ushered into the jungle with the cacique's house-hold some hours before, without being told the reason why, but after hearing the gunfire and realising that European forces must be on hand, he had slipped away from his captors and hastened to the town to seek his salvation.

'We were told you were a castaway,' Sandoval said, 'but how did you come to be here in Mutul, so far from the coast?'

'By many long and bloody twists and turns,' said Aguilar. 'In the year 1511 I was in Darién, involved in the wars and quarrels and mischances of that villain Pedrarias. I set sail for Hispaniola with some others to acquaint the governor with what was going on. We got as far as Jamaica when the caravel struck on shoals and twenty of us barely escaped in the ship's boat, without sails, without water, without bread, and with only one miserable pair of oars. We drifted in this fashion for thirteen or fourteen days, when we were caught in a current running very fast and strong to the west that brought us to the shores of the Yucatán. Eight of us had died of thirst by then, but matters only became worse. Soon after we made landfall we fell into the hands of a rascally cacique named Taxmar. He sacrificed five of us to his idols and had their flesh prepared for the pot, making a fiesta of it and offering a share to his friends—'

'Dear God,' Sandoval interrupted. 'What horrors you have faced.'

'I and the six others who remained alive,' Aguilar continued, 'were placed in a cage to be fattened for the next banquet. To avoid such an abominable death we broke out of our prison and fled to the jungle. It was God's will that we should find our way to Mutul, for Aquincuz, the cacique of this town in whose hands I have been ever since, is a powerful man and a mortal enemy of Taxmar. He is no less a cannibal and a sacrificer of humans, but I think he found us a curiosity, and besides we had escaped from his enemy – so he sheltered us and spared our lives, though he kept us in servitude. One by one over the years since then my companions died, until no one remained but myself. I'd all but given up hope when I heard your guns . . .'

As Sandoval and Aguilar talked, the other Spaniards in the squad listened in, and from time to time added comments of their own. Hard-bitten men though they were, they were plainly astonished by the castaway's account and filled with fear at the thought that the people they had come to conquer were in the habit of sacrificing and eating men.

When the telling was done, the gates of Mutul's prison were forced open and its wretched inmates were permitted to come forth. They were all, Aguilar confirmed, to have been eaten in a month's time at the next full moon when one of the great Mayan festivals was to be held.

'Tell them they're free to go,' Sandoval said. He looked with more sympathy than he would have believed possible a few moments before on Star embracing his sister and added generously: 'Those who wish to return with us to Cozumel may do so.'

Aguilar put the offer to the freed captives, more than half of whom instantly said they wished to accompany the conquistadors. The rest hurried off towards the jungle. 'Most will be recaptured before they get back to their home villages,' Aguilar said wistfully, 'but they're too afraid of you to stay. They heard the guns – we all heard the guns! For them it was the sound of terror. For me it was the sound of hope.'

In preparation for the five-hour return march through the jungle to the waiting brigantines, Aguilar led the conquistadors to the town's main water supply. It lay in the midst of a shady orchard and proved to be not a river, or a lake, as Sandoval had expected, but an almost perfectly circular sinkhole, a bowshot across, which plunged straight down into bedrock to a huge crystal-clear pool fifty feet below. Such natural wells, Aguilar explained, were fed by underground rivers. They were called *conots* and were the main source of water for the Maya throughout much of the northern Yucatán.

Using buckets and ropes left in place by the townsfolk, the Spaniards drank their fill and replenished their empty flasks, while the dog handlers saw to the needs of their hounds. Meanwhile, under Hope and Star's direction, some of the women prisoners they'd freed had busied themselves preparing a meal of stewed meat, cooked with chillies, and delicious flatbreads called *qua* made from freshly ground maize. Though hungry, the conquistadors initially looked askance at the stew, and some asked if there was human flesh in it, but all scruples were cast aside when Aguilar assured them it was nothing more than a medley of venison and turkey, requisitioned, like the maize, from the town's stores.

The question of what was to be done with the Mayan fighters

captured in the battle weighed heavily on Sandoval's mind. They were, for the present, bound hand and foot and locked in the prison. Brabo remained adamant that they must all be put to death.

'What do you say, Aguilar?' Sandoval asked. But the tall castaway, who claimed never to have been fed properly by the Maya, was eating with intense concentration, stuffing his mouth with the rich stew which dribbled down his chin and onto a linen shift he'd taken from the home of his former captor.

'What do you say?' Sandoval urged.

Aguilar gestured towards the prison. 'They are savages,' he mumbled through a mouthful, 'but that doesn't mean we must also be savages. Let them live. Leave them there.' He returned to his chewing.

'They'll break free and come after us,' Brabo objected.

Aguilar considered it. 'You don't know these people,' he said finally. He looked to the sun, hanging low in the sky. 'Our march to your brigantines must be done for the most part after dark and the Maya are a superstitious people. They don't like to fight at night when the spirits of the dead walk abroad. Besides, the jungle is a dangerous place, patrolled by great beasts. Even if the captives break free they'll not follow us until morning . . .'

'By which time we'll have sailed.'

Aguilar was chewing ferociously. 'By which time, God willing, we'll have sailed,' he agreed.

'But what of these beasts?' asked Sandoval.

'They are a species of panther. Some are tawny, with black spots. Others – truly they are devils – are all black in colour. They are as large and heavy as the biggest hound and they're very fierce. The Maya call them *B'alam*. They hunt by night.'

'Are they a danger to us?' Sandoval asked.

Aguilar shrugged: 'Not if we stick together. They hunt alone, never in packs. Besides, the dogs will scare them off.'

'Still,' Sandoval glanced uneasily at the late afternoon sun, 'the sooner we get on the road the better.' He turned to Brabo: 'I'm sorry, García,' he said, 'I respect your advice but I can't bring myself to order the deaths of our captives. They will remain in the prison, tied as they are but alive. Do you accept?'

374

'It's not for me to accept or deny, sir. Command is a lonely business, suited to a gentleman such as yourself. You must carry its burdens.'

As the sun dropped low it swelled into a vast orange disk, alien and somehow menacing, streaked with smears of cloud. Lying poised on the horizon where the sky met the ocean it cast a glittering path across the ripples of the bay.

Pepillo and Melchior had been dismissed for the evening by Cortés, who was in a foul and sullen mood. They had made their way to shore and found a hiding place in the thick undergrowth of a palm grove a bowshot from the water's edge that gave them a fine view of the sunset and overlooked the spot where the launches from the ships usually came to load and unload cargo and passengers. They were both armed, Melchior with his long rusty dagger and Pepillo with a small hatchet that his friend had procured for him and insisted he thrust into his belt. The idea that he might actually have to use this weapon to kill Muñoz made Pepillo feel sick, and a little light-headed. Yet this seemed to be Melchior's only plan. 'We'll wait and watch here,' the older boy said, 'and if the devil comes ashore we'll follow him and do away with him first chance we get.'

With a little luck, Pepillo hoped, the wicked friar would not come ashore! It was certainly beginning to look that way since he was preaching a seemingly interminable sermon to a few bored men on the main deck of the *San Sebastián* – and had been doing so for the past two hours at least. His loud but somewhat fluting, high-pitched lisp had carried across the water to the *Santa María* and now, amongst the palms, his proclamations against the common sins of soldiers and sailors could still be heard clearly: 'And they shall say unto the elders of his city, this our son is stubborn and rebellious; he will not obey our voice; he is a glutton, and a drunkard. And all the men of his city shall stone him with stones, that he die: so shalt thou put evil away from among you; and all Israel shall hear, and fear . . .'

More admonitions and dire warnings followed, but then, quite suddenly, Pepillo realised with a lurch of alarm that Muñoz was winding himself up to a conclusion: 'Dearly beloved, I beseech you as strangers and pilgrims, abstain from fleshly lusts, which war against the soul, and follow righteousness, faith, charity, peace with them that call on the Lord out of a pure heart.'

'Abstain from fleshly lusts!' Melchior gave a bitter laugh. 'Follow righteousness! A pure heart! That's rich coming from a murdering sodomite! I can't wait to give him what he deserves.'

'Suppose he doesn't come?' Pepillo asked, trying to keep the hope he felt out of his voice.

'We'll get our chance. Maybe not today. Maybe not tomorrow. But we'll get him sooner or later. It's just a matter of time.'

In the last of the light, the two boys saw the friar's tall, angular form stride across the deck of the *San Sebastián* and go below.

Another hour passed, the night grew black as pitch, bloodsucking insects buzzed and whined, lanterns were lighted across the fleet and there came the sounds of raucous laughter as food was cooked and served. Some of the men had begun drinking, bottles clinked, a few songs were struck up, a long and plangently beautiful guitar riff rang out, a drunken fight got started and was equally quickly stopped.

'Listen!' whispered Pepillo, nudging Melchior in the ribs. 'What's that?'

'What's what, you silly mammet?' Melchior growled.

'There! Don't you hear it?'

Pepillo strained his ears and there it was again – a faint, almost inaudible splashing in the bay. There was no moon but the starlight was bright. By its silvery luminescence, and the reflected glow of the ships' lanterns, the breaking line of surf where the wavelets lapped against the shore was clearly visible.

The hairs on the nape of Pepillo's neck and along his forearms suddenly stood on end as he saw the figure of a naked man, gleaming ivory in the starlight, slowly and stealthily emerge from the sea. The man carried a bulky object – a bag! – and in a moment had pulled a dark garment over his head and all but disappeared.

Then he came padding up the shore, taking the path that ran through the palm grove, towards the hill and the lights of the Indian town.

As he passed within an arm's length of their hiding place, Pepillo and Melchior both recognised Muñoz.

'Let's get after him,' Melchior whispered after the friar had gone by, heading up the hill towards the Indian town.

'Are you sure we're the right ones to do this?' Pepillo asked, hearing and instantly regretting the anxious, childish tone in his voice.

'Course I'm sure,' said Melchior. 'If we don't do him now and he kills other children, I for one will never forgive myself. We'll not get another chance half as good.'

In the darkness Pepillo nodded. He was afraid, but he remembered how Muñoz had beaten and tortured him, the madness in the friar's eyes, the feeling of his teeth and his wet lips at his ear. If there was justice in the world the man had to be stopped and it seemed that Cortés, for whatever reason, was not prepared to act against him.

Melchior was already in pursuit, hunched forward on the path through the palm grove, running uphill in the direction the friar had taken.

With a pounding heart, tugging the little hatchet from his belt, Pepillo followed.

Chapter Fifty

Moctezuma was awaiting his dinner and taking some comfort in the prospect. Tonight the dishes would include one cooked from the thigh of a delicate young boy he had sacrificed at dawn in an attempt to coax Hummingbird to visit him again. The attempt had failed, as had every other since the holocaust on the great pyramid nine days before, but at least he could enjoy the tender flesh of the victim.

There was little else that gave the Great Speaker pleasure. His stomach was constantly disturbed, busily moving, inclined to strange rumblings and howlings, as though it had taken on a life of its own. Only when filled to satiety did it fall quiet for a short while and give him peace.

Another problem was also beginning to trouble Moctezuma greatly. Although he continued to have intercourse with his legitimate wives in the hope of siring an heir healthier than his weakling son Chimalpopoca, he greatly preferred the company of his many mistresses for solace in the bedroom. Since the holocaust, however, his *tepulli* had ceased to function as it should and neither his wives nor even the most appetising females in his harem had coaxed him to an erection. Sometimes – quite often – Moctezuma had the sinister feeling he was being *watched* as he attempted to perform. He'd consulted his magicians but as yet they had been unable to offer a solution.

He was in the spacious, high-ceilinged dining chamber on the first floor of his palace, seated on a soft, richly worked stool in front of a low table covered with a white cloth of the finest cotton on which were laid a selection of long napkins of the same colour and material. To his right, at a distance of some twenty paces on the far side of the

378

chamber, the three grey-haired dignitaries who would dine with him tonight stood with their heads respectfully bowed.

Moctezuma decided to keep them waiting a little longer while he gave thought to the matter of Guatemoc. He had received two irritating visits from Mecatl today, the first in the morning to announce that the troublesome prince had refused his 'medicine' and a second unscheduled visit in the afternoon to report continued lack of success. This non-cooperation was a setback to what had, until today, been solid progress, and if it continued there was a danger that Cuitláhuac would return and take his son from the hospital before the *cotelachi* had done its work. Urgent measures were called for, and Moctezuma had not hesitated to accept Mecatl's offer to prepare a new batch of poison from a large *cotelachi* butterfly – large enough to kill Guatemoc with a single dose. It would be best if the dose were swallowed willingly, but if not he had authorised the physician to use force.

Guatemoc was feeling very much better, and far stronger than he had believed would ever be possible again.

Perhaps it was because he had successfully avoided Mecatl's poison all day.

But he could not get out of his mind the incredible sensations of warmth and healing that had filled his body, and the instant relief from pain he had been granted when the goddess Temaz had placed her hands upon his wounds the night before. Despite the exhausting effort of fending off Mecatl without arousing his suspicions, Guatemoc's conviction that a miracle had put him on the path of recovery had not left him for a single moment.

It was one of the reasons he remained certain his encounter with the goddess in the still of the night had been real and not some fever of his imagination.

But the more powerful proof was the little bottle Temaz had given him, a physical thing quite outside the realm of imaginings. He had passed it on to his mother that morning, without explaining how it had come into his hands, telling her only that it was a medicine Mecatl kept pressing on him, that he suspected poison and that his father must be summoned back at once to Tenochtitlan to help unravel the plot. His mother had wanted to confront Mecatl herself, but Guatemoc had forbidden it. The doctor was part of a wider conspiracy. They must trap him in such a way that he could be forced, by torture if necessary, to reveal its instigator. Only Cuitláhuac had the power to see such a drastic initiative through, and until he arrived they must give no sign of their suspicions.

The day had worn on. In the mid-afternoon Guatemoc rebuffed Mecatl yet again but the physician refused to leave the room. 'I cannot,' he said. 'it's more than my life is worth. The Lord Speaker himself commands you to drink this medicine.'

'My respects to the Lord Speaker,' Guatemoc replied wearily, 'but my body commands me to sleep, so please *go away.*'

The physician had tucked the bottle inside his robes again – a good sign. 'You put me in an impossible position, sire,' he said, wringing his hands.

'Come back tonight,' Guatemoc replied. 'I will, for the Lord Speaker's sake, attempt your elixir then.'

'Do I have your promise on that, sire?'

'You have my promise.'

'Very well. I will return tonight.'

Shortly before sunset came the news that Cuitláhuac had reached Tenochtitlan and was making preparations to infiltrate the hospital in secret with a few of his most trusted men.

The trap was baited and set. All that remained was to wait.

Two hours after dark, Mecatl entered Guatemoc's room, moved to his bedside, produced the medicine bottle and bent over him, oozing false concern. 'The night is well advanced, lord. You must drink the elixir again.'

Guatemoc gave him a stony glare: 'Clear off, you toad. I've told you a dozen times today I don't have the stomach for it.'

'Against my better judgement, sire, I have allowed you to postpone your medication, but you promised me you would drink it this evening.'

'*Allowed*, you say? Allowed *me*? You little quack. I'm a prince of the realm and I do as I please.' And with that Guatemoc thrust out his hand from under the covers, gripped Mecatl by the throat and drew the doctor's fat, sweating face towards his own. 'Get out of my sight!' he bellowed, and tightened his grip for a moment before shoving the other man away.

The words 'get out of my sight' were the agreed signal; behind the doctor, Guatemoc saw the door open – saw his father Cuitláhuac and three men at arms silently enter the room. Unaware of the threat, Mecatl straightened and gulped in air, a look of real anger for the first time crossing his face. He'd held on tightly to the medicine bottle, which he now unstoppered. 'I am afraid I must insist,' he said. A muscle twitched at the corner of his mouth. 'The Great Speaker is deeply concerned for your welfare. My orders are to ensure, by any means, that you drink the elixir.'

'And how, may I ask, do you propose to do that?'

Behind Mecatl, Guatemoc saw another man slip into the room. He recognised Acamap, Cuitláhuac's personal physician.

Mecatl was too busy digging his own grave to notice. 'If I must,' he said with more self-confidence than he usually expressed, 'I am author-ised to call for assistance . . . I will have you restrained, young Guatemoc, and I will pour the elixir down your throat with a funnel. My master the Speaker requires it.'

'Oh does he indeed?' said Cuitláhuac in a cold, quiet voice. Rushing forward, the men at arms pounced on Mecatl and held him still while Cuitláhuac prised the medicine bottle from his hand.

'My lord.' A note of hysteria had entered the doctor's voice. 'This is an outrage.'

'Yes, I agree,' said Cuitláhuac. 'It is an outrage that you threaten my son with violence.'

'The noble prince is stubborn, lord. What am I to do when he refuses medication that will save his life?'

Ignoring him, Cuitláhuac passed the bottle over to Acamap, who sniffed its contents and made a sour face.

'Well,' said Cuitláhuac. 'Do you recognise it?'

'One moment please,' said Acamap. He poured a drop of the liquid onto his finger, very cautiously tasted it with his tongue, spat violently, rinsed his mouth with water from a flask at his hip and then spat again. 'It is *cotelachi* poison,' he said. 'A very strong dose – much stronger than the sample your lady wife asked me to test this morning. Had the prince drunk the entire contents of this bottle, he would have been dead in a few hours.'

His face contorted with rage, Cuitláhuac turned on Mecatl. 'What do you say to that?'

'I say it is a lie, Excellency. This medicine is an elixir of wondrous virtue that I prepare for the Lord Speaker.'

'Then you will no doubt be happy to drink it yourself.'

Mecatl's face drained of colour. 'I . . .' he said. 'I . . . No, sire. I prefer not to.'

'Force his mouth open,' growled Cuitláhuac to the men at arms.

Mecatl struggled, with surprising strength, Guatemoc thought, but the soldiers were all over him. Soon enough they got a dagger between his teeth and levered his mouth open, wounding his lips and cheeks in the process. As blood spattered down his costly robes and pooled on the floor at his feet, he let out a stifled sob and shook his head wildly, cutting himself further on the blade.

Cuitláhuac loomed over him holding the bottle. 'So what's it to be?' he said. 'Death by this Zapotec butterfly poison you were going to kill my son with? Or you tell us who's behind all this and maybe we let you live?'

Moctezuma's stomach rumbled as a zephyr of delicious aromas wafted from the adjoining kitchen, and he glanced up to see four serving girls, selected from the daughters of the nobility for their cleanliness and beauty, enter the dining chamber carrying a large, deep gourd. As they approached they did not – dared not! – look at him, but kept their eyes downcast, ladled water from the gourd onto his outstretched hands and skilfully caught the overflow in special basins. None of the water was allowed to drop to the floor; it was considered bad luck, punishable by the death of the offending servant, if any did. Taking the greatest possible care, the girls then towelled his fingers dry as two more noble daughters entered, bringing him white maize cakes. Finally the women retired and a host of male retainers, all chosen for the honour from amongst the nobility, entered the room carrying thirty earthenware braziers on which were arrayed three hundred small red and black ceramic dishes heaped with a fantasia of cooked fowls, turkeys, pheasants, partridges, quail, tame and wild duck, venison, peccary, marsh birds, pigeons, hares, monkeys, lobster, shrimp, octopus, molluscs, turtles, thirty different varieties of sea and river fish, a dozen different vegetables and, in pride of place, seasoned with salt and chillies, little cubes of meat sliced from the thigh of the sacrificed boy.

When the feast had been set out, all the retainers withdrew, with the exception of Moctezuma's steward Teudile, a man of the most refined noble birth who, because of his proximity to the ruler, stood amongst the highest lords of the land, ranking seventh after Moctezuma himself, the Snake Woman (a position still unfilled since the death of Coaxoch), Cuitláhuac, the lords of Tacuba and Texcoco, and the new high priest, Namacuix. Tall, gaunt and hollow cheeked, Teudile's temples and brow were shaved, his long grey hair gathered in a top-knot at the back of his head and his cherished personal dignity enlarged by the star-spangled robes of office that he alone was permitted to wear in the presence of the Great Speaker. He held sole responsibility for all matters concerning the running of the royal household, and at dinner it was his particular honour and privilege to describe the dishes to the Speaker and hand him whichever took his fancy. First, however, he drew a gold-inlaid wooden screen around Moctezuma so that his three dinner guests, who were now invited to draw close, could not see him eat.

This was the part that Moctezuma always enjoyed the most – for tradition required that the guests must be barefoot, must remain standing throughout like beggars at his gate, must speak only when he spoke to them and might eat only if he chose to offer them a morsel of this or that from behind the screen. It was an excellent system for reminding the nobility of their subservience to him and to keep them at each other's throats by bestowing honour on one and humiliation on another.

Even as he sampled the first juicy chunks of the sacrificed boy's inner thigh, however, Moctezuma looked down and saw with horror that a drop of water had somehow splashed to the ground at his feet while his hands were being washed. It was a terrible omen, and as though in immediate fulfilment of it he heard the familiar voice of

383

Cuitláhuac, not in Texcoco as he was meant to be but at the door to the chamber and speaking loudly and urgently to the guards. The names Guatemoc and Mecatl were both mentioned.

With a roar of anger Moctezuma threw his plate to the floor and dismissed his guests and Teudile.

This could only be about one thing.

Chapter Fifty-One

The route Muñoz had taken led through an area of terracing on the
lower slopes of the hill where the Indians of Cozumel grew vegetables
for the town, and although well camouflaged in his black habit, the
friar had left deep sandal prints in the rich red earth that were easy
enough to follow in the starlight.

'Quick,' said Melchior, 'he's too far ahead of us. We're going to lose
him if we don't get closer.'

'But not too close!' Pepillo felt compelled to warn. 'If he hears us
we're done for.'

'Silly mammet!' hissed Melchior, increasing his pace. 'We've got to
get close to kill him.'

Pepillo scrambled after his friend, doing his best to keep quiet even
though he was already panting with the effort and his heart pounded
frightfully against his ribs. *You must be mad*, he said to himself as he
ran. *You're going to get yourself killed.* Every rational instinct, every
bone in his body, every straining, terrified nerve urged him to turn
and slink back to the ship. But he couldn't do that, could he? Because
if he did he would let Melchior down in the worst possible way and
reveal himself for the coward he was.

They were out of the terraces now, speeding up an open grassy
slope. There! Ahead! A surging column of darkness deeper than the
rest. That had to be Muñoz! Melchior had seen him too and raced
faster, fairly pounding up the hill, widening the gap between himself
and Pepillo who was thinking, *Even if we do kill him, what then? Won't
my soul be damned forever for the murder of a religious?* And he heard

inside his head, like a drum roll, a deep, portentous voice that seemed to say over and over again, *Damned! Damned! Damned!* and *Murderer! Murderer! Murderer!*

A hundred paces above them loomed the ominous, massy gloom of a swathe of woodland, and with a chill Pepillo recognised it as a different quarter of the same wild copse in which they'd found the body of the murdered child two days before. The shadow that was Muñoz slipped amongst the trees and was gone.

'Melchior!' Pepillo wanted to shout as he ran. 'Stop, for pity's sake! We dare not follow him there.' And he thought – *It would be like tracking a lion to its den.* But he couldn't call out for fear of giving their pursuit away, and to his horror he saw his friend, so far ahead now that he too seemed little more than a shadow, making straight for the spot where the friar had vanished.

Twenty seconds later Pepillo reached the edge of the trees and skidded to a halt.

By the uncertain glimmer of the stars he saw the entrance to a path, no wider than the span of his arms, leading deep into the wood.

He squinted but he couldn't see Melchior.

In fact he couldn't see anything!

The darkness amongst the close packed, thickly tangled trees was near total. Worse still, although the forest was alive with all manner of strange and frightening crepitations, rustlings, clicks, squawks and snuffles, he couldn't identify any sound that was obviously Melchior pushing ahead through the undergrowth.

'God help me,' Pepillo whispered, and felt he was about to be sick as he took his first step on the path. Immediately something clutched his face and he slapped it away, gasping with horror before he had time to register it was nothing more than a creeper hanging down from above. The urge to vomit grew stronger, but the fear of being judged a coward by Melchior, and worse still the fear that his friend might be in danger and in need of his help, was stronger than the fear of what lay ahead, so he pressed on, carefully testing the ground at his feet with each step, sensing the soft detritus of fallen leaves, feeling the brambles tugging at his ankles. On both sides now the trees seemed to close in and when he looked back he found he could no longer see the start of the path.

He held tight to his hatchet, pushing branches and thick clusters of rough leaves and clinging tendrils aside as he walked. Then with no forewarning he heard a slow, vibrating *whirr* – very close! – and something about the size of a small bird flew right over the top of his head, disturbing the air with the flap of its wings. There were bats here, the sailors said, that drank human blood – yet surely such creatures were the least of his worries when a true monster like Muñoz lurked in this terrible close darkness, and when Melchior, on whose strength and courage he depended, was nowhere to be seen.

'Melchior!' he hissed, risking all. 'Where are you?'

Nothing.

Deciding he would take ten more paces before making his way back to the ship, Pepillo began to count – one . . . two . . . three . . . four – when suddenly he heard . . . what? A footstep? A crackle of branches compressed under a heavy sandal?

'Melchior?' he croaked. 'Melchior?' Icy terror gripped his bowels and a strangled whimper rose in his throat. He turned to run but a strong hand fell on his shoulder out of the night and held him in place.

'Ahhhh!' Pepillo shrieked. 'Let go, let me go.' He struggled desperately, flailed and lashed out but it was useless. 'Please,' he begged, 'please, Father, don't kill me.'

A hand was on his other shoulder now, shaking him, and he heard a deep, familiar chuckle. 'Don't shit yourself, you daft mammet,' said Melchior. 'It's only me. Muñoz has gone. We're not going to catch him tonight.'

In an instant Pepillo was wildly angry, and planted a kick on his friend's shin that sent him hopping amongst the bushes. 'You swine!' he yelled at the older boy, 'you scared me. Creeping around like that! What were you thinking of?'

'Just a jape. Don't take on so!'

'A jape? A *jape*? You'd jape about this?' Pepillo felt indignant, foolish and furious all at once, but most of all, he realised, he felt relieved. 'Come on,' he said, 'let's get—'

He didn't finish his sentence. Something came *whoosh* out of the darkness, there was a solid *clunk* and he sensed rather than saw Melchior crumple to the ground beside him. A second of mute incomprehension followed, and then a moment of sudden, horrific realisation before a blow crashed into Pepillo's jaw, lifted him off his feet, exploded bright lights inside his head – strangely reminding him of the time, years before, when he'd run full tilt into a stone wall – and plunged him, finally, into absolute, enveloping blackness.

As he swum up into consciousness, Pepillo couldn't at first remember where he was or understand why he was lying naked on a surface of broken branches and leaves, on his stomach, gagged, with his knees bent, his wrists and ankles bound together behind his painfully arched back, and a noose around his neck seemingly connected to the tether at his ankles so that any attempt to struggle or straighten his body brought on immediate strangulation. It was very dark but the flicker of some faint light nonetheless reached his eyes. He heard a man's voice, lisping, horribly familiar – *Muñoz!* – and the events of the night came back to him in a stupefying flood. A great cry burst from his throat, only to be stifled by the thick bundle of foul-tasting rags that stuffed his mouth.

The Dominican was speaking in an almost pleasant, conversational tone. 'See blackamoor! Your young accomplice awakes to witness your punishment. By the time I have him he'll be *oozing* with fear.'

Pepillo thought – *Have him? Have him? What does that mean?* – and heard an incoherent, choking roar which he understood must be Melchior, gagged like himself. He thrashed his head left and right, tightening the noose, coughing and wheezing, as he strained to find his friend whose own struggles he could hear somewhere behind him.

But he saw Muñoz first, sitting two paces away on the thick trunk of a fallen tree, his hand resting on a Bible, his black habit drawn up exposing the knobs of his knees and his face hellishly illumined by the quivering gleam of two altar candles positioned on either side of him.

'Ah,' the friar said, 'allow me to oblige.' Suddenly standing, he loomed over Pepillo, raised a foot, placed the sole of one heavy-duty sandal on his shoulder and gave him a powerful shove, spinning him round half a turn on his belly until Melchior came into view, facing him, also naked and hogtied. Unlike Pepillo, the older boy showed no fear, only a brooding anger that burned through the reflected candle flames in his eyes and contorted his proud features.

With a strange chuckle Muñoz crouched and put his mouth close to Pepillo's ear – the same ear he'd bitten in Santiago, brushed now with the same soft heat of his lips. 'See how your friend hates me,' he said. Casually he placed his open hand between Pepillo's hunched shoulder blades, moved it slowly down his body, caressed his trussed wrists and brought it to rest on his buttocks, making him flinch as though burned with a hot iron. 'Why do you think he hates me so?' the Inquisitor continued.

Because you're a wicked sodomite, Pepillo would have said if he wasn't gagged, but Muñoz clearly didn't expect an answer. 'He hates me,' he mused, his voice instantly raised to a shout and ringing in Pepillo's ear, 'because I had him *for a peso* in my cabin when we sailed with Córdoba. He'd do anything for coin when he was a slave – *wouldn't you, blackamoor?* – but now he's free the poor boy can't bear the shame.'

Another furious roar from Melchior, who was struggling desperately, hopelessly, against his bonds, the noose biting so hard into his neck it had drawn blood.

'That's why he wants to kill me,' Muñoz sneered. 'With *this*.' He held up Melchior's rusty dagger, then pushed his mouth closer to Pepillo's ear. 'I expect he told you otherwise, yes? Some high-principled story about defending the Indians? Was that what brought you out here tonight? Well, now you know the truth, boy! *Now you know the truth!*'

He cast the dagger aside and suddenly he was on his feet again, pacing about the clearing where he'd obviously dragged both of them after knocking them out, shadows dancing across his coarse features as the candles glimmered. 'The great dragon was hurled down,' he said, his voice rising, 'that ancient serpent called the devil who led the whole world astray.' As he spoke he strode close to Melchior and kicked him twice in the ribs with such incredible violence that Pepillo distinctly heard something crack followed at once by a terrible groan of pain. 'You are tempters,' Muñoz boomed, '*tempters*, I say, who have wickedly tempted me, and the flesh is *weak*.' He raced across the clearing, drew back his foot and Pepillo winced and moaned as two kicks now thudded into his own ribs. He felt a gush of vomit rising up his throat and bit it back, fearing he would choke and die.

But of course he was going to die anyway. They were both going to die, he and Melchior, here in the dark woods at the hands of this evil madman.

Muñoz was muttering to himself, and this was even more frightening than his shouts and yells. 'In that day,' he intoned, 'the Lord with his sore great and strong sword shall punish leviathan the piercing serpent, even leviathan that crooked serpent, and he shall slay the dragon.' Through the tears pouring from his eyes, Pepillo saw the friar's hand disappear inside his habit and emerge holding a straight razor. Then in a single step he surged back to Melchior's side, planted a hand in his thick hair and flicked the razor open so that its long steel blade glittered in the candlelight. 'A man who lies with a man,' he said, 'has committed an abomination and shall surely be put to death.'

As he placed the blade at Melchior's throat there came a rush of footsteps and a huge sword lanced in seemingly from nowhere, pierced the Inquisitor's back and emerged through his belly. The man wielding it was tall, bearded and powerfully muscled. He dipped the hilt of the weapon and, holding the friar impaled, forced him screaming to his feet.

'Mercy,' Muñoz shrieked. 'Mercy! In God's name.'

Two other men had closed in around him, their faces grim. They held daggers which they now used to stab him repeatedly, while he still wriggled on the sword blade like a gaffed fish.

It took some minutes, and a great deal of blood, before he was finally still.

The bearded, hard-eyed soldiers who had killed Muñoz were Bernal Díaz, Alonso de La Serna and Francisco Mibiercas, the latter being the owner of what Pepillo would ever afterwards think of as the sore great and strong sword. Although they sailed with Alvarado, Pepillo remembered Díaz from his visits to the *Santa María*, most recently over the matter of the murders in Cozumel, and it seemed that Melchior knew all three men from the Córdoba expedition.

The first thing they did after they had cut the boys free and allowed them to dress was very strange. 'Are these yours?' asked La Serna, holding up Pepillo's hatchet and Melchior's dagger.

They admitted ownership of the weapons.

'And what did you plan to do with them?'

Melchior looked at Muñoz's gashed and bleeding corpse lying face down on the forest floor. 'We followed him here,' he said. 'We were going to kill him.'

'Why?' asked Díaz.

'We hate him,' said Pepillo. 'He is – I mean he was – a murderer. Two days ago we saw him track and kill an Indian child. He killed another last night and he . . . he . . .'

The three soldiers shared meaningful glances.

'He was a filthy sodomite,' said Melchior.

'He said he was going to "have" me,' Pepillo added, 'after he'd killed Melchior.'

La Serna held out the dagger and the hatchet. 'Right, boys,' he said. 'Take your weapons and do what you came here to do.'

'What do you mean, sir?' asked Pepillo. The hatchet weighed heavy in his hand. Heavier than he'd remembered.

'You came here to kill him,' said Mibiercas, who was cleaning the blade of his sword on Muñoz's habit. 'Now's your chance.'

'But he's already dead, sir,' Pepillo objected.

'Just do it,' growled Díaz. 'Do your part.'

Melchior needed no further urging. His breath was already coming in short fast gasps, low moans rising in his throat, and now he fell on Muñoz in a rage, burying his dagger over and over again in the friar's inert, bloodied back. Pepillo saw tears running down his friend's cheeks and great sobs racking his chest. Before he was done La Serna nodded. 'You too, boy,' he said.

'Me, sir?' Pepillo asked in a small voice.

'Do you see any other boys here?' snapped La Serna.

Pepillo turned to Díaz and Mibiercas but there was no give in their eyes. Feeling sick, he joined Melchior by the body, knelt and raised the hatchet but at first couldn't bring himself to strike a blow. 'Do it!' Melchior snarled, his face so livid with violence and fury that Pepillo started back in shock. 'Do it if you're my friend!'

Suddenly something broke inside Pepillo and he chopped the hatchet down into Muñoz's shoulder, then again – hack! hack! – into his neck, feeling the vertebrae separate, and finally, in a frenzy himself now, into the back of the friar's head until the bones of his skull splintered.

'Good enough,' said Díaz. He stood behind Pepillo and Melchior, put his big, strong hands under their arms and lifted them to their feet. As he did so the swordsman Mibiercas favoured them both with a grim smile. 'Well done, lads!' he said. 'We're all in this together now.'

The world spun. Pepillo doubled over, clutching his stomach, and vomited.

A few moments later, still feeling faint, Pepillo sat on the trunk of the fallen tree where Muñoz had perched triumphantly not long before, and watched as Melchior helped the three soldiers tidy various items away into a knotted canvas sack lying empty and open on the ground. When he'd waded naked through the sea from the *San Sebastián*, it was presumably inside this sack that the friar had bundled his habit, his sandals, his bone-handled razor, his Bible, several coils of rope of different lengths and the two altar candles he'd used to illuminate the scene. Now one by one, with the exception of his slashed and blood-sodden habit, which was left to cover his body, they all went back into the sack.

'Did he know you were going to follow him up here?' Díaz asked.

Pepillo and Melchior both shook their heads. 'He couldn't have known. We didn't tell anyone what we were planning.'

'He must have been onto you,' said Díaz, coiling away the last of the lengths of rope, 'because he came prepared – right down to candles so he could see what he was doing.'

Pepillo felt a shiver run down his spine. 'How did *you* know we'd be here?' he asked.

'We didn't,' said La Serna. 'We were waiting for our chance and tonight was it – which was good luck for you boys.'

'We were with Córdoba,' explained Mibiercas. 'A lot of good men died because of Muñoz. He had this coming to him.'

'And more good men would have died if we'd let him live,' added Díaz. 'At least now Cortés can run this expedition the way it should be run, and make us all rich, without having to take a meddling Inquisitor into account.'

'Does Cortés know about this?' Pepillo asked.

'No, lad, he knows nothing,' said Díaz. 'And he must not learn of it. What happened tonight didn't happen. You will never speak of it again and we will never speak of it again.'

Mibiercas, his great sword now slung in its scabbard across his back, was more emphatic. 'If word of this gets out,' he said, glaring at Melchior then shifting his gaze to Pepillo, 'I'll have your heads. Remember that.'

'Word won't get out, sir,' said Pepillo. 'We're truly grateful to you for saving our lives and we'll keep our mouths shut.'

Melchior nodded his agreement: 'It's like you said, Mibiercas. We're all in this together and we all have to watch each other's backs.'

Pepillo was impressed by Díaz and his friends, and not only because of the rescue. They could have left Muñoz in the clearing but they wouldn't do so because the Indians of Cozumel would certainly be blamed if he was found, and another bloodbath might result. Instead they'd decided to dump the corpse in the sea off a remote headland they'd reconnoitred more than a mile away from the fleet's anchorage. 'It's better we have a mystery than a murder,' La Serna explained with a lopsided grin.

Most of the night had passed and dawn was beginning to lighten the sky in the east by the time they reached the headland. Gulls wheeled and squawked, waves crashed and burst against jagged rocks with a strange booming echo, and a strong wind was blowing as the soldiers gathered heavy stones and used the ropes from the canvas sack to tie them securely to Muñoz's body.

'Anyone want to say a few words on behalf of the deceased?' asked Díaz.

'He was a wicked man,' said La Serna. 'May his soul rot in Hell.'

'He asked for mercy,' said Mibiercas, 'that he never showed to others.'

'We gave him a bad death,' said Díaz, 'and he must account for himself before his maker now. When we're judged for what we've done, as we surely will be when our own time comes, I pray the Lord does not deal too harshly with us.'

Just before they rolled the corpse into the deep water, Pepillo caught a glimpse of Muñoz's broken skull and pale, blood-smeared face.

The friar's black eyes were wide open and they seemed to glare back at him with a fierce and living hunger.

393

Chapter Fifty-Two

Tenochtitlan, Saturday 20 March 1519

'I've had a report from my informant in Cuitláhuac's household,' Huicton said. 'It seems Guatemoc makes daily offerings to the goddess Temaz for her miraculous intervention. Would you consider paying the prince another visit?'

Tozi's heart raced at the thought. She could not forget poor, lost Coyotl but she had ceased her fruitless search for him and during the twenty days since the dramatic events in the royal hospital, Guatemoc had been more on her mind than she cared to admit. 'Pay the prince another visit?' she asked, feigning nonchalance. 'What would be the purpose? We achieved our goal of disturbing Moctezuma's household. Suspicion is everywhere now. A rift has opened between him and his brother that can never be mended.'

'We must think ahead to when Moctezuma is gone . . . We must look to his successor.'

'Quetzalcoatl will succeed him.'

'So you believe. But we must live in the real world of men where gods do not descend from the sky every day. I pray you're right, but I must plan for the possibility that you're wrong.'

'I'm not wrong, Huicton! You'll see.'

'Very well, Tozi. You're not wrong. But humour me. Imagine for a moment that Quetzalcoatl does not return but that we succeed in driving Moctezuma mad – and so far we have done rather well – and bring about his downfall anyway. His son Chimalpopoca is sickly and, even if he lives, will be too young to take the throne for many years. There will be a struggle for power . . .'

'And surely Cuitláhuac will win it,' Tozi said begrudgingly. She disliked any line of thought that didn't involve Quetzalcoatl.

'Cuitláhuac may not *want* power. He's not a natural leader and there's every sign he knows his own limitations. If Moctezuma falls, Guatemoc will become a contender. Let's take this opportunity to make him our man . . .'

'Guatemoc? Our man? That puffed-up Mexica bully? You must be even crazier than Moctezuma if you think we can do that!'

'Far from it, Tozi!' Huicton rested a gnarled hand on her shoulder. 'Recent events have put us – you! – in a unique position of influence. Not only did you foil Moctezuma's plot but also my informant tells me that the prince holds you responsible for the healing he has experienced. After the goddess Temaz warned him of the poison, it seems she placed her hands on the battle wounds Guatemoc received fighting the Tlascalans. He felt a warm glow suffuse his body. At once his injuries, which were of the utmost seriousness, began to close up, as though by magic, and within days the sepsis had vanished. He is still in a great deal of pain, I am told, but his doctors say he will make a complete recovery and he attributes all of this to you—'

'To Temaz you mean!'

'There's no difference. You *are* Temaz in his eyes! Go to him again in the regalia of the goddess. Appear to him. Work your way deeper into his affections and into his trust so we can use him for our own ends when the right time comes.'

'That all sounds very clever,' Tozi said, 'but it could easily go wrong. Suppose Guatemoc sees through my disguise? Catches me out in some way? Then instead of making an ally we'll make an even worse enemy.'

'I don't see why you should get caught,' the old spy said. 'You're confident of your invisibility now?'

'Yes, completely confident!'

'More to the point, *I'm* confident of it after what you did with Guatemoc, Mecatl and the poison. When you make yourself invisible no one can see you, no one can seize you. So if anything does go wrong you simply slip into invisibility and escape.'

395

Seeing her chance, Tozi admitted: 'There's something I haven't told you.'

'Oh?' Despite their milky opacity, Huicton's eyes could sometimes be very expressive and now was one of those times.

'It isn't just what I was able to do at the hospital that's made me confident,' Tozi said. 'I've been going into Moctezuma's palace as well.' She giggled. 'I've watched him a few times while he's been eating his meals. I've even been in his bedchamber!'

'You've what?' Huicton looked startled, and genuinely angry. 'I told you to stay away from the palace. It's too dangerous there.'

'Well you were wrong.' Tozi stuck out her lower lip. 'And I was right. You said Moctezuma had sorcerers who might magic me but they're useless. I've slipped past them and they haven't noticed a thing and I've been there with him, right beside him without anyone knowing – and I've been *torturing* him, Huicton!'

'Torturing him? Whatever do you mean?'

'The gift Hummingbird gave me. To magnify my enemies' fears? I've been using it on Moctezuma the same way I used it that night on the great pyramid.' Tozi giggled again. 'He's troubled by his bowels and I've been working on that. Quite a lot actually. His stomach never gives him peace. Oh, and I've stopped his *tepulli* working . . .'

'His *tepulli*?' Huicton was choking with surprise. 'What do you know of *tepullis*, young lady?'

'What do you mean, "young lady"?' Tozi asked scornfully. 'Girls of my age are married with children. Of course I know what a *tepulli* is!' Another giggle: 'And I know what they have to do if they're going to work!'

Huicton just looked at her through his cloudy eyes.

'They have to stand up!' Tozi shrieked, 'and I've made Moctezuma's *tepulli* as limp as a little worm so he can't enjoy his wives and mistresses. They mock him behind his back. He's *very* upset about it.'

Huicton was laughing now, a great rumbling, rolling guffaw of sheer pleasure. 'Oh Tozi,' he said, wiping a tear from his eye, 'you are a prodigy.'

She didn't want to admit she didn't know what a prodigy was so she said: 'About Guatemoc? When do you want me to start?'

Chapter Fifty-Three

Potonchan, Sunday 21 March 1519 to Wednesday 24 March 1519

It was the auspicious morning of the Vernal Equinox, Sunday 21 March 1519, when Alaminos piloted the *Santa María* into the wide bay at the mouth of the Tabasco river and Cortés gave the order for the fleet to drop anchor. He would require no work of the men today, only prayer. Tomorrow, Monday 22 March, they would sally forth against the town of Potonchan to punish the Chontal Maya as Saint Peter required.

Not that the men knew of Cortés's dreams! He'd kept his real motive secret, even from Alvarado, and sold the planned attack on Potonchan as a reprisal for the humiliation of the Córdoba expedition the year before. Most of the survivors of that debacle were here, after all, and itching for revenge; many others who'd lost friends and relatives were equally enthusiastic; for the rest, the pride and honour of Spain and the hope of treasure provided ample incentives.

Much had happened in the twenty days since young Gonzalo de Sandoval had returned in triumph to Cozumel with the shipwrecked Spaniard Jerónimo de Aguilar. After eight years spent amongst the Maya, the castaway knew their language with complete fluency and quickly began to prove his worth as an interpreter. Even his skills, however, which allowed a thorough interrogation of the chief and notables of Cozumel – and in due course almost the entire population of the island – could not solve the mystery of the sudden disappearance of Father Gaspar Muñoz.

The Inquisitor had preached a sermon on the deck of the *San Sebastián* on the evening of Saturday 27 February. He had then gone below to a small cabin Alvarado had ordered constructed for him in the hold – and thereafter had not been seen again. Since his habit and sandals, his Bible, two altar candles, his razor and other small personal items were missing from his cabin, it was presumed he had left the ship of his own volition, something he was known to have done on the night of the 26th when he had told the sentries he was going to a secluded spot on the island for contemplation and prayer. On the night of the 27th, however, no one had witnessed his departure.

Had he somehow slipped by the watch, made his way to shore – no doubt to sodomise and murder another child, Cortés surmised – and ended up being caught and killed by the Indians instead? This seemed the most likely solution, but there was absolutely no proof and no hint of any Indian involvement to be had from the interrogations. Indeed Aguilar had made it clear that in his opinion the islanders were not hiding anything.

So perhaps Spaniards had been responsible? This could by no means be ruled out. The Inquisitor had many enemies amongst the conquistadors after his part in the disaster of the Córdoba expedition. The page Pepillo also had a legitimate grudge, and for a while Cortés had even suspected him and his friend Melchior – the boys were behaving strangely and both had bruises and cuts on the morning of 28 February which they claimed, unconvincingly, were the result of a fight between themselves. But again proof was lacking and, on reflection, the notion they would have been capable of murdering a grown man like the Inquisitor seemed absurd.

It was an unsolved enigma, and when the repaired and revictualled fleet sailed out of Cozumel on 6 March, a week after Muñoz's disappearance, Cortés had already concluded it was for the best if it remained unsolved. Two weeks later, anchored in the bay at the mouth of the Tabasco river, he felt Saint Peter by his side as he prepared to lay his vengeance on the Mayan town of Potonchan, and conjured in his mind's eye an image of that infinitely greater city whose name he did not yet know, that jewelled and shining city with its golden pyramid, built upon the waters of a far-off lake, surrounded by lofty mountains wreathed in snow, that beckoned to him from his dreams.

'All these things God will give you,' Saint Peter had told him, 'when you have done the thing I require you to do.'

And what the saint required, right here, right now, was the humbling, the punishment and the utter destruction, until their dead lay thick upon the ground, of the Chontal Maya of Potonchan.

It was on the day of the great spring festival, when the hours of light and darkness are equal and the sun rises due east on the horizon, that Malinal at last came within sight of Potonchan. Approaching from the south on the broad white road running through fields of young maize, she hardly recognised the town of her birth from which she had been expelled five years previously, betrayed by her own mother, cast down from her noble lineage, and sold as a slave to a passing Mexica merchant. Compared to the massive scale, elegance and complexity of the Mexica capital where she'd spent the intervening years, it was, she saw at once, nothing special. But compared to the Potonchan of her memory – just a few dusty streets, a market and her father's palace – this town that now loomed before her had grown very large, and sprawled for a great distance along the bank of the Tabasco river. She might have thought she had lost her way and arrived at some other place entirely, had it not been for the nine sheer terraces of the ancient pyramid that soared up out of the central plaza and towered unchangeable over the warren of streets and houses. The pyramid had been built by King Ahau Chamahez in the long ago, so long ago that no one could possibly remember; yet his archaic prestige still shone down on Potonchan like the rays of the sun and made it a place of sacred pilgrimage to all the Chontal Maya, eclipsing even the greatest towns of the region, for the special celebrations of spring.

The sight of the monument reminded Malinal of that other infinitely greater pyramid, dedicated to the Mexica war god Hummingbird, where she had come so close to losing her life and yet been reprieved at the last moment, through the mysterious intervention of the war god himself. She did not know exactly how long she had been walking – at least thirty days, she thought, perhaps a little longer – since she had left Tenochtitlan behind on that night of horror. But her bruised and aching feet bore witness that there had not been a single day since then when she had stopped moving, not a single day when she had allowed herself rest, as she put ever greater distance between herself and the cruelty and madness of the Mexica.

Dusty, battered and travel-stained though they were, she still wore the embroidered blue cotton blouse and skirt and sturdy sandals she had been given on leaving Tenochtitlan. The heavy, fur-lined travelling cloak she'd also been given – of little use to her after she'd come down out of the mountains into the tropical lowlands – had been exchanged for food twelve days before and her backpack was gone too, its contents bartered and consumed. The journey had burnt her courtesan's skin brown and taken such a toll on her expensive clothes and general appearance that she'd long since ceased to stand out from the countryfolk and other travellers she met along the way. And now she was almost home and found herself amidst pilgrims flocking into Potonchan for the spring festival, which must already have been under way since the previous night and would continue for another three days. As she had many times on her long and hazardous journey, when she'd avoided bandits, or Mexica patrols, or found unexpected shelter in the midst of a storm, or been given a bed for the night by a kindly family, or found a willing guide when she was lost, Malinal remembered Tozi's claim that some divine plan was unfolding in which she had been chosen to play a part. Her return here exposed her to great danger from her own family, a risk she had decided she was prepared to run, but the joyous crowds seemed like yet another gift from the gods, making it so much easier for her to blend in, anonymous and undetected, while she sought tidings of the god Quetzalcoatl.

As she drew closer, however, she began to realise that something was amiss. Although multitudes were indeed still making for the town, equally large numbers had begun to pour out of it, heading south in the direction from which she had come. Judging from their style of dress, most were visitors who, for some reason, were hurrying away before the festivities could even have got into full swing, but it was also obvious there were some residents amongst them. As more and more of the travellers in both directions crossed paths and exchanged words, she saw that increasing numbers of those heading for Potonchan were turning back.

Puzzled, she stopped a family on the road – mother, father, grandparents, five children – and asked them what was happening. The grandfather, grey haired, lean, bent, supporting himself on a walking stick, made her heart leap when he told her: 'The white strangers have returned.'

'White strangers?' she asked, masking the excitement she felt. 'Who are they?'

The old man gave her a hard look. 'The same strangers we fought with before, of course! Where have you been, girl?'

'I've been . . . away. I've been five years in the lands of the Mexica.'

His expression softened. 'Then you won't have heard because it was just last year the strangers came to Potonchan. They came in huge boats that move by themselves without paddles. They demanded our food, our gold and tried to make us worship their god. They even burnt some of us on great fires! So in the end we went into battle against them. They were few but they possess fearsome weapons and they killed many before we drove them off. Now Muluc urges us to resist them again but anyone with any sense is leaving.'

Malinal hid the instant surge of anger that the name Muluc evoked in her. 'You say the strangers tried to make you worship their god but the way you describe them makes them sound more like gods than humans themselves. Do you not think they are gods?'

The elder kept silent as he appeared to consider her question. 'Some believe that,' he answered finally, 'but they eat like men, they shit like men and they smell like men, so I would say they are men, even though they seem very different from us.'

As he plodded off with the rest of his family, Malinal called after him. 'These strangers – are they in the town already?'

'They're in the bay in their great boats,' the old man answered. 'But they will come. You can be sure they will come. Take my advice and leave while you still can.'

Malinal pressed on, hardly registering now how many other large parties of pilgrims all around her had begun to turn back. She was so completely absorbed in the news she had been given that she was trembling – although whether it was with joy or with fear, she couldn't say.

Through all these days of hard walking, it had been the hope planted in her by Tozi that Quetzalcoatl and his retinue of gods were about to return that had kept her going. Even so, part of her – perhaps the larger part – had continued to doubt the whole story. But after what she had just heard, how could she doubt it any longer?

And how could she doubt Tozi's other assertion that she, Malinal, must in some special way be part of the gods' plan? For not only had they made their first appearance in Potonchan, the town of her birth, but now they had returned here on the very day that she too had returned after five long years of absence.

Such a conjunction, she thought, could hardly have come about by accident. It must have been fated. It must have been written in the stars – and by the hands of the gods themselves, long ages before.

She was so deep in these reflections that she failed to notice how close to the town she had approached and that she was no longer one amongst many now that almost all the other pilgrims had turned back. But suddenly her flesh crawled and she looked up with a start to discover two soldiers from Muluc's palace guard drawing a temporary barrier of thorns across the road less than a dozen paces in front of her.

'Hey you,' said one of them, the younger of the two, a gangling youth with bad acne. 'Where do you think you're going?'

Malinal stared him down. 'Into town for the spring festival, of course.'

'Well you're wasting your time. Haven't you heard? The festival's been cancelled.'

'Since when?'

'Since now. Muluc's orders. There's an emergency.'

The older of the two soldiers, who had wattles of wrinkled skin hanging loosely from beneath his chin like a turkey, was studying her closely, a calculating look in his hooded eyes. 'Don't I know you?' he asked. He had a distinctive, croaky voice.

Malinal's heart was racing. 'I don't think so,' she said. 'I'm from Cintla.' She named the regional capital two hours' walk to the south through which she had passed earlier. 'I've never been to Potonchan before.'

'Are you sure of that, my pretty? Because you look very familiar to me somehow.'

'Yes, quite sure, and I suppose I'd better be getting back now since you say the festival's been cancelled.'

She turned and began to walk in the direction she had come, resisting the urge to break into a run, keeping her pace slow and measured as the soldiers talked urgently behind her. She knew exactly where turkey-neck remembered her from – had known the instant he spoke to her. His face had aged a lot in the five years but she couldn't forget that voice.

'Come back here, my pretty . . .'

She ignored him, kept on walking.

'Hey you! Halt!'

There was a scramble of running feet and in a moment they were on her.

'You're Malinal!' turkey-neck said as he grappled with her. The slyness in his eyes had turned to triumph.

The soldiers brought Malinal straight to the palace and insisted on showing her to Muluc in person. 'We'll get a good reward for catching this one,' said turkey-neck, whose name was Ahmakiq. 'I was there five years ago when they put her into slavery – handed her over to the merchant myself. They sold her to the Mexica to be sure she'd never come back. Princess of the blood like this – she could have caused them a lot of trouble.'

'Well she's back now,' said Ekahau, the younger soldier.

'Exactly! And that's why they'll be grateful we caught her.'

Waiting in the palace courtyard for Muluc to appear, Malinal found herself reliving the events of five years ago.

Her beloved father, Kan-U-Ueyeyab, the late chief of Potonchan, had died suddenly and unexpectedly when she was fourteen years old. She was his only child and should have succeeded to his position when she was sixteen. Meanwhile her mother Raxca ruled as regent and swiftly took a lover, the lord Muluc, whom she equally swiftly married. Shortly after Malinal's fifteenth birthday, the couple had a child, a boy they named Nacon, and from the moment of his birth Muluc doted on him and detested Malinal. His influence on Raxca was very great, for she was besotted and weak, and he conspired with her to get rid of Malinal so that in due course Nacon could inherit the chieftainship. Raxca had baulked at having her own daughter murdered, the solution

Muluc preferred; instead Malinal was sold to a Mexica slave-trader and taken off to Tenochtitlan, that city of terrors from which none who were sent in bondage ever returned.

Now no longer an innocent girl but a woman of the world herself, Malinal felt quite certain her mother must have been intimate with Muluc long before her father's death. Worse, it was depressingly obvious that Kan-U-Ueyeyab had been murdered, most probably poisoned, by the pair – for he had been strong and radiant with health until the very moment a mysterious affliction struck him down, brought blood pouring from his nose and mouth, plunged him into unconsciousness and killed him within a day.

And all this for what? Was absolute power in Potonchan, and putting Nacon in a position to inherit it, really worth such betrayal, such scheming, such wickedness?

Malinal looked up. The palace was as she remembered it, with two storeys and a floor area of a dozen or so rooms. She had once thought it big and impressive – and it was, indeed, very much larger than all the surrounding buildings. Accustomed to the beautiful and luxurious dwellings of the Mexica nobility, however, she now saw her childhood home for what it really was – the rude and rustic seat of a minor tribal chief.

A woman's voice raised in anger could be heard within, a child crying, a man speaking in indistinct, urgent tones. Shuffling to attention, Ahmakiq and Ekahau tightened their grip on Malinal's arms and she prepared herself for the first sight of her mother in five years. She supposed she had loved her once – doesn't every child love her mother? – but all that had long ago been burnt away and she was surprised to discover she felt nothing for her, not even hatred any more, not even curiosity, just cold and disdainful contempt. All the rage she felt was focussed on her loathsome stepfather! He'd got the better of her five years ago and most unfortunately it appeared he was going to get the better of her again today.

However, it was not Muluc who emerged from the door of the palace but the worried-looking steward who'd been sent to fetch him, closely followed by Raxca whose attention was focussed on a bawling babe swaddled in her arms. Trailing behind, and gripping a fold of

Raxca's skirt tightly in his chubby fist, was a fat and exceptionally ugly little boy – he took after his father! – with the sniffles and a smear of snot drying on his upper lip. He looked to be about five or six years of age and could be none other than the usurper Nacon.

Despite the danger of her predicament, Malinal enjoyed that special pleasure that sometimes comes from another's discomfiture as her mother looked up from the babe. Clearly the steward had summoned her without daring to mention who was at the door, but now she gave a startled shriek and stepped back sharply, standing on her son's foot and eliciting a high-pitched yowl of protest. 'Gods!' she gasped.

Once thought a great beauty, Raxca had grown plain and dumpy, with greedy eyes and the puffed-up cheeks of an agouti. Her jaw trembled and her complexion turned fish-belly pale as guilt, shame and fear fought a brief skirmish on her face. 'Is it Malinal?' she asked over the sniffles and incessant grizzling of Nacon.

'Yes, mother,' Malinal replied wearily, 'I've come back to haunt you.' She wasn't sure why she said that, except that she did, somehow, feel like a vengeful ghost returned from the dead.

It was a bizarre situation. Malinal had been sent into slavery by Raxca five years before, yet here she was, in her mother's audience chamber on the first floor of the palace, drinking a bowl of chocolate with her in the late afternoon as though nothing had happened!

Well, not quite nothing, perhaps, because there were guards at the door and Raxca was in the process of making it very clear that Malinal remained a prisoner. 'We shall have to wait until Muluc returns, then we will decide.'

'Mother, let me go!' Malinal said urgently. 'I have no interest in the chieftainship of Potonchan. Nacon may have it when he matures, for all I care. I'm no threat to him, or you, or your darling Muluc. My only interest is in these white men, or gods, or whatever they may be.'

'Well Muluc is interested in them too,' Raxca said severely. The colour had returned to her chubby face, which was set in its usual mode of fanatical devotion to her husband. 'He's making plans to attack them if they dare to come here. I don't think he'd want you to contact them directly. No. I'm afraid you must stay, my dear.'

She had been breastfeeding the baby, but now Nacon stamped possessively to her side and pawed at her teat, and to Malinal's amazement she hugged the little boy close and allowed him to suckle too. Raxca smiled as she settled back on the couch, cradling her children. 'Tell me about Tenochtitlan,' she said, as though Malinal had returned from a sightseeing trip instead of five years of slavery and prostitution. 'I've heard it's a very beautiful city.'

Little by little as the afternoon wore on, and Raxca steadfastly refused to be drawn into anything other than small talk, Malinal began to realise something she had never fully appreciated as a child – that her mother was a very stupid, small-minded, parochial woman. No wonder Muluc had found it so easy to manipulate her to his own ends!

Shortly after nightfall he stormed into the audience chamber, as ugly as she remembered him, muscular and scarred, with beetle brows and bulging eyes, dressed in full war regalia of body paint and feathers. 'You!' he said pointing a finger at Malinal. 'How dare you show your face in my palace!'

'I wouldn't have done so,' she replied modestly, 'if your guards hadn't arrested me and brought me here by force. They seemed to think you'd reward them well for doing that. I can't imagine why.'

With a few harsh words, Muluc sent Raxca and the children from the room. 'Tell me your purpose here,' he said when they were gone. 'Surely you can't imagine you've any claim to the chieftainship after all this time.'

'I have no claim,' said Malinal, 'and no interest.'

'Then what do you want?'

Malinal saw no need to tell the whole truth to this oaf. 'I was sent from Tenochtitlan,' she said, 'to make contact with the strangers . . .'

'But how could anyone in Tenochtitlan know the strangers would be here? They only returned in their boats today . . .'

'The Great Speaker heard of their visit to Potonchan last year,' Malinal said carefully. 'He believes they are gods in the retinue of Quetzalcoatl and wonders if Quetzalcoatl himself is about to return. He sent me to find out more . . .'

Muluc's mouth twisted into a sneer. 'The Great Speaker sent you?' he laughed '*You*? A mere slave?'

'I'm a slave no longer,' Malinal bluffed. 'I've been gone five years and much has changed.' She was making up the lie as she went along. 'I work for the Great Speaker now.'

'So you're what? His ambassador? Show me your papers and insignia then.'

'I have no papers and insignia.'

'Ha!'

'I have no papers and insignia because I'm on a secret mission to treat with the strangers.'

'I wonder why I don't believe you?' said Muluc. He laughed again. 'You know, you should stop wasting my time! Just admit you came back to oust me, but you got caught and now you're making up stories about the strangers to try to wriggle out of the trouble you're in.'

'I've told you already,' Malinal protested, 'I'm not here to oust you.' She tried flattery. 'I know I have no chance against a powerful man like you.'

Muluc rolled his eyes. 'I don't have time for this,' he said. 'I've got a full-blown emergency on my hands.' He gave a loud whistle and the two guards Ahmakiq and Ekahau marched into the room. 'Put her in the palace jail tonight,' he told them. 'I'll review her case tomorrow.'

'Have a care before you go into battle with the strangers,' Malinal called over her shoulder as they dragged her out.

'Why?' scoffed Muluc.

'Because if they are gods they will kill you all.'

'Bah!' said Muluc. 'I'm not afraid of them. We've killed them before and proved they're just men like us. If they choose to fight, they're the ones who will die.'

The Spaniards rowed upstream against the swift current of the Tabasco river, sweating in the close morning heat and fending off clouds of tiny bloodsucking insects. The river was broad and smelled of rot, winding in serpentine fashion between banks lined with the stunted swamp trees called *manglars* in the native Taino language of Cuba and Hispaniola. Sprouting from multiple exposed roots, like interlinked tripods, these ugly trees were filled with gaudy, shrieking birds and grew promiscuously in thick clumps out of rich, glistening, silty mud.

Amongst them, with angry glowers, uttering hostile whoops and yells, moved immense crowds of Indians.

An arrow struck the deck of the brigantine but failed to penetrate the stout timbers. It bounced, slid and skittered to a halt at Cortés's feet. Curious, he picked the little projectile up, studied its head of brittle obsidian – quite shattered by the impact – and threw it dismissively overboard. He considered for a moment firing a few rounds of grapeshot into the massed foe but relented. King Charles would expect more restraint from him than that and, besides, if he wished to engage the Indians, he was legally obliged to read them the *Requerimiento*, a tedious piece of bureaucratic nonsense that gave them the option of avoiding battle by accepting the authority of the Spanish crown.

He was certain there was going to be a fight – in part because that was exactly what he had come here for, but in part also because these savages, in their body paint and feathers, armed only with crude weapons, seemed completely unafraid of the invaders. And little wonder! They knew the Spanish were mortal, having given Córdoba such a sound thrashing last year, and thousands of them had mustered here on this morning of 22 March to repeat their victory – ten thousand, at least, visible on the river banks alone, and God alone knew how many more were waiting in the hinterland.

Córdoba had come here with a hundred and ten men and left with forty.

Although Cortés had five hundred men, he'd only been able to bring two hundred with him this morning because the river wasn't deep enough for navigation by the carracks and caravels which he had therefore been obliged to leave at anchor in the bay, with most of his army still on board. The two brigantines did have a sufficiently shallow draught and were, in addition, superbly manoeuvrable under oar-power, so he had crowded fifty soldiers onto each, taking temporary command of one himself and giving charge of the other to Alvarado. The rest of his flotilla consisted of five good-sized longboats, borrowed from the largest ships, each carrying twenty soldiers.

Until a beachhead could be established and reinforced, the odds weren't much better than Córdoba had faced, but mistakes had been made in the debacle of 1518 that wouldn't be repeated in the event of a massed enemy attack today.

Most notably, Córdoba had been ill equipped, being able to bring only two small, outdated cannon to bear on the foe, whereas Cortés had loaded five good falconets, and their gun carriages, on each of the brigantines, and had many more besides waiting to be ferried out from the ships in the bay. He had also brought along Vendabal with the first thirty of his armoured war dogs – Córdoba had none – and these, Sandoval assured him after the battle he had fought to rescue Aguilar, would terrify the Maya.

Potonchan lay less than three miles upstream, where a long straight stretch of the river began; even battling against the current, the Spanish flotilla came in sight of it before noon. Alarmingly the town was large – far larger than the Córdoba veterans had remembered it, unless it had grown enormously in the past months. Sprawling for more than a mile from west to east along the bank and half a mile inland to the south, it consisted, Cortés estimated, of some twenty-five thousand houses. Although these were for the most part built of adobe thatched with straw, he spied many substantial stone structures amongst them, including a towering stepped pyramid standing at the heart of a great ceremonial plaza.

He turned to Sandoval, Brabo and Aguilar who stood by him on deck. 'Looks quite impressive,' he said. 'One might almost imagine these people possess a culture.'

'Not as we know it, Don Hernán,' Sandoval replied. 'As I've come to understand the matter, their ancestors were indeed civilised, with many great achievements of architecture and engineering, but the Maya of today have fallen far from that high estate . . .'

'They are brave enough warriors though,' added Aguilar, pointing to a fleet of thirty large canoes, each with ten armed men on board, paddling down towards them. 'I don't suggest you underestimate them.'

The Indians surrounded the Spanish boats while they were still almost a mile west of Potonchan. Again Cortés was tempted to disperse them with grapeshot and again he decided to wait. Let them make the first move.

Amidships the largest canoe, a tall painted warrior now got to his feet. Aged about forty, he had an air of authority. He was dark and muscular, with many scars on his body, straight hair falling in braids over his prominent brows and fierce, rather bulging eyes. He leaned on a long spear and shouted a harsh challenge up to the brigantine where all the conquistadors were at action stations, lining the rail, swords drawn, muskets and crossbows levelled.

'What does he say?' Cortés asked Aguilar.

'He wants to know our business here,' the castaway replied. 'He says we look like the men who tried to force the Chontal Maya to worship their god last year. He says the Chontal Maya don't want any gods except their own, so they put those men to flight. He asks if we would like them to teach us the same lesson.'

'Cheeky bugger,' said Brabo.

'Tell him I heard a different story,' said Cortés. 'Tell him we know the Spanish were few yet it was they who put his people to flight.'

'I'm not sure that's wise, Don Hernán,' said the interpreter.

'Tell him.'

'He says let's not waste time talking about past events,' Aguilar translated when he'd received the warrior's reply. 'If we wish to force our god on them again, and test their mettle, then they're ready to fight us now and we will see who flees and who stands at the end of the day.'

Cortés frowned. 'When this is over he will accept our God! But don't tell him that yet! Tell him instead we are only an advance party and that we have many more men and much larger ships out in the bay. He knows this already but I want you to tell him anyway, and tell him if we're attacked that the rest of our force will fly to our aid. Tell him not to start a war or he'll be sorry, but also tell him – and convince him of this, Aguilar! – that we don't seek battle. You're to say we've been long at sea and we require only provisions – fresh water, for the river here is salt, and meat for our men. Tell him we'll gladly pay for these things.'

A long exchange followed and at the end of it the Indians applied themselves to their paddles and the canoes shot back towards the town.

'Well . . . ?' said Cortés.

'I've persuaded Muluc – that's the spokesman's name – that they'll have more to lose than gain by fighting us,' Aguilar replied. 'He's gone to put the matter to their chief. He says we're to anchor midstream and wait for their return.'

'Right!' said Cortés, rubbing his hands. The riverbank here, so close to the town, had been cleared of *manglars* and was more sandy than muddy, with flat fields of young maize growing beyond. There were crowds of Indians about but it looked a good place to set up and fortify a camp. He ordered the brigantines and longboats into shore and the cannon unloaded.

'They'll attack us,' Aguilar advised. 'They don't want us to land.'

'I'm betting they won't attack,' said Cortés. 'I think Córdoba hurt them last year more than they want us to believe, but if I'm wrong,' he raised his voice so it carried to the soldiers on deck, 'we're ready for a scrap, aren't we, men?'

A ragged cheer went up.

The Indians did not attack but drew back a few hundred paces from the bank as the Spanish made their camp. Two hours later a small fleet of canoes put out from the town and paddled down to them. The fierce-eyed warrior Muluc exchanged angry words with Aguilar but the upshot was that small quantities of food were delivered – some of the delicious maize flatbreads called *qua*, a few turkeys and some fruit – all in all, hardly enough to feed more than a dozen men. This, Muluc said, was a gift.

Cortés gave thanks but pointed to his two hundred self-evidently rough and violent soldiers, every one of them armed to the teeth, who were now fortifying the camp. He reminded Muluc that hundreds more like them waited in the big ships out in the bay. 'In view of their great hunger,' he said, 'these few fowls and fruits are not enough if my men are to go away satisfied. Some might even see such a "gift" as an insult. I prefer to think, friend, that you have simply not understood our needs but I give you fair warning – I cannot be responsible for the actions of my warriors if you do not bring us adequate provisions soon. We will do you no mischief if you simply allow us to enter Potonchan to purchase everything we need there.'

'Attempt such a thing,' Muluc replied, 'and every one of you will die. We have fifteen thousand warriors already arrayed for battle and thousands more have been summoned from neighbouring towns. We will destroy you.'

'Perhaps,' said Cortés. 'Or perhaps we will destroy you. But such threats are a waste of your breath and mine. Only bring the provisions we need and we'll leave your town alone.'

While this was being put into the Mayan tongue, Alvarado, who had been supervising the emplacement of cannon, strode to Cortés's side and interrupted Aguilar. 'Tell him our needs include jewels and gold as well as food,' he said to the interpreter. He rested his hand menacingly on the hilt of the heavy falchion he now often wore.

'Don Pedro, you go too far,' Aguilar protested.

'No,' said Cortés. 'Don Pedro is right. Tell Muluc that we Spaniards suffer from a disease of the heart that can only be cured by gold. When he brings us food he must also bring us gold and jewels, or we *will* be forced to enter Potonchan.'

As Aguilar translated, the Mayan warrior's face contorted with rage and he took a sudden step forward, putting both hands on his spear as though about to thrust. In the same instant Alvarado, whose left arm was still in a sling, had the falchion out of its scabbard. 'Come on, my lovely,' he said. 'Just you try it.'

Seeing the joy of battle dancing in his friend's eyes, Cortés put a restraining hand on his shoulder. 'Not yet, Pedro,' he said quietly. 'Not yet. You'll get your chance.'

Aguilar and Muluc spoke in raised voices for some time and then the Mayan delegation returned to their canoes and paddled furiously away.

That night, Monday 22 March, Cortés used the cover of darkness to reinforce his beachhead, sending the longboats back in relays to ferry out more cannon, supplies and soldiers from the carracks and caravels. The new arrivals, numbering more than a hundred, included all the remaining crossbowmen and musketeers. Cortés also sent Brabo out with a small scouting party to gain a thorough sense of the lie of the land between the camp and the town, which lay about a mile to the east. In the small hours of the morning, the sergeant returned with vital intelligence. As well as the obvious approach, more or less directly due east along the bank and into the western side of Potonchan, he had found a good track that led inland through the fields, and then through dense brush, and eventually looped back into the town on its east side. When the time came, therefore, a squadron could be sent along this path to attack the town from the east while another marched straight up the bank to attack from the west. Brabo had also been able to reconnoitre the river, observing the currents, and recommended the brigantines be used to land men on the waterfront on the north side of the town. Such a three-pronged attack, if properly timed, was likely to be devastating. It would leave an escape route to the south for refugees, but this was surely better than forcing the enemy into a corner and a desperate last stand in which many Spaniards might also die.

Cortés congratulated Brabo on a night's work well done, but the sergeant admitted it had been easy. 'The Indians weren't keeping proper watch, sir. They were too busy evacuating their women and children.'

'Sounds like they definitely mean to put up a fight then.'

'I'd say so, sir, yes.'

Muluc returned soon after first light on the morning of Tuesday 23 March.

This time he brought eight plucked and dressed turkeys and some maize, but only enough to feed ten people. He also brought some carved green stones and a gold mask of good quality, thickness and weight. The mask's features, which were finely worked, seemed to be a mixture of human and feline – perhaps some species of lion. 'This should be worth a pretty penny melted down,' Alvarado announced as he held the piece to his face and glared out through the eyeholes at Muluc.

'How much, do you think?' Cortés asked.

'Five thousand pesos,' said Alvarado. 'Maybe a little more . . . The stones are worthless though.' He picked up one of the carvings, shaped like a small axe head, and skimmed it out across the river, eliciting a gasp of horror from Muluc as it bounced and sank.

'What's the matter with you?' Alvarado challenged. 'Filthy monkey!'

Even though he could not understand the Spanish words, and Aguilar chose not to translate them, it was clear Muluc knew he had been insulted. Shaking with anger, he told Cortés through the interpreter that the Spanish must now leave.

'Certainly not!' Cortés replied. He cast a sour glance at the little heap of provisions. 'You can see I have a hundred more mouths here to feed than I did last night, but instead of offering us friendship, which would be wise, you offend us with these paupers' rations. As to the gold,' he took the mask from Alvarado and weighed it in his hands, 'it's a pretty enough piece but quite insufficient for our needs.'

The turkeys had been carried in two large baskets, four carcasses to a basket. Cortés ordered the birds removed for cooking, picked up the empty baskets and thrust them at Muluc. 'If you don't want us to come into your town to trade,' he said, 'you must fill both of these with gold and bring us four hundred more birds, twenty deer – no, make that thirty – and sufficient maize to feed all my men, not only those you see here but those who remain on my great ships. If you refuse to offer us that hospitality, then we will enter your town in force and help ourselves.'

When Aguilar had put all this into Muluc's tongue, the Indian laughed. It was a harsh and bitter sound. 'We do not wish to trade with you,' he said, 'and we have no more gold. I'll see to it that you receive some more food from us tomorrow, the last we will bring you. After that you must leave our land or we will kill you all.'

After dark, Cortés sent out three scouting parties, but all returned within the hour to report a large Indian force massing in the fields between the camp and the town. He therefore sent the longboats back to the bay to bring out further reinforcements, several more pieces of artillery and all the remaining dogs, leaving little more than a hundred of his soldiers with the fleet. Although he would have liked the option of using cavalry, Cortés judged the riverbank at the temporary encampment too steep to land the precious animals, which were stiff from the long voyage, so they, too, remained on board ship.

Posting a strong guard, Cortés slept in his armour and ordered all the men to do the same. It meant a night of great discomfort, but the whispers of the Indians taking position in the fields were menacing enough to banish all complaints.

For two days Malinal had heard sounds of increasingly frenetic activity from the palace, and the shouts and footfalls of huge numbers of people on the move throughout the town. Neither Raxca nor Muluc visited her, and she remained in solitary confinement in the jail, largely ignored even by her guards. When they pushed food through the bars and took out her toilet slops, they spoke only a few harsh words, refusing to tell her what was happening or give her any information on the where-abouts or activities of the strangers.

But now, when her third night as a prisoner was already well advanced, Ahmakiq and Ekahau came for her and dragged her out into the courtyard. Dozens of torches – fixed to the walls and in the hands of retainers – lit up the night, and Malinal saw that all the palace slaves, numbering more than fifty, had been gathered as bearers for the portable treasures of the household, which were already being apportioned amongst them. Beautiful statuettes, pectorals, earspools, ornamental weapons, face masks, belts, plates and serving vessels, all carved from the most precious jade, a few small gold and silver orna-ments, fine ceramics, costly wall hangings, bales of rich fabrics, heaped jaguar skins, and much else besides, were hastily wrapped and placed in bundles on the shoulders and backs of the slaves. No doubt to make certain none of them attempted to abscond, and to protect the treasures wherever they were about to be taken, a hundred warriors wearing Muluc's personal livery stood watchfully around, armed with spears and obsidian-edged *macanas* – the Mayan version of the deadly weapon known by the Mexica as the *macuahuitl*.

Ahmakiq and Ekahau gripped Malinal firmly by the upper arms as they marched her across the yard, almost lifting her off the ground in their haste, and now manoeuvred her round the pile of treasures to a corner under a flickering torch where, with something of the manner of a dragon guarding its hoard, Muluc himself stood watching. He was once again dressed for war and his muscular body glistened with oil and paint.

'Ah,' he said, 'Malinal! I don't believe your story about working for Moctezuma. The white men certainly aren't gods and the Great Speaker of the Mexica wouldn't be such a fool as to imagine they are. All in all I think you're here to cause me trouble . . .'

She tried to protest but Muluc held up a large, grimy hand to silence her. 'No! I don't have time to listen to any more of your lies and excuses. Count yourself lucky I'm not ordering your execution – you've your mother to thank for that – but tomorrow I'm going to destroy the white men and then we'll send you back to Tenochtitlan with the next Mexica trader who passes through. There's one visiting Cintla now who always pays a good price for ripe female flesh.' He laughed as though he'd said something funny, and Ahmakiq and Ekahau sycophantically joined in. 'Meanwhile, as you can see' – Muluc's tone was becoming pompous – 'I'm rather busy! We've decided to evacuate the palace ahead of the fighting and send some things of value down to Cintla, so I thought I might as well put you to use as a bearer with the rest of our slaves.'

'I am not,' Malinal said very slowly and deliberately, 'your slave.'

'You're whatever I say you are,' said Muluc. He gave her an appraising leer: 'Including my bed mate, should I give you that privilege.'

'I imagine my mother might oppose such a . . . privilege,' Malinal said acidly.

Muluc's hand shot out and grasped her left breast as though it were a piece of fruit on a tree. 'Your mother,' he said rubbing his thumb roughly over her nipple, 'respects my needs.'

'Well I don't,' Malinal yelled. Thirty days of walking had made her lean and strong. With a twist of her body she broke free of Ahmakiq and Ekahau, clawed Muluc's face and felt a rush of satisfaction as her long nails raked deep through his flesh. He yelped and jumped back, releasing her breast, then surged forward again and punched her hard in the belly. As she doubled over he took her by the hair and dragged her to the ground, roaring with rage.

'Muluc!' It was Raxca, wailing from an upper window of the palace. 'You promised she wouldn't be hurt!'

On the morning of Wednesday 24 March, Muluc was back. Four parallel scores, deep and still bloody, disfigured the left side of his face. 'Looks

416

like he's had an argument with his wife,' said Alvarado. Cortés laughed and asked through Aguilar: 'Are you well, Muluc? You seem to have been in a fight.'

The Indian ignored the question and again presented eight turkeys and a small amount of maize. He pointed to the fields now seething with Mayan warriors, thousands of whom had approached within a few hundred paces of the camp. 'Go now,' he said, 'or die.'

As Aguilar translated this, Alvarado drew his falchion and showed Muluc the edge of its heavy steel blade. 'Do we look like the sort of men to take orders from a bunch of savages like you?' he said.

The Mayan emissary didn't flinch. 'Leave our land,' he insisted.

'Come, come,' said Cortés. 'Where are your manners? Where is your hospitality? I tell you what – if you allow us to enter Potonchan, and provide food for my soldiers in your homes, I'll give you good advice and teach you about my God.'

'We don't need your advice,' Muluc replied stiffly, 'we certainly will not receive you in our homes, and we heard enough about this god of yours last year to know we prefer our own.'

'Ah, but you don't know what you're missing,' Cortés said. 'If you'll only listen to me, you'll prosper. Besides I *have* to enter your town. It's my responsibility to meet your chief so I may afterwards describe him to the greatest lord in the world . . .'

'And who is this great lord?' asked Muluc with a sneer.

'He is my king,' replied Cortés, 'who sent me to visit you here. He desires only peace and friendship with your people.'

'If that is what he desires,' replied the Indian, 'then you should leave and not play the bully in our land.'

'Enough!' barked Alvarado. 'Let's stop sparring with this fool.'

'I'm nearly done,' said Cortés quietly. 'Make certain all the cannon are primed and loaded with grapeshot.' Alvarado grinned. As he set off around the perimeter, where a dozen falconets now pointed towards the advancing Indians, Cortés repeated his offer of peace and friendship, knowing it would be refused.

He had prepared carefully for this moment. The expedition's hundred war dogs were caged below deck, fifty on each of the moored brigantines. Their barks and howls echoed through the camp but it was clear the Maya had no idea what sort of animals were producing these sounds. Vendabal and his assistants had orders to bring them ashore after Muluc's departure.

Earlier Cortés had put a squad of fifty soldiers on board each of the brigantines and placed them under the command of Díaz and Sandoval. Men were ready at the oars to row the boats upstream to Potonchan as soon as the dogs had been disembarked. Each brigantine was also armed with three falconets, one amidships, one at the bow and one at the stern. Cortés had given firm instructions to Díaz and Sandoval to set human feelings aside and use all six cannon to enfilade the town with two full salvos of grapeshot before landing.

Once again, as he'd expected, Muluc refused to accept the perfectly reasonable request that the Spanish be allowed to enter Potonchan peacefully. On the contrary, the stubborn Indian turned his back and stalked down to the river's edge, where his retinue waited in a small fleet of canoes. They paddled out to midstream and held still, then Muluc put a conch to his lips and blew a mighty blast.

It was, as Cortés expected, the signal for a general attack. Giving vent to chilling shrieks, yips and ululations, the massed Indian ranks surged across the fields, unleashing slingstones and spears, some of which reached the camp despite the extreme range. What Cortés had not expected was the second large force in canoes concealed amongst the *manglars* on the opposite side of the river that simultaneously put out into the water and began to paddle rapidly towards them.

Even so, correct form had to be followed. With a yell, Cortés summoned the expedition's notary, Diego do Godoy, and ordered him to begin reading the *Requerimiento*.

Chapter Fifty-Four

Moored by the steep bank below the Spanish camp, Bernal Díaz was in the foremost of the two brigantines commanding fifty soldiers. His force included five musketeers and five crossbowmen. He had three falconets on board, each cannon loaded and fired by a two-man crew. Sandoval, who also had three falconets at his command, was right behind him in the second brigantine with an identical force. Their task, after disembarking the dogs from their cages below decks, was to row the mile upstream to Potonchan with the greatest possible despatch, bombard it from the river with the falconets and then force entry. Meanwhile, Cortés would lead a charge of the main land force of some two hundred men, supported by the armoured dogs, directly along the bank into the town's western suburbs. Pedro de Alvarado and Alonso Davila would lead a subsidiary force of a hundred men on a flanking manoeuvre through the fields to the south of the town and then round behind it into its eastern suburbs.

This was the theory.

But as he heard the loud blast of the conch, Díaz realised that Muluc had seized the initiative and that matters would not be going to plan. As though conjured into sudden existence by some sorcerer, a thousand howling Indians in a hundred canoes were on their way across the breadth of the river, homing in shockingly fast on the port side of the brigantines. Already spears and arrows were arching up out of the canoes and, if they were falling short now, they would not do so for much longer.

At this range, a broadside of grapeshot from his three falconets, and the same from Sandoval's three, would sweep the river clear of attackers in an instant. Unfortunately, however, all the cannon were arrayed on the starboard side of the ships, ready to enfilade the town, and while their crews swivelled and moved them, losing precious seconds, Díaz ordered the rest of his force to port to repel boarders, and the musketeers and crossbowmen to open fire immediately. A glance from the corner of his eye showed him that Sandoval had done the same and the ten muskets roared almost simultaneously, with the crossbows firing a second later.

Sandoval had reported the almost magical effects of gunfire during the rescue of Aguilar from the town of Mutul, but Díaz had no such expectations here. The Indians of Mutul had never faced firearms before, whereas these devils of Potonchan had not only faced muskets and cannon but had faced them down and driven Córdoba's forces, Díaz amongst them, back into the sea.

Cortés was not Córdoba, however. His army had fifty musketeers, against Córdoba's lowly seven, and fifty crossbowmen against Córdoba's five. Another crucial difference was artillery. Córdoba was able to deploy only two ancient hand cannon, whereas Cortés had eighteen of the small, mobile falconets and three great lombards designed to demolish castle walls.

As the musket balls whirred amongst the Indian canoes, ploughing through flesh and blowing heads apart in explosions of blood and bone, the awful boom of the percussion rolled and echoed. It was gratifying, despite having knowledge of guns, that hundreds of the attackers panicked at once and threw themselves into the water or wheeled their canoes and began to paddle furiously upstream towards the town. Even as they did so, however, there came a gigantic rolling crash from the shore as the twelve falconets defending the camp were fired in a single barrage – at what target Díaz could not immediately see. The effect of these new detonations, a thousand times louder than any musket, and of the accompanying eerie whistle of grapeshot, was to disrupt and bewilder even further the attack the Indians were attempting to mount from the water.

Still enough of them came on to overrun the ship. Díaz drew his broadsword.

* * *

Godoy didn't finish reading the *Requerimiento*, and of course there was no time for Aguilar to translate any of it into Maya. After the notary got to the part explaining how Pope Alexander VI had given all the lands and peoples of the New World to Spain and Portugal, the Indian horde charging across the fields was at point-blank range and really had to be stopped, so Cortés was obliged to order the falconets fired.

As the smoke began to clear, he surveyed the harm done to the massed enemy and felt inspired to offer a short prayer of gratitude for the incredible advancement of science that God had permitted to the European powers. Without their twelve small cannon, the Spanish in the camp might easily have been overwhelmed by the five thousand homicidal savages who had poured in on them. But now, instead, the front ranks of that vast attacking force had been transformed by the maelstrom of grapeshot into an eerily silent, bleeding ruin of mangled bodies cut down in swathes before the guns, the fallen lying in indiscriminate heaps of guts, dismembered limbs and shattered skulls, the living stumbling dazed and addled over the dead, and great smears of gore splashed through the young maize as though by some giant paintbrush.

The Indians' battle experience against Córdoba's two pathetic little hand cannon hardly stood them in good stead for this! Seized by panic, the middle ranks, though quite unscathed, had dissolved into a full and chaotic retreat, yet the numbers committed to the attack had been so great, and the mass and momentum of their charge so huge, that the rear ranks were still coming on. A fearsome, tangled collision ensued across a wide front, from which piteous screams rose up as hundreds were trampled and crushed.

It was, Cortés thought, as though the horsemen of the apocalypse had descended upon that place and the last days of the world had come. Even Alvarado, falchion in hand, was impressed. 'God in heaven,' he said, 'that's as fine a sight as ever I saw.'

Still there were thousands of survivors, most already in flight along the riverbank back to Potonchan. Wanting to press home his victory at once before they had time to regroup and mount a proper defence of the town, Cortés whirled towards the brigantines. '*Vendabal!*' he yelled, as he grasped the extent of the parallel attack that was under way there, '*Get those dogs amongst the enemy!*'

His eyeline into the camp obscured by the steep riverbank, Díaz had only the haziest idea what was going on there and little time to care. More than a hundred Indians, plumes of bright feathers in their hair, their bodies and faces fearsomely striped with black and white paint, had boarded the brigantine and hand-to-hand fighting raged all across the deck. Ducking low, as a swarthy, sweating, wild-eyed savage swung a huge club at his head, Díaz backhanded the edge of his broadsword across the man's naked belly, spilled his guts, stepped in and trampled him down. Now two more were coming at him, flanking him. He felt something strike his right thigh hard and sharp, ignored the pain, cut the legs out from under the man on his left, put the point of the sword neatly through the second man's chest, and with a roar shoulder-charged a third, sending him cartwheeling over the rail and into the river.

In a second of breathing space he saw that not a single Spaniard was down. Although hard-pressed they were winning the fight! The enemy were for the most part naked but for loincoths, and their flint daggers and wooden batons edged with obsidian were little better than children's toys, quite unable to penetrate the plate and chain mail with which the Spanish were armoured – and no match for Toledo steel. He saw Mibiercas wade into a mass of the enemy, ignoring spear thrusts that slid harmlessly off his cuirass, swirling his great longsword before him, hacking left and right, left and right, cutting a man clean in half here, taking an arm off a shoulder there. Right behind him came La Serna, who'd snatched up a pike and was jabbing its vicious point down overhand into the faces of the attacking warriors, piercing one through the eye, tearing the throat from another.

'To me!' Díaz yelled, 'to me! Avenge Córdoba!' And in twos and threes his men rallied to him, formed up almost automatically into a square bristling with steel and harm, and swept forward along the deck in an armoured mass. The Indians still outnumbered them, but they lacked coordination and were already wavering, on the brink of panic, when Vendabal appeared like an evil genie from the hold with fifty of his armoured dogs streaming before him. He'd starved the animals the night before and now Díaz understood why. As they leapt, snarling and baying upon the enemy, as lions upon lambs, the huge animals spread the contagion of utter terror amongst them, tumbled at least a dozen on their backs and began at once to devour them. All the courage and bravado drained out of the rest in an instant. With howls of despair they threw themselves overboard onto the muddy bank and into the water, where Cortés and a hundred conquistadors from the camp waited with swords drawn to slaughter them.

In the rush, Cortés had forgotten his buckler; he fought with a dagger in his left hand, a broadsword in his right. He had also lost a sandal somewhere on the riverbank, but hardly noticed it as he closed with a glowering, barrel-chested savage, chopped off his arm at the elbow with a firm downward sword slash and slit him open from groin to navel with the dagger. The man gave a horrible yell and lurched forward – absurdly still trying to grapple with him! – but Cortés contemptuously swept him aside and advanced through the cloying mud towards a slim, long-haired Indian youth who stood hip-deep in the river with his back turned. Armed with a sling and a bag of stones, this veritable David had, in the past few moments, singlehandedly brought down three conquistadors on the deck of Sandoval's brigantine, where the last of the boarders were still being dealt with. The youth was whirling the sling above his head again, concentrating, taking careful aim, inexperience making him oblivious to danger, when Cortés hacked the edge of the sword into his neck where it joined his shoulders, releasing a spray of arterial blood. As the muddy water blossomed red around him, the boy turned and sank down into it, still gripping the sling, his eyes rolling in horror.

Cortés stalked on in search of new prey, but the fight had become a mopping-up operation. Those of Vendabal's dogs that could be separated from the Indians they were eating on Díaz's brigantine – now joined by the other dogs from Sandoval's hold – had been set on the fleeing remnants of the very large force that had attacked the camp. They would pursue them to the outskirts of Potonchan before Vendabal finally called them off. The last of the Indians who'd infested Sandoval's brigantine had also been killed.

As Cortés searched for and retrieved his lost sandal from the mud, he resolved to press home the attack on the town at once. Muluc's pre-emptive strike across the river had taken him by surprise and caused some disruption to his plans, for which indignity he intended to make the inhabitants pay dearly.

Action at last, thought Alvarado as he led his force of a hundred men at the double through the fields of the dead. The effects of the cannon fire on the enemy had been spectacular, but there was no substitute for cold steel and the press of battle. He grinned as he remembered the surprised faces of the five Indians he'd cut down in the fight around the boats – the heavy blade of the falchion was perfect for the brutal slaughter of such foes with their puny stone weapons and no concept of the science of warfare. But his blood was up now and he was in the mood to kill more.

According to Brabo's scouts, the track he was following would lead first to a point about three miles south of Potonchan and then a mile to the northeast across fields before looping back again a further two miles or so through dense forest and brush into the town's eastern suburbs. Alvarado was to begin his assault there as soon as the sounds of muskets and cannon told him the other two prongs of the attack – from the river to the north and along the bank to the west – had begun. To avoid the danger of Spanish troops being hit by their own guns, it had been agreed that the falconets on the brigantines, and with Cortés, would fire only two salvos before the offensive was pressed home simultaneously on all fronts.

Alvarado had marshalled his men into two columns of fifty, each consisting of ten ranks of five, but had them bunch into a defensive square of ten ranks of ten as the track approached a major thoroughfare. Here, some three miles due south of Potonchan, and close to a range of low hills, they encountered large groups – hundreds – of Indians in disorganised bands, many injured and bleeding, some missing limbs or so badly wounded they must be borne on stretchers, evacuating the town. A few of the refugees carried pathetic bundles of belongings, none offered any challenge, and those who were able broke into a shambling, panicked run at the sight of the Spaniards. Alvarado was tempted to give chase and kill as many as possible before they could shelter in the hills, but Alonso Davila, to whom Cortés in his wisdom had given joint charge of the flanking party, dissuaded him. 'There's no honour in it, Pedro,' he said, 'and it's not what we're tasked with. Let's press on.'

A mile further on, having turned northeast, the track left the open fields behind and narrowed sharply as it entered the forest Brabo had warned of, obliging the conquistadors to break formation into double and even single file in places. Here the enemy might easily come at them unseen out of the undergrowth, ambuscades were to be expected and Alvarado ordered a full alert. Yet still there was no attack. 'Cowards!' he said to Davila. 'They dare not confront us.'

'Judging from those refugees,' said the other man, 'their spirit's broken . . . Still, the real test won't come till they're forced to defend their town.'

Two hours' hard march from the Spanish camp, the track emerged from the forest and the eastern outskirts of Pontochan came into view across a strip of cleared land two hundred paces wide. There was no sign of any defending enemy forces, absolute silence reigned, and the empty streets leading due west towards the ancient stone pyramid and the rich structures around it in the main square beckoned Alvarado to gold and glory. 'You know what?' he said to Davila. 'Why don't we just go in and seize this shithole ourselves before the others get here?'

As he spoke they both heard the sound of distant musket fire.

For speed of movement, Cortés made the difficult decision to leave all but two of the falconets in camp with fifty men and twenty of the dogs to guard them. He gave Alvarado and Davila a head start of more than an hour because of the long indirect route they would have to follow to get their flanking party into position, then set Díaz and Sandoval on their way upriver in the brigantines and ordered his own force of two hundred men to advance the mile directly along the bank to the western edge of the town.

At first the Indians were silent, and it seemed they might all have fled, but soon a great mass of warriors, some two thousand or more, rushed out to meet them, shrieking their war cries. As they ran they

425

sent up clouds of arrows and spears, which seemed fearsome but could effectively be ignored since they did little damage against Spanish armour and shields and were no match for the riposte that Cortés had prepared. Ten musketeers were on the brigantines, and ten with Alvarado, but the remaining thirty out of the expedition's entire complement of fifty were with him. Shouting rapid orders, he brought the infantry square to a halt and arrayed the musketeers to the front with one rank of fifteen kneeling and one rank of fifteen standing. As the enemy closed, both ranks fired simultaneously into their midst, shattering their charge, and stepped back into the protection of the square to reload while thirty crossbowmen strode forward, fired and likewise retreated. The foe were increasingly used to gunfire, and not all broke and ran when the muskets crashed, but, as Cortés ordered the square into motion again, those hundreds who came on were met and utterly destroyed by the massed pikes, swords and axes of his disciplined and unbreakable infantry. Cortés himself was fighting in the front rank of the square, using his buckler to protect the man to his left just as the man to his right protected him. A huge warrior came at him, brandishing a flint-tipped spear, but before he could get close a pikeman in the rank behind reached over Cortés's head and killed the attacker with a thrust to the chest. Two more of the enemy rushed in. Cortés smashed one away with his buckler, knocking him dazed and bleeding to the ground, and ran the other through with his broadsword as the square surged onward, trampling over both of them and many others who had fallen, reducing them to broken, bloody pulp.

Now the musketeers and crossbowmen had reloaded. Picking their aim carefully over the shoulders of the infantry, they began to fire independently from within the moving square – which Cortés realised must seem like some great armoured beast to the Indians, a myriad-legged monster spitting fire and death. And at its very heart, trundled along by their gun crews on wheeled carriages, were the two falconets – those even more terrible instruments of destruction – and with them eighty war hounds, still leashed and held in check by Vendabal's handlers, but baying and barking furiously, maddened by the smell of blood.

Neither dogs nor cannon would be needed, Cortés decided, until

426

the next stage of the assault, but this would come very soon. The initial fury of the Indian attack had already been broken, and moments later he smiled with satisfaction as the survivors turned in a mass and fled back along the bank, taking shelter behind crude barricades and fences of heavy timber set up to protect the town.

As he brought the infantry to a halt a hundred paces from the enemy, slingers darted out through gaps in the defences, sending a hail of stones towards them, and he saw two of his men drop stunned and bleeding from heavy blows to their helmets. 'Shields!' he shouted, 'Shields!', as flights of arrows and spears followed. Again there were a few injuries, none of which looked fatal. Shrugging off the hail of missiles, he ordered the falconets loaded with ball.

Following Díaz in the lead brigantine, Gonzalo de Sandoval scanned the banks of the river for more fleets of canoes, but perhaps through fear of the cannon only a handful came out against them and these were easily kept at bay by musket and crossbow fire. One that approached too close was ploughed under the water by the bows of Díaz's ship and all the Indians in it disappeared from view; another became tangled in Sandoval's starboard oars and managed to unleash a few futile arrows before its crew were shot to pieces.

In this way, facing little opposition, the two brigantines drew level with Potonchan and dropped anchor midstream, from where they observed Cortés's square break the massed attack of the Indians and come within striking distance of the town's western limits.

Sandoval studied the waterfront where he and Díaz must soon land their forces. It was thick with Indian warriors carrying their primitive weapons, blowing trumpets and conches, beating tattoos on their drums and yelling defiant war cries. He felt almost sorry for them in their naïve bravery, for even having seen and experienced the deadly effects of cannon they seemed not to have learnt their lesson and were obviously intent on stopping the Spaniards getting ashore.

Defended from a hail of arrows, spears and slingstones by a line of soldiers carrying big *adarga* shields, the gun crews on the bank were now rolling Cortés's two falconets forward. Though their target was concealed from him by rows of simple native houses, Sandoval had a good view of the crews and saw they were feverishly unloading canisters of grapeshot from the barrels of the weapons and reloading with ball. He would not do the same with his own three cannon since he judged grapeshot – unfortunately for the savages – to be the right ammunition to clear the waterfront.

He was about to signal to Díaz so they could order their crews to fire simultaneously when he noticed that Cortés, again braving arrows and spears, had walked in front of his own guns with another conquistador – Aguilar! – and seemed to be attempting to address the foe within the town.

What in heaven was the caudillo doing?

A few more moments passed and the salvos of cannon fire that were to signal the general attack on Potonchan had still not been heard. The muskets had also fallen strangely silent. 'Damn it!' said Alvarado. 'Let's take this town while the others are dallying.'

'No, Pedro,' Davila insisted. He was handsome and daring but argumentative, with a habit of disputing every point. 'You know I'm as eager as you are for a fight but we must wait. We'll end up getting our men killed by our own guns if we go in now.'

'In war,' said Alvarado, 'it does not pay to hesitate. Think, Alonso! What if the other attacks have run into unexpected trouble? Our assistance may be needed.'

Davila was biting his lower lip, his hand resting on the hilt of his sword. 'Bide awhile, Pedro,' he said finally. 'Those are our orders. We'll hear the signal soon enough.'

'Bah! Orders!'

Twenty of the hundred conquistadors in the flanking party, top-flight swordsmen every one of them, belonged to Alvarado's personal squad. He called them to him and, without another word to Davila, led them out of hiding in the undergrowth and across the open ground to the eastern edge of Potonchan. They had not gone fifty paces into the town, however, when war cries rose up all around them and Indian warriors, grimacing furiously, burst forth from the adobe houses on both sides of the seemingly deserted street.

* * *

428

From his position, Cortés could see both brigantines clearly with Díaz and Sandoval on deck. All that remained was for him to fire his own guns and they would enfilade the town with grapeshot.

But he hesitated.

Despite an intense, restless desire to inflict mayhem on Potonchan, as Saint Peter had commanded in his dreams, it troubled him that Godoy had not finished reading the *Requerimiento* before the earlier engagement and that there had been no time for Aguilar to render the text into the Mayan tongue. His Royal Highness and Most Catholic Majesty King Charles V of Spain was known to be a stickler for such matters and, without the monarch's support, the conquest would ultimately be doomed. Godoy had the *Requerimiento* in his possession and had remained in camp, now almost a mile behind them, but Cortés wanted to be able to claim justification for the harm he intended to do. Since Aguilar had accompanied the infantry, though not in a fighting role, he therefore summoned the interpreter to join him in front of the guns.

A slingstone whizzed past Aguilar's head as he came ducking and weaving forward, and one of the curious darts – launched from the clever little spear throwers with which the Maya were so handy – smacked into the earth between the two men. 'Tell them,' Cortés told the interpreter, gesturing towards the feathered and painted Indians who could be seen in dense ranks peering through gaps in their hastily erected defences, 'to let us enter their town, buy water, buy supplies and speak to them about God and His Majesty.'

'There's no point, Caudillo!' Aguilar protested. 'They're determined you will not come in.'

'Tell them anyway.'

The interpreter raised his voice and bellowed a few sentences in Mayan, which were answered by laughter, hoots of derision, drum beats and more flights of missiles from behind the barricades. With considerable force, an arrow bounced off Cortés's helmet and three infantrymen came forward with adarga shields to offer protection.

Cortés waved them back. He would not show fear or weakness. 'Tell the Indians,' he said to Aguilar, 'we are going to enter their town whether they like it or not. If they attack us, and if in self-defence we have to kill or hurt more of them, it will be their fault not ours.'

429

Aguilar's speech was met by a renewed hail of slingstones and both men were hit about the body, though their armour protected them. 'Very well,' said Cortés, taking the interpreter by the arm and leading him back behind the falconets, 'I commend their souls to God.' As the Indian drums beat more wildly, conches blew and the howls of the warriors went up in a continuous wall of sound, he called Vendabal and the dogs forward and ordered the gunners to fire.

An instant after the first salvo from Cortés's two falconets, Sandoval signalled to Díaz on the forward brigantine, received his answering signal, and both men simultaneously ordered their crews to fire. The wheels of the gun carriages had been jammed to stop the weapons careening back across the deck, but Sandoval, who had his hands pressed to his ears to shut out the mighty sound, felt the whole ship rock under his feet with the recoil. Fire and smoke belched from the barrels, the smell of sulphur filled the air and the murderous barrage of grapeshot, like some deadly hurricane, spread out as it whistled the two hundred paces across the river and tore into the enemy ranks massed on the waterfront, reducing them to blood and offal, shredding the adobe walls and thatched roofs of the houses beyond and bringing many down to their foundations in a whirling avalanche of dust and masonry.

There was no time to conduct more than the most cursory assessment of the damage. Cortés's orders were clear that a second barrage must follow as closely as possible upon the first. Already the sweating crews had covered the fuse holes and the ends of the falconets' barrels to suffocate any residual burning matter. Now, with huge bursts and hisses of steam, they pushed damp sponge rods into the barrels to cool them and clean out any hot debris. Next, bags of powder were forced down to the base of the barrels with ramrods, then the clusters of grapeshot in their canvas tubes and, finally, after the weapons had been aimed again at the shore (and no great precision was required at this range), new fuses were inserted and lit, and with a tremendous roar the killing wind burst forth again upon the unlucky Indian town and its doomed inhabitants.

'To shore!' yelled Sandoval to the rowers as the anchor was pulled up, and the brigantines surged across the current to the devastated waterfront, piled high with the broken and dismembered dead.

Alvarado cursed his broken arm that meant he could not hold a buckler and fell automatically into the swirling Talhoffer style of *messer* combat he'd learned in Zurich years before and practised many times on board ship since he'd set himself the task of mastering Zemudio's falchion. Though crude, with the weight of a battle-axe, the heavy steel blade offered a skilled user – such as he had become! – all the flexibility and speed of response of a sword, and he used it now to carve a broad, bloody path through the heaving mass of filthy Indians who'd surrounded his twenty and who continued to pour out, in vast, unexpected numbers, from the adobe houses lining both sides of the street.

He'd made every one of his men an expert with the sword in the years they'd been with him; they were all heavily armoured and, though they were outnumbered at least ten to one, Alvarado was confident they would win through. He delivered a killing blow slanting right to left, cutting an opponent down from the base of his neck to his ribcage, then immediately reversed the blade and slashed another man's belly open, brought the point up in a ferocious lunge into the face of a third, withdrew and began a new cycle of blows with a clean decapitation of a fourth. '*Yes!*' he yelled, '*yes!*' as he saw his foes backing warily away from him. 'This is what I live for!'

He was enjoying himself so much that he'd completely forgotten about Davila and the other eighty men hidden in the undergrowth, but now there came a tremendous crash of musket fire. Bullets whirred through the air, passing perilously close to the Spaniards, ploughing into the mass of their attackers and – predictably! – causing consternation amongst them. What was it with these Indians, Alvarado wondered, that made them so afraid of a few loud bangs? The actual killing power of the muskets was, in his opinion, fairly negligible; they were hard to aim and they took an unconscionably long time to reload, but their terrifying effect on the natives could not be denied.

A few well-aimed crossbow bolts followed, and then Davila's men, coming on in a compact square, hit the Indians from the rear with all the force of a battering ram.

Alvarado killed and killed again, the remaining Indians fled, and suddenly there was no one left to fight. Davila swaggered over wearing an I-told-you-so look.

'Well?' said Alvarado.

'Got yourself in a bit of a tight spot there,' said Davila disapprovingly.

'I've been in tighter.'

'Perhaps,' – a sneer – 'but I'd say it's just as well the rest of us were here to get you out of this one.'

Pompous fool, thought Alvarado. Hot words rose to his lips but, before he could utter them, Davila held up his hand and gestured: *Listen*.

There could be no mistaking the rumbling roar of the cannon salvo that echoed forth from the western side of Potonchan.

As they broke into a run, their men streaming after them, the guns fell silent and shouts and musket fire carried to them on the sluggish afternoon breeze.

Then the falconets boomed again, signalling the start of the general attack. 'Santiago and at them!' yelled Alvarado. 'Santiago and at them!' yelled Davila. 'Santiago and at them!' yelled their hundred men in unison, now at a full charge towards the distant sounds of battle.

Cortés had watched with satisfaction as his falconets billowed fire and the pair of one-pound balls exploded into the centre of the barricade, smashed apart a section of heavy fencing and transformed it into a deadly weapon from which a hail of lethal splinters and shrapnel tore into the enemy ranks and plunged them instantly into ferment.

Followed by the infantry in a disciplined mass, the gun crews hurriedly wheeled the cannon forward, swabbed out the barrels and reloaded while the musketeers and crossbowmen picked off milling, terrified Indians through the breach. Amidst clouds of smoke and the fearful din of battle, the second volley from the falconets, now at point-blank range, demolished two further segments of the defences and set off a terrified, stampeding retreat.

'Santiago and at them!' Cortés yelled at the top of his voice. His men wrenched apart what remained of the Indian defences and he led the charge into a broad street beyond. At the end of it, a hundred paces

432

distant, stood another row of barricades, barely waist-high and much flimsier than the first, behind which, and atop the neighbouring houses, the Indians – poor fools that they were – had rallied.

There was no time or need to bring up the falconets. As the infantry square once again formed and surged forward, Cortés gave the signal to Vendabal, and eighty ferocious war dogs raced ahead. Some, following their noses, found entry to the houses that lined the street, from which wails of terror were immediately heard; others leapt the barricades and tore into the defenders, snarling and snapping like demons from hell. The infantry followed, swords flashing, pikes and battle-axes gleaming in the sun, and fell upon the scattered and broken enemy, squads peeling off to root them out of the houses, others tearing their miserable barricades apart.

As quickly as it had formed, the square disintegrated into ever smaller units, each pursuing separate objectives in what seemed to be a generalised rout of the enemy, when suddenly – a trap! – fresh war cries were heard and a thousand or more Indians converged in great masses from three different side streets and charged down on the conquistadors, seeking to exploit their temporary loss of coherence and pressing them hard.

'Square!' Cortés yelled, 'Square!', making himself a focal point in mid-street to which his men could rally, but also attracting the attention of dozens of the enemy who seemed to recognise him as the Spanish captain and surrounded him with single-minded intent, jabbing at him with spears and knives. For an instant he stumbled and nearly fell as a great wooden club smashed into the side of his head, but surged up with a roar, rammed his buckler into his attacker's face, hacked the edge of his broadsword at the man's knee and killed him with a thrust to the heart. As more of the enemy closed with him he heard a voice – 'I'm with you, Hernán' – and his friend Juan de Escalante fought his way through the melee, long black hair hanging loose to his shoulders, broadsword dripping with blood, to stand at his side.

Precious time was lost mooring the brigantines, detailing skeleton crews to guard them, and disembarking the rest of the men as the sounds of battle from the western sector of town into which Cortés

433

had led the main attack grew fiercer and more urgent. 'Santiago and at them!' Bernal Díaz was at last able to yell, and led the charge across the waterfront – though at first the Spaniards struggled to make headway, so high and so tangled were the heaps of dead and dying Indians left by the ships' guns.

During the action this morning, Díaz had been shot in the muscle of his right thigh by an Indian arrow. He had pushed the barbed head through, broken off the shaft and extracted both pieces of the little missile, so he was reasonably sure, if he could dress the wound cleanly in the next few hours, that there would be no infection. Meanwhile he ignored the pain, as he had long ago learned to in the heat of battle, and let his ears and sense of direction guide him towards the sounds of heavy fighting, charging through Potonchan's deserted main square and past the looming stepped pyramid into a maze of mean alleys and small adobe houses. Finally, rounding a corner with Sandoval at his side and seasoned troops behind him, he saw Cortés's infantry barely a hundred paces away at the convergence of four streets. By some misjudgement or accident they had lost their formation as a proper fighting square and were beset by a large Indian force. 'Santiago and at them!' Díaz yelled, and at the same moment, to his immense relief, he heard the ancient battle cry of his forefathers echoed not only by Sandoval and his own men but by another Spanish contingent – Alvarado and Davila! – charging into the fray from the east.

In an instant the tide turned and the enemy, losing heart, fled in a mass towards the south.

Díaz heard Cortés shouting, 'Get me prisoners!' and saw a dozen warriors who'd not yet broken out of the melee tackled and brought down. Exulting in their sudden victory, a large squad of conquistadors set off in hot pursuit of the rest, but the caudillo called them back. He looked strong and cheerful though blood dripped from beneath his helmet. 'We've done enough for one day,' he said. 'We'll finish this tomorrow.'

Cortés strode into the main square of Potonchan as the afternoon shadows lengthened and brought his troops to a halt before the forbidding terraces of the pyramid where a giant silk-cotton tree grew.

434

Pointing to it he asked Aguilar if it had any significance, and the interpreter replied that it was sacred to the Maya. 'For them it is the tree that connects the underworld, the earth and the heavens.'

'Pretty idea,' said Cortés thoughtfully. He looked up into the branches for a moment, made certain that Godoy, the royal notary, whom he'd summoned at the double from the camp, was present to witness the act, then drew his sword and slashed three deep cuts into the tree's broad trunk. Speaking loudly, and in a firm voice, he said: 'I have conquered and I now take possession of this town, and this land, in the name of His Majesty the King. If there is any person who objects I will defend the king's right with my sword and my shield.'

Huge shouts of 'Hear, hear!' followed from the mass of the men, passionately affirming that he did right and that they would aid him against any challengers. But, he noted, some of the friends of Diego Velázquez, lead by the glowering, lantern-jawed Juan Escudero, had gathered in a tight group and were plainly offended that Cortés had failed so conspicuously to mention the governor. 'See the upstart,' he heard Escudero bark, 'who usurps Don Diego's rights. Something must be done to stop this treachery.' The man had made no attempt to lower his voice, but the other Velazquistas around him, including Diego de Ordaz, Cristóbal de Olid, and the governor's cousin Juan Velázquez de León all averted their eyes when they saw they were observed.

Cortés smiled cheerfully and pretended nothing was amiss, but a reckoning was coming – and not only with the Indians. Sensing trouble, his own close allies, Pedro de Alvarado, Juan de Escalante and Alonso Hernández Puertocarrero came to stand on either side of him as, in the distance, from the surrounding countryside, they all heard the sound of drums and the ululations of warriors. 'The town is ours,' Cortés said, clapping his friends on their shoulders, 'but it seems our fight here is far from over. Time to bring the horses ashore and get them exercised. I'll wager we'll have need of them tomorrow.'

Chapter Fifty-Five

Four days after agreeing the plan with Huicton, Tozi left Tenochtitlan and crossed the Tacuba causeway amongst busy early evening crowds. She was visible, but invisible, a dirty beggar girl of no consequence who came and went as she pleased. No one noticed as she made her way into the warren of side streets off Tacuba's main square, blending in amongst the other beggars. With night falling she followed a narrow, dark alley choked with rubbish and came at last to a green gate in a wattle fence. She knocked and the gate swung open. Looking neither left nor right, Tozi passed through the gate, nodded a greeting to the burly middle-aged woman who admitted her, made her way across a yard where sheets, blouses, loincloths and a threadbare cotton cloak hung drying and entered the simple dwelling. A lantern flickered in the single large room that served as bedchamber, kitchen, dining area and parlour, and here Huicton was waiting, seated at a rough-hewn table sipping from a cup of pulque.

'So, Tozi,' he said. 'Are you still willing to charm Prince Guatemoc?'

'I'll do my best,' she replied.

An hour later she was ready, dressed up in the finery of the goddess Temaz, her cheeks painted with yellow axin pigment, her lips reddened with cochineal, black bitumen applied to her eyelids.

'Gods!' said Huicton. 'I myself could believe you are Temaz. You have the look of a woman of twenty – a wise and beautiful woman! – not a girl of fourteen. You know what to say? You know what to do?'

'You've prepared me well, Huicton. I'll go to Cuitláhuac's estate at Chapultepec, wait until after midnight, enter the mansion, climb to the second floor and find Guatemoc's room in the south wing. I'll do all I can . . .'

'He's deeply estranged from Moctezuma after the attempt to poison him. It shouldn't be too difficult to work on his mind and detach his loyalties further.'

'I'll do everything in my power . . .'

'The only thing I ask you, Tozi . . .'

She frowned. 'We've been through this already. You don't want me to speak of Quetzalcoatl. But why should I not?' She was aware her lower lip was sticking out in a stubborn, childish way.

'It would be too soon. It might scare him off.'

'Tonight I am a goddess,' she said. 'I will speak of what I wish.'

Huicton shrugged. 'You know my mind on this; I can only pray that you will listen to me.' He leaned forward and embraced her. 'I wish you luck, little Tozi.'

'So I'll see you on the fourth day then?'

The arrangement, unless anything went radically wrong, was that Tozi, in her disguise as the goddess Temaz, would visit Guatemoc tonight and for the two nights following, returning to Tenochtitlan to report to Huicton on the fourth day. But that had changed. Huicton's arrangements often changed.

'I regret not, little one,' he said. 'I'll be gone when you return. My master Ishtlil has entrusted me with a mission. I'm to go to Tlascala and meet the famous battle king Shikotenka.'

Tozi made a face: 'I met many Tlascalans in the fattening pen when I was waiting to be sacrificed. I didn't like them at all.'

'No one likes the Tlascalans! They're fierce, prickly, downright difficult, but they've kept Moctezuma at bay until now and for that reason Ishtlil intends to make an alliance with them.'

'Make an alliance or don't make an alliance – either way Moctezuma is going to fall. Quetzalcoatl *is* coming, Huicton. He's coming right now. So you'd better tell those Tlascalans to be with him not against him.'

Huicton cupped her face in both his hands and kissed her on the nose. 'I believe you,' he said, 'about Quetzalcoatl. But no one else will until they see proof of it. That's why it's best to keep quiet about him for now.'

437

'Like you want me to keep quiet with Guatemoc?'

'Exactly! Quiet as an owl in flight. Will you promise me you'll do that, Tozi?'

'I promise,' Tozi lied.

438

Chapter Fifty-Six

Wednesday 24 March 1519

Melchior had been sullen and uncommunicative since that night on Cozumel when they'd taken their part in murdering Muñoz and disposing of his body. Pepillo thought he knew why. It was the Inquisitor's claim to have 'had' Melchior for a peso – surely also over-heard by Díaz, Mibiercas and La Serna – that had shamed him and made him withdraw so far within himself.

Pepillo now had a clear idea of what 'having' someone meant, and it was horrible and disgusting, but even if Melchior had once allowed Muñoz to do that abominable thing to him, he could not and would not look down on his friend because of it. God alone knew what other indignities he must have suffered as a slave, but he was good and brave and true and this was all that mattered.

Throughout the long voyage, hugging the coast from Cozumel to Potonchan, Melchior had gone about the work that Cortés had assigned to him without any of his usual laughter, bravado and cynical jokes, and whenever Pepillo had tried to talk to him he'd responded with a 'yes' or a 'no' or a grunt, or simply said nothing, but now, suddenly, there was a change in him.

Again it wasn't difficult to work out why.

Since anchoring at the mouth of the Tabasco river on Sunday 21 March, the caravels and carracks of the fleet, the *Santa María* amongst them, had sat idle in the bay while the brigantines and longboats ferried soldiers, guns and supplies ashore to reinforce a beachhead that it seemed Cortés had established on the riverbank near Potonchan. Pepillo had learned what he could by listening to the talk of the men as they came and went, but had been able to establish nothing first-hand because he and Melchior had been confined to the ship with nowhere to go and nothing to do except attempt, as best they could, to exercise the stiff, torpid, fearful horses on the bobbing deck. In a curious way, Pepillo thought, the condition of the horses seemed to mirror Melchior's own depressed inner state.

Since this morning, however – it was Wednesday 24 March – all on board ship had heard the distant sounds of cannon and musket fire that spoke of a sustained battle, and now, as evening drew in, a longboat had come out from Potonchan. Its crew brought news that the town had been captured, and orders from Cortés to prepare the ropes, pulleys and harnesses to lower the horses into the brigantines, which would follow directly. Pepillo's heart leapt when he heard that he and Melchior were to accompany the horses, he bringing parchment, quills and ink – for there were certain matters the caudillo wished set down in writing – and Melchior paying special attention to Cortés's own mount Molinero. With a flash of insight Pepillo realised it was his friend's sense of being needed again, the prospect of action and, last but not least, freedom for his beloved horses, that had brightened his dark mood.

With the deck of the *Santa María* the height of a man above the deck of the brigantine, lowering the horses was difficult and risky work. Fortunately the sea was calm and the big moon, just past full and still bright in the clear sky, made lanterns almost unnecessary. Still Melchior fussed like an old maid over Molinero and cursed the crew like a trooper as one by one they cinched all ten of the great destriers into their leather harnesses, raised the derricks and swung the quivering and blindfolded animals down to the close-moored smaller vessel.

Bundles of long cavalry lances followed, their lethal steel warheads enclosed in leather sheaths, and finally several large, very heavy wooden chests that had to be handled with almost as much care as the horses themselves.

While this was being accomplished, the second brigantine collected the five horses from Alvarado's *San Sebastián* and the three from Puertocarrero's *Santa Rosa*, together with more lances and chests, and finally the two ships made for shore.

Pepillo saw how Melchior stayed with Molinero, stroking his sweating flanks, calming him with whispered endearments as their brigantine entered the mouth of the Tabasco and rowed steadily upstream. There was an atmosphere of hushed expectancy on board and the musketeers and crossbowmen who had come along as guards watched the banks fiercely – as though they expected an attack at any moment. Thickets of *manglars*, weird and otherworldly in the moonlight, pressed down to the water's edge, transforming the wide river, in Pepillo's eyes, into the haunt of devils and spirits. No one talked and for a long while the only sounds to be heard were the splashes of the oars, the nervous whinneys of the horses, mysterious shrieks rising and falling from all quarters of the night, and the distant, spine-chilling thunder of a thousand native drums.

'What do the drums mean?' Pepillo asked Melchior. 'What are those cries?'

'They mean trouble,' his friend replied. 'We heard them when we were here with Córdoba just before the Indians threw ten thousand men at us.'

Pepillo looked down at the deck. It was obvious the brigantine had seen action earlier because the moon's glare showed smears of blood and arrows still embedded in the planking. 'Looks like there's been plenty of trouble already,' he said.

Melchior shrugged. 'Sure. There's been a big fight for Potonchan and Cortés won. But the enemy have towns and villages all over this region, hundreds of thousands of people, more warriors than you can imagine. They'll be gathering their men and then they'll be back.'

'So we could die here?' Pepillo wondered.

Melchior seemed not to have heard his question and fell silent for a long while. Then abruptly he spoke. 'About Muñoz,' he said, but so quietly that men even a few paces away would not hear him. 'There's something I want to tell you.'

Alvarado was in a furious bad temper as he crashed, lantern in hand, through the empty, echoing rooms, devoid even of wall hangings and furniture, of the big two-storey building identified by the prisoners as the chief of Potonchan's palace. Like the shrine on top of the pyramid, and the three stinking temples he'd already searched in the plaza, there wasn't a single item of value in it. The Indians had used the time while

441

Cortés had been strengthening his beachhead to remove all the treasures from the town!

Not only that, but as the prisoners had revealed through Aguilar, the painted savage called Muluc – who'd presented himself merely as an emissary of the chief – was in fact the chief himself! These swine had a sort of low cunning that Cortés had not anticipated, and had taken liberties that they must not be allowed to repeat.

Feeling murderous, Alvarado stormed out of the palace, across the plaza, back to the spot under the silk-cotton tree where Cortés was still patiently interrogating the prisoners and announced: 'Nothing, Hernán! Not a jewel, not a ring, no gold plate. Nothing at all! They stripped the town bare before they left.'

'Ah well,' said Cortés mildly, 'it's as I expected. But don't be put out, Pedro, our work has just begun. I've learned there's an even larger town to the south called Cintla where the chief of the whole region – a far more important man than Muluc – has his seat. I'm certain when we take Cintla that great wealth will fall into our hands.'

He turned his attention back to the prisoners whom, to Alvarado's horror, it appeared he was about to set free. 'Go to Cintla,' he said, speaking through Aguilar, 'and tell its chief I know the truth of many great mysteries and secret things of which he'll be pleased to hear. Tell him we do not want war. Tell him we sorrow at the injuries and death we've been forced to inflict on the people of Potonchan. We would rather not have done so, but it was their own fault because they attacked us and gave us no choice. Tell him we come in peace to teach him about our God who has the power to grant him immortal life.'

'You're not really going to let them go, are you?' said Alvarado.

'Yes I am, so the big chief in Cintla can have the opportunity not to repeat the mistake Muluc made in Potonchan today.'

'And what if he chooses not to seize that opportunity?' sneered Alvarado.

'To be quite honest with you, Pedro, I am gambling that he will not – because then, by the rules of war, we have the right to destroy him. Today we faced thousands, yet the cost to us was small. Twenty with slight injuries – some hit in the head by their slingers, a few with spear or arrow wounds, but they'll all mend soon enough. Not a single man killed, Pedro! Not one! And tomorrow we'll put horse in the field and teach these savages a lesson they'll never forget!'

Footsteps. The sound of clothing being adjusted. A hoarse whisper: 'Don Pedro! A word with you if we may.'

Alvarado had walked out from the campfires for a piss and now found himself flanked in the moonlight by two other men, all likewise clutching their privy members – Juan Escudero to his right, Velázquez de León to his left.

'Gentlemen!' Alvarado commented as he sprayed a great arc into the bushes, 'this is passing strange.'

'Nothing strange about a full bladder,' muttered Velázquez de León through his beard as he too made copious water.

Escudero had so far summoned forth not even a dribble. 'You seem to be having some trouble there, Juan,' Alvarado observed.

'I'm not here to piss,' replied the ringleader of the Velazquistas, his voice seething with resentment. 'When we last talked you gave us to believe you were ready to join us, yet I saw you stand by Cortés tonight.'

'And I'm standing by you now, Juan, am I not?' Alvarado shook his member, being sure that a few fat drops flew up to hit the other man in the face.

With an oath Escudero stumbled back, but to his credit retained his composure. 'We've been watching you, Don Pedro,' he said. 'You found no gold in the palace . . .'

'No gold anywhere,' Velázquez de León added.

'It's clear Cortés has brought us here for reasons of his own,' said Escudero.

'Which would be what?' Alvarado asked.

'Power? Glory? Personal aggrandisement? Revenge? Who knows? But certainly not the interests of this expedition. These are primitive savages we're fighting and it seems they have no treasure. We're wasting blood and strength here for nothing. Córdoba's reconnaisance last year showed richer and easier pickings further inland . . .'

'So you want me to do what?' Alvarado asked. 'Turn on Cortés now, when we're surrounded by the enemy? Arrest him? Truly, gentlemen, I do not think this is the right moment.'

443

'On this we agree,' said Escudero. 'Cortés has made this bed for us and we must lie on it. But when we're done here, if God gives us victory over these barbarians, then the time will come to choose. Cortés is not the right man to lead this expedition. You know it in your heart, Don Pedro, and we ask you to be ready to join the friends of your friend the governor of Cuba and help us return this expedition to legitimacy.'

'What's in it for me?' Alvarado asked.

'Gold, Don Pedro. All the gold a man could possibly want. Put this expedition on the right side of the law, win over Cortés's supporters to our side, and we'll make you a rich man.'

'I'll think on your offer,' said Alvarado. He was already walking back towards the light of the fires. Out of the corner of his eye he saw Escudero and Velázquez de León walking in opposite directions, one to the left, the other to the right. Soon both disappeared amongst the shadows.

Last night, after Malinal had gouged Muluc's face, Raxca's intervention had saved her from a beating at his hands, but had not stopped Muluc forcing her into the column of his household slaves carrying the palace valuables from Potonchan to the safety of Cintla. The slaves had reached the regional capital in the small hours of the morning where they'd been put to work in the great palace of Ah Kinchil, the wizened and ancient paramount chief of the Chontal Maya. Malinal had been assigned lowly duties in the kitchen under the watchful eye of Muluc's steward Ichick, who had roped her ankles and allowed her no possibility of escape.

Muluc himself had turned up in Cintla early that evening and since then had been ensconced with Ah Kinchil in the dining chamber of the palace. Malinal had not even considered appealing to the paramount chief's sense of justice, since he was Muluc's uncle and had been in on the plot to displace her five years before. But the kitchen adjoined the dining chamber and the two men talked loudly enough for her to eavesdrop their conversation even when she wasn't shuffling in and out with their dinner dishes.

It seemed the white strangers – the companions of Quetzalcoatl as it was Malinal's habit to think of them – had resoundingly defeated Muluc's forces in Potonchan. But in the time bought by the negotiating and fighting there, Ah Kinchil had called in tens of thousands of additional warriors from Cintla, Xicalango and other neighbouring towns. As a result, a new force, a truly exceptional force of more than forty thousand men, was now mobilised and stood ready for battle. 'With such numbers,' Muluc crowed, 'we will devour them.'

'So long,' Ah Kinchil corrected him, 'as they are not gods.'

'They are not gods!'

'Yet their weapons seem not of this world, Muluc,' the old chief said in a voice dry as bones. 'I have been hearing accounts all day of what they did to the men you left in Potonchan after you yourself fled.'

'I did not "flee", uncle!' Muluc blustered. 'I fought hard and remained in the field until the end.'

Ah Kinchil waved a hand as though dismissing him. 'I am told they have fire serpents,' he continued, 'that spit flame killing hundreds at a single blast. I am told ferocious beasts whose skin cannot be pierced by arrows obey their commands and tear out the throats and bellies of our warriors. I am told these white men – or gods – are themselves impervious to our weapons and cannot be killed. Is none of this true?'

'They have powerful weapons, that much is true, but we have known since last year they are men who can be killed, just as we can be killed, and their weapons are of this world though made with great skill and cunning. We defeated them before and we can defeat them again!'

'You defeated them before but it seems these new ones are more dangerous even than their predecessors. If you are mistaken about their powers it could cost us dear.'

Malinal, who was bringing a steaming bowl of chocolate to the table, saw a glint of triumph in Muluc's eye. The evil toad, she realised, had something up his sleeve. 'I am not mistaken, uncle,' he said. 'Last year when the white men came to Potonchan they captured one of our warriors and carried him away in their boats to certain islands they have occupied that lie far off our shores.'

'Islands?' Ah Kinchil seemed almost offended. 'I know of no white men living on our islands.'

'I don't speak of the nearby islands we can reach in our canoes, uncle. I speak of the faraway islands of legend where the people called Taino and Arawak are said to live. It seems the legends are true, for the white men found those islands twenty years ago. First they destroyed the Taino and the Arawak and seized their lands, then they brought in countless settlers from their own even more distant country far off across the great ocean, and now they've come here intending to inflict the same doom on us.'

'I don't understand how you can know this.' Ah Kinchil sounded peevish but also, Malinal thought, afraid.

Looking repulsively pleased with himself, Muluc clapped his hands, the outer doors opened and a short man of middle years with a pronounced stoop, long unbraided hair and crossed eyes entered the chamber, made the obeisances appropriate to great lords, and came padding barefoot across the floor. 'This is the warrior the white men stole from us last year,' Muluc announced proudly. 'His name is Cit Bolon Tun.'

'He doesn't look like much of a warrior,' Ah Kinchil said.

'Perhaps not, uncle; but with respect that is not my point.'

'Well, what is your point then?'

Muluc sighed. 'My point is that Cit Bolon Tun has spent many months living with the white men! They taught him their language, always intending to use him to communicate their wishes to us. They kept him under guard, but this afternoon in the confusion of battle he escaped and returned to our side. It is because of what he has told me about them that I know these white men are not gods. I ask you to hear him.'

Now it was Ah Kinchil's turn to sigh. 'Nephew,' he said, 'I am confused . . . In all your reports about the white men before tonight, you have said that one of them is a fluent speaker of our language and that it is through him you talk to their chief. Now suddenly you present this Cit Bolon whatshisname to me and say that he is their interpreter. Which is true?'

'Both statements are true, lord,' interrupted Cit Bolon Tun, making further obeisances. 'The white men did kidnap me when they came here last year. They did take me back to the islands they have seized from the Taino and the Arawak. They did attempt to teach me their horrible language. And they did bring me to serve as their interpreter. But on their way here they heard that one of their own, a man named Aguilar, was living amongst the Yucatec Maya . . .'

'How can that be?' asked Ah Kinchil.

446

'Eight years ago a boat of theirs sank in the great ocean and this Aguilar was washed up on the northern shores of the Yucatán. He became the prisoner of Acquincuz, the lord of a small town, who kept him as a slave. The Spaniards – that is the name by which the white men are called – heard of this and sent some of their soldiers to seize Aguilar from Acquincuz. They succeeded and he became their interpreter, displacing me. When we came finally to Potonchan I sought the first opportunity to escape, took off the Spanish clothes they made me wear and hung them in a tree, fled away naked and sought sanctuary with Lord Muluc . . .'

'I see,' said Ah Kinchil, rubbing his chin, 'I see.' His rheumy eyes were fixed on Cit Bolon Tun. 'Very well,' he said, 'tell me about these Spaniards.'

'That thing Muñoz said about me . . .' Melchior's voice was so low as to be barely audible, even to Pepillo who stood right by his side.

'He was lying!' Pepillo whispered. 'I know he was lying . . .'

Another long silence from Melchior and then: 'Well, no . . . he wasn't. Not exactly. That's what I want to tell you.'

You may want to tell me, Pepillo thought, *but I'm not sure I want to hear.* 'We don't need to talk about this,' he said. 'We don't need to talk about Muñoz! He was evil but he's dead and he'll never hurt anyone again.'

Melchior's face shone in the moonlight and he shook his head as though denying something. 'The fact is,' he continued, 'the bastard was telling the truth. He *did* have me. But it wasn't for pay, like he pretended. It wasn't for a peso!' A great sob heaved in his chest and he struggled for a moment to stifle it. 'They beat me half senseless,' he said finally, 'and then they both had me.'

Pepillo's face was suddenly burning and his head reeled. What in heaven was Melchior telling him. '*They?*' he asked. 'Who were they?'

'Why Muñoz and his page, of course, the devil. His name was Angel! Can you believe that? He was a year older than me. Bigger too. Muñoz had corrupted him and they worked together, hunting down Indian boys for the Inquisitor's pleasure. They kept after me – after my *arse* – but I always managed to give them the slip. Then the Maya killed seventy of

Córdoba's men here in Potonchan. That was Muñoz's fault, too, burning "lapsed converts". Poor souls! How could they have been converted to anything when he could only speak to them in signs? And if not truly converted, then how could they be said to have lapsed? He pushed these people to the limit in his zeal for God, so no wonder they attacked us in the end. There were barely enough of us left alive to sail the fleet back, and most too sick or injured to notice what was happening with the high and mighty Inquisitor and his rat-faced bastard page. We were eighteen days at sea, long enough for mischief to be done. One night, when no one was looking, they dragged me into his cabin, beat me until I could not stand and held me down over his table. That was how Muñoz had me! And when he was done Angel had me too.'

Pepillo felt a great ache of compassion. 'Oh Melchior,' he said. 'Now I understand! No wonder you hated Muñoz so . . .' Without thinking he reached out to touch his friend's arm.

'Wait!' Melchior said, shrugging him off. 'I don't want your pity and there's more to tell. After they raped me I wanted revenge and I swore, Pepillo, I swore to everything that's holy, that I would kill them both or die in the attempt. Two nights later – we were far out to sea – I found Angel on his own on the aftcastle. We struggled but my anger made me strong and I threw him overboard. No one saw it happen, just as no one saw what happened to me.'

Pepillo gasped. 'But you told me . . . You said—'

'That Muñoz had killed his page? Yes, when Angel disappeared that's what everyone on the expedition believed and I saw no need to correct them. But they were wrong! I was the one who killed him, and proud of it too! As for Muñoz, I didn't get the chance on the rest of that voyage and I thought I might have to wait years before fate crossed my path with his again. So when I heard he'd been appointed Inquisitor to this expedition, I couldn't believe my luck . . .'

Pepillo was thinking things over, vividly reliving the events of the past weeks. The way that Muñoz had behaved, the way Melchior had so obviously hated him, the way he himself had been drawn into the plot to kill the Inquisitor, all made perfect sense in the light of what he now knew.

'Well,' said Melchior, as the brigantine slowed and the lantern-lit waterfront of Potonchan loomed ahead on the bank of the dark river, 'I've given you the truth. I owed you that after nearly getting you killed. I won't blame you if you think the less of me.'

'I don't think the less of you,' Pepillo said. 'I think you're brave and you've righted an injustice and I'm proud to count you as my friend.' He hesitated, turned his gaze to the great dark shape of Molinero standing quietly nearby and added: 'You did nearly get me killed, though – so the least you can do is teach me how to ride a horse.'

Eavesdropping from the kitchen, Malinal heard almost every word of Cit Bolon Tun's story.

She found herself rebelling against it and at the same time was persuaded by it.

Perhaps, she supposed, even though she had always doubted, this was because some other part of her – the part still deeply connected to Tozi – did very much want to believe that these white men, these 'Spaniards', were indeed the companions of Quetzalcoatl, returning to right all the injustices of the world, and that perhaps their leader could even be Quetzalcoatl himself.

Her mind was in flux on the matter. First she had joyfully abandoned her doubts when she recognised the hand of the gods in bringing her back to Potonchan at the exact moment of the strangers' own return. But now, as she listened to what Cit Bolon Tun had to say, all her scepticism flooded in on her again with renewed force. This was because the men he described were undoubtedly *men*, not gods, who had taken him to their island where he saw many strange and wondrous things that were, nonetheless, quite clearly the work of men – very clever men, very cunning men, but certainly not gods. And when Cit Bolon Tun related how these strange-looking white men had seized that island twenty years before from its native inhabitants, a people known in the legends of the Maya as the Taino and seemingly still called that today, her blood ran cold – for rather than bringing peace, harmony and progress with them, the 'Spaniards' had inflicted terrible massacres and tortures upon the Taino, burnt them to death in fires, stolen all their lands and all their possessions, and for the most part obliterated them from the earth, except for a few survivors whom they kept as slaves.

449

She did not think Cit Bolon Tun was lying about any of this. His words had the ring of authentic experience and truth.

Moreover the powerful, remarkable, incredibly dangerous weapons of the 'Spaniards' were just that – weapons, made by human artifice – and not godlike devices endowed with unknowable supernatural properties. The shining 'skin' that the stone-tipped spears and arrows of the Maya could not penetrate was nothing more than armour! There was nothing godlike about it, and without it, or if struck in vulnerable, unprotected parts of their bodies, the white men could be killed like any other men. Both the Maya and the Mexica used armour made of padded cotton, so there should be no surprise or awe here. The only difference was that the Spaniards' armour was better, harder, stronger because it was made of metal. It was not even as though the Maya and the Mexica did not know of metals, because they did, and boasted skilled workers in soft copper and bronze. It was just that the metallurgy of the white men was far more advanced than theirs and extended to exceptionally hard and durable metals called iron and steel, which their clever artificers were able to fashion not only into armour but also into axes, spear-tips, arrowheads, daggers and the terrible long knives they called 'swords'.

Then there were the weapons spitting flame and death that Ah Kinchil thought were *Xiuhcoatl* – the deadly 'fire serpents' with which, according to legend, the gods of both the Maya and the Mexica were armed. Once again, Cit Bolon Tun explained, there was nothing godlike about these white men's weapons, which were called 'guns'. They were certainly not fire serpents! In fact these 'guns' were not so very different from bows and arrows – which the Spaniards, indeed, also possessed – or from *atlatls* used to launch darts. Like bows, and like *atlatls*, guns were simply weapons designed by men to send projectiles flying through the air over long distances at high speed. They took the form of metal tubes and, instead of using the tension of a bow-string, or the leverage of an *atlatl*, they achieved their objective by means of a black powder which exploded when lit, produced great force and propelled balls of various sizes made of metal or stone into their enemies' bodies.

As to the ferocious war beasts of which Ah Kinchil had received reports, these were of two types, and Cit Bolon Tun had taken the opportunity of his time with the white men to study both closely.

The first were about the size of jaguars and appeared to be unnaturally large and ferocious members of the dog tribe. They had huge jaws and sharp teeth and they went into battle dressed in metal armour like the white men's own. This was why Muluc's warriors had been deceived into believing that the beasts could not be killed by spears or arrows. Untrue! Remove their armour, or strike some part of their bodies that was left unprotected, and they could indeed be killed in the same way that jaguars – which the Maya knew very well how to hunt – could be killed. However, there was one thing that made these 'dogs' far more terrible than any other beast, and this was that they were trained by the Spaniards to obey their commands and execute their will. They were fleet of foot, had an exceptionally sharp sense of smell, and could detect the presence of their prey by scent alone, so that even if a man had fled far away and concealed himself in some remote place, dogs would be able to follow his scent over the ground, find him and kill him. Cit Bolon Tun had witnessed horrible scenes in which, for nothing more than their own amusement and sport, the Spaniards had arranged for native Taino of the islands to be hunted down and torn to pieces by their dogs.

The second type of war beasts were about the size of large deer and were called 'horses'. The Chontal Maya had not yet met them in battle, but it was only a matter of time before they did because the leader of the Spaniards, whose name was 'Cortés', was a great expert in their use and Cit Bolon Tun had often heard him boast how the Maya would be unable to stand against them.

Like the dogs, these 'horses' wore metal armour, and if the dogs ran fast, the horses ran even faster, as fast as the wind, as fast as an avalanche. What was more amazing was that the white men knew how to mount themselves upon the creatures' backs and attack their enemies from there, at terrifying speed, using their lethal spears and swords. 'You must prepare our warriors,' Cit Bolon Tun urged Muluc and Ah Kinchil, 'for the shock of encountering the enemy mounted in this way. I myself have yet to see the Spaniards use their horses in battle, but I have seen them ride them in practice often enough. The air thunders with the beat of their hooves, the ground trembles as they charge, and the massive weight and momentum of the beasts is a weapon in itself, capable of

451

smashing down any who stand in their way. Our men will lose courage at the very sight and sound of them and this will be all the worse if they are deceived into believing they confront supernatural beings, part-man, part-deer, as I myself believed when I first saw them. They are frightful, they are formidable, they are something quite beyond any foe the Maya have ever encountered before in battle, but *they are not supernatural.* They are men mounted upon the backs of creatures, and like other men and other creatures, they can be killed.'

As these words were spoken, Malinal came into the dining chamber with beakers of water and tobacco tubes for the men to smoke. There was a sheen of sweat on Cit Bolon Tun's face – undoubtedly from the effort of communicating all the terrible things that he knew. Muluc's mouth gaped. Ah Kinchil sat staring blankly straight ahead, as though he had seen a ghost.

'How many?' the old paramount chief asked Cit Bolon Tun eventually.

'How many what, lord?'

'How many of these "horses"? How many of these infernal "Spaniards"? And what do you advise me to do about them?'

The face of Cit Bolon Tun was grave. 'My lord, I advise you to fight them night and day, without mercy and without fear while they are still few enough in number to be destroyed utterly. I have counted their horses. They have only eighteen! I have counted the white men and their entire force does not much exceed five hundred soldiers, of whom some have been left to guard their boats and some have undoubtedly been injured today. I very much doubt if the lord who is called Cortés will be able to put more than four hundred of his warriors into the field.'

The ghastly triumphant smile that Malinal so hated was back on Muluc's face. 'Four hundred!' he chortled. 'Four hundred! When we have forty thousand.' He turned to Ah Kinchil: 'There, uncle! You see! It is as I said. These are not gods but men who have come so boastfully into our lands – and tomorrow, when we meet them in battle, we *will* devour them!'

452

Chapter Fifty-Seven

Cuitláhuac's estate, Chapultepec, small hours of the morning, Thursday 25 March 1519

The moon, waning but still close to full, cast its light through the open window of Guatemoc's bedchamber where the prince lay on his back, his eyes open, staring up at the ceiling. Though his recovery had been remarkable (his doctors described it as a miracle), his wounds still pained him deeply and he was wide awake, thoughtful, his mind restless.

Everything that had happened since Shikotenka had expertly ripped him apart on that hillside in Tlascala all those weeks ago had been extraordinary, wondrous and inexplicable.

He had met Hummingbird, the god of war, and been told that it was not his time to die.

And he had met Temaz, the goddess of healing, who had brought him back to life.

Impossible to believe these two divine encounters were not connected!

'A great battle lies before your nation,' Hummingbird had told him, 'but the weakling Moctezuma is not competent to fight it.'

While for her part the Lady Temaz had urged him to defeat the plot against him and find the one who was truly responsible for it.

Well, he knew the answer to that now!

It had been Moctezuma himself who had sought to poison him. Mecatl had merely been a puppet in the royal hands. Of course his uncle had responded with feigned outrage when Mecatl revealed the truth under torture. He'd ordered the fat physician flayed alive and presented his skin to Guatemoc – as though that could possibly make any difference.

No one dared challenge the Great Speaker, but the truth was the truth and it could not be divided. The only question now was what was to be done about it.

As Guatemoc lay on his bed, silent and still, for the first time in his life seriously contemplating rebellion, a voice spoke to him out of the darkness.

'How fare you now, Prince?' the voice asked. The voice of a goddess.

'Better than I could have hoped,' Guatemoc replied, not allowing the sudden excitement he felt to reveal itself in his tone. 'Perhaps better than I deserve.'

The moonlight traced a bright path across the floor and in the midst of it there came some disturbance of the night, some ripple and sway of the empty air. A small, slim form emerged from nothingness, a hand reached out to touch him and he felt once again the mysterious radiance of divine power.

There was a moment of communion, almost of bliss. So this was what it meant to be caressed by a goddess! Guatemoc attempted to raise himself on one elbow, but soothing warmth was pouring into his body in a great flood and he groaned and lay back.

'Rest, Prince,' said Temaz. 'Do not struggle. I bring you the gift of healing. You must only accept it.'

For a long while he felt her working on him, first removing his bandages, then delicately probing and touching with her fingers, all the while sending this incredible glow, this splendour, this tingling, revivifying heat into his wounds. She did not speak but sang softly under her breath, half a whisper, half a chant, as she continued these gentle ministrations and, little by little, trusting her utterly, he fell asleep.

When he awoke, hours had passed, the moon was set, grey dawn was breaking and the Lady Temaz was gone.

Leaving Guatemoc asleep, Tozi had returned to the safe house in Tacuba and now lay stretched out on a reed mat on the floor as the lakeside town awoke noisily to the new day.

She had gone to the prince intent on talking to him about many things, and most of all about Quetzalcoatl, though she had promised

454

Huicton she would not. But when she had seen Guatemoc in the moonlight, seen how wounded and vulnerable he still was despite his remarkable recovery from poison and from his dreadful injuries, she had known she must help him first before any talking was done.

And she'd known she *could* help him. The healing spell had come to her unbidden, from some hidden depth of her heritage, and she had sung it for him in the moonlight all the night long.

It was strange. Hated Mexica prince though he was, scion of a cruel and murderous family, a killer and a sacrificer himself, she nonetheless found she was strongly, indeed almost irresistibly, drawn to Guatemoc. She realised now that the attraction had begun the moment she'd first set eyes on him weeks before when he lay gaunt and wasted in the royal hospital, on the edge of death. She'd wanted to cut his throat but had ended up saving his life.

There was good in him, that was why!

She must have known it, she must have seen it, even then.

And since there was good in him, she resolved, it was her job to nurture it and turn it to the cause of Quetzalcoatl.

A thought crossed her mind as she drifted off to sleep. This attraction she felt for the prince, with his handsome, hawk-like face and his beautiful copper skin so warm under her hands? It wasn't, was it, that foolish attraction a woman sometimes feels for a man?

'Gods forbid!' Tozi muttered, her eyes fluttering closed. She had no time for such nonsense.

Chapter Fifty-Eight

Thursday 25 March 1519

Thursday 25 March was the day of the Feast of the Annunciation of the Blessed Virgin and it started badly.

After a night loud with the drums and whoops of the very large Indian force massing in the countryside south of Potonchan, an uncomfortable night during which the Spaniards once again slept in their armour with their swords by their sides, Cortés rose before dawn to inspect the horses and found them stiff, listless and not yet fit for battle. 'They've been too long on board ship,' Melchior complained from his perch on Molinero's back, 'and we couldn't exercise them properly last night in the dark. Give us a few more hours to run them and get some more of this good grass into them and we'll have them right for you.'

The good grass in question was, at least, plentiful amongst the fruit trees of the walled orchard – now heavily guarded – that extended five hundred paces from the rear of the chief's palace to the river. Already all the other grooms were up and about their business, some brushing down their masters' horses, some leading them by their reins, some riding. Young Pepillo was there, too, following Melchior around as usual the way a puppy follows its master. 'I'll have secretary's work for you tonight,' Cortés told the boy. 'King Charles must be informed of what we've accomplished for him here.'

'I'm ready, sir,' replied Pepillo. 'And . . . sir . . . would you object if I were to try a ride on Molinero while we're exercising him?'

Cortés laughed: 'It's not my objections you'll need to worry about, lad! Molinero has a mind of his own. He'll have the final say in the matter.'

Leaving the orchard as the sun rose, and hurrying back through the palace to the main square where the men would be mustering, Cortés was stopped by Gonzalo de Sandoval, who brought him the morning's second piece of bad news. Little Julian had not been seen by anyone since the capture of the town yesterday afternoon, but during the night a sentry had found the interpreter's shirt and Spanish breeches draped over the branch of a tree. Eventually the matter had been reported to Sandoval and now here he was reporting it to Cortés. 'Looks like he's gone back to his own people,' Sandoval guessed.

Cortés felt a surge of anger. 'Damn!' he said. 'I should have anticipated this and had the squint-eyed cur killed weeks ago. He was a useless interpreter anyway, but all these months he's been learning our strengths and our weaknesses, counting our numbers, and now we let him just prance back to the Maya and tell them everything he knows. They couldn't hope for a better-informed spy.'

'Most unfortunate,' said Sandoval. 'What do you think the damage will be?'

'Less fear of us, better understanding of our weapons and our tactics. He'll tell them about our cavalry, which I would have preferred to have been a surprise.'

'If they've never seen heavy horse in action, Don Hernán, no amount of telling will prepare them for the shock.'

Cortés laughed, his mood suddenly improving, and clapped the younger man on the back. 'Let's hope you're right!' he said and then asked: 'How is it you don't own a horse yourself, Gonzalo?'

'Can't afford one,' said Sandoval honestly, 'but I grew up on horseback before my family fell on hard times.'

'You've trained with the lance? You've practised the charge?'

'I have, Don Hernán, more often than I can count.'

'Well, who knows? You may find yourself in the saddle again before too long.'

With just twenty soldiers now assigned to guard the ships in the bay, made up of a few who had fallen sick and a dozen too badly injured to go immediately into battle again, the troops mustered in the main square of Potonchan numbered some four hundred and eighty determined,

457

filthy, bearded men, formed up in sixteen ranks of thirty at the base of the pyramid. After they had heard Father Bartolomé Olmedo say Mass, Cortés reminded them it was the feast of Our Lady, thanked them fulsomely for their efforts the day before, which had been crowned with success, and told them to look forward to an even greater victory today. Cupping his hand to his ear at the drums and ululations of the Indians beyond the town, he said: 'Hark to the noise the heathen make! We gave them a beating and they ran but now they're back full of bluff and bluster, building their courage to attack us again. I say we don't stay cooped up here to await their assault but take the battle to them instead. Do you agree, men?'

There was a ragged cheer, some of the soldiers thumped their spear shafts into the ground, others beat their swords against their bucklers.

'Very well,' Cortés continued. 'For those who missed the activity last night, our horses are all offloaded from the ships' – he gestured towards the palace – 'and put to pasture to get the aches out of their joints. They'll be ready for battle in a few hours – I expect by noon. Meanwhile I want two companies of a hundred men each – volunteers all! – to conduct reconnaissance in force and learn the number and dispositions of the enemy.'

From the reports of his spies, who'd been out around the campfires during the night, Cortés knew that some of the Velázquez faction had been busy sprinkling the wormwood of fear and doubt on the courage of his stalwart troops. Juan Escudero in particular had been working on the faint of heart, suggesting that further action against the Maya was ill-advised, that there was no gold to be had from them, and that it would be better to move on elsewhere rather than risk annihilation here. But Cortés had also been doing the rounds during the night and was reassured that the majority of the men were still solidly with him, their caudillo, and believed his leadership would bring them victory, honour and wealth. He therefore felt inspired to end his address with some verses from the eleventh psalm.

'In the Lord I take refuge,' he recited, sending his voice ringing out across the square:

how then can you say to me: 'Flee like a bird to your mountain.'
For look, the wicked bend their bows; they set their arrows against
*   the strings*
to shoot from the shadows at the upright in heart.
When the foundations are being destroyed, what can the righteous
do?
The LORD is in his holy temple; the LORD is on his heavenly
*   throne. He observes everyone on earth; his eyes examine them.*
The LORD examines the righteous, but the wicked, those who love
*   violence, he hates with a passion.*
On the wicked he will rain fiery coals and burning sulphur; a
*   scorching wind*
will be their lot.'

There was no shortage of volunteers for the reconnaissance in force. Appointing Alonso Davila to lead one company and Alvarado the other, Cortés summoned Francisco de Mesa, his chief of artillery, a short, stocky, middle-aged man with thinning hair, a spade beard and a broad, unemotional, sunburned face. After the horses had been brought ashore last night he had taken a brigantine out to the bay and returned with two of the lombards and sixty Taino slaves who would be needed to move the heavy cannon into battle positions. Mesa's expression was, as usual, deadpan: 'I expect you'll be wanting me to arrange the fiery coals and burning sulphur to rain down on those wicked violent Indians,' he said.

Bernal Díaz, who judged the wound in his thigh to be superficial, had refused evacuation to the fleet and felt moved enough by the caudillo's speech to volunteer for Davila's hundred. Mibiercas and La Serna came with him, for what La Serna described as 'a breath of country air'.

Well, it was proving to be a great deal more than that. About three miles from Potonchan, the great north–south highway they were following skirted an outcrop of low hills, concealing them from the town, and a mile further south they were approached and attacked by a band of a thousand howling warriors. Huge numbers of arrows, darts and slingstones began to hail down on their armour and shields and they soon found themselves completely encircled.

Having tasted Toledo steel the day before, Díaz understood why the Indians were avoiding hand-to-hand combat and preferred to harm the Spaniards from afar. Moreover, the strategy was working, since half a dozen men already bore minor injuries and one, knocked senseless by a stone, had to be carried by his comrades, slowing everyone down. Making a virtue of necessity, Davila brought the square to a halt, had ten of his twenty musketeers move to the flanks and ordered them to fire on the enemy. Every bullet found its mark but what was noticeable, and worrying, was that the flash and roar of the heavy muskets had nowhere near the same terrifying effect on the circling horde as it had yesterday. To be sure ten fewer Indians were now on their feet, but that still left nine hundred and ninety of them, none of whom were running away as Díaz had hoped!

Further volleys from the muskets and crossbows produced no better results and the arrows, spears and slingstones continued to pour in.

'Damn,' Díaz heard Davila mutter. 'We should have brought a pack of hounds.' Indeed the idea had been discussed and turned down in favour of mobility. Too often the dogs would stop to eat their prey and it took time, and kicks and blows from their handlers, to call them off.

'Let us be the dog pack,' Mibiercas yelled to Davila. 'Let me take a flying squad and get in amongst them.'

Davila nodded and, moments later, after another crashing volley from the muskets, Mibiercas, Le Serna, and ten others drew their swords and sprinted towards the mass of Indians. Too slow for such a mission because of his thigh wound, Díaz felt faintly guilty as he watched his friends go.

Since Davila's squad had marched south, Alvarado reconnoitred towards the east. He passed for about a mile along the same forest track he'd used to enter the town the day before, but where it looped back towards the south he left it and continued, as Cortés had ordered, in an easterly direction. For some hundreds of paces his men had to cut a passage through heavy bush with their swords. By the time they emerged into the open again Alvarado was itching to impale a few Indians with his new Nuñez rapier, which he'd strapped on today for the first time since besting Zemudio back in Cuba.

Annoyingly, however, there seemed no immediate prospect of running anyone through. Extensive fields of young maize stretched ahead, vanishing in the distance into the morning haze, with not a single enemy formation visible anywhere.

Alvarado yawned with frustration. Overnight he had removed the splint and cast from his left arm and confirmed to his relief that he could move the limb, though it was somewhat wasted from a month of inactivity. He made a fist. God's blood! He was weak! But he had sufficient grip to hold the reins of Bucephalus for the cavalry attack that Cortés had promised for this afternoon.

And just as well, he thought, since there was no action to be had here. After advancing a further mile through the fields he was so thoroughly bored that he decided to do his reconnoitring in force elsewhere and turned his men back the way they had come.

Where the falconets fired ball or grapeshot weighing about a pound, the lombards fired ball or grapeshot weighing up to seventy pounds. Not for nothing, thought Cortés, were these heavy smoothbore cannon called 'wallbreakers'! He had brought three of them as the main artillery of the expedition, and of these two now stood in Potonchan's main square. Alongside them were the eighteen falconets that had already seen service against the Maya the day before, but whereas the latter could be fired, and even moved if necessary, by their own two-man crews, the lombards were so unwieldy that each required teams of thirty bearers to haul their massive carriages and transport their prodigious ammunition and bags of gunpowder.

'I'd stick to the falconets if I were you,' Mesa was saying. 'This country's too broken with irrigation ditches to move the big cannon – especially with bearers as reluctant as these.' He jerked his thumb towards the sixty Taino slaves, who were sitting under the silk-cotton tree in their loincloths looking sullen and stupefied.

'I know,' said Cortés, 'it's going to be difficult, but my mind's made up on this. We'll be badly outnumbered today, and the Indians have

461

already seen the falconets in action. I want something that's really going to surprise them and I expect the lombards to do that.'

'Ball or grapeshot?' asked Mesa without comment.

'Oh . . . both I think,' said Cortés. 'You know, horses for courses . . .'

Mibiercas's flying squad hit the circle of Indians in wedge formation and Díaz saw his friends start the work of killing: Mibiercas, the angel at the east of Eden with his flickering, whirling *espadón*, La Serna beside him, his gleaming broadsword licking out to taste the enemy. A huge Indian, transformed into a piebald demon by the striped paint of his face, came at Mibiercas with a long two-handed weapon, one of those batons edged with sharp flakes of obsidian that Díaz had encountered the day before. They seemed equally matched in size and strength but Mibiercas was a master of the longsword, a man who had made this weapon his lifework, and he fell upon his foe like a landslide, split his skull from crown to chin with a single blow, snatched out the glittering blood-smeared blade and cut down two more men before the first yet knew he was dead.

In this way the twelve valiant Spaniards, confronting the enemy hand to hand at last, wrought havoc amongst them, while the archers and musketeers of the main squad reloaded and let fly another devastating volley. Yet Díaz saw that the Indians had courage and determination in no smaller measure than the Spaniards, and they did not fall back, despite their losses, but rather rallied and pressed all the harder around Mibiercas and his men, who all of a sudden seemed like rocks hemmed in on all sides by a rushing, roaring murderous tide.

Seeing that they would soon be engulfed, Davila yelled, 'Santiago and at them', and led the whole squad pounding across the field to their rescue. Díaz's thigh pained him as he ran, the ground beneath his feet rough and uneven, filled with the brittle stalks of young corn. 'Santiago and at them!' he bellowed raising his sword. 'Santiago and at them.'

Melchior hauled Pepillo up in front of him and, with a click of his tongue, set the huge stallion to a walk. Unnerved by the peculiar, rocking gait, Pepillo looked down. The ground seemed very far below!

'Hold on,' said Melchior as they passed beneath a tree. Pepillo sensed

462

his friend's heels knock once, twice, against Molinero's sides and suddenly the animal's progress became even stranger, bumpy and uncomfortable, nearly jolting Pepillo from the saddle as its back dropped between steps, rose rapidly with the next, and dropped again. 'That's called a trot,' Melchior said, 'nice for the horse; not so nice for the rider.' His arms extended forward on either side of Pepillo, his hands loosely holding the reins. 'Now we'll try a canter.' His heels urged Molinero's flanks again and at once they were moving much faster, Molinero's hoofs hitting the ground in a staccato three-beat rhythm, Pepillo clinging tight to the pommel at the front of the saddle, feeling nervous but at the same time excited, wanting to laugh. They'd crossed to the side of the orchard during the trot and there was now a clear avenue ahead of them between the wall and the trees as far as the river. 'Want to try a gallop?' said Melchior.

'Yes!' shouted Pepillo, for the wind was already whipping past his ears.

Melchior moved his hands, still holding the reins, and lifted Pepillo a little. 'Then here we go,' he said. The horse surged forward and all at once they were flying.

Flying!

All the jolting unevenness went out of the ride and the great destrier tore towards the river at unbelievable speed, so fast that the trees and the wall blurred as they shot by, so light and free and boundless that joy bubbled up in Pepillo's chest and he couldn't stop himself whooping and yelling his excitement to the wind. Then before he knew it the muddy brown expanse of water lay ahead and he thought for a moment they would soar across it like winged Pegasus, until he felt Molinero hesitate a fraction, lean into an exhilarating, sweeping turn, then straighten again in the wonderful mile-eating four-beat gait of the gallop, the river flashing past beside them. In what seemed no more than seconds, the other wall loomed up; Melchior gently twitched the reins, letting Pepillo drop back into the saddle, and the horse slowed its pace through canter and bumpy trot and came to a halt.

'My goodness!' said Pepillo after a moment to catch his breath. 'So that's riding!'

Melchior was stepping down. 'It is what I who was a slave truly call freedom.' Holding the reins he began to adjust the stirrup. 'Stay in the saddle if you like.'

Pepillo's heart, already thudding, beat a little faster. 'On my own?' he asked.

'Yes, silly mammet. Is anyone else up there with you?' Melchior moved round to the horse's other side and adjusted the second stirrup. 'Use these. I'll lead you for a bit.'

Pepillo lodged his small feet in the huge iron stirrups and found that by pushing down he could raise himself up in the saddle as Melchior had done for him when they galloped. Whispering encouraging, gentle words to the stallion, Melchior moved to the front of the enormous animal and began to lead him forward by the reins.

Looking down at Molinero's great head, ears twitching, long chestnut mane flapping a little with each step, Pepillo felt a tremendous rush of excitement and pride. He was riding! The smell of the horse was in his nostrils and he thought there was no finer scent in all the world. He reached forward to pat the animal's powerful neck and suddenly, offering no explanation, Melchior thrust the reins into his hands and stepped away.

'What?' asked Pepillo, as the horse continued to amble forward. 'Why?'

Melchior grinned. 'Stay on as long as you can,' he said, and slapped Molinero on the rump.

Blood ran freely from a deep cut in Mibiercas's face, he and La Serna were desperately holding off a mob of Indians who sought to capture and draw away a fallen man, and the rest of the small group of Spaniards were struggling to form a defensive circle when Davila's full squad reached them at a run, rapidly absorbed them, reformed as a square and turned back towards Potonchan, which lay four miles to their north, concealed behind the range of low hills they had passed. The Indian attack did not cease but pressed on all the harder, hundreds – it seemed thousands – howling their monstrous war cries, vicious spears jabbing at exposed faces and legs, obsidian-edged swords slashing, while the pikemen fought mightily to thrust them back and the musketeers and crossbowmen at the centre of the square hurriedly reloaded.

Díaz was in the front rank, buckler defending the man next to him, broadsword arching down over the shield of the man to his right, his muscles aching with the strain of the unrelenting effort, sweat soaking his shirt and breeches beneath his armour as he hacked and stabbed at foes so close that the alien odour of their dusky bodies filled his nostrils. The square continued the fighting retreat towards Potonchan, but it was slowing with every pace, losing momentum like a carriage mired in thick mud, when all the muskets crashed again at point-blank range. Discouraged by this, or perhaps at some command from their captain, the Indians seemed to lose their taste for the close melee and broke away to a safer distance, where they began to put up a great din of drums, trumpets, whistles and shouts and at once resumed their barrage of slingstones, arrows and wicked fire-toughened darts, launched with great force from spear-throwers.

More of the enemy could be seen across the fields, flocking to reinforce the attackers, and it seemed to Díaz the worsening odds made it impossible for the Spaniards to fight their way back to Potonchan. There was a real danger they would all lose their lives here unless Cortés came out to relieve them – a prospect made improbable by the stunted hills that blocked the view and a strong breeze blowing steadily from the north carrying the sounds of battle away from the town. Because they were fully encircled, there was no question even of sending a fast runner to summon help, but a large, barn-like structure standing in the fields to their east at a distance of six or eight hundred paces seemed to offer some hope of respite. Although somewhat in ruins it was built of stone, its thatched roof was still largely intact and it looked defensible, so it was with a renewed sense of hope that Díaz heard Davila shout the order and the whole square wheeled ponderously and charged towards it under the unceasing and implacable hail of missiles.

The next ten minutes – it could not have been much longer – passed like an hour for Díaz, the agony of his injured leg slowing him, his breath heaving in short hot gasps as the square fought a running battle against the massed foe, forcing every footstep through the rough impeding growth of the young maize. Three times, large companies of Indians swung in towards them, making concerted efforts to close and stop their flight, but Davila had the shooters working in continuous

465

relays, five musketeers and five crossbowmen along each flank now, moving in and out to fire and reload, fire and reload, so although the attacks hindered their progress, they could not stop them, and at last, all winded, two score at least bleeding from flesh wounds, they reached the shelter of the building. A few dozen Indians had already occupied it, but the Spaniards ignored their spears and arrows, crashed in on them and slaughtered them in a frenzy of pike and sword thrusts.

It was a large, bare rectangular structure they'd taken possession of, twenty paces in length and ten wide with an earthen floor and transverse rafters supporting the thatched roof at about twice the height of a man. The walls were of stone, badly broken on the north and south sides, offering good cover for the shooters but unfortunately dilapidated enough to allow sufficiently determined attackers, should they choose to come on in overwhelming numbers, to break through. There were also many window slits, the remnants of ten each amongst the rubble on the north and south sides, five more to the east side and a wide, unprotected gap where a door had once stood on the west side.

All in all, a good, naturally defensible position. It would have served, Díaz thought, as an excellent fortress when it was intact, and still offered the Spaniards a refuge that they might hope to hold for many hours at little cost to themselves and great cost to the enemy. Davila had already ordered musketeers and crossbowmen to take up positions at every breech in the masonry, through which it could be seen that all around, just out of range, the Indians had drawn to a halt. Díaz found Mibiercas and they joined Davila at the doorway while Le Serna with two musketeers and crossbowmen and a few others climbed up into the rafters, cut through the thatch and forced their way onto the roof.

Reinforcements had been joining the foe all morning. 'How many do you see?' Davila called up.

'Counting,' La Serna shouted back. They heard him moving around over the thatch.

'Still counting,' he said a moment later.

'How many?' Davila insisted.

'Two thousand,' said La Serna finally, 'and you know what? Absent a miracle, we're all dead men.'

Even as he spoke the drums of the enemy, which had fallen silent, began beating again, their trumpets and whistles blew in a violent cacophony and the front ranks surged forward with blood-curdling screams.

Davila ordered a volley fired, ten muskets, ten crossbows, and the men began to reload feverishly as the second volley crashed out.

Potonchan was seven miles north of Cintla and fast messengers, who could run that distance in less than an hour, had been scurrying back and forth all morning to keep Muluc and Ah Kinchil fully informed. For some perverse reason of his own, Muluc seemed to want Malinal to witness the humiliation of the white men, whom he insisted on calling 'your precious so-called gods', so he kept her in attendance in the main audience chamber of the palace.

She knew as a result that no all-out attack had yet been ordered. During the night, ten thousand warriors had been camped in an arc less than a mile south of Potonchan, but around dawn Ah Kinchil had drawn them back to Cintla, leaving only a few thousand skirmishers in place to harry the white men should they attempt to push along the *sacbe* towards the regional capital.

Malinal couldn't help thinking, with so dangerous an enemy as these 'Spaniards', that she herself might have suggested a different strategy – for example, massive, overwhelming force right from the start. But Muluc, for all his bravado, was cautious, even cowardly, and Ah Kinchil was old, indecisive and deeply afraid of the white men, whom he still in his heart believed might be gods, despite the advice Cit Bolon Tun had given him.

So their decision was to wait and see what the Spaniards would do.

What they did was surprising and contradictory.

On the one hand they had released prisoners, captured during the battle for Potonchan, and sent them to Cintla in the night with a message of peace for Ah Kinchil, to whom it appeared they wished to offer immortal life.

On the other hand, an hour after dawn, a tight, disciplined unit of the white men, a hundred strong, had marched out of Potonchan along the *sacbe* obviously spoiling for a fight. They had been engaged by skirmishers about four miles south of the town – just three miles north

467

of Cintla itself! – where the Xaman hills concealed them from the Spaniards' main force.

'Do these hundred have the weapons called "guns" that make a great noise and kill men at a distance?' Ah Kinchil had asked the messenger. The answer was yes, but not, it seemed, the terrifying big guns on wheeled carriages deployed the day before. Even so, the white men had defended themselves well with their smaller guns and their long metal knives. The skirmishers, for their part, had kept their nerve and called in reinforcements. When the messenger had left the scene, the hundred Spaniards had been fought to a standstill and were completely surrounded in open fields by two thousand Mayan warriors.

Muluc and Ah Kinchil argued for a long time about what they should do next. Ah Kinchil was convinced it was a trap. These hundred must be bait intended to provoke him into committing his main force, which the Spaniards would then destroy. But Muluc reminded him of Cit Bolon Tun's information. The army of the Spaniards did not exceed five hundred men, of whom not many more than four hundred would be available for combat today *and they had no reserves to call on*. So if a hundred of them had failed to overcome two thousand skirmishers, it stood to reason, *regardless of whatever desperate trap they might hope to spring*, that four hundred – even five hundred! – must fall like the ripe maize at harvest if Ah Kinchil would only throw his forty thousand warriors against them, now, in one massive blow.

Malinal had to admit she could find no fault in Muluc's reasoning and was not surprised, in the face of his insistent bullying, when the paramount chief eventually gave way. Being too old to go into battle, Ah Kinchil seemed almost grateful to pass command to the younger man and agreed to travel with the rearguard as an observer only.

Before he hurried from the audience chamber to lead the army of the Chontal Maya north in a great mass towards the fields of Potonchan, Muluc turned on Malinal. 'Remember that Mexica trader I told you about,' he said, 'the one I'm going to sell you to?' He smirked as he saw her face drop. 'Well, you're about to meet him.'

Malinal thought she had never seen her stepfather look so pleased with himself.

* * *

468

Having returned to the passage they'd cut through the bush, Alvarado led his men onto the track he'd followed in yesterday's flanking manoeuvre. It continued through forest for about another mile, and then a further mile through open fields to a point about three miles south of Potonchan, near a range of low hills, where it intersected with the great highway that Davila's squad were reconnoitring today. He had it in mind to cross the highway and head west towards the coast and the manglar swamps to see if there was any sign of the enemy there but, soon after emerging into open fields again, with the long white strip of the highway in sight, he began to hear musket shots. The sounds were coming from somewhere further to the south, beyond the hills, and reached him faintly at first because of an adverse north wind. Still, there was no doubt in his mind. That smug bastard Davila, who'd rescued him yesterday, had run into trouble with the Indians.

Alvarado ordered his squad to turn south across the fields. Proceeding through the maize at a forced march, and skirting the hills, he soon had a better idea of Davila's predicament. Half a mile ahead, somewhat to the east of the road, stood a large building completely surrounded by a great horde of the enemy. The crash of musket fire was unmistakable now, so too the mad discord of drums and pipes with which the Maya liked to accompany every attack, and snatches of wild yells reached him between gusts of wind.

'Keep low, men,' Alvarado ordered. 'Let's see how close we can get without being seen.'

It was uncomfortable bending over almost double, carrying weapons and running through the maize, but well worth the effort. The enemy, and there were thousands of them, had their backs turned and were so intent on the waves of assaults they continued to throw against the well-defended building that they remained for a long while perfectly oblivious of the squad's fast, stealthy advance.

Alvarado raised his arm and brought his men to a halt less than five hundred paces from the outer ranks of the enemy encirclement. A small force of Spaniards still held the roof of the beleaguered building, shooting down on the attackers at point-blank range, pushing them back with pike thrusts, and seemingly as unaware as the Indians themselves of Alvarado's approach.

Keeping his voice low, he called his twenty musketeers and twenty crossbowmen forward and ordered them to spread out into a single skirmish line with the rest of the square formed up behind them. 'Pick your targets,' he said, 'and at a hundred paces, sooner if they spot us, put a volley into their backs, all the muskets and all the crossbows together, then countermarch at the double back into the square and draw your swords.'

'What about reloading, sir?' one of the shooters asked.

'We're going to cut our way through and join Davila's men. You can reload at your leisure once we're inside that barn they're defending.'

Alvarado drew his rapier and slashed its blade satisfyingly through the air. He rather wished he'd brought the falchion after all. This Nuñez steel was too good for riffraff like the Maya.

The Indians were getting better at timing their charges in the intervals between musket and crossbow volleys, Díaz realised. He was defending a gap in the masonry on the south side and this was now the sixth or seventh wave of attackers who had hurled themselves furiously against weak points all around the structure and repeatedly tried to scale the walls whence they were thrown back by the shooters and pikemen on the roof. Again came the hideous shrieks and yells of the attackers; again strong hands scrabbled at the crumbling blocks, tearing down the wall stone by stone; again snarling painted faces loomed up through the breach, their rank breath reaching Díaz. He gave a hard thrust with his sword, saw it smash a man's front teeth in a burst of blood, felt it slip through the void of his mouth and catch as it severed his spine. Another suicidal warrior was already climbing over the back of the first, offering his face to the blade, and Díaz withdrew and stabbed again.

A great weariness began to overmaster him. From the position of the sun he guessed the time at around eleven in the morning, which would mean they'd been marching and running and fighting for only four hours.

Four hours! It felt more like four days!

Yet how much longer could they hold out before the sheer numbers of the enemy overwhelmed them?

Already a new charge was coming in but, as the Indians ran screaming towards the walls, Díaz heard excited shouts from the roof

and the sweet sound of muskets roaring, not from within the beleaguered structure, but from somewhere to the northeast outside the
encircling ranks of the attackers.

'Thank God,' he breathed as he killed another man. 'We are saved.'

From a hundred paces the twenty musket rounds and twenty crossbow
bolts tore into the backs of the surprised Indians with devastating force
and a huge gap opened in the circling mass. The shooters retired within
the square and Alvarado led the charge with his personal squad of practised swordsmen thirsting for blood right behind him in the front ranks.

The Indians milled in dazed panic as the armoured square hit them
at a run, Toledo blades carving limbs and heads from bodies with no
more difficulty than slicing bread. In moments a hundred – two
hundred! – of the enemy were down, stone dead or writhing on the
ground, trampled underfoot by the advancing squad and stabbed by
the pikemen as the Spaniards found themselves traversing the circle
of clear space encompassing the building.

'This way, this way!' Alvarado heard men shout as grinning faces
peered through gaps in the masonry and the defenders on the roof
beckoned his men round to the west side of the redoubt. Groups of
Indians who'd been assaulting the walls tangled with them and were
mercilessly despatched, then they rounded the northwest corner, climbed
heaps of the enemy slain by the defenders and poured in through the
ragged breach in the west wall where once a door must have stood.

'Ho there, Davila!' said Alvarado to the exhausted, blood-smeared
captain who came forward to greet him. 'I see you've got yourself in
a bit of a tight spot here. Just as well my men and I happened along
to get you out of it.'

'*Touché*,' admitted Davila with a weary smile. To Alvarado's surprise
the other captain then stepped forward and embraced him warmly.

Bernal Díaz stood at the doorway poised for the breakout with
Mibiercas and La Serna by his side. 'Funny how things turn around,'
said La Serna. 'One minute you're looking death in the face, the next
a long life beckons.'

'We're not home and dry yet,' observed Mibiercas softly as he ran a whetstone down the edge of his blade. The long diagonal cut on his cheek was still dripping blood.

'I fancy our chances though,' said La Serna. 'That Alvarado's a tough one. What do you reckon, Bernal?'

'We'll make it,' Díaz grunted. He had the shakes, something that didn't usually afflict him no matter how tough the fight.

'You OK?' La Serna asked him, concerned.

'Not so good,' Díaz gestured to his thigh which was now so swollen he'd had to cut the seam on his breeches.

'That arrow you took yesterday?'

'Yes. Didn't think much of it at the time.' Díaz shivered again. 'Some kind of fever setting in.'

'Bad day for it,' said La Serna. He was just stating facts.

'I'll get through.'

Half of Davila's squad were injured, but all – *except maybe me*, Díaz thought – were fit enough to march. Even those stunned by the pestilential slingstones had regained their senses, and none, thanks be to God, were dead. For their part, Alvarado's men were fresh and in high spirits. Better still, a quick inventory had found that the musketeers and archers in his squad had sufficient powder, ball and bolts to replenish the near-exhausted stocks of Davila's shooters.

So La Serna was right, Díaz thought. Whereas a fighting retreat drawn out over the four miles to Potonchan had been out of the question just moments before, it was now, thanks to Alvarado's timely intervention, a viable option. Indeed it was not too much to hope that the combined strength of both squads, with forty archers and forty musketeers amongst them, would be sufficient to drive off the few thousand Indians surrounding them.

Water skins were passed around, powder and ammunition were shared and checked one last time, a few men muttered prayers and then, with a great roar, the two hundred Spaniards burst forth from the stone shelter and set out at a jog across the fields.

Every jolt was agony for Díaz, but he'd withstood far worse than this in his soldiering career. As the hail of Indian missiles began to pour down again he kept his buckler above his head, set his teeth and ran on.

* * *

472

Pepillo had fallen off Molinero four times, and was bruised from head to foot, but he thought at last he was beginning to get the hang of it. 'We'll make a rider of you yet,' Melchior said with a grin.

They hadn't seen Cortés since dawn but around noon a messenger came from him with orders that Molinero was to be barded at once. The caudillo expected to have need of him within the hour. All across the orchard, similar instructions were being delivered to the other grooms.

'What's "barded"?' asked Pepillo.

'It means armoured,' said Melchior. 'Barding is armour for horses – plate and mail and boiled leather; it protects them from arrows and spear thrusts and sword cuts and such . . . It's the barding that was in those sea chests we offloaded last night. Come on, you can help me.'

They led Molinero over to the south side of the orchard, directly behind the palace, where all the chests brought from the ship were lined up. Melchior went directly to one of these. 'This belongs to Cortés,' he explained, adding proudly, 'he stores his personal armour in here as well. It's my job to keep it and Molinero's barding polished and free of rust.' With a flourish he sprung the chest's catch and opened the heavy lid. The sun, directly overhead now, shone down on the dazzling contents of gleaming steel.

'We'll start with the *champron*,' Melchior said. 'That's what protects Molinero's head and eyes – though he doesn't like it much, do you, boy?' He stroked the stallion's quivering neck then reached into the sea chest and pulled out a fearsome-looking steel mask.

'It's a sort of helm, but for horses,' Pepillo said.

'That's right.' Muttering soothing words, and with many gentle clicks of his tongue, Melchior strapped the *champron* over Molinero's head. It ran from his ears to his muzzle, with hinged extensions covering the jowls. There were holes, protected by flanges, for his eyes, and a great spike, like a unicorn's horn, now projected from the centre of his forehead.

Melchior returned to the chest and extracted a set of segmented steel plates. 'These are called the *crinet*,' he said to Pepillo. 'Go to the other side. We're going to put them over Molinero's neck.' Once in place and fixed by straps to the *champron*, Pepillo saw how the plates of the *crinet* would protect the stallion's neck and throat – not completely, because there were gaps between them to make the armour flexible and allow him to move his head freely, but enough to ward off most attacks.

Melchior was pulling out more large sheets of plate armour. 'Now the *peytral*. It's heavy – you'll have to help me again; there, take that side – but Molinero's so strong he hardly notices the weight.' Working together they buckled the *peytral*, which was designed to protect Molinero's chest and extended back almost as far as the saddle, to straps hanging down from the *crinet*.

The last and largest piece of armour, a cunning combination of steel and leather, was called the *croupiere* and protected the hindquarters of the great war horse. 'There you are, boy,' Melchior said when he was done, standing back to examine the stallion. 'Now you look fearsome!'

As though he understood the words, Molinero responded with a whinny, blew air from his nostrils and pawed the ground.

He did look fearsome, Pepillo thought.

Gazing up at the huge animal decked out in his gleaming armour and ready to charge into battle, he could hardly imagine that he had ever sat upon his back.

The trader, Malinal immediately saw from his clothing, belonged to that elite stratum of Mexica society, ranked just below the nobility, known as the Pochteca. As well as being the principal traffickers in exotic slaves, these Pochteca merchants dealt in chocolate, jaguar pelts, quetzal plumes, metals and other luxury items from the most far-flung tributaries of the empire, and from more distant lands like the Yucatán that were not subject to the Great Speaker's rule. Such long-distance commerce, over much of which they exercised a strict monopoly, had made the Pochteca extremely rich, though they were forbidden to flaunt their wealth in Tenochtitlan or other cities of the empire except within the confines of their secretive guildhalls. They travelled in large caravans with hundreds of servants and bearers, well protected from marauders and outlaw bands by detachments of seasoned Mexica warriors, and were themselves frequently highly skilled in the martial arts. Many, in addition, cultivated connections with foreign rulers and served Moctezuma covertly as spies and intelligence-gatherers.

Many, thought Malinal, such as this one, Cuetzpalli by name, to whom Muluc planned to sell her on the morrow and who would take her back to Tenochtitlan – just as she had been taken there five years previously by another visiting Pochteca. This afternoon, however, Cuetzpalli was evidently in the mood for a spectacle, not business, having been invited by Ah Kinchil to witness the destruction of the white men by his great army of forty thousand warriors. Like so many Maya chiefs, Ah Kinchil was in awe of the power of the Mexica and would go to great lengths to please and impress their representatives in the hope he would never be obliged to pay tribute to them. While no doubt providing some grand entertainment to the influential Pochteca, therefore, the looming battle was clearly also being taken as an opportunity to demonstrate to him – and thus to Moctezuma whose spy he most certainly was – the full extent of Mayan military readiness.

Cuetzpalli meant 'lizard' in the Nahuatl language and, with his hooded gaze, long perfumed hair and slithery manner, this merchant was, Malinal decided, aptly named. She did not know him, since her services in Tenochtitlan had been reserved exclusively for the higher nobility, but he was much younger than those few in the guilds with whom she had come into contact, being no more than twenty-seven or twenty-eight years of age. No doubt, since membership of the Pochteca was hereditary, he had inherited the position from his father. He had a long, narrow face, prominent nose, high cheekbones, good teeth and a strong jaw and would have been the very image of classic Mexica comeliness were it not for the furtive, sliding-away quality of his gaze, which had never quite met her own since Ah Kinchil had required her to serve as his interpreter on this seven-mile jaunt down to Potonchan.

Both men were being carried shoulder-high in comfortable, cush-ioned litters and had their bodyguards – a dozen Mexica Cuahchics in the case of Cuetzpalli – arrayed around them. Malinal walked between the litters, translating the occasional formal pleasantries and observations of the wizened old chief and the smooth young merchant, but with her mind hardly on the task. What preoccupied her instead was the coming confrontation with the white men and her hope, still in part touched by Tozi's prophetic zeal, that something extraordinary was about to take place. She could sense Ah Kinchil's nervousness and uncertainty even while he boasted to Cuetzpalli of the ferocity of his warriors who marched just a mile ahead in five regiments of eight thousand men each. Their forty thousand pairs of feet had stirred up a dust cloud so vast it seemed to stretch from horizon to horizon. Despite the Xaman hills, which lay in the way, this immense cloud must surely be visible from Potonchan, now barely five miles from the advance units.

In her imagination Malinal's mind soared up over the hills and flew to the side of the leader of the white men. She felt sure, after everything she had heard Cit Bolon Tun say the night before, that he must indeed be a man, like any other man . . .

And yet . . . and yet . . .

The lookouts had called Cortés to the top of the pyramid around noon when Alvarado and Davila's squads, united in a single large square, had emerged from behind the cover of the hills three miles south of Potonchan and proceeded at a forced march towards the town, harried by a large mob of enemy skirmishers. Although Cortés could not understand why the two squads were now together when they'd set out on separate missions, they did not seem to be in any danger of being overrun and were proceeding in good order. He'd sent out a hundred men to reinforce them anyway, but the Indians had immediately disengaged at the sight of the new force and fled back towards the hills. In the past half-hour Alvarado and Davila had crossed most of the remaining distance, joined up with the relief column and were already approaching the southern outskirts of the town. It was obvious, now, that they'd fought a major engagement, since there were many injured amongst them, but though bloodied they appeared to have suffered no losses.

Of much greater concern was the huge cloud of dust that had begun to form much further south while Cortés had been watching Alvarado and Davila's progress. He couldn't see details because the range of little hills blocked his view, but he estimated that the cloud's leading edge was presently about five miles from Potonchan and that it stretched back at least a mile from there, almost as far as Cintla. It could only be the product of a great army on the move, an army tens of thousands strong, advancing to make war on him.

The good news, after a morning's light exercise, was that the horses were frisky and full of grass, all the stiffness gone from their limbs. Cortés had already sent orders for them to be barded for battle. He turned to the artilleryman, Francisco de Mesa, who stood at his side. 'If we bring the lombards up here,' he said, indicating the wide platform at the top of the pyramid, 'what will their range be?'

Mesa's eyes widened. 'Up *here*, Don Hernán?'

'Yes, you heard me, up here. Put those sixty slaves to work!'

Mesa raised his eyebrows. 'Well, I suppose it can be done.' He looked speculatively at the advancing dust cloud. 'And from this altitude, with the barrels at maximum elevation, I judge we'll be able to put ball into the midst of enemy formations anywhere up to two miles from the town.'

Cortés whistled. 'Two miles, eh? Couldn't ask for better! Well, get on with it then, Mesa, and at the double. We're very short of time.'

Cortés had already decided who would ride with the cavalry today, and they were not in every case the men who owned the horses. For example Ortiz, nicknamed 'the musician' and Bartolomé García both owned fine destriers that were presently exercising in the orchard, but both men were poor riders; their mounts would go to Miguel de Lares, whom Cortés knew to be a superb horseman, and to Gonzalo de Sandoval, whose story of a lifetime in the saddle before his family fell on hard times rang true. Likewise, Diego de Ordaz owned a fast grey mare, but it would be ridden today by Pedro Gonzalez de Trujillo – not, in this case, because of any lack of horsemanship skills on the part of Ordaz, but because Ordaz, despite his Velazquista sympathies, was undoubtedly the best officer to take command of the infantry in the coming engagement while Cortés himself led the cavalry. Ordaz's field experience in the Italian wars was second to none and he was, in addition, an excellent swordsman. Besides, Cortés hoped, giving him this important role, which he had accepted with pleased surprise this morning, might help to detach his loyalties from the pro-Velázquez clique.

As he reached the foot of the pyramid Cortés had Ordaz put out an urgent summons for an immediate muster of all the men and, while he waited for them to fall in, and for Alvarado and Davila to arrive, he gathered the rest of his selected corps of cavalry around him – Cristóbal de Olid, Alonso Hernández Puertocarrero, Juan de Escalante, Francisco de Montejo, Juan Velázquez de León, Francisco de Morla, Miguel de Lares, Gonzalo Dominguez, Pedro de Moran, Pedro Gonzalez de Trujillo, Juan Sedeno, Jerónimo Alanis, Pedro de la Mafla, Juan Rodriguez de Salas and young Gonzalo de Sandoval. Moments later Alvarado and Davila, both excellent horsemen, joined the group, while the two hundred men they had led in this morning's skirmishes, and the hundred from the relief column that Cortés had sent out to support them, milled in the square. Alvarado and Davila's men were evidently grateful to be out of danger, even if only temporarily, attending to their injuries, eating and drinking from their packs and telling the rest of the gathering force what had happened to them.

Cortés now climbed eight steps up the stairway of the pyramid, where Mesa was already organising his Taino slaves to carry the first of the two great cannon to the top, and called to the men for silence, which fell instantly, without complaint. Even the Velazquistas, it seemed, were willing to hold their tongues at this grave moment.

'I'll make this brief,' said Cortés. 'As some of you who've been up the pyramid in the last half-hour already know, a huge force of Indians is heading our way. I'll not put any gloss on this – I'd say we're facing thirty thousand men.'

At the figure of thirty thousand, which Cortés knew in his heart to be an underestimate, a gasp of alarm passed around the square. 'But this is not like facing thirty thousand battle-seasoned Moors on the plains of Granada,' he continued, waving the men to silence again, 'or thirty thousand of any European army. These are thirty thousand savages, armed with stone weapons and with no concept of the science of warfare. In addition to our discipline and *esprit de corps*, which they lack, we have three outstanding advantages that we will turn against them. First, our cannon.' He pointed to the huge barrel of the lombard in its cradle of ropes, supported by a team of thirty slaves, now halfway up the steep steps of the pyramid. 'Second, our hounds' – a gesture to Vendabal and his assistants who were busily cinching the armour to the snarling dogs. 'And third, and I believe the factor more than any other that will tip the balance in our favour, our cavalry.' He waved at the group of horsemen gathered at the base of the steps.

Turning back to the infantry, Cortés paused, saying nothing, for ten . . . twenty . . . thirty seconds. It was a technique of oratory he had long ago mastered, the effect of which was to cause all the men to lean slightly towards him, anxious to learn what was coming next. 'I know,' he said at last and in a deeply sympathetic tone, 'that some of you brave fellows have fought hard already this morning, risked your lives, taken wounds, and I know I ask much to expect you to go out into the field, surrounded by overwhelming numbers of the foe, and do it all again this afternoon. Nonetheless, this is what I ask of you! For if we do not all fight for our very lives today, with every bit of our strength, then we will perish here.' Another pause: 'But we will fight, and we will *not* perish!'

A great cheer arose from the men.

'We will fight and we will *not* perish because we are courageous men, *heroes all*, and because God and His saints and all His angels fight on our side this day!'

There came another cheer, more rousing than the last, and Cortés saw how many of the men's eyes gleamed with emotion as they fixed their gaze on him, relied on him, counted utterly on him as their leader who would bring them salvation, and – God willing – victory.

'So here is what we will do,' he said. 'Our enemies approach us from the south at a fast march. They will be upon us in a little more than an hour but we will have a trap prepared for them. The infantry will be the bait of this trap and the artillery and cavalry will form its two jaws.'

He beckoned to the stocky, bearded figure of Diego de Ordaz who was standing nearby in a chain-mail tunic, his broadsword hanging from a baldric and a grim look on his face. Ordaz nodded and climbed the steps to stand beside him. 'I will lead the cavalry today,' Cortés continued, 'and Don Diego here will lead the infantry. You will march out *at once*, pausing only to gather all necessary supplies of powder, ammunition and water, and you will challenge the enemy by blocking their way one mile south of the town. Eight of the falconets will remain here in a battery to kill any of the foe who may slip past you, but the other ten will go with you, and all the dogs, and there you will stand and there you will fight while the Indians fall upon you in their thousands.'

Cortés paused again. Close to five hundred strained, dirt-streaked, in many cases blood-smeared faces leaned towards him. 'While you hold and engage the enemy, Francisco de Mesa, our artilleryman –' he pointed to Mesa who was overseeing the progress of the second lombard on its way up the pyramid – 'will be preparing a bombardment the like of which these Indians cannot possibly conceive. Yonder lombards fire seventy-pound balls a distance of two miles, and when Mesa sees that the enemy are closing in on you he will begin firing over your heads and into the depths of their ranks, spreading terror and panic amongst them. Many will seek to flee to the south, back towards Cintla where they have come from, but at this point they will find our cavalry behind them – for we will have gone out by the east side of town and worked our way south from there following the same track that Davila and Alvarado took yesterday – and we will hit them at a full charge and destroy them utterly.'

As he dismissed the men to a resounding chorus of cheers, Cortés wished he felt as confident as he had sounded, and wished he could persuade himself of the merits of his simple plan as successfully as he seemed to have persuaded everyone else.

For the truth he knew at the bottom of his heart was that this plan of his had been hastily stitched together and was as full of holes as a threadbare sock. There were at least a dozen ways in which it could rapidly unravel, leaving his men and his cannon horribly vulnerable to being flanked and overwhelmed, and his precious cavalry cut off from all support amidst numberless foes.

Offering up a silent prayer to Saint Peter, who had so often promised him victory in dreams, Cortés turned with a smile to his cavalrymen. 'Brothers,' he said, 'ours will be the first charge of horse ever witnessed in these new lands. Today we make history.'

Chapter Fifty-Nine

Thursday 25 March 1519

Cortés feared the lombards on the pyramid would be vulnerable to a sneak flanking attack by the Indians after the infantry had marched out of Potonchan and taken up its position as the 'bait' in his trap. Yet if the enemy were to be drawn into a fight that would last long enough to expose them to the 'jaws' of the trap (his cavalry to their south, Mesa's lombards to their north), he couldn't afford to reduce the strength of the infantry squares.

The Taino slaves who moved the big cannon could not be relied upon – indeed they would be more of an impediment than an asset – so there was no point in looking to them to help solve the problem. But more than fifty of Davila's men had been injured in the morning's heavy skirmishing and Cortés now had Mesa choose the forty who were most badly hurt, the ones who'd be the least use to Ordaz on the plain, to garrison the pyramid. He also put eight falconets under Mesa's command and told him to use them either to support Ordaz or for the defence of the lombards as the need arose.

'Does he need eight falconets?' growled Ordaz. 'When the fight gets hot we'll wish we had them with us.'

'Nothing's more important than protecting the lombards today,' Cortés insisted. 'Without them our trap will fail. Besides, you'll have ten falconets with you, a good number, and the eight with Mesa can be turned on any enemy units that get between you and the town. I think in the end you'll be glad of them here.'

Ordaz made a sour face but nodded his agreement.

'I have a question,' said Mesa. 'How long do I continue the barrage with the lombards? I don't want to hit your cavalry, Don Hernán.'

Cortés laughed. 'Believe me, Mesa, I don't want you to hit us either!' His expression became suddenly grim. 'Do the maximum harm you can to the enemy. Stop when you see us amongst them and not a moment before.'

He turned back to his cavaliers who were waiting nearby. 'Gentlemen,' he said. 'Shall we to horse?'

Watching the eighteen cavaliers dress in their armour, strap on their swords and remove the scabbards from the warheads of their lances was, for Pepillo, like witnessing the romance of *Amadis de Gaula* come to life. Here was chivalry! Here was adventure! Here were heroes! He might easily imagine that Cortés was Amadis himself, the Knight of the Green Sword, on his way to kill the giant Endriago whose monstrous body was covered with scales – that courteous, gentle, sensitive but invincible Amadis, who emerged victorious from every battle, drenched in his enemies' blood.

Cortés was already wearing a steel cuirass but, with Melchior's help, he unbuckled and removed its breast and back plates, donned a hauberk – a shirt of chain mail that fell to his thighs – reaffixed the cuirass over it and belted on his sword. Although the hauberk had mailed sleeves, additional items of steel plate were now added – *pauldrons* to protect his shoulders and armpits, *rerebraces* to protect his upper arms, articulated metal joints called *couters* to protect his elbows, forearm guards called *vambraces*, and gauntlets made of a cunning combination of plate, mail and leather to protect his hands. Next Melchior turned to the caudillo's legs, attaching *cuisses*, articulated *poleyns* and greaves to protect his thighs, knees and shins, and strapping mailed *sabatons* over the toes of his boots. Finally he fixed a *gorget* of multiple articulated steel plates around his master's throat and handed him his gleaming open-faced helmet, called a *sallet*, with armoured flaps at the side and back to protect his neck.

While all this was done Cortés, who was in high good humour, laughed and joked with the other knights, pausing from time to time to explain the names and functions of the different pieces of armour to Pepillo, who felt his eyes must be as big as saucers as he looked on. Then, mounting Molinero, the caudillo placed his *sallet* on his head, reached down to take the twelve-foot lance that Melchior now passed up to him and leaned it jauntily over his right shoulder. All around the other knights were doing the same.

Cortés was looking at the boys. 'We'll win the fight today,' he said, 'but there's a risk the enemy may try to infiltrate the town before it's over. If that happens I don't want the two of you ending up in their cooking pots!' He laughed, but Pepillo could see that at some level he was serious. 'So get yourselves over to the pyramid,' he continued. 'Make yourselves useful to Mesa and see if he can't find you a weapon or two to defend yourselves with.'

'I have my knife sir,' said Melchior.

Cortés nodded. 'Keep it handy, but get Mesa to arm you with a spear.' He turned to Pepillo: 'How about you, boy?'

'I'm not armed, sir.'

'Then take this.' Cortés reached into the top of his boot and pulled out a small, wicked-looking dagger.

'Won't you need it, sir?'

'I carry a second,' said Cortés, patting his other boot. He passed the knife to Pepillo. 'Use it on yourself if you have to.' With a raised finger he mimed the motion of a man cutting his own throat. 'Believe me, it will be better than letting the Indians capture you.'

Pepillo gulped. 'On *myself*, sir?'

'Yes, if you have to.' A confident chuckle: 'But you won't have to! We'll win today, you'll see. I want you to observe everything that happens – the top of the pyramid will be a good place for that – and tonight you'll help me write to the king.'

The rest of the squadron had already formed up two by two behind him, their armour glittering in the sun. Cortés waited for Alvarado to fall in at his side, raised his left hand above his head, signalled 'forward' and nudged Molinero into a trot.

Holding the little knife, testing its keen edge, Pepillo stood dumb-founded at the thought of taking his own life with it as he watched the riders file out through the gate of the orchard and clatter across the square. They increased their pace to a gallop, scattering dust, and turned onto the main avenue leading east out of Potonchan.

* * *

Ah Kinchil and Cuetzpalli had decided to watch the battle from the Xaman Hills, really nothing more than a fold or a wrinkle in the plains. The tallest peak in the little range was barely a hundred feet high, but offered an excellent vantage point across the maize fields that stretched three miles north from here to the outskirts of Potonchan. There was a copse of ancient ahuehuetl trees on the summit to provide shade, and even a little bubbling spring. All in all it could hardly have been more idyllic.

'We will devour them,' said Ah Kinchil, echoing Muluc's comment of the night before.

'I don't doubt it,' Cuetzpalli replied. Having been carried up here by their sweating litter-bearers, the two men were now standing side by side at the edge of the copse with their retainers gathered nearby and Malinal placed between them to translate their every word. Ah Kinchil had detached two hundred warriors from the rearguard of the immense army Muluc was leading into battle, posting them around the base of the hill and keeping his personal bodyguard on sentry duty amongst the trees. Muluc's steward Ichick was present – primarily, Malinal suspected, to keep a close eye on her and make sure she had no opportunity to escape before being sold to Cuetzpalli tomorrow and sent on her way back to Tenochtitlan. All twelve of Cuetzpalli's Cuahchics were in attendance, along with a scribe and an artist whom he had instructed to keep a record of the main events of the battle.

Malinal was unable to imagine any way in which the situation could fail to be utterly hopeless for the white men – unless they really were gods. Their entire army, which they had divided into four small square formations of a hundred men each in ten tightly bunched ranks, had marched one mile south of Potonchan and taken up position between the town and Muluc's advancing army. Each of the squares looked to be about thirty feet wide and thirty deep and even though they were divided one from the other by horizontal gaps of approximately twice that width, their entire combined front still stretched no more than three hundred feet across the fields. Moreover Malinal realised that the little squares were not even deployed in a single formidable row, but in two pairs, with the second pair some distance behind the first and offset diagonally, creating a front that was staggered rather than straight. Why, she wondered, would the Spaniards have adopted such a vulnerable formation? Surely being divided like this into four tiny, isolated units would only make it easier for Muluc's men, who formed a block two thousand feet wide and a thousand deep, to surround and 'devour' each one? Indeed each of the eighty Mayan ranks contained five hundred men, thus alone outnumbering the entire Spanish force!

It was almost as though the white men were offering themselves for sacrifice!

Out of the corner of her eye, Malinal noticed Cuetzpalli's artist rapidly sketching the scene. Here they were on the Xaman hills with Muluc's army a mile and a half to their north, marching rapidly across the open fields and already manoeuvring into a vast convex formation to flank and engulf the Spaniards. Approximately half a mile of empty fields came next and then – appearing even smaller in the painting than they did in real life – the four squares of the unlucky Spaniards.

Her first intimation that things might not go the way that numbers and common sense suggested came a moment later when she saw five clouds of dirty grey smoke rise up a little distance in front of those tiny squares. This interesting phenomenon was followed almost instantly by some ripple or perturbance in the Mayan front ranks; though she could not see the cause, it was obvious that men had fallen. Finally, a fifteen count after the smoke had appeared, she heard a tremendous rolling, crashing blast, a sound like the thunder of doom, and knew she was witnessing in action the weapons the white men called 'guns'.

Well, Muluc's men were prepared for this. They now knew – for the intelligence Cit Bolon Tun brought had been passed to every one of them – that there was nothing supernatural about these 'guns'; they were just weapons like any other, albeit very dangerous ones. After they had been fired they had to be reloaded, which took time, and during the intervals the white men would be vulnerable.

As she had expected, the entire Mayan force, which had been approaching at a fast march, surged forward into a wild charge. Immediately, five more clouds of dirty grey smoke rose up from before the squares.

Had Cit Bolon Tun been lying?

No, Malinal thought. The more likely explanation was that the

485

Spaniards had ten 'guns' and were reloading the first five while the second five were fired.

Again she saw that mysterious perturbance in the Mayan ranks – more noticeable this time than before; it seemed that many men had fallen and that these powerful weapons worked their harm not only on those directly facing them but in long narrow strips extending five or even ten ranks back into the charging mass. Even so the charge did not break – and it still had not broken after a fifteen count when the devastating reverberating roar of the guns reached her.

What was becoming obvious, however, was a distinct closing-up, a definite *compression*, of the forty-thousand-strong army. To Malinal's eye it seemed that the front ranks had slowed their onward rush somewhat while the rearmost ranks had, if anything, increased their pace, and the result was that the whole force had now become more dense, compacted into a space somewhat less than a thousand feet deep, as it bore down in a mass on the white men's squares.

That was when Malinal saw two much larger clouds of smoke billow from the top of Potonchan's ancient pyramid and sensed a blur in the air as two objects, moving incredibly fast, crashed into the very heart of Muluc's army.

What was this? She blinked, trying to make sense of what she was seeing. There! And there! Two glinting objects bouncing and rolling with unbelievable force, mowing down hundreds – hundreds! – of Mayan warriors amidst bright splashes of blood, spreading disorder and rampant terror amongst them. Cuetzpalli gasped and leaned forward, shading his eyes with his hand; Ah Kinchil's face turned grey and his toothless jaw sagged.

And then came the sound . . .

A sound beyond imagination and nightmares.

A sound like the end of the world.

Pepillo pulled his fingers from his ears, shook his head to clear the infernal ringing that had set in and surveyed the damage that the first two seventy-pound balls from the lombards had done to the massed enemy. Already visibly discomfited by the ten one-pound rounds from the falconets, he saw they were now in a state of some distress, not

486

exactly falling apart but definitely lacking the aggressive certainty and cohesion they'd shown moments before.

He and Melchior had very little to do and looked on in amazement as Mesa's gun crews worked like demons, swabbing out the big barrels and loading new charges. Down on the plain the enemy front line, still manoeuvring from a block into a horned formation, was quarter of a mile from the four Spanish squares and coming on at a full run. But the falconets had been reloaded and now Ordaz fired all ten at once, a concentrated salvo that smashed through the advance, cutting deep swathes into the ranks, raising screams of confusion and terror, causing some men to halt and others to turn back, transforming the Mayan army almost instantly from an organised coherent force into a melee. Meanwhile the crews were reloading the little cannon and, from now on, Melchior explained, they would fire grapeshot at point-blank range, doing terrible damage.

But the Maya did not lack courage and large elements of their wavering front line still pressed forward, now less than a thousand feet from the Spanish squares. Behind, in a seething, tumultuous, curving band, seven hundred feet deep and two thousand wide, the rest of the huge force struggled with itself, some advancing, some retreating – a giant flux of close to forty thousand men into the midst of whom, keeping the seventy-pound balls as far from the Spaniards as possible, Mesa must concentrate his fire.

The lombards were ready again. Melchior and Pepillo returned their fingers to their ears.

Ah Kinchil, Cuetzpalli, the scribe, the artist, the Cuahchics, Ah Kinchil's guards and retainers, Malinal, even the litter-bearers, in short everyone on the hilltop regardless of rank or station, had now pressed forward to the edge of the trees and stood silent, riveted in place by the events unfolding on the plain below. Whereas moments before it had seemed certain that Muluc's army must sweep the white men away like saplings before an avalanche, it was now obvious that the forty thousand Maya warriors were in some kind of serious, unprecedented, unknown trouble.

Malinal saw the smoke plumes that told her the ten guns in front

487

of the Spanish squares had fired again, all of them together this time, felt in her viscera the hammer blows that struck the Mayan front ranks, making them reel back, and sensed the shock waves radiating rearwards from there through the whole army, causing men far from the impact to stumble and fall as though pushed by giant, invisible hands while others – thousands! – turned in blind panic and ran.

'Fight!' Ah Kinchil croaked, 'Fight!' – as if anyone could hear him; as if it would make any difference if they did! But perhaps in some way the paramount chief's feeble command had got through, for those who ran on towards the Spaniards, Malinal realised, still far outnumbered those attempting to desert.

Cuetzpalli was whispering urgently to his artist – 'Paint everything! The Lord Speaker will reward you!' – when Malinal saw two huge plumes of smoke rush up again from the top of the distant pyramid and, in the same instant, with intimations of horror, witnessed the same shimmer in the air she had seen before, presaging the same mysterious phenomenon of shining metallic spheres tearing through the Maya ranks, bowling over whole rows of men twenty or thirty deep, crushing some, decapitating or dismembering others, bouncing high, crashing down, bouncing and rolling again.

'Fight!' Ah Kinchil was still screaming, spittle running out of his mouth and down his chin. 'Fight for the honour of the Chontal Maya!' Cuetzpalli looked on, his fists clenched so tightly that the knuckles had turned white. Malinal saw that the chaos in the midst of the ranks was multiplying out of control as the metal spheres spread their doom and those running away collided with those running forward. Yet so huge was the army that tens of thousands at the front were still swept onwards by the vast momentum of the charge – onwards like some great ocean wave that must crash down on those tiny, seemingly defenceless Spanish squares and wipe them utterly from the face of the earth.

Bernal Díaz knew he should have stayed behind with the injured men assigned to defend the pyramid, but his pride and his infernal sense of honour had got in the way when Mesa made his selection. Instead of admitting he could hardly walk, let alone stand and fight for hours on the plains, he'd kept his head down and let the dour chief of artillery choose others, fitter than himself, for the garrison.

Worse still, he'd said yes when Ordaz had picked him to lead the hundred men in the westernmost of the four squares. Well, how could he refuse? Most of the officers were away with the cavalry – and where the hell *was* the cavalry, come to think of it? – leaving precious few with enough experience to command large groups of infantry.

Ah, pride! Ah, honour! Díaz winced and closed his eyes for a moment against a wave of dizziness as another stabbing pain ran the length of his throbbing, hugely swollen leg. When he looked again the onrushing mass of Indians, like some turbulent, surging tide, was just five hundred feet away, their shrill cries and whistles and the terrible beat of their drums ringing in his ears, and he saw Ordaz's sword come slashing down, the signal to the gunners, and the ten falconets ranged in front of the squares again fired in unison amidst clouds of smoke, their coughing, booming roar echoing forth, their charges of grapeshot spreading out and tearing into the massed enemy, cutting them to bloody ribbons as though a thousand keen-edged knives had been hurled at them. The attack faltered but did not break and the gun crews wheeled the little cannon back on the double, three into the protection of Díaz's square, two into the next, three into the next and two into the last, just ahead of the Indian front rank, which threw itself against the Spanish pikes with suicidal fury.

Gods! Díaz thought, sweeping aside a spear thrust and hacking his broadsword into a screaming, painted face. *Are these men or devils?* And suddenly his square was engulfed – all the squares were engulfed – by countless thousands of the enemy. The fighting was so intense, so furious, so close that Díaz forgot the crippling pain of his leg, forgot the fever and nausea that shook him, and fought like a madman for his life, aware as he parried and thrust that the crews of the three falconets inside his square were feverishly reloading.

'Musketeers!' he yelled. 'A volley! A volley *now!*'

Cortés was finding it difficult to stay calm. For the past quarter-hour he and his riders had been hearing cannon fire, yet they still remained stuck on the track that ran east and then south out of Potonchan, curving through forest and dense bush for two miles before reaching open fields. There had been no musket fire, which meant the Mayan and Spanish front ranks were not yet engaged, but he knew the clash could not be delayed much longer. He cursed under his breath as, for the seventh or eighth time since leaving the town, the whole troop was forced to dismount in order to clear trees that had been felled across their path.

This was a bad development. Alvarado and Davila had both made use of the track yesterday, and Alvarado again this morning, and they had reported it narrow but free of obstacles and passable by horses riding in single file. It followed that the enemy – Cortés could not guess how many – had penetrated the forest within the past few hours. Might there be enough of them to stage an ambush? The dismounted riders were vulnerable. Or might they be planning a flanking attack on the town?

Both possibilities loomed large in Cortés's imagination; however, the greater worry was the time it was taking to get his cavalry into the field – far, far longer than anyone had anticipated! Once battle was joined in earnest in front of the town, the foot soldiers could not hold out indefinitely against the overwhelming numbers of the Maya. Cannon might delay the inevitable but only a decisive charge of heavy horse could swing the balance and demoralise the enemy completely enough to give victory to the hard-pressed Spaniards.

Sandoval and Escalante wrestled aside the last of the felled trunks and the troop mounted up again.

'I don't like this,' said Puertocarrero, glancing nervously into the dark mass of trees pressing close to the track. 'Forest is no place for cavalry.'

'Who cares whether you like it or not?' growled Alvarado, touching his heel to Bucephalus's flank and causing the white stallion to surge forward into the rump of Puertocarrero's silver-grey mare.

'Silence, gentlemen, please,' said Cortés. In the distance they all heard the bark of muskets.

Where was the cavalry? This was the question at the forefront of Díaz's mind. Despite the carnage wrought by the cannon, the gigantic, howling torrent of Mayan warriors had engulfed all four of the squares, flowing round them as a river in spate flows round islands in its midst, hammering at the Spaniards on every side. He smelt them – rank, fetid, like dead meat; saw their furious eyes, their bared teeth, filed to sharp points, their brown skin glistening with sweat, their lean, painted bodies, the barbaric splendour of their plumes and standards, the flash and gleam of their primitive stone weapons – here an axe, here a dagger, here a spear – lunging and battering at his men, breaking against armour, deflected by good Spanish shields. He was sorely tempted to unleash the twenty-five war hounds held barking and straining at the centre of his square, but the signal Ordaz had arranged, three blasts on the bugle, had not been sounded, and there was more work yet for gun and sword.

Responding to his command, his twelve musketeers had pushed their way forward, three on the north, three on the south, three on the east, and three on the west side of the square, and now fired a volley in unison, tearing holes in the press of the enemy, creating points of weakness and confusion into which his swordsmen charged, hacking and slashing wildly. The madness of battle was on him, the agony of his leg wound dulled, and Díaz found that he too had surged out of the protection of the square to attack the disrupted enemy ranks, shield in his left hand, sword in his right, a lunge to a man's throat, a slash across a bare abdomen, smash his shield into another's face, hack down with his blade to take off a leg at the knee . . .

Then suddenly he was cut off, alone, surrounded by a wheeling knot of the foe, and he felt a spear thud and shatter against his cuirass. In the next instant a flint knife somehow found a way through his *pauldron* and embedded itself in his left armpit with a shock of intense, burning pain, and some great club smashed against his helmet, knocking him sick and dizzy to the ground, stars flashing before his eyes.

What was this? *What was this?* Dirty bare feet, hairless brown legs, a man's crotch bound in a breechclout, strong hands gripping his upper arms, dragging him away, excited voices jabbering in the barbarous tongue of the Maya.

The realisation dawned on Díaz that he was being taken. *Dear God!*

491

They'll sacrifice me! They'll cut out my heart! But just then he heard a great roar of 'Santiago and at them!', saw an Indian's head go thumping and rolling, the stump of a neck gushing blood, long black hair cartwheeling, saw a hand sliced off, an arm amputated at the shoulder, saw another painted warrior hacked clean in half as Mibiercas, like the angel of death, did terrible butchery with his longsword, yelling furious insults with every massive blow, clearing a wide space into which La Serna and three others charged and bore Díaz aloft and carried him back into the square.

There was no let-up, the press of the enemy resumed at once, but then someone shouted '*Now!*' and Díaz sensed rather than saw the three falconets trundled forward to the edges of the square, heard the roar of their percussion and the whistle of grapeshot and the terrible screams as their tempest of fire was unleashed.

At point-blank range, the effect of the shrapnel storm was calamitous for the Maya. Huge gaps a dozen men wide opened up in their ranks into which, once again, poured the flying squads of Spanish swordsmen, Mibiercas to the fore. They hacked mercilessly at their dazed foes until they began to form up again and then withdrew to the protection of the squares.

Ignoring the thudding pain in his leg, ignoring the hot blood dripping from under his left arm, Díaz was on his feet near the middle of the square where his friends had set him down, using his height to get a sense of the ebb and flow of the battle. He saw that wherever the Maya kept their discipline and dashed in good order against the outer ranks of the Spanish formations, they were met by solid walls of shields over the top of which long spears and pikes were thrust into their faces from the ranks behind, while the men directly confronting them gutted and hamstrung them with sword blades. Meanwhile the musketeers and crossbowmen, firing sequentially in groups of six, kept up almost continuous withering volleys that tore yet more holes in the Mayan ranks, which were again exploited by groups of swordsmen until the falconets were once more ready to fire, restarting the whole cycle of death and destruction.

Díaz felt proud of his comrades, so proud that tears leapt to his eyes and his breath caught in his throat. They were men of the finest mettle, men who refused to break, no matter what fearsome odds they faced, men who would not give way, men who did not know the meaning of defeat.

Yet even men such as they could not possibly survive this terrible onslaught. Had they killed a thousand of the enemy with their cannon and muskets and swordplay? Two thousand? It did not matter. They could kill three thousand or even five thousand and the odds would still be close to a hundred to one and the final outcome certain.

Unless the will of the foe broke – and only the cavalry, Díaz was sure, had the power to bring that about.

Mesa was ready to fire the lombards again and Pepillo put his fingers back in his ears. He could see the shots were becoming more difficult for the artilleryman now the enemy swirled so close to the Spaniards. Still, they were legion, stretching back in a disordered mass at least five hundred feet south of the squares.

The two huge guns bellowed flame and smoke, sending the lethal seventy-pound balls whistling low to crash down amidst the Mayan ranks just a hundred feet south of the Spanish formations.

My goodness, thought Pepillo, *that was a close thing!* But again the cannon balls and the massive roar of the big guns had a stunning effect on the enemy, causing even those locked in direct combat with the squares to pause and look up.

Some were pointing at him! Then his eye was caught by a horde of warriors, a thousand strong, leaving the centre of the battle and pouring north across the intervening mile directly towards the town.

Directly towards the pyramid.

'Captain Mesa!' he yelled. 'There! Look there!'

Seeing the threat, the artilleryman scrambled to crank down the elevation of the barrels as the gun crews frantically reloaded.

Malinal watched spellbound as the battle unfolded. If they were not gods, she thought, these Spaniards were certainly proving themselves to be brave men with exceptional, indeed almost superhuman, fighting skills. Against all logic and reason, their squares would not break before the overwhelming numbers of the Maya, and somehow continued to hold out against them in the midst of the ferocious scrum of hand-to-hand combat.

'Look,' Ah Kinchil suddenly gibbered to Cuetzpalli. 'Look!' Despite his great age the paramount chief of the Chontal Maya was far-sighted and was now dancing up and down with joy and pointing towards Potonchan. 'My warriors go to recapture the pyramid of King Ahau Chamahez from the invaders! The white men there will die! Their terrible weapons will be thrown down!'

Stupid old fool! thought Malinal. *What do you know?*

Weirdly she found her loyalty to the Maya had become so detached she actually *wanted* the Spaniards to win! Well, why not? What had her own people – even her own mother! – ever done for her? They had sent her into slavery and humiliation and danger and when she had returned they had slaved her again! They deserved the punishment the white men were inflicting on them. They deserved to lose this battle!

Except it still did not seem possible that the huge Mayan army could lose, even in the state of chaos the white men's guns were reducing it to, because Ah Kinchil was right. At least a thousand warriors had formed up into a block and were pouring across the open fields north of the battleground and making for the town. It wouldn't take them long to reach the pyramid and the white men on its summit.

In minutes they covered half the distance. Malinal watched anxiously with her knuckles pressed to her mouth, daring to hope that more Spaniards might usher forth from the town to intercept them; but none appeared and Muluc's triumphant words echoed in her head – *'they have no reserves!'* It seemed that nothing could stop the attack on the pyramid when the guns on its summit billowed smoke again, and she almost cheered as glittering death crashed down amongst the charging warriors, pounding them, crushing them, annihilating them, scattering the survivors like chaff.

Yet, even as she admired the Spaniards, she could not suppress the pride she felt in her own people's courage when she saw that some of the shattered column still ran on towards the pyramid, while others picked themselves up from the ground and followed.

* * *

'Good shooting, Captain Mesa!' yelled Pepillo. Though it had been worth the attempt, he'd doubted the artilleryman could hit the fast-moving Mayan column with even one of the huge cannon, but in the event both had been perfectly on the mark, causing bloody mayhem.

Even so, hundreds of enemy warriors were still coming on and were now so close – less than quarter of a mile away – that the lombards couldn't be depressed far enough to target them.

Mesa had placed four of his eight falconets around the base of the pyramid, deploying the other four to the southern outskirts of Potonchan, overlooking the battlefield. It was unlikely they'd be enough to stop what was left of this attack completely, but the Maya must be demoralised by the colossal losses they'd already suffered, and anything was possible. The guns were hidden from Pepillo's view by the buildings at the edge of town, but now he heard their choking roar and saw the onrush of the enemy falter as the four one-pound balls smashed into them.

Dozens of men went down but not enough, not nearly enough. 'Reload!' Pepillo found himself shouting. 'Reload with grapeshot!' But just then Melchior came charging by, grabbed Mesa by the elbow and pointed east.

Just minutes away, their war cries already audible as they approached along the east–west avenue running through the centre of Potonchan, was another band of Indians, at least two hundred of them, armed with spears and clubs and obsidian-edged longswords.

Mesa bellowed a warning to the falconet crews around the base of the pyramid, called to arms the squad of forty injured men waiting in the shade of the little temple on the summit platform and led the way down the eastern stair.

Somewhere Melchior had found two round wooden bucklers and two eight-foot spears and thrust one of each at Pepillo. 'Know how to use these?' he asked.

Pepillo shook his head dumbly.

'Well you'd better learn fast,' said his friend.

At last, after throwing aside three more hurdles, Cortés led his cavalry out into the open fields. Though they had several times caught glimpses of painted warriors moving amongst the trees, no attack had materialised – perhaps because the steel-clad horses and riders appeared so alien and menacing to the Indians. What was certain, however, was that Potonchan was entirely unprotected at its east side and that the force mobilising in the forest must be there to attack the town. For the hundredth time, Cortés found himself wishing he had left Mesa with more than forty men – every one of them injured! – to defend the lombards. But the Spaniards were stretched so thin he'd been unable to spare a larger number and now the only hope for all of them was a stunning coup by the cavalry.

Cortés saw the battle raging just two miles to the northwest, where the Spaniards were perilously hemmed in on every side, but the fields here at the edge of the forest were broken and treacherous, cut through by irrigation ditches that the horses couldn't leap without risk of serious injury. Any charge attempted across such terrain was doomed to failure. Cursing inwardly, he ordered the troop to ride another mile due west to the foot of a ridge of low hills where the track intersected the main highway running into Potonchan from the south.

From there, finally, they would be able to bear down unimpeded on the enemy masses where they swarmed, and now threatened to overrun, the four beleaguered Spanish squares.

Malinal had watched the thousand Mayan warriors – charging across the fields to Potonchan – reduced to hundreds when the big guns fired down on them from the pyramid. Moments later they were struck again as plumes of smoke revealed four smaller guns positioned at the southern edge of town. Finally they were struck a third time in some devastating way that felled almost all the survivors, leaving barely a hundred to press home the attack as she lost sight of them amidst the streets and houses.

She heard an urgent sound, like the rapid beat of some great drum, and a gasp from one of Cuetzpalli's Cuahchics who babbled in Nahuatl the words 'men of silver' as another said, 'deer-men!' She turned towards where they were looking, a little to the east on the plains below the hill, and her eyes fell on something extraordinary, something unbelievable, something enchanted with the most powerful magic, something truly belonging to the world of the gods. This something, which she could barely comprehend, took the form of fifteen or twenty giant figures in a tight group racing at supernatural speed towards the Xaman Hills, and the figures moved on four legs, with an appearance somewhat like white-tailed deer, except their bodies were three times the height of the largest stags of that race, and rising up from the midst of their backs – though whether seated upright upon them or actually one creature with them it was hard to be certain – were gigantic human forms. Both the human and animal parts of these beings, which must be the 'horses' Cit Bolon Tun had spoken of, were covered from head to foot in some metal that shone brighter than burnished silver, and they held in their human hands long lances with tips of the same shining stuff.

Ah Kinchil had been growing steadily more deranged all afternoon, but now he uttered a high-pitched scream and threw himself to the ground, covering his head with his arms while his skinny legs kicked and thrashed. The Cuahchics, who usually knew what to do in any situation, seemed bewildered and confounded in ways wholly out of keeping with their status as ferocious warriors. The artist had stopped painting and stood gazing, not exactly in fear, more in awe and in puzzlement, at the onrush of the strange group of beings. Cuetzpalli was stumbling back into the shelter of the trees, apparently trying to get out of sight as quickly as possible, his handsome face filled with horror, and the slippery, evasive quality of his gaze transformed into frank, unabashed terror. Taking their cue from him, Ah Kinchil's guards lifted the paramount chief bodily and ducked into the undergrowth with him, followed by his retainers and Muluc's steward Ichick. The guards at the foot of the hill had fled and it seemed there was nothing to stop the metal beings charging right up the steep slope and destroying everyone.

Malinal stayed in the open, refusing to hide. 'Come to me!' she shouted. 'Come to me! I am here because of you!' And it seemed to her for a moment that the leader of the beings had heard her words, for he turned his metal head towards her and she saw his white, bearded face – the face of Quetzalcoatl! – and his eyes fixed on her and filled her body with fire, and rooted her to the spot.

497

But then in a roll of thunder and a storm of dust he was past, they were all past, and they turned onto the *sacbe* and charged north along it towards Potonchan, their lances levelled before them.

'Aim for their faces!' Cortés yelled. 'Spit them but don't waste time spearing fallen men. Just charge them and keep on charging them, put the fear of God into them, break up their formations, scatter them and ride them down!'

He glanced at the smooth white surface of the road flying by beneath Molinero's hooves, saw his brave cavaliers flung out in a fighting wedge behind him, every one of them burning for battle, urging their mounts onward at a tremendous pace. They had covered the ground in a matter of minutes and the huge mass of the foe sprawled just five hundred feet ahead, already in a state of turmoil, boiling with confusion at the havoc wreaked by the lombards. These now belched fire for the last time from the top of the pyramid and sent a pair of seventy-pound balls into the midst of the enemy, bouncing and crashing, mowing men down like ripe wheat before the thresher, even as the falconets sewed death in their front line from the shelter of the squares.

The Maya were so preoccupied with the fight ahead, which they were close to winning by sheer numbers despite their terror of the cannon, that none of them even seemed to have noticed the doom that was bearing down on them from behind. 'Santiago and at them!' Cortés bellowed as Molinero thundered across the rapidly closing gap, and then, with a fearsome crash, the wedge ploughed deep into the already chaotic enemy rear. He felt the jolt as his lance took a turning man in the side of his face, and was filled with brutal joy at the terrified howls and screams that rose up all around him and at the shockwave that passed through the milling throng ahead. He jerked the lance free, speared another man, and spurred Molinero onward, the great destrier's iron-clad hooves trampling the fallen, Alvarado riding Bucephalus roughshod over the huddled foe to his left, Escalante to his right, and there was Puertocarrero, and there Lares, there Olid and there Morla on his dappled grey, there was Montejo and there young Sandoval, a spearhead of armoured men sweeping out a great swathe in the very heart of the Mayan army, painted warriors fleeing away from them in all directions in panic-stricken mobs. Again Cortés's lance struck; again he pulled it free as he smashed his heavy iron stirrup into an enemy's face and impaled another so hard through the chest that the lance protruded a yard from the man's back and for a moment he thought he might not retrieve it . . .

Alvarado saw Cortés struggling to withdraw his lance. He had already lost his own, buried in a savage's head somewhere in the fray, but he didn't care. As they were arming in the orchard, he'd once again set aside his Nuñez rapier, not at all a suitable cavalry sword, and brought along the falchion instead. *Good choice!* he thought, *good choice!* – for what a weapon the long heavy cutlass was proving to be in this pounding, trampling charge through the dense mass of a hopelessly undisciplined foe. Most were utterly demoralised and fleeing in every direction, but some, he was pleased to discover, pressed round him and still had the guts for a fight. He slashed left, opening a screaming warrior's face in a great bloody gash from cheekbone to jaw, slashed right, taking a man's head half off his shoulders, felt some pitiful stone blade shatter against his armoured thigh, hacked down the enemy who had wielded it and laughed out loud in sheer, mad, murderous joy as he urged Bucephalus forward . . .

Gonzalo de Sandoval saw the excitement, the sheer pleasure on Alvarado's face and knew that he did not and never would love killing in that extraordinary, murderous, almost insane way. Although he had killed no men at all until a few weeks ago, Sandoval found himself surprisingly calm and collected as he killed again now, not because he wanted to, not because there was any satisfaction or relish in it, but simply because it was the job at hand, the job he was born to do and, now that the caudillo had given him his chance, it was a job he was determined to do well. He thrust forward, impaling a man through the throat, snatched the lance free in a single fluid movement and wheeled the chestnut mare to strike another warrior, plunging the tip of the weapon vertically down through the soft, vulnerable flesh between his neck and collarbone and into his heart.

Sandoval had practised such manoeuvres a hundred times in training exercises, when his Hidalgo family still had some remnants of wealth and power, and was amazed at the way everything was coming back to him now. The extra height that one gained on the back of a great destrier accorded the rider exceptional advantages over the foot soldier – and especially over foot soldiers such as these Indians who had never before faced mounted men, who indeed had never even seen horses before and were for the most part in a blind, superstitious funk.

Not all of them though! Twenty paces away, two wild, half-naked savages, who seemed to have identified Cortés as the leader, were swarming him in the midst of a dense pack of the enemy; one had leapt up behind him and was sawing at his throat with a flint dagger – but getting nowhere because of the steel *gorget* he wore – while the other clung to his left arm and sought to pull him down. Sandoval spurred his horse to a gallop, scattering groups of the enemy left and right, levelled his lance and killed the warrior on the ground with a massive thrust which swept him away, while Cortés, his left arm now free, reached inside his boot, pulled out a dagger and used it to stab the man on his back through the eye, drawing a gush of blood.

'Well done, Sandoval!' Cortés shouted. As he stood in his stirrups to throw down the dying man, whose blood poured in gouts over the shoulders of his armour, his elevated view showed him all four of the Spanish squares, the nearest only a hundred paces away, still beset on all sides, and all but overwhelmed, by great mobs of Indians. But now a bugle sounded and, out of the squares, held back until this critical moment, baying and snarling like so many demons released from hell, raced the four packs of dogs. The steel armour of the hundred furious, ravening animals glittered, and their great mouths, filled with jagged teeth, gaped wide, spraying saliva, as they fell baying and snarling, maddened with bloodlust, upon the press of the dismayed foe. Throats were snatched out in an instant, bowels worried from naked bellies, thighs and groins seized and ripped open, heads clamped and crushed.

His lance levelled, Cortés charged on towards the squares, vaguely aware of the other horsemen around him, smashing down and trampling groups of Indians in desperate flight away from the dogs – Indians who, indeed, no longer constituted a proper fighting force anywhere across the battlefield.

Quite suddenly, as though communicated by some mysterious

telepathy, their spirit had broken, and what had begun as a fight, and come very close to total victory for the Maya, was ending as a rout.

Ah Kinchil, Cuetzpalli, Ichick and the guards and retainers emerged from their hiding places in the trees soon after the men of silver had thundered past. Thereafter, Ah Kinchil sat slumped, spittle drooling from his mouth, seemingly aware of nothing, but Cuetzpalli very soon regained his composure and watched the final stages of the battle keenly, giving a running commentary to his scribe and his artist who industriously set down everything that happened.

When it was clear, against all the odds, that the Spaniards had won the day and the immense Mayan army was in full flight across the battlefield, pursued, charged and speared at will by the terrifying silver beings, Cuetzpalli stood up, brushed grass and a few leaves from his rich tunic, and snapped his fingers for his litter to be brought. 'Give the paramount chief my regrets,' he said to Malinal with a gesture to Ah Kinchil, 'and tell him I could not stay. Pressing business calls me back to Tenochtitlan.' A sly smile: 'Tell him I much appreciated the afternoon's . . . entertainment. It has been – how can I put this? – most instructive. I am sure the Great Speaker of the Mexica will be eager to hear of these events.'

As the merchant turned to go, Muluc's steward Ichick thrust himself forward, dragging Malinal by the wrist. 'But lord, do you not want to buy this woman? You had an agreement with my master to take her off his hands.'

'Your master,' said Cuetzpalli coldly, 'led forty thousand men into battle against four hundred . . . and lost. Quite an incredible achievement, wouldn't you say? He has dishonoured the name of the Chontal Maya and, if he lives, which I rather doubt, he should kill himself. Entirely his choice, of course, but either way my agreement with him is void.'

With that he stepped into the litter and was carried off down the hill in the direction of Cintla, his Cuahchics jogging protectively along beside him.

Ah Kinchil remained in a stupefied state, but his retainers wasted no time bundling him into his litter too. On Ichick's orders Malinal's hands were tied, a noose was placed around her neck and two soldiers were detailed to guard her. Then, in great haste, the whole column wound its way off the hilltop, also heading south to Cintla.

There was no time to lose, for below on the plains the defeated Maya were likewise fleeing south in their thousands. Casting a last glance back, Malinal saw the men of silver abruptly break off the chase and turn away, thundering towards Potonchan. 'Come for me,' she whispered as she lost sight of their leader in the dust cloud of their charge. 'Come for me.'

So vengeful were his cavalrymen, so furious in the wild hunt, that Cortés had great difficulty persuading them to break it off. But the battle was won and he feared for the men in Potonchan. There had been firing from the falconet battery he'd left with Mesa, but the guns had fallen silent and now, ominously, he saw Indians swarming up the flanks of the pyramid.

The squat figure of Ordaz was before him, sword mired to the hilt with blood, a look of triumph on his face as he surveyed the rout of the enemy. Cortés reined in beside him, pointed with his lance to the pyramid. 'It's not over yet,' he yelled. 'Bring two hundred men. Bring them fast!' As he spurred forward again he saw Vendabal and swerved by him. 'Dogs!' he shouted. 'I need dogs now. Tear them loose from the foe and bring them to the aid of our comrades.' Vendabal followed his gaze to the pyramid, his eyes widened, and he bellowed for his assistants.

Cortés urged Molinero to a full gallop, furious to see Alvarado and some of the other cavaliers hanging back, so keen to punish the thousands fleeing the battlefield that they were oblivious to the danger in the town. But Escalante, Puertocarrero and Morla on his left, Sandoval, Velázquez de León and Dominguez on his right, had seen what he saw, and others were wheeling away to join the charge.

'Santiago and at them!' Cortés yelled, thrusting his lance forward. 'Santiago and at them!'

Darting here and there behind the line, Pepillo saw everything and could do nothing. He saw a black-and-white painted warrior, his face twisted with hate, exploit a gap in the thicket of spear points, bound up the last three steps and break his stone dagger against a bearded soldier's mailed hauberk, while to his right another of the foe also found his way through, somehow grabbing the ankles of a defender and tugging wildly to unbalance him. Both attackers were dead within seconds, the first with a dagger thrust to his heart and a shove that sent him rolling and tumbling down the side of the pyramid; the second with a thudding blow from a war hammer that split his skull and spilled his brains.

Following Melchior's example, Pepillo held the heavy buckler above his head to ward off the missiles – arrows, fire-hardened darts, sling-stones – that showered down constantly on the summit platform as he dashed to and fro, his heart drumming, ready to spear any man who broke through the line.

It had all happened suddenly. One minute he and Melchior had been spectators only, safe on top of the pyramid watching the lombards rain death on the enemy, the next minute Melchior had spotted two hundred Indians approaching the square from the east and Mesa and his troops had charged down to stop them. But no sooner had they placed the falconets to enfilade the attackers than the crews of the other battery, positioned on the south side of town, had appeared in the square, hotly pursued by a further hundred of the foe, the remnant of the large column that had approached from the south and been torn apart – though unfortunately not completely destroyed – by the lombards. This changed everything and Mesa was only able to get off one salvo of grapeshot towards the east before abandoning the little cannon, wheeling his men to the defence of the fleeing gunners and fighting a desperate retreat up the pyramid steps against the combined force of the two Indian bands.

In addition to himself and the Taino slaves, who'd been herded into the temple and would not take part in the defence, Pepillo counted sixty-four defenders now ringing the summit platform – forty injured soldiers, sixteen gun crew from the falconet batteries, six further gunners who had fired the now silent lombards, the artilleryman Mesa, and Melchior.

Despite the many injuries they'd already suffered in this morning's battles, they held the high ground and were better armed and equipped than the far more numerous Indians attempting to storm the summit platform. Morale was high, too, because even as they fought with all their strength to prevent the summit from being overwhelmed, and thus save their own lives, all the defenders had seen the huge Maya army out on the plain break and fall apart as Cortés and his cavalryman entered the field and the war dogs were unleashed from the squares. Then a great cheer went up and someone shouted: 'The caudillo's seen us! He's coming.' And another man said: 'God be praised, I knew Cortés wouldn't leave us in the lurch.'

'Five minutes more,' Mesa bellowed as he lunged his twelve-foot spear into the face of another attacker. 'Five minutes more and the cavalry will be in the square and then we'll have these devils on the run.'

Pepillo watched the infantryman next to Mesa on the south side of the platform swing a great double-headed axe, sending two more of the Indians hurtling and screaming down the steep steps to the ground far below. 'I do believe,' said Melchior, 'that we may live through this after all.' But just then, perhaps because they too had seen what had happened on the plain, the Indians redoubled their assault, huge numbers of them pressing up the steps at once, and the defenders on the west side suddenly buckled and gave way; an infantryman with a bandaged leg was pulled down and a crazed savage burst through, stabbed another man in the neck with his flint knife and opened a gap for more attackers to follow. In an instant a knot of half a dozen Maya fighters gained the summit, screaming ferocious battle cries, laying about themselves mightily with clubs and obsidian-edged blades.

Melchior didn't hesitate but ran at them with his spear and thrust it under the ribs of the warrior who'd first broken the line. He hit him with such force that the man was thrown back over the lip of the summit and tumbled out of sight, taking the spear with him, even as another lean Indian, smeared with blood and paint, forced his way forward. Melchior drew his knife and two more attackers closed with him, stone blades flashing. For an instant longer Pepillo stood frozen with his back against the wall of the little temple at the centre of the platform, his hands shaking; then the spell was broken and he dashed forward, thrust his own eight-foot spear at the mob of invaders and felt the impact as its tip hit bone and it was snatched from his grasp. Where was Melchior? For a moment, in the screaming, bellowing scrum, amidst the press of bodies, he couldn't locate him, but then he saw he was down, grinding his rusty old dagger between the ribs of a long-haired warrior who straddled and stabbed at him repeatedly with a flint blade. Pepillo sensed a rush of feet and heard the roar of Mesa's voice as men from the south side, where the line still held, charged in to throw the invaders back, but his only thought was for Melchior. As he hurtled across the intervening space at his friend's attacker, Cortés's knife gripped in his fist, something huge and heavy smashed with dreadful force into the side of his head and he tumbled instantly into darkness.

When Pepillo awoke, blinking, with the taste of blood in his mouth and the sounds of screams flooding back into his ears, he didn't know how much time had passed, or even, for the first few moments, where he was. He sat up groggily to see a massive wolfhound feasting on a dead Indian whose throat it had torn out. Other dogs were here, and more fallen Indians – most dead, some wounded; they were the ones doing the screaming. He recognised Sandoval, in armour, a bloodied broadsword gripped in his hand, talking quietly to Mesa. And there was Cortés, his armoured back and shoulders drenched in gore, crouched over a sprawled, still form.

Melchior!

Dread seized Pepillo as he crawled and clambered over bodies, shoved a snarling mastiff out of his way and dragged himself to his friend's side.

Melchior's eyes turned towards him. 'Pepillo!' he whispered. 'You did well. I saw you spear that Indian . . .'

'I tried to get to you,' Pepillo sobbed. 'Something hit me in the head, knocked me out. But thank God, you're alive.'

Melchior reached out his hand, rested it on Pepillo's arm and held him in a fierce grip. 'Silly mammet!' he said. 'Of course I'm alive. Who else is going to teach you to ride?'

Chapter Sixty

Thursday 25 March 1519 to Sunday 18 April 1519

In the aftermath of the battle, though he had won an astounding victory against overwhelming odds, though he had destroyed the Indians of Potonchan utterly, as Saint Peter had required him to do, Cortés was seized by an immense weariness and a fall in his spirits. It was almost, he thought, like the feeling one has after sex, when one has anticipated the joys of a woman's body, seduced her at great length, got her between the sheets and finally spent one's seed in her only to discover, when all is said and done, that the act was a little less pleasurable than one had imagined it might be.

A sense, somehow, of anticlimax rather than culmination.

A sense of melancholy and a vague, restless, gnawing hunger for something more . . .

Something . . . better.

In this mood, leaving Alvarado in charge of the mopping-up operation, not pausing even to wash or take supper, Cortés threw himself down on his bed soon after nightfall in the former palace of the chief of Potonchan, now commandeered as his own headquarters, and fell immediately into a deep sleep.

Deep, but not dreamless.

For it seemed very little time passed – no time at all – before the beloved figure of a tall strong man of middle years, very handsome and commanding, with golden hair and dazzling bright skin, appeared to him and drew his soul out of his body and lifted him, high, high, into the evening sky under the flickering stars and carried him off over the field of battle where countless thousands of the enemy lay dead.

'The Lord God smiles upon you,' Saint Peter said. 'He celebrates your victory. We all do.'

'You *all* do?' Cortés asked.

'We the saints, and the congregation of angels. The Lord is pleased with you, Cortés. I am pleased with you. We are all pleased with you.'

And it was true. The keeper of the keys of Heaven, the very rock upon whom Christ built his church, beamed with joy as they descended to the battlefield and walked together, their feet bathed in blood, amongst the heaped and mutilated dead. 'Look, Cortés,' Saint Peter chortled, 'look what you have done for your God. Look there, and there, and there.' And he showed him the bodies, some ripped apart by the fangs of the war dogs, others trampled by the horses, some hacked and stabbed to death by the swords and pikes and spears of the Spaniards, others with their heads blown off, many torn limb from limb or burst apart into unrecognisable fragments of flesh and bone, where storms of grapeshot and musket rounds had struck them or where the heavy cannonballs fired by the lombards had bounced lethally through their ranks, striking them down in swathes. 'You have won,' said the holy saint, 'a great and terrible victory over the heathen; you have laid my vengeance upon them as I asked, and now your reward beckons.'

An image took shape in Cortés's mind of the city in the lake surrounded by mountains that Saint Peter had shown him weeks before, the jewelled and shining city built upon the water with an immense pyramid of pure gold towering at its heart.

'Yes,' said the saint, smiling encouragingly, 'that's the one. That's your prize. Shall we go and take another look?'

'Yes, Holy Father, you have read the secret yearnings of my heart.'

'You have no secrets from me, for I know all your yearnings, all your hopes, all your dreams, and in the fullness of time I will satisfy every one of them.' So saying, the saint swept Cortés up into the sky again and showed him the way, a hundred miles and another hundred, and yet another hundred, and a hundred miles more across jungles, across rivers, across snow-capped mountains, between two immense volcanoes and down into the distant, verdant valley beyond and the gleaming lake that lay at its centre and the shining city that stood in the midst of the lake, and the massy pyramid looming at the very heart of the city.

But what was this?

'The pyramid is no longer of gold, Holy Father,' Cortés protested, 'as you showed me before.'

'Oh,' said Saint Peter, 'is it not?'

'Well, see for yourself,' said Cortés, hearing the disappointment in his voice as he pointed to the hulking structure beneath them. Though splendidly made, and monstrous huge, it was of common stone with its four levels painted respectively green, red, turquoise and yellow.

'Ah,' said the saint. 'You are quite correct.'

Then what, Cortés wanted to ask, *do you propose to do about it?* Part of his plan for keeping the demands and insurrections of the Velazquistas in check had involved the golden pyramid. To be able to offer them a share of such a bounty, at the right moment, would have quieted all dissent. But a pyramid of stone? What use was that to him or them?

'There is gold here aplenty,' said Saint Peter, as ever reading his thoughts. 'Gold in the treasure houses of the emperor, gold in the temples, gold around the necks of the nobles, gold in the emporia of the merchants – more than enough to satisfy the greed of your opponents, more gold than you can possibly imagine – and all of it I will make yours.'

'An emperor rules here?' Cortés asked.

'A great and wealthy emperor, whom I give you leave to plunder for the glory of the Lord, whose temples you must bring low, whose idols you must destroy, whose pyramid you must take apart block by block.'

'But why,' Cortés asked, 'did you show me the pyramid of gold when in truth it is made of painted stone?'

The saint's smile was somehow fearsome, and his black eyes glittered. 'Therein lies a great mystery,' he said, 'and it will be your fate to discover its meaning.'

There came a clap of thunder, the heavens split, darkness descended upon the scene like an inkblot and Cortés awoke in his commandeered bed in the midst of the night and for a long moment he had no idea where he was.

Tozi's second visit to Guatemoc in his bedchamber at Chapultepec began much as the first. Entering the darkened room after midnight she emerged into form and offered him healing.

He seemed childlike in his trust. She said 'turn here', and he turned; she said 'face there', and he obeyed, all the while groaning with relief as her fingers gently caressed and probed his wounds.

It was not until close to dawn that the encounter became scary and unpredictable. Tozi thought him asleep and was about to leave him to his rest when suddenly he reached out to her and drew her close. 'Is it permissible,' he asked in that soft, aristocratic drawl of his, 'for a mortal man to kiss a goddess?'

She was flustered, afraid, her whole body was trembling, sweat broke out on her brow. It was all she could do not to render herself invisible at once and fade away like smoke between his hands. 'No, Prince!' she exclaimed. 'Such a thing is impossible. You would be turned to stone!'

'I think I would be willing to endure that fate,' he said, 'and remain eternally a statue, in return for one taste of your sweet lips.'

He was, Tozi had to admit, very persuasive. She felt the heat of his body, felt herself blush. Thankfully it was still too dark for him to see. But he mused: 'What is this? Even a goddess trembles?'

'I tremble that you do not die for this sacrilege! Release me at once, Prince, or never see me again!'

Guatemoc nodded. 'So slim,' he whispered, 'so warm . . .' His forehead rested against hers before he let her go. 'So moist . . . So very human . . .'

Feeling his hands unclasp from her waist, Tozi stepped back sharply from the bed and faded into invisibility.

'And yet not human,' she heard the prince add as she disappeared, 'for surely no human has such powers.'

'Who else is going to teach you to ride?'

Those words, so full of hope and promise, were the last Melchior spoke. Moments later he slipped into unconsciousness, his fierce grip slackening, and did not wake again. Pepillo sat vigil with him through the night in the makeshift field hospital that Dr La Peña had set up for the injured, but as dawn was breaking his friend drew a final laboured breath and died.

'He's gone to a better place, lad,' said Bernal Díaz, who lay on the next mat, his right thigh swollen and septic where an arrow had struck him two days before, the left side of his chest bandaged and seeping blood where a knife thrust in yesterday's fighting had got past his armour.

'What's so good about being dead?' Pepillo shouted angrily. 'Nothing's better than being alive!' Then he remembered that if it hadn't been for Díaz he and Melchior would both have been dead, killed by Muñoz, weeks before. 'I'm sorry,' he sniffled. 'I didn't mean to shout.'

'And I'm sorry you've lost your friend,' said Díaz. 'He was a good lad and a brave one. He didn't deserve this.'

'He was teaching me to ride,' Pepillo said. Suddenly, the emotions he had held in check all night, trying to be strong, trying to be a man, overwhelmed him, and he found himself doubled over, sobbing disconsolately, snot running out of his nose. 'He put me on Molinero's back. Yesterday! Just yesterday, Don Bernal. And we rode, and we felt so fine and Melchior was so happy. Even after what Muñoz did to him – the bad memories, the horror, the pain – he'd overcome all that. I know he'd overcome it, and he was smiling again. And he loved his horses, Don Bernal. He loved his horses. He told me how he'd been a slave and how riding like the wind was the true meaning of freedom for him. And now he's dead. Just dead! It's not right! It's not fair! What kind of God would allow a good person like Melchior to die in such a way?'

'The same kind of God that let an evil person like Muñoz live for so many years,' said Díaz quietly. Pepillo looked up and saw only kindness and concern in the ensign's eyes, but when he looked down again, nothing had changed, for there was Melchior, cold and still.

Outside morning had broken and a new day had begun.

During the night after the battle, Ah Kinchil recovered his wits and refused Muluc's request to raise another army from surrounding towns to do battle with the white men again.

'Are you mad?' the old chief spat at him incredulously as Malinal served them an early breakfast in the palace in Cintla. 'I saw what happened. I saw how they defeated us. Don't forget I was *there*, Muluc! I witnessed the whole battle, from beginning to end, and it was unbelievable. Something impossible even to imagine. Whether they are men or gods, it's obvious we can't fight them.'

At that moment, Cit Bolon Tun, the cross-eyed former captive of the Spaniards, was brought in by the palace guards. The man's nose had been broken by some brutal blow and was still bleeding freely.

'There you are!' said Ah Kinchil. 'You knew they'd beat us and you told us to fight them anyway. I call you a traitor! A *traitor*, do you hear? It was you who misled us and brought this disaster down on our heads. Without your advice I would never have gone to war.'

'I'm no traitor, sire,' said Cit Bolon Tun, falling to his knees and sobbing pitifully, drops of blood from his nose spattering around him on the polished floor. 'The Spaniards are very dangerous. I made no secret of that! But I gave you my best, most honest, most truthful advice when I urged you to fight them, while they are still few in number. Wait a few more months and there will be many more of them. Wait a year and there will be thousands. Our only chance was a swift, decisive victory now . . .'

'Liar!' roared Ah Kinchil, spraying spittle. 'We had no chance at all! I say you knew that all along.'

'No, sire. I swear it . . .'

Ah Kinchil gave a curt nod to one of the guards who pulled a long dagger from his belt, walked up behind Cit Bolon Tun, wrenched the wretched man's head back by his long hair, and sawed the blade back and forth across his throat as one might slaughter a deer. Blood spurted freely as the major vessels were severed, the victim's horrible screams and gurgles were abruptly silenced as his vocal cords were cut, and the guard didn't stop until he'd decapitated the poor man. The whole procedure took about a minute. When it was over, Ah Kinchil turned to Malinal and the other serving girls. 'Well?' he said. 'What are you waiting for? Clear this mess up at once.'

Not surprisingly, Muluc's plans for a further battle with the white men evaporated like mist after that and he readily agreed to Ah Kinchil's suggestion that he should go to Potonchan at once at the head of a peace delegation, seek out the Spanish leader Cortés and present him with the abject and total surrender of the Chontal Maya.

'He will require gifts,' said Muluc.

'Take him gifts,' said Ah Kinchil with a lofty wave of his hand. 'You may empty the palace treasury.'

'The gods only know why,' said Muluc, 'but these white men have a particular lust for gold.'

'Then take them all we have,' Ah Kinchil replied with a sniff. The smell of Cit Bolon Tun's blood was thick in the air. 'Not that it amounts to much.' Another sniff: 'Why would they want gold anyway?'

'They say it's the specific remedy for a certain disease of the heart they suffer from. Silver also seems to help it.'

'I hope they will not be angered that we have so little of both.' Ah Kinchil turned thoughtfully and directed his ancient rheumy gaze at Malinal, busy scrubbing the floor. 'This women is quite fetching,' he said. 'I suggest you take her as well. In fact, take twenty women, the most beautiful you can find, and present them all to the Spaniards. All men, and even gods, suffer from a certain need –' a lecherous, toothless grin – 'and women are the specific remedy for it.'

'You said you returned to us to meet the white men,' Muluc told Malinal gleefully, 'so now you're going to get your wish – and good riddance to you; I hope you're as much trouble to them as you've been to me.'

Malinal found it hard to conceal her joy. She had walked all the way from Tenochtitlan to find these white 'gods', only to be diverted from her quest by Muluc – yet fate had now conspired to make him the very instrument that would put her into their hands!

The peace delegation, with the twenty women in its midst, and bearers carrying fifty heaped bundles of jaguar skins, two hundred bundles of embroidered textiles and three large treasure chests, was ready to depart by midday and reached Potonchan, seven miles to the north, three hours later. The route, following the *sacbe*, led directly across the battlefield between the Xaman hills and Potonchan itself, and Malinal was now able to see close up the effects of the devastation she'd witnessed from afar the day before.

The Spaniards' 'guns' had torn men limb from limb, smashed them, crushed them, turned them inside out. Those grim glittering spheres launched from the top of the pyramid had cut long lanes of carnage through the Mayan ranks – here ten, twenty, even thirty warriors in a row had been mowed down; then there was a gap where the ball had bounced into the air, then another lane of demolished corpses, all rotting already in the hot afternoon sun. Closer to where the Spanish squares had stood there were countless sword and axe and spear wounds. And everywhere there were men who'd been ripped to bloody ribbons, their guts dragged out of their bellies in stinking, slimy, flyblown piles, by the Spanish war animals. Some species of dog, Cit Bolon Tun had hazarded? Some species of demon or dragon more like, Malinal thought, judging from the dreadful butchery of the wounds.

And what of the animals, like deer, called 'horses'? The huge beasts on which Malinal had seen the Spanish war leader and his troop thunder past the foot of the Xaman hills on their way to battle? The hoofprints of these creatures were everywhere, in the churned-up soil and imprinted on the bodies and faces of fallen men, and where they had charged into the thickest press of the Mayan ranks, crowds of corpses lay hunched and heaped one upon the other, as many killed as they'd fled in blind panic as had been struck down by the weapons of the Spaniards.

The trail of bodies led all the way into Potonchan, through the narrow streets and up towards the plaza, where the ancient pyramid overlooked the sacred silk-cotton tree. Long before this, the Mayan delegation had been shadowed and flanked by Spanish scouts, hard-faced, bearded, pale-eyed men wearing metal armour, carrying metal swords and spears – some of the terrifying 'guns', too, Malinal noted – but Muluc had shown by signs that his intentions were peaceful and the caravan had been allowed to proceed.

Now at last, in the mid-afternoon, they came into the square and, up ahead, in the shade of the silk-cotton tree, seated regally on a throne, looking relaxed, confident, handsome – gods he was handsome! – the Spanish leader awaited them. Malinal recognised him at once and felt again the special connection she'd felt with him yesterday as she'd watched him ride into battle. The way he had turned his bearded white face towards her then, the way his eyes had seemed to fix on her and root her to the spot, had filled her with hope and a strange yearning, and she now had a sense, as she'd had so often in the past month, that she was swept up in some divine scheme and that her fate was about to be fulfilled.

But how to talk to him? This was the problem. How to communicate to him her special purpose? How to let him know that she was the one who had been chosen by the gods, and spared from death, to bring him to Tenochtitlan and end forever the cruel and gluttonous reign of Moctezuma?

Strangely – a blow to Malinal's conviction that a divine plan was about to unfold – this man, if he was a man, or god if he was a god, this Cortés, did not even acknowledge her existence as she stood roasting in the sun with the other twenty women, amongst the bearers of the treasures and jaguar skins and textiles, while Muluc alone entered the shade of the silk-cotton tree. Through the intermediary of the black-bearded interpreter Aguilar, whom Cit Bolon Tun had spoken of, and who sat on a stool at Cortés's right hand, a long conversation then ensued. Very long. Malinal was only able to grasp snatches of what was said, as her hated stepfather was made to grovel and squirm. At one point another Spaniard even more beautiful than Cortés himself, a man who it seemed was called Alvarado, but who resembled the sun brought down to earth with his yellow beard and hair, stepped forward and beat Muluc about the buttocks with the flat of his huge metal sword.

All this was very enjoyable and diverting, but it still brought Malinal no closer to Cortés, the avatar, she yet had reason to hope, of the god Quetzalcoatl, whom she had travelled all this way and risked so many dangers to see.

The solution, of course, was the interpreter Aguilar. Malinal must simply speak to him in the Mayan language, which he appeared to have complete mastery of, tell him of her mission, and he would immediately translate what she had said into the language of the Spaniards and Cortés would understand.

She leapt forward. A Spanish guard got in her way but she bowled him aside, swords were drawn all around her – *swish, swish, swish*

– and she found herself on her knees at the very feet of Cortés, strong hands holding her, forcing her head down.

'How *dare* you, woman?' Muluc shrieked, reaching out to strike her, but his hand was kicked aside by the Spaniard Alvarado, who stood over him, hand on the hilt of his sword, his pale eyes glittering, saying incomprehensible words in his strange language. 'You're to leave her alone, Muluc,' snapped the translator Aguilar. 'Back off! My masters want to hear her.'

Snarling and snapping, Muluc backed away.

'What's your name?' said Aguilar in faultless Mayan.

'Who, me?' asked Malinal.

'Yes, you. Who else?'

'I am Malinal.'

'Very well, Malinal, state your business here.'

'I must speak with the Lord Cortés,' she said. 'I have been seeking him out these last thirty days. I have walked all the way from Tenochtitlan to find him. I . . . we . . . my friend and I, we believe he is the Lord Quetzalcoatl, returned to claim his kingdom. I have come to guide him to his home.'

'His home? His home is in Spain.'

'No, lord. We believe him to be the human manifestation of the great god Quetzalcoatl, whose rightful home is Tenochtitlan, capital city of the Mexica. I am here to guide him thither. I am here to help him to overthrow the usurper Moctezuma and claim back his throne.'

'Nonsense, woman. You are talking complete and utter nonsense!'

'I have heard,' Malinal said, desperate now for anything that would sway this dog-faced translator on whose good graces she depended utterly to speak to Cortés, 'that you Spaniards have a great need for gold. Well, you will find precious little here amongst my people the Maya, for whom gold holds no meaning. If you want gold, whole rooms full of gold, a city of gold, then only allow me to lead you to Tenochtitlan and I will place in your hands all the gold you want. Please, I beg you, Lord Aguilar, convey what I have said to the Lord Cortés.'

Aguilar seemed to think about it. A muscle twitched in his bearded cheek. His upper teeth appeared and nibbled his lower lip. 'Do you,' he asked, 'speak the language of the Mexica?'

'I speak it fluently,' Malinal replied, 'like my mother tongue. And through me, and through you, Lord Aguilar, the Lord Cortés also may speak to the Mexica, and convey to them his commands. You will put what he says into the Mayan tongue and I will put it into the language of the Mexica. I will put what they say in reply into the Mayan tongue and you will put my words into Spanish. It is a good plan, is it not?'

'No,' said Aguilar cruelly, 'it's a terrible plan, it's a stupid plan and I'll have nothing to do with it.' Abruptly he turned to Cortés and spoke to him at length in Spanish, and the next moment guards took rough hold of Malinal and dragged her out into the sun again, and threw her down, sprawling amongst the other women, while from the shade of the silk-cotton tree Muluc leered at her in triumph.

What followed was, if anything, worse. Despite the connection she felt certain they enjoyed, that special connection that had drawn him to her and her to him as he rode into battle, the Lord Cortés continued to ignore Malinal – completely, as though she did not even exist – for the rest of the afternoon.

His primary interest was the treasure, and truly he did not even seem greatly interested in that. The bales of embroidered cloth and jaguar skins meant nothing to him. He looked at them as though they were excrement.

Only the three wooden chests attracted his attention, and when they were opened he rifled through their contents before giving a great sigh and turning away in disgust. Behind him followed the Spaniard Alvarado who, if anything, seemed even more angered and frustrated by Muluc's gifts.

That was when the pair of them noticed the women again. They walked over, fingered the girls, squeezed their breasts, slapped a buttock here or there, all the while speaking to one another harshly and cruelly in their mysterious foreign tongue. Then other Spaniards gathered round, lean men, hungry men, who looked on the women as vultures might look on carrion, and there was much laughter and nudging and lewd gestures, all of them perfectly comprehensible to Malinal.

This was about sex now, that eternal obsession of men.

Finally the women were divided up, this one to that man, this one to another. Cortés still showed not the slightest interest in Malinal and gave her finally to a vulgar beast with a bushy red beard.

She learned soon enough that his name was Alonso Hernández Puertocarrero.

Melchior had died during the night, as Cortés had known he must the moment he'd seen his injuries, and was buried just hours later on the morning of Friday 26 March. Four good Spaniards who'd also lost their lives on the plains of Potonchan were buried alongside him in a moving ceremony, at which Cortés gave a reading, attended by all who were fit to walk. The death toll was small, all things considered, but more than a hundred of the men had been wounded in Thursday's great battle, a few so severely that even the best efforts of Dr La Peña would not save them. Still, there was much to be thankful for, Cortés decided. He'd faced down and defeated a giant army while his own small force was still almost entirely intact.

That same afternoon of Friday 26th, a delegation of Indians appeared, led by the creature Muluc, whom Cortés now knew to be the chief of Potonchan – though he'd pretended otherwise. He came bearing the seal of Ah Kinchil, the paramount chief of all the Chontal Maya, to offer a complete, abject and unconditional surrender, which Cortés was happy to accept. His men had taken a hammering over the past few days and badly needed time to rest and recuperate.

As a token of the peace, Muluc brought twenty fine, clean women to serve the Spaniards as slaves or, he said with a lewd grimace, 'for any other purpose you wish'. Amongst them, Cortés noted, was the same striking, graceful beauty whom he'd seen the previous afternoon, watching the battle from the hills south of Potonchan. He'd been strongly drawn to her then, her magnetism reaching out to him as he'd thundered by on Molinero, and he felt her spell again now, but resisted it even when she rather dramatically threw herself at his feet and yammered away at Aguilar in her exotic tongue for some minutes.

She was, the interpreter assured him, completely mad. It seemed she was convinced he was some pagan god! In Aguilar's opinion she was best ignored if he did not want trouble. Cortés was tempted to take the matter further, but ultimately decided against it. With rebellion brewing amongst the Velazquistas it was important to keep his friends sweet, and a sex slave as decorative as this was an easy way to satisfy Puertocarrero, who loved women at least as much as he loved gold.

On the matter of gold, the peace offerings presented by Muluc were less satisfactory. Other than the heaped skins of some unknown animals, and two hundred bundles of embroidered textiles, costly but inferior to silk, he brought only three chests, admittedly large, packed in the main with little statues, face masks, pectorals, belts, ear and lip decorations, ornamental weapons, plates and serving vessels, all made of the curious, somewhat translucent green stone that had been offered before at the riverside in Potonchan. There were in addition a good number of pearls, various gemstones resembling rubies, cornelians, emeralds, agates, topazes and the like, but pitifully little gold – four diadems, some ornaments shaped like lizards, two shaped like fish with finely worked individual scales, five resembling ducks, a handful of earrings and necklaces, two gold soles for sandals and a few items of silver, pretty to look at but of small value. Alvarado thought the gold, silver, pearls and gems worth less than fifteen thousand pesos, a sum – he declared with a sour face – that was by no means worth the battle fought to obtain it. He suggested they put Muluc to torture and burn the town of Cintla where Ah Kinchil had his seat. 'It's the only way we're going to part these swine from their treasure.'

But Aguilar disagreed. 'The Maya don't share our idea of treasure,' he said. 'They place little value on gold.' He pulled a carved green stone from the chest. It was similar to the piece, shaped like an axe head, that Alvarado had thrown in the river some days before. 'This is the stuff that matters to them. 'They call it *ik'*, and they regard it as precious beyond any jewel or metal. It speaks to them of breath, fertility, the maize crop, vitality. It's their ultimate symbol of wealth.'

'Looks like shit to me,' said Alvarado. 'Let's burn some towns. They'll show us their gold soon enough.'

When questioned, Muluc protested that the chest contained all the gold of Cintla and Potonchan. There was no more to be had in either place, and while other towns and villages in the region might be able to offer some pieces, they would be of poor quality and the quantity would not be great.

'We'll see about that,' Alvarado growled.

Muluc then launched into a lengthy account of another people, a people called the Mexica who were ruled by a great emperor named Moctezuma and whose capital city, Tenochtitlan, stood on an island in a lake at the heart of an immense green valley hundreds of miles to the northwest, protected by ranges of huge, snow-capped mountains.

Cortés was at once entranced; he sat forward, listening intently as evening drew in and the first stars appeared in the darkening sky.

Mexica traders, Muluc continued, frequently visited the Maya, and some of the Maya had made the journey to Tenochtitlan. Indeed Muluc claimed to have made a visit to it himself. It was, he said, a city of fabulous wealth and power. If the Spanish wanted gold, that was where they should go, for its temples and treasuries were stuffed with gold and every other precious item they desired. Indeed, all the gold ornaments he had brought as gifts today had been acquired by the Maya – who had no gold mines of their own – through trade with the Mexica.

'He's lying,' said Alvarado, 'just trying to send us on a wild goose chase to get us away from here.'

But when the Mayan delegation had been dismissed to return to Cintla, and the Spaniards sat down to their supper, some taking to their beds soon after to enjoy the women they'd been given, Aguilar confirmed Muluc's story to be essentially true. Even the distant part of the Yucatán where he had been held as a slave was occasionally visited by Mexica merchants. It was generally understood that the far-off land from which they came was enormously rich and that their emperor, Moctezuma, ruled over huge territories populated by millions and commanded a vast army.

Tozi was filled with trepidation as she entered Guatemoc's bedchamber in Chapultepec for the third and final night – her last chance on this present mission to make the prince 'our man'. She wasn't sure exactly what Huicton had meant by that strange phrase, but she was determined to achieve something, to make some breakthrough before returning to Tenochtitlan tomorrow to resume her haunting and torture of Moctezuma.

As she stood watching Guatemoc in the moonlight, his eyes closed, his chest rising and falling evenly with his breathing, looking so much stronger than he had on the two previous nights, indeed positively *glowing* with health and vitality, it occurred to her that she had perhaps already achieved much. She had, after all, given the prince healing and freed him from the pain of his wounds and won his trust, and these gains might surely be bartered to some valuable advantage when the right time came.

She moved silently to the bedside and faded into visibility, watching Guatemoc uncertainly for a moment longer before waking him. His attempt last night to kiss her had taken her by surprise but had not, she had to admit, been entirely unwelcome. He was a stunningly handsome man, even *beautiful* in his way, and she was flattered that so powerful and important a personage should be attracted to her at all.

Although, of course, she had to remind herself, it was not her, Tozi, he was attracted to, but her in her guise as the Lady Temaz, goddess of healing and medicines – a completely different matter. A prince who might abase himself and do foolish things to win the attentions of a goddess would not even spare a glance at a little beggar girl!

Feeling a burst of annoyance and indignation, she reached out her hand and touched his muscular naked shoulder.

'Hello, sweet goddess,' he said immediately. 'I was waiting for your visit.' He opened his eyes and in a single graceful movement sat up, swung his bare feet over the side of the bed and arranged the sheet – just so – to cover his manly parts.

Ha! So he hadn't been asleep after all. Just pretending. He was tricky, Tozi realised. She would have to be careful. 'You must not,' she said, 'attempt to kiss me again.'

'Or you'll turn me to stone?'

Was he mocking her?

'Not I, Prince, but the universe itself will punish you if you transgress the sanctity of the gods. Now lie down again, please. Let me complete the work of healing.'

'No,' he said. 'Not yet. I want to talk first.'

'We can talk as I work.'

'Oh, very well,' he grumbled. 'I can hardly object.'

He lay on his back. He wore no bandages tonight. His wounds were clean and dry with no sign of infection. As she ran her fingers over the jagged scars for the last time he asked: 'Why are you doing this for me?'

'A great battle is coming,' she said. 'The world as you know it will cease to exist and a new world will arise to take its place. You are a powerful figure amongst your people, Prince Guatemoc, an important figure, one to whom many look up. It will be good if you are on the right side.'

'Strange that,' said Guatemoc. He paused: 'Shikotenka of Tlascala gave me these wounds.' He moved his hand down to touch her fingers where they rested on the series of great puncture marks across his belly. 'Afterwards, as I lay dying on a hillside, the war god Hummingbird appeared to me and he too told me that a great battle is coming.'

Tozi's mind was in turmoil. Hummingbird, who had reprieved her from death on the sacrificial stone and touched her with his fire! And Shikotenka of Tlascala, the very man with whom Huicton had been sent to negotiate an alliance! Both brought together in this single utterance of Guatemoc's! It could hardly be chance.

'I suppose,' Guatemoc said, 'it is your privilege, Lady Temaz, to see the face of Hummingbird every day in the council of the gods?'

'I have seen him,' said Tozi, 'and I do not like him. He is a cruel god with a lust for suffering . . .'

'Whereas your work is healing?'

'I heal the wounds that war makes—'

Guatemoc seemed to ignore her. 'Hummingbird told me,' he continued, 'that Moctezuma is a weakling, not competent to fight the battle that confronts us.'

'That is true,' Tozi agreed.

'And he told me – I think he told me – he had brought me back from the dead to fight that battle in Moctezuma's place.'

Tozi's mind was racing. 'It was I, not Hummingbird, who brought you back from the dead,' she exclaimed, 'and I am here to tell you another thing . . .'

The prince looked at her expectantly.

'The god of peace is coming,' Tozi continued, 'the god Quetzalcoatl, the Feathered Serpent. It is with him and his retinue of gods that Moctezuma will very soon find himself at war, and Moctezuma will lose that fight and be cast away forever. You must not, Guatemoc, *you must not* place yourself in opposition to Quetzalcoatl! You must be on the right side. You must be on the side of peace.'

'Peace?' The prince seemed genuinely puzzled. 'Peace? I am a warrior, my lady. I can never be on the side of peace. Besides,' a sly look crossed his handsome face, 'what sort of god of peace would fight a war in the first place? Surely if he wishes to rid the world of Moctezuma he will find a way to do that by peaceful means?'

Tozi thought about it. It made sense! But it would never work. 'Moctezuma is evil,' she said, 'and sometimes evil overwhelms good, and when it does it can't just be wished away peacefully. It has to be fought and it has to be stopped, and that's what Quetzalcoatl is returning to do.'

'So Quetzalcoatl, then, is a god of war, just like Hummingbird?'

'No . . . Yes!'

'Which is it to be, my lady? Is this Quetzalcoatl of yours a god of peace? Or is he a god of war?' The prince laughed. 'He can't be both!'

'Then he is a god of war! But his war is against Hummingbird himself, the wicked ruler and authority of the unseen world, who contaminates and pollutes everything he touches with evil and darkness, whose puppet Moctezuma is, just as the physician Mecatl was Moctezuma's puppet in the plot to poison you . . . So the question you must ask yourself, Guatemoc, is this – will you, too, be Hummingbird's puppet in the great conflict that is to come, or will you fight on the side of the good and the light?'

Guatemoc's lean, handsome face was serious. 'Lady Temaz,' he said, 'if you are asking me to fight against Moctezuma then I will tell you now I am ready to do so! He is a weakling and a fool and he sought to murder me! But if you are asking me to fight against Hummingbird, my lady – well, that is quite another matter and by no means so easily done.'

'The time will come, Prince, when you will have to choose,' Tozi said. 'I can only hope you choose wisely.' She pressed her fingers one more time against the wounds that scarred his lean, naked belly, sending healing warmth into his body. 'I will see you again,' she said, straightening, relinquishing the contact, 'but now I must return to Aztlán.'

Quick as a striking snake, Guatemoc sat up on the bed and threw one arm around Tozi's waist and another around her neck. 'Not so fast, Lady Temaz,' he said. 'I still want my kiss.'

'Well you shall not have it, foolish boy! I am a goddess and you a mere man. Do you wish to be turned to stone?'

'I'll take that risk,' said Guatemoc, and pulled her face down to his, crushing his lips against hers. Her mouth was open, perhaps with shock, perhaps something else. She felt his tongue enter, pass the barrier of her teeth, and – *what was this?* – her own tongue responded! For an instant she was lost in a delicious, roiling, wet warmth, tasting this man, smelling this man, melting into him, and then she remembered herself and focussed her intent and *whoosh*, with a whisper of reluctance she dissolved into smoke and vanished and left him embracing empty air . . .

In the few seconds she remained invisible in the room with him, she saw him look with astonishment at his hands, at his arms, and press his fingers to his lips.

'Well at least,' he said finally, 'she didn't turn me to stone.'

Guatemoc stood by the open window of his bedchamber in the dawn light, listening to the chorus of morning birds amongst the trees of his father's estate.

What just happened? he thought. *Who is she? A goddess, as she claims? Or something else?*

He touched his lips again, glowing, alive, tingling with sensation. But when he brought his fingers away he saw they were smeared with red.

He frowned. What was this? Blood? He tasted his lips with his tongue. No! Not blood! Something else. Something familiar.

He found an obsidian mirror and examined himself. This red stuff, whatever it might be, was not confined to his lips but smeared all round his mouth. He tasted it again and suddenly he had it. Tincture of cochineal! Rare and exotic, yes, but quite definitely a woman's makeup.

What would a goddess need with makeup?

As the sun rose on a new day he pondered this question, but could come to no definite conclusion.

As the sun rose on the new day, Huicton was ushered into Shikotenka's presence.

The battle king of Tlascala, he was pleasantly surprised to discover, had no pretensions whatsoever. Rather than insist on meeting him in some overblown audience chamber in the royal palace, he'd invited him to his home where his beautiful young wife Zilonen, doe eyes, high cheekbones, bee-stung lips, silky dark hair hanging to her waist, pert bottom, perfect hips, was personally cooking breakfast. 'Your eyes are clouded, father Huicton,' she said, noticing his scrutiny, 'but I think you see everything.'

So . . . not only stunning to behold but clever, feisty and direct as well!

'I see,' he replied, 'everything I need to.'

Shikotenka entered the room. He wore only a colourful length of cloth wrapped around his waist that covered his legs to just below his knees. His black hair hung in knotted braids around his broad shoulders. His eyes were shrewd and intelligent, weighing his guest up. He was not handsome in the way his wife was beautiful, but there was a roguish forthrightness and charm about him, and his hard, muscular body was inscribed with the pictographs of a hundred old scars – all to the front, Huicton noticed, none at all on his back. Deduction: this was a man who stood and fought. This was a man who did not run away.

'Good morning, Ambassador Huicton,' said Shikotenka. 'To what do we owe this honour?'

Huicton decided to be honest. 'To your remarkable success in your recent battles with the Mexica, Lord Shikotenka. Your destruction of the great field army of Coaxoch has attracted the attention of my master Ishtlil of Texcoco. He would like, if you are willing, to propose an alliance between your people and his.'

'You say "his", not "ours". Can I take it you are not a Texcocan yourself then?'

'I am Mexica.'

'Yet you work for Ishtlil against the interests of your own people?'

'As I worked for his father Neza before him. I do not see myself as Mexica, or Texcocan, but as a citizen of the one world, and in that capacity I strive honestly, I strive truly, I strive with all my heart, for balance. For a generation now, the power of the Mexica has been too great. It has introduced distortions into the one world. It has created a nation of cruel and arrogant bullies in Tenochtitlan. I have done my best, played my part such as the gods allow, to restore that balance.'

'And this is why you now seek an alliance with Tlascala?'

'My master Ishtlil seeks that alliance. I am merely his messenger.'

Zilonen had laid out a stack of maize cakes on the table and a bowl of richly spiced venison in which green chillies floated. There were goblets of foaming chocolate and plates of succulent fruit. 'Sit down,' she said, 'break your fast. No good business gets done on an empty stomach.'

Huicton licked his lips. 'Very true, my lady.' He took his place at the table, broke off a handful of bread and gathered up an ample mouthful of stew. 'Ah, excellent,' he commented as he chewed, smacking his lips. 'Truly excellent.'

'So this alliance,' Shikotenka asked, 'what's the purpose of it?'

'Why, to defeat Moctezuma, of course, once and for all. Even for his most loyal, arselicking vassals,' an apologetic glance at Zilonen, 'his endless demands for human sacrifices have become too burdensome for any reasonable person to stand. And you in Tlascala, who have never submitted to vassaldom, have borne the cruellest burden in the incessant wars and raids of the Mexica – until, that is, you smashed Coaxoch's army.' Huicton helped himself to another dripping mouthful of stew. 'That, I can tell you – *that* gave Moctezuma something to think about!'

'So much to think about,' Shikotenka said, 'that our Senate does not believe we'll be troubled by him again for many a long year. Which raises the question – if we've got Moctezuma off our backs, why do we need a pact with Ishtlil? As you know, Huicton, we in Tlascala go our own independent way. We've never been very keen on alliances.'

Huicton chewed in silence for a moment. He would not speak of Tozi and her prophetic utterances. He could hardly expect a pragmatist like Shikotenka to believe any of that. But he didn't see now how he

525

could avoid the subject of Quetzalcoatl. It was impossible to understand Moctezuma's motivations, and his insatiable quest for ever more sacrificial victims, without taking the legends of the plumed serpent and his return in a One-Reed year – this very year! – into account.

'I'm afraid, Shikotenka, it is not so simple. Not nearly so simple. And I much regret to inform you that your victory over Coaxoch will not be an end to the matter "for many a long year", as your Senate naively imagines. There is another factor at work, one you may not even be aware of, but I have reason to believe that because of it you and your people will face more – not fewer – attacks from the Mexica in the months ahead, and the same will unfortunately be true for Ishtlil's people and for many others. So, contrary to your commendably proud and independent stance, the truth is there has never been a time when an alliance would be more expedient or more worthwhile for Tlascala than it is today . . .'

Shikotenka took a long draught of chocolate and wiped his mouth. 'Very well, old man, I'm here to listen.'

Huicton dipped another handful of bread into the stewpot and transferred it to his mouth, smacking his lips with satisfaction. 'It's a long story,' he said, 'and I'm an old man, as you rightly say, and much given to prolixity, so please bear with me while I tell it . . .'

Melchior had been buried with full honours alongside the four Spaniards also killed in Thursday's fighting. The graves lay in a shady corner of the orchard behind the palace, the same orchard where the horses had been exercised before the battle, and on the morning of Saturday 27 March Pepillo returned there carrying the little dagger Cortés had given him. He knelt, whispered, 'I miss you, Melchior,' and then very carefully carved four words onto the wooden cross that bore his friend's name. The words were:

RIDE IN GREEN PASTURES

'A fitting epitaph,' said a gruff voice behind him, and Pepillo turned to see Bernal Díaz standing there leaning on a stick. The ensign's thigh looked less swollen than before and the bandages around his chest were clean. He was holding a hessian sack with some object inside it.

Pepillo, who'd been crying again, sheathed the knife and rubbed the back of his hand across his eyes. 'Don Bernal. I'm happy to see you on your feet.'

'Dr La Peña has done well by me,' Díaz replied with a smile. 'He tells me I'll be fit for battle in no time.'

Pepillo shuddered. 'I hope there'll be no more fighting!'

'I'm afraid there will be, lad, it's what we're here to do . . . Now, look . . .' Something moved in the sack he was holding and he glanced down at it. 'There's a kindness you could do for a poor orphaned creature . . . If you're willing.'

'A kindness, sir? I don't understand.'

'It concerns the war dogs.' Another wriggle of the sack. 'Amongst them when we sailed from Santiago was a pregnant wolfhound bitch. She gave birth to a litter of six pups on the voyage and was nursing them, but Vendabal dragged her away from them on Thursday and put her into the pack for battle. She was one of his best fighters, so he said, but she was killed. The pups are barely weeks old, too much trouble to feed by hand, so Vendabal and his handlers destroyed them all . . .'

Pepillo's face fell.

'. . . Except this one, which I managed to save. I was thinking you might have time to rear him. Goat's milk, I'm told, is a good substitute to feed an orphaned pup when its dam is lost. And, well, we have plenty of goats on the hoof with us. A veritable farm! I should know, since I requisitioned them from Santiago's slaughterhouse the night we sailed! Here, take a look.'

And with that the ensign hobbled forward, reached into the sack and lifted out by the scruff of its neck a surprisingly large, furry, brindled puppy, which opened its toothless jaws in a yawn and licked him with its pink tongue. 'Here, lad, he's yours if you want him,' Díaz said, passing the animal over. 'He's not a purebred wolfhound. From the look of him Vendabal says he was likely sired by a greyhound.'

Pepillo cradled the puppy. It was quite heavy, as long as his forearm and wonderfully warm. He could feel its heartbeat. It gave another yawn and a small contented whimper.

'Well?' asked Díaz. 'Will you keep him?'

'Oh yes, sir!'

'And what will you call him?'

Pepillo already knew the answer to that question. 'Melchior,' he said fiercely. He stroked the soft hair of the puppy's head. 'His name is Melchior.'

Sunday 28 March was not a day of rest for Cortés. After an early mass he left Potonchan two hours before dawn with two hundred men, proceeded at a forced march and reached Cintla by sunrise to pay a surprise visit to Ah Kinchil. Both the paramount chief and Muluc were detained under armed guard and the royal palace was ransacked. Other than a few small items of little value, however, no gold was found.

It was the same story in every other town and village searched during the days that followed – lean pickings or nothing at all. Gradually, after Cortés had given Alvarado a free hand to use torture (Muluc had been blinded in one eye with a hot iron, and Ah Kinchil had died, foaming at the mouth on an improvised rack), it became clear, even to Alvarado, that the Maya must either be extremely brave, stubborn and good at hiding their treasure, or – more likely – they were telling the truth and had none. This, anyway, was what Aguilar, who grew increasingly distressed at his role as interpreter during the interrogations, had been saying all along. The Maya were, in his view, a fallen people, whose once great and prosperous kingdoms had lapsed into obscurity, poverty and barbarism hundreds of years before. Nothing now remained of their former glory, except the mighty pyramids and temples, many already in ruins, they had inherited from their ancestors.

With the Velázquez faction complaining bitterly that the whole story of the rival Pedrarias expedition had been a trick to procure a hasty departure from Santiago, and demanding to know why they were wasting their time in this godforsaken, gold-bereft land, Cortés began to feel the lure of the fabled, indeed almost legendary, empire of the Mexica ever more strongly. Why, it was rumoured to possess so much gold that even its children's toys were made of the precious metal! Moreover, although the mysterious city of Tenochtitlan, standing in its lake beyond snow-capped mountains, was always spoken of as far away, repeated questioning of traders made it clear that it could in fact be reached by forced march within as little as thirty days.

And there was something much more important, much more significant, much more *meaningful* to be considered.

From the moment under the silk-cotton tree when Muluc had first spoken of it, Cortés had known it was Tenochtitlan that Saint Peter had revealed to him in his dreams. The mountains wreathed in snow that must be crossed to reach it, and its distinctive location in the midst of a great lake at the heart of an immense green valley, left no room for doubt. This was the jewelled and shining city that was to be his reward.

Even while Alvarado rampaged far and wide across the lands of the Chontal Maya in the fruitless quest for gold, therefore, Cortés sent his friend Juan de Escalante out in his carrack to conduct reconnaissance. Although Tenochtitlan lay deep inland, it was said to possess certain vassal states and tributary towns along the coast – one of which, Cuetlaxtlan, had been settled by the Mexica and was ruled by a governor who, the Maya said, had been appointed directly by the great Emperor Moctezuma himself. Several Potonchan merchants knew Cuetlaxtlan well and Escalante took two of these with him, who claimed they would be able to identify the town from the sea.

While he was gone, Cortés redoubled efforts he had already begun to fulfil God's will by converting the Chontal Maya to Christianity. To this end, speaking through Aguilar, he preached several lengthy sermons to the assembled populations of Potonchan and Cintla, urging them to destroy their idols, which were not gods but evil things and images of Satan. From now on, he said, they must worship the Lord Jesus Christ and believe only in him. Soon afterwards, perhaps expedited by Alvarado's activities, which had spread great fear throughout the region, there was a general destruction of idols, with those of stone being rolled down pyramid steps and smashed while those of wood were heaped up into fires and burnt. Several hundred people, many leading nobles amongst them, also came forward for baptism at the hands of Father Olmedo, who conducted the ceremonies but nonetheless confided in Cortés that he did not think their conversion would last. 'We're moving too fast,' he said. 'They act out of fear of us, not because the faith has taken root in their hearts.'

'What then would you have me do, Father?'

'Teach them by example. Show them the meaning of Christian love.'

Cortés cast a glance at the crowd of converts. 'What we have achieved here will have to serve for the present, Olmedo. These New Lands are vast, time presses, and this is but the beginning of our conquests. Praise be to God, all things will prosper for us, and wherever we go we will spread the word.'

After a voyage of just eight days, Escalante returned. Although the Maya said twenty days were required to reach Cuetlaxtlan on foot, through the dense jungles of the Yucatán, the journey by sea proved much shorter. Escalante did not land, but observed the well-ordered streets and grand buildings of the Mexica town from the deck of his carrack, and judged it to be rich, far more prosperous than Potonchan and Cintla, and linked by good roads to several other equally impressive settlements further along the coast.

Cortés embraced his friend. 'Well done, Juan,' he said. 'This is welcome news!'

'So, shall we go there?' Escalante asked.

Cortés nodded. 'By God, yes! And from Cuetlaxtlan we march on those good roads you saw to the golden city of Tenochtitlan!'

Indeed the news had come just in time. During Escalante's absence, the Velazquistas never stopped bellyaching and spreading dissent and the men had grown mutinous with inaction, complaining that Cortés had brought them across the sea to fight battles with savages for no pay. Now, at last, he had a target to distract them and the gold of the Mexica to dangle before their eyes.

It was Thursday 15 April. 'We sail on Sunday,' Cortés said.

It would be Palm Sunday. An auspicious day.

Puertocarrero rolled over in his sleep, flung out a hairy leg, mumbled incoherently and let rip another colossal fart, filling the bedroom that Malinal was obliged to share with him in the palace at Potonchan with a hideous, miasmic stink. When she'd first been given to him, part of her had still been open to the possibility that he and his fellow Spaniards might be gods, but she'd since learned better. Indeed, even if it were not for Puertocarrero's uncouth manners and his constant demands for sex, she would have known from the smell of his farts alone that he was a man, as they all were, with every weakness, folly and stupidity to which the male sex was prone. To be sure, they looked very different from the Maya or the Mexica, and their language – which Malinal had already begun to learn – was quite unlike any other she had ever heard. Admittedly, also, their customs and behaviour were strange, they were unusually disciplined and determined, and their weapons and trained animals were extraordinary. Nevertheless, when all was said and done, they were men and nothing more than men and, as such, no matter how fearsome and alien they might seem, they could be understood, manipulated and managed.

All of them, that is, except their great war leader Hernán Cortés, who spent much of his time out of Potonchan, often in the company of his cruel but handsome second-in-command Pedro de Alvarado. Malinal soon learned – from servants Muluc had sent to work for them in the palace – that they were ransacking all the towns of the region for gold, which seemed to obsess them as much as it obsessed the Mexica. It was even said that Ah Kinchil and Muluc had been tortured to surrender stores of gold the white men believed they had hidden – but of course they had none to give. Malinal neither knew nor cared if these reports were true; the two chiefs had conspired to ruin her life and, in her opinion, deserved whatever bad things came to them.

When not hunting for gold, Cortés's other favourite activity – to which he showed great dedication – was destroying the idols of the gods in the temples and preaching to the people of Cintla and Potonchan about his own strange and incomprehensible religion. Since everyone was terrified of him, he won many converts.

On the occasions when he was not preoccupied with these activities, Malinal several times asked Aguilar's help to approach Cortés and speak to him. As he had done on the very first day, however, the Spanish interpreter continued to rebuff her.

This evening, for the first time, she'd understood why.

Cortés had made an announcement to the assembled army, which Aguilar had been required to translate for the benefit of all twenty of the female slaves who would be accompanying them, that the Spaniards had concluded their business with the Chontal Maya and would soon be moving on to the lands of the Mexica. They would go first by ship to the coastal town of Cuetlaxtlan – everyone must be ready to embark in just three days' time – and from there they would strike inland to Tenochtitlan, the Mexica capital. This they would seize by force, take its Emperor Moctezuma 'dead or alive', and help themselves to the vast hoard of gold his empire was reputed to have amassed.

Reputed? Malinal thought. *Reputed!* If she'd been allowed to talk to Cortés, she could have told him weeks before that it was not just a matter of 'reputed'. The Mexica were the richest people in the entire world, Tenochtitlan overflowed with gold and Moctezuma's treasuries were stuffed to bursting point with it.

Clearly Aguilar had acted so strangely because he knew Malinal was fluent in Nahuatl – which he spoke not a word of – and could see she was clever enough to learn Castilian and learn it quickly. The foolish man must fear, since it was inevitable that the Spaniards' lust for gold would sooner or later lead to the Mexica, that she would then usurp his privileged place at Cortés's side. While not actually lying to Cortés about the fabulous wealth of Tenochtitlan, the interpreter had therefore done all he could – notably by keeping Malinal away from him – to divert and delay this important intelligence and prevent him from discovering how indispensable she might prove to the Spanish cause.

Perhaps Aguilar had even hoped the slaves would be left behind when the Spaniards continued their journey, but this evening's announcement had put paid to that! There was no way Puertocarrero or any of the other officers who'd been given women were going to do without their all-purpose cooks, cleaners and bedroom companions, and Cortés had made a point of confirming they would accompany the army in its advance on Tenochtitlan.

So once again Malinal realised that she had been reunited with her fate. Very soon Cortés would meet the lords of the Mexica and find he was unable to talk to them. When he did, no matter how Aguilar might try to block her, she would be there to take her rightful place in history.

It was Palm Sunday, 18 April 1519, and Pepillo stood with Cortés and the pilot Alaminos on the navigation deck of the *Santa María de la Concepción* as the great flagship raised sail under scudding clouds and led the fleet north out of the bay at Potonchan.

It was exactly two months to the day, Pepillo realised, since he'd left Cuba on a night of storm to begin the journey that had brought him to this place and this time.

He remembered how he'd imagined the journey would be – a noble quest through faraway lands in the company of gallant warriors to achieve a sacred purpose. Yet in reality he'd taken part in the murder of a wicked friar, seen chivalry thrown to the winds in the lust for gold, and found a true friend only to have him snatched away again so cruelly he thought his heart must never mend.

That journey had ended at Potonchan. The quest had never been noble, chivalry was dust and Melchior lay cold and dead in the ground, but the slap of the waves against the keel, the whistle of the wind through the rigging, and the crack and whip of the sails spoke through Pepillo's sorrow to an adventure that had only just begun.

'Well, lad,' said Cortés. 'What do you think? This great Emperor Moctezuma we're going to see commands an army of two hundred thousand men. Can we beat them?'

Pepillo fondled the ears of his new Melchior. Part wolfhound part greyhound, the pup had thrived on goat's milk, was already eating flesh with his new sharp teeth and had grown beyond all recognition in the past three weeks. He was proving to be a fine companion – strong, brave, endlessly inquisitive and loyal – and Pepillo was determined he would never be put to war with the rest of the pack.

He was thinking about the question. Glimpses of the Cortés he'd met on the road to Santiago harbour could still be seen from time to time, but the caudillo had grown harsh and cruel since then, with sudden dark moods and dangerous rages. It was not always wise to speak the truth to him but rather to divine what he wished to hear and say that instead.

'Let there be two hundred thousand men, sir,' Pepillo answered finally, 'or twice that number. It makes no difference. You lead the army of God and even the greatest empire of these lands will not stand against it.'

For a moment Cortés seemed lost in thought. But then he nodded his head. 'I may have to deal with Moctezuma severely,' he said quietly, almost to himself, 'but when we do God's work I'm told there is no sin in it. Would you say that's true, Pepillo?'

'I'm certain it must be true, sir,' Pepillo replied. 'For if God is good then surely no evil can be done by those who serve him?'

It was the right thing to say.

Time Frame, Principal Settings and Cast of Characters

—◆—

Time Frame and Subject Matter

War God: Nights of the Witch unfolds in the two-month period between 18 February 1519 and 18 April 1519. The book deals with the opening events of the Spanish conquest of Mexico. Five hundred Spanish adventurers led by Hernando Cortés pit themselves against the might of the Mexica (Aztec) empire. The empire is ruled with an iron hand by the feared Moctezuma, who has two hundred thousand brutal and experienced warriors at his command.

Principal settings

(1) **Tenochtitlan**, capital city of the **Mexica** (Aztec) empire of ancient Mexico, 1325 to 1521. Built on an island in the middle of a huge salt lake (Lake Texcoco) in the Valley of Mexico. The Valley of Mexico is ringed by distant snow-capped mountains. At the heart of the valley is Lake Texcoco. At the heart of Lake Texcoco is the island on which Tenochtitlan stands, accessed via three huge causeways (varying in length between two and six miles), extending to the southern, western and northern shores of the lake. At the heart of Tenochtitlan, surrounded by a vast walled enclosure (the grand plaza, or sacred precinct), is the Great Pyramid, which is surmounted by the temple of Huitzilopochtli ('Hummingbird'), War God of the Mexica, to whom tens of thousands of human sacrifices are offered every year.

(2) **Santiago**, capital city and principal port of **Cuba** during the early

period of Spanish colonisation of the New World. It is from here that the expedition to Mexico embarks.

(3) Mountain country within the borders of **Tlascala**, an independent principality at war with the Mexica. Tlascalans captured in raids and battles are a prime source of sacrificial victims for the Mexica.

(4) **Cozumel**, island off the northeast coast of the **Yucatán Peninsula**, Mexico. First landing point of the Spaniards in their conquest of Mexico.

(5) **Potonchan**, town on the southwest coast of the Yucatán Peninsula, Mexico. Second landing point of the Spaniards in their conquest of Mexico and site of their first major battles. Their opponents in these early (and brutal) pitched battles are not the Mexica but the Maya.

Point-of-View Characters

(1) **Tozi.** A witch. Age, fourteen. We meet her amongst the victims being fattened for sacrifice in the women's fattening pen at the edge of the grand plaza in Tenochtitlan. Tozi never knew her father. Her mother was a witch but was cornered and beaten to death by a mob when Tozi was seven, at which age Tozi's own training had just begun and her powers were not fully developed. She survived as a beggar on the streets of Tenochtitlan for the next six years until captured and placed in the fattening pen at the age of fourteen to await sacrifice. Tozi has certain magical talents, of which the most important is the ability to make herself invisible. However, at this point of the story she lacks skill and experience, and if she attempts to maintain invisibility for more than a few seconds she suffers catastrophic physical consequences. Tozi's origins are mysterious. Her mother told her they came from **Aztlán**, the fabled homeland not only of the Mexica but also of the Tlascalans and other related 'Nahua' peoples who speak the language called Nahuatl. But Aztlán is a mythical and legendary place, the home of the gods, where masters of wisdom and workers of magic are believed to dwell; although the Mexica say their forefathers came from Aztlán, no one knows where it is any more, or how to find it.

(2) **Malinal**. A beautiful courtesan and sex-slave of the Mexica. Age, twenty-one. Malinal is Maya in ethnic origin and is fluent both in Nahuatl, the language of the Mexica, and in the Mayan language. We

meet her in the fattening pen in Tenochtitlan where she, like Tozi, has been imprisoned awaiting sacrifice. How and why she is there becomes clear to the reader as the story develops. When we understand the roots of her intense hatred for Moctezuma and the Mexica, we understand why, when she escapes the fattening pen, she travels to the Yucatán, where Cortés has landed, intending to use him as her instrument to destroy Moctezuma.

(3) **Pepillo**. Spanish, fourteen years of age. An orphan, he was given shelter, reared and taught numbers and letters by Dominican monks, who brought him from Spain to the New World, first to the island of Hispaniola and then to Cuba, where he worked as a junior bookkeeper and clerk in the Dominican monastery. When we meet him he has just been appointed page and assistant to the mysterious **Father Gaspar Muñoz** (POV character number 8) the Dominican Inquisitor who will travel with the expedition of **Hernando Cortés** (POV character number 9) to Mexico – referred to as the 'New Lands' – on a mission of conquest and evangelism.

(4) **Moctezuma**. Emperor – his official title is **Great Speaker** – of the Mexica. Age, fifty-three. We meet him performing human sacrifices on the summit platform of the Great Pyramid in front of the temple of the War God Huitzilopochtli (Hummingbird). These sacrifices take place in full view of the fattening pen, at the edge of the grand plaza, where Malinal and Tozi are imprisoned awaiting sacrifice. Moctezuma frequently enters a trance state induced by the use of hallucinogenic mushrooms in which he communicates directly with the War God – demon – Hummingbird. The demon, whose purpose is to maximise human misery and chaos on earth, urges Moctezuma on to ever crueller and more brutal mass sacrifices.

(5) **Shikotenka**. Battle-king of Tlascala, sworn enemy of the Mexica. Age, thirty-three. We meet him concealed on a mountainside in Tlascala (two days' march away from Tenochtitlan), spying on a gigantic Mexica army gathering to attack his people. The army is there to capture thousands of Tlascalans as victims for human sacrifice. Shikotenka has a plan to stop them.

(6) **Guatemoc**. Prince of the Mexica. Age, twenty-seven. Nephew of Moctezuma (he is the son of Moctezuma's brother Cuitláhuac).

(7) **Pedro de Alvarado**. Age, thirty-three. Close friend and ally of **Hernando Cortés** (POV character number 9). Alvarado is handsome, excessively cruel – a charming psychopath. He is also a brilliant swordsman and a notorious lover of gold. When we meet Alvarado he is with **Diego de Velázquez**, the governor of Cuba, who is attempting to bribe him to betray Cortés. Velázquez wishes to remove Cortés from command of the expedition to Mexico and replace him with **Pánfilo de Narváez**, who is more amenable to his will. He seeks Alvarado's help in this scheme.

(8) **Father Gaspar Muñoz**. Age, late thirties. Dominican friar who has been appointed (by Diego de Velázquez) as Inquisitor on the expedition to Mexico. Munoz has a reputation for burning 'heretics' to death on the slightest pretext. He is also a sadistic paedophile and serial killer and exploits his position as Inquisitor to indulge his perverse appetites.

(9) **Hernando (Hernán) Cortés**. Commander of the Spanish expedition to Mexico. Age, thirty-five. A brilliant military commander and political operator, he is clever, Machiavellian, manipulative, utterly ruthless, vengeful and daring, but with a paradoxical streak of messianic Christianity. He hates Diego de Velázquez, the governor of Cuba, whom he has conned into giving him command of the expedition and whom he intends to betray. Some years earlier, Velázquez imprisoned Cortés on trumped-up charges to oblige him to marry his niece Catalina. Cortés went through with the marriage to escape prison, but has been plotting his revenge on Velázquez ever since.

(10) **Bernal Díaz**. Age, twenty-seven. Down-to-earth, honest, experienced Spanish soldier on the expedition to Mexico. From farming stock, no pretensions to nobility, but literate and keeps a diary (even though he self-deprecatingly refers to himself as an illiterate idiot). Admires Cortés, who has recognised his potential and promoted him to ensign rank.

(11) **Gonzalo de Sandoval**. Age twenty-two. From *Hidalgo* (minor nobility) family but fallen on hard times. New recruit to the expedition to Mexico. Promoted to ensign in same ceremony as Díaz. Unlike Díaz, Sandoval has a university education and military and cavalry training but no personal experience of war.

Supernatural characters

Huitzilopochtli (referred to throughout the novel as Hummingbird), war god of the Mexica. The full translation of the name Huitzilopochtli is 'The Hummingbird at the Left Hand of the Sun'. Like all demons, through all the myths and legends of mankind, the purpose of this entity is to multiply human suffering and corrupt all that is good and pure and true in the human spirit. He appears to **Moctezuma** when the Mexica emperor is in trance states induced by his frequent consumption of hallucinogenic mushrooms. A tempter and a manipulator, Hummingbird deliberately stokes the flames of the conflict between the Mexica and the Spaniards, and ultimately backs the Spaniards because he knows they will make life in Mexico even worse than it has been under the Mexica. It is a historical fact that within fifty years of the Spanish conquest, the indigenous population of Mexico had been reduced through war, famine and introduced diseases from thirty million to just one million.

Saint Peter, patron saint of Hernán Cortés. As a child, Cortés suffered an episode of severe fever that brought him close to death. His nurse, María de Esteban, prayed to Saint Peter for his salvation and the young Cortés miraculously recovered. Ever afterwards, Cortés felt he enjoyed a special relationship with this saint and believed he was guided by him in all the great and terrible episodes of his adult life. Like Moctezuma, Cortés encounters Saint Peter in visionary states – in his case, dreams.

Quetzalcoatl, 'The Plumed Serpent', the god of peace of ancient Central America. Described as white-skinned and bearded, an age-old prophecy said he had been expelled from Mexico by the forces of evil at some time in remote prehistory, but that he would return in the year *1-Acatl* ('One-Reed'), in ships that 'moved by themselves without paddles' to overthrow a wicked king, abolish the bloody rituals of human sacrifice and restore justice. And as it happened, the year 1519 in our calendar, when Cortés landed in the Yucatán in sailing ships that 'moved by themselves without paddles', was indeed the year One-Reed in the Mexica calendar. Whether this was pure chance or whether some inscrutable design might have been at work, **Malinal** would eventually teach **Cortés** how to exploit the myth of Quetzalcoatl. What followed was a ruthless and spectacularly successful campaign to dominate Moctezuma psychologically long before the Spaniards faced him in battle.

Whether in some mysterious sense real, as I rather suspect, or whether only imagined by Moctezuma and Cortés, Hummingbird and Saint Peter played pivotal roles as agents of mischief in the events of the conquest, while the prophecy of the return of Quetzalcoatl was equally fundamental.

Secondary Spanish characters who appear frequently in the story

Melchior. An African, aged about sixteen. Formerly a slave. Freed by Hernán Cortés and now his manservant. Becomes Pepillo's close friend and ally.

Diego de Velázquez. Age, fifty-five. Governor of Cuba. Appoints Hernán Cortés to be captain-general of the expedition to Mexico (which he has jointly financed), but has a change of heart and plots to remove Cortés before the fleet departs from Santiago and to replace him with Pánfilo de Narváez, a man he can manipulate more easily.

Zemudio. Expert swordsman and bodyguard to Diego de Velázquez.

García Brabo. Age, forty. Tough sergeant who leads a squad of men dedicated to Hernán Cortés. He does Cortés's dirty work whenever required.

The Velazquistas. The name Cortés gives to senior figures on the expedition to Mexico who remain loyal to his enemy and rival Diego de Velázquez, the governor of Cuba. Cortés must either bribe, manipulate, or force members of the Velázquez faction to change sides. They include **Juan Escudero** (ringleader of the Velazquistas), **Juan Velázquez de Léon**, cousin of Diego de Velázquez, **Francisco de Montejo**, **Diego de Ordaz** and **Cristóbal de Olid**.

Significant allies of Cortés on the expedition. In addition to **Pedro de Alvarado** (POV character number 7) Cortés can rely on **Alonso Hernández Puertocarrero** and **Juan de Escalante**. An additional figure, **Alonso Davila,** is at least neutral; he does not like Cortés but he does not like Diego de Velázquez either.

Alonso de La Serna and Francisco Mibiercas. Soldiers on the expedition. Friends of Bernal Díaz (POV character number 10).

Dr La Peña. Doctor hired by Diego de Velázquez to drug and kidnap Cortés. Instead Cortés captures La Peña and kidnaps him to serve as the expedition's doctor.

Antón de Alaminos. Pilot and chief navigator of Cortés's fleet.

Nuno Guiterrez. Sailor.

Father Bartolomé de Olmedo. Mercedarian Friar, a gentle, good-hearted man who participates in the expedition to Mexico. Opposed to forced conversions.

Jerónimo de Aguilar. Spanish castaway in the Yucatán. Spent eight years as a slave amongst the Maya and became fluent in their language. Rescued by a squad sent by Cortés and led by Sandoval, Aguilar joins the expedition and becomes Cortés's first interpreter and, later, Malinal's rival for this role.

Francisco de Mesa. Cortés's chief of artillery.

Diego de Godoy. Notary of the expedition.

Telmo Vendabal. Keeper of the expedition's pack of one hundred ferocious war dogs.

Secondary Mexica, Tlascalan and Mayan characters who appear frequently or have prominence in the story

Coyotl. Little boy, six years old, castrated in infancy. Held in women's fattening pen with Tozi and Malinal awaiting sacrifice. Protégé of Tozi.

Ahuizotl. High priest of the Mexica and devotee of the war god Hummingbird.

Namacuix. Deputy high priest of the Mexica.

Cuitláhuac. Age, forty-eight. Younger brother of Moctezuma and father of **Guatemoc** (POV character number 6).

Coaxoch. Age late forties, holds title of 'Snake Woman'. Second most senior Mexica lord after Moctezuma himself, and the most important general in the Mexica army. We meet Coaxoch leading a massive force of thirty-two thousand men into Tlascala to snatch victims for human sacrifice. This is the force that **Shikotenka** (POV character number 5) plans to destroy.

Mahuizoh and **Iccauhtli**. Eldest and youngest of Coaxoch's sons. All four are generals in the Mexica army, but appointed above their skills through nepotism.

Acolmiztli, Chipahua, Tree, Etzli, Ilhuicamina. Commanders in **Shikotenka's** squad of **Tlascalan** warriors whom we meet as they are about to mount an attack on Coaxoch.

Tochtli, 'Rabbit' (**Shikotenka's** cousin). Also in the squad that will attack **Coaxoch**.

Shikotenka the Elder. Civil king of the Tlascalans (**Shikotenka**, his son, is the battle-king).

Maxixcatzin. Deputy to both **Shikotenka** and **Shikotenka the Elder**.

Huicton. A spy working to destroy **Moctezuma**. Huicton is in his sixties and passes unnoticed through the streets of Tenochtitlan disguised as an elderly blind beggar. However, he is not blind. He is the mentor and protector of **Tozi** (POV character number 1).

War God and History

War God is a novel about an extraordinary moment in history but it is not a history book. Rather it is a work of fantasy and epic adventure in the tradition of *Amadis of Gaul*, the post-Arthurian tale of knight-errantry in which the conquistadors of the early sixteenth century saw their own deeds reflected as they pursued their very real and perilous quest in the strange and terrible lands of Mexico.[1] Wherever I felt it served the interests of my story, I have therefore not hesitated to diverge from a strict observance of historical facts. Let me give a few examples.

Malinal (who was also known as Malinali, Malintzin and La Malinche and whom the conquistadors called Doña Marina) was more likely a Nahua woman of the Mexican Gulf coast who had learned the Mayan language than a Mayan woman – as I have her – who had become fluent in Nahuatl. On the other hand, her biography as I relate it – daughter of a chief, disinherited and sold into slavery by her own mother after her father's death (because her mother favoured a son by her second marriage) – conforms to the facts as they have been passed down to us.

Likewise, while I write of the disastrous Córdoba expedition that visited the Yucatán prior to Cortés, I make no mention – it would have been too cumbersome to do so – of the second expedition, under Juan de Grijalva, that also preceded Cortés. I have, however, conflated some details of the Córdoba and Grijalva expeditions, and in doing so I do not think I stray far from the spirit of the facts.

In a similar way, and for similar narrative reasons, I have telescoped the story of the departure of Cortés's fleet from Cuba into the single dramatic night of 18 February 1519, when in fact it was a more long-drawn-out affair. The fleet did leave Santiago precipitously, Velázquez

543

did try to prevent this, and Cortés did confront him from a small boat, much as I describe these events.[2] The story that I tell of Velázquez sending a messenger cancelling Cortés's command and putting another man in charge, together with the killing of this messenger *en route* by one of Cortés's allies and delivery of the papers he was carrying to Cortés himself, is well attested in historical sources. The same goes for the raid on the slaughterhouse and seizure by Cortés's men of all the meat and livestock on the hoof.[3] However, these events did not occur on 18 February 1519 but on 18 November 1518, Bernal Díaz does not admit in his memoirs to leading the raid on the slaughterhouse,[4] and the killing of the messenger was not done by Alvarado (although he was certainly capable of such an act and responsible during his lifetime for many like it), but by Juan Suarez, another of Cortés's close associates.[5] It is correct that the fleet did finally leave Cuban waters on 18 February 1519, as I state in *War God*, and that it was that night scattered by a storm,[6] but it had first spent three months sailing around Cuba, evading Velázquez's authority by various means while Cortés collected further supplies, men and horses. I saw no need to burden my story with these details and complexities.

Other similar examples could be cited here (for instance Guatemoc was probably Moctezuma's cousin, not his nephew) but, by and large, while responding to the narrative needs of a fantasy adventure epic, I have worked hard to weave my tale around a solid armature of historical facts. This is not to say that the fantastic and the supernatural are not prominent themes in *War God* – because they are! – but there is nothing 'unhistorical' about this. Such concerns were of prime importance both to the superstitious Spanish and to the Mexica. Indeed Mexico-Tenochtitlan has, with good reason, been described by Nobel Prizewinner J. M. G. Le Clezio as 'the last magical civilization'.[7]

Take the case of Tozi the witch, one of my central characters. Some might think that an obsession with sorcery, animal familiars (even transformation into animal forms), the ability to make oneself invisible, the concoction of spells and herbal potions by women and the persecution of women for such practices were purely European concerns; but in these matters – as in so many others – the Spanish of the sixteenth century had much more in common with the Mexica than they realized.

Witchcraft was widespread in Central America and endemic to the culture of the region.[8]

Then there is the matter of human sacrifice, a recurrent theme throughout *War God*. Do I make too much of this? Do I dwell on it at a length that is not justified by the facts? Honestly, no, I don't think I do. The facts, including the fattening of prisoners and their incarceration in special pens prior to sacrifice, are so abhorrent, so well evidenced and so overwhelming that the imagination is simply staggered by them. In saying this I recognise that the prim hand of political correctness has in recent years tried to sweep the extravagant butchery and horror of Mexica sacrificial rituals under the table of history by suggesting that Spanish eyewitnesses were exaggerating for propaganda or religious purposes. Yet this cannot be right. Let alone the mass of archaeological evidence and the surviving depictions of human sacrifice, skull racks, flaying and dismemberment of victims, cannibalism, etc, in Mexica sculpture and art, we have detailed accounts of these practices given to reliable chroniclers within a few years of the conquest by the Mexica themselves. Both Bernardo de Sahagún, in his *General History of the Things of New Spain*,[9] and Diego Duran in his *History of the Indies of New Spain*,[10] based their reports upon the testimony of native informants, and both give extensive descriptions of the grisly sacrificial rituals that had been integral to Mexica society since its inception, that had increased exponentially during the fifty years prior to the conquest, and that the conquistadors themselves witnessed after their arrival. The historian Hugh Thomas sums up the matter soberly in his superb study of the conquest.[11] 'In numbers,' he writes, 'in the elevated sense of ceremony which accompanied the theatrical shows involved, as in its significance in the official religion, human sacrifice in Mexico was unique.'[12]

Political correctness has also tried to airbrush out the Quetzalcoatl mythos of the white-skinned bearded god who was prophesied to return in the year One-Reed, and Cortés's manipulation of this myth, as largely a fabrication of the conquistadors – but this too cannot be correct. Again Sahagún's immense scholarship in his *General History* contains too much detail to be ignored.[13] But there are many other sources too numerous to mention here, and we should not forget the universal iconography of the 'Plumed Serpent' throughout central America. Some of it – for example at La Venta on the Gulf of Mexico – is very ancient indeed (1500 BC or older) and is associated with reliefs of bearded individuals with plainly Caucasian rather than native American features.[14]

Other 'fantastical' aspects of my story, such as Moctezuma's visionary encounters under the influence of hallucinogenic mushrooms with the war god Huitzilopochtli (Hummingbird), and Cortés's conviction that he was guided by Saint Peter, are also thoroughly supported in numerous historical sources.

Last but not least, there is the matter of the incredible disparity of forces – the few hundred Spaniards against vast Mayan and later Mexica armies and the apparent miracle of the conquistadors' triumph. But, as I show in *War God*, this 'miracle' was really science. The guns and cannon the Spaniards were able to deploy, their terrifying war dogs,[15] and the stunning impact of their cavalry gave them decisive advantages. No dogs larger than chihuahuas had previously been known in Central America, and whereas European infantry had accumulated thousands of years of experience (and had developed specialized tactics and weapons) to withstand charges of heavy horse, the armies of Mexico were completely unprepared for the seemingly demonic beasts and supernatural powers that Cortés unleashed on them.

But there was something else, ultimately more important than all of this, that brought the Spanish victory.

If Moctezuma had been a different sort of ruler, if he had possessed a shred of kindness or decency, if there had been any capacity in him to love, then he surely would not have preyed upon neighbouring peoples for human sacrifices to offer up to his war god, in which case he could have earned their devotion and respect rather than their universal loathing, and thus might have been in a position to lead a united opposition to the conquistadors and to crush them utterly within weeks of setting foot in his lands. But he was none of these things, and thus Cortés was almost immediately able to exploit the hatred that Moctezuma's behaviour had provoked and find allies amongst those the Mexica had terrorised and exploited – allies who were crucial to the success of the conquest. Of particular note in this respect were the

Tlascalans, who had suffered the depredations of the Mexica more profoundly than any others and who were led by Shikotenka, a general so courageous and so principled that he at first fought the Spanish tooth and nail, seeing the existential danger they posed to the entire culture of the region, despite the liberation from Moctezuma's tyranny that Cortés offered him. Only when Cortés had smashed Shikotenka in battle did the brave general finally bow to the demands of the Tlascalan Senate to make an alliance with the Spaniards, an alliance that soon put tens of thousands of auxiliaries under Cortés's command and set the conquistadors on the road to Tenochtitlan . . .

These events, and many others even more remarkable, will be the focus of the second volume of this series, *War God: Return of the Plumed Serpent*.

References

1 See, for example, Hugh Thomas, *Conquest: Montezuma, Cortés and the Fall of Old Mexico*, Simon & Schuster Paperbacks, New York and London, 1993, pp. 61–62 and 702.

2 Ibid, pp. 141–142.

3 Ibid, p. 141.

4 Bernal Díaz, *The Conquest of New Spain*, translated by J.M. Cohen, Penguin Classics, London, 1963, p. 49.

5 Thomas, *Conquest*, p. 141.

6 Ibid, pp. 157–158.

7 J. M. G. Le Clezio, *The Mexican Dream: Or The Interrupted Thought of Amerindian Civilizations*, translated by Teresa Lavender Fagan, The University of Chicago Press, Chicago and London, 2009, p. 41.

8 See for example, Jan G. R. Elferink, Jose Antonio Flores and Charles D. Kaplan, *The Use of Plants and Other Natural Products for Malevolent Practices amongst the Aztecs and their Successors*, Estudios de Cultura Nahuatl, vol. 24, 1994, Universidad Nacional Autónomo de México. See also Daniel G. Brinton, *Nagualism: A Study in Native American Folklore and History*, MacCalla and Co, Philadelphia, 1894. And see David Friedel, Linda Schele and Joy Parker, *Maya Cosmos: Three Thousand Years on the Shaman's Path*,

William Morrow and Co., New York, pp. 52, 181, 190, 192–193, 211, 228. See also Le Clezio, *The Mexican Dream*, pp. 104–108

9 Fray Bernardo de Sahagún, *General History of the Things of New Spain* (Florentine Codex), translated from the Aztec into English by Arthur J. O. Anderson and Charles E. Dibble, School of American Research, University of Utah, 1975. See for example book 12, chapters 6, 8 and 9.

10 Fray Diego Durán, *The History of the Indies of New Spain*, translated by Doris Heyden and Fernando Horcasitas, Orion Press, New York, 1964. See, for example, pages 99–102 (from where the oration given to sacrificial victims in chapter 28 of *War God* is quoted), pp. 105–113, 120–122, 195–200 and many other similar passages.

11 Thomas, *Conquest*, pp. 24–27.

12 Ibid, p. 27.

13 Sahagún, *General History*, see for example chapters 2, 3, 4 and 16.

14 See for example Graham Hancock and Santha Faiia, *Heaven's Mirror: Quest for the Lost Civilisation*, Michael Joseph, London, 1998, pp. 38–42.

15 An excellent source on the conquistadors' use of dogs trained for war is to be found in John Grier Varner and Jeannette Johnson Varner, *Dogs of the Conquest*, University of Oklahoma Press, 1983.

Acknowledgements

First and foremost I am grateful to my wife and partner Santha, my fiercest critic and constant companion who has read every word of this book and of the two subsequent volumes that follow it and who never lets me get away with any short cuts. My children Sean, Shanti, Ravi, Leila, Luke and Gabrielle, as well as my son and daughters in law Lydia, Simone, Jason and Ayako, have all also been helpful and inspiring presences, reading draft after draft and offering encouragement and advice.

My literary agent Sonia Land of Sheil Land Associates has, throughout, played a most important role in this book, giving me the benefit of her professional judgement and her kind and wise guidance at every stage of the process, and championing my new career as a novelist with tremendous verve and energy. I'm very grateful to you, Sonia, and can't thank you enough. Deep appreciation also to Gaia Banks and to all at Sheil Land, the best literary agency in Britain.

Others who have read and been kind enough to comment on the manuscripts of the evolving *War God* series and who have given me much valuable advice, but who are of course not responsible in any way for the shortcomings of what I have written, include Chris and Cathy Foyle, Luis Eduardo Luna, Father Nicola Mapelli, Jean-Paul Tarud-Kuborn, Ram Mehen, Ileen Maisel, Sa'ad Shah and Volker Westphal. I'm grateful to each and every one of these good and true friends of mine for their generosity with their time and their many constructive suggestions.

My editor Mark Booth at Coronet has been brilliant as ever, seeing what needed to be done at each stage of the writing process and keeping me on the right course with amazing professionalism and insight.

My communities on my Facebook author page (www.facebook.com/ Author.GrahamHancock) and on my Facebook personal page (www.

facebook.com/GrahamHancockDotCom), and also my website community (www.grahamhancock.com) have been incredibly supportive of me through the several years of my life that *War God* has dominated my writing and my creativity.

Last but not least I want to put on record my appreciation for those Spaniards and Mexica of the sixteenth century who were caught up in the events of the conquest and wrote about it at first hand, leaving accounts luminous with the spirit and terror of the time that I have been able to draw on in creating this book – sometimes even putting the exact words of the individual concerned into the mouth of his or her character in my story. A number of modern scholars have also written important works on the events of the conquest without which I would not have been able to develop a full appreciation of the period and again I am grateful for the tremendous job they have done. Needless to say none of them are responsible in any way for the shortcomings of *War God* but if the book has strengths it is in large part owed to them. Many more works of reference on which I have drawn could be cited here, but I list in particular the following texts to which I have most frequently had reference as primary and secondary sources for this first volume of the *War God* trilogy:

Primary sources

Hernan Cortes, *Letters from Mexico*, Translated and with a new Introduction by Anthony Pagden, Yale University Press, New Haven and London, 1986.

Bernal Diaz, *The Conquest of New Spain*, Translated by J.M. Cohen, Penguin Classics, London, 1963.

The Bernal Diaz Chronicles, Translated and Edited by Bernard Idell, Doubleday, New York, 1956.

Fray Diego Duran, *The History of the Indies of New Spain*, translated by Doris Heyden and Fernando Horcasitas, Orion Press, New York, 1964.

Patricia Fuentes (translator), *The Conquistadors: First Person accounts of the Conquest of Mexico*, The Orion Press, New York, 1963.

Francisco Lopez de Gomara, *Cortes: The Life of the Conqueror* by his

Secretary, Translated by Lesley Byrd Simpson, University of California Press, 1966.

Fray Bernardo de Sahagun, *General History of the Things of New Spain* (Florentine Codex), translated from the Aztec into English by Arthur J.O. Anderson and Charles E. Dibble, School of American Research, University of Utah, 1975.

Miguel Leon-Portilla (Ed), *Broken Spears: The Aztec Account of the Conquest of Mexico*, Beacon Press, Boston, 1990.

Secondary sources

J.M.G. Le Clezio, *The Mexican Dream: Or The Interrupted Thought of Amerindian Civilizations*, Translated by Teresa Lavender Fagan, The University of Chicago Press, Chicago and London, 2009.

David Friedel, Linda Schele and Joy Parker, *Maya Cosmos: Three Thousand Years on the Shaman's Path*, William Morrow and Co., New York, 1995

C. Harvey Gardner, *The Constant Companion: Gonzalo de Sandoval*, Southern Illinois University Press, 1961.

John Eoghan Kelly, *Pedro de Alvarado, Conquistador*, Kennikat Press, Port Washington, N.Y., and London, 1932.

William H. Prescott, *History of the Conquest of Mexico*, The Modern Library, New York.

Karen Sullivan, *The Inner Lives of Medieval Inquisitors*, University of Chicago Press, 2011.

Hugh Thomas, *Conquest. Montezuma, Cortes and the Fall of Old Mexico*, Simon & Schuster Paperbacks, New York, and London, 1993.

Hugh Thomas, *Who's Who of the Conquistadors*, Cassell & Co., London, 2000.

John Grier Varner and Jeannette Johnson Varner, *Dogs of the Conquest*, University of Oklahoma Press, 1983.

WAR GOD: RETURN OF THE PLUMED SERPENT

The War God epic continues with volume two of the series, *War God: Return of the Plumed Serpent*, published October 2014. Having destroyed the Maya at Potonchan, Cortes now marches on Tenochtitlan wrapped in the aura of a returning, vengeful god. But the Mexica armies are vast, battle-hardened and trained for war and between them and the Spaniards stand the ferocious Tlascalans led by the hero Shikotenka. Cortes imagines the Tlascalan battle king, sworn enemy of the Mexica, will join his side to bring Moctezuma to his knees, but instead discovers he has a fight for his life on his hands. The supernatural and history combine in this tale of love, courage and the triumph of the human spirit in the darkest of times.

October 2014

CORONET